PIERRETTE FLEUTIAUX

We Are Eternal

A NOVEL

TRANSLATED FROM THE FRENCH
BY JEREMY LEGGATT

LITTLE, BROWN AND COMPANY
BOSTON   NEW YORK   TORONTO   LONDON

First English-Language Edition

This is a work of fiction. Names, characters, places, and incidents
are either the product of the author's imagination
or, if real, are used fictitiously.

The author is grateful for permission to include
the following previously copyrighted material:

Excerpt from "Domination of Black" from *Collected Poems of Wallace Stevens*
by Wallace Stevens. Copyright 1923 by Wallace Stevens; © renewed 1951
by Wallace Stevens. Reprinted by permission of Alfred A. Knopf, Inc.

This work was published with the support
of the French Ministry of Culture.

Library of Congress Cataloging-in-Publication Data

Fleutiaux, Pierrette.
  [Nous sommes éternels. English]
  We are eternal : a novel / by Pierrette Fleutiaux ; translated by
Jeremy Leggatt. — 1st English language ed.
      p.   cm.
  ISBN 0-316-28617-6
  1. Man-woman relationships — Fiction.   2. Brothers and sisters —
Fiction.   I. Title.
PQ2666.L43N6813   1994
843'.914 — dc20   94-202

10 9 8 7 6 5 4 3 2 1

MV-NY

*Published simultaneously in Canada
by Little, Brown & Company (Canada) Limited*

Printed in the United States of America

To Anne Philipe
To A. Wagneur
And to all the Helleur family

Contents

I

At G.

ONE

"He's Your Brother"

*A*s FAR BACK as my mind's eye can see, my brother's face was there. As if he had been always by my side. Always, even before he came into this world.

Which perhaps explains my reaction when they first showed him to me.

"He's like a little monkey," I said.

He was yellow, wrinkled, and diminutive in the nurse's white-sleeved arms. But I knew this was simply a disguise he had donned before arriving so as not to overwhelm me.

He was calling out, making strange little whimpers nobody sought to calm.

And those calls too I recognized for what they were. No need for translation. "Hang on, Estelle," they told me. "For the time being this is the only way I can communicate with you. Because we're not alone, because there's nothing else I can do, because I don't know what, but in any case it's me, it's me, Estelle!"

I pretended to be annoyed that he was disturbing the grown-ups' conversation.

But already I knew that he was the most beautiful creature in the world, and that life had just begun in this corner of the planet where I had waited alone for five long years.

"He has jaundice," said the nurse.

She was speaking to me. Nobody else seemed interested in her comments.

"It isn't serious," she said. "We can put him in an incubator if he weakens."

In an incubator? My brother? Not to be seen for days and days? One of those incubators that look like small glass coffins?

Once again, the nurse had been speaking to me.

She seemed curiously distraught, as if put out that the only one listening to her words was this five-year-old standing there in her white collar, her ribbons, her pleated skirt, and her disapproving look.

I could feel she was upset. I could feel everything that was going on.

I had never been in a hospital before, yet I knew that a nurse was someone whose words we should have been listening to. We should have been grouped respectfully around her as she stood beside the crib — with my brother in the center of the group, with the nurse next to that center, and with us all around her, drinking in her words. And then perhaps my brother's illness might have receded, he might not have been so yellow and wrinkled. He might have given us a real baby smile.

"You may go now, miss," said my father to the nurse.

"Should I take the baby?" she asked in the same uncertain voice.

My head swam, and the room was suddenly flooded with whiteness, dense, choking whiteness. At the heart of the whiteness were three dark shapes, one by the window, one near the door, the third against the wall. To keep myself from falling, I clutched at a nearby pillar, the nurse, who still held my brother in her arms.

Later on, my brother and I often experienced this affliction. We called it our "vaypigo." (We must have heard our doctor speak of "the vapors" and "vertigo," and we must have gotten the words wrong, as we so often did. But we had been impressed, and the expression had stuck.) Vaypigo played a big part in our growing up. We were careful to keep it secret, so sure were we that it belonged to us alone and that we alone could nurse each other through it, with me taking care of Dan, and Dan taking care of Estelle.

Vaypigo affected all parts of your body, it swept your whole being. It was something we knew intimately, and something profoundly mysterious.

"Should I take him away now?" the nurse asked again.

Since no one seemed to have heard her, she had once more turned to me, the five-year-old.

The dizziness left me, and with it all pretense of not caring. Because now I had to fight. In that room and in the whole wide world, I was the only one truly and wholly concerned.

I looked at the nurse as steadily as I could, and my look was the one she must have been expecting, the look of someone eager for her wisdom and her reassurance, and also the look of someone giving orders. Without another word, she put the infant in his crib and left the room.

I had just won our first battle. I bent over my brother, and he smiled. "Well done, Estelle," said the expression on his little face. "You got the better of them!" But I knew very well that it was his own strength that had prevailed. That his strength transmitted through me, his older sister, would always prevail.

Always.

I believed it, I believed it right up to the last second, I even believed it afterward, and sometimes even now I believe it.

In that moment our partnership was born, although in the secret places of my heart I am sure it dates from a moment or two earlier, when I clearly saw that his look of a tiny archaic being was just a disguise (we alone knew the truth), and perhaps from earlier still, from before the time of his birth . . . But I want to be reasonable, I want to keep our story within bounds accessible to ordinary reason. In fact I wanted it even then, which is why I quickly shrank back from him and said again, "He's like a little monkey." At once he began to scowl in earnest, his wrinkles turned red, and he let out piercing wails that I alone seemed to hear.

No one spoke. My mother Nicole, her back to the crib, looked paler than usual. She wore a shift I had never seen her wear. It was white, but by a curious reversal it looked black to me, for I had never seen her except in clothing of lively colors, most often bright blue. She seemed to be staring into space.

Tiresia sat by the window, her back to the light as was her habit, but I knew all the shapes her body could assume.

The positions of Tiresia's body were my alphabet, and my brother's too. No one had to teach them to us. The language of her body was written directly into the memory of our awareness, weaving a network of signs up which we grew like vines on a trellis.

We could read Tiresia's body before we were able to read anything else, and thereafter every book we read suffered by comparison with that first book, Tiresia's body. Subsequent books could be only reduced or amplified or distorted echoes, only translations, always somewhat foreign compared to the original, which had been our mother tongue.

Yes, the books we read later always seemed to us a sort of trans-

lation. Perhaps that is why we turned away from literature despite
our passionate love for it. And perhaps that is why today, when I so
desperately need to write, I cannot entrust myself with the task but
have to find a writer.

I do not believe Tiresia had yet ceased to speak. But I have a
feeling so strong it takes precedence over the truth, that we had
never known her anything but mute. Mute, she who said the most
to us.

Standing in that room, stifled by its whiteness and its silence, I read
something in Tiresia's body, in her still form backlit against the
window.

"He's not very pretty," I went on, thinking to soften my previous
remark.

"He's your brother," my father snapped.

His words cracked out. It was as if a sudden squall had sprung up
out of nowhere and filled the room.

I staggered as if I had been slapped.

Our father was standing at the foot of our mother Nicole's bed
(which presumably reached the door). He stood very straight. He
too was wearing black, it seems to me, but it may just have been his
everyday clothing, made blacker by the relentless whiteness of the
room.

Slapped — by our father! Highly unlikely. No, quite impossible,
more impossible even than a giraffe on an ice floe . . .

"He's your brother," my father said again. His tone was no longer
harsh, but his voice was tense, without a hint of softness to cushion
the words.

That hellishly white room, the grown-ups' dark shapes, the crib
that imprisoned my brother . . . A new and unfamiliar sensation
welled up inside me. Today I know its name — indignation. If
there is one strong feeling that characterizes childhood, it is indignation.

Love of my brother was so great within me, and love of me so
great in my brother, why was my father reproaching me in this way?

Suddenly he took me in his arms. He looked frightened. He spoke
to me gently, patiently, as he always did when speaking of things
beyond our understanding, this time no doubt telling me about jaundice in babies, the soft spot in their skull, their helplessness. But I
was not listening.

It was enough for me to be in his arms, rocked by the gentle flow of his voice, which was once again my father's real voice.

In the room a girl was arranging flowers, or perhaps just moving them. Nicole wanted all the flowers she had received to be moved to the other end of the room, then put out in the corridor, and finally given to some other new mother. The smell bothered her, she said.

Then, once we were more or less calm, with me in my father's arms, the flowers finally gone, and Nicole dozing, there was a knock at the door and a delivery man came in with an enormous, an amazing bunch of flowers in his arms.

The delivery man and my father bent over the box, looking for a card, a letter, a paper, something apparently not there, for they both seemed puzzled. "I can deliver them to your residence," said the man, but Nicole suddenly sat up in bed.

"No," she said, pushing back her damp fair strands in a mechanical attempt to restore her everyday hairdo.

The look on our mother Nicole's face just then was extraordinary. For years and years I tried to describe that look of hers to my brother. I never really succeeded, even though he asked me again and again. After a while, the look faded, as if it had been the dying breath of the flowers, and now only those flowers remained to recall the look that had evaporated like a perfume. They were enormous black tulips — blue-black, really, since black tulips do not exist. They are so rare that despite our occasional attempts we never saw them again, except perhaps once in New York, but we couldn't be sure.

"I'll keep them," said Nicole with that look which reached out and transfixed me where I sat in my father's lap.

Tiresia at once rose and went over to our mother. With her dexterous fingers, her superb strong pianist's fingers, she combed the hair, plaited it into a single long braid, and with a movement so quick you saw only its final result, she twisted it around and pinned it in a flawless bun on top of Nicole's head. She let her hands rest there a second, cupped around the fair chignon, then withdrew them.

And at last I recognized my mother Nicole again, recognized the graceful head that she carried like a rare object on her delicate neck.

All over again I recognized my mother's bearing, the regal carriage of her head that made her stand out among thousands, the way she did, for example, in our town when she stood out in the midst of the busiest crowd on the busiest of streets on the busiest of market days.

It seemed to me that very soon she would get out of bed and look around for a bar, or a railing, the rail at the foot of the bed would do, and resume her ballet exercises. My brother and I would watch her practice every day. We would try to copy her movements, only to collapse in pitiful, grotesque heaps. It seemed to me now that this was what she was about to do, and I had a sudden glimpse of our future horseplay, of my little brother and me trying to do the splits like our mother, of our falls and our helpless laughter.

The black tulips stood at my mother's bedside, and my mother wept.

Our father and Tiresia had left. I stood alone in the middle of the room. My mother did not look at me or at my little brother. He had stopped crying. I went over and took his small blue wrinkled hand, and both of us listened to our mother weeping, her back hidden by the white sheet, her face in the shadow of the big black tulips.

When our father returned he had our old family doctor with him and another man, probably the hospital doctor. This second man told her she would be able to dance very soon, that she would be able to resume her exercises gradually over the next few weeks.

Nicole listened, not believing him. In her eyes was the strangest of looks. The look did not leap outward and grow as it advanced, but slowly spread over the opaque, vitreous basin of her eyes. And there, trapped on that surface, the look began to metamorphose, began a chain reaction, a series of transmutations — oh, that look in my mother Nicole's eyes.

My father must have been listening to advice from the hospital doctor, for he had somewhat shakily reverted to his usual bluff self. Perhaps he had been told that familiarity might erase some of the fear that was within our mother, a fear so overwhelming that nothing could destroy it. Perhaps he had been told you could ward it off, for a moment, with patience.

"Very well," Nicole said crisply.

Nonplussed, the hospital doctor silently consulted my father. Had he heard "Go to hell"? Or just "Very well"? "Mr. Helleur," his look implored, "please help me, how should I handle this?" But we paid him no attention.

As we always did when something was beyond our understanding, my father and I turned to Tiresia, to Tiresia's body, just to see what it was saying. Her hands lay on her black skirt, the fingers locked across her stomach and squeezing so hard they were white at the joints.

She had assuredly heard still another meaning in our mother's curiously terse reply, a whole long sentence full of anguish and entreaty and fathomless terror . . .

Our old doctor too looked toward Tiresia.

"Let's get her up right away!" he said suddenly.

His tone was breezy, as if to minimize the importance of his suggestion, because of the other doctor, I think, so as not to irritate him. Our good family doctor was a wily old fox.

"It would make her feel better," added the wily old fox, neatly shifting the problem from medical to psychological grounds — grounds he must have known the other doctor, the hospital doctor, discounted.

"It's not the usual procedure," he said.

"No, but after all, a dancer isn't your usual maternity patient," said our doctor with a laugh.

Our mother got up and essayed a few steps in the center of the room, humming the first bars of Ravel's *Bolero*. Suddenly, before our eyes, she raised her gown. She had removed her underwear. I saw her soft round stomach, the way it had always been, with its blond fleece usually flattened by tights but now looking tousled (she had persuaded them not to shave her). The three men, who until then had been curiously still, at once began to fiddle about. One adjusted his stethoscope. Another (probably my father) straightened his tie. The third (it must have been our doctor) bent over an object on the floor, rummaging in his ever-present bag. But Nicole was oblivious to their embarrassment.

The face she sought to read was Tiresia's, her veil, her black glasses, the hands resting on the black skirt, all those things no one else could have deciphered but that spoke volumes to us.

Then my mother began to laugh.

"Not bad at all," she said.

And she tried a few more steps, the same ones she had so doggedly rehearsed despite her swollen belly before leaving for the hospital.

"Not bad, not bad at all," she said again, delighted.

*   *   *

Naive little Nicole, always so ready to be delighted, to be overjoyed, and therefore obliged always to leap too high, high up into the empty sky. Once there she could of course only fall. But what did it matter, she would begin again, she was young, her hope bore a thousand blossoms, her hope could never die.

Her body swayed and she struck a final pose, with back held straight and arms uplifted. Then she erupted into activity.

She had all the banished flowers brought back into the room, while others arrived in such numbers we did not know where to put them. She threw them in armfuls on the floor, on my little brother's crib. She pulled me down on the bed and covered me with kisses (my mother Nicole's kisses, butterflies, clouds of tiny yellow downy butterflies), and told me she would make me a prima ballerina, a star.

"Estelle, do you hear me, do you hear your name, stella, estrella, stellar, star?" She said I would shine so brightly we would no longer need lights. She said even Tiresia in her shadow world would see me. She told me mad, intoxicating things.

"What about my brother?" I yelled.

"Your brother will be the handsomest of all brothers, you will love him to distraction, he will be the most gifted musician on earth, he'll write the most splendid ballets for you and me, and we'll dance together before kings and queens."

"And what about my father?" I cried.

"He will watch us," said my mad, elated mother Nicole.

"And Tiresia?"

"She will watch us."

"But she's blind."

"She will see us, believe me. We will shine so brightly that she'll see us."

TWO

"I'm Going to Marry Nicole"

S URE you are," said my brother. "That's about as likely as a giraffe standing on an ice floe!"

We were on our side of the gap in the dividing wall, and from the other side our little neighbor Adrien had announced to us that he would marry our mother Nicole when he grew up. My brother had just read (with my help, for he wasn't yet in school) Kipling's *Just So Stories* and Jack London's *Burning Daylight.* But Adrien hated reading and had no idea where our images came from.

A giraffe on an ice floe.

Adrien was taken aback by the idea. Not just the pairing of terms, but also each term on its own. There was after all neither cinema nor zoo in our town.

After that, he said no more about marrying our mother Nicole.

Our metaphor for improbability had cut him to the quick, in some still vulnerable recess of his child's heart. From that day on our relationship was defined: with Adrien withdrawn, sulky, and malevolent, and my brother and me wary and contemptuous.

Was a slap from our father more improbable than the sight of a giraffe on an ice floe?

Far more!

Far more improbable, even though that disoriented giraffe was for us the height of improbability.

A slap would have been not improbable, but impossible, not even remotely related to reality!

Only the violence of my love for my newborn brother could have thrown me off balance so and called forth another excessive and unfamiliar emotion — fear — to make me perceive such an absurd thing, perceive my father's words lashing out like a whip!

Adrien, sometimes it seems to me that you are the one cackling and whispering this nonsense that so wounds me. For you know how to hurt us, don't you, our neighbor, our constant companion who knew us better than anyone.

I need someone to blame, and once again you are my choice for that sordid distinction. Yes, you again, Adrien, after all these years, and all because of that incongruous comparison that came back to me. In fact, of course, the idea of an African animal on an ice floe, however improbable, is nevertheless possible: all you need do is think up the right set of circumstances; indeed, perhaps they have already come about spontaneously. But even this suggestion of possibility is more than I can bear, for the thought of our father losing his temper with us is utterly inconceivable.

Nor do the conditions exist that would make it possible. I can see a giraffe on an ice floe, but it is categorically impossible to imagine my father slapping us.

His kindness to us was constant, even when he returned exhausted from his trips to the capital or from interminable hearings in our town courthouse. His voice was always calm and attentive, never one word louder than another, a trait that might seem unusual in a lawyer, yet that had strangely enough been of some benefit in his career. "Not a career," he would say with a gentle laugh, "a job, a second-rate job, and with no hope of divine intercession."

Of course my brother and I did not believe him, we thought he was the greatest lawyer on earth, that he held the scales of good and evil, that he had no need of God, that he himself was God as far as justice on earth was concerned.

Our admiration for him was boundless. It was only much later, at the stormy onset of our adolescence, around the time of the brutal irruption into our life of five young people from elsewhere ("Your cousins," our father announced, but what cousins? we had no family), that we began to realize one or two things. Only one or two things.

Then we saw fairly clearly that our father was just a modest country lawyer, called upon to handle the occasional important case in Paris only because he was trilingual. "I am not trilingual," he would say, "I speak French and I still have my English, which isn't the same thing. And the less said about my German the better," he would add with a glance at Tiresia.

He did not like to say how he had learned German. Nor did he want people to know he was born English. He had changed his name from Heller to Helleur, because the spelling seemed to him more French. As for the challenging legal cases in Paris that required his help, he did not solicit them. "My heart can't take it," he said. "They need younger lawyers, ones who haven't experienced all those horrors in the flesh."

And he would suddenly go pale and have to sit down. "Rapid heartbeat," he would say, and then seeing our anxious look he would add, "Crybaby talk — that's what Minor calls it." But we looked at Tiresia, who sat withdrawn, her face as usual veiled. We looked at her, and anguish clutched our hearts.

At night we took turns standing watch outside our father's door.

One night when we were both outside his door (of course we never really managed to take turns, since we possessed no alarm clock and naturally did not dare ask for one, so both of us stayed awake all night, one of us a little more alert and the other a little sleepier at different moments), both of us together, legs bare, numb with fear, necks stiff from listening through the open door to make sure our father was still breathing.

Now, if there was one thing we did not want, it was for our mother Nicole to catch us there, to witness our fear. In fact it was our second-biggest fear, second only to our father's rapid heartbeat. But if Nicole ever caught us, then it would be her reaction to that discovery we would fear most, even more than our father's rapid heartbeat.

But it wasn't Nicole who caught us.

It was Tiresia.

She had merely leaned forward through the half-open door, for she was still seated, you could see the chair against the wall beside the doorjamb. The rest happened very quickly. As always with Tiresia there was no need for words. She made a little sign to us, and we understood that she was watching in our place, that we could go back to our beds.

No scolding, not a sound. Direct understanding.

Our father was not in danger. Our mother Nicole was not having her nightmare.

We went off hand in hand, immensely relieved.

THREE

Nightmare

*I*T WAS raining hard and the windows had fogged over. I rubbed the cold pane with my hand and pressed my forehead against the wiped area to try to see outside. It was already dark and the wind battered the big chestnut trees in the garden. I could imagine leaves being torn off and whirled away through the air before tumbling to the sodden ground, what a cruel fate to be ripped from your parent tree and flung earthward to rot.

Even the light from the street lamp looked sodden, seeming to flap in the wind like a forgotten rag. You could no longer see the lights in the houses nearest us, everything was drowned in darkness, and the wind and rain led the night a ferocious dance, at times sending a pallid wavering glow like moving shadows through the darkness, at times sending out harsh swift glimmers that fleetingly touched this or that corner of our garden as if they were themselves the questing eyes of the storm, as if they sought some unguessed-at place among the familiar landmarks of our garden, as if they were reconnoitering on behalf of some obscure and terrifying power that would one day return bent on havoc, oh, Dan, my brother Dan, my love.

At intervals the squalls died down, the rain abated, and then I heard a desolate moaning, the thin and exhausted cry of something dying. A black leaf flattened itself for a second against the windowpane, causing me to cry out. But nobody heard me. Tiresia must have been with our mother upstairs and my brother . . .

Terror and desolation overwhelm me when it rains so hard, when the wind gusts through the black air, lifting sodden, already rotting leaves, when the wet eyes of the street lamps seem to weep. Something pierces me, bending the very axis of my life, and the strengths that might help me resist this possession are eroded by the rain and crushed by the wind, and the leaves that rise up and subside are like the shreds of my ragged soul.

Yet I tried. I told myself these were only feelings, that they would pass. I told myself my brother would come, and when he did, the rain would become a gentle shushing behind the windowpanes; the wind, the night, and the whirling leaves would become a nest where we could snuggle and play. But what if my brother could not come?

I was waiting for our father.

He had gone to the capital on one of those missions that left him more troubled than usual, on one of those jobs he called "my duty cases," jobs that brought him no joy, unless it was the gloomy satisfaction of carrying them to a successful conclusion. His heartbeat was affected by these stressful cases, and one case in particular. But I did not learn of all that until much later, when I heard Tiresia's story. My father never spoke to us of his duty cases, still less of the two cases that preoccupied him above all else.

I missed his presence. I feared for my brother. He was weak, and gaining no weight. At the hospital he was the smallest of the babies born that day. I was angry with our mother Nicole for making him so frail. It seemed to me that she had done it unwittingly but deliberately, if such a thing is possible. Without my father and his big gray car and his quiet confidence, I felt we were vulnerable. Who would go for help if Dan grew smaller inside that little wrinkled skin of his, if his body started growing in the wrong direction, shrinking and shrinking until it disappeared? That could happen if we relaxed our vigilance.

I listened for the crunch of car wheels on the gravel of the driveway. My mother had long since given up driving, and Tiresia, of course, could not drive.

When my father was in the house, I had every confidence in Tiresia. In fact she was the only one I trusted. She was our secret strength, our undefined but constant bulwark, the blind focal point of our household. But when my father was absent, when he was held up far away, for long periods, then this beacon of our strength clouded over and I no longer knew what emanated from it. When our father was absent, I would sometimes catch a glimpse of Tiresia's veil and glasses in some corner of the house, I would see them as a mask, and I would suddenly be afraid.

Our house was at the end of town on a secluded road leading to the cemetery. Just before you reached the cemetery a narrow lane, a little more than a footpath, dropped down to the stream and then climbed up again to cross the highway. My father took this shortcut when he drove back home from out of town. So did our neighbor, who owned a transport business. However, this did not deter either of them from petitioning the town council to close the little trail, for it was truly dangerous when it iced over in winter.

Before it reached the stream, the path skirted the big meadow behind our house. Beyond were the hills.

When we were children our house seemed huge. On blustery days when clouds raced across the sky, my brother and I held hands and stared at the gray slate roof topped with an iron weather vane. Sometimes it seemed to us that the house tilted under the weight of the rushing wind, that it was about to fall. My brother and I huddled close together, straining backs and necks to hold each other as upright as possible, and by the power of our concerted will we managed to prevent the house from collapsing altogether.

We could stay that way for long periods, locked in a kind of trance. Neither of us wanted to be the first to relax, I because I was the elder, my brother because he was the boy. And on a deeper level, we held on because each of us wanted to protect the other to the end.

Tiresia would call and we would not answer, then we heard her come out on the porch and walk down the steps. Our hearts pounded. Would she find us? She had to, if we were ever to be released from our task, but the rules did not allow us to call out to her. We held our breath, we kept our eyes fixed on the weather vane, and we squeezed each other's hands so hard they ached.

Tiresia always found us. I now know that she was not totally blind. But when we were children we knew nothing about her, nothing concrete, nothing precise. She always wore her glasses, which seemed black but were really only tinted. To us, they were Tiresia's eyes. Where others had blue or green or sunken or protruding eyes, Tiresia had dark glasses. But we had no idea what could be seen with dark glasses. This uncertainty about Tiresia's vision colored our entire childhood, but I realize it only now, now that everything has become so clear. So clear, and then to disappear so completely.

Tiresia found us, and suddenly we were free.

We danced around her, transported with joy, embracing everything that we could get hold of around her, great armfuls of air that felt so much a part of her they seemed almost tangible, we told her what we would never have dared tell our father or our mother: "We love you, oh, how we love you."

We were so thrilled, so relieved, to be restored to our childhood, to our life, to our house.

We told her what happened, what we had seen, how the house had tilted, how we had strained to hold it up, and how silly it really was because after all, as we knew perfectly well, and as our father had explained, it was only an optical illusion. "But still, Tiresia, the house was falling down, it was! the house was falling down . . ."

We could tell Tiresia everything, and were sure we heard her answer. In that answer our words swung open, like doors accidentally pushed, and beyond them was a fleeting glimpse of a world in which houses toppled beneath raging skies, in which two children who loved each other joined forces to prevent the toppling, in which love was helpless and yet in which you could be yanked to safety and know a frightening joy.

Still caught up in our excitement, we romped unrestrainedly about her. After a time we realized that she was protecting herself against our boisterous behavior, that she was shielding her belly. We calmed down, we stepped back a little from her but continued to hold on to those armfuls of air that floated about her like scarves as we returned, appeased, to the house.

I did not hear my father arrive. By the time he came home I had been put to bed. I fell asleep in the roar of the storm, listening for the car wheels or my brother's crying. But suddenly I woke. At the far end of the corridor my mother Nicole was screaming.

Her screams were bloodcurdling, unlike any I had ever heard. Doors slammed, I thought it was the storm. I thought that my mother's voice was part of the storm, that she and the storm were one, forever. Then I was fully awake.

The corridor was in semidarkness, but my parents' bedroom door was ajar. My mother was dashing back and forth, her hair disheveled, bent double as if protecting herself against kicks or punches. Nicole, who always carried herself so proudly, her small haughty head borne aloft like a precious jewel! These frenzied movements were hideous, this horribly broken creature was not Nicole, it could not be Nicole, I had never seen anything like it.

Then I was sorry about her dancing and her endless exercising at the bar. I was angry at myself for poking fun at her, for teasing her, for pestering her while she was trying to absorb herself in what she called her art. She loved dancing, but we sometimes hated it because it absorbed our mother's time and took her away from us. How I missed her dancing now: it would have been a hundred times better than this horrible, mindless rushing about.

I was only five, but I believe I understood in a brief flash what my mother was, understood that dancing was her way of struggling, that without dancing there would be only this terrifying ugliness.

If that fleeting intuition had remained within me, had expanded, had shed a broad peaceful glow over my love for Nicole and then cast an even broader light, revealing to our gaze . . . But almost at once it was drowned in fear, fear for my brother, and resentment toward Nicole because she might wake him, terrify him, inflict this horror upon him.

My father had returned. He grabbed my mother by her waist, threw her on the bed, and held her down as she continued to thrash about. He was wearing his robe and beneath it a sort of nightshirt with long tails that my mother disliked because it seemed to her like an old man's garment. She was naked, as she often was, proud no doubt of her dancer's body. And proud perhaps for other reasons I didn't understand.

It was a sight I was not supposed to see. I sensed that it was not right for a child to see her parents sprawled thus grotesquely on the bed, bones grinding together, pale flesh draped incongruously over bones. Forced to go on watching, afraid to slip away lest they notice me, I stayed in the dark behind the door.

My mother sobbed strange and terrifying things. "I'm scared, Thérèse, help me, I'm scared . . ."

I listened in amazement. I knew the names of all her friends and some of her relatives, all dead, but "Thérèse" I had never heard.

And she kept on calling it, ceaselessly, interspersing her calls with screams of fury or of love for that person or for my father, still crouched over her as she continued to thrash about.

I have no idea how our doctor got there.

When he switched on the hall light, I whirled around, startled by the sudden glare erupting behind me. He spoke to me. I did not understand what he said; there was a harshness in his voice that prevented me from hearing his words.

But he really was our old family doctor, the one who spent long hours with us, who stayed to chat with my parents or play with me during his visits. He was part of the family. He had his own key and sometimes paid social calls at night (I once saw him coming down the stairs with his bag). He had a marvelous Russian accent that enchanted me because I thought he put it on only for fun and only with us, just to amuse us. But now he did not really seem to see me; I was just an obstacle he had to get past to get into the bedroom, but first he wanted me to answer a question, and finally I understood what he was asking:

"Where is your mother?"

That was what our old doctor was asking: "Where is your mother?" and his rolling *r*'s no longer sounded like a game.

My mother?

Couldn't he hear her screaming in the bedroom? Was he deaf not to hear that demented raving a few feet behind the door, with my father's voice cutting in every now and then?

Couldn't my mother hear my father begging her to calm down?

Couldn't my father hear the doctor repeating his absurd question?

Had we all gone deaf?

And where was Tiresia? Why didn't she come?

"My mother?" I said.

Then our doctor was his old self again. He bent over me and stroked my hair as he always did.

"Never mind, little one," he said.

And suddenly he did something strange. He set down his bag and knelt . . .

FOUR

Letter from Sister Beatrice

Convent of A. at V.

My dear Estelle,

Six years already. But we have not forgotten you.

You are still one of us, and today the community has asked me to write to you.

The sisters who were closest to you want me to be sure to give you their news. Here it is.

The Mother Superior you knew is once again our Superior. In fact we have adopted a four-year rotation system, but with renewable tenure. Sister Marie-Marthe has done wonders with the fields; thanks to her harvests, our community is now virtually self-sufficient. We have managed to bank up the slope where our little cemetery was in danger of sliding downhill. Several of our older sisters have died. We have an arrangement with the local school, and the pupils come with their teachers to pick limes and gooseberries, as part of their practical education. They are also learning how to make herb teas and jam. Sister Madeleine and Sister Madeleine-Marie, as you might have guessed, are in charge of this practical work. They are still here, still pillars of our daily life. When we pray for others, you are the one for whom we most often implore God's light.

Can you believe it? Our priest Dureuil, whose sermons were so strict, left the priesthood to get married. Now his wife is dead, and because of his exceptional qualities he has been ordained again and is now a bishop. Which means we have his company sometimes for seminars. He sleeps in the cell you first occupied. His visits remind us of you, for he smokes a pipe and when he leaves we have to put the object that so distressed you back on the table.

Sister Marie-Marthe insists that I include these lines concerning her. She has been through a painful crisis, which the doctors called a nervous breakdown, but which she knew very well was a crisis of vocation. She weathered it, and has become more essential to us than ever.

She wants you to know that because of it she thinks of you with compassion. Even a protracted crisis can be overcome, and it is never too late to return to the bosom of the Church. I should add that her faith has been strengthened by the ordeal, and that, alas, she is soon to leave us, called to higher duties in our order.

Notice, my dear Estelle, that this time I have refrained from inflicting any philosophical or theological ruminations on you!

I have often reproached myself for having been of no help to you. I was new as mistress of novices and did not know how to get beyond the conflict I perceived between us, and we lost you. I have performed several mortifications, and thanks to you I believe I have progressed in humility.

We all wonder what has become of you.

We were deeply hurt that it was your neighbor who called to tell us of your decision. And we were even more wounded that you had decided not to return.

We have not forgotten the tragic circumstances of your departure, the death of the person dear to you, the only one left from your former circle of friends and family, according to your neighbor. Of your circle in the "outside world," dear Estelle, for here we were all around you, and we still are.

We learned from the same source how deeply the death of this woman affected you. And so, my dear Estelle, we made up a prayer for you. Mother Superior wrote the words and I composed the music. We called it "Prayer to Tiresia," and we sing it often.

In this prayer we ask the dead not to pursue the living but to leave them in peace, so that they can forget all attachments and woes here below, and turn their souls toward Him who alone is love and consolation.

The whole community joins me, and it is with this prayer in our heart that we write to you.

Sister Beatrice

FIVE

I Need Your Help So Desperately

I CANNOT write Tiresia's story, madame. I hear the music that these words make, I even hear the words, but when I try to approach them the words no longer resemble the music I hear. They turn into nothing, into little pebbles that fall apart as soon as I put a few of them together.

Tiresia, that veiled woman from my childhood, dressed in black, mute, talked without stopping for five days and five nights, the five days and five nights it took her to die. She slept a little too, as I watched her.

In her weakened condition she could no longer wear her veil. It slipped from her face to the floor beside her bed. I picked it up and she did not ask me to put it back.

I studied her face.

This woman had never been absent from my childhood. Perhaps she had never left my thoughts, yet I had never seen her face.

I had to wash her too, and I saw her belly.

It is important that you understand. We had never touched Tiresia. We had come close to her, she was the one we were closest to, no one in the world was closer to us, yet we did not touch her.

I do not believe anyone, least of all Tiresia, had forbidden it. But from the very first, my brother and I knew everything about her.

Neither of us could have said what we knew, or even that we knew, but Tiresia was inside us.

When I say "from the very first," I mean of course from the first moment of my brother's birth. What came before, my five years of life before him, I do not recall.

We touched our mother Nicole, who was just a pretty girl, blond and tiny, with skin soft as rose petals. Don't laugh, it's what our father used to say: "Nicole's skin is soft as rose petals." In fact there was a rosebush in the garden whose yellow flowers he called Nicole roses. That the rosebush was called Nicole, and that Nicole had rose-petal skin, were for us on the order of revealed truths, and it is too late now for me to subject this truth to the test of my adult scrutiny.

Not because my parents would be older, not that our father would have grown less fanciful or our mother's skin lost its luster, but because they are both dead.

Why they died — our mother Nicole, who was such a lively, pretty girl, and our father, who was scarcely older than I am now — all that is in Tiresia's story.

And Tiresia's story also tells why my brother died, why I survived, madame, and why today I need your help, why today I need your help so desperately.

SIX

The Doctor's Bag

OUR DOCTOR called his bag a reticule. Along with his samovar, it was one of the few belongings he had brought with him from Moscow.

Our doctor was Russian. Exiled with his aunts, he lived for a few years in London, then in Paris, then had settled for good in our town. He wanted a quiet life, patients who were also friends, time to devote to them, time to stay and chat after his calls, to play with the children and stroll around the garden before leaving.

By the time my brother was born, the doctor was already talking about retirement, but he remained our family physician. My father did not want anyone else.

Could have had no one else.

He came by almost daily. At the end of his visits, he and my father would stroll around the garden and talk and talk about things that had happened long ago in the doctor's country and our father's country and in other places. My brother and I loved seeing them walk

like that. "There they go again, conducting Mass," said Nicole, bored
to tears by their talk. But my brother and I enjoyed listening and
watching, and we mimicked them from a distance, walking with our
hands folded behind us, solemnly, not venturing too close. It was
not time for us and we knew it.

Our time came later, back in the house, when we opened the
doctor's bag and he called us his little Pandoras. And meanwhile, he
and my father would go on with their self-deprecating jokes about
their "second-rate" jobs, my father's perennial status as "second coun-
sel" and the doctor's as a "Band-Aid dispenser."

I almost forgot that other source of humor, the doctor's name:
Minor.

"Minor's the word, all right," the doctor would say.

"Not at all," our father protested.

"It's quite true," said our doctor, "what's more, I know my Major."

We assumed vaguely that this Major was some ferocious military
man who had ground our doctor under his boot in one of the wars
he endlessly discussed with our father.

When they were on their after-visit walk in the garden, we kept
our distance, content just to follow, happy and secure. But sometimes
our father and our doctor sought privacy, and then we could neither
follow close nor at a distance. Curiously, they did not shut themselves
in our father's study but in the car, the big gray Citroën, which was
almost always parked in the street outside our front gate. Now and
then one of them would lower a window for some fresh air and then
immediately raise it again. And we would know that they were having
that quarrel of theirs, no echo of which ever reached us.

At such times, everything in the house seemed to congeal, stand
stock-still and silent. Once we thought we saw Tiresia behind the
clump of hydrangeas beside the gate, but when we drew near, across
the lawn, barefoot and silent, there was no one there and we ran,
terrified of being spotted in the rearview mirror.

Another time the car door suddenly opened and Minor leapt out.
"Lies!" he yelled, and the word slammed simultaneously with the
door. We thought the street was going to open up and swallow
the houses, the car, and ourselves. Minor strode furiously away. The
other door opened and our father got out and ran after him, the
black bag in his hand. The doctor turned around, saw what our father
held, and stopped. As if in slow motion we saw our father stretch
out his arm and the doctor stretch out his, and their hands joining
over the bag.

*   *   *

All this must have been when our doctor was thinking of retirement, when their quarrel was at its peak. Perhaps Minor tried to make this official step a pretext for breaking with us, for withdrawing from the quarrel. I don't know. And yet I do know . . .

Minor's young replacement was most thorough and devoted, but I can still see my father coming back up the garden path after walking him to the gate. He stopped on the steps and turned suddenly to me. He was in one of those moods when he seemed to forget I was a child, when he spoke to me as if to an equal, in fact as if to his wife, indeed in a manner that he never adopted with his wife.

"What can you expect?" he said, "it all goes so much deeper . . ."

He moved his hands helplessly.

"Isn't that so? So very much deeper . . ."

"Yes, Papa," I said.

He glanced at me with a nod, his tired features relaxing slightly, with the beginnings of a smile, as if my presence were already a consolation, the comfort of a companion, a trusted friend, no matter how small (although I do not believe he saw me at that moment as a child).

Of course I had no idea what he meant, and yet in a certain sense I was already beyond the need to know.

At these moments a shift occurred, not of time, but of space. My father and I found ourselves in a domain in which we fully understood each other, because in inexplicable ways and along different paths and moving in opposite directions, we had made the same journey.

And then he would move away, and I would become a child again, with a strange tightness in my throat. For in truth I was only a little girl, and I always had to return from that place in which I was a grown-up and my father's closest companion. And then I felt sad and forlorn, felt it without knowing it or being able to say it or complain or weep.

I would go and look for my mother Nicole in the garage she had converted into a dance studio, its walls lined with sky-blue fabric and equipped with a polished wooden bar.

She was almost always to be found in that garage of hers. She had designed it to resemble the sky, and so strong was the power of suggestion that she actually saw the sky there, the purest, most virginal of expanses. Her hair caught up in a ponytail, her feet in ribboned dance slippers, she was light and utterly absorbed, absorbedly dancing, and so very young . . .

I dared not disturb her. In my mud-caked rubber boots, my pleated schoolgirl skirt, my too-tight sweater, I dared not even go in. Soon, very soon, I would be taller and heavier than my mother. She would look like a little girl next to me, she was so tiny. Whereas I was tall, like my father, but unlike him, I was also broad-shouldered.

So I would look for Tiresia.

I never had to go far to find her. She was always somewhere about the house and would appear as soon as I started to seek her. She did not have a study like our father or a dance studio like our mother. She had a piano in the drawing room and her bedroom at the very top of the house, opposite the door to the attic, but she did not linger at the piano or stay in her room. She was always somewhere about the house.

So I found Tiresia, and my sadness at last retreated. She listened to me, looked at me with those dark glasses, her fingers lightly touching my sweater. I was wearing that sweater I complained of, too bulky in the shoulders, the heavy shoes that made me clomp heavily along, and the socks that kept me from looking like a pretty girl, from looking like my mother. And a little later that sweater might disappear and then be returned to me, reknitted in a different style, the style I had described to Tiresia as my ideal sweater. I never saw her at such work, and she never said a word to me. She must have done it in her top-floor room during those long evening hours in our quiet little town when we were with our father and our mother Nicole in the living room after dinner. Her room was a place we never went. I do not remember our parents telling us not to, and yet at some point we could not recall they must have, for we never went to her room, and the idea of doing so never even entered our heads.

The person who altered my sweater could only have been Tiresia. My father never noticed what we wore, nor would we ever have bothered him with such trifling matters. My mother would have shaken her head unconcernedly and said:

"Just take one of my sweaters, Estelle, whichever one you like best."

My mother Nicole was generous, as generous as a bird randomly dropping its pretty feathers. It was just that her sweaters were too delicate for me, would never fit me, and I dreaded hurting her by refusing her gift. Nor did I have the courage to tell her why her sweaters wouldn't do, for that would have obliged her to examine me, obliged her really to see this daughter who lacked her own grace and her own talent, this daughter who would never be a dancer. I was ashamed.

So I found Tiresia and my sadness receded. But it did not leave me altogether. Nobody could really get close to Tiresia. There was an invisible barrier around her that none of us could cross. I could not snuggle up to her, rest my head against her tummy, wrap my arms around her waist. That sort of thing we did with Nicole, although she did not like to be touched. Tiresia, who for us was the very essence of close contact, we never touched. I loved Tiresia with all my heart, but that love had to stay at arm's length.

But of course it was neither my father nor my mother Nicole nor Tiresia I really looked for.

It was my brother.

Only with him could I be truly a child at last, and he all by himself would be my real father, my real mother, and so much more besides.

My tiny little brother, who on that night of my mother's nightmare was just a newborn in his crib.

In my anxiety, in my haste, I am leaving things out, skipping around, confusing things.

I no longer have the needed strength in me, madame. It has been eroded by the sands and downpours of those long lonely childhood hours before my brother arrived, those squalls and downpours that were like the future arriving prematurely, mistaking the time, that future in which my brother would be no more. I am afraid of falling into the sobs I feel splashing deep down within me. I no longer possess the simple steely strength my father tried to instill in me, the strength I long considered part of my very nature. It was my father who inspired me to study law, and my inner strength helped me dedicate myself steadfastly to that pursuit. I believed in those studies. They allowed me to believe in a world of justice in which aberrations and horrors were but accidents you could observe and limit and even prevent.

That purposeful strength has left me. All I can do is move forward as fast as possible, in sporadic surges as unpredictable as the waves. Only speed can save me. And perhaps at the end of my forward flight I will find solid ground and will be able to slow down. I long to slow down, and sometimes I can almost imagine it. But I dare not even glance at such a hope, for looking at it would destroy it. I must act as if the hope did not exist, avoid training upon it my inner gaze that frightens even me. If I can do all that, perhaps one day I will be granted a measure of slowness, the ability to live at peace in the present, as well as another love or something, if such a thing is possible, that might resemble a love.

The doctor suddenly set his bag against the wall. The old creased leather bag he called his reticule, and because of which he called us his little Pandoras . . .

Madame, madame, let me go on talking about the doctor's bag. I know I am clinging to it so as to put off the moment of return to my mother's nightmare. How can I return to my mother's nightmare without that bag of the doctor's? It meant so much to us, his "reticule." It protected us. I now hear so many meanings in that word . . .

All this was later, of course, when my brother was already walking.

The doctor would pretend to scold us, to keep us away from his bag. He spoke of grave dangers, of caged microbes, viruses in irons, bacteria in cells. "Worse than any zoo, children, this bag, worse than any prison." It made us howl with laughter. We listened delightedly to the litany of tortures he said were visited on these pathogens. As soon as he had finished talking about them all, he allowed us to open his bag, sighing, throwing up his hands, calling us naughty little Pandoras.

And I used to think that the "little Pandoras" he saw in us were small mountain goats with hard little horns.

Little goats foraging for the candies hidden amid the thickets of syringes and thermometers on some ledge of a steep cliff to which only the good doctor could give us access.

Now that old creased bag of our doctor's sits squarely in front of me, demanding all my attention. An enigmatic object, commonplace yet terribly strange.

I have already encountered this kind of object.

In a picture, floating in midcanvas, I see a small crate, just an apple crate built with ordinary strips of wood — yet all of a sudden this thought comes to me: "ordinary strips of wood, just like the planks of a coffin." It was an art opening in Paris, my brother was still back in the first room. I worked my way back to him and told him I wanted to leave. "But I haven't seen the rest, Estelle." "There's nothing to see, Dan." And we turned right around and left the gallery. "Where are you going?" shouted Vlad, following us out into the street. "We've been called away," my brother answered, pulling me along faster. Late that night Vlad phoned; he was angry. "Who was calling you?" he demanded. "Happiness," my brother said, and unlike Adrien, who would be infuriated by that kind of answer, Vlad roared with laughter. "You're so unpredictable," he said as he hung up. *And that remark cheered us up, madame, as if being unpredictable might be a desirable asset. As if we needed assets to help us outwit fate, but had so far simply groped blindly forward . . .*

I see a photo, taken by one of Dan's friends in New York. It shows a row of jars on a windowsill, just a photo of some jars. But I think my soul is trapped in them, and I am reminded of those human fetuses preserved in formaldehyde on a dusty shelf in our city museum in G.: they never showed them to us during our school visits, but we knew they were there, and we always managed to sneak back to them, their huge closed white eyes mesmerized us . . .

SEVEN

"Run Away Now!"

THE DOCTOR set his bag against the wall, sank to his knees, took both my hands in his, and in a voice I did not recognize, an old man's voice, infinitely sad and pitying, he said:

"Forgive me, little one."

In the gloom of the corridor, he looked deep into my eyes as if he detected behind my child's gaze a deep knowledge that was already there, knowledge that he himself had perhaps put there, but could no longer bring to light.

Suddenly he raised my two hands to his lips and planted a kiss on them. Then he closed my hands as if to enfold within them the imprint of that kiss, to leave it with me as a talisman. And for a moment, a moment that seemed like an eternity, that seemed to cover all the years we had known each other, all the years of my childhood, he kept his forehead pressed against my clasped hands.

In later years to come, whenever I did not know which way to turn, I would cup my hands and stare intently at them. I had the mad idea that if I did it suddenly, at a moment when the powers that be were not paying attention, it might take me back in time to that moment when our doctor nearly said something to me, or I nearly heard it.

Later still I would do the same thing but with a different goal. Cupping my hands, I would stare at the bowl they formed, and it would seem to me that a little of my bitterness trickled into it. When I felt that it was full I opened my hands and that was that. I could resume life's activities. More recently, I have surprised myself performing the same gesture, but now it is to catch the strength I finally feel welling and bubbling up about me.

I have never really tried to shake off these strange compulsions. Sometimes I fear that they will drive other people away from me, that they will even alarm me and thus lose their power, degenerating into dead and repugnant rituals. But the years have washed over me, slowly wearing away the layers that separate us from others, almost wearing them through in places, and I have come to realize that when all is said and done, strange behavior is everywhere. It sometimes affects an appearance of normality, but if you look just a little deeper you will see that it too is a matter of strange compulsions, scarcely more surprising than my absorption in my cupped hands.

Suddenly the doctor picked up his bag and rose. He pushed me impatiently aside. "Run away now!" he said. "Off you go!"

My father stood in the doorway.

"Minor, thank you for coming. I shouldn't have bothered you . . ."

"You did the right thing," said the doctor, walking past him.

My father noticed me.

"Run away now," he said. His tone was one of cold command, as at times of emergency or danger.

"Run away now." Ever since that night, when those three words surface in the present — and they are never far away, an acute pang in my memory — I feel a faint fluttering inside me. Sometimes I think I hear "Run away now" as "Run along," the way the doctor meant it, and sometimes it is the other meaning I hear, the warning, clear as a bell in my father's voice: "You are in danger, my child, take care!"

* * *

I went to my room and then — despite the raging storm, and my
mother's screams breaking every now and then through the gusts as
if great whirling birds had suddenly been struck down by the wind,
and the clattering of shutters against their metal frames, and the
ceaseless creaking of the giant chestnut trees, and the terrifying commotion engendered within me by the storm and my mother's screams
and the shutters and the trees and the words tossed about among
them — despite all this, I heard my little brother.

No sound came from his room, yet I knew with the utmost certainty that he was crying. I saw his eyes wide open in the dark, and
his distress was within me. I was suddenly my brother, alone in that
crib as if at the bottom of a vast black well.

No logic could undermine the power of that feeling: in that moment, I was my brother, my brother was in me.

When I reached his crib his eyes were turned toward me like two
reflections at the bottom of the dark well. They looked exactly as I
had imagined them, wide open and brimming with a storm-tossed
water suddenly welling up through the hidden fissures of the house
and filling him with terror.

I raised him delicately and held him to me, supporting his head,
and I felt his body mold itself to mine as if he recognized it, as if
that were just what he had been waiting for and why he had come
to this earth. At once we both grew calm. I stood there perfectly
still with my little brother held tight against me, while outside the
storm raged and inside doors slammed, people screamed, and feet
raced down corridors.

On my child's breast an indelible mark was imprinted, the mark of
my brother's body. I felt a whirlwind of still unformed and unfamiliar
forces seeking one another, seeking for a channel to the surface. I
felt my nipples on my flat child's breast. Sensing my brother's presence, my nipples had risen like antennae, they would never acknowledge anyone but him. And my brother's breast would always seek
mine, seek to mold itself to mine, to crush itself on mine, and his
head would always seek rest in the hollow of my neck, our fused
bodies vigilant as we listened together to the pulse of that strange
life.

EIGHT

The Dream Conductor

*I*T WAS a dream," my father said on the morrows of night-mares.

I did not know whether he meant Nicole's night or mine.

Many storms, many dreams. They certainly did not all take place at once, but I have mixed them all indissolubly together.

Dreams roamed the skies above our part of the country, some-times descending savagely upon us.

"What are dreams?" I asked my father.

"They are storms inside our heads," he said.

So why did we not have a conductor to ward off dreams?

From afar, filtering through walls, came the sound of the record player our mother used for dancing, almost always Ravel's *Bolero*. Joyous, unfettered, Nicole was dancing in her garage.

"Dreams come and go, like storms, you know," said my father, his face haggard with fatigue. I still did not know whether he meant Nicole or me.

"What attracts dreams?" I asked.

I could see the black rod of the lightning conductor high on our roof.

"What attracts dreams?" my father echoed worriedly.

There are black rods in houses that attract dreams the way lightning conductors attract storms. That was what I replied to my father, who said hastily, almost stumbling over the words:

"Yes, but like lightning conductors they protect us too."

And Tiresia, who until then had been seated (something in the way she sat also suggested extreme fatigue), stood up.

Her black, upright, sequestered shape, suddenly rearing up inside our house . . .

She walked away.

We listened, unbelieving, to the sounds from the entranceway.

She left the house. Soon we would hear the squeak of the garden gate, the small side gate that opened onto the deserted stretch of road leading to the cemetery or the hills.

"I really must oil those hinges," my father muttered.

He stood a little back from the window, looking out.

"How do they protect us?"

But my father could no longer answer. He was down on the road where Tiresia was disappearing from view, and now the words he tossed out at my insistent questions were hollow as soap bubbles. They too would vanish on contact with the skin. They would not feed me, they would let me starve.

Again we were alone. My little brother huddled against me. He too wanted to hear what kind of lightning rod would protect us from nightmares, he too had seen Tiresia rise and leave through the garden gate, he too had seen our father turn as transparent as mist before our eyes. And like me he heard the notes of the record player, stripped of their flesh by distance and repetition, hollow notes carrying through walls to let us know that down in her pale blue garage our mother pursued her dream of an immaterial invulnerable body that the most relentless nightmare on earth could never harm, of an arabesque faultless in the infinite blue of the sky.

Tiresia did not come back. Our father shut himself in his study, our mother continued her exercises, dinner hour was long forgotten. My brother and I went to the kitchen.

First we listened in the hall, not breathing, unsure of the evening's lines of force, watchful for disturbances and doing our best to anticipate them. But no new development seemed to be afoot. The garden gate did not squeak, our father's footfalls did not sound in the corridor, the little hollow notes we knew so well went on gasping for air as they filtered through walls, and soon we were reassured.

Nobody would be wondering about us tonight.

Then we went into the kitchen, silently closing the door and pushing home the small bolt positioned near the floor. It was hard to work, because we were the only ones who used it and it was not kept in working order. In fact it had almost certainly been forgotten. But this bolt was our height, I mean my brother's height, and it was small, as if it had been made for us, perhaps by the invisible beings Nicole believed in. Unless they bent down, grown-ups would not see it.

It moved only a fraction of an inch. Perhaps it did not really cross the gap between door and wall; perhaps it did not really enter the tiny bolt hole on the other side. Yet to us it seemed as strong as the soundest of bolts.

Once we had forced our little bolt home, we felt safe, together in our own home.

And suddenly we were happy.

My brother had the maddest ideas. He would give me orders and I — staggered by his boldness and at once experiencing it as my own — obeyed.

I stood firmly on my brother's boldness, as I might stand on the solid bottom of a boat. And since I no longer had to seek that solid bottom on which to plant my feet, I too experienced a kind of boldness, untrammeled, assured, and I was able to focus all my attention on carrying out my brother's orders.

I went about it effortlessly, for in the momentum he gave me, movements came unbidden, movements observed in grown-ups in the kitchen, as if my brother's wish were all that was required for them to take up residence in me.

He wanted me to break eggs, and although I had never done it I knew how. He wanted me to make "grated cheese" with chocolate, so I found the grater and the chocolate and scraped away until my knuckles were raw, until my brother decided the fine brown scrolls were heaped high enough on their silvery foil wrapper. And then, although it was strictly forbidden, I turned on the gas and lit the burner under the pan.

My brother wanted the biggest one, the one that was never used because it was not really a pan at all but a tray our mother had bought to decorate the wall. Then of course she had given up the search for a nail to hang it up, and the tray had remained on a shelf. But she liked to stare mesmerized at the deep golden glow of the copper. "Look, look." "Look at what, Nicole?" "The way it shines." "Yes, Nicole." "How cheerful it makes this house," she said.

Cheerful?

That had not occurred to us.

Sometimes Tiresia took the tray off its shelf to clean it with a curiously evil-smelling product.

As if aroused by this smell our father would appear. He would look at Tiresia and her fine hands, stained black by the loathsome product. She went on rubbing with an expression that we did not understand but that seemed to be of the same color as the product and to have the same curious smell. As if at that moment Tiresia were in the power of a genie who dwelt in the bottle, as if she were obliged to rub away endlessly at that copper, which was already too bright for the faded paint of our kitchen.

"No!" our father said.

And Tiresia stopped, as if suddenly coming back to her senses.

"No," said our father, "that isn't work for you."

She raised her face to him and they seemed to be challenging each other. What did our father see behind Tiresia's veil and dark glasses? And what did she see of him from the other side of that veil and those glasses?

A moment later she put the tray down. Our father hesitated, then took it, rinsed it quickly under the faucet, looked for a cloth, still hesitating in these unfamiliar kitchen surroundings — out of pure carelessness, Nicole was constantly moving things around — and then he dried the shining object with the acrid smell and replaced it on its shelf.

"Good," he said, looking at Tiresia, "good."

Then he said:

"I just don't want you to do that, look at your hands."

And he turned to us:

"Tiresia has lovely hands, hasn't she, children?"

We concurred. We thought Tiresia's long white hands were lovely indeed, particularly when flying over the keyboard and making the keys leap like a tiny ballet company in full cry and seething, over-flowing to comic degree with energy. But how long was it since she had put on such a display for us?

"Go and play the piano," he said very softly, almost fearfully. "Please . . . I would like to hear you in my study."

A murmur.

"Please, I would like to hear you in my study." That meant, as we very clearly understood, "I can't stand that other music, the music from the record player, I want real music, music from our grand piano, the music only you can play."

Our father still hesitated. He was out of place in this kitchen, and we felt that something was prowling inside him like a restive beast he could not tame. It worried us, his feeble disciples, the ones who relied on him to adjudicate good and evil, to bring about the defeat of evil and the victory of good. So my brother and I strained bodily toward him, offering him all we possessed in the way of strength, and he felt the succor radiating from us.

A gentle breeze seemed to ruffle his face and soften his features, and his voice became once again the voice we loved, kindly, somewhat amused, evenly pitched.

"Why don't you make them a cake, Tiresia?" he said.

Tiresia's reaction was striking. She threw back her head in a pose in which we suddenly saw, as plainly as could be, as if in a photo from some glorious past, the outline of a beautiful woman, acclaimed and loved. How clairvoyant were our children's eyes! Quite unwittingly, we were permanently aware of another Tiresia behind the black-veiled one who lived with us.

That fleeting image sped by like a benevolent spirit, sowing in its wake the gentle impalpable seeds of solace.

"A cake!" my brother shouted delightedly, throwing his arms around my waist and burying his face in my tummy as if unable to believe in such happiness.

"Ha-ha!" cried my father in the manner of an inventor finally stumbling on his great discovery.

And as if tickled by that voice my brother wriggled even harder.

"But you know I always burn cakes," said Tiresia in that strange voice, veiled like her face. It did not sound like a voice meant to carry words but a wounded crystal on which the echoes of another world still tinkled, echoes that she alone could monitor and that we heard in her voice always.

All through our childhood, we heard those echoes in the wounded crystal of Tiresia's voice, tinkling around us as if in a fog, mysteriously shifting position. We had no idea what they meant, but an alarm system that was within us and that never left us homed in on those echoes, until the day they fell almost utterly silent, and then we still had her body to home in on.

"I burn cakes," Tiresia said again with that almost joyful astonishment that occasionally seized her and that made us joyful in our turn.

Now I know the meaning of that astonishment that filled her with simple and unhoped-for happiness. It was astonishment at hearing her voice carry words, ordinary everyday words. Her voice could do that, could be an innocent tin pail carrying sentences as good and as wholesome as milk!

"A burnt cake!" shouted my brother with tenfold enthusiasm, rolling his eyes and clutching at me as if overcome with vertigo.

He was so funny then that my father started to laugh, and that laugh of our father's, which was so rare, drove us wild. My brother swarmed over me like a little monkey, I grabbed him and set him astraddle around my waist, but he bounded upward and molded himself to my chest. I staggered beneath his weight, yet I too was stronger in that moment because he was my shield and breastplate, and one day my breast would seek out this haven, would nestle against it, would be unable to exist without its sheltering walls.

Tiresia started to busy herself in that kitchen, deftly groping for the articles she needed. We helped her, and very soon we too were at work. My father watched the confusion, sighed, ran water over his hands, and left.

Then Tiresia's movements slowed.

We felt that a kind of chill had entered the kitchen. The stove's extrovert warmth had retreated, shrunk back into the oven, where it did no more than mechanically obey the temperature-control buttons. Every article seemed to have returned prudently within itself, inside the bounds ordinarily assigned it. The silvery chocolate wrapping no longer had its magic-star glitter, it had the wrinkled shabby look of something destined for the waste bin, dried egg white clung to the bowl, flour caked the tabletop.

Despite the heat, the kitchen had that chilled feel we were familiar with, for this was not the first time.

My brother sucked his thumb, my heart thudded, distress once more had hold of us.

I tried to ward off that distress, kicking up a racket, rattling the whisk against the sides of the bowl containing the egg whites. If Tiresia happened to notice, if she asked me not to be so rough, showed me how the glaze on the bowl was getting chipped, it would mean we still had a chance of holding on to her, keeping her and the kitchen's real warmth here with us. But it seldom worked.

Tiresia gave us a few vague directions, then left.

We listened to her steps. When we could no longer hear them, I ran to shut the door.

My chief concern, my enormous concern, was to keep my brother from falling into the cold lake of distress that had risen around us.

I was uncertain what to do. The kitchen suddenly seemed the seat of a chaos beyond the two of us. I thought longingly of our neighbors' maid Nanou, who sometimes came over to give us a hand (I know today that she was sent by them). It must have been Adrien who sounded the alarm. He was our age, I mean younger than I was and older than my brother, exactly in between. He was often in our house, watching everything with a cold and critical eye. But I could not get Nanou to come over all on my own.

For our father must not be allowed to know that Tiresia had left us in the midst of preparing the cake, that the seeming enthusiasm she had shown in his presence had little by little died after he left, and that the combined strengths of us children had been inadequate to rekindle that enthusiasm.

Our father must not know; of that Dan and I were in tacit but total agreement. But if asked why, we would have been unable to answer; we did not even know that that was what we wanted. And if I think back and ask myself, "Why were you so anxious to keep this thing from your father, so anxious not to let him know that Tiresia had left you alone in the midst of the little party he himself had set in motion?" I would of course find answers, since I now know everything that was hidden from us at the time. But behind all those possible answers there is only one.

I wanted a ring of warmth and well-being for my brother, I wanted no horror to intrude on the territory he occupied. It seems to me that I never stopped struggling, never stopped overturning situations in order to maintain a kind of warm and gentle glow around him, but no doubt I was too anxious, too mechanical.

For in the end it was he, my tiny tiny brother, who rescued us from the distress I sought to spare him.

It was as if he dwelt at the wellspring of my being, in the place where real desires took shape, and that he leapt outward from that wellspring, swiftly and unerringly, to accomplish what I was still struggling to understand.

When I think of it now, tears scald me. If only I could weep, could hurl out tears like a bucket of slops and with them some of my rage. But I know they will remain there, around my eyes, refusing to flow, and tomorrow and for days after that my face will be strangely swollen.

My brother was at the wellspring of my being. Now that he is no longer there, the spring is tainted, choked with rotting vegetation.

Then he began to hop about in the deserted kitchen, rattling everything he could lay his hands on, giving me outlandish orders with comical authority and determination. I was too worried to perceive the source of this comical vein, but it made me laugh till I cried. It was reassuring, and the relief it brought allowed my laughter to escape.

Never since have I laughed the way I laughed with my brother. If I could have that laugh back . . . I could also sleep. I could live.

My little brother was a mimic. He mimicked the members of our household, our doctor, but also our neighbors: Adrien, his parents, their maid Nanou, as well as people we had only glimpsed, our father's clients, for instance, and the creatures he had seen in our picture books or in my history books. He could mimic everything, but he hopped so quickly from one expression to another that you had no time — or at least I, so much slower, duller, more earnest, had no time — to identify the model.

Hearing these cries, warmth once more leapt from the stove and spread through the kitchen. The chocolate's silvery wrapping forgot the waste bin and glittered like a star, the pots and pans clattered merrily in our unskilled hands. With Tiresia no longer there to guide us, my brother wanted to stir everything up together, everything that was not too hard, too dry, or too inaccessible. He blended it all with a sure instinct, for despite our ignorance and our clumsiness we ended up producing what looked like a cake, which we then took in solemn procession to show our father.

We merely showed it to him, the two of us standing in the half-open door of his study, "Tiresia's cake, Papa." He was by now deep in his work, and we were almost sure of not being caught. He looked up, "Splendid," he said, "save a big slice for me," "Yes, Papa," we said, already beating a retreat, "And shut the door," he added. No need to worry, the big slice was already forgotten.

Then we went out onto the front steps with our cake.

Adrien appeared. He had been spying on us from his garden.

"Disgusting," he said after one mouthful. Whereupon we instantly decided to eat it. Furious, Adrien watched as we sat side by side chewing our cake, in the peace of short-lived relief.

I thought I was rescuing my brother, but he was always the one who rescued me.

And now, as I prepare for a rendezvous with the man who is not my brother, perhaps he will again be the one to rescue me.

Yet I resented him so bitterly. My hatred was as powerful as my love. Even now, so many years later, in the midst of my love for him

I feel hatred rising like molten lava, burning the love all around it, leaving it charred and black.

I hate my brother for living and then abandoning me. I hate him for retiring from the world and leaving me on this stupid planet where I know neither how nor where to turn.

But perhaps he was merely rescuing me yet again. Perhaps I had to make contact with both these extremes, with this limitless love and this utter absence of love, in order to stand at midpoint between the two, in order to fulfill my life on this planet the way it is commonly fulfilled in the age I now live in.

I shall not mention my brother to Phil, to this man who is not my brother, and I shall change my name. I shall no longer be Estelle, the name my mother Nicole chose, which means star, and which in her mind meant star ballerina.

I will be anonymous, a piece of flesh manufactured by the age and dimly reflecting it, mingling with all the others, squeezed against them in the press of subway, traffic jam, and sidewalk.

Philippe, a name like any other. I call him Phil because then I hear "friend," yes, and also because I hear "fill." And in this age it seems to suit love in the age and to suit me the way I am today. A friendship that is only filling in time.

Phil sent me a cassette in the mail after our bike ride. I was pleased that he made this second contact. On the cassette were songs he had recorded for me, songs he had been surprised to hear I did not know. I did not tell him that I had not listened to music with anyone for years and years. I make do with what my little pupils play — and they can barely tell one note from another when I correct a piece for them.

It is music of the age, just filling in time, no doubt.

I shall listen to his cassette. I shall talk to him about it in a friendly way. Another way of filling in time.

NINE

"Smell . . . Tell . . . Estelle"

TIRESIA had put out a plate of pastries. Nicole had her deeply bored look. She was wearing the dress she disliked, a navy blue schoolgirl dress.

The day after our mother had a nightmare — how many nightmares and how many next days there were! I remember the first one, after my brother was born. And I also remember this particular one.

"This is just wonderful," she said grumpily to me. "All these people coming, and to think it's such a beautiful day and I could be dancing with the doors wide open!"

Our father looked worried.

"They're our neighbors," he said to me, "we have to ask them over, you understand, don't you, Estelle?"

My father and my mother explained things to me in turn, and I listened first to one, then the other, giving each my full, careful attention. Then I went to help Tiresia, and we brought in trays and placed them around the room. Absorbed and silent, I rushed back and forth between the kitchen and living room. I can still feel that strain in my neck; it did not come from the trays we were carrying.

At one point, Tiresia leaned over and stroked my cheek, and instantly the two of us were sitting at the piano. Oh, how happy our fingers were on the long row of white keys, keys flying up to meet fingers, literally bearing them aloft, each key slipping a finger onto its back and taking wing like wild geese bearing Nils Holgerson away. We played, Tiresia and I, amid those rustling wings and that gentle honking, soaring up into the wide spring sky.

And Nicole, who had been moping about, all at once skipped up the stairs as if she too were carried away by the exuberance of the music.

In no time at all she was running back down the stairs and whirling around the room. We stopped playing and watched her.

Nicole had changed clothes, and was now wearing a real party dress, oh, I see it so clearly, Nicole's yellow paneled dress, the top panel sweeping from one shoulder to the other, her waist caught in a wide belt of the same fabric, a grosgrain belt, she explained to me, with a big knot whose ends fell lower than the hem of her skirt, a skirt made of two or three overlapping panels.

"Nicole," my father exclaimed, "you look like a butterfly!"

His voice was suddenly full of joy. From then on we called it his butterfly voice. We heard in it the fluttering of countless tiny, downy wings in a bubble of light, wings that must have tickled his throat, for in his voice we also heard a little laugh. Then Nicole ran to Tiresia, dropped to her knees, and passionately kissed the hem of her skirt.

"This is the dress Tiresia wore for her first concert," Nicole announced very loudly, as if she wanted to launch her words into the sky and there record them on a vast undulating banner that would float forever above our house, "the dress she wore for her very first concert. And she had it altered for me. Do you hear, Estelle, for *me?*"

And my father said with a quiver in his voice:

"Well, in that case I'm going to put on my white suit."

He dashed to the staircase. Stopping halfway, with tears in his eyes, he said to me:

"You see, Estelle, my ladies are so beautiful, I have to look my best to be worthy of them."

And he took the stairs four at a time to hide the emotion that had caught him by surprise. How young my father was at that moment, going up the stairs four at a time, how impetuous he could be . . .

Now I see him coming back down in that white suit that suddenly made him so different.

"Oh!" gasped Nicole, "you look like a camellia!"

"A camellia?" said my father, and I saw a blush rise to his cheek.

"Yes, a camellia," Nicole replied, louder than ever, and she too blushed.

It confused and worried me to see my father and mother blush. My father noticed and scooped me up in his arms.

"I may look like a camellia, Estelle, but I'm still your papa."

Nicole shrieked with high-pitched, nervous laughter. "Your papa!" she tittered.

My father hugged me.

"Nicole!" he said, reproachfully.

"Sorry." Nicole hung her head and pouted, but it lasted only a moment. "What about Estelle?" she suddenly exclaimed.

"What about her?"

"She can't stay dressed that way!"

"Oh!" said my father. "You're right."

I heard the instant relief in his voice, and from the way he hugged me I felt he was grateful to me for existing. I existed to bring him relief during those eerie moments that sometimes swept over us like sudden winds, stifling or icy, gusting in from foreign lands, eerie breezes wafting in whispers and secrets from unknown territory.

I so wanted to be that Estelle, to be the one who comforted our father on this strange, unpredictable path we traveled.

"Yes indeed," said my father, setting me back down with exaggerated ceremony, "if Nicole is wearing Tiresia's first concert dress and I am wearing the white suit I wore to my graduation, then Estelle too must have a dress. But do we have a special dress for her?"

Tiresia knew of one.

She went to her room, where we never went, and after a while returned with a voile dress with ruffles and pink feathers, a frothy cloud of a dress, which she shook out to restore its fluffiness.

"Oh," said Nicole, "I haven't seen that one before."

"I was so slim then," said Tiresia's hands as they slipped the dress over my head, "it will almost fit her."

"It's funny," my father said, "I never saw either of those two dresses before."

"Hah," said Tiresia's look, "there are many things you don't know."

"After all," said my mother, "you weren't always there; it's a dress from before your time."

Meanwhile, Tiresia was pinning the dress at my waist and tightening the wide belt, which, like Nicole's yellow one, was also of grosgrain. I cannot forget the word because I did not understand it. Sometimes I thought it referred to sprouting seeds, but surely that could not apply to such a beautiful dress. So the word dangled like a question mark from those two wide belts. Perhaps that is why I have not forgotten a single detail of that scene. And the dress looked good on me.

"Why, Estelle's a young woman already!" said my father.

The dress enveloped me like a cloud, slowing every movement I made.

I felt I was the handmaiden of the person wearing that dress. It gave me a curious sense of dignity — and of sadness, for now there were two of us, one only a handmaiden, and the other someone I was meeting for the first time, someone who intimidated me. But I desired her, because she too was me.

My father kissed Tiresia's hand, then he offered his arm to that hand of Tiresia's and led her ceremoniously forward among the chairs that sat scattered in pools of light flooding in through windows open for the first time since winter. Tiresia too wore an evening gown, a long dress of dark red taffeta.

But was that really possible? We had always perceived Tiresia as someone dressed in black. Could we have been mistaken? Had we endowed her clothes and her veil with what we sensed inside her?

I still see that red-purple dress, vivid enough to be incongruous in the feather-light springtime glow. Tiresia's gait was regal. She was used to long dresses, she paced with care so as not to trip on the folds.

"You look just like a queen," Nicole said wistfully, "and I'll never be anything but a butterfly."

"But when you dance, Nicole," said my father, "when you dance, you're the queen!"

Nicole burst out laughing. In those days it took so little to make her laugh.

What tickled her now was the idea of our neighbors stumbling in on this midafternoon costume ball, clutching their flowerpot offering. Mr. Neighbor would be sporting his turtleneck — "trying to look countrified," according to Nicole — and Mrs. Neighbor would be "just out of her curlers" (again according to Nicole, who often had her very own expressions). She spluttered with mirth, laughing so hard she burst the yellow taffeta belt.

"Ooohhh!" she cried in what sounded like ecstasy.

"What is it?" we all wanted to know.

"Wee-wee! Look!"

I looked, and was astonished to see a little yellow puddle under the yellow dress, next to the yellow belt, which had dropped to the floor. Nicole laughed again.

And at that precise moment, our neighbor's hairless skull went by outside the window. "They're here," my father hissed in panic. Tiresia dashed to the kitchen, Nicole fled to the bathroom, and my father hurried to the front door.

Bearing their spindly potted offering, our neighbors were almost upon us. Inside the living room, whose windows we had thrown open to let in the garden air, we all stood waiting, like great hothouse blooms swaying over the small puddle. Our neighbors trooped in, plant in hand and Adrien in tow. He carried a bag of sweets, a present for me. Seizing me by the hand, my father leapt forward to head off their advance.

"How elegant you look!" said Mr. Neighbor.

"Oh no," said my father, "but this was my first real suit, the one I wore to my graduation. It's too small for me, but the ladies . . ."

"Are you sure we aren't disturbing you?" said Mr. Neighbor.

"No, no," said my father, "on the contrary . . ."

"You make us look like bumpkins!" said our neighbor's wife. "I kept telling my husband, good taste matters to these neighbors of ours — but you know what he's like, determined to play the country squire . . . As for Adrien, it's just impossible to get him to dress decently, what a ragamuffin, not like your young miss here . . ."

From behind his mother Adrien stuck his tongue out at me. My father stood in the doorway with the potted plant in his hand, rooted to the spot as if terrified that our visitors would push past us into the living room. I caught his entreating glances and slipped past him, holding up the hem of my tulle dress (Adrien laughed sneeringly), to see how Nicole and Tiresia were coming along. Seeing that they had finished wiping up the puddle, I dashed back to the doorway, delighted to be the bearer of the good news my father craved. I tugged at his coat, and at once he turned and came into the room, with the neighbors on his heels and Adrien bringing up the rear.

Nicole sat in the little low armchair she adored, her dress spread around her. In that tiny chair with its invisible armrests, with those huge panels lying open about her, she now looked like a big yellow rose in full bloom. "Nicole roses," my father used to call them, because of the yellow rosebush in our garden. She wore the solemn expression of a little girl smothering laughter and trying to behave.

Tiresia sat as usual in her big chair by the rear window, dimly lit
from behind, Stygian in the blackness of her chair.

No, I am wrong: it is the days following this one, the long procession
of days following it, which now weigh on this particular day, rough-
shaping it to fit their own meaning.

In fact Tiresia was not wearing her black dress, nor was she seated
in the chair with her back to the light. She leaned like a tall rose
against the grand piano, the folds of her dress cascading to her feet.
For Tiresia too looked like a rose, a tall purple rose, tall and straight
against the black of the piano. And what about her veil? Was it too
dark red? Suddenly I see a red spotted veil with a velvet strip, itself
deep red, pinned to a small hat and wound around her neck. But
am I dreaming all this? I can no longer ask Tiresia, nor our father
nor our mother, nor of course can I ask Dan.

"Go and play with Estelle," said our neighbor.

But Adrien refused.

"No one can play with a girl dressed like that," he said.

"Why can't you behave, Adrien?" his mother scolded, and no one
knew what else to say.

Then Tiresia went to the piano and played a short passage from
Ravel's *Bolero*. Our mother slid to the floor and curled up like a bud.
Then she very slowly unfolded and arose, her whole body straining
upward, her gaze turned to the sky outside as she danced a short
passage from her own dance, utterly absorbed, without a thought for
our neighbors, while Tiresia went on playing softly, almost chastely,
while my father looked on, himself absorbed and oblivious to our
visitors.

Adrien was staring hard at me, and I knew what that black stare
said. "You little fool," it said, "you're all crazy here, and the only
reason we're staying a little while longer is my parents are polite —
if it was just me I'd have been out of here long ago. To think I could
have been in the cemetery kicking a ball around with Alex." And I
stiffened inside my tulle dress. How I wished it could have whisked
me from the ground like an ascending rocket and removed me from
his sight!

Then our neighbor cleared his throat and formulated a compliment,
and his wife followed suit. Our mood of near-intoxication (like
breezes blowing in on us from unknown lands, sometimes the bearers

of crippling heat, sometimes of mists and cold spells, and always the bearers of strange inexplicable sounds) slowly faded. Nicole fell back into her low armchair, smoothing the panels of her dress. The piano lid came down. And my father and our neighbor were back in their usual argument about the failures of our local government and the continued existence of that dangerous back road to the cemetery, so tempting as a shortcut. Tiresia brought in the pastries, and Adrien suddenly looked less rebellious.

"That dress is okay," he said between mouthfuls, "but it wouldn't do for soccer."

"It isn't my dress," I said, "I was only trying it on to show my mother."

"Your mother's beautiful," said Adrien, "more beautiful than mine. But she's weird."

"No she isn't," I said.

"Yes she is. My parents say so too."

"She is not weird," I repeated despairingly. "You've never been around a dancer, that's all."

And Adrien went on:

"Anyway, she's the most beautiful woman in town, my father says so. You're weird too, but I think you're also the most beautiful girl in town."

Looking important and serious — the way he would look almost constantly in adulthood — he went on: "Anyway, your father's doing pretty well, your house is bigger than ours, even though we belong here and you don't."

Once again we had survived. Out on the garden steps our neighbors said good-bye to our parents, and my father walked them to the gate at the bottom of the path. They all shook hands again, then we realized that Adrien had disappeared.

"Where is Adrien, Estelle?"

"He left earlier to play soccer," I said.

"The little rascal, he must have escaped through the hole in the wall beneath the lilac," said his mother.

"No," I said, "I opened the side gate for him."

"We really must fix that gap," said his father.

"Yes," said my father, "we'll have to fix it. Although it doesn't bother me, you know . . . anyway, whenever you like."

"Doesn't bother us either . . . But whenever you like," said our neighbors.

Everything was fine, goodwill on both sides had dispersed those breezes blowing in from afar . . . (They had of course blown in, but our neighbors had pretended not to notice them and the winds had died down quicker than they had arisen. The town had accepted us, we had passed the test fairly well.)

And Adrien would be my ally on the morrow at school because I had kept quiet when he slipped out through the hole in the wall beneath the lilac. When Tiresia came to get me and the other children started to jeer, "Here comes the witch," Adrien punched them and told them to shut up. She wasn't a witch, he said, but my mother. "Then she has two mothers!" the others said. "How dumb you are," answered Adrien in his most scathing voice. "When you're too dumb to understand, you should just keep your mouth shut."

Yes, we had survived yet again, despite the breezes blowing in from so far away. On this day, for reasons accessible only to them, those breezes had chosen to transform us into enormous flowers — Tiresia a purple rose, Nicole a yellow rose, our father a white camellia, and their daughter Estelle a cloud of pink petals.

When I returned from school our house would still be standing there under the sky. Deep inside the house I would hear my father's voice in measured conversation with a client in his study. From the garage would come the patter of Nicole's ballet slippers. Tiresia would release my hand, and soon I would hear her too, hear her at the piano, and there they would all be, whole and alive, the musical accents that were a part of the soul of our house. And in later times, even after Tiresia had permanently ceased to play, I would still hear her when I came home from school. I would stop outside our house and at once be alerted to Tiresia's presence, a presence that would always be Tiresia's, in some mysterious fashion carrying the whole house. There it would be, whole and alive, and I could walk up the path, climb the steps, cross the patio, and go inside to where my brother waited for me . . .

Madam —

My mind is drifting across time zones, getting snagged on disconnected moments. I meant to mention the apple tree in the meadow and my brother crawling toward the apple tree, but then those dresses swam into my vision . . . I am helpless to resist such digressions, but they must have a reason for occurring.

Nothing is false . . .

          *   *   *

Madame —
 I hear the rustle of those dresses, Nicole's yellow dress, Tiresia's purple dress, and the rustle of that apple tree and my brother crawling through the bright grass.
 That is true music.
 Different moments can be part of the same music . . .

Madame —
 Sequence of events, probability . . . how difficult it all is!
 Forgive me for rambling in this way, but I am sure you will be able to make the connection . . .

Our neighbors had come in with their wilted plant. Tiresia sat in her chair, her face in the half-light. My father and our neighbor sat discussing local affairs. In her low armchair Nicole played at being the gracious hostess while our neighbor's wife complimented her dress and her dancing and Adrien made faces at me behind Nicole's back.

Where was Dan?

I cannot situate him in that moment . . . Perhaps he had been entrusted to Nanou, our neighbors' maid. Perhaps the two of them were sitting on a blanket out in the meadow . . . Yes, that is possible, that is what must have happened, but I cannot visualize my brother Dan in that moment — and if I cannot see him it means that there was unhappiness all around me, that I was hemmed in alone by that unhappiness.

"They're our neighbors, you see, Estelle," my father had told me. But it was not enough. The hellish breeze was upon us, I sensed it. Nicole was uttering inanities, Tiresia was not getting up to offer pastries to our guests, my father was casting sidelong looks at me, "They're our neighbors, Estelle, don't you see."

Father, I cannot go on trying to understand what you won't explain to me, I cannot go on taking this nameless thing, this beast, in my arms, and holding it like a kitten because you ask me to, Father, because you believe your daughter has this gift, because you need her, because you don't really want to be troubled with her.

You have already given so much thought to Tiresia and Nicole that you can no longer think about Estelle.

Nicole sat more and more woodenly in her chair, Tiresia's silence became deadening, our neighbors' voices periodically chipped in, and you spoke in your most imperturbable lawyerly tones. And yet: "You see, Estelle, you do see, don't you?"

I went out to the meadow and sat under the apple tree and began to cry. Who would save us this time?

Out on the meadow something was moving: a very small child, dragging itself along on its stomach. I wept, hemmed in by my unhappiness. The child raised its head and went on crawling toward me through the grass, its face round and smiling, twittering like a bird amid pools of liquid sunlight as it crawled toward the budding apple tree. Through the mist of my tears, I did not recognize this undulation out on the meadow. He wriggled in under the first branches, a movement in the foliage shook out a shower of petals, he laughed aloud, stretching his arms toward the bright downpour — and suddenly I was myself again. I recognized him, Dan, my little brother, his eyes laughing in the sun, his chubby little arms reaching for the petals, and I picked him up so that he could clutch at a small cluster of blossoms. He tugged. Again blossoms fell, and we were haloed in white. His body was warm and round and heavy in my arms, his eyes stared and laughed into mine and he waved the tiny bouquet in front of my mouth. I nibbled at a flower, oh, how Dan my brother laughed, and suddenly all my sadness disappeared, I was no longer alone, I remembered that I would never again be alone. "Oh, Dan, Dan," I buried my face in his plump shoulder and one little arm slipped around my neck while the other arm went on shaking the branch above us and bringing the white petals raining down. I was weeping and laughing at once, "Dan, oh, Dan."

Shouts came from the far end of the meadow.

I did not stir. My happiness was so complete that nothing could break in. How could I have forgotten that I was no longer alone, never again alone? Dan was chirruping, it was the first time he had ever threaded sounds together, and I basked in their music.

Our father ran up, white as a sheet: "We looked everywhere for him." Behind him, Nicole was irritated. "Your father was afraid he had fallen in the pond," she said. And our neighbor's wife added, "Mr. Helleur, children always turn up again in the end." "Tiresia is always right," Nicole interjected nervously.

Then we were all going back up to the house. "How could he have wandered so far?" they were asking. Our neighbor's wife smacked Adrien's head: "I wouldn't be surprised if it was you who let him outside," she said, "do you realize he could have drowned?" Adrien, his cheek red and smarting, began to yell, "That rotten kid, that rotten little Dan, I'll get my own back someday," and at once received another slap. At that he fled, howling, and disappeared through the hole in the wall beneath the lilac. Suddenly my father noticed that Dan was talking.

"Why, Nicole, your son, he's saying something, listen to him!"

Everyone stopped. We were in the garden now, on the lawn. Nicole set Dan down on the grass, and we all stopped talking and listened to his chirruping.

"Do you hear," said my father, "do you hear what he's saying, Nicole?"

Nicole listened, looking doubtful and already on the verge of giving up, as if this whole scare had been too much for her, a taxing administrative procedure of the kind that disturbs you for nothing and deserves nothing more than to be instantly forgotten, its place taken by something else, by something really worthwhile . . . Yes, but by what, Nicole?

Suddenly we heard Tiresia's voice. She had stayed behind in the living room but now joined us, and made us hear what we were not hearing.

"He's saying 'Tell, tell, tell,' isn't he . . . Or perhaps 'Smell, smell, smell . . .' Or could it be 'Estelle, Estelle, Estelle . . .'?"

And indeed that is exactly what my brother was saying. He was saying "Smell, tell, Estelle" — and I was hearing my name the way nobody would ever say it again, everyone oohed and aahed at the baby saying his first words . . . "Astonishing," said our neighbor, "usually children begin with Papa and Mama," and my heart swelled with joy, my name was the first word my brother ever said, he had come to say it to me under the flowering fragrant apple tree, he had come into the world to say my name so that I should never again be alone.

TEN

Little Vermin

*U*NTIL my brother said his first word I had never noticed that apple tree. But thenceforth we were both bound to it.

*   *   *

We went back there all the time. Sometimes it was good to us, sometimes bad, and we modified its name accordingly. When it was good we called it the "sweetree," when it was bad, the "sourtree." We could thus refer to the tree at all times and in all company without fear of discovery — which, as we shall see, could be very useful.

We liked it when it was good to us, but we also liked it when it was bad.

And in fact (although we never explicitly perceived the connection) it was bad only when Mr. Raymond was perched in its branches. So when we talked about going to the sourtree, we meant the apple tree plus Mr. Raymond. And going to the "sour-troll-tree" meant going to watch Mr. Raymond pick apples. But it could in consequence also mean playing hooky.

On sourtree days we prowled around the tree, strangely aroused, as if the tree itself contained an answer — and that was strangest of all, because we had no inkling of any kind of question: as I have said, we lived in a state of non-question, yet it always seemed to us that our apple tree would have an answer. And so, although by definition we could have no curiosity about that answer (having no urge to ask a question), we nonetheless felt arousal. At the time it seemed wicked: we dared not tell our parents of those moments beneath the apple tree. Not for anything in the world would we have wanted our parents to hear about them.

Because of this secret knowledge of ours, our arousal was wicked. But beyond it, beyond the flow of time that carried away our house and the meadow behind it and the apple tree in the meadow and us under the apple tree, our faces raised to the unseen man rustling among the leaves, there seemed to be a place where that wicked water reached a vast still cove, spread itself expansively there, and then, purified and appeased, lay glittering and transparent under the sun. And because of that place that dwelt suspended above the confused currents of time, our arousal too was good.

In our minds, my brother and I were unaware of all this. But in our all-knowing bodies we were at once happy and ill at ease. And when this man came, when this Mr. Raymond came to pick the apples from our apple tree, we dropped everything and followed him, skipping school and paying him not to give us away.

For that was our understanding with this man who did not like us. (Or who perhaps did like us — all these years later my view of things has come full circle.) His limping gait still fills my heart with pity: it was merely one sequel of a childhood spinal affliction that bent him double as he walked. I think now that perhaps he did like us, that in his rough twisted way he was straining to warn us of something he half sensed . . . Quite possibly we were his only admirers, perhaps the only people who ever spoke to him . . . Today I think that Mr. Raymond was a poor lonely old wretch, and that all the unpleasantnesses he showered down on us from the boughs, instead of the apples we hoped for, were words of friendship and affection.

The apple tree stood near the center of the meadow between the back of our house and the wooded hills that fringed our side of town.

Dan and I had the run of that meadow, but when the apple tree was in fruit this man came and rang our doorbell. Tiresia asked him in and took him to the big ladder we kept along the wall of the rear porch. Wordlessly hoisting it to his shoulder, he walked with heavy deliberate steps to the apple tree in the center of the meadow, his rubber boots sinking into the earth.

But the apples were not for us: he picked them for someone else. We thought it was for the "disabled" (we had been struck by this word, which people so often applied to him), but since then I have learned that my father not only paid him to pick these apples but also allowed him to keep them.

So when he came to our place he was paid three times.

By the apple tree, in kind.

By our father, in paper money.

By my brother and me, in coins.

(And a fourth time after that, since he sold what he gathered to anyone who would buy.)

As soon as the first apple fell from the tree we watched for his arrival. If it was a holiday we waited for him at the garden gate. If it was a school day, we hid in the ditch at the bottom of the field. The field sloped downhill, and whether we were in the ditch or behind the tree, nobody could see us from the lower floors of the house. At least, that is what we told ourselves. Only Tiresia, whose bedroom was on the same floor as the attic, could have seen us and known we were not in school — and then only if she had been standing at the window at just the right moment.

She must occasionally have gone to her window in that room nobody ever went up to. She must have seen us from that window, or else how was it that our absences from school never reached our parents' ears?

There are so many things I could have asked Tiresia in those days she lay dying, when she finally started talking, talking . . . *But those questions come to me only now, madame, questions about this or that detail, all those tiny questions that, once attempted, would have led me step by step up to the great terrible question crouched like a sphinx in the innermost sanctum of my grief, would have let me take the sphinx by surprise, and then Dan would not have died. Why, why, Tiresia?*

At a distance, we followed Mr. Raymond.

He scared us with his short twisted legs and his back, so bent he seemed unable to see you and had to twist his mouth sideways in order to throw his voice outward, as if his voice too were twisted, like his body.

He was jetsam from the Great War, carried in the womb of a Polish woman who died soon after his birth, a half-wild woman who had a shack in the hills and lived by odd jobs and the kindness of people who were sorry for her.

Who of course included our parents.

Our eyes never met. Yet there was nothing wrong with his eyesight. He knew, for example, if apples had disappeared from the apple tree. He would call down to us.

"You there, the big one. And the little one!"

We drew near, shaking with terror yet longing for the terror he offered so prodigally.

"Did you take this apple?"

He pointed to a small unhealed wound on a twig peeping from between two leaves.

"There was an apple there, and now it's not there."

"Perhaps it fell off," I suggested.

Dan immediately dropped to all fours and scanned the tall grass.

"There are ants," he said (an indestructible column marched permanently past our house), "perhaps they took it away."

"They'll take you away too, little liars!" said the man.

Dan clung to my legs and I clasped his shoulders. We were frightened.

"Good-for-nothings," he grumbled. "Little vermin . . ."

That particular word, which came back again and again, we turned over in every direction, for hours on end, and after every visit, always with the same total absorption.

"Perhaps he means Germans?" I said to Dan.

Not that we were very clear about what German meant, either, but it seemed awful enough to match our detractor's vindictive tone. And there was no denying that in a way that Mr. Raymond knew and that we did not, we were indeed vermin.

He fascinated us.

We remained rooted beneath the tree, watching him adjust the ladder until he found the right angle.

"You'd like to make the old hunchback fall, wouldn't you, little vermin? If I didn't scare you, you'd give the ladder a kick!"

Thus we learned, to our horror, that felony and murder dwelt within us. We did not question his insight, not for a second, for as long as we stood under that tree. If he had asked us to fall to our knees and beat our breasts with branches we would have done it.

"Hey, you with the ribbons, and that brother of yours, looking so innocent! I tell you, if I could I'd kick both your asses, but I can't . . ."

"Why not, Mr. Raymond?"

"I can't. Hand me that basket, vermin!"

Mesmerized, we passed him the basket.

He climbed into the heart of the tree. He was already lost to sight among the leaves when suddenly a large bough was thrust downward and part of his face emerged just a few feet above us.

"Don't you dare try moving the ladder, little vermin."

We shook our heads vigorously. I believe he simply wanted to make sure we were still there, to make sure his power over us still worked. We were probably the only creatures on earth over whom he had power.

Perhaps that was the source of his rage. We were creatures he could dominate — but that was just an added humiliation, since we were so weak.

The branch leapt violently upward again, almost slashing our faces in its flight. We jumped backward, then returned to our posts and waited. Soon we heard only the sharp click of apples being plucked, the dry plop of apples falling into the basket, a rustling in the leaves.

*   *   *

As he worked Mr. Raymond panted and continued to grumble (it kept us aware of his presence, and maintained his hold), but we no longer heard what he said.

"Let's go," I whispered to Dan. "Now's our chance. He can't see us."

At once the branches were thrust aside and his voice dropped heavily on us.

"What are you cooking up now, you good-for-nothing little vermin? Oh, I can see you there, girl, with your surprised look and your combed hair. Who combs it for you, huh, the blond prickteaser or the crazy woman in black? What a family, what a family!"

He disappeared again.

I tried to pull Dan away but he resisted, rooted with fear and fascination, and the apple picker reappeared through another gap in the foliage.

"And what about him, yes, you, the choirboy there! You were carried in your mother's belly, ha ha, just like me. Except that you've had it soft, real soft, at your age I was already in rags."

Dan looked at his pants. He was very proud of them. His lower lip began to quiver, and I said very loud:

"Don't cry, Dan, that's just what he wants, to make us cry. Don't cry, he'll enjoy it."

The man laughed.

"The big one's smarter than she looks. I like you two little vermin. Well, why don't you go and snitch to your father if you're so scared. Defending people is his job . . ."

"No," Dan said, "we're staying."

The man cackled and went back to his apples. Dan and I sank to the ground and gazed at the big blue sky with its scattering of small white clouds. We plucked a few blades of grass. Time seemed immense, endless: we floated in time, like small white clouds in the sky.

There was a violent rustling in the foliage overhead, and we realized that the man was climbing back down the ladder. He cursed as he came: with twisted legs and head bent to the waist, it could not have been easy for him. We leapt to our feet: this was our chance, the moment we had theoretically waited for as we sat there under the tree.

Without a word, the man handed us the full basket. I took it. It was heavy; inevitably, I spilled a good third of the apples.

"Clumsy brat, spoiled kid, dolled-up ninny, useless bitch!" he said.

But Dan was already busily returning the spilled apples to the basket. That was his own special job. Then I took the basket, emptied it into a sort of bin roped to the rear of a motor-powered bike near the fence at the bottom of the meadow, and brought it back.

"There you are, Mr. Raymond."

"Sure you didn't eat one?"

"Yes."

"You're not allowed to, you know. You have the run of the meadow, but you don't get any fruit."

"Yes, I know, Mr. Raymond."

Dan fumbled in the pockets of the offending trousers (short woolen pants that had appealed to Nicole because the plaid pattern reminded her of her own taffeta dress) and handed Mr. Raymond a fistful of coins so that he would not tell anyone we were not in school.

Not once did he give us an apple. But after we left we would see that some had been left lying on the ground. We gathered them up with great zeal.

We never ate them.

At first we took them up into our garret, but its proximity to our parents bothered us, so we carried them to the cave, our own cave in the side of the nearest hill.

We lined them up beneath the picture painted on the wall.

"This one's for . . . ," said Dan.

I nodded.

Yes, that one was for the blond prickteaser.

"And this one's for . . ."

For the crazy woman in black.

And the third?

For the one whose job was defending people.

Another apple each for the little vermin. Then we lined the others up behind the defensive screen of the first five fruit.

Only then could we examine them with our flashlight, nibbling the chocolate we kept in one of Nicole's shoe boxes on a little rock overhang in the cave.

As the end of the school day drew near, we selected a few apples from the second row, left the cave, took the hill path and a narrow alley between two garden walls, and rejoined our own road.

Already we could hear Alex and Adrien ahead, banging their

schoolbags as they walked home, banging them against walls and lampposts and against each other, schoolbag against schoolbag. Then we heard Alex — who was more gifted at that particular game — saying, "Time it! Time it!" and Adrien's unvarying reply: "Shit!"

By now they were almost at the mouth of the alleyway where Dan and I crouched. Breaking into a wild run, Alex burst into view, head thrust so far forward in his haste to see us that he sometimes literally dropped at our feet like the exhausted hero of Marathon. And indeed he bore news, breathless news, from the battlefront:

"Adrien told the school you were vomiting all night after you went out on your own mushroom picking because you wanted people to think you're smart but you didn't know anything about mushrooms . . ." Or else, "Adrien told them you went chasing rabbits in the hills and ran into a wild boar and it didn't attack you but scared you so much you had a heart attack . . ."

These reports were of the utmost importance to us. Alex gasped them out, so terrified that Adrien would learn of his treachery that he swallowed half his syllables. But even if he had only managed one syllable per word, we would have understood.

Yet to Adrien it seemed we were truly clairvoyant. For just as clairvoyants need only a nail paring or a hair in order to see the whole gamut of their subject's personality spread out before them, so we seemed to need only the beginnings of a hint from Adrien (his expression, a twitch of the hairline, one word) and at once we knew what the score was. He knew it, and the word "shit!" was constantly on his lips like an exorcism.

The more outlandish the excuse Adrien had given the school to explain our absence, the more we paid him.

We reasoned as follows: surely, faced with such an improbable tale, the school authorities would hesitate to bother our parents. It was hard to imagine our little shy-as-a-mouse principal saying to our father: "How could you let your children eat poison mushrooms, perhaps we should inform the police!" or else: "Poor things, a heart attack at their age, are you going to hunt down that wild boar?" Obviously not.

The people of our town were not without malice, but they were deeply reserved.

In which case, of course, all the onus was shifted to Adrien. A black mark would appear against his name in the class register (a given number of these black marks brought you close to the dreaded frontier of expulsion from school). Only we didn't trust him, and Alex was our only means of checking on him. And Alex could not tell us the truth in Adrien's presence. Whence Alex's last-minute dash to the alleyway, his painful falls.

And here is how we paid Adrien.

We gave him a first apple.

"This one will wipe out your black mark."

First point. The prediction never failed, for a week of consistent good behavior from Adrien was enough to cancel the black mark.

Second apple

"This one will give you a goal against Alex."

That too came to pass, for Alex, whether consciously or not, would let Adrien beat him at soccer that week.

Third apple.

"This one will get you the truck you want for Christmas."

Here we were taking a risk. But not really, either, for we were inwardly certain that despite his strictness and his constant threats of reprisal (Adrien was always up to some kind of horseplay), Mr. Neighbor would yield and Adrien would get the truck he asked for.

In our cave too, in front of the indecipherable picture on the wall, our five "sacred" apples enjoyed fates as varied as they were mysterious. They shriveled up or they fell apart, they dried or rotted away. Once they had clearly reached the end of their appointed paths, what was left to do?

Declare them ordinary apples and throw them away . . . What else?

ELEVEN

"Look Out, Dan!"

*B*EHIND the house, where we stacked the winter firewood, was a slope. At its foot was a gravel strip, and then the meadow, which led up into the hills. Driven from the house by a sense of deep unease, we wandered forlornly over the meadow, as lost as if enveloped in fog, not knowing where to go, lacking the courage to look at each other.

Now and then we jostled each other as we walked, surprised almost to feel a leg yield or a foot stumble on an irregularity in the ground. Almost at once we felt better to be thus borne along together side by side, to have our wandering attention guided back to earth. Like a span of oxen, we rode out every obstacle on our path, every clump, pebble, or hollow. The clouds dispersed. Suddenly all was adventure again.

From the feel of the ground beneath our feet we realized we had stumbled upon a path, and our existence was at once restored to us. My little brother began to laugh, and at once found the strength to turn around.

He spread his feet, folded his arms, and studied our house.

I too turned, and looked intently.

That was our house down there. From where we stood on the meadow there was not a sound to be heard. I don't know how many times we stood up there, with my little brother in front and with me a little behind him, glued together, gazing at our house, and always much too absorbed to say anything.

Two figures on a raft, gazing at the tall ship, their ship, away down below. Was it near or far? On that boundless sea it was impossible to say with any certainty.

And suddenly one day my brother called out:

"Look!"

"Look at what?"

He was wildly excited.

"Up high, Estelle, up high."

"I don't see anything, Dan."

But already he was dragging me.

What he had seen was a door just above the roof of the lean-to storeroom at the back of the house, a door of unusual shape, square and small. It did not seem made for grown-ups.

"Do you see it, do you?" asked Dan. "That's our place," he told me, and as usual I instantly believed him.

"We can't climb up to that door," I said.

And indeed it opened directly onto the steep gray tin slope of the lean-to roof.

Perhaps we could reach it from inside the house, through the main attic — but that we did not want. If we had to go past our father's room, then Nicole's, then Tiresia's, it would never be our place. Dan would not have been able to say "That's our place."

We had considered reaching it through the attic, then rejected the idea. In a few seconds, wordlessly, our two minds had together followed that short trail, explored its possibilities, scented its dangers.

Like two swift hunting dogs, our minds raced along the same trail, sniffed the same scents, and together had returned to the point of departure without our needing to whistle them back, give them orders, move a muscle. Without our even knowing that they had gone forth and loped back to us.

And now that I am alone, my mind no longer hunts in company but wanders by itself along paths where it continually loses its way. Now I know that this restless questing of two minds racing side by side through the world and sniffing at myriad possibilities is the rarest of occurrences, a wildly improbable freak of nature. An irreplaceable treasure, which I possessed and which I no longer possess.

Now, today, no matter what I do, even the most down-to-earth things, panic overtakes me.

For the hound has lost her mate, and the thousand twists and turns she once accomplished in a twinkling are quite beyond her. Trembling, fearful, she hugs my side. And the surrounding countryside is all fog: it no longer sends back echoes. My antennae are gone, my bearings lost. And panic overwhelms me.

At the time I did not realize how concertedly my brother's mind hunted alongside mine. I thought we were always at loggerheads. And in truth we never stopped arguing.

"Those children bicker all the time," our mother Nicole said distractedly, then fled. She could not bear disagreement. To her, each of our quarrels was the equivalent of a false step in a dance, a break in the smooth seamless flow she so obstinately sought. Our mother strove for oblivion, or rather for a death of the memory (but perhaps only our doctor really understood that), hoping to find it in the formal perfection of a sequence of movements, in a perfect, flawless moment of dance. The rest of existence for her was probably chaos, and she reacted to it most of the time with apathy.

Our intense squabbling must have been painful to her, but the nature of that pain we could not imagine. In any case, she never scolded us.

A smooth seamless flow: that was what she aspired to, like a plant yearning for oxygen.

"Those children bicker all the time," said Nicole as she moved away.

My father, listening from a distance, would reply, "Those children are inseparable." And both were right.

Tiresia said nothing, but her eyes followed us everywhere. It seems to me now that Tiresia's eyes were always on us, on the two of us together, holding us together as if in a net. But at the time we could not know what the mesh was made of.

"We won't be able to climb that far," I told my brother (the lean-to, the gutter, the sloping roof, et cetera) . . .

But all the time I knew we would: the door was meant for us, a child's door, beckoning. But I had my father's cautious, circumspect mind (and here of course I don't mean the fleet hounds of the mind, those superb and invisible hounds Dan and I unleashed, but my own mind, which was not a bit like my brother's); I had to weigh the problem from every possible angle. My brother did not burden himself with such considerations but went straight for the goal.

He did it always and in all things — all except one. And because of that one hesitation we lost everything. Because of it, I have been weeping deep inside for all these long years.

"You're crazy, Estelle."

"You're the crazy one. The lean-to, the gutter, the sloping roof . . ."

"So what?" he said.

"Do you want me to give you a leg up?"

"No, no. How would you get up yourself?"

I returned to the attack:

"We can't. The lean-to, the gutter, the sloping roof . . ."

He laughed. And for that laugh alone I would gladly have pretended to be the dumbest girl in the world.

"I don't need a leg up, Estelle, I need two legs up."

As soon as I heard a joke coming, I was caught. So was he. ("Dan, Dan, talk to me, don't leave me outside that tiny castle you're hiding in, just like a tiny mouse, don't leave me outside its tiny walls . . . I hear you laughing in there: I'll scratch and I'll scratch and I'll scratch if you don't let me in . . .")

"Get me Mr. Raymond's legs, Estelle."

"His legs?"

"His ladder, stupid!"

The solution he had hit on — the apple tree ladder — was almost as daunting as our objective. More than twelve feet long, it was wooden and heavy. Since I was the bigger one, it was my job to lug it, teeth clenched, to the back of the house.

To an unconcerned observer, I would certainly have looked like any small girl on the point of physical collapse. Our gardener moved it only with my father's help, or (if he was around) Mr. Raymond's.

But to me it did not seem an effort at all. For Dan raced around me, sometimes behind, subtly shifting the ladder's course so that it skirted obstacles I could not pull it over, sometimes in front, where he guided me like a pilot fish, his authority total, his enthusiasm unflagging.

If he had said, "Estelle, let's put this ladder up against the moon," I would have said, "Dan, that's silly, you know that's impossible," and he would have said, "Why?" and I would have answered, "The ladder is too short and the moon isn't even in our atmosphere." Naturally — yet it would have been only my voice speaking, my voice and my literal nature. Deep down, I would have believed him at once, my seemingly unassailable arguments would have seemed piffling, and the impossibility of putting that ladder against the moon would have seemed a weakness in me, or a weakness in the world, but not an impossibility in itself, not an impossibility in the only area that counted, the one my brother created.

Madame, I am speaking of a world that was immense and has become tiny, a world that existed in another dimension, a world whose existence no one remembers, and of which I alas am the only survivor.

How am I to live with other people, to come to terms with the realization that nobody, nobody in the world, will ever be my brother? Nobody.

How am I going to build a life with Phil, who is not my brother, who is and always will be a stranger, to whom I shall never say "I love you" without hearing death's taunting laugh in my head and hearing death whisper "You lie"? I cannot see him walking by my side or lying on my body without a mind-numbing astonishment. Phil, who is nothing to me, nevertheless lives in the world of today, and without knowing he is doing it, teaches me how to live there, stay there, say things there.

He will never know that I am not at home in this world in which he moves with such casual ease. He will never know that every one of his utterances is completely foreign to me even though I understand them; in fact because I understand them.

Every moment spent with him is an immense effort to hide my origin, I mean the origin of my essence, which was in my brother.

But I want my brother Dan's ivy-grown gravestone to stay behind in our world, which was once vast and is now so small. I want it to stay there, as if on an uninhabited planet drifting far out in space, and I will not look at it again. Except sometimes in the evening. I might spy a distant star in the cold sky when I am out in dark streets, before turning toward the lights of the building where this man of today will be waiting, this Phil, a man I can scarcely find words to describe.

And then we will truly have exchanged names, Dan and I.

He will be Estella the star, but the kind of star that is only a shimmering speck high in the vast ink-blue vault. And I will be Dan, a name so like the French word for "in," "inside." For Dan will be out in the cosmos, and I, Estelle, will be in among the living on this planet of ours and in this age of ours.

All the strength you invested in a quest for what shines, for a star, for your star, Dan, I will put into a quest for the earth, the most ordinary earth, the kind of earth on which everyone has a foothold.

Do you know that I recently bought a TV set and a videocassette recorder, that I now take an interest in everything in the outside world? Oh, I work at it, Dan.

I am learning by heart (I nearly said "by head" since it is decidedly not with my heart that I learn but through my "headstrong" will), I am learning the names of popular singers and the songs they sing, good, not so good, terrible, it doesn't matter to me (except for one, Dan, the lyrics are almost exactly the words you used when you tried to explain your dance. That song is on the tape Phil sent me, his first present and the occasion of our second meeting. Does that mean something, my love? Later, later . . .).

I go onto subway platforms and into fast-food restaurants where screened videos turn my mind into a shattered windshield. I walk along Avenue de C. with its secondhand-clothes stalls and appliance stores that look more like warehouses for the debris of some planetary disaster, the loudspeakers yammering as if determined to destroy what remained of thought in people's brains.

Yes, Dan, as if a small personal thought can no longer be anything but a single cell inside the skull, a high-security cell subjected not to sensory

*deprivation but to saturation . . . A childhood like ours could have no place
in such a world, and if it ever did exist it would be inside those skulls,
like a cell undergoing sensory saturation to the point of being crushed,
annihilated.*

*I walk among new crowds, crowds eager to knock at the door of the
modern world, the most accommodating of doors, the most dazzling of doors,
you wouldn't recognize our old Avenue de C., Dan.*

*But I am not very often in this neighborhood, my love; usually I am
at Phil's. Wherever he happens to be is the ground I must cling to. If I
can. Perhaps . . .*

I carried that ladder. It hurt my shoulders and hands. I was like those
ants we had so often watched (the very same indefatigable column
that marched around our house despite the equally indefatigable
counsels of our neighbor) bearing burdens five or six times their
size, and I was utterly happy.

For although the task was quite clearly beyond my strength, I was
managing it.

A miracle, a special dispensation. And as with all miracles, ordinary
laws did not apply. To me the weight was slight, effort was converted
into joy, the ability to overcome pain, aching muscles, and bruises
engendered a sense of power, the vast distance between the apple
tree and the lean-to steadily shrank, and the onerous chore was
transformed into heroic adventure.

Heroic, and joyful too. For Dan chanted an accompaniment to
our trek across the meadow, an accompaniment drawn from our
childhood reading. True to his nature, he did not narrate or recite
it but mimed it. Danced it. So that he and I took turns being Sancho
Panza, Don Quixote, a sled dog, Tom Thumb, Little Drop of Water
pushing her wooden log, and many more.

We hauled the ladder to the bottom of the meadow, tipped it over
the low wall into the backyard, then propped it against the lean-to.
I held the ladder while Dan climbed. Then he was crawling up the
tin roof, rising to his feet, clutching at the door for support. And
still he was not home, because the door refused to open. His hands
felt it all over, seeking the magic spot. "Open sesame" and it yielded.
I climbed up and joined my brother.

The ladder was high. It sat shakily on the pebbly ground. The tin
roof was steep and slippery.

When my brother left for the United States and all of us thought he would never return, I wanted to seek out this first refuge of our childhood, to shut myself away there as if in a cloister, to pray there until my pain was gone. But I could not reach that door. The base of the ladder kept slipping, and when I finally managed to prop it up, precariously, and reach the top, scaling the roof seemed beyond me.

The top of the ladder rested against the gutter running below the roof. The gutter was covered with a fine slippery moss that denied me a firm foothold, and the gutter itself seemed shakily attached, ready to fall apart.

I was afraid, but I forced myself to hoist my body as high as I dared onto the roof without letting go of the ladder. But my weight pulled me back down the slope, and I was unable to stretch high enough to get a grip on the stone ledge under the little door.

The rain began to fall, and with the morbid fervor of despair I hoped it would pull me down with it, like a dead leaf in the gutter, pull me down in a blind endless flow. I wept uncontrollably on that roof, racked by my tears and the rain and the incessant wind until I almost went mad.

Next would come pneumonia, and our doctor again, and my mother more unconcerned than ever, and my father buried ever deeper in his cases, and Tiresia wandering more and more distractedly about the house.

It was a strange kind of vacation, so soon after my marriage (itself most strange: why had Yves not come with me for this first visit to my family?).

But with Dan, I flew up that ladder and over the roof. For years we accomplished the feat, several times a day. In all kinds of weather, which in our part of the world often meant stormy weather.

In fact especially during storms, for you heard the rain better from that room in the attic than from anywhere else. The tin roofing of the lean-to just under the sills made every drop reverberate, sweet and strong. We could have listened forever. It was music with just one theme encompassing the subtlest of variations, giving us a sense at once of eternity and immediacy. It put us into a trance of astonishment, akin almost to fear, as if in this private sanctum of ours we had stumbled upon one of the world's closest-kept secrets.

When we tried to express this to our father one day, he said, "The English have a word for that feeling: 'awe.' " It was the first English word we ever learned, and I sometimes think that if my brother left for the United States because he wanted to flee us, to flee me, it was in the unconscious hope of finding a place that would reveal another of the universe's secrets, one that could put him into another overpowering trance, one that might even save him.

As soon as it rained we ran to our ladder. The ladder everyone had given up for lost (for when we no longer needed it we hid it among the bushes behind the low wall). The denizens of our family world were so preoccupied that when they stopped seeing it under the apple tree they forgot all about it. And if they had chanced to see it propped against the lean-to, I am not sure they would even have noticed it.

When Tiresia finally saw it, it had already been replaced in the apple orchard with a new aluminum ladder, of much more up-to-date design, and nobody dreamed of depriving us of the old one. Nor did anyone think it might be dangerous for two children to climb it several times a day in wind and rain.

Of course, the thought must have occurred to our father, who always worried so much about us, but there was no room inside his weary head for any more horrors. He had to contend with the ones buried in his files, horrors from his past and horrors too that survived into the present.

Our mother was absorbed in her dream. When she finally saw us perched on that ladder, I am sure it meant no more to her than figures in a ballet. My brother was so agile, so graceful in his smallest movements, instinctively transforming every gesture into dance. And I, if only out of mimicry, must not have been too clumsy.

When she was shown the scene of our exploit (and we agreed to give a demonstration, obligingly, just for her), she laughed, that laugh which was so young and fresh.

"Just like squirrels," she said with delight, and then again, as if to encourage us, "Veritable squirrels."

She looked at us with that far-off look of hers, and I knew she was not seeing Dan and Estelle, her children, but two small animals dancing nimble-footed on a bough.

And my heart would tighten. I suffered when she spoke to us or looked at us in that way. I did not feel at ease until I heard her back in her garage, far from the house, her familiar limbering-up music floating up to us.

I was tall and broad-shouldered, so how could she compare me to a squirrel? There was only one answer: when confronted with Dan and Estelle, she saw only Dan. And in Dan, she saw the dancer of her great dream. (It was already clear by then that I did not possess the true gift.)

I wanted my mother to be concerned for my safety, the way other mothers I saw on the street or at school feared for their daughters. But what I could not see was that our mother Nicole was a little girl, the star dancer of an eternal ballet. How could I have been her daughter?

Tiresia knew the ladder was dangerous. I felt it in the depths of my soul, where convictions dwell. I perceived it through something in her body, that body we ceaselessly consulted but never deciphered.

One day, there she was. It was pelting with rain, the kind of weather we liked. Dan was just propping the ladder against the roof; I was still on the low wall, wiping my hands on my skirt. I turned and there she was. It was the first time we had ever been caught. Her face was looking up at Dan and at once, without any possibility of doubt, I knew she expected an accident, she expected him to slide down the slippery, wet roof, bounce on the low wall below it, and then fall again to the stones piled up on the far side. And I was so frightened that I screamed, "Look out, Dan!"

Startled, Dan turned and of course he slipped. In a flash, Tiresia was under the gutter and had a grip on his feet seconds before he could fall. Dan immediately climbed back up the ladder again. And I began to sob, overwhelmed by a quite disproportionate anguish that seemed to come rolling in from far beyond me.

Tiresia came over, seized me almost roughly by the hand, and pushed me onto the bottom rung of the ladder. Her eyes behind the glasses were unfathomable. Oh, how I questioned her! One of her hands covered my hand on the ladder, and I felt something in that hand, a lesson, a warning, something tragic. I sensed the violence in Tiresia that day, the horror and the passion in her which produced that stillness of hers we knew so well and which was simply the precarious equilibrium of two terrible opposing forces.

"You made him fall," said a voice that must have been mine but that I did not recognize.

"I caught him," she said quietly, and her words too seemed to belong to someone else.

And those two people who were not us stared at each other from either side of the dark veil.

Perched on the sill of the little door, my brother listened to the voice that was not Tiresia's answering the voice that was not his sister's. And his own voice, bold and ringing, came down to us, sending a beam of iridescent light through the strange rain-filled blackness that held us motionless at the foot of the ladder, both of us by now drenched.

"She caught me, Estelle," he called, half-teasing, half-serious. "You're the one who made me fall with your owl hoot."

We had an owl, at the far end of the meadow. People said that hearing it hoot at night meant a death. Admittedly it was not night, but my brother never spoke false. He went on:

"Your owl hoot, Estelle, your owl hoot. You scared me."

And suddenly I understood my brother's luminous laugh, what he was telling me that was beyond Tiresia's understanding, beyond our own understanding, which was undeveloped at the time, being that of a boy of nine too mature for his age and a girl of fourteen who was too much of a dreamer.

He was telling me:

"Estelle, my sister, you have just seen my death, hovering not far from us in the invisible realms, having traveled here from a time and a place we do not know. It moved furtively, feeling its way along the invisible frontier, seeking a crack to admit it to our own world, in order to find me and carry me off. It was looking, looking, and you thought you sensed that the crack was there, hidden inside Tiresia. Now that thing you saw has moved away, let's forget it, we've won for now."

We sat cross-legged on the old carpet we had hauled up there and smoked the cigarettes we had stolen from our doctor. For there were not just candies in his bag, but cigarettes too. I believe he knew we smoked at his expense, and of course he disapproved but he did not have the heart to forbid us.

And why did he not have the heart to forbid us?

It did not occur to us to ask ourselves that question, or to ask him. But we felt it with the same certainty I have already described. We felt that our doctor had a strange kind of pity for us. Like Nicole's nightmares, his pity derived from a world beyond our comprehension that bristled with terrors, sometimes nearby, sometimes almost forgotten, but there, always there.

On the other hand, while we might not know the reasons for his pity, we knew how to manipulate it. And that was how we came to possess cigarettes without our father and mother knowing.

Tiresia knew we smoked. Miraculous things would happen: a pack getting dangerously low (when we were reduced to saving halves and then halves of halves because Minor's last visit had been a long time back) would be less empty one day when we got back from school. And while Minor smoked brown tobacco, these would be Virginia cigarettes, the Camels we revered because they seemed to bear the prestige of our American saviors, the winners, as we knew, of a recent war.

We stared at each other, my brother and I, but the miracle left us unsurprised. It seemed part of a whole universe full of strange things, unspoken, indirectly felt, which was ours.

We were children and we had no thought of intervening in that universe. We assumed it was like all others.

TWELVE

I Will Find You

I TRIED to throw Tiresia's story to the winds.

I was weak. I was almost someone else but incapable even of guessing who that someone else was.

I did throw it to the winds.

But the winds fell flat.

And Tiresia's story has returned to me, breathless and tearful. I cannot stand it, madame. Tiresia was tearless and of almost indestructible strength.

Her story had become that of a hired village mourner. I heard it at her grave the day after her death, and it seemed to me that death had already taken her into its maw and was beginning to suck her, soften her, prepare her for its secret digestive processes.

I do not want to tell it to anyone today, for fear that it will come back to me again, deformed by whoever might have heard it, deformed by me. Madame, I trust myself as little as I trust others, I have never liked to speak, my brother spoke for both of us, and what he said was my truth.

How should I speak, now that I no longer have a voice?

Madame, I want you to write Tiresia's story. That is why I have sought you out.

Our father believed in justice. Perhaps he wanted to believe in it, perhaps he no longer had a choice. He was a lawyer (not a judge — he could not have been, the moral disorder of nature shattered him, just seeing a thrush gulp down a worm in our garden could bring on tears despite our neighbor's scoffing, for then, madame, all his knowledge was of no use). He was just a lawyer and we, his children, thought he controlled the scales of good and of evil and thus gave every act its own precise identity.

I want you to fix Tiresia's story in its exact place and give it its exact identity so that I may recognize it again exactly as I heard it during the five days and five nights she lay on her deathbed, the story of a tearless woman of almost indestructible strength.

My brother and I lived by our truth, our father by his justice, Tiresia by her vision, and our mother Nicole, the frailest, by her dreams.

A story must stand or fall by its writing. And just as our father was to us the sole repository and guarantor in matters of good and evil, you are for me the sole repository and guarantor in matters of writing — since you are a writer, madame.

Thus Tiresia's story will have its identity, its place among all the other stories that history picks up and sweeps along, who knows whither. But what does it matter where it goes, madame, or even if it goes out to nothingness. Whatever happens, Tiresia's story will have been put right.

My brother said to me one day: "Our mother Nicole was trying to right a wrong, a great wrong . . ." Our mother Nicole was not strong, and she died while she was still slender and blond and graceful on the eternal points of her dance slippers, but she tried.

I was unable to help Nicole in her great struggle, but perhaps I shall at least succeed in putting Tiresia's story right.

* * *

For a long while now I have lived "in seclusion from the world," as one of the friends I have mentioned expressed it (the expression amused me, for to me that "seclusion" was first of all the convent, and for the nuns there the convent certainly wasn't "the world" either, only my friend Vlad and the nuns do not mean the same world), but I will find you.

I will find you and you will be able to translate and rebuild . . .

If I can manage it, if I can manage . . .

I am afraid, madame . . .

THIRTEEN

A Foretaste of Invasion

OUR FATHER periodically told us that strangers would be coming to stay. "Your cousins," he elaborated resolutely — but we had the distinct impression that he edged closer to Tiresia in order to make the announcement, that he actually stood at attention by her side.

These cousins lived on another continent. They were supposed to spend their summer vacation with us. But for one reason or another that instantly slipped our minds, they would fail to come, and we would be relieved, safe for another summer, safe for the whole year.

But it was a close shave every time. We all saw the letter with the Canadian stamp, Tiresia was unusually agitated, our father once again trotted out the phrase "Your cousins" — and we once again caught the strange insistence in his voice and felt his body stiffen to attention. We crept off to the attic to calm ourselves with our purloined cigarettes and exhale some of our resentment with the smoke.

"Canada is big," said Dan. "It should be enough for them."

"Maybe they want to see us," said Estelle.

"They even have the Arctic, and Eskimos," said Dan, still deep in Jack London.

"Or maybe they think they *have* to visit," said Estelle.

"Who asked them?"

"Nobody asked us what we think."

"And four of them!" said Dan, appalled.

"Five of them."

"Oh yes, the girl too," said Dan. "A girl cousin, can you imagine, like poor old Adrien."

Poor old Adrien, our neighbor who was two and a half years younger than me and two and a half years older than Dan, had cousins who visited every week, one of them a dolled-up girl. We watched wide-eyed as she teetered down the road on heels that visibly pinched her feet and wearing a tight blouse with great dark halos under her arms.

Perched on a stool by the bull's-eye window in our attic, we watched for that moment in midafternoon when they all spilled out onto the road, doubtless chivvied out by parents who wanted to finish their Sunday dinner in peace.

Their numbers astounded us: five boys, plus Adrien, plus this girl. Seven in all, seven children kicking their heels out on the road. It irritated us. We would never have dreamed of joining them, and they would never have ventured as far as our gate.

Adrien we tolerated. He was our neighbor, and besides, he never waited to be invited.

Dan dealt with the girl, I took care of the boys.

"Can you imagine her climbing the roof, Estelle, or going up to the cave!"

I knew exactly what he meant. He meant the girl cousin's gleaming white high heels and black stockings, her tight-to-bursting girdle, the bra straps peeping from beneath her blouse, the halos at her armpits. All that girly paraphernalia.

Let me try to picture that girl again. For that was all she was, really — a girl very much like every girl back then. Gingham skirt, *broderie anglaise* blouse, and nipped waistline like those worn by the newest of the starlets featured in *Paris-Match* (Adrien brought it over to shock us; his mother was a subscriber). Only the stockings and high heels betrayed the small-town girl. But pretty, I believe, and friendly. So why were we so merciless?

Perhaps because she (and her brothers) were there on a Sunday visit and because such Sunday visits took place all over town and all over the country, on this same day and in every family. In every normal family. It aroused contempt in us, a sort of ill-defined distaste.

"So next Sunday," said Dan, "Adrien will be going to their place. How boring for him!"

And methodical Estelle would set herself mathematical problems.

"What do they do if there are other cousins in other branches of the family? If there are more than four branches of the family, I mean, how do they work that in with four Sundays a month?"

"They rotate."

"But what if there are more than four branches?"

"In that case," said Dan, "they decide there are more than four Sundays in a month."

"They can't do that."

"Why not?" asked Dan.

And so on.

Then it was my turn to attack the boys. I took them all on at once.

"Look at them with their protruding ears, and whistling at all the girls!"

"They whistled at you?"

"Well . . ."

The idea that these oafs might have whistled at his sister Estelle filled Dan with cynical joy. That's what normal families were like — the kids scurrying down the road like chickens or whistling like policemen. While indoors their crimson-faced parents stuffed themselves and drank too much and shouted each other down, their voices (we could hear them at that very instant) swelling to a roar: they sounded as if they were butting into a head wind of laughter, laughter with hysteria close to its surface. "Tipplers' voices," said Dan, who must recently have heard the word.

Certainly no one in our house had a tipplers' voice. And our parents did not stuff themselves. Besides, where were they? On this Sunday, as on all other days, our father sat in his study surrounded by his files (his duty cases on Sundays), our mother Nicole danced to the music of her record player, and Tiresia . . . Well, you couldn't really imagine Tiresia "doing" anything, she was somewhere in the house just "being," probably neither at her piano nor in her room. And her way of being wherever she was in no way resembled Adrien's parents' way or Adrien's cousins' parents' way, that was certain.

"So what did you do, Estelle?"

"Well . . ."

Of course Estelle had done nothing. Nor in all likelihood had Adrien's cousins. And in the event they actually had whistled at her, Adrien had certainly shut them up at once with a terse "She's my neighbor." But perhaps not, on the other hand — perhaps Adrien had experienced a sly pleasure at seeing his neighbor the butt of his cousins' whistles, perhaps he had even instigated the whistling . . .

But now that the ball was rolling I could not stop.

"What did you do?" said my brother's insistent voice.

He danced for me. I told stories for him. That was the way it was throughout our childhood, and for years afterward.

But still I hesitated a little, because of the word "lies" our doctor shouted as he slammed the car door, and because of that same word "lies" that our father had repeated in such strangely wounded tones as he chased him down the road, holding the bag at arm's length. Was it lies to invent something that did not really exist?

Was that what had infuriated our doctor and affected our father's voice so strangely?

"Go on, Estelle."

"Very well . . ."

Dan changed my heart's truth. He needed a world of shifting intensity; he forced me to make it up, in response to the slightest change in his voice or his eyes, as I went along. The resulting fictions became our truth, the truth of our own world.

Dan still crouches in the recesses of my heart. What I am doing now is simply continuing to lie in order to become the truth of what crouches in my heart.

"Well, then, Estelle?"

"I went up to them . . ."

My brother began to glow! This was what he craved, a confrontation with giants, a swashbuckling adventure that would somehow, however improbably, wind its way back to our own life, where it would approach us, orbiting alongside us like a twin planet, and for a little while we would be able to believe ourselves upon that other planet where history evolved according to the wishes of those who had willed it into being and had eyes to see it.

He glowed. Without needing to look at him, I felt the animation on his face, shot with swift flashes that spread a powdery electric halo around him.

I made the leap . . .

"I went up to them and asked what they wanted."

"How did you ask?" said Dan.

"Coldly, like this: 'May I help you?' They started to blush, and their jug-handled ears flapped in the breeze like sails in distress. I said, 'Forgive me, gentlemen, but I fancied I heard a whistle.' 'No, no,' they stammered. I said . . ."

"Don't forget the subjunctives, Estelle," Dan whispered, his voice much lower than my words so as not to interrupt the story.

"I said, 'Heaven forbid you should fall into unwitting violation of some stern statute. I should be most unhappy were ill luck to hound you, most unhappy were you to find yourselves in prison.'"

I stopped, out of ideas, exhausted by the subjunctives.

"And then, Estelle?"

"I said, 'I should be most unhappy were ill luck to visit you, most unhappy were you to find yourselves in prison, above all were I to be the cause. I should be unable to deny that you had alas indeed'" ("Had alas indeed!" Dan echoed respectfully, his voice still flowing with my own discourse) "'had alas indeed been whistling at me for some considerable time, and as you must know, the law severely punishes . . .'"

"Corruption of minors," hissed Dan.

We had heard our father use the expression; he often talked legal business at table. If we asked, he would discuss all his cases except the duty cases. Legal language enchanted us, particularly Dan, who saw it as ordinary language in strange and seductive disguise, a new kind of ballet performed by words.

"Also incitement to vice," he added at once.

"Of course," said his sister, fearlessly accomplishing every twist and turn in his wake, continuing on her new course as solemnly as was her custom in everything she undertook.

"And public solicitation."

"I said to them: 'The law severely punishes corruption of minors as well as incitement to vice and public solicitation.'"

"What did they say then?"

"The oldest one said to the others, 'Watch out, her father's a lawyer.' And they started to tremble uncontrollably; they said, 'What are we going to do?' And the oldest one said: 'There's only one thing we can do — surrender unconditionally.'"

Out of ideas again. Another pause.

Dan leapt to the rescue:

"You said to them: 'Approach me one by one and go down on your knees and, and . . .'"

Following his mimed directions, I came up with a discourse that went roughly like this:

"'. . . and utter the following words: "Mademoiselle, be so kind as to accept our apologies for our crude behavior in whistling at you in the street as if at a woman of easy virtue. In our defense, we would plead that we are not acquainted with any young ladies, being much too repulsive, and in consequence have so far been obliged to pay for the embraces of professionals, which is the reason the dividing wall between Adrien's house and yours has never been repaired, our cousin Adrien's father having had no other recourse but to come to our rescue to pay the debts we incur in the course of such insalubrious encounters. Given these several distressing circumstances, mademoiselle, we hope you will overlook how hairy and repulsive we are, how our ears flap and our noses bulge, how stupid we are in every way, which are not in themselves crimes and which we earnestly beg you to take into account as extenuating circumstances." ' "

By this time we were both making gigantic efforts not to explode into laughter (it was out of the question for Adrien's boy cousins and girl cousin to notice our presence at the window). We were writhing so uncontrollably we almost fell off our stool. Because in Dan's voice we heard the intonations of our father when he was discussing his business, or of certain clients of his we had spied on from behind the privet shrubs outside his office.

He was also mimicking Adrien's father, and the conversations we had heard on the subject of that dividing wall. And then the girl cousin came back onstage: of course she had to witness the defeat of her camp and the victory of ours, for now Dan had joined me in the adventure.

Their final humiliation was awful to behold. The eldest cousin was literally unable to make the required amends, but remained petrified in the middle of the road: in his distress he had been unable to control his natural functions, and now dared not move lest he reveal the horror. But in vain: the horror glittered like an ice patch on the road between his feet. A hospital ambulance came roaring up at full speed (the ambulance we always feared seeing at our own front door), but it skidded on the puddle and he escaped by a hair as the ambulance crashed into the ditch. Numb with terror, the brothers froze in place, like their sister, whose heels had sent her toppling facedown on the ground. We raced to the help of the ambulance crew and their patient (who was a man well known in our town), tugged them out of the burning wreck, our hair in flames. But we rescued the victims, and a few days later we received a medal for our courage. The leading doctor in all of France presided over the ceremony, and then, moved by our entreaties, agreed to cure our mother of her nightmares. In secret, of course, so that our good Doctor Minor might believe himself the healer. Our mother stopped having nightmares, and simultaneously stopped wanting to be a dancer (we vaguely sensed that the two were linked). Henceforth we could kiss her from morning till night, twist the small curls on the nape of her neck in our fingers, and she could bake us real cakes, and sing us songs at the piano.

There was another version.

Our mother stopped having nightmares and simultaneously became the great dancer she dreamed of being. She was world-famous. Our house was permanently heaped to the ceilings with gigantic bouquets.

"No," Dan suddenly said, "that's too much like a cemetery."

"Like a cemetery?" I echoed.

We were horribly struck.

The story was over. We stayed there leaning against each other, hands glued to the windowsill, weighed with cares we could not fathom, unable even to get off the stool, wearied to the marrow of our children's bones. The cousins had long since left the road.

It was an attack of what we called our vaypigo. It would pass. But we could not leave things there. Anxiety had settled deep inside us, together with a strange curiosity. We wanted to know all about gravestones and wreaths. Could all kinds of flowers be put on graves, or were only certain varieties allowed?

I thought of my mother Nicole's tulips, the ones that arrived on the day my brother was born, flowers that seemed black, a monstrous black bouquet in that white, white hospital room. And Dan was obsessed by the word "tuberose." He thought that if there was indeed a cemetery flower, it had to be the tuberose.

Tiresia! Sitting bent over a book with the light behind her, one hand supporting her glasses as if she could not get used to their presence, their weight, and would be well advised to manipulate them like binoculars or household appliances. Then her veil slipped and she set down the book in order to replace it. After a time (was she unable to follow the text or were glasses and veil too much for her?) she gave up trying.

A humdrum activity had become an insurmountable task. She let go gently, like a mountaineer seen from a distance sliding down a cliff face.

We watched, Dan and I. We saw Tiresia slide far from her book, the two of us silent at our end of the living room, motionless, utterly absorbed.

There were many books in our house and apparently no one read them. Yet it seemed that everybody had read them. Our father and Tiresia constantly referred to this or that setting or situation to be found in a book. They discussed them as if those things really existed, as one discusses one's family. But allusively, so that we could never clearly identify people and places and events. We dwelt in a fantastic world of fleetingly glimpsed beings who made a powerful impression on us — and whom we then transferred (in response to the inspiration or the needs of the moment) to the territory the two of us shared. So that for us Don Quixote could quite credibly be in love with Mary Queen of Scots, and because of that impossible love find himself metamorphosed into the horrid beetle Samsa, or tumble from the famous bridge that was hard, that was cold, that was a bridge, a bridge spanning a ravine.

But when, when had they read all these books? we wondered.

The question alarmed us, occasioned real physical distress. We felt ill. Our vaypigo returned.

Dan and I often fell suddenly ill in this fashion. I am not referring to visible illnesses. Of them we had the regular quota, and our Doctor Minor handled them most competently. I mean what to us was *true* illness — those attacks of dizziness that seemed to well up from black swamp water, suddenly reminding us of the unstable bottom within us, a bottom of silts and quicksands where finding a footing was impossible. Nevertheless you kept trying — and all at once something like an animal emerged, lashing back and forth. This was the peak of the crisis. Now all we could do was let ourselves be buffeted from side to side: this thing was inside us and we had but one urge, to emerge from ourselves, where this awful thing that so terrified us dwelt.

Our father and Tiresia often brought books into their conversation, and our mother Nicole listened, seeming to know what or whom they were talking about, but left to herself she never asked all those books to join us at the dining room table. She never called upon the ghost world that seemed to surround our father and Tiresia as tangibly, as concretely, as the walls and the people of our little town.

When our father and Tiresia talked together, that ghost world seemed perfectly real, and the phrases that flowed between the two of them made solid sense. We listened to them the way children always listen to grown-ups, apparently distractedly but beneath the surface all ears, utterly believing.

And then our mother Nicole spoke, and suddenly we sat up straight, wide awake. Her words seemed utterly incongruous.

"Samsa could be a dancing role," she said one day. Reflective, remote, her voice cut short the serene but busy flow of dining room talk.

I remember it well, for her words fell upon us as if a meteorite had crashed into the middle of the table.

I recall it too because of my father's irritated rejoinder:

"What an idea!"

And our mother went on, her eyes filled with tears:

"Yes, yes, those little legs waving on the bed and when he climbs the wall, and when he crawls closer to his sister to hear her play the piano, how wonderful for a dancer, taking up the whole space, the floor, the walls, above, below, moving your limbs to resemble waving feelers . . . Not for me, of course, but for a modern dancer, for Dan . . ."

And she rose sobbing, saying something, something we were unable to grasp, something about culture and our father and Tiresia, suddenly she was leaving the table, and Tiresia rose, our father rose as well, seizing Tiresia by the arm to prevent her leaving in pursuit of Nicole, and Tiresia turned back to our father. They stood there motionless and rigid, and as usual we read something in Tiresia's body — a command, an entreaty — that was addressed to us.

That entreaty said: "I cannot move, nor can your father move, for we are swayed by a destiny of which I can tell you nothing. If we acted, no one could predict what might happen. But you children are free. Hurry to your mother, find her, and do what children can do. Go on, hurry, otherwise we are all lost."

And we would go, we would look everywhere for our mother. It was not easy, for she did not want to be found right away. Perhaps she wanted to test the extent of our determination, perhaps she did not want to be seen in her distress. And then we would hear her laugh, a laugh still moist with tears but rapidly drying, for our search had become a game of hide-and-seek, and we ran to her, hugged her hard enough to suffocate her, stroked her hair and the curls on her neck, so small and blond. Dan licked her, just like a little animal. Now was our chance, and we had to seize it, for this was one of the few times she gave herself to us, let us do what we wanted.

I see clearly now that even in those moments she did not give herself to us like a mother, but as if she herself were a little animal. Dan and Nicole, two little cats, and beside them a kind of dog, in other words me, not really daring to do too much, for I was intimidated by my mother. I too caressed her, but furtively: she looked so fragile, her eyes endearing and always a little shadowed in the pallor of her face. I was afraid of making her fade, I think. Afraid of seeing her fade suddenly before my eyes, like the flowers our gardener's clippers let blindly fall upon the heap of branches and leaves waiting for the bonfire.

Dan would pretend to raise her in his arms, indeed a little later (he was growing fast, he had always been the tallest in his class) he actually managed to raise her, then to carry her. I followed, excited and terrified. He bore her, he held her aloft as in a cage, this mother of ours so like a bird, always seeking the open immensity of the sky. Not for a second did I (still dwelling in that wellspring inside myself where Dan lived) believe he could drop her — but she twisted as she laughed, she twisted so, couldn't she see how small Dan was?

My heart pounded with fear. I was angry with our mother for being so careless, for taking such little care, for not caring that Dan was in danger of falling, not caring about the injury he might do himself, of the injury his pride might suffer if he were to stumble with our mother's weight in his arms. And almost in the same breath I remembered Nicole's nightmares and was angry at myself for censuring her heedlessness and high spirits. By the time we reached the front porch, a hole had dug itself deep inside me and my strength had fallen into it.

Our mother had already forgotten all about us. She had dismissed us in her careless way, and I called to Dan, wordlessly, with every fiber I still possessed. More accurately, I imagine I must have been leaning over the garden steps, my head resting on the rounded stone. I can feel that rounded edge pressing against my cheek, rough enough almost to bruise, but solid (the stone of the stairway reminded me of our doctor's hand when he was steadying us for an examination).

And Dan heard my appeal and looked at me: "You have vaypigo," he said, and his look revived me. He had stopped playacting. Dan took these attacks most seriously, and soon, thanks to that intense seriousness of his, I no longer felt so ill. After a few more attentions from him of the kind I have already described, and others I have perhaps forgotten, childish but effective, our world returned to normal.

And then we could return to the dining room and face the sequel to the incident.

Our father was no longer there, nor Tiresia.

We finished our meal alone, mixing up the dishes the way we always did when there was no one to supervise us. But no one ever supervised us anyway. It was we who supervised ourselves, in the presence of grown-ups, of our own volition. Instinctively, so as not to add to their worries. For we sensed that something was worrying them.

But as soon as Dan and I were alone together, we just did what we wanted, like unsupervised children. Our meal became the occasion for every kind of blend, and after we put everything away as best we could, our father would drop by briefly, see how hard we were working, and pay us a compliment or two. But there was a faraway look in his eye, and I felt the effort he made to keep us standing on the outer limits of his awareness. His compliment shamed me, though, and I came close to telling him, "Papa, don't give yourself all this trouble," but one glance at Dan and I held my peace. There was no question of betraying Dan.

Evening fell, a chill crept over the kitchen, the smell of things reasserting their authority after the fleeting busyness of human beings.

As he went out, our father had switched off the light without realizing it, and at once a somber mass loomed behind the windows, the whole huge darkness of outdoors, alive with mysterious movement. Struck motionless, we watched. Night deepened.

Then we turned our heads: the staircase light was on. There someone had equally thoughtlessly forgotten to switch it off. Soon we could no longer tear our gaze from the glow stealing in as if on tiptoe from the hallway, laying an enigmatic triangle on the kitchen floor.

We grasped hands.

It was our house that huddled around the vertical shaft of the stairway, and we were safe inside.

FOURTEEN

"The Earth Is Calling Us"

I DANCE because the earth is calling, Estelle, because the earth is calling us, and I'll dance for other people to make them feel that call and teach them how to answer it. Oh, Estelle, my beloved sister, what else is there in life?"

Dan, my brother, so young, where could you have learned how short life can be? Where did you learn that life can be but a brief dash across the face of death?

Dan knew about death's trappings.

We would often watch from our attic fanlight as funerals snaked their slow way to the cemetery. I would be busy somewhere inside the house and Dan would come up, wild with excitement: "Estelle, come quick!" "What is it, Dan?" "Come on, come and look!" And I followed him, as I would have followed him anywhere, and we climbed together onto the little stool he had pulled beneath the window. He had already lifted the pane and propped it open with the rusty iron arm, and we rested our chins on the ledge as Dan pointed to the white cemetery wall: "Look, a burial, Estelle!" Then he stopped talking, his excitement subsided, and he watched, deeply absorbed.

And I watched him. It was on his face that I saw the dark serpent slide up the road, saw the gates swing open and the hearse roll in. On his mobile features I saw the procession wind through the graves, and by his face I knew whether we would be able to see the ceremony or whether it would take place out of sight. If the grave was within view Dan stayed to the end. And I watched him.

It seemed to me that through his familiar features something was attempting to take shape, something vast seeking ingress through that moment which was much too small for it to enter by.

*   *   *

Madame —
    The things I am trying to say are unsayable . . .

Madame —
    Television noises float across the street, blaring commentary on the elections from the apartment of an elderly neighbor who leaves his window open and his set turned on all day long, even when he goes out. I believe he is deaf and lives alone. And someone is fighting out in the street as well, over a parking spot, I believe . . .
    All that noise from the outside world . . .

Madame —
    I am checking through these notes I've made for you, how inadequate they are. They are not Tiresia's story. They could as easily make me laugh as cry . . .
    Don't forsake me . . .

What I saw on my brother's face was the road up which a corpse was traveling, the gaping earth at the end of that road waiting to close over the corpse, and ourselves with our chins resting on the sill, cheek to cheek, watching it all, cheek to cheek and still among the living.

"I'm going to dance, Estelle," my brother said as the gates swung to and the procession dispersed.

Suddenly his voice changed:

"Hey!"

"What?"

"See that?"

Once more we glued ourselves to the sill. A dark shape seemed to be seated behind the mound by the grave.

"What is it?"

"I don't know."

Mysteriously impressed, we spoke in low tones. All at once I said:

"Dan, it's a man!"

The man held something in his hand, which he lifted from time to time to his face.

"It's Alex's father, Dan!"

"What's he doing?"

"He's drinking . . ."

We pulled the fanlight down and climbed off the stool. "I'm going to be a dancer, Estelle," Dan said again.

* * *

We closed the fanlight, shutting out the outside air, which bore on its breath the white cemetery wall and the black procession and the grave and Alex's father getting drunk, all alone, beside his most recent corpse.

That same day Dan told our mother Nicole that he could no longer work with her, that he wanted to take lessons at the new conservatory that the municipality had just opened at the urging of charitable organizations.

Until then Nicole had kept him working in her blue garage. He was lazy and moody and thought only of playing pranks. Even though I possessed no gift at all, I worked more seriously than he did.

"But Dan, why don't you want to dance with Nicole anymore?" I asked him, stricken at the realization that he was leaving her and leaving me for somewhere unknown.

I heard Dan's reply. But at the time, as with so much of what he told me, I failed to understand him. Nor did he himself realize that he had understood something. An intuition spoke through him and sank into me: it went through us both like a small comet through a dark sky, leaving in its wake only a tail that to our eyes flashed like a signal. The trail it left was illegible, inconsistent with a reading. Yet it was there.

"Nicole dances for the angels. I want to dance for the earth."

We stared at him, astounded. We were at the dinner table, I believe. My father emerged from his private thoughts.

"What did you say, Dan?"

And my brother, half-surprised himself, said again, "Nicole dances for the angels. I want to dance for the earth."

Dan could talk like that, unsuited to his years. They seemed to emerge as if they had always been written down inside him. After that, we always called Nicole's work dancing for the angels. Nobody even remembered where the expression came from, our father himself used it, surprised at his own perceptiveness. "Of course, dancing for the angels, poor Nicole," he would say, tears starting to his eyes. Dan did not recall inventing it. The phrase was so obvious to him that he must have believed he had found it along the way one day when he needed it. I alone knew that it was Dan who had first used the expression, but it never occurred to me to tell our father. I sensed confusedly that it would have scared him.

*   *   *

Dan wordlessly watched the funeral procession enter the cemetery, then almost at once reverted to the fanciful mode we all knew so well. He pinched my arm.

"Estelle, how come you're still here?"

"I'm watching the burial."

"You mean you think funerals are fun?"

"But you're the one who called me to watch."

"Just for a quick look, not to go on rubbernecking for hours and hours . . ."

"But Dan, you're the one who . . ."

I was astounded, outraged. Dan watched me, then suddenly hugged me, squeezing so hard he nearly suffocated me, kissing my neck and my arms.

"Estelle, my little sister, you're going to cry."

Eyes brimming, I denied it.

"No, I'm not going to cry, are you crazy, who do you think I am?"

His finger softly traced the hollows of my eyes.

"You think I'm making fun of you, that I've betrayed you. Don't ever think that, Estelle, I'll never betray you, never, do you hear?"

And one day while he was hugging me hard, he suddenly whispered:

"When I'm dead, Estelle, I want you to come and see me."

"What do you mean, Dan?"

"Come and see me in my grave — once, just once."

"What do you mean, what do you mean?"

But already he had moved away and was laughing.

"Estelle, you take everything so seriously, come and play."

Their roots hopelessly tangled, time and places blur and intertwine and send out forests of new shoots. How am I to cut through them, madame, how am I supposed to separate them out? They are my life. Don't forsake me, I beg you . . .

I looked at my brother. The whole world lay on his face like the open pages of a book — our life, our death, the long, tortuous path leading from one to the other, and how to negotiate that long, tortuous path that stretched before us.

All I had to do was look at my brother, and I saw where we were on that path and what we were doing there.

*   *   *

I look too at Phil. But I see nothing on his face. I watch him when he is driving and I am in the passenger seat. He keeps his eyes on the road and doesn't know I am watching him.

But there is nothing to see on his face but a combination of male features I have learned to desire, and I turn away with such sadness, oh, Dan, I want to tell him to turn around, to put a stop to this travesty, to return me to my home.

Could it be that this is where I am now on that long, tortuous path — sitting in a moving car beside a man whose face I have learned to desire but on which there are no signals for me to read?

That face of Phil's. Can anyone understand what it means to love the face of one who is not your brother? It is monstrous and meaningless.

That face torments me. I no longer possess the proper implement for recording it in me, and even if I did possess such an implement there is no longer a surface within me to receive its imprint.

Ever since we met, it seems, Phil's face has hovered in the air before me, triggering in me an astonishment that combines repulsion and attraction. I cannot put his features together, they swim all amorphous in my memory.

I watched my brother because his face showed me meaning, and I consistently had to watch it to acquire reassurance. I watch Phil because his features show me amorphousness; each time I need to rearrange it in some sort of order, which will last only for the precise duration of that encounter.

But I have seen that face in love, I want to see it in love: not very long ago, turning toward him on the crowded street, I suddenly realized that this face of his possessed beauty, that Phil was a young and attractive man. And I felt a new pain, Dan, because he was attractive *and yet* he was not my brother, and because at any moment that chance-met love could trickle away in the cracks between the paving stones.

That is how they live, Dan. Everyone is afraid all the time. Not afraid of losing their loved one to death, Dan, but afraid of losing him to life. Afraid of mutating desire, which moves first in one direction, then another. That is what they talk about. They do not talk of dancing or of music or of justice, but of that — of love, which betrays. And I, in the street, now that I have returned to their world, I too am afraid, oh, Dan, my brother, my little brother, why did you send me to this world where I am now?

Phil is not my brother, I do not have love for him, my love is anxiety — anxiety lest as I walk by his side he suddenly move out of step and find himself walking beside another woman. Can you understand that, Dan? Can you imagine that life could be like that?

I went away with Phil for the weekend. Not the way you and I used to, because we had finished our work and wanted to take a trip together before going back to it. I left with Phil "for the weekend" because we had become lovers, and lovers leave for the weekend.

I had not dreamed of going away: I had already traveled so far, and it had taken me so long to get back. Phil talked about a vacation and I wanted to laugh, it was as if I were listening to a radio announcer, Dan. And suddenly I recalled my new first name, Claire, and within me this Claire spoke. "Estelle," she said or rather begged, "be quiet!"

We went to the seashore.

With what in mind I was not really sure, Dan, to "weekend by the ocean."

On the balcony of the apartment we rented, looking at the sea and the setting sun, I tried really listening to Phil. I clutched the flagstone that moves about ceaselessly inside me, sometimes resting on my heart, sometimes my eyes, sometimes my ears, preventing me from hearing. I tried to shake myself, to live that moment, Dan, as if you had never existed, to live it with this stranger as warmly as I could. I tried, but I have such trouble hearing him.

"In May of 1968 we tried to make revolution. Then we tried to make families. Now we don't know what . . . We just move on . . . Yes, that's it, we move on and look around us . . ."

The whole time he was speaking, leaning on that balcony in the fading sunlight over the sea (and what he said suddenly moved me, tugged at my attention), there was a pain inside me.

Because I was waiting for your voice, Dan. In love, I always wait for your voice, but instead I find only detached words that settle where they can, like small stray parachutes never sure of being retrieved by anyone anywhere.

From the other side of the bay, in the ruddy twilight, the city looked like a cliff of bleached coral soaring above a sumptuous mirror ("Ugh, all those concrete blocks to replace what was destroyed in the war," said a disgusted Phil), and then the sun sank and the lights went on. Now the city was like a diamond necklace displayed on a backcloth of dark silk with long gray delicate liquid reflections, such a display of beauty: I had the sorrowful sense of error, of deceit. Then Phil crushed out his cigarette. "Enough lofty talk," he said vigorously, and left the balcony to get the meal started.

FIFTEEN

"This Woman Who Wanders About at Night"

IN THE EVENING Dan would come to my room, where I was already in bed, and spread his mattress out on the floor. We began to talk and to fall asleep as we talked; night came in through the window on which we never closed curtains or shutters. It slowly penetrated the house, which seemed to grow hollow and deeper and to change in secret ways in order to receive it. It impregnated our words so that we heard sightlessly, guessing rather than seeing. Then I would slip down to the floor, to the rug, pulling a blanket off the bed, and without opening our eyes, without interrupting our whispering, we finally fell asleep, Dan on his thin mattress, and me on the even thinner rug, camping out in my bedroom for another night.

Never was my sleep more precisely that — "sleep" — than on those nights we spent on the floor, usually without sheets, for bedding under those conditions was too complicated. We lay under our blankets, which fell away to leave us naked and shivering by dawn. But these were the only real nights of my life, firm, intact nights in which the hours fit together like boards on a well-made floor.

Yet I did not sleep deeply; we never slept deeply. I believe we kept our ears open for what might come from our mother Nicole's bedroom. We feared her nightmares, and I am sure that every night we heard almost every hour toll on the grandfather clock she had insisted on putting on the landing so that everyone might hear it.

"But it's all worm-eaten and the pendulum's stuck," said our father.
  "I'll have it fixed."
  "Where will you put it?"
  "Outside the bedrooms."

"The bedrooms?"

"That way," she said, "I can be sure that you will never altogether go away."

"Go where? Go where, Nicole? Where do you think we'd go?" our father said.

And she looked at us all with her frightened look.

"To . . . to sleep," she answered.

Just as Nicole had planned, we never altogether went to sleep. We always heard the clock chime, but that did not mean insomnia: it meant a solid connection between the hours of the night, the chimes fitting the hours closely to each other. And despite our fear of our mother's nightmares, we had true sleep with us, we were at the very heart of true sleep.

Because as long as we were together and the house was quiet, those nightmares had no hold on us. They did not assume full strength until they actually assaulted the house. The rest of the time it was as if they were shut away in a trunk; as long as we did not hear that trunk's clasps snapping open, we were at peace.

For me those nights were a solid foundation on which I could rest the whole of the following day.

I have never since known such sleep.

Not after Dan's death throes, when I believed all my feelings were spent. Not in my cell at the convent, where the silence was so deep that my own breathing frightened me. Not when I came back to our house, bereft of both living and dead. Not when I sleep by Phil's side.

I fall asleep beside Phil, I touch his warm thighs, I feel his strong hand on my hip. Our bedroom is peaceful, and I know he will be first up in the morning to turn on the heat and make coffee, I know that after the piping-hot coffee and the bread he slices for me himself, he will sit at the head of the bed with his back to the wall and hold me to him for a few minutes in silence, only breaking the silence to inhale and tap the ash from his cigarette into the ashtray, and then we will separate for the day. All that I know, and I repeat it to myself, and I feel surges of feeling, of gratitude, welling up into my head, into the place where such things take shape. But it does no good.

Sooner or later I will awaken.

The night will have that horrible black whiteness. In my ears will be a strange calm, which is not that of the bedroom where I used to sleep with my brother. The room will be foreign, every noise will be hideously foreign, and I will turn onto my side so as not to see the face that is not Dan's face.

There are no doors between the rooms of this apartment and I do not know where to turn.

Those naked hinges mounted on doorless jambs struck me like a blow. "Where's the door?" I asked Phil. "I don't know, in the basement, maybe," he answered distractedly. "But why?" I persisted, something within me beginning to moan. I thought he would hear what was moaning inside me, I thought that when I returned, the door between the two rooms would be there, but there were only the hinges, laid bare, and the same emptiness between the lintels.

A brutal urge to run. "Get the hell out!" shouted the former Estelle. It seemed impossible to stay since he had not heard me and my pain had not reached him. But suddenly the other voice said softly inside me: "Be careful, Claire, this man is not your brother."

I heard that voice clearly.

Phil is not my brother. How could he hear what I am not saying?

But I do not want to tell him that I no longer know how to sleep, that the convent put stiffness into my limbs, that I can no longer bear a body next to mine. Oh, how I would love to be able to bear it. But death, which watches within me, forbids it.

I will not say any of these things.

In my letterbox was an envelope addressed in unknown handwriting. I turned it over and over. There was no longer anyone who would write to me; the last letters I had received were from Vlad and Michael several months ago, and they had stopped writing. I had forgotten the convent's handwriting, but this hand, open and straightforward, had nothing in common with Beatrice's cramped fist. It was a letter from Phil.

Or rather a note. I saw only one phrase: "this woman who wanders about at night . . ."

The woman who wandered about at night was me; she was what Phil sees in me.

And once again I thought I would not be able to return to him.

*   *   *

Dan knew what it meant to wander about at night.

Even when we slept so happily together on my bedroom floor, we knew all kinds of wanderings.

Those set in train by the first scream of our mother's nightmares, those that followed the severest onsets of our vaypigo, and later on those that seized us unpredictably, no matter when, and hurried us out onto the streets, in the middle of the night, arms around each other and a little unhinged, because that was how we were, because everything we did together seemed natural to us, because our love made every act of madness natural and normal.

I needed time to see the rest of Phil's letter. "Claire, I'm thinking of you. Lots of work today, I got away from the site to scribble this note. I can hear that happy laugh of yours, I can feel your skin. And then I think of this woman who wanders about at night, this woman I don't understand. But it doesn't matter. I want to be with you again. Come over tonight if you want to, I'll be waiting. Phil."

Phil sleeps at night, rises early, makes coffee, doesn't understand sleeplessness. That is what he lets you see of himself; that is what I saw of him and believed in and loved.

Phil, my ally, my medium in the world where I must live without my brother.

But I no longer see things quite in that way. For since receiving his letter I realize this: every time I move, however slightly, Phil too moves, and when I get up I sense his mind getting up too and following my movements from room to room.

I have no idea how to talk to Phil, I have no idea how to listen to him, I have no idea what to do with what we say.

Perhaps only thousands of years together could give us what Dan and I had from the very first second. But will we still be seeing each other in a week's time?

How do creatures who are not brother and sister love? What gift will time give them? What stars watch over them? Are they abandoned to chance, sundered by every passing breeze, by the slightest breath of air? Is that what the love of such beings is like? Is that what I will know with Phil? Will that be the "human love" that the priest who visited our convent described with such dismissive compassion?

If it is so, then I insist that the love of Dan and Estelle was not human love. I insist that it was another kind of love, the only kind nothing could weaken because it sprang from childhood and no one can change his childhood.

(And if you were here, "our" priest Dureuil, you who were so stern to the silent nuns in chapel, you who married only to return at once to the Church and become Bishop Dureuil, sterner if possible than before, I would tell you that this love was greater than the love of God for His creatures, for God and His creatures are not on an equal footing.)

Claire, never speak in this way to Phil or anyone else. You have "returned to the world," as they said in the convent, and it was permanent — so be careful. Learn the language they speak there and the love they live there, or else you are lost, or else you will have to return to that ivy-covered grave — this time to lie on it forever.

SIXTEEN

"I Know Those Diamonds"

OUR FATHER spoke:
"Your cousin Sara can sleep with Estelle in Dan's little bedroom. Your cousins Sam, Olivier, Paul, and Frank will sleep with Dan in Estelle's big bedroom. I've ordered sleeping bags and inflatable mattresses; you can put them in the attic during the day so that you can use the bedrooms if it rains."

He added somewhat grudgingly:

"I got them in that sporting goods store . . . where the name Helleur is apparently well known."

But we weren't listening.

I heard Dan's voice, his high-pitched innocent's voice, the voice he used when he ventured onto dangerous ground. My heart leapt. Here is what Dan was saying in that innocent high-pitched voice, a headlong flight of birds sweeping overhead in full formation:

"And why shouldn't this cousin Sara sleep with Tiresia? After all, she's from Tiresia's family, not Estelle's."

I was hot with perspiration. Dan, how could you say such seemingly harmless things that were really so terrible? Had you forgotten that nobody ever, ever went into Tiresia's bedroom? And just look at Tiresia's body, don't you see her hands trembling, her beautiful pianist's hands that no longer play, Dan, how could you do this to Tiresia, who is the heart of our family? Dan?

But nothing terrible happened. He had touched the sightless heart of our family, and nobody realized the trick he was attempting; neither his parents nor Tiresia reproved him.

On the contrary, our father suddenly pulled him onto his lap.

"Yes, Dan," he said, "yes, little boy."

I can still hear him saying "little boy," and then, more gently, "My little boy."

His voice sounded almost painful, and we understood clearly that his yes meant no, meant "Dan, I must refuse what you ask, and I cannot tell you why, but my refusal is full of sadness and regrets and pain."

"If Sara is a member of Tiresia's family," he said, "it's the same as if she were a member of our family, you know that, Dan, don't you?"

"Yes, yes," Dan answered eagerly.

But he had turned to look at Tiresia.

"Oh, Tiresia, I don't know anything about families, and if I did know anything, it would certainly be that you belong to our family more than any of us, but please, please, let me sleep with Estelle . . ."

"Oh Tiresia, I know nothing of what lies behind your words, and if I did know anything I would try to be more helpful to you, but please, please, let me sleep with Estelle . . ."

"But please, please, let me sleep with Estelle . . ."

And Tiresia heard that mute plea.

Unlike our father, she did not live in the past's dusty files. Neither did she live in the mists of the future, as our mother did. She who had lost past and future must have understood the fearful passion of children who possess only the present.

For Dan, a night without Estelle was black abandonment, black starless night terrifying to all who sensed its approach.

*   *   *

But Tiresia could do nothing. There she was, wordless, motionless. I thought I heard something rip open deep inside her.

"Stop it, Dan," I screamed suddenly, "stop it!"

My voice echoed in front of me. There was no calling it back: it ran like a maddened wolf straight across the snow to the horizon, jet black and howling in the vast whiteness, and at its heels a huge fire gulping down the air . . .

Oh, I have no idea how to say all these things, there were so many enormous things in our house that sent us staggering, that sometimes seized us and tossed us abject and naked into the vat where their monstrous secret boiled and bubbled.

I could feel Tiresia's body, the light from the window as usual at her back, and the ripping deep inside her continued, and I continued to shout, "Stop it, Dan, stop it . . ."

Tiresia came over and put her hands on my face, just her fingertips on my temples, but at once the horror subsided.

Oh, Tiresia, your hands, it seemed to me that I knew them like no other hands in the world, my skin recognized them again from an age-old acquaintance, they soothed base terrors buried in the most ancient recesses of my being, and I raised my hands to my face, to the place where her hands had just dwelt, and I sobbed.

"I'm sorry," I said after a moment.

"It doesn't matter, Estelle," my father said, but he was looking at me with a kind of astonishment.

Could this be his Estelle, his elder child to whom he spoke as if to a wife? I was usually so poised. I do not believe he had perceived the crisis of nerves that had overcome me.

Dan too was looking at me with astonishment. I had never screamed in that way, and my scream had been directed toward him.

It was the first break of our life and our cousins had brought it about. Our hatred for these uninvited strangers burned more fiercely still.

But it was simply the beginning of our woeful teens. I mean Dan's teens, for I was of course already eighteen. But what did age matter between us? In the space we shared, we were the same age, an age not numbered in years.

"Well," said Nicole, who had so far said nothing, "since Dan is sitting on his father's lap, why don't you come and sit on my lap, Estelle, my daughter?"

Nicole! We had forgotten her. Yes, we did occasionally forget our mother. She was so often elsewhere, dancing in her garage, or at dance class, or lost in her dreams of becoming a star dancer, dreams so luminous they surrounded her with dazzling light and hid her from our gaze.

But she was there, and she had watched our whole scene, and now she was suggesting that I — who was so much taller and heavier than she was — should come and sit on her lap. Her voice had a strangely rigid edge to it, which froze the blood in my veins, for as a rule our mother Nicole was nothing if not grace and harmony.

And again Tiresia put her hands to my temples. I really heard those hands murmuring softly to my skin: "Go and sit on her lap, Estelle."

And at once she was moving away, returning to her seat in the chair with its back to the light from the window, vanishing into the shade of the large armchair. Tiresia had subsided into shadow and I was alone.

Horribly embarrassed, I rose and went to sit on my mother Nicole's lap.

Every detail of that scene was hammered into me; the passage of time has modified them, but their impact endures, like a crater you can dig around in forever without making the slightest change in its outlines.

I had on a plaid skirt of coarse wool, rubber rain boots, and one of those shapeless, too-tight pullovers Tiresia had probably not yet had time to alter.

In those days there was no such thing as versatile flattering fashions deliberately tailored for the young. All that came later, when I was already a young woman, and married — and then I threw myself indiscriminately on everything that came out, changing styles the moment fashions changed. At twenty-five and at thirty I was dressing like a fifteen-year-old, and my husband, this husband of mine, found this habit both absurd and costly. No doubt he was terribly in love with this dress mania, but he was much too unsubtle to realize it. I have totally forgotten the boy, I have never even felt like thinking about him, he was the man I married because Dan left for another country, and farther than another country. Yet he did exist, and nowadays I do think of him and would like to make amends. Everything I do with Phil is also an amends toward that young man, Yves. He did not deserve the betrayal I inflicted on him.

*   *   *

"There," Nicole said in that same curious voice, as if she spoke to beings who were not in the room, or who were there but invisible to me, unknown to me, beings that brought with them turbulence, even perhaps loathing.

"There, since you're *my* daughter you have to sit on my lap. Dan is sitting on *his* father's lap. So you must sit on *your* mother's lap."

That was what she said (stressing "my" and "his" and "your"), and they were not the words of a mother. Yet I could feel that the arms around my waist were without malice. Nicole, our young young mother, I loved you too! And I turned to kiss her.

She was wearing a Guerlain perfume, L'Heure Bleue, which my father brought her from Paris and which she loved because of the color in the name . . . I intended to kiss her on the hollow of her neck, on the place the perfume came from, but only there, so as not to annoy her, for she did not like our untidy caresses.

In other words, pretend I was seeking the source of that perfume and yet really kiss her, to show her I loved her despite my rough skirt, my sturdy body, my face that lacked the delicacy of her features and the translucid pallor of her complexion.

I turned toward her, slightly shifting my seat on her lap, feeling her slender legs under my thighs, and bent my face toward her.

She did not pull away. I think she loved me too, our mother Nicole; there was even a kind of compassion amid the bellicose reflections of her green eyes. I saw that compassion, can still see it — and with the same remorse I can never atone for, for I never completed my movement. I did not kiss my mother, because something stopped me: the diamonds I saw in her ears, or rather the diamonds that stared out at me.

They gazed at me like two eyes that had journeyed from a distant, unknown, terrible land. Their fires burned inside my head.

Instead of murmuring "Mother Nicole, darling little mother" to her, the way I had planned, I heard myself say:

"Where did you get those diamonds?"

In the depths of the green gaze compassion drowned. In its place, like some dreadful fish rising from those waters, I saw mistrust and rage, and I knew that black tide was not for me, or else I would have leapt from her lap and out of the house, bounded to the farthest reaches of our meadow, to the hills, to the road, anywhere, if only I could escape a world in which my mother could harbor such mistrust and such rage toward me.

"They are mine," she said. "They were given to me and I am fond of them. Very fond. You know nothing about such things, but let me tell you that they are very valuable, and that I have others, a necklace that you have never seen either, it was given to me at the same time, a diamond choker, you won't see many of them, believe me! Usually diamonds are strung rivière-style, but I didn't want them that way. I had them reset just to fit my neck, and when I wear it it's like a chain, do you understand, Estelle, like a chain, but it suits me, it makes me very beautiful."

My mother always spoke in short bursts. Yet now all of a sudden here was this long speech — and I did not listen! If only I had been able to listen, oh, Nicole, why didn't you shake me, slap me, force me to hear? "Like a chain," poor Nicole, so young, so young, "like a chain."

"I know those diamonds," I said, suddenly stubborn, with a childish obduracy that came I knew not whence but of such strength I could not let it go.

"That's impossible," my mother snapped, "this is the first time I've worn them."

And she laughed:

"Just to see if they make a splash with your cousins. With your wonderful cousins. I'm going to have to dazzle them, because I have a feeling they may not like me."

And I went on saying, "I know those diamonds." I came close to saying, "They're mine."

Oh, the hellish winking of those tiny facets!

"Estelle, please!" my father said. "What's got into you tonight?"

And at last Dan came back, capering about in the middle of the room, saving me from the whirlwind sucking me up into its belly.

"She's angry because they're taking her bedroom," he cried.

My irritation vanished at once. I rose. Nicole patted her dress, already far away.

"Is that true, Estelle?" said our father. "Does lending your bedroom to all those boys bother you?"

How I loved my father for putting his question that way, for giving me the means of defending myself!

Thinking back to that phrase that floated quietly onto the bubbling vat of our emotions, I want to smile: our father was a lawyer after all! "And never one word louder than the next — that's really what you owe your career to, my dear Helleur" was the mocking comment of Minor, who was never able to tame his own unruly verbal flow.

"Yes, Father" (despite everything, something of the solemnity of the courtroom must have reached me through his voice, I had called him Father, which was not my habit; generally I called him . . . no, I called him nothing, I gave him no name).

"Go on, Estelle," urged Dan.

With an effort I went on:

"Yes, it bothers me. I don't know these boys, and I'm used to my bedroom."

Our father looked worried. His earlier quiet authority disappeared. I think he could not bear hurting me, or hurting anybody, perhaps unfortunately for him.

"The thing is, Estelle" (and once again he was addressing me as an equal, as he usually did, as if addressing a wife), "I see no other solution. These cousins have asked to come here, I always worry that you and Dan may be lonely, and I thought it might be a good thing if you, if you . . . if you weren't so alone."

Our father hesitated. How much all this must have cost him!

"But we already have the neighbors, and the neighbors' cousins, and our school friends," Dan shouted, "we're never alone, you don't understand, Father."

And he added disgustedly, with the odd leaps and falls of his new teenage voice:

"In fact we never have the chance to be alone!"

Our father gave a faint smile.

"Is that so, Dan?"

"Absolutely," my brother repeated forcefully, "never a chance to be alone!"

"But I had young people from your own family in mind," said our father. "Tiresia and I might disappear" (he suddenly seemed disoriented, then caught himself), "Tiresia and your mother and I could disappear, and we wouldn't want you to be left alone. Isn't that so, Estelle, you wouldn't want your brother to have nobody?"

"He would have me," I said.

But our father knew he had won. His Estelle could not but share his views, could not but want what he thought was right and what would spare him anxiety.

"You are a good girl, Estelle," he said. "And I'm glad Dan has you for a sister."

"So what are we going to do about the bedroom?" repeated Dan, who had no love for such sentimental exchanges.

("Simpering like a sister!" he would say to me later, "yes, that's right! It was like a conversation in a convent between a priest and a sister, it made me sick, Estelle!" and I had to defend myself tooth and nail to prove to him that I was not a sister out of some convent, oh, Dan, if you could only have seen me all those years later, in that chapel and those corridors, and our long silences, oh, Dan.)

"Forget it," I said, "it's no use, we have to do what Papa says."

For I sometimes used to find myself on our father's side. Particularly at that time, when I was eighteen and Dan thirteen. My age, the age of a young woman, sometimes distanced me from Dan, who must assuredly have looked like a boy who had shot up too fast, even though I can never manage to see him in that light. Perhaps photos could tell me if it was indeed so, but not my memories.

But never, never was the distance so great as that night.

"All right," said Dan, abruptly closing himself off. The cloud that passed across his face must abruptly have darkened it, for despite his absentmindedness our father noticed.

"Dan, I believe you're starting to grow a beard," he said.

"Screw my beard," shouted Dan, and raced away.

It was not burgeoning whiskers my father had seen on Dan's face (they had already appeared, and were in fact rather fair), but something black, the harbinger of the cloud that was to lower upon our life and darken it for so many years.

Dan fled, and it seemed to me that night had suddenly fallen. It was dark in the living room, everyone was seated in his place, shadows were slowly engulfed in night, and I was finally the one who got up to turn on the lights.

SEVENTEEN

"There Are Things I'm Not Allowed to Tell You"

OUR COUSINS came. They were nothing like the neighbors' cousins.

Sara had long wavy hair that she wore in all sorts of surprising styles. To me it seemed like the first time I had really seen a girl my own age. I could not help shooting sideways glances at her as we undressed at night.

"Why don't you take a real good look at me, Estelle? You're dying to."

I was dying to look at her? She had guessed it? Something inside me suddenly lurched, and I blushed scarlet.

We were in Dan's little baby bedroom, the one where I first felt him against my chest right after he was born, the bedroom where I had so often held his hand, sitting on the floor beside his crib with my arm stretched between the bars. The bedroom where my thoughts stayed all day long, where I spent every night, falling asleep on the floor after my numbed arm slipped from the crib, where I awoke later in the midst of a great black silence edged with white, shivering, terrified, yet flooded with happiness.

I was no longer alone, no longer the only child in the world. I had a brother and he was there next to me, I rose and watched him sleeping. And it seems to me (but I must be wrong) that every time he opened his eyes and saw me and smiled, I leaned over him and kissed him and at once he fell asleep again. Then I removed the storage-room curtain, and wrapped in that curtain I finally slept my own sleep at the foot of my brother's crib.

I know I am repeating myself. I know I have already said these things. They are of no weight in the world. Even as I write these notes, a nuclear power plant has already leaked its radiation over our planet; countrymen of ours languish month after month in captivity, hostages in a part of the world where nobody has a hope of extricating them . . . Yet all I can do is go on parroting these little phrases:

> *I touched his hand,*
> *I lay down next to him,*
> *I fell asleep, I woke up,*
> *there he was, smiling at me,*
> *I kissed him,*
> *it was nighttime,*
> *I slept my own sleep.*

There was never ever anything down deep in my heart but those words, those small phrases. Everything else I articulate only by an effort of will. But if you journeyed to the end of the corridor of my being, raising one after another the thousands of tapestries of speech, those would be the words you would find at the very end, simple and unknowing in the gloom. And when I die those are the words I must have on my grave, and if there is no grave, then they are the only ones I want to see whirling in the icy universe amid the planets, the only ones I would have wanted present at the very first breath of life in the world. I know, I know, I am regurgitating every absurd image that comes to me, but what do I care? I have paid my dues to silence, to years of silence, now I want to seize all the words, the most bombastic, the bloodiest, the maddest . . . How can you hope to understand? You do not know silence, what do your irritation or your contempt matter to me, words are no longer precious things to me, they are embryos whelped out just as they are, perhaps dead, perhaps alive . . .

"Estelle, be careful!"

Yes, yes, Claire, my twin in this present time, I hear your voice, I will calm down, but don't expect to prevail every time.

And you, Phil, don't assume you will always have this clear-eyed Claire at your side. The torrent will well up all over again, I feel it inside me, sometimes scalding, sometimes icy, and yet I want to go the whole hog, I want to return to our murderous adolescence. To save myself, Dan. To save myself, Phil.

My cousin unpinned her hair, which shone with red highlights. She washed it in camomile and brushed it a hundred times every night, her head thrown back to air it. I had never heard of such things.

"But everyone knows that, Estelle!"

She stood before me in pants and bra, bent double, and shook her head energetically.

"I'm airing it."

I was sitting on the bed.

"Don't just sit there, Estelle, come and brush for me."

And this unknown cousin straddled a chair in the middle of my brother's little bedroom, and I went over to her and brushed her hair. I could have brushed it for hours as she talked and talked from beneath the waterfall of her hair, telling me how girls our age lived. Fascinated, woebegone, I listened to her; I was no longer myself but an envelope emptied of everything that had been me and being refilled with the light down of my cousin's carelessly and perversely scattered words, and all next day I moved about half-somnolent, my head packed like a pillow with that down.

What my cousin was stuffing me with was not for me, struck no corresponding chord in my innermost self. Her words did not stick to my walls but floated in a void. The whole time my cousins were there I remained in that half-sleeping state.

But her hair attracted me. And when my arm was numb she said: "Your turn now, Estelle."

And in her turn she sat down behind me and undid my barrettes and brushed my hair. Under her nimble fingers and siren words I sank into drowsiness.

"Estelle —"

It was Dan outside the door.

"Don't come in," shouted Sara, "we're in our panties."

"Estelle, Estelle —," shouted Dan from under the window.

I could not answer. I did not want the stroking or the golden words to stop.

Those words of my cousin's!

Down and gold and magic, assuredly it was all that at once, in a soporific blend. It must have been so — otherwise how can I explain that I questioned neither Sara nor any of our male cousins, that they came and they left without telling us, and that what might have saved us merely precipitated our misfortune?

"Estelle," Sara said, "there are things I'm not allowed to tell you. I'd like to, but I've promised."

And I did not ask.

I did not ask my cousin Sara what she was not allowed to tell me. She was obviously aching to tell me, but that drowsiness held me and I was unable to react to her words.

I know now that I asked nothing because in a sense I had no need to ask. I already possessed all the necessary information. I am sure I had known everything since the beginning, since my brother's birth.

But that knowledge remained coiled up upon itself. The magician who guards the secrets declined to touch it with his wand and open up its coils. And Sara, my cousin, said nothing to me, apart from the insinuations that piled up on the fringes of my understanding like algae, and for years I splashed through those algae without seeing them, feeling only strain and impediments and obstacles, and the pain that piled up in the darkest corners of my being.

                                 *   *   *

I never saw my cousin Sara again. She went back to Canada and did
not write to me, and I lost her address.

And yet, in that eighteenth year of mine, as she combed my hair
in that little bedroom where Dan was no longer admitted, I thought
I had at last found a sister; I thought a sister of my age was preferable
to a brother who was after all — as Sara pointed out — just a kid.

"Estelle," cried Dan through the door.

"Estelle," cried Dan from under the window.

I still hear that voice. It has been sinking down inside me ever
since. "Estelle," it called, and I made no answer.

For years I had the same nightmare.

I was in a house that resembled a city, with thick fortress walls.
Outside it was bitterly cold, the night black, the snow whirling white
and soundless about the ramparts. Suddenly I heard a voice calling
me. I went to the window, my heart transfixed, as if I were guilty of
monstrous neglect, and there was a child out there, a tiny near-naked
child, who could not get in and who wandered calling around the
walls in that bitter night on that hellishly white snow.

My horror was so great that I awoke, and at once broke into sobs,
for I had not had time to let the child in, I had awakened too quickly,
I had been too weak, and I was convinced that somewhere out there
in that kingdom of death the frozen child was still calling out, still
looking for the gate in the walls and I was no longer there to help
him, oh, Dan.

Dan, tonight it is snowing, the first snow for three years. The papers
say it has been unusually cold, that temperatures will fall to levels
lower than for years and years, perhaps for a whole century. I looked
outside and it has already covered the sidewalks and made round
anonymous humps of cars and trash cans. It is not melting, and the
snowflakes are still falling, glittering as they sink down through the
glare of the street lamps, and the moon itself looks like a lamp giving
off a very soft yellow light, a snow moon.

Dan, can you imagine all this snow falling all over town, all these
flakes falling through the night, and Phil not calling me, not phoning,
not coming?

You remember, Dan, every time snow fell we went crazy. Once
you were at dinner with some people, important people from the
university, and I had stayed behind alone in our apartment. I was

working at the table by the window when something at the window-pane made me start. I hurried to the window, thinking there had been an explosion, an accident, I hadn't had time to think properly, and there you were out in the street, Dan, coated in white, and you were shouting and laughing up at me:

"Estelle, it's snowing, it's snowing, my little sister."

I had not noticed a thing. I had just sat there recopying scores, bored and gloomy without even knowing it — and suddenly here was this avalanche of beauty, and you, Dan, out in the street below the window, the snow splendid under the street lamp, and your laughter.

I opened the window and leaned out dangerously far.

"Dan, what are you doing there, what about your dinner?"

"I came to tell you it's snowing," said my brother out in the street.

He was standing right below the window, head thrown back, laughing, brushing constantly at the flakes tumbling into his face. I saw his eyes glittering, his whole face glittering, even his words glittered.

"I came to tell you it's snowing, little sister, I wanted to be the first to tell you. Am I the first, Estelle? Am I?"

"Dan, I was working, I didn't notice a thing."

"So I am the first, truly the first," my brother shouted, laughing for joy. "I knew you wouldn't see anything unless I came. I bet you never even moved from your chair."

"Oh, Dan, you're crazy, and what about the dinner, and those people, and . . ."

"I told them I had to buy cigarettes, I told them any old thing. I took a taxi here and I have to get back right away. But come and give me a kiss first, Estelle."

"Go, Dan, they'll be wondering where you are."

"Come and kiss me first."

There we were, talking to each other all alone in that silent street, with me at the window and my brother sparkling in the light under the snow.

He had thrown a pebble at the window; we found out months later that the pebble made a crack. The glazier told us the pane would soon break, but the crack is still there and the pane never broke.

I went down into the street, just as I was, without a coat, and my brother took me in his arms and we kissed wildly under the falling snow and suddenly we wrestled each other into the entranceway and we made love lying on the floor tiles with the snow gusting in, under the magic light of that street lamp, almost without undressing and in insensate joy.

Dan raced away. As he rounded the corner a taxi was moving slowly by. It picked him up and he was gone. All that was left of him on the snow covering our little street was his footprints. I kicked off my shoes and went out to walk on those prints, to step in each of his steps, setting my naked feet down one after the other to fit exactly in the prints left by my brother's shoes. At the end of the street the tracks had been obliterated by the taxi's wheels, and I came back home and lay down just as I was, covered with snow, my feet soaked, my thighs slick with my brother's sperm. I stretched out on our bed so as not to lose what remained to me of him, so as to wait for him with all those traces of him still on me. By the time he returned I was frozen. I had left the window open so that I could go on watching that miraculous fall of snow in the glow of the street lamp, and in that dazzlement watch for my brother's return.

But I fell asleep and suddenly there was my brother, rubbing my feet, kissing my feet and my blueish legs, my thighs that bore our mingled smells. We took a bath together, and talked and laughed and ate, and went back outside to roll in the snow and then had another bath. But our bathtub was too big, and there wasn't enough hot water, so we brought our camping stove into the bathroom and heated pan after pan of water. When we finally lay down and fell asleep in the midst of the act of love, too exhausted to finish, one inside the other, it was dawn.

That was our best time, those brief years long after our teens and after my absurd marriage, the time when we were so fearfully happy.

Dan, can you imagine it? Can you imagine that a man of today, a man barely older than you were, would not call the woman he loved to tell her it was snowing? Yet such people exist, Dan, I promise you, that is what love in this time is like, can you understand these things, Dan, in your grave under the ivy? Oh, my love, how I still miss you, who, who can I talk to?

I happen to know that tonight Phil too is having dinner with someone. He will notice the snow on the way there and on the way back, and that will be all, Dan. Winter will go by, one season, then another, does he see them, does he feel them, does he know how intimately connected they are to love? I do not know, I know nothing of such men, Dan.

No doubt he will call me in a day or two and we shall talk of winter and of the cold, and of our next meeting. That is how things are, Dan, in this world where I live without you.

And you will never come again to call me from below my window, the way you did that evening at the Helleur house when my cousin Sara was combing my hair, or many years later when you came in the splendor of your youth, my love, to be the first to tell me it was snowing. Never again will you throw pebbles at my window. Never again will I hear the crack of a pebble on the windowpane in the silence of a snow-falling night.

If anyone threw a pebble today, the pane would finally shatter, would finally confirm our glazier's prediction. And the only thing for me to do would be to pick up the splinters on the street and in the apartment and look for scissors and glue paper over the broken pane . . .

EIGHTEEN

"Don't Wear Your Bra"

$\mathcal{M}$Y COUSIN combed my hair, and as she combed she talked to me about her life in Montreal, and about New York, where she had driven with her brothers. She talked about the great snow-covered wastes where the highway faded into the distance. At one point they had been rescued from a snowdrift by an army helicopter and been housed together with other blizzard-bound motorists in a Lutheran church. Her three elder brothers already had driving permits. She had also done some hitchhiking. A truck driver who picked her up had driven her to a back road and asked her to undress in front of him. She had been on the point of complying — "Poor guy, all he had in his cab was paper girls." "Paper girls?" "Yes, pinups!" — but a police car had followed them because the truck driver was exceeding the speed limit, "he was pushing sixty!" Sixty did not seem much to me, but I was too shy to say so. What else had she done? Things that astonished me: she went to a summer camp where they roasted marshmallows speared on sticks and where she practiced with a bow and arrow.

"Have you ever kissed a boy, Esty?"
    "Estelle, Estelle," Dan called from outside.

Suddenly the old weakness was back, but how could you talk about vaypigo to someone like Sara?

It was clear that Sara knew nothing about that kind of illness, that it was no use trying to explain it to her. And after looking on it all these years as a natural occurrence, something to put up with and forget, I suddenly felt hatred for it. I fought it.

It was the kind of illness that could stop anybody from hitchhiking, roasting marshmallows around a fire in the evening, shooting off a bow.

And at that very moment it stopped me combing Sara's hair. I had to throw myself down on the mattress, as if I had suddenly had enough of her hair, but really it was to fight my vaypigo, to keep Sara from noticing it. Luckily, like most people who can feel in others only what they themselves have experienced, she noticed nothing. She just went on talking.

"Boys kiss us in the backseat of cars — our cars aren't tiny like yours — they get on top of you and jam their mouths on yours and they try to push up the hem of your panties with one hand and unzip their fly with the other. Some of them must practice, because it isn't easy to do all that at once," said Sara seriously. "We buy panties with tight hems and throw them away if the elastic gets too slack, because we don't want them to go any farther, understand. Have you ever gone farther, Esty?"

The vaypigo was baffled by my resistance, baffled at the realization that it was wasting its time. I was afraid I would be unable to conceal it, I was gasping for breath, I would have liked some cold water.

Dan was back outside again.
    "Estelle, Estelle," I heard him call.

"What's wrong with that kid, yelling like that?" said Sara. "Doesn't he ever let go of your apron strings? You're not his baby-sitter, are you?"

*   *   *

It was the first time I had ever heard such expressions. They scared me.

And now another kind of affliction swept me. It was not our usual vaypigo, which came from within and which properly speaking did not hurt. This particular affliction affected me alone, and it was implacable. Neither cold water nor any of our other little medicines could have tamed it. I did not even know where it came from, but it knew how to hurt. Bathed in sweat, I shut my eyes.

"You're weird, Esty, you never answer," said my cousin.

And all of a sudden, out of the blue:

"You have pretty breasts too, why don't you show them off?"

Apparently my cousin Sara never let herself be put off. Only what did she mean, showing off my breasts?

Neither Tiresia nor my mother, even though she was beautiful, nor anyone else in our little town ever showed off her breasts.

Oh yes, one did! Our neighbor Adrien's girl cousin, whose blouse revealed her bra straps and rolls of fat in front and rings under her arms. "She lets it all hang out!" Mr. Raymond once said, and this way of disassociating one part of the body from the rest in order to flaunt it, far from the center, far from the soul, seemed to us a ridiculous kind of display. But it only happened on Sundays, not the best of days as we knew, and perhaps because of a curse peculiar to that day the girl cousin was obliged to "let it all hang out"?

Of course we had also seen our mother Nicole's breasts. But she did not let them "hang out"; they conformed to all her movements, were a part of the line her body described in space, they danced with her. She never sent her breasts out on detached patrol, outside herself, away from the dance.

The fluid lines of our mother's body and her silky skin were well known to us, and her breasts were simply a part of it all. I saw Nicole naked almost daily at one moment or another, but I am unable to isolate her breasts, to root them in my memory. Nicole was so incredibly beautiful.

Perhaps beauty is just that — a quality that cannot be broken down, that enters you at one single stroke. Can I recall my brother

Dan's body at this very moment? I cannot, a painful glare neutralizes my vision, and I perceive the glare but not his body.

Since then, nothing has entered me in one single stroke.

Either I am no longer able to perceive beauty, or else there is no more beauty to see and everything on earth is equal. I do not know which of these alternatives would be worse for me.

And Sara? She wore a half-cup bra (with her breasts packed tightly in to give them "uplift") and a most clinging shirt, a T-shirt, she called it. She wanted us to look at our breasts in the mirror. I liked hers better because they were small, the kind of breasts that let you be a dancer, but I could see she envied me mine.

(And now we are on the subject, what were mine like? Once again I am at a loss. Hers I gave a half-glance, mine not the hundredth of a glance, the rest of the glance being dissipated across the room. At about that time there was talk of fitting me with glasses. But what kind of optical science could have palliated the special mathematics of my eyes? "You don't need them with me," Dan said, and he was right: I saw straight only in his company. But nobody in the house and nobody at the optician's or the oculist's realized this.)

"If only my brothers could see you, Esty! You shouldn't even wear a bra. Don't put on a bra, and put on my T-shirt, and just wait till you see their faces!"

We quarreled about it, I thought she was making fun of me, and at the same time I clearly saw that she was not.

The idea of parading before my cousins braless and in a T-shirt made me instantly sick, dizzy and nauseated, with a touch of vaypigo to boot. But I was scared of losing Sara's friendship.

I wanted her to go on combing my hair, in panties and bra, telling me her crazy stories and studying me and telling me I was beautiful. That I would be beautiful if I did this or that.

She held my face over a bowl of hot water, rubbed my hands with lemon and my eyelids with ice cubes, and as she did all those things, bathing me in a pool of delicious shudders, I wondered fitfully about the things she had promised never to tell me. But the pleasurable shudders nibbled at the outlandish notion and drove it away. I was unable to think.

"What a pity you're not my real cousin, Sara," I said.

"Oh yes!" said Sara in a voice that was suddenly distant but strangely vibrant, as if she were answering me from the moon with a loudspeaker.

But now I had hold of one small corner of that outlandish notion and I tried to hold on to it.

"I wish you were my real cousin."

I really wanted to say "sister," but did not dare.

I dared not tell Sara I wanted her for my sister, because that would have been a declaration of love, and I did not love Sara. How in those years could I have hoped to untangle such confusion?

I was without a guide. Confusion would prevail and would sweep us all away, Dan and me, our father, Nicole and Tiresia. Confusion had wormed its way, small and unassuming, through the crack of our teens, of our silly run-of-the-mill teenage concerns — but it would take root and prevail. And little by little it would loop its thread around an enormous thing that had once remained far off, and then it would be all over with us.

"I mean," I said by way of consolation, and because that outlandish notion was already escaping me, "Tiresia's family is the same as ours."

I was merely repeating what we had so often heard. It seemed so obvious, I uttered the remark mechanically and it triggered no particular reaction in me. That was simply how it was.

"Your parents are really weird," said Sara.

"You find our parents weird?"

"You're all weird."

I said nothing.

"They told me you would be," Sara added.

The floor under my feet grew steady again. Weirdness we were familiar with.

But other people's weirdness: people's families visiting each other on Sundays, noisy parents stuffing themselves with food, masses of kids underfoot, cousins underfoot, girls "letting it all hang out," the weirdness of all those who did not dedicate their lives to justice or beauty or mystery, of those who did not work on their cases on Sundays, who did not dance in their ballet slippers to the record player, who did not know how to remain still and soundless at the center of things.

My cousin's remark wrenched me out of my stupor, invigorated me. My affliction passed, all my afflictions. I was once again in my home and eager to expel the intruder. The idea of spending the night beside this stranger, one girl cousin among so many girls, now seemed impossible. I wanted to see Dan; I felt as if I had not spoken to him for years. But he had stopped calling. Almost the whole afternoon had gone by, where was he, what had he been doing?

He and my male cousins had gone for a walk in the hills behind the house.

Our cousins were climbers and were anxious to see if there were any rock faces worth climbing in the area. They were also kayakers, and were hoping for a downriver run with Dan. Alas, we had no river to offer them, just a stream with a few gudgeon in it. And no rock faces, just a few big boulders.

Our cousins laughed, and finally settled for going fishing since there was nothing else to do.

First Dan had to take them into town to buy fishing poles and other gear. Our cousins laughed at him because he had no driver's license, and they too told him the story about the girls you kissed in the backs of cars. They apparently gratified him with all kinds of other stories as well, although he did not tell me exactly what, since our quarrel, or more precisely the suspension of our friendship, also began that very week.

The eldest cousin was studying what he called abnormal psychology, the second was in his first year of medical studies, the third was getting ready to enter medical school. The fourth, the most fun of them all, did not like studying; he wanted to be a mechanic, "first on cars and later on planes." Sara was doing her classes over again. All of them.

It was our neighbor Adrien who told us all this. We were not unaware of it, no doubt, but neither did we truly know about it. There is a space between being aware and not knowing, a sort of vacant lot, invisible from the outside. My brother and I were the natural inhabitants of that space.

But Adrien required details. To relay them to his mother, who then passed them on to her husband. These (Canadian) cousins were with their neighbors (us) on a visit (the vacation). Routine situation. The same thing as a Sunday family visit.

Thus my brother and I were dragged willy-nilly from our vacant lot and tossed down into the world of the others, to be blended with them, mixed, homogenized, and one day destroyed.

It began one evening, the first evening of the irruption of our cousins.

We had all eaten dinner with our parents. Being together in a bunch like that made Dan and me feel so odd . . . each at his own corner of the table, separated, unhappy and desperate, lost.

We ate dinner with that great mass separating us, our parents a part of it. They were animated and they too told lots of stories, even Tiresia, who seemed almost to glow behind her veil, even our mother Nicole. Our cousins looked at her; she had put on her plaid taffeta dress with its beautiful deep colors, as well as the little diamond earrings, which sent small incandescent sparks flashing deep inside my eyes, painful sparks flashing in darkness that lay at unfathomable depths.

I was in Sara's T-shirt, very embarrassed, and I saw Dan watching me, a fitful sidelong look, his gaze never directed straight at me. He seemed angry. But perhaps that was around the second or third evening of our cousins' visit.

The end of dinner came. Nicole shone brighter and brighter, and our father had stopped asking questions. He suddenly looked tired, a look I well knew; I could hear floating inside my head the words he had once used, "It all goes so much deeper, doesn't it, so much deeper . . ." Tiresia rose, and we understood that the day was over, that it was time for night.

On the stairway as we trooped upstairs Dan slipped a note into my hand. I took it to the bathroom to read. *"Estelle,"* it said, *"I can't spend the night with all these guys. Meet me in the cave."*

And now I was hearing Sara's voice in my head: "What's wrong with that kid, yelling like that? Doesn't he ever let go of your apron strings? You're not his baby-sitter, are you?"

I threw the paper into the toilet bowl, flushed, and at once bent to retrieve it. But the swirling water sucked it out of my grasp, and then there was only a round still mirror that did not even reflect my image at the bottom of the bowl.

I looked at that mirror and it seemed to me that my being had just drowned in it. I had the certain knowledge that one day I would again look at a place like this one, familiar and squalid, associated with secret functions, with the body's vital functions, and that this place too would be emptied and that my being would be swallowed up in it. In that moment I knew exactly not what was going to happen but what I was going to feel. It came and went very quickly.

And it was our little neighbor Adrien — whose company we never sought but whom we never turned away, who must at that moment have been spying on us from his toilet window, Adrien who was almost without intuition and who hated feelings — it was Adrien who years later suffered the repercussions of that fleeting incident.

And so I wonder which, future or past, influences the other, or whether time is not rather an immense flat plane covered with threads intersecting from all directions, and whether those seeking a coherent story do not simply become entangled with it and thrash about until they have extracted one structure that might just as easily have been another.

I wanted to see myself, to see my face. While Dan and I were together I had not needed a face.

Now that I had been without him for hours that were not just hours but a laceration, a laceration fast yawning open to the possibility of absence, and that absence stretching out like a perspective into infinity, I needed a face.

I was miserable about what I had just done. I had thrown a letter with Dan's handwriting, Dan's words, into the bottomless well of that toilet bowl whose surface yielded me nothing, not even my reflection. I had to find myself again, even if only from the outside. I went into our bathroom and Sara was there. I dashed to the mirror: I was no longer thinking of her, she could go straight to hell, but naturally she did not move an inch, and as an excuse for looking at myself I began to remove my makeup.

"That's a funny way to remove your makeup," said Sara.

"I'm not removing it."

Removing my makeup! I hated her in that moment. She was preventing me from going to find Dan, to find myself, in other words my brother, find my universe, my life, my soul.

But how could I get away? What was Dan up to? I was in despair.

It must seem such a little thing, two girls in a bathroom, washing and spying on each other, and one of them desperate for a teenage rendezvous. But childhood despairs are not simply infantile non-sense: they echo the humming of destiny's top, just beginning to spin on its tiny sharp point, and they know it even if the humming is ever so faint, as faint as the movement itself, even if nobody yet notices the enormous mass of the top above the spinning point — and for me it was death beginning to spin upon its axis and my body knew it.

I closed my ears to what Sara was saying. I strained to hear the noises from the bedroom opposite, the big bedroom, mine, which all the boys were sharing. They were kicking up a din, I could hear our cousins' big male voices, they were talking very loud, I realized — or rather I realized how softly we usually spoke in our house.

Our cousins had normal voices, the clear loud voices of people used to space and the outdoors, while we had the voices of people who shared a cramped cell with a being whose name was torment.

Outside, the moon shone harshly, stridently as a declaration of war. The window stood wide open. Sara wanted me to lie on her mattress with her. She kept up a stream of mindless complaint:

"It's no fun sleeping alone."

And when I made no answer she started up again:

"It's no fun having only brothers. You always sleep alone."

And when I thought she had finally dropped off, the litany resumed:

"And then when you get the chance to sleep with someone . . ."

Followed by:

"Some people say they want to be your sister and then they won't even sleep with you."

I nearly shouted, "Liar, I never said *sister*," but from her sleepy whine I sensed that she was dropping off, speaking as she drifted down the sleep slope, that in a few moments I would be free and able to leave.

I rose. At once Sara sat up on her mattress.

"Where are you going?"

"For a walk," I answered as casually as I could.

"Don't leave me alone," Sara begged, "this house scares me. You all scare me. Tiresia scares me. So does Nicole. And your father. And Dan, he has such a funny way of looking at you."

I lay back down, defeated. The moon loomed enormous through the window. To me it seemed to bar the exit like a heavy polished-steel door. Perhaps I was dreaming. And in the midst of the dream I thought I heard Dan's voice calling me, but very softly, and suddenly someone really was calling me. It was Tiresia.

She was leaning over me.

"Estelle, come."

There was a terrible shouting in the house. It was our mother, and her nightmare. But why had Tiresia come to get me? Usually, our father called Minor, Minor came, and Tiresia remained leaning on the rail in the dim bend halfway up the stairs, where nobody noticed her. But this time I sensed that she was beside herself. And our mother was screaming and screaming. As usual the same words came up again and again, words to which we were so accustomed that we did not really hear them; we perceived only the maelstrom of suffering that spewed them out into the house, the crackling of a fire that heated them and spat them all over the house like glowing embers.

"Estelle," said Tiresia's body, leaning over me, "go and talk to your cousins, don't let them come here, they mustn't see Nicole, keep them away . . ."

A flood of tumultuous pleadings flowed from Tiresia's body, eddies that swirled in upon themselves and moved off again, uncertain where to go. I had never felt such agitation in her, and she was looking at me differently too, as if a particular complicity between us were revealing itself for the very first time. She was putting herself in my hands.

Even our father never behaved toward me in this manner. He spoke to me, as I have said, as if to a spouse, but a spouse of whom he expected nothing except that she listen to him and sustain him through her listening.

In Tiresia's body I read unusual anxiety, anxiety unrelated to our mother's condition. Nicole was screaming as she always did. Our doctor would soon arrive, in a few moments she would get her shot, our doctor would speak to her and she would calm down. We knew it all.

Tiresia's fear was not for our mother but for that interlude in which our cousins might emerge, might come out into the corridor, might go to our parents' bedroom door and see what was to be seen there — see what I first saw shortly after Dan's birth and had probably seen several times since.

"Dan isn't there," she was saying as well. "There's only you, Estelle, please hurry . . ."

Already the door of the bedroom opposite was opening. Behind me Sara got up and approached me with sleepwalker's eyes. Tiresia had disappeared.

It felt as if I were dreaming, as if I was smack in the middle of a nightmare that also included Tiresia's nightmare, which in its turn included our mother's nightmare, and I felt that all those nightmares could go on fitting endlessly one into the next, that you left one only to enter the next, each nightmare bigger than the following one until the last which swallowed the world . . .

But even inside nightmares the sun can suddenly shine, and that particular nightmare contained a gift for me. The two middle cousins, the one in his first year of medicine and the one in premed, and the eldest, the one studying mental illnesses, seemed quite calm. All three stood in the soberly lit corridor outside the bedroom, bare-chested, in shorts, the rough shadow of new-grown beard on their faces, and suddenly I was tranquilized as if I were the one getting the shot, a satisfying state in which I could experience and tell myself things — for example, that I had never seen anything so extraordinary as these three calm and resolute young men standing in our corridor in shorts.

"Sara and Esty," said the eldest, "come into our bedroom."

"What's happening?" whimpered Sara.

"It's nothing," said Paul. "Aunt Nicole has nightmares, you know that, you've been told."

"But it's awful," said Sara, "it's awful, nobody told me it would be like this."

"Yes, they did. Stop whining and come in with us."

We followed them into the room and they began a Monopoly game with us. But the screams paralyzed us.

"Isn't there another part of the house we could play in?" the eldest asked. "Esty?"

He was speaking to me. He was looking straight into my eyes. That beard-darkened face, still shadowed by our midnight awakening, that masculine face, a man's face in which I thought I recognized Tiresia's features even though I had never seen them, penetrated deep inside me and its grown-up gaze drove out the old Estelle and brought a new one to light, an Estelle created there and then for the grown-up world in which he lived.

My mind was suddenly very clear.

What I could not know was that this clarity was right and good in his world, but wrong and bad for me.

"Yes," I said, still in that state of almost medicated tranquillity. "I know a place, but it's not easy to get to."

"Don't worry. Show us. You shouldn't be hearing those screams."

By "you" he meant Sara and the youngest boy cousin, Frank. He did not mean me, and I felt absurdly proud.

"It's not that they worry me," our cousin added, "but you shouldn't be hearing them."

"What worries me most is that Dan's disappeared," said another cousin.

Dan's disappearance did not worry me at all. I knew where he was. He had gone to the cave, and I was sure he would stay there all night and perhaps next morning, sulking because I had not joined him there.

And in that moment his flight to the cave of our childhood seemed to me so futile, so childish, ridiculous. Great things were happening in the house, and he was not there, he was in his hiding place like a kid!

But it was he who was right. If I had joined him, if only I had joined you that night, Dan . . .

"I know where Dan is," I said. "He's fine, no need to worry."

And the night-long vigil with our cousins began. First, sandwiches in the kitchen: they worked efficiently, schooled in the summer camps they had all attended for years. Then they sent me to get a flashlight and we assigned bearers for the sheets and blankets, and soon we were straggling up to the tin roof, to Dan and Estelle's attic, and it was Estelle who led the party.

When I was at the top of the ladder in my white nightgown under the hellishly white moon, in the front of the line and perfectly conscious of my cousins' eyes on my bare legs and thighs, I again had the sense of betrayal. And this time, instead of being ashamed, I was horribly glad.

The moon was huge; it seemed to have come down closer to watch us. I literally felt the halo of white light encircling us.

Keep that light shining on Estelle's legs so the cousins can see them, Estelle doesn't love her brother anymore. Keep it shining on those legs, Estelle's a witch, too bad her brother can't be there, her brother has been found wanting. I climbed slowly toward the top of the ladder, the moon giving off a flat and sickly light; love's white leprosy spilled onto my skin.

At one point I turned. Bathed in supernatural light, the meadow looked like the surface of a still pond, with the apple tree like a ghost ship in the middle, sails frozen in the windless air. The hills formed a somber arc beyond. The eldest, Sam, who was just behind me, grabbed my thighs.

"Hey, Esty, you'll make us all fall," he muttered. "What are you staring at?"

From the lean-to you could hardly hear Nicole. We all clambered up the tin roof, our cousins laughing as I described our initial difficulties: they knew all about climbing and would never have needed a ladder. I saw in the paper recently that one of them was medical officer on a skiing expedition to Annapurna in the Himalayas, but I was unable to distinguish which cousin it was of the three who studied medicine, and I did not recognize the face in the photo.

We set up camp in the attic, even making a fire, and resumed our game of Monopoly. I thought of those marshmallows you toasted on sticks, it all seemed terribly desirable to me, and I forgot about my brother in his gloomy cave.

Between moves, our cousins talked about "aunt Nicole."

"What a pity," said the eldest, "such a pretty girl."

"It can't be much fun for her," said another, "this whole situation."

"If it wasn't for the situation," said another, "I wouldn't mind at all."

"Shut up," said the eldest. "You're not alone here."

I heard their words as if in a dream. They were speaking low-voiced rapid English between comments on the game, and what they said was not intended for me. I did not know enough English, yet I heard, I heard as if I had grown antennae. The antennae picked up all those words, then brought them back and deposited them, translated, in a neat little heap in a corner of my brain. And meanwhile, I was passionately involved in Monopoly.

The eldest, Sam, sat next to me. Whenever he leaned across me to choose a card or move a house, he put a hand on my thigh to steady himself. The fire threw off brief flashes that sent strange lights across our faces. Through the flashes our looks met and separated.

NINETEEN

The Dance on the Lawn

MOTIONLESS, legs dangling, my brother and I sat on the front steps.

Our cousins were busy with Tiresia, writing letters to Canada, our father was in the garage watching our mother dance, our mother was dancing to the sound of the record player.

The house breathed without us, at peace. Perhaps that was something that rarely happened, perhaps we were most often anxious and watchful.

We felt peace of a kind such as we would never again feel. A kind of gift came down upon us.

Much later we tried to recapture this sensation, which must have been the last happy sensation of our youth. "I must have been thinking about dew," said Dan. "I felt as if some kind of dew was soaking into me, and everything was clear as glass, and cool." And Estelle? "I had the feeling that a rough sea had subsided, that the waves had slowly flattened, that everything was calm and flat and I could walk within myself without having to be wary."

And then one of us said, "What if Sara could have heard us!" and we laughed.

In the happy period of our lives, my brother and I lived with metaphors. They were our shared staple, we made them up, rolled in them, consumed them like the scalding teas Minor had taught us to like or the ice-choked Coca-Colas we formed a taste for in New York, shared them like pastries. We could never get enough of them, we could never resist improving on them, they piled up inside us, the oldest of them becoming references for those that followed, and so on ad infinitum.

They were our life's echo chambers. Through them we lived a thousand lives, ten thousand lives.

When Dan disappeared, my life shrank back abruptly to my size, a most run-of-the-mill size, as if a vast sky that had been our natural canopy burst and dropped its canvas folds about me, closing me in, imprisoning me.

At the beginning of our encounter I had no idea how to address Phil.

And if our first rendezvous had been in a café or indoors, no doubt that would have been the end of it. After a few minutes I would have left.

I was afraid every moment of the day, afraid that my words would escape me and grow twisted and tangled before my eyes, that something appalling and wrong would happen, afraid of making the smallest utterance.

But we did not go to a café. We did not stay indoors.

"Claire!" came a shout from the street below.

It was late summer, just a few months ago. I was hearing my new name for the first time.

Phil was outside.

Perched on a bike in the middle of the street with one foot on the ground, he was shouting in the general direction of our house-front. I think it was at this moment I began to love him.

His body looked extraordinarily vigorous, with a vigor that seemed to flood the whole street, forcing windows to fly open, yanking apartment dwellers from their lairs, making dogs run and pedestrians look up and smile. An animal vigor that made me shout "I'm coming," seize my bike (in fact, one belonging to one of my piano students), and run down the stairs, awkwardly and too fast, the frame chafing my thigh, the chain dripping grease.

I know now that this was the first time a living being had broken into the vault where I had sat immured with my brother's death. In this vigor of Phil's my body at last perceived the presence of a living being.

It took all my concentration to breast the flood of cars, trucks, and motorbikes we encountered as we crossed Paris. When we reached the Canal de l'Ourcq the towpath was too narrow for us to ride abreast. Phil went ahead, and for several hours we pedaled gently along the unencumbered trail. I kept my eyes on Phil's back. It mesmerized me. It was the back of a powerful, living being, with great dark patches of sweat already staining the shirt, and soon it seemed to me that I was pedaling effortlessly. I was glued to that back: it was there that all movement began, with his movement pulling mine along. Only when we stopped to picnic did I notice how tired I was. We felt little need to talk; it was hot and we ate. Close by sat an angler. The sun bore down on us through the foliage — sweat trickled down Phil's forehead and I felt my own making a rivulet between my breasts — our sweat did duty for words between us, as did the dance of light on leaves, the shimmering reflections on the canal, and the incongruous flotsam the angler patiently removed from his hook. Then we were off again. We rode until nightfall, and it was because of that wordless day, with only the crunching of our wheels on the towpath, that I felt I might at last have set my feet on the road once again. I did not immediately realize it, of course. But that evening as we rode back in the direction of the city, my eyes glued to the rhythmic rolling of Phil's back and shoulders, the first murmurings of gratitude arose inside me.

And then night came on. We caught a Paris-bound train at Meaux, hanging our bikes on hooks in the goods wagon, and in the train Phil talked of the death of a friend he had seen through his final illness. I do not remember exactly what he said. The motion of the train and fatigue drowned his sentences, but there were all the words I knew so well — death, hospital, disease. He sat across from me, his open shirt exposing his broad throat and upper chest. Rich glittering sweat trickled through the blond fleece in the opening. He did not look at me and I had trouble hearing him, but it was like a fishing line cast in hopes of catching whatever still lived in me — and for the first time, very far away yet not so far, I felt my convent years shift ever so slightly.

They shifted, edging back toward the past. The train was racing through residential suburbs thick with houses; it was a very ordinary evening, my first ordinary evening, and something inside me seized hold of that ordinariness, quaffed it, gulped it greedily down. I looked at that train and those suburbs, at those housefronts and their sweaty family intimacies almost within touching distance, and all that ordinariness filled chasms of emptiness inside me. Oh, Dan, only you could understand what I am talking about and of course it was you being covered over by this ordinariness, it pushed you under, pushed you under, piling up on you as lightly as eiderdown, sweet ordinariness, oh, Dan, more metaphors . . .

And to push you away and to transform me I filled myself with that ordinariness. I drank it like a philter so as to mutate, Dan, to become a mutant.

The philter would have to be potent.

Phil's face was before me during our picnic on the towpath. It had looked opaque, impenetrable, not reflecting the shimmering canal water, the trembling leaves, or the angler, not reflecting anything of what was there.

And I had had a sudden desire, the kind we used to have, Dan, I wanted to throw myself on his body, hear his stomach sounds, eat grass with him, touch the earth, roll with him in that warm moving light. An urge from so very far back, Dan, but of course I controlled myself, I stayed within myself, as if there were nothing amiss.

That is how these creatures are, Dan, they live as if nothing were amiss. And now I accept it. Henceforth I shall look no farther, my spirit will no longer yearn for distant skies, it will stay soberly inside me and I shall be happy, Dan, always happy.

*　　　*　　　*

We sat side by side on the front steps, and suddenly the moon emerged from a rent in the clouds.

"Do you see, Estelle?" said Dan.

"The moon?"

"It's speaking to us," said Dan.

"What do you mean?"

"I mean we can see it, that's all. You and me, at this very minute, we can see it. That's all it's telling us. And Tiresia is with our cousins, and our father is with Nicole, and you and I are sitting on these steps, and it's now and not some other time. Estelle, promise me you'll never forget this moment, this moment right now."

My voice began to shake.

"You promise too, Dan."

"Oh, Estelle, I don't need to promise," said Dan, "but how will we know when it's time to remember this moment, Estelle, how will we know?"

"I'll promise, Dan, if you like."

"But Estelle, it's not enough not to forget, we have to remember too, and it's not the same thing. And not just remember this moment, but to remember all the time . . ."

"Remember what, Dan?"

"Remember that I'm here, that you're here, that everything is here and we're here as well."

The things my brother said! They had the whole world in them, sent shudders through all our surroundings from the dark soil of the garden to the sky where the moon rode, were the very substance of tremulous twilight, *and this is what they become, madame, when I attempt to pass them on to you, they grow thin and naked, oh, madame, I'm losing hope, perhaps words for such things no longer exist.*

We spoke softly, close to each other and close to the garden, the moon, the hills, the toad chirruping under the bottom step. We were not alone, we were with each other, and with us was all the rest, the garden gliding out into the town, into the forest, into the ocean, into space, out into the vast night in which the moon swam.

"Look," said Dan, "a moonbeam just touched us."

And I swear we had felt something, the impression of a moonbeam brushing us, if such a thing can happen. That moonbeam was something more than itself: the universe's finger had assumed its form in order to descend and salute us, and my brother and I had both felt it together.

We went mad.

"Come on," said Dan, "let's get something going . . ."

We jumped down off the steps, and Dan knelt. "Look," he said, "our footprints, our footprints on the stone," and he kissed the convex stone of the steps. We went down backward, kissing each step — "Put your lips where I put mine," and I complied; "Stone, the stone of our own house, Estelle," Dan said — and it seemed to me too that something tremendous was afoot. Then we were on the bottom step, and Dan kissed the ground as well — "The earth too," he took my hand and pressed it against the earth, "Can you feel it, Estelle, can you feel the earth's heart beating?" — and I did feel it, even though I knew it was really my own blood pumping along its channels of flesh — "Oh, the earth feels cold, it's been so long since we kissed it," and then we sucked the grass, the rough grass blades, and soon our lips were slashed and split. "You're bleeding, Estelle, so am I, but that's just what the grass wanted — a little blood for dew." We hugged the tree trunks, we stroked their bark, we raced around the garden and Dan insisted on including the fence railings — "The railings too!" he yelled — and I knew he was thinking of the cemetery at the far end of our road, where we had so often watched funerals from our attic vantage point, yes, we had to touch every bar in the railings that surrounded our garden because on this moonlit night they looked like the cemetery fence and because that too we had to possess.

Everything my brother undertook that night was real to me. I followed him blindly. Even the wildest of his acts had meaning — and I can no longer express that meaning.

His wisdom was profound. In his child's way he knew of his death, of my death, and he wanted to keep us together in that death which would last us longer than our lives. Of that I am certain. Because of what I felt that evening, and because of what happened ten years later, in that same cemetery at the end of our road.

And suddenly we heard our father's voice:

"These kids are quite mad!"

But we were not frightened, because Nicole was beside him, laughing, and our father, bathed in her laughter, was neither afraid nor condemnatory.

Nicole's laughter had briefly dissolved the anxiety that lived permanently in him, leaving him so light that he seemed literally to float before our eyes.

"Take it easy, you two!" he said.

But his words lacked the power to stop us.

"No, no," said Nicole, "they're dancing too. Come here, Dan, come and dance for me."

Dan walked onto the lawn, tugging me by the hand.

"Dance for me, Dan," said Nicole.

I was suddenly sober; I was such a mediocre dancer. But Dan would not let me go, pulling me into the middle of the lawn.

"Let her go," said Nicole, "you know she doesn't want to dance."

"Stay here," Dan whispered, "sit on the grass and I'll dance around you."

"I can't, Dan," I muttered.

"If you're scared, just put your head in your hands this way," he murmured, pushing my head down, "but I have to dance around you."

"If you don't want to dance, Estelle, come over here with me," said our father. "We'll sit on the steps together."

"No, no," Dan whispered into my heart, "stay here, Estelle, I can't dance without you."

I buried my face in my hands, for I did not want to go to my father and Nicole. Soon my embarrassment faded.

I had no need to look up to see what Dan was doing. I felt his every movement, I still feel that dance now, but how can I ever take possession of it? It is not written down anywhere, there is no score, no picture, no medium, not even my memory, just a persistent and pellucid nervous echo for which I can find no words.

My brother danced for me and for the earth that bore us, his movements weaving circles around me, and soon I felt at peace, quite simply at peace, and then our father spoke again, his voice very low. I should not have been able to hear, but I did, and his words sounded so strange that I can still hear them today.

"Do you call that dancing, Nicole?" he asked.

"Shh!" said Nicole.

"But is that what he learns at dance class?" muttered our father.

"Of course not," said Nicole, "he's improvising."

"Well, you don't dance like that, do you?" said our father.

"Because I can't. He can!"

"Yours is real dancing."

"No," said Nicole, "mine is just steps, real dancing is what he's doing."

"But is that what he'll do for a living?" said our father.

"Not here, of course," said Nicole, "but in New York, certainly."

"You're not going to send him to New York, Nicole? Nicole?" said our father.

"Shh!" said Nicole. "Don't spoil this evening."

Like a handful of tiny pebbles, their words whizzed through the net of my brother's dance, lodging in my heart and there embedding themselves.

They must have often discussed the dance classes my brother attended. My father had probably been reluctant and Nicole correspondingly enthusiastic. She believed that with the right teachers my brother could become a great dancer.

Dan attended dance class several times a week but no longer practiced in the garage with Nicole. At the time that seemed natural enough to me: my brother went to the conservatory, our mother danced in her blue garage, our father worked in his study, and Tiresia too had her room where nobody went. It was an order of things we never questioned. And now that I know everything that was hidden from me at the time, I still find it natural.

And then suddenly the front door was thrown open, framing us in hard white light, and our cousins came out onto the steps. Dan stopped dancing, our father and Nicole suddenly moved apart, each of them, I believe, withdrawing up his own side of the stairway as if ripped apart and extinguished by our cousins' rude arrival. Tiresia was behind them, it seems to me, but she at once pulled back inside the entryway. Under our cousins' mocking gaze we came forward into that unwelcome light, and Sara exclaimed:

"Ooh, how disgusting! They're filthy. Dan, do you realize how filthy you are? Estelle?"

One of our cousins said:

"Genuine savages!"

We went upstairs in silence. I was ashamed, and I suppose Dan was as well. We washed, then went our separate ways, me to Sara, Dan to the boys.

Our world was defenseless against theirs.

*   *   *

For several days I hardly saw my brother. Our cousins had joined forces with our neighbor Adrien and his cousins and were exploring the hills. Sara and I and the girl cousin from next door did girl things, I no longer remember exactly what. Inside me a deep hole had been torn and my life was leaking from that hole. When I returned to school after that vacation, my grades, I remember, were very poor. Our father, who never worried about our studies, assuming that everything was going well, became concerned. He received a letter from the new high school in the neighboring town where I was doing my pre-college baccalaureate year over again.

"Estelle, is something the matter?"

"No, Papa, it was our cousins, they upset us."

"Of course, of course," said my father.

And at once he was a thousand miles from my school and my grades.

"Their visit did Tiresia good," he suddenly said. "The visit did her good, and now it's doing her harm."

"Yes, Papa," I said. "Everything will be all right."

"Yes, yes," he muttered with that helpless flap of the hand I knew so well.

Everything was not all right, though I failed to see it.

For on the eve of our cousins' departure, my alliance with Dan was shattered. It was the year of my baccalaureate exam, which I took and failed in September, obliging me to repeat the year in the town next door to ours. After that I left for the university to study law, and whenever I returned home during those years of study the break between Dan and me refused to heal. On that mined and dangerous battlefront all my energies were consumed.

I saw nothing of what was happening to Tiresia.

Our cousins were packing. Sara alternately wept and laughed. Sam never let me out of his sight; he followed me up the stairs, waited for me outside the bathroom door. "Estelle," he said, "this is your last chance to make love this year." "Do you think you're the only boy in the world?" I said, and he answered, "I know you, you'd never make love with a stranger." "What do you know about me!" I raged and he replied, "You're a primitive, Estelle, I know you better than you know yourself." We wrangled furiously, to the point where we no longer even knew what we were arguing about and Dan prowled ceaselessly about us, forcing us to separate. Sara too spied on us.

She and I still combed each other's hair; she wanted to sleep against my breasts and I would have liked that too, but Sam used to inch our door open in the middle of the night and I could not have stood it if he had caught us lying naked together. "If you don't make love soon, Estelle, you're going to turn into a lesbian," he told me, but I went on refusing. "Why not, Estelle, why not?" My incomprehensible refusal enraged him. "There's no danger with me, I'm a doctor, after all." "It's not that," I said. "What is it, then, Estelle?" Finally there was nothing left to say: after hours of pleading and refusal I was haggard and so was he. "I can't," I insisted, "I want to but I can't," and then "Not here . . ." "So let's take the car and go to the country," he said.

But the country was still "here," the whole earth was still "here." Sam was my first desire, but it would have taken another world for my body to be able to join in love with his.

TWENTY

"Please Let's Make Love, Please"

I HAVE long since lost touch with those cousins. My memories of them are vague, and I believe I mix the two middle ones up.

The eldest, Sam, was quiet and thoughtful. The fourth, the future aircraft mechanic, who was closest in age to my brother since he must have been about sixteen, was a good-looking boy, straightforward and action-loving.

Those two I see most clearly because both made what my father (who could be surprisingly sentimental, not to say sloppy) called "calves' eyes" at me. I was in love with them both.

"Sam and Frank are making calves' eyes at Estelle," said my father with a laugh.

Nicole seemed to drop back suddenly into our midst.

"A pity they're cousins," she said, "it might have led to matrimony."

She spoke in that strange "interplanetary" voice we so disliked.

"But we're not real cousins!"

"Of course," said my father, "of course . . ."

Then he moved away, as he often did, but taking me with him, and went on with what he had started to say:

". . . of course, marriages within families, whatever they are, I mean, whatever the family structure might be, are never a good thing. It would be endogamy, the worst kind of selfishness, no, no, not really advisable . . ."

Our poor father was soon hopelessly tangled in his explanations, and since the conversation was not to my liking either, neither he nor I ever returned to it. He had addressed me out there on the garden path exactly as if he had been speaking to his car; no one had heard us; it was as if the subject had never been mentioned.

And yet . . .

Our cousins had given up their forays into the hills with the neighbors. They stayed at home. We all stayed at home, despite the fine summer weather.

At last our father noticed. One day he appeared on our landing, breathless from climbing the stairs four at a time and in most unusual garb (I had never seen him, even at home, in anything but a business suit, and I believe he had simply swapped shirt and tie for a heavy sweater, but my surprise was so great that I failed to take in a single detail of this sartorial revolution).

"Right, I'm taking you all out," he announced in a voice pitched so high above its everyday volume that it cracked and he had to say it all over again.

"On your feet, all of you," he went on.

All seven of us had come out onto the landing and were gazing at him in dismay.

"Into the car," he added. "You need fresh air and something to do . . ."

By now he was almost begging.

None of us moved. We did not want to hurt him, but we had no wish to go out. At last Sam spoke.

"You know, Helleur," he said (that was how he addressed our father; his brothers called him "Uncle"), "in Canada we spend our lives out-of-doors. We're really very happy to stay in the house with Dan and Estelle . . . as long as we don't bother you."

"No, no, you don't bother me, I just have to shut my door, my study door, it's padded, you know . . ."

Suddenly he looked very relieved.

"Are you sure? I was quite prepared to take you. Sam?"

"Quite sure. Thanks a whole lot," said Sam with enormous politeness.

Our father smiled unexpectedly, a child's smile, as if he were putting himself in a grown-up's hands.

"Fine, I'll go and tell Nicole that we're leaving without you."

"Helleur," shouted Sam from the head of the stairs, "we'll take care of Tiresia."

"Thank you, thank you," our father shouted from below.

"So much for that," said Sam, turning back to us.

My brother Dan's eyes shot down the staircase where our father was off to find Nicole, up the stairs to where Tiresia must be, then back to us, to me, to Sam. But he said nothing.

I saw my brother's eyes, but I thought only of Sam's victory.

We no longer did anything but play hide-and-seek.

That was why we no longer wanted to go out, why we stayed in the house.

Hide-and-seek meant two of you squeezing into tight corners where you were forced to huddle close and deathly silent while in the house all around you a thousand small stealthy sounds made you jump, any of them possibly made by the approaching seekers, and you had to gulp the air back into your lungs in order not to yell "Here we are" and have done with it.

We split into clans, seekers and hiders, and squabbled over who ended up with whom. I was usually with Sam, or with Frank.

Sam took me in his arms, squeezing me in his dreamy way, seemingly unaware of anything at all. I got cramps and wondered what he might be thinking of.

With Frank it was simpler. When we were together, half lying in the space under the stairs, he worked his way on top of me and sought my mouth. I turned away. His mouth missed its target, he kissed my eyes, the corners of my lips, my neck, but I could not let him kiss me squarely on the lips. I wanted it; my whole body wanted it. But I could not. I thought it was because I preferred Sam.

Meanwhile the others, in teams of two, were seeking us all over the house. I heard Sam calling with both anger and amusement in his voice: he knew very well what his young brother was up to.

A great urge to make them jealous entered me, as if from outside myself: I tried to do what it commanded, but the commands were not clear and I did not really manage. I believe in fact that the two of them were in cahoots, that they had even made a bet on which of them would make me give in. They must have been surprised at my stubbornness, particularly Sam, for whom this was not the first affair and who had no doubts at all about the desire racking me. Despite that dreamy look of his, his hand had wandered under my skirt:

"Estelle, you're dying to make love," he said in his calm, amused voice.

I wanted to hit him, to hit him until my arms were numb, for it was true, and I did not want it to be true.

"Estelle, Estelle," said Frank, "I want you so badly, please let's make love, please."

And I was angry at him too, but less so, for he was trembling a little, and that reassured me. Sam was too strong for me. And saw things too clearly. It frightened me.

"Estelle, I know why you won't make love," he said. "Want me to tell you why?"

We were in the cramped broom closet, amid the dusty smell of brooms. He held me tight from behind, his mouth on my neck, and from all sides and on different parts of my body I felt the rigid contact of the broom handles. Among them was my cousin's member, which must have been what was pressing so hard against my buttocks.

"I'll tell you why you won't make love, Estelle," my cousin continued.

"Who asked you?"

"I'll tell you anyway."

Although it was raining we had wandered far across the meadow, far enough to reach the trench the previous owner had dug during the war to protect himself from bombs.

"What bombs, what war?" Sam asked. "I don't know, *the* war, I guess," I answered irritably. My brother and I did not like history: rejection of it was in our bones. While studying for my exams I had barely skimmed the First World War and virtually skipped the Second, which seemed an incomprehensible affair to me. In fact, I owed my failure in the baccalaureate to the two great wars of my century.

"Don't get mad," said Sam, "all we expect of the old geezer is a trench deep enough to hide us."

We had decided that because of the rain the others would never think of looking for us there. The trench was deep and covered over with planks, presumably to prevent an animal or a human being from falling in. At one time, before we discovered our cave, Dan and I had covered the walls of the trench with lengths of oilcloth.

"It's because of that kid Dan. He trails you everywhere, he watches over you like a dog. That's why you won't make love. Say it!"

When my cousin Sam said those words — he was probably twenty-one or twenty-two at the time — there was an explosion inside me. No, my cousin had not managed to open up my body, but he had certainly opened a chasm in my soul, and violence of an intensity I would never have suspected erupted with unstoppable force.

I slapped him and punched him, and far away at the other end of the field I heard Dan calling "Estelle, Estelle," I heard Dan's voice the way I had never stopped hearing it since our cousins' arrival, distant, heartbreaking, as if from beyond mountains, from the bottom of a gorge.

Before our cousins' arrival we had always been together. Or if not, each knew exactly where the other one was at any moment of the day or night. We had never needed to call each other.

But that summer we were as good as lost.

Sara in her fashion pulled me away, as did Sam and Frank in theirs. They took Dan away too, so that we never knew where the other one was. We were lost along paths not of our choosing. Our usual trails had been obliterated, our territory invaded by strangers. We could no longer find our tracks; we had had to resort to that crude device, calling out, and it did not work.

Partly because of playing hide-and-seek, and because naturally they put us on opposing teams, we could not answer each other. And the rest of the time I felt paralyzed, prevented by the presence of one or another of my cousins from answering Dan's calls. It was their sneers, I suppose, and the poison Sam had poured into me.

Sara did not want me to answer either. She wanted me for herself alone, for me to comb her hair or for her to comb mine and for us to examine each other's breasts and bras and panties. I had become an indispensable looking glass for her. And what about me?

My desire was so strong it went everywhere with me, my nameless desire, unable to follow its true course, overspilling its banks like a stream in spate, submerging whatever lay in its path. Sara in the evening, for instance.

"Estelle, Estelle," Dan called, and I remained hidden away in the little bedroom, drowsy from the feel of Sara's fingers in my hair, my eyes on her breasts and hers on mine. I did not answer him.

Soon there was something else. Sara too began to talk to me about Dan, but in a different way.

"Your brother isn't the little kid you think he is," she said one evening.

That word "kid" again! I could not bear it. It was a word from the outside; it had nothing to do with my brother or with me; it was a word from the vast outside world peopled by beings who might as well be extraterrestrials, and Sara spoke their language. Except that this extraterrestrial language was insinuating itself into our world, licking around the outskirts of our lives, probing for an opening.

I felt my mouth go dry. Vaypigo was settling in, I was about to feel ill, but I did not want to, not for anything in the world did I want Sara to see my distress, for that would have forced me to see myself.

"Go on, tell me."

"I can't," Sara whimpered. "It's his secret, and you're his big sister, anyway, you know what I'm talking about."

"I said go on!"

I was surprised by my voice. Authoritative and icy, it was like no other voice I had ever heard; it seemed to belong to someone else, to the creatures that peopled my mother's nightmares, perhaps. But I realized at once that I would never get anything out of Sara like that. You had to be cunning with extraterrestrials.

"He's a kid, Sara, I don't see what he could do, you're the one who's imagining things."

Oh, the pain she inflicted on me! I do not know whether her stories were true or whether she wanted to make herself interesting, hold my attention. I think now that it must have been the latter. Sara wanted me for herself and had sensed that in order to hold on to all of me she had to talk to me about Dan. And how she invented, my cousin Sara! She loved seduction, she loved stories abounding in stolen glances, stealthy caresses, the thousand and one tiny exchanges of flirtation — they were like glittering spangles she yearned to adorn herself with. Without them life was a dull gray rag. I was very surprised to hear that she has since become a good mother, if a little overweight, and with no cares in the world beyond her offspring.

What she told me hurt me, and what made it even more unbearable was that I had no idea why it hurt me.

My logical mind told me that Dan was developing as he should, that he was game and full of charm, thank goodness, and that in any case I had already noticed these things myself. But in the dark depths of my warm clay, jet-black serpents writhed ceaselessly, never stopped writhing throughout that short cousinly stay that nevertheless lasted an eternity and spawned the gravest consequences.

Those serpents lunged forth from me in that trench where my cousin held me tight against the member digging into me through the cloth, they flew into his face, those clawed monsters from another age like the beasts carved on the porch of our town church. Sam defended himself as best he could, probably recognizing it for the nervous outburst it was, and not unduly alarmed. Yet I must have been alarming.

The rain fell in vertical streams. I heard Dan calling, still at a distance, he knew this hiding place and I knew he would find us.

No matter how cleverly I hid in or around the house with one or another of the cousins, Dan was bound to find me, adding a strange and unbearable agony to the excitement of the game, something resembling the indefinitely deferred spasms I encountered when I started to masturbate, very shortly after this episode. Indeed, it seemed to me that I was reproducing this very situation.

Sam and I rolled in the mud at the bottom of the ditch. By this time, I believe, he was slapping me to calm me down, but at the same time he was kissing me, and I was kissing him and hitting him at once. Every one of Dan's calls, floating in through the rain from one corner or another of the field, seemingly from all points of the compass, renewed my violence and fury. We must both have had an orgasm, in my case without really knowing it, but it only made me angrier, with one surge of fury rolling in after another as if it would never abate. We were plastered with mud and blood, cut perhaps by broken planks and branches, or else by our questing biting lips and teeth, or it could have been my period. "Calm down," Sam kept gasping, but soon he too was out of control. And suddenly Dan loomed above us.

"Scram!" Sam yelled at him.

But Dan dropped on him like a stone — hardly a metaphor, for it was as if Dan had lost consciousness, regressed back through the ages, petrified, become stone. He dropped straight onto Sam. Sam tried to catch him, but his hands were slippery, and Dan was already scrambling out of the ditch. Then again he was falling, unconscious, compact, rocklike, on our cousin.

My fury died. At the sight of Dan my habitual concern returned. I was afraid he would hurt himself.

"Dan, be careful, stop!" I cried.

And Dan must have recognized my old voice, the voice from before our cousins. His stone carapace shattered and I heard his normal voice, my brother's real voice:

"I'll stop if you get out of here."

TWENTY-ONE

The Little Drop of Water

*A*LL RIGHT, I'm leaving."

We were ourselves again. Ourselves, but not quite.

My brother did not help me climb from the trench. He stood on the edge, stiff, not extending a hand. I felt a stab of pain.

My brother had just inflicted pain on me. Deliberately.

For years we had played in that ditch, and had always climbed out of it in the same way: I gave Dan a boost to lift him to the edge, and there he held out his hand to me and helped me out.

Clambering clumsily out of that trench, getting filthier by the second as I flattened myself against the mud walls, forced to crawl on my belly to hoist myself over the edge, I felt all the weight of those piled-up moments when we had helped each other hand and foot to emerge from this same trench.

Those tiny superimposed instants made up a fragile column, but its base sat far back in time, deep inside our flesh. Our present rested upon hundreds and hundreds of fragile columns of this kind, and Dan my brother had just deliberately shattered one of them.

Sam had already climbed out on the other side. He had not helped me either.

It rained on.

I stood motionless as the water trickled down my neck. I focused on that rain, the feel of the trickles running down my back, I threw myself into its arms, I loved it, I ran off with it to its kingdom where human beings have no place. How joyfully I would have turned into a drop of water: indeed, the Hans Christian Andersen story about a drop of water was actually in my thoughts at that moment. I could see the drop of water leaving her cloud to visit the earth of men and animals, and I saw her returning, with the sun's help, to her original cloud and to all her sister drops. The story had made me cry when I was little, and I badly wanted to cry now.

Thus from that first wound my brother had ever inflicted on me I sought flight by trying to become rain, water, a drop of water in order to join sisters — beings not similar to me but identical — and lose myself in them.

Years later, when my brother inflicted the ultimate wound on me, the irrevocable wound, I would seek flight in the same way, seeking beings not similar to me but identical, beings in whom I could lose myself. Beings who were also sisters, nuns, beings who melted into their God like drops of water melting into their cloud.

And that second time, like the first time, of course, it would be madness, and I would be mistaken.

We gazed at the rainbow that had appeared. By the time it faded, our cousin Sam had vanished. We slowly climbed back up the meadow. When we reached the house, Sara and Frank were waiting for us. "They're covered with mud!" she exclaimed, and Frank said, "They've been at it again!"

Sam (no one had seen him) appeared behind them, already changed and clean. He leaned against the stair rail and said calmly:

"Apparently it's a habit with them."

Oh, why did I not look at my brother with the new eyes of a girl in love, of a girl who has been caressed, who has just climaxed? Why oh why was I unable?

The forces flickering between us would have found their proper pathways. We would have been able to grab them, lean on them, make them our allies, oh, Dan, who knows what might then have happened when I was eighteen and you thirteen?

If I had only looked at you, Dan, as I emerged from that ditch with another's sperm on my skirt and the damp warmth of my orgasm between my thighs, if our eyes had only met, we would have understood. This is the thought that tortured me through the years, all my lost convent years.

Instead we gazed at the rainbow.

"My God, let me retrace my steps to that waterlogged ditch, to the edge where I half knelt, head lowered, where I fled in the flow of the rain, just for a second, my God, just the tiniest of miracles. All of time stretches before you and that moment is so tiny, my being is so tiny; if you are unwilling to reach down to me, if you are unwilling to act, then simply revoke your power over me and I will flit swift as a dragonfly over the water and alone, all alone, find that moment again in the vast weft of time."

That was what I used to say in the convent, fool that I was.

And so great was the power of my desire that I actually felt close to success. Not for a second could my mind stand still at that word "God." It was simply an object — x — in no way my concern, an object to give my mind support. Should this object x elect to remove itself from the world, should it elect to leave me in the confusion of a time bereft of its presence, I would at once have leapt upon that minute. And Dan would be there. Once again I would see his mud-splashed rubber boots, I would raise my eyes and at last know whether the world is one or multiple, whether there is an immensity of possible worlds all spread out at once as if segments of an immense fan. And the very second our eyes met, Dan, you and I would leap lightning quick into another of those worlds.

Day after day among the nuns I looked forward to that moment. I never thought of their God; the prayers they read slid over me, unable to enter me. For my whole body was nothing more than a prayer, and my prayer used theirs: I wanted to return to that moment on the edge of the ditch, to that moment of our youth, there to undo the death approaching us.

One day, in the after-lunch hour when we were allowed to break silence, the sister looked up at the clock, then leaned against the draining board and said, in that solemn childlike way of theirs that at another time might have made me smile:

"We have to seek annihilation of self."

She had just pulled the plug to drain the scalding dishwater from the sink. Her reddened hands steamed in the cold air and she dried them on her apron.

"That was a big wash," she went on as if in the same sentence.

The barred window was steamed over, obliterating our view of the hens pecking about in the backyard. Another nun came over to take the tall tin containers draining under the other window. She hung them on their hooks, then left. The first nun had removed her apron. Something in my stillness must have struck her. The last of the washing-up water drained away with a deep gurgle.

"— to open a horizon on which God's light can rise," she said as the sink gave a final loud belch, the obscene sound almost drowning her voice and sending a blush across her scrubbed face.

There was a problem with the sink, she explained, a bend in the pipe that forced the water back and made the surrounding wall damp.

But my heart had made a leap. So I was not mistaken — this annihilation of self was surely what I had come here in search of. I too sought to open up within me that vast horizon in which I would at last see again that grass shimmering in the sun and flattened by the rain and that muddy ditch, with my brother standing beside the ditch and our cousin already gone, and myself half kneeling on the edge and raising my eyes not toward the rainbow, not toward that many-colored specter, but in that field of shimmering grass to meet the gaze of my brother Dan. So then the convent was not a mistake and I had indeed come where I was supposed to . . . The nun's words had long since gurgled away with the greasy washing-up water, but I was now ready to do all the community's washing up, day after day, in that old-fashioned, damp, cold, wonderful convent kitchen . . .

All those hours in the convent, in the chapel, in my cell, in the oratory!

In the end I no longer even sought you out. I no longer had the strength, all that remained to me was that obsessive need to know, to know whether other worlds existed, alongside ours at all times, like the segments of an open fan. That would have been enough, that would have cooled my fever; I could have told myself that Dan and Estelle were alive somewhere, without me but together; it would have been a consolation, infinitesimal compared to the fever that burned me — but a beginning of consolation.

Perhaps there had been a time when our life did not have to be the terrible devastation it became; a time when I could have fallen asleep next to you every night as I did for the brief duration of our happiness, lying next to you, Dan, like a limpet clinging to a rock, and in the middle of the night we both turned over and then you became the shell and I became your inner flesh. The whole time we slept together, we slept that way.

Every evening, Dan, until our bodies disintegrated together, and then we would together have gone into the earth as you so dearly wished.

How can one explain such things, madame? How strange and disconcerting they must seem. Do people speak of such things in the world you inhabit, madame? They are things that belong to the body, not to words, not to language . . .

I rely neither on words nor on language to make them intelligible. I rely on others, on those who one day fell asleep next to a being they loved, on those who one day lost that being, on those who have seen a coffin filled with the flesh of their loved one sinking into a sodden ditch, on those who for the rest of their days try like unnatural beings to live their lives backward.

I smell out these pitiful monsters in subways and streets. I smell the struggle against nature that twists their lives out of shape; all my senses are alert for them, for I am myself one of them. They are many, and I have no idea what task they perform in time's vast weft. But sometimes it seems to me that they must nibble away at the weft like moths and that time will one day fly away in a cloud of dust . . . That sometimes is how I see the end of the world.

TWENTY-TWO

"*My God, It's Physical*"

I MOVED from the arms of one cousin to the arms of the other, then rejoined Sara, who talked to me about my brother, her brothers, our neighbors. We studied our bodies. Sara said she had made love with my brother — "and believe me, he knows everything, Esty" — I listened but those words did not penetrate my mind. They merely bumped about in the turbulence that had overtaken us. My breasts hurt constantly, I left Frank only to stumble upon Sam, and every night there was Sara beside me, with her ivory body and half-open legs in the light of the moon.

"Don't close the shutters, Esty, it's like closing your body."

We left the shutters open and the window too, and discussed all the day's encounters, endlessly examining every smallest amorous manifestation from every possible angle, with Sara commenting and me asking questions. We were half-asleep when we heard footsteps under our window. "Esty, prowlers," hissed Sara into my ear. I woke up, we listened with thudding hearts. "Let me close the window," I begged. "No, no, Esty," murmured Sara, holding her breath, "no, I like being scared." I heard her with amazement: "You like being scared?" "Of course, so do you, you'd like us both to be raped together by whoever is walking around outside." I put all my soul into attempting to convince her that she was wrong — "No, Sara, no, I don't like being scared." My heart was beating an insane tattoo; was I lying, did I really like being scared?

Convincing Sara was quite beyond me. She was a siren who lured me into states of near-madness; I was powerless to resist. We argued in low voices, hers mocking, mine desperate, but today I know I was right: I could not love being scared because I lived in fear.

In that sheltered house of our childhood, among people who loved us, my brother and I had always been surrounded by fear. It was a monstrous shadow lying in wait for us. And one day it caught us, as we sensed it would.

For Sara, fear was a minnow that occasionally nibbled at her legs in its freshwater habitat. But how could I have explained such a thing?

My own mind attacked itself voraciously, from all sides. We could not sleep more than an hour at a stretch, then Sara was back on the attack.

"Esty," she whispered, half lying on top of me, "there's someone outside, I swear."

There were footsteps in the garden.

Suddenly Sara's excitability, which I had held at bay with all the strength of my logical mind, took hold of me. I pushed her away and sat up.

"Let's see," I said.

My voice was trembling.

"But first we have to wake the boys," said Sara.

That of course was uppermost in her mind.

But I feared the dark corridor, and even more I feared knocking at our cousins' door. My brother? I did not think of him. He was of my cousins' constellation, as if drowned there. I felt as if I had been delivered up to Sara and to her world in which everything was foreign to me. Since she said so, yes, there could well be prowlers in the garden; they could get in through our window or through another window elsewhere in the house.

"We don't have time," I whispered.

We got up stealthily and went to the window, one to the left, the other to the right, hearts racing at every misstep. What if we came suddenly face-to-face with the intruder before we had time to swing the shutters closed and shoot the bolt?

That was what Sara was whispering. "What will we do if there's already someone at the window?" she hissed. "Be quiet," I said, for now that my physical contact with her had been broken for a few seconds I had found myself again. All of a sudden it was my own fear that returned to me, the old fear that had long cradled Dan and me. I felt it there close by, and wished I could go back.

I felt that we should not be going to that window, nor hearing those footsteps, they had nothing to do with our girlish fears, but already Sara was calling out in a loud whisper:

"Good Lord, come and look!"

Relieved, but more excited than ever, Sara had come to my side of the window and was steering me by the back of my neck.

"It's your father, Esty, your father!"

Yes, it was my father, walking slowly as he always did, except that his hands were not clasped behind his back.

Both hands held someone else's. He walked carefully with this person: the two of them moving so strangely you would have sworn they were ghosts from a vanished world, a pair of ghosts profiting from the relaxed vigilance of the present to steal back to a lost past. They moved like refugees, fugitives certain they would soon be recaptured.

All this I felt in a flash. But it was unimportant, for it was not a discovery to me.

What I wanted more than anything was for Sara not to probe and pry, not to ask questions. I wanted us to return swiftly to the un-questioning state in which Dan and I had managed to ensconce our lives. But Sara could not contain herself.

"Esty, can you believe it, it's her, it's Tiresia."

*　　　*　　　*

And then I actually saw my little cousin get a grip on herself.

She was making a violent effort to curb her excitement. How sternly she must have been admonished, how hard it must have been for my plump sensual little cousin, so greedy for gossip and spicy tales, a pretty little leech from the here and now, dying to fasten on whatever that here and now set before her and suck it up in one go.

But there was something stronger here than she was. She pulled back, drew the curtain, slowly so as not to make the rings click. We returned without a word to our respective mattresses and at last fell asleep.

And then I woke up.

I awoke brutally and totally, as if a trumpet had sounded inside me.

Sara was sound asleep, snoring, her nightgown pulled all the way up to her neck, but her body no longer interested me. I was on the alert and had no idea why. I told myself I was thirsty. The house seemed utterly at peace; my cousins too must have been asleep; in any case I gave them not another thought. I felt that the way to the kitchen was clear, and almost without realizing it I found myself out on the landing at the head of the stairs.

Along the corridor every door was closed. On the floor above too the silence was heavy. I was sure Tiresia was in her bedroom and asleep. I was almost supernaturally sure of it — but that was how it always was with Tiresia.

Abruptly very thirsty, I went down the stairs, my thoughts on the kitchen and the cool water that would flow from the faucet. I was already in the hallway — where it was dark but not totally black, for the kitchen door was ajar and a little moonlight filtered through it — when suddenly I bumped into someone.

It was my brother. He too no doubt had been thirsty and was leaving the kitchen, where he had not even turned on the light.

I said we bumped into each other but that cannot be accurate. I must have seen his shape against the open kitchen door, outlined in the faint moonlight. He too must have seen me as a dim shadow at the foot of the stairs. We must have been a full yard apart, and yet we collided violently, as if we had stumbled, as if the earth had moved beneath our feet, as if someone behind us had shoved us roughly forward.

That moment, which was to destroy our youth, happened very quickly.

My brother held me tight in his arms. He was so tall in the darkness, he was no longer my brother, he was exactly the one I had been expecting, the one neither of my cousins could ever be, the one I had at last found in this darkness, and I pressed myself hard against him, swept away by this violent end to my waiting. My breasts thrust at his chest, I felt his member stiff against my belly, and his mouth sought mine. I hesitated for a fraction of a second, out of terror, out of love, and it was over.

I recognized my brother's features, he recognized mine, and he pulled roughly away from me. I heard his voice say "My God, it's physical," just those four words, gratingly uttered, and for years that voice went on like a razor cutting fresh strips from my heart that I went on trying with all my strength to sew back again.

Excessive images, perhaps, but don't reject them, do not laugh, madame, they are not false, simply "misplaced," left somewhere that exists because I have been there, somewhere with naked red flesh and razors slashing viciously, endlessly.

"My God, it's physical."

In a second, we had become enemies.

Analyzing those words did not help: they could only tear me endlessly apart.

If one of our cousins had uttered those same words, my mouth would have relayed them to Sara, Sara's mouth would have taken them up, we would have dissected and discoursed upon them for hours on end.

"My God, it's physical."

My brother's words were an arrow whose flight was brief and swift. It struck home and was lost to sight.

I do not know how Dan and Estelle got back to their respective rooms. There is no memory between the two shores of that moment. A compact silence fell on Dan's words, on our brutal embrace, a silence seemingly substantial but not truly of this world, the silence of a meteorite.

Next morning our cousins left. They sent a few postcards from Montreal in the months that followed, then we lost sight of them altogether. In September I failed my baccalaureate, and left first to repeat the year in the adjacent town and then to Paris, to the university. Dan stayed on at home. I knew from my father's letters that he was no longer interested in anything but dancing. But instead of keeping him at home, like our mother, his passion kept him away. He now spent every evening at the new conservatory at the other end of town, and my father did not think he would be returning to school. Between the lines I understood that Dan was almost never at home, that he had a group of friends my father disapproved of, that our family unit had disintegrated. Our mother sank into her dream. "I do not believe she has been chosen to go on her company's tour," said my father, and I knew as a certainty that in fact my mother no longer belonged to any dance company at all. "Tiresia has arthritis in her hands and suffers pain if she sits up too long," said my father, and I understood that Tiresia had practically stopped playing the piano, that her link to the world, whatever world that might be, was slowly dissolving. "I spend more and more time on my duty cases," wrote my father, and I understood that he too in his way was sinking, that he had returned to confront himself in the most arid, the most painful area of his work, and that in it he found the extinction of his hopes, and perhaps also a kind of peace. For his duty cases spoke to him in a language that the depths of his heart understood, and that was doubtless a comfort to him. My father no longer had the strength or the urge to measure himself against the new and apparently more frivolous world emerging from the womb; he was returning to the past, to the place of mortal and terrifying issues, the issues that had scarred his and his family's life, and the rest of the world no longer concerned him.

There, in a certain sense, I was mistaken. For among those duty cases were two on which my father was working ferociously and which directly concerned the future, my future and Dan's. But we at the time knew nothing of those things.

I was studying law, and my father was glad of my successes. Although I was hardly brilliant, I moved steadily from exam to exam, each step in my degree course familiar to him, and that gladdened him. And then I married a law student. *"I am happy with the life you are creating for yourself,"* he wrote to me. *"Selfishly happy, for as you know you are the only member of our family following the path I chose, which makes me feel less alone and stronger. It gives me great joy to hear you talking of your courses, your assignments. I go to check back in my own books, and that makes me younger. I am so grateful to you for all the details you give me. I only hope that keeping me up-to-date on everything going on in your university and your studies does not add too greatly to your burden. But if the going is heavy — and I'm sure it must be heavy at times — know at least that it is not in vain. Your letters are at present my greatest joy; in a way they keep me intellectually fit: without them I'm sure I'd quickly degenerate into an old outdated attorney. But, my dear Estelle, I am not just selfish. I cherish the hope that the path you are following will steer you away from life's dangers. Your marriage to someone who shares your interests can only stabilize your life, and then I am still a lawyer, and I think too that this training will help you to defend yourself should the need one day arise. As you know, I do not have quite the same certainties in Dan's case. His mother has no worries about him and I strive to emulate her wisdom."*

I sometimes returned to the house. I never brought my husband, and nobody found this surprising.

Well, one person did — my husband. But I told him it was better that way, that he would never understand, and that in any case my home visits bored me to death. He did not press the question overmuch. Neither was our marriage one in which we pressed issues. There had been no question of "pressing" priorities at our wedding, just a few recent university friends for lunch in a neighborhood Vietnamese restaurant, and there was a problem with the city hall ceremony, but I at once forgot it.

On my returns to the house I rarely saw Dan. He had become extraordinarily handsome, staggeringly handsome, which I found awkward almost. We exchanged formalities. We no longer had anything to say to each other. And yet a few days later my father would write, *"Thanks to you, we saw more of Dan than usual,"* and for days my head swam strangely when I thought of that remark of my father's; I sought for it in his letter and reread it, and for days I would be unable to concentrate on anything.

"Estelle on walkabout again," said my husband Yves, who picked up a lot of such expressions from his reading. I secretly resented him for it.

TWENTY-THREE

"I Want You to Go to New York"

A PIGEON has built its nest on Phil's balcony. The nest sits against the dividing rail behind a number of discarded boxes. There were two fledglings at first, but one died. The second is now al-most full-grown, its dirty yellowish wings are turning gray, only a few of its original feathers remain, encircling its neck like a disin-tegrating fur collar. The mother no longer spends much time there. The fledgling is alone nearly all the time on the dropping-spattered remnants of its nest. I offered it some bread crumbs, but it does not seem to want them, shrinking back against the railing when I come close.

It is not very beautiful. Its mother has already abandoned it, its twin is dead, and soon it will take wing and join all the other city pigeons, dying, hatching, reproducing. If I saw it pecking about on the sidewalk I would not recognize it. Small trembling thing (you can see its heartbeat in its skull) huddled in its corner of the balcony, a tiny corner in a big city. It will blend in with its own kind and then disappear.

I could not take my eyes off that pigeon.

Phil was in the kitchen replacing a washer. I went out to the balcony, one of those narrow balconies you often see on the facades of turn-of-the-century buildings, one on the third floor, another on the sixth. Phil's is on the sixth.

At first I was afraid to be at his place because of it.

After my return from the convent, I lived in a second-floor apart-ment. I needed to hear the street conversations that floated up to my window, and without making an effort, an effort of which I would have been incapable, I found myself living in a floating vegetation, sometimes dense, sometimes sparse, of words. The weather, health matters, the dog's problems — such were the topics of neighborhood people on the sidewalks below, but there were also the conversations of people passing through, like ships glimpsed and then at once lost to view, leaving behind them a wake of speculations that briefly buoyed me. Lives went by under my window. I wished I could go out, a white flag in my hand, and hail them.

Once I thought I heard "Helleur," although perhaps it was "feller" or "teller," or else something completely different, and I almost ran after those people shouting "What? What was that?" In the morning the garbage truck made such a din it seemed to be right inside my bedroom and I thought how lucky I was to live along its itinerary, to live amid the grinding roar of its hydraulic tipper, the terse shouts of the garbagemen and the insults of motorists. And several times a day there were the small urgent footsteps and excited yells of children from the nearby school.

I felt lucky that life should come and gather me in right where I lived.

The sixth floor would have been too high.

That was how it was, madame, after my return from the convent: piano lessons for my material needs, street conversations for my social needs.

On a fine day you can see the hills around Paris from Phil's balcony. Yesterday there was a wonderful warm sun, perhaps the first of the year. I realized that I had come several times to this apartment, that I had known the hours of the day and the hours of the night here, and already the changing seasons.

In short, I was so far successful in the new contract I had signed with the living.

Only, instead of a strengthening, I felt a weakening of my body. I at once feared the common vaypigo. What would become of that tenacious visitor of ours in these strange surroundings? My brother and I could tame it, and in the convent the nuns paid no attention to creatures of its kind — but here? Would it feel rage at not being recognized, at not finding its accustomed landmarks?

Leaning on the wrought iron railing, I felt the weakness creep over me.

I thought of Phil, who might come out at any moment. I raced to the kitchen, almost slipping on a women's magazine spread out on the floor. "Phil, I'm going to smoke a cigarette at the window while the sun's still out there." He was busy with his toolbox and did not look at me. "You have about a quarter of an hour," I heard. Inside me all was disturbance, but he did not notice, it did not show. I took a book of matches from a shelf and went out again as if nothing were the matter.

As if nothing were the matter. That was the attitude I had to learn.

My vaypigo receded. It was still there, still fighting for my attention, but it had left me space in which to concern myself with it. Again I leaned on the balcony railing.

The trees stretched green to the end of the boulevard. On the sections of sidewalk visible between the clumps of foliage were walkers, their arms bare, their gait leisurely, strolling calmly alongside the noisy river of traffic. A few seconds on the sidewalk, then they vanished under the next bunch of vegetation, while other similar passersby emerged. The housefronts too were full of bustle, of easygoing Sunday bustle.

And on Phil's balcony I saw her, the woman I wanted, Claire, one among the thousands of women who had risen late that morning and were now wandering about their apartments, vaginas sated, luxuriating in the first warm sun, consumed by small feminine thoughts, perhaps with spring dresses or with suntans, of the kind you see in magazines, while their lovers tinkered in the kitchen or took a shower.

I said to her, "Look at all that, those fine housefronts, this boulevard with its cars and trucks going anywhere they want, and that long line of trees growing as many leaves as they want, and those passersby, and that wide generous sky without a single cloud to be seen. That's your city, your life, your love."

And I added: "Take it, go for it, you're Claire now, nothing behind you but what you see right in front of you."

I tried to fill her up with these things, to fill her up with that nothingness, with that empty ghost that had chanced to materialize on this balcony, but Estelle behind her was dizzy, the sun made her head swim, set those excessively beautiful splinters of life to glittering. But between those splinters nothing, vertigo . . .

The pigeon had backed into its corner. A tiny white feather floated in the blue void. An airplane. I believe it was the first I had seen in the sky here in Paris.

In New York, when I used to lie down on the parapet above Riverside Drive or the wall at East River Park or anywhere else during my marathon walks up and down the length and breadth of Manhattan, I saw an aircraft a minute, making wide turns in the direction of Kennedy Airport.

My father had written to me:

"*We have very little news of Dan. I ought to go over there myself to see him, but you know how I suffer from claustrophobia. I don't know if I would be up to the flight, even a sea crossing, for so long. And of course I would not be able to take Tiresia, and our doctor doesn't think she should be left alone. I have always avoided doing so. When I have left it has been for a day or two at most, and then you were always there, you, my daughter.*

"*Nicole talks of going, then drops the subject. Frankly, Estelle, I'm not keen on her going back over there. That city was never good to her, and just now her own plans are faring so badly that I'd have little confidence in her. She has not been selected for her dance company's coming tour: although she tries to hide it, it's clearly a blow. I believe she is dancing less well, you know how it is, you need faith, and to have faith you need* a little encouragement. My own encouragement carries little weight, and perhaps I too lack faith. Some days she tells us Dan is becoming a great dancer. She tells us that we understand nothing of Dan's talent, that we're willing him to fail, that we're making him fail the way we made her fail. I don't want to distress you, but of course that is just what my letter is going to do. Don't be too angry with me, Estelle; sometimes I feel a little bit alone, especially now that Tiresia has almost stopped playing the piano and Nicole dances so much less.

"I realize, Estelle, that that was my happiness. Hearing Tiresia play the piano in the living room from my study, hearing the pitter-pat of Nicole's slippers in the garage. Yes, that was my happiness: as long as I could hear those two sounds I felt that I had won, that I had won my greatest case, that my defense had been sound, that justice had been done, and that the world had resumed its business. You and Dan I simply took for granted; I must have believed that your happiness, your stability, would come about naturally. I must have been mistaken. Perhaps I should have concerned myself more with you and Dan. Particularly with Dan. I still cling to the idea that you, Estelle, will always come through, will always be there to hear my words, with that thoughtful, serious look of yours. Perhaps that too is an illusion. I sometimes think that I have not treated you as a child and I fear that one day your life could change violently. And that would destroy me, Estelle. I do see clearly that I count heavily on you, that I take your support for granted, that I have always done so, bless you. Oh, damn it all, please don't pay too much attention to all this confessional blather! Put it down to premature senility, no, you won't accept that, I can already hear your voice reproaching me . . . very well, then, put it down to my concern for Dan.

"In fact, Estelle, I do worry about Dan, and if you agree I want you to go to New York and see him, try to bring him back here, at least bring back news of him. Nicole's reactions tell me nothing useful, and I do fear that city. You were too little to remember, but it shattered Nicole; she was in a terrible state when she returned. Luckily I was still young and so was Tiresia, and of course you were here. But if Dan too comes back damaged, I don't know who will be here to take him in and help him recover.

"It is quite possible that I'm exaggerating, that I am letting myself be led on by these two overemotional women. Mrs. Neighbor says boys are like that and they get over it. And she tells me all over again about Adrien's troubles with the bar owner. I just don't know. If you agree to go and see your brother I'll send you money for the trip. We have friends over there, you could live with them . . ."

I at once wrote back to tell my father that of course I would go to New York to see Dan, that he should not worry about a thing, that it would be a pleasure.

My father replied:

"Estelle, my darling, I'm so happy, you'll never know how happy. But please don't pretend it will be a pleasure. I believe that as usual you want to help your father, who's never been too good at handling things. But don't think I'm totally blind about you. I've noticed the distance that has grown between you and your brother. I don't know the reason for it, perhaps you're simply too different.

"But I incline to the notion that it's Dan who has changed. He has not been the same since your cousins' visit, as if the intrusion of the outside world into our somewhat closed universe had opened new roads for him. Perhaps even revealed him to himself. He had been so bright and he became so somber. I felt he no longer loved us. People talk of the 'onset of puberty,' of course. But this was no 'onset.' It was something that took up residence during that visit of your cousins' — and never left. Some days he was just as he had been, as if the thing had disappeared, but it always came back, sometimes stronger, sometimes less strong.

"I felt he no longer loved us. Particularly his mother. At least it was most obvious with her. You remember how he loved to dance with her, how happy they both were in the blue garage, you remember his dance on the lawn.

"But I know nothing about dancing. I thought it was like the piano. Tiresia was a great pianist, my sweet Estelle, she was barely twenty-five and had every hope of becoming one of the very greatest. I don't know whether I have talked to you enough about all this, it was so difficult, and I was afraid of hurting Tiresia: whether I had brought up her talent and successes or not, I would have been hurting her either way. Afraid too of hurting Nicole, who did not have the same gift and would never succeed as Tiresia did.

"I had always known Tiresia healthy, in full possession of her art, and that art blossomed in elegant concert halls packed with attentive appreciative audiences. Yes, Estelle, that is what I have not told you and your brother enough about: those beautiful concert halls, full of happiness. We have photos. If you come back together, if Dan has done what he set out to do over there, I'll show them to you. In any case, as far as Tiresia's art was concerned, it grew with her and she grew with it. Time was on her side, and so was art.

"To me, dancing seems very different. I find the dancer so isolated. It seems to me that he sets himself up against the laws of nature. I am probably babbling, Estelle, but after all I have no experience beyond what

I have gleaned through Nicole and now Dan. He says he must fight the earth with his body. You know what I often think, Estelle? A dancer has to drag onstage the bag of excrement he calls his body and then has to make it glitter like a diamond. To me it's like a conjuring trick.

"Yes, when I look at a dancer, I always think sooner or later of those yards of intestines stuffed with shit, only just hidden by the skin, intestines he is obliged to haul along through every one of his movements. When I talk to Minor that way he says, 'That's my department, may I remind you that it is I who dissect, not you,' or if he is in a good mood, 'Fine, fine, how about a small sedative, Helleur?'

"A piano is clean as a whistle inside. It is a friend to the piano player. I was often afraid for Tiresia the night before, or else as she walked across the stage just before performances, but as soon as she sat on the stool and I saw her hands, my fear subsided (I always brought my binoculars to get a clear sight of her hands at that moment, even from the front row of the stalls, you didn't know that, Estelle), I felt at peace, and the music flowed into me as if into a space yawning between tall columns.

"The dancer has no friend and nothing to support him but the ground, which seeks only to hold him back. You cannot imagine how it hurt me to see Nicole stumble during a performance. When she fell, Estelle, it was like a bursting dam or an earthquake, something monstrous, as if nature were reasserting her rights, tossing poor pretentious humans aside like broken dolls. Well, I suppose I feel these things so strongly because that's the way Nicole feels them. She lacks the solid temperament Tiresia possessed. I believe she is too frail to be a real artist; her art dominates her instead of her dominating it.

"I don't know how it is with Dan. I had the impression that he was stronger than Nicole, you know what I mean, Estelle. I know how sensitive Dan is, how easily swayed by emotion, but he always struck me as stronger than all those things. It's a feeling I can't really account for, yet Dan seemed to me different, innocent, and no doubt possessing genius. Perhaps, though, that is an impression stemming from his youth. He was such a beautiful child, such a seducer.

"And I told myself that he would be strong enough for New York, that in the city that had crushed his mother he would be able to express himself and grow, and that that would have a positive effect on Nicole, cure her of the pain that took root in her over there — as if she needed pain! So I didn't object too strongly to his departure.

"In fact, to be quite candid, perhaps I wanted him to leave, Estelle. Temporarily, of course. It's strange to say it at my age, but the non-love of others is almost unbearable to me. I sense a kind of injustice in it. Only, *unlike other human failings, there is no court to which you can bring your grievance. And that is why non-love hurts me so much. You know, Estelle, how much I need to 'right wrongs,' as you put it when you are making fun of me. But in this case, no righting of the wrong is possible. Dan did not love us much those last months. He watched his mother's dancing with a critical eye, and did not bother to hide it. He was never a deceiver.*

"There was an ugly scene, Estelle. He told her that he had to leave her if he ever wanted to become a real dancer. Well, I just took it as a son's rebellion against his mother, but poor Nicole was so little of a mother, in a sense she did not deserve that. To Tiresia he said nothing, but he had a way of looking at that piano when we were at table, Estelle, such a strange way of looking. He would stop eating altogether and just stare. 'What are you looking at, Dan?' said Nicole. 'At the piano.' But there were so many things in his voice, it sent shivers up my spine, I swear it, Estelle. I wonder how he dared. Sometimes I felt like explaining certain things to him, you know, Estelle, painful things . . . But we long ago decided never to mention them, and it did not seem the right time to bring them up. I just wanted to shut him up, I couldn't stand him anymore. And that's not a feeling I find particularly honorable.

"In those last few months he had no love for me. I don't know why, unless it was because I understand nothing of dancing; he must have found me dull and pedantic. One day he said to me, 'You arrive with your heavy equipment after the fire has started, which does no good. What I want is to go through the fire.' Or something like that; I was so shaken I didn't hear clearly. Another time he said, 'I want to move absolutely straight, like lightning.' He muttered something about Hannibal's elephants and about birds ineffectively flapping their wings. Anyway, the kind of things teenagers say.

"But now that he's gone I think of him all the time. It's strange, Estelle, but I have the impression that with him gone we are just lost souls. Your absence did not affect me the same way. You write to us, as if you were still here; you've never really left us — besides, look at this monster letter I'm writing now!

"Let me tell you this before I close. I'm not just the selfish and demanding father I seem to be. I am working on your and Dan's behalf, on a case I can't tell you about just now. But if anything happens to us, you'll find all the information you need with our attorney. Actually you already know him, he's your old philosophy teacher's brother. If you want to take up music again one day, or if Dan decides to go back to school, I want you to be able to do so whatever happens to us. Don't be angry with me for

being mysterious, it's a money matter and that's all there is to say about it, except that I don't want you and Dan to go without it.

"For now, I'm sending you the promised sum to cover the flight and your stay. I think Tiresia would like you to go to Montreal to see her cousins, and in case you want to I'm enclosing the addresses.

"I'm sending enough for two tickets, for I assume you'll want to take your husband with you. I hope he'll want to go, tell him I'd like that, that I would feel safer to know he was over there with you.

"Adrien has been to see us. He has turned into a good-looking man. The wall under the lilac is more tumbledown than ever, we still talk about repairing it, but neither our neighbors nor we ever make a start. Adrien still comes through the gap and his mother continues to scold him as if he were a small boy. He told me he would like to pay you a visit now that he has his own car (a kind of convertible missile that looks altogether dangerous to me and in which I would hate to see you ride) and enough money to 'make a maître d' drool' (his exact words, Estelle), but that he has no wish to entertain your husband too because he can't stand 'legal eagles' (his term for lawyers, I suppose!). I should perhaps have taken that last shaft personally and voiced indignation, but I believe he is simply a little bit jealous. Over you, I mean. And then you know how Adrien is, he says irritating things so coolly that you almost feel like applauding. And when all is said and done he's not unlikable, with that cool manner and his disarming candor. All the same, I'd rather not have him for a son-in-law. His political ideas are a little basic! I should add that he was ready to go to New York with you ('At my own expense, Mr. Helleur, in fact I'll pay for Estelle and for me' — I'm sure you can hear his tone), but I didn't encourage him."

Another letter from my father arrived by the same post, full of anxiety and cares: *"Above all, Dan mustn't think we're pursuing him,"* *"I'm so afraid he'll fall into bad company over there,"* and this phrase: *"Estelle, I am so undecided and there is no one to put me on the right road."*

II

New York

TWENTY-FOUR

The Airport

*M*Y BROTHER was waiting for me at the airport. "Kennedy Airport," I had specified over the phone. "Yes, yes, JFK," he answered. I had hung up, suddenly ice cold, not recognizing the initials pronounced American-style.

I did not see him but at once sensed his presence in the bewildered throng crowding the vast terminal hall. He was hidden by a compact group of travelers with long side curls, just off an El Al flight, all in black and huddled tight. Nor was it my eyes that picked him out, for he was a different person, he did not look like my brother Dan.

We exchanged rapid glances, he patted my shoulder, words tumbled out, phrases like "How tanned you are," "Well, you're very pale," "We have to get your baggage," "Where?" "Right over there," and we walked over to where the suitcases paraded along a conveyor belt. There we stood side by side, faces directed stonily at the moving belt, occasionally jostled by other passengers but not once turning to face each other.

All those cases parading by. I gaped at them.

Each one was like a soul belonging to someone, and this was where that soul and that someone were reunited. An arm would cleave the crowd clustered before the belt, a body would push through, and a case would be hoisted aloft while the articulated sections of the belt went on their way. The traveler withdrew with his case from the immediate vicinity of the carousel and at once, because he had retrieved his soul, was at liberty to continue his journey. Soon he would be surrounded by family and friends and the noisy group would move out to the exit.

The strange language intoxicated me. Never had I felt so dispossessed.

But a curious thought occurred to me — regret that my husband was not with me. My father had sent money for his ticket but I did not want us to leave together.

*   *   *

"Nice flight?" said Dan.

Tears came to my eyes because I could find no reply.

"Nice flight?"

That was how my brother spoke to me now, his words so vague they could mean anything, anybody's words, waiting to be borrowed, just like those handcarts you find at airport entrances; you load them up and then you leave them behind.

That was what he was offering me, borrowed words, which others had already used and others would use again. Words a stranger might have used to me — which would have been much simpler, because a stranger could only have been asking about strictly technical aspects of the flight, and then I could have spoken of mid-Atlantic turbulence or of our smooth landing.

Or was it a question for me, only for me, a question meant to reopen the old paths we had once walked together? Oh, Dan my brother, what do you mean?

"Well?" Dan said absently.

"Yes," I said.

He had grown even taller. Or had all that training propelled his body upward? He had to stoop to talk to me — but he did not stoop, he stood ramrod straight, hands stuffed carelessly into pockets, and addressed me from on high, from where there were fewer human faces crowded together, where the air was purer, more refined, where I was denied entry.

He was twenty.

His face radiated beauty and raw fresh youth, accentuated to the point of insolence by a contrary quality that I was unable to pinpoint because I dared not look squarely at him.

I saw later that it was a wrinkle on his face, a line of pain, and that even when the pain slept the line remained, waiting to be awakened. Later still I saw that where the line had dug itself a channel down the center of his cheeks, Dan had acquired a sort of tic that occurred whenever he stared into space. At such moments he crinkled his eyes, and that had caused this mark that set such a dissonant seal on his youth.

The other disconcerting thing was the color of his skin.

It was dark gold, a deep warm hue that made him a stranger to me, something out of a magazine. This was a beauty foreign to me, born elsewhere, in realms unknown, in that megalopolis set down on the ocean shore, bisected by two great rivers, extended by vast beaches, secretly sown with penthouses riding high on luxurius buildings with terraces like gardens. It was born in repeated excursions to those islands that float like huge water lilies in the Caribbean. And from something else as well, perhaps, from artificial sunlamps in men's clubs. All this I guessed at confusedly. It was not us, it was not our life, and Dan had not written to tell us of it.

And my skin was pale; my body knew not where to turn, it was grievously hobbled. The desire that had been impelling it forward now seemed to have reversed direction. And that disconcerted me most terribly.

My body wished to remain on ground it already possessed — indeed, it longed if possible to beat a retreat, back down the corridor along which it had followed the other passengers, back into the plane where it had sat like all the other passengers neatly installed in their boxes, and ever farther back, farther and farther . . . And the point of departure it really was straining for, the destination it desired without daring to divulge that desire, was the garden of our house, the lawn, the center of that lawn where Dan had planted a deathless root, that day of his wild and exuberant dance, his first dance of love.

"No," Dan suddenly said. "Not a nice flight."

He still did not look at me. He was studying the conveyor, where there were now only a few cases left, manhandled by strangers who had thrust them aside to seize their more fortunate neighbors, thrown them aside and abandoned them like great limp corpses, few and far between, and appearing again and again, banging into the sides at each bend and lurching into even more awkward positions. Those cases made me want to weep.

There were still people waiting around the conveyor, but the remaining cases and travelers seemed unable to join forces. I heard the grinding heartrending hum of the rollers, the faint flop of the rubber pads rising and falling in the distance as another case emerged onto the belt, and something else, a diffuse impalpable buzzing that hovered in the air, floating over everything, permeating everything. The sound of foreignness, the sound of this foreign country.

*   *   *

"Oh, Dan," I said.

But our wing tips barely touched before we were once again lost to each other.

"Damn it, Estelle, I can't believe it, there's hardly any baggage left, we're going to have to fill out a claim, what a drag!"

Although our exchanges had been meager I had been unable to follow them, unable to follow my brother.

This was not Dan, and yet Dan too was there, the Dan who had once unerringly picked up on everything I thought or felt — just a second ago, in fact, with that "No. Not a nice flight." Or had I heard wrong? Already there was no one there to confirm it.

Why was he not looking at me, why had he not kissed me, why had we not thrown ourselves into each other's arms in warm and unruly embrace, like the other travelers?

I could not question him, I could think of nothing to ask.

Did he resent my visit? Did he see me as a spy for our parents? Did he see me as the bearer of an order, an ultimatum, did he suspect that I had been delegated to see what he was doing with the money he received from home? No, none of that seemed likely; I had never seen a child in Dan, and now less than ever. It seemed equally unthinkable that he should see in me an elder sister dispatched to scold him.

I stood rooted to the spot, looking at that sorry conveyor belt.

But Dan had said something. And then, as if by delayed action, as if his words had themselves been borne into view by a wheezing dilapidated conveyor belt, I heard: "Damn it, Estelle, I can't believe it . . ." and I knew too what had delayed his words, prevented them from reaching my hearing directly.

It was nothing, really, no more than a speck of dust. Just my name, my first name, at long last in Dan's mouth: Estelle.

How strange to hear my name in that mouth that now belonged to a stranger. And now the rest of his words followed their leader in: "I can't believe it, there's hardly any baggage left."

But it had to be believed, for I had brought no baggage. Just a handbag, my regular handbag, which I had carried aboard the plane.

*   *   *

No baggage because I had not wanted to arrive loaded down as if for a long stay. I had not wanted to give any kind of impression; I simply wanted to leave the plane like a ladybug, settle on his sleeve, and be carried off without his even realizing it to the places where he lived and had his being.

One day a few weeks later we were on a Long Island beach where Michael, one of the dancers, had taken us in his taxi. Michael had raised a finger. On its tip was a ladybug and he asked us if we knew its name in English. Neither of us did. "Well, it's a lovebug," he said, blowing the delicate creature toward us, and I thought back to the day of my arrival, when I had longed so hard to be just that, a small creature bearing love on its wings. I thought back to that first day, and at once the thought stopped short, as all our thoughts did at that time, leaving us the helpless prey of invisible lightning bolts. "What faces you make," laughed Michael, "real weirdos!"

I certainly must have looked like a weirdo, standing under the sign flashing the number of our long-arrived flight in the vast deserted baggage-claim area. But I had never flown, I had no idea of the unseen connections that kept airports running, and now I dared not say we were waiting for nothing, that there could not possibly be any baggage for me on this sinister conveyor belt, empty and increasingly creaky. I had brought no baggage, and I had not realized what we were doing, standing here in this place, and why was my brother not showing me the way out?

"There was hardly anything in it," I said, "it was an old case, let's go."

"We'll have to fill out a claim," said Dan, "what a drag, and Alwin is waiting."

"Not a claim, Dan, I don't want that case anymore, it's worn-out and damaged, I'd have thrown it away anyway."

"What's got into you?" said Dan. "You want to throw away your case and your things?"

"I want to buy new things, American things, let's go, please!"

"No," said Dan, "you're entitled to reimbursement. What's the good of studying law if you don't know that!"

Dan knew exactly what to do. It was not the first time he had picked up friends at the airport ("friends," he had said; was I now a friend, and what exactly was a friend?). This had already happened to one of them, a South American; they had claimed a fur coat and jewelry, and the friend had been generously reimbursed, although all the time there had only been some old jeans and T-shirts in his baggage, along with his dance photos and press clippings (of which he always kept copies on his person anyway).

Dan, Dan, this whole life you have built and of which I knew nothing, which you have never mentioned, not a letter, nothing.

We had reached a smiling young customs officer. My brother began a long conversation with him. "Thanks a lot, Kenny," he said at last, and turning to me: "He's one of Alwin's dancers, he let me through to meet you, it's not allowed . . ." But I was not listening.

"Why didn't you write to me?" I said suddenly.

We were in the claims office and I was being shown a card depicting different kinds of baggage. I was meant to check the picture most closely resembling the one that was supposed to be lost. I had the card upside down, as if it had been covered in cabalistic signs.

"You have the card upside down," said Dan.

"Why didn't you write to me?"

I had found a question, something of my own. How dear those words were to me. They gave me back my substance and strength and I wanted an immediate reply, right there in that tiny room, which was scarcely big enough for the enormous airport official, so enormous that he appeared to be balancing his desk on his stomach. We had taken our seats one to the right and the other to the left of this bulk, and now our words flew back and forth from side to side of the huge close-curled head, which rocked back and forth from one side to the other like the arm of a saturnine scale.

"Because I didn't know what to write, that's why," said Dan.

"You didn't know what to write?"

"No. Not a word. Nothing."

The claim was so staggering that I almost thought I had rediscovered the old Dan, the way he used to be when he was playing tricks on me. I put down the card.

"There isn't any case."

"What do you mean, there isn't any case?"

"I didn't bring one."

"You didn't bring one!"

"I didn't know what to pack."

"You didn't know what to pack?"

"No. Not a single solitary idea."

"You only have that handbag?"

"Yes."

"You didn't check any baggage?"

"I didn't realize what we were doing just now in the baggage-claim area."

Dan stared at me for a second, as if looking at me for the first time since my arrival.

"You didn't realize what we were doing in the baggage-claim area?"

Then he began to laugh. He said something to the enormous employee with the little desk perched on his stomach, the big head stopped following our words and came forward to retrieve the card, and we left, we finally left the airport.

TWENTY-FIVE

The Taxi

*I*N THE TAXI Dan laughed again, unpleasantly.

"You're just a small-town girl after all. My sister is a little small-town girl like my mother. Hey sir," he said to the driver, "my sister is a real simpleton, and my mother is just about worse."

The English words were recorded inside me, to be understood later, but the French!

Nicole, my Nicole, a small-town simpleton! I did not matter, I could live with it, but Nicole, who wept as she danced on the tips of her perennially new slippers in her garage lined with sky-blue fabric, a fabric now faded almost to gray . . . Nicole, who wept because she would never be a great dancer, because her son had the gift she lacked, because he had left for the city that had crushed her, because he would not return or send news . . . Nicole, dancing all alone, and weeping for other, hidden reasons I could not even guess at, her frail little-girl body racked with sobs, bent at the bar, limbs awry! It was thus I had last seen her; I had opened the door to say good-bye, but she did not hear it open and she did not hear it close.

I had seen Nicole's secret: a rag doll hanging on to a bar and shaken apart by sobs.

I turned and of its own will my hand flashed out.

Of its own will, without my consent. I had never slapped Dan, even as a child when he could seem unbearable.

I would have been unable to slap him. Dan had never been a child to me but my equal, my only equal, of an equality unrelated to age or to rights but to the fathomless depths of genesis, and because of which he was my bulwark, as I was his. Nor had he ever been unbearable to me, since I entered into all his moods, which were also my moods, which were my life.

My hand was on its trajectory, speeding toward Dan's face to give that face a message only my hand could convey, a message that could be delivered only to the skin, and its landing on the threshold of that skin had to be hard enough for the whole body to hear it, for the sound of the impact to reach the bottom of the cells in which my brother's soul was hunched.

How deep down my brother's soul sat hunched, how hard the blow had to be.

But Dan's face, forewarned by the secret signals our bodies had exchanged since childhood, swung around at almost the same second, just as I, finally realizing what I was doing, transmitted the recall order to my hand. Abruptly checked in its trajectory, it swerved off course. But my brother's face, which had turned in anticipation of that approaching message from my body in order to arm himself against it, suddenly encountered its full force. Blood spurted on his lips, droplets fell to his shirt.

"You must be crazy," he shouted.

"Your shirt," I said stupidly.

Suddenly I saw only the shirt.

When Dan left home a year earlier he was still wearing the short-sleeved shirts Nicole bought for him, small-boy's shirts still, except a little bit bigger. In such things he had been a malleable boy who wore what he was given, without a thought.

I had left him looking like a small-town boy dressed by our small-town mother. I suddenly saw how different he now was.

He was wearing the clothing of another continent, not just another continent but another life, cut on lines that were not those of bodies as we conceived of them in our little town and with colors more vehement than I had ever seen on our streets, and he was handsome dressed thus, provocative and glowing. But on his shirt were these droplets of blood, turning brown as they fell, unsightly brown stains like a skin disease.

Something blazed in Dan's face. He seized with the speed of a bird of prey the hand that had struck him, seized it where it had fallen, limp and trembling, and raised it to his mouth to bite it and draw blood in his turn.

I felt Dan's teeth close on my hand and quiver on my skin, ready to bite into the flesh, quivering with eagerness, awaiting a command, their points already sinking in. They waited and my hand shook, my whole body shook with the tension, with the expectation.

I had almost slapped him and he was going to bite me.

"Leave her alone, sir," the driver said.

And my brother dropped my hand.

Smashed to pieces, our bodies tumbled about inside the taxi.

The driver looked like the employee in the claims office. He too was black and enormous. His drawling voice flowed like an ancient river.

"Leave her alone, sir," he said again, wearily, as if repeating the chorus of a very old song.

His voice drew us onto the banks of a dark, hidden river. By now we had managed to get a grip on ourselves. Our eyes did not meet, we were still enemies, but the two of us drifted toward the banks of the river where this voice flowed.

"One should not speak ill of one's mother," he said next, "she will soon be dead, will be dead before you know it."

"She hit me," said Dan, hunching low on his seat.

"She hit you because you spoke ill of your mother. And right she was."

"I'll say what I want of my mother," muttered Dan.

"But your mother is her mother too."

"And how do you know that?"
"Because you're brother and sister."

Where was New York?

We were in the great American metropolis, racing along the Van Wyck Expressway, then Grand Central Parkway, going through the Triboro Bridge toll, heading for the fabled island's towers, but all that was nothing, mere adventitious, irritating details, to be shut outside the windows of this taxi that now contained my whole life.

The Atlantic journey was shriveling into a parenthesis, and so were Dan's long absence and my marriage.

It seemed to me that this malevolent exchange was an extension of an earlier malevolent exchange, interrupted years earlier in our little native town. As if we had leapt straight through the gaping wound of our teenage years and into this vehicle. As if our old house had been incongruously transformed into this rocking yellow vehicle. As if, however tortuously, the link had been reestablished.

I was on my guard, my back turned to the window, turned to the city, turned entirely toward the interior of the cab.

And yet this was New York.

This was the city our mother Nicole had come to before Dan was born, the city she had told us so much about.

". . . brother and sister," the driver had said.

"And how do you know that one, Mr. Know-Everything?" my brother Dan continued.

"Well, sir, a cabbie knows those things. I have been a cabbie for the best part of my life and I know things. And if you're not brother and sister, you're . . ."

"We're what?"

"This I'm not allowed to say."

"Not allowed by whom?"

"By the one who watches everything and foresees everything."

"And he does not allow you to say who we are?"

"No."

Our driver would say no more. His silence was as dark and massive as he was. It was my brother who insisted, who asked him crazier and crazier questions, about me, about our family, about his future, about our future.

Dangling from the dashboard were images that made up a labyrinthine yet vaguely familiar theme. By staring at them, I finally recognized portraits of Christ, all the same but stuck in every direction and overlapping one another, whether by accident or design I could not tell.

The driver remained silent. From time to time he looked in his rearview mirror, not to study us but to check the traffic. We were already in Manhattan, on the FDR, where oily puddles forced drivers to swerve suddenly, the vehicle lurching and groaning over potholes.

"Well, sir, tell me, since you know everything."

Still the driver remained silent, and still Dan pressed him, while the city raced past like an unwanted stage set.

"And meanwhile you took the long way?" he said suddenly.

The driver gave him a brief look. Cynical, amused?

"Just what I thought," my brother grumbled, "he could have taken the Long Island Expressway or the tunnel, but of course this route means more money."

I had turned back to the window.

Dan, you're showing me nothing and telling me nothing of this city you left us for, letting these landscapes slip by all around me like wrong-way-round scenery, and all you can think of is putting these obsessive questions to this man we shall never see again.

Dan, speak to me.

"What about your husband?" he said abruptly.

"What?"

"Your husband."

"He's coming a little later because —"

"He's coming?" he exclaimed.

"I told you on the phone."

"You didn't tell me a thing."

"You didn't listen to me, Dan."

Dan had turned to face me, and he had his old look, the look that went back to our childhood, but wounded, badly wounded and laden with reproach I was unable to decipher.

"I always listen to you, Estelle," he said.

Suddenly he was Dan, my long-lost brother. I could not stand the pain in his eyes, my gaze rushed to meet his, to embrace it, to comfort it, but once again our timing failed to coincide, and in that same moment Dan leaned toward the driver and in a voice that was once again truculent said to him:

"Well, sir, what do you think of that? She says she told me her husband was coming too, and I say she never mentioned anything about any husband coming. Who's right, tell me, who's right?"

Our driver made no reply.

"Dan," I pleaded.

"So I'm going to have both of you at my place? It's not very comfortable, Estelle!"

"We'll stay with friends."

"Friends? Estelle has friends in New York?"

"Not me, you know that, but Yves does."

"Who is Yves?"

"My husband, Dan, you know that. I wrote to you."

"Your husband's name is Yves?"

"Yes."

"Yves, truly?"

"You know it is."

"Yves as in poison?"

"What are you talking about, Dan?"

"Will you tell her, sir, what poison ivy is?"

The driver did not answer.

"It's a kind of ivy they have here, it grows at the foot of trees and it's pretty virulent. It grows in Central Park. You'll have to be careful."

Then:

"And how is it that Poison Ivy has friends in New York?"

"Don't call him that, Dan. He's very, very —"

Just at that moment something strange happened to me. It was to recur several times subsequently, and I feared it almost as much as the chronic vaypigo that afflicted our childhood.

Suddenly I could no longer remember my husband; I just felt a kind of exhaustion concerning that precise point in my life. I recalled nothing of his face, of our marriage, of our apartment, of our plans: everything seemed blotted out by that name whose exact meaning was as yet unknown to me, but that rang obsessively and maliciously in my ears — "Poison Ivy, Poison Ivy."

The very name was venomous; my tongue turned leaden in my mouth.

"Your husband's just fine, Estelle. There are lots of young French people here, all of them just fine, fresh out of the best schools. Your husband is from one of the great schools, isn't he, Estelle? He'll know everything about New York, oh what a drag it's going to be! Anyway, I'm counting on you to show him around."

*   *   *

Poison Ivy . . .

It was the first time I had ever heard the words, but I knew that with them poison had stolen into the cab, was already in us, would never leave. I knew it with the strange certainty with which we know things in childhood. And I knew too that only some kind of shock could expel this poison, a shock that would at one stroke demolish us, blow us to smithereens; only then would the poison be released to evaporate in the open air. But what about us, where would we be then, and what kind of shock would it be?

Hideous formless things swirled inside me and the city flowed by, the city of which I would see so little.

I stayed there six months and saw none of the sights.

Right from the start I was in a place that belonged to me. My soul took residence there; it belonged to me as simply and straightfor-wardly as our little native town.

Oh, madame, I know these words would be laughable if you read them in a book, but I cannot think how else to say it: being in that huge city, New York, for the very first time, yet not looking at its streets, its old and new skyscrapers, its old brownstones, the cast-iron-framed buildings in our neighborhood, not looking at anything in particular because I was there with my soul and not with a tour guide, and because it was my soul and nothing outside it that kept me busy.

It never occurred to me to "do" New York. I lived there because Dan was there and because Dan too was my soul, and the life that was mine — it had simply been transported from one place to an-other — was enough to occupy me.

When I talked to people later about my six months in New York, they would ask if I had seen this or that, if I had visited the West Side, or the North or the South or whatever. What could I answer? I knew the city from inside me; I had no very clear idea of what it looked like from the outside, resplendent with its illustrious sky-scrapers, girdled by its two great rivers, arrayed at night in its glit-tering lights, the jewels of its bridges around its neck: I was unable to see it in its ceremonial garb as the capital of the world.

Not long ago Phil, who is an engineer with the highway department, talked to me about those bridges, about the Gothic towers and the web of cables on the Brooklyn Bridge, tossing himself crumbs of history — "fourteen years and twenty deaths, including its designer, Roebling" — and comparing it with the Williamsburg and Manhattan bridges. He moved on to the Verazzano — "I'd love to take a camera there someday" — then interrupted himself: "I must be boring you, Claire, you know them all!"

No, I truly did not know them all.

"Has Father met Poison Ivy?" Dan suddenly said.

"No," I said reluctantly, hurt by this surrender, this betrayal of my husband, whose name was Yves and who did not deserve to be called Poison.

"Ah," said Dan.

Then he continued:

"But he's a lawyer too, isn't he?"

"I thought you knew nothing about Yves."

"I must have read it in Nicole's letters."

"Nicole has written to you?"

I was surprised and hurt. Nicole never wrote. I had never received a letter from her.

"Well, she must have phoned."

It was my turn to say "Ah!"

I am in despair tonight, madame. Why, why am I remembering these things? Everyone in this story is now dead, except for me and Adrien. Adrien doesn't read books and is even less likely to read disjointed notes made up of telescoped memories, of details blown up out of proportion, all of it in handwriting he says is indecipherable. "You write like the village idiot," he used to say gleefully. In elementary school he was always first in handwriting and I was last. But I did better in composition, which was another cause of friction between us. "It's much better to write just a little in good handwriting than write a whole bunch of stuff in a scrawl like yours," he decreed on the subject of an essay in which we were asked to describe our cat. "My cat has four feet, a tail, and whiskers" was the entire content of his composition. But of course the essay could have been shorter still; he could have written "My cat is a cat." *And thinking about all that still makes me angry today, madame, "My family had three grown-ups and two children and four are dead," will that do, madame?*

Adrien! I can just see him opening up this bundle of notes. Perhaps he would briefly skim them for our childhood's sake, for the sake of that coffin we dragged together one night, and for the sake of our brief and ugly coupling under the lilac. Yes, he might perhaps make an effort, but what good would it do? None, Adrien can do no more for me now than when we were children, and I do not even know his new address.

The notes serve no purpose and help no one. Not even the ones who lived through the things they describe. They will vanish into the great gulf of time along with all our absurdities, but here am I trying to fish them up again, like many others, all of them unsuccessful fishermen. I see us all lined up on the moving riverbank of our hopes, hunched over our pathetic tackle, with one of us occasionally leaning too far forward and toppling with his small catch into a pool of ripples that at once vanish.

I cannot bear your silence, Dan, my own dead one, and bitterness returns to me. Wherever you are, how can it be that you have not yet found a way of sending me a sign? Subtle and cunning as you are, why haven't you found a way to fool those who have you in their power?

But perhaps you have already sent me such signals, perhaps you are the one despairing in that place, wherever it is. Perhaps you are already exhausting your powers, whatever they may be, devising signals. In which case your calls are ringing all around me, Dan, flocking about me like birds, and I do not hear them.

The pain will not leave me. It finds new paths.

Infinite are pain's paths.

Phil booked seats for a show. It was a surprise: his office entertainment committee had bought the tickets and he decided to take me. A whim. He said, "I'm taking you out tonight!" and I laughed because of the cheeky air he likes to put on.

I had forgotten that the living go to shows, that they take their girlfriends along, that they call it "taking you out." "Where are we going?" I asked. "Surprise!" he said in the same cheeky tone, and I laughed again. But we were already there. Phil was locking our bikes.

It was the Théâtre de la Ville. A ballet.

The ballet was in two parts. In the first, the dancers' movements followed seemingly haphazard configurations against a backcloth of translucent blue, creating strange and beautiful figures like mathematical equations randomly birthed in a space that might have been a universe in the throes of creation. They clustered into constellations, then broke apart into specks of matter floating free, and all you heard between the rare bursts of sound from John Cage's music was the noise of their feet and their breathing.

The noise of their feet and their breathing, that was all that reached me, and to prevent those feet from pounding my skin, to prevent that breathing from seizing my heart and making it thud and driving it mad, I had to fight back by freezing right down to the very core of my being.

Intermission. Phil was applauding.

"Don't you like it?"

"Yes . . ."

He looked happy. He was leaning toward me and talking more volubly than usual.

"The movements don't tell any story, do they, it's restful, don't you think? No demands . . . All you have to do is look . . ."

Phil was talking about dancing.

Phil, talking to me about dancing . . . Phil . . . dancing . . . it was all I could tell myself.

Phil, who is not my brother, talking to me about dancing.

I am sitting with Phil, who is not my brother, watching a dance.

With Phil, who is not my brother, I am watching this dance company, which was once Dan's, which Dan admired so much.

The translucent space grew dark and an old man stood alone onstage. He moved first his arms and then his legs; although still slender and smooth-flowing, his limbs were slowed down by osteoarthritis, and his movements were strangely angular, a crawling solitary progress against the dark translucent blue. Little by little other dancers appeared, great rumblings swept in from the wings like earthquakes, like storms, stormy comets from the dawn of time. The old man moved out to center stage, hands held out before him, groping for a path amid cosmic collapse as the other dancers, quicksilver swift, darted first to one side, then the other, like flights of frantic birds.

That old man was Alwin.

"Phil, my brother was a dancer."

"What was that, Claire?"

My brother was a dancer . . . My brother was a dancer . . . My brother was a dancer . . .

My lips moved and it seemed to me that the words emerged, disturbed our neighbors, exploded inside my head. But Phil simply raised his eyebrows and then turned back to the stage. A tiny instant that he would forget before the show ended. A negligible jumble, three or four tiny movements and words, such as every moment contains. Swept away like a puff of dust.

In that puff of dust was my life, my brother, Nicole, Tiresia, our father, our childhood, my pain, the convent, death, death: all that was there, swept away and unnoticed, while onstage the show continued, with the red glow of the synthesizers in the orchestra pit and the dark bank of the auditorium filled with people who like us would in a moment pour out into the lobby, chat animatedly, jostle their way through the doors, and go out to swell the throngs in street and subway.

"My brother was a dancer, he was a member of this company . . ." We too would leave the theater, and Phil would not have heard Claire. Let Claire hold her peace, let her smile and accept a beer at the brasserie and all that. And above all let her go and wash her eyes and repair her makeup to hide her ravaged face.

Let Claire remain silent, but let Estelle never forget Estelle.

That broken form groping blindly forward on the stage, hands outstretched, had looked to me like Tiresia, and behind her came all the others, all my other ghosts, emerging from their other world to call me, groping their way toward me through Alwin's movements, searching for me. But when they reached the floodlit stage the woman they sought was hidden in the darkness of the auditorium; perhaps that was all they could manage, perhaps that had been their only option. Alwin's body had opened this crack for them into our world, Alwin's body had let them come almost to the door of our world.

No, let Estelle never forget Estelle.

I watched my ghosts follow Tiresia. I saw them advance down a very long and narrow gallery opened up for them by Alwin's dancing. And Alwin's body was dancing the slow approach of the dead up the secret escape route they had found; slow and broken, Alwin's body moved upon the stage, and my dead would come no closer, could come no closer to the light . . .

And then and there I swore to myself that I would open a real passage for them, that if a stage was the place they felt able to approach, I would find them a superb stage, where they could be bigger and more beautiful than our own miserable world had ever permitted, where their shattered dreams could open like huge flowers, where their nameless voices could radiate in music and song, where Nicole could have endless cascades of taffeta dresses, where Tiresia's veil could at last drop away down her long purple gown, revealing her flawless face, its strength resplendent over the great burnished piano. And there Tiresia's fingers on the keys would start Nicole's slippers to tapping.

And a tall fair figure would appear in the night outside: my father, his face deeply attentive, standing still halfway up the garden path, listening as the two musics he loved best in the world floated out from the open windows. Then they would all three unite at the top of the garden steps, my father youthful in his white suit, Nicole, his yellow rose, on one arm and Tiresia, his purple rose, on the other. And at the foot of the garden steps the lawn would climb supernaturally green in the moonlight, every grass blade delicately touched with silver, and from beneath the earth the most living, most dazzling flesh would burst forth, oh my brother . . .

TWENTY-SIX

The Loft

I DID NOT GO to see Alwin after the show. It was his last performance in Paris. He was probably leaving the very next day; I knew his habits.

Outside, it was pouring. We drank a beer in the brasserie and waited for the rain to die down. Then we set off on our bikes. Down dark, near-deserted streets with Phil whistling as he pedaled, racing ahead of me, then letting me overtake him. He was unusually exuberant.

His exuberance was not just unusual, it was unbearable.

My mind was troubled and heavy, as though its weight had dragged it right down to the bicycle wheels, where it had stuck to the spokes like a bramble attaching itself to your trousers and was slowing the bike down. All the weight of my mind seemed to be in my leg muscles.

"Keep going, keep going," Phil whistled, shooting ahead yet again.

Claire, be careful, prowling death is near, and clutching at you.

My bitter mind wanted to lead me away from that bike zigzagging around it, from that whistling from which it shrank in horror.

"Phil, my brother was a dancer."

"What was that, Claire?"

"My brother was a dancer."

"What was that again, Claire, my little sweetie pie?"

"My brother was a dancer."

"Speak louder, Claire."

My brother was a member of that company, Phil, the finest dancer in the company you just took me to see, Phil, how can you not know what you took me to see, how can you not hear what my voice is saying?

The wind blew down the deserted streets and our wheels hummed on the wet asphalt.

"Claire, I'm sorry, I didn't hear you."

Phil drew level with me, leaned toward me, and tried to catch my handlebars. I swerved abruptly, the wheel struck the curb, I fell, and my head hit the ground.

"Poor Claire, poor Claire . . ."

Phil was kneeling beside me, rubbing my head.

The pain in my temple was as sharp as if the impact were being repeated every second; it felt as if a stone hurled with great strength had struck my skull.

"It's the rain," said Phil, "your tires are too smooth." He was studying my bicycle wheel. "Almost bald, in fact, but it should hold till we get home." He turned the bike over and busied himself with the chain.

Prowling death had flung a stone at me, had essayed this strange assault.

And suddenly it came to me that my brother had sent me this warning, through the only intermediary he possessed: death. And that I should recognize the other message hidden in that parody of a stoning, the message that said, "Estelle, my love, I have only death to send to speak to you, and what I want to tell you is to be on your guard against it. Death is prowling, lying in wait for you. And now that you've understood my message, Estelle, my love, send the envoy back to me, send death back."

And it seemed that the pain in my head was turning into strength. At that precise moment as I sat there on that sidewalk, still quite near the theater where we had seen Alwin's company dance, with that light drizzle falling on our two gleaming bikes and with Phil calmly smoking one cigarette after the other as he waited for me to get up, I felt the true power of my decision, my decision to become Claire, and swore that nothing would be allowed to dislodge this new name of mine.

Let Estelle take care of Estelle.

"Hey," Phil said, leaping from bed next morning, "I'm going to turn on the radio, maybe they'll say something about the ballet. Shall I?"

I watched him get up, watched his broad, strong back. The strength in those buttocks had nothing to do with dancing . . .

For him the distance between bed and radio was just a space to be annihilated and his body crossed it in one unbroken movement. No, nothing to do with dancing. No difference between his first and his last step, just the mechanics of transportation, of repetitive animal movement. No, no, nothing at all to do with dancing.

Dancing was neither point of departure nor arrival but the time between them, a time my brother would have brought into glorious being so that life, from being sulky and bored, would have leapt to sudden wakefulness, would have thrown itself into that flesh and made all those movements bear seed and flourish as luxuriant, inexhaustible jungle.

I watched Phil's sturdy back go straight to its goal, to the radio, which might offer a discussion of Alwin's ballet. And indeed there was some talk of it, and then of other things. From the kitchen Phil cheerfully disagreed with the radio and made breakfast for us. In a few minutes he would return with the tray of steaming coffee and a new topic flipped out by the radio, and as we ate our bread and butter and jam we would nibble at that topic together. No, my boyfriend Phil was no dancer. His body was made for him alone and served only his personal needs. He laid the butter on thick and scooped out heaping spoons of jam, and I would do the same, I too would eat thick slabs of bread and butter . . . What did it matter, dancing had deserted me, it was another world.

And then we would be off down bike trails in the woods around the city and be back at nightfall for dinner and listening to the radio again. Just an ordinary Sunday, bearing us toward night. And then our bodies would give each other warmth before drawing apart, and next morning we would rise in the gray and probably wet (but perhaps sunny) dawn to face the working day. That was human life, without dancing. Your life, Claire.

I did not go to see Alwin after the show. I did not tell Phil about Alwin.

"You didn't enjoy last night all that much, Claire?"

"Oh, yes I did, enormously."

What I enjoyed, Phil, was you: the surprise you planned for me, your applause, your strong hands on my bike chain, the smoke from your cigarettes in the mist, and of course your beloved radio the next morning when you got up and your noisy cheerful comments from the kitchen, which I couldn't hear too clearly, naturally, but which I heard clearly enough.

You, living next to me.

I mentioned neither Alwin, nor that company I once knew so well, nor New York.

The pain I suffered there through the months I was both with my brother and apart from him had returned with the sharp impact of my head against that sidewalk — and there it would have to stay, for there was no one with whom to leave it.

I thought the pain had self-destructed when Dan and I finally found each other again. I thought our season of happiness had well and truly dissolved it. Not so. It had simply pulled back a little, letting me forget it for a while. I had not had time to show the pain to Dan, to put it in front of him for him to blow on it and banish it forever.

Our season of happiness was too short. We were not granted the luxury of growing old together, even briefly. Had we been granted this we might have been able to experience together every twist and turn of the madness that poisoned those six months before our parents died. We might have ground the madness down to nothing on the millstone of our new life. Together, I believe, we might finally have killed it.

And I still believe that with my brother I could have killed pain, every kind of pain.

But we were not granted the time, and the pain — the particular pain of those New York months I spent beside my brother and foe — has returned. It seeks recognition: be careful, Claire, it seeks a hearing, seeks the opportunity to infect beings unaware of its existence. And now this voracious pain is eyeing Phil, longing to feast upon him, for the ballet and Alwin's company with Alwin himself onstage are too good an opporunity to miss.

All that evening as we made love, all of Sunday, I was tempted to speak to Phil, to tell him who Alwin was, what the company we had seen was, and the suffering he had unwittingly caused me. Too much past, incommunicable past. Phil must be my present.

We shall remain two separate planets. Never will I be anyone's sister again, never someone whose past you possess, someone whose existence like your own you take for granted. Never again will I have a brother.

Sometimes it occurs to me that Phil too possesses a past, an existence. It is an idea I do not yet have the strength to harvest. Let us remain in the moment, in the motion of our bikes, which leave no wake on towpaths or trails or streets.

Let Claire be Claire, and let Estelle take care of Estelle . . . madame, can't you see how desperately I need you . . .

My brother's New York apartment was in disused industrial premises, what the Americans call a loft. Spacious, unfurnished, the walls unpainted but the floor sanded and clean, a bar in front of a big mirror, stereo equipment in a corner, a machine with asymmetrical bars, health club–style.

At the far end of the loft, at the street side, was a rectangular wooden structure with a big mattress on its upper tier and two unmatched sofa beds and a TV set on the tier below. Against the wall beside the grimy sash window were a shower, a toilet, a stove, an oven, a refrigerator, lined up side by side as if they had stood there ever since the movers set them down.

"You can sleep on the platform," said Dan.

"And where will you sleep?"

"I'll go to Alwin's."

To Alwin's?

At home we always slept in the same bedroom.

"Don't look at me like that, Estelle. Don't forget, you're married."

How the contempt in his new voice stung!

"Anyway, Alwin lives just across the landing."

And then and there I saw Alwin.

He was leaning in the doorway at the other end of the loft, staring at me. I had not heard him arrive, but there he was, staring at me.

"She doesn't look like you," he said.

I did not know what it was about that harsh voice, but I feared it at once. Many people who approached Alwin, even back then when he was just a fringe dancer and choreographer, said his presence "put you on the defensive." The expression had bothered me. My law studies inclined me to believe that being put on the defensive was something quite different. Now I understand that it was exactly what I felt in that moment. He was several yards away and I could not see him properly, but I felt as if I were being examined under a glaring light. Doubtless only a dancer would have been immune to that invisible blast, able to move effortlessly through it.

"She doesn't look like you," he said to Dan.

Alwin did not address me directly. He spoke always to Dan, and referred to me as "she."

"She" was myself, the sister, in other words, the old continent, the small town, family, the one who did not dance, who was a woman.

Who did not dance.

Who was a woman.

But Estelle, who had been a star in that family buried in that small town in that old continent, would need six months to understand all that.

"Coming?" Dan said to me.

"Where to?"

"To the studio, of course! I told you in the taxi."

"She's coming?" said Alwin.

"Don't you want to come?" said Dan, turning toward me, almost surprised.

"She needs to rest," said Alwin.

I was drunk with fatigue. I had only one ambition, to throw myself on the mattress or one of the sofa beds, and I hated this unknown man for offering me what I desired.

"It was a long flight, Dan," I said.

"It was a long flight?" said Dan.

That voice I had loved so much, dancing and pure, how twisted it had become.

"A long flight, huh?" he repeated in this new, strange, hurtful voice.

Suddenly he was at the door with Alwin, conversing rapidly and concentratedly, then they were gone.

Dan had not even thought to give me his keys. I was locked in.

TWENTY-SEVEN

The Studio

$\mathcal{A}$LWIN'S later career is today the subject of countless books — specialist studies, illustrated texts for general readers, the "spiritual autobiography" he himself recently published, with sketches by his own hand and the famous diagrams he ceaselessly worried and battered into shape. Recognizing them in a book displayed in a Paris bookstore window behind the Senate, I at once crossed to the other side of the street. I have read none of these books, and of Alwin, as of New York, I saw little.

In his presence my eyesight grew blurred.

Yet he was not then widely known. His studio — for obvious financial reasons, he moved frequently from one to another — was enormous but unheated, on the top floor of a dilapidated building scheduled for demolition, in which he was the last, and I believe illegal, occupant. From here too he would soon be obliged to move when a section of ceiling collapsed.

I went to see my brother work at the studio the day after my arrival.

"Does she want to work too?" said Alwin when he saw me in the doorway.

"I came to watch Dan," I said.

"Sit over there," said Dan, pointing to a rolled carpet in a corner.

I remember how embarrassed I was by the impression that these few words and my footsteps and even my unobtrusive occupation of the carpet created a disproportionate disturbance in that vast bare room, cutting short the sequence of movements I had indistinctly glimpsed as I came in, breaking a rhythm — and not really for their own sake but apparently because of the noise they caused. It was a noise out of all proportion to its cause, that is to say, to myself, for I closed the door softly and glided along the wall and sank silently onto the carpet, my body the least obtrusive and least bothersome of all the bodies moving about in that vast space bathed in cold light, moving about virtually under the open sky or rather (for the sky in a certain sense belongs to our earth) moving in a kind of interstellar space where what you could see of neighboring buildings resembled angular chunky meteorites traveling at the same speed infinitely far away.

I sat on that carpet, more alone than I had ever been.

In my head, very faintly, the sixteen bars of Ravel's *Bolero* rippled out.

As I slowly became aware of this presence of *Bolero* within me my distress abruptly increased. It felt as though someone in my head were humming or playing it, someone who was myself, one of the members of my tribe, one of those I did not know well, and for that reason I lacked the strength to distinguish why he had come forward, like the old flute player, to bring these familiar sounds out onto the streets of my consciousness.

And the other members of my tribe shuddered on hearing the intoxicating melody and wanted to follow it, but it was so faint.

And contradictorily, afraid too that it might suddenly explode, I sat frozen, unable to move a muscle. "You looked just like a hyper-realist sculpture," Dan told me — but it made no sense to me and it never occurred to me to ask him if there really was such a thing.

Still that fog between us, where the trivial and the important loomed with the same massive, inscrutable, disquieting power.

I was still affected by the hubbub I thought I had caused while coming in.

For there was no music in the studio. Nothing but small, isolated noises, bodies at work, Alwin's voice, the creaking of the floor.

Alwin worked without music. Music bothered him: he was unwilling to interrupt a movement to follow a musical sequence or, on the contrary, to prolong a movement that in his opinion had reached its end. Music came "later," and it was composed by one of the two or three musicians who counted among his intimates and who like him would be making their name a few years later.

Madame, I am speaking of Alwin and of his musicians and other famous people.

If I could, I would not mention them at all.

I would have preferred never to mention them; I would have preferred the circumstances that brought me in contact with them never to have materialized.

I found myself part of the group — merely the "group" — around a handful of people who are now household names. This happens to all kinds of anonymous people and everyone deals with the situation as best he can.

I mention these people only because of my brother Dan, and my brother Dan is dead.

I saw nothing of them, I know nothing of them, less even than anyone else, for every normal person living in these times would inevitably be intrigued sooner or later by one of those famous names.

But I turn away from them.

Not deliberately. I cannot even say that it is a conscious decision, that like Chopin I want to "know nothing, see nothing, experience nothing."

Alwin cherished that trait of Chopin's. When one of his dancers started to talk of plans — travel, marriage, a child, whatever — he became sullen, he cut short all effusiveness with a single word. "Chopin," he said. Nothing more, but all the dancers knew what he meant.

(As usual, the American accent had led me to construct a full-scale, complex, and wrongheaded hypothetical scenario around the word. It was Michael who explained the reference to me one day. But he did not know the composer, and after I gave him a few cassettes to listen to in his taxi, he expressed astonishment that so gifted an artist could have had such "limited" ideas. And I remember thinking sadly, "Well, Michael, that's exactly why Alwin thinks you'll never be a great dancer.")

What I meant, madame, was that I cannot mention their work. I try and it's like hammering at an armor-plated door. I cannot.

The dancer my brother had gone to New York to find was Alwin.

I could not see my brother clearly either. He worked in spandex shorts and stevedore-style T-shirt, like all Alwin's students, and I think my eyes were afraid to distinguish him from them.

In the ballet I was recently dragged to see, I was struck by the muscularity of the men, the extraordinary indecency of their bodies, sculpted by their trunks, the sweat glistening on arms and in the hollows of chests, the loving revelation of a human body's secret possibilities.

And my brother? My brother at Alwin's studio in New York? It was the first time I had seen him for a long time and he was almost naked and only a few yards from me, in the flower of his youth and strength, and no, I do not recall his body. But I know full well I am deceiving myself: someone within me, some member of my tribe, must have seen him, must have drunk in every detail of his body. And months later, when he came to me in that black night of our heart, his body seemed so familiar to me, so familiar to my touch.

And on the other hand I saw how hard it was for my brother to bend to the strict discipline Alwin demanded of him. His capricious mind rebelled, and Alwin seemed to attach particular importance to controlling him. They had terrible quarrels.

My brother yelled, beside himself with rage, "You feel nothing, you don't want to feel anything, you'll end up dancing like a marionette or a robot. And I don't feel anything anymore either. To make your goddamn back muscles work you need a motive, an emotion, something, and I've lost it since I've been here, lost it, you hear me, Alwin?"

And my brother threw himself on the floor and beat the boards with his fists.

"This floor doesn't speak to me, we might as well dance on a grave."

"And if you go on punching it like that," said Alwin, "it will speak to you even less because there'll be a hole in its place."

And he was right, for that was exactly what happened a few months later. In its fall the ceiling carried away a section of floor as well.

"A hole," Dan echoed him, "a hole. Good, fine, then maybe we'll have a chance of seeing the ground, the earth. I'm fed up with playing the clown on a floor of dead wood a hundred feet above the ground."

"Because in your darling little provincial birthplace you didn't work on a floor made of dead wood?"

"Not a hundred feet above the ground!"

"And what would you like to work on?" said Alwin.

"On the earth!" my brother yelled. "But you wouldn't understand! I dance for the earth, not for a string of numbers!"

And Alwin stopped, suddenly intrigued, his anger gone.

"What do you mean, Dan, the earth?"

And my brother's anger also faded. He got up and stood straight in the middle of the room, silent, his features perturbed. It seemed to me at that moment that a paralyzing cloud had settled on him; I literally felt the presence of that cloud around him, and I knew where it came from.

It came from that long-gone lawn where my brother danced his own dance for the first time, it came from what he had felt beneath his feet: a living, mighty force that had written a message on his skin, and that message had propagated itself into his muscles, his blood, his whole body, and all my brother's dancing was simply the attempt to decipher that enigmatic message, that message from the earth.

This excitable, mercurial youth, Dan Helleur, who had arrived unannounced from the Old World with old-fashioned technique and ill-defined ambitions, had everything the god of dance can bestow on a human being to make him a great dancer, a dancer after Alwin's heart.

"You've got it all," he muttered, except that in that gloomy mutter I heard the unspoken sequel: "All, except for one thing," and I did not know whether that one thing was something my brother lacked, in which case it was a head for figures, or something he did not need, in which case it was me, Dan's sister. But in both cases it meant that all the gifts lavished by the god were canceled out because of this one thing he lacked or had too much of.

Whereupon, sensing that it was Dan's very being that Alwin rejected, I longed to leap at his throat.

Yes, the picture that now relentlessly assailed my mind's eye was of the dog we saw literally leap at Mr. Raymond's throat one apple-gathering day when as usual he had come in without ringing. Luckily, Mr. Raymond had his fork in his hand and our father was a few yards away. "I'll have it put to sleep," my father, still shaking, said right afterward. "Bah! Let it go!" the old hunchback rumbled enigmatically. "They're all alike except for one thing, that's what causes it. He'll get over it." But our father had been scared. He had the stray dog, which we had taken in and to which he was already somewhat attached, put down.

Those first times in the studio, my mind was wholly mobilized and haunted by Nicole.

All I knew about dancing came from what Nicole had been able to show me, and what went on in this studio had practically nothing in common with what Nicole did.

For us Nicole had been dancing incarnate; I had spent years of my life admiring her graceful body, made even more slender by the slippers on whose points she soared or swooped, her arms always an extension of a body in desperate search of the endless curve, the arabesque, free of corners and free of an ending . . .

Our mother Nicole, who was not like the other mothers in our town, who looked nothing like those short, squat women, their black hair in tight permanent waves, their knitted shawls tugged around their necks, their bodies bulging in too-tight coats, standing four-square outside the school on their thick legs and in their shoes the color of dead skin and with scuffed heels, neither high nor low. And Nicole arrived, late as usual . . .

We watched her approaching from the very end of the street, with that dancing gait and in ballet slippers too light for the cold or the rain that so often blanketed our town, or else in the stiletto heels she loved, perhaps because they gave her something of the upward spring she derived from the points of her ballet slippers.

The other mothers, who had already bundled their children into raincoats, bonnets, scarves, turned to watch. It was raining and Nicole was bareheaded, the blond knot perched high on her head beginning to dissolve into golden rivulets.

She noticed none of them. She came from her blue-lined garage, from that azure dream of hers where birds drew lines so pure that only the eyes of angels perceived them. And we, shivering and anxious, the last children left outside the school fence, were suddenly happy: still shivering from standing about in the rain without raincoats and of course still anxious, but so proud, because the herd of other mothers had turned and was watching Nicole irrupt into the gray street like a gilded apparition, slender and ethereal . . .

"Botticelli's Venus," our Doctor Minor used to say. We did not know what he meant except that Venus was a bright planet our father had pointed out and named for us one luminous night, and since Nicole was all those things, bright and beautiful and luminous, she became Venus, and Venus was our mother.

And at one stroke we forgot everything, our day in school, our classmates going home on the sidewalk opposite and still waving to us, our teachers leaving the school, locking up, bidding us farewell. We walked home beside Nicole, flanking her like bodyguards, the bodyguards of Venus, marching with gravity and with an ecstasy that was not exactly happiness but that was . . . oh, who knows what it was exactly . . .

Moreover, "Venus" had been here, in New York, in this studio of Alwin's. Perhaps back then it was another studio, but it must have been similar to this one, unheated, in a dilapidated abandoned building, on the fifth or sixth floor, accessible by means of a freight elevator expiring under creaking chains. And Alwin too must have been the same as now, cold, stubborn, exacting, already knowing precisely what dancing must be — which was not at all what Nicole wanted or what Nicole could accomplish.

Nicole was my mother, Dan's mother, but in this studio I had now been attending day after day I felt her constant presence, like a furtive shadow. It was the presence of a broken young woman who had come here not in quest of "growth," as she believed, of a leap forward, but of a regression, of a little girl's dream, which was really a baby's dream, even a fetus's dream, and further back still, an unborn's dream, an angel's dream.

Nicole could not and would not learn anything anywhere about dancing, and her blue dream of heaven had shattered upon the hard rock of Alwin's determination.

She had come here, had submitted to this discipline of Alwin's, had lived here — where? Any other dance school would have been better for her than this one. There were so many in New York: how had she landed in this one? Why had Alwin accepted her?

She had come here and then left, ashamed and rejected. And now in his turn her son was here, and over there in her small town in the Old World she was waiting.

The notes of *Bolero* entered my head in obsessive unending procession, muted, painful, as if Nicole were trying to call me across vast distances, but the notes were too faint and I was unable to get a grip on myself, to move in one direction or another.

My father wanted to know what Dan was doing in this great strange city, whether what he was doing was good for him, and why he sent no news.

And now I too was unable to send news.

I wrote, of course, but I did not allude to the things my father had sent me to investigate. I asked him to stop sending money orders, explaining that Dan had found a way to make a little money by giving French lessons — and here suddenly I was all endless detail. He gave lessons, I said, in a small French school that had just opened on the second floor of a hotel, the Croydon Hotel, on West Eighty-sixth Street. As yet the school boasted very few pupils, but it had hit on the promising name of Cours Victor Hugo and inspired great hopes in its young founder-principal-headmaster-teacher, Louis, a Haitian my brother had bumped into on the ferry that shuttles night and day between Manhattan and Staten Island.

I had hit here upon what might be called an epistolary thread, and I worked the thread diligently. My brother, I said, had been on his third or fourth crossing that particular Sunday, and had finally noticed a young man (handsome, intelligent-looking, et cetera) who, like himself, never went ashore but remained leaning on the rail, eyes turned toward the Statue of Liberty, solitary and pensive, while the ferry swallowed or regurgitated passengers. They had several times found themselves alone on deck together and — surprise — they both spoke French and — another surprise — they were both on this ferry (on which tickets cost twenty-five cents) to "think about the future." Twenty-five cents to be able to think all day long was not bad at all: that was the first thought they shared. With the Statue of Liberty but also Wall Street as a particularly propitious backdrop: that was their second shared opinion.

At this point I sidestepped Dan's future and ducked straight into the Haitian's, which gave me the chance to dwell on his past. He was an opponent of the Duvalier regime who was trapped in his house one night by the Tontons Macoutes and had escaped by releasing a whole coopful of his father's fighting cocks into their faces. He was so frightened that he had dived into the sea and swum blindly for the horizon, but he was picked up by a boat and granted political asylum in the United States. He was sure that the Cours Victor Hugo would be a success. For one thing, he was not targeting the same clientele as the solidly established Lycée Français, and so on and so on.

And one day my father, who so disliked the telephone, called.

There was great embarrassment in his voice. He feared my brother might be overtaxing himself, he did not see how a school could be run from a hotel, and then: "Estelle, this young Haitian, we're a little worried, is he . . . ? Do you think . . . ? Yves . . . I'd hate to think . . . It isn't that . . . ." "But Father, he's married, he has two daughters, besides, I've never seen him."

Flabbergasted, I realized that this Louis — whom I had indeed never seen — monopolized my letters. And I was submerged in uncontrollable distress.

I never managed to discuss what Dan had come to New York for. It would have meant saying, for example, "What Dan is doing is not good for him," and in that case bringing him back. But I was incapable of making a judgment, let alone of taking action. Or else saying, "What Dan is doing is good for him, I can vouch for that, so my task here is done and I'm leaving." But I did not want to leave, in other words, to leave him.

Paralyzed without understanding why, I dashed off brief notes to my father and Nicole without ever mentioning what they had sent me to New York to do. But I no longer spoke of the Haitian (and besides, it was clear that the Cours Victor Hugo would not last the year).

I wrote about places.

About places I never looked at. I could not look. The multiple landscapes of the great city flowed directly from my eyes to my pen without lingering in my memory or my thoughts.

But even this is not quite accurate. How bottomless is the truth when you seek it! In fact I was repeating what Nicole had told us about New York when we were small, on evenings when she was relaxed and came into our bedroom and was willing to answer our sleepy avid questions.

She would come in and shut the door behind her in a special way, and at once we remembered that she and we possessed a secret, oh, we refrained from pouncing on it, we pretended we had noticed nothing, we just followed her with our eyes. We knew her little ritual. "Shh!" she would say, standing motionless by the door, looking so seriously and convincingly vigilant that we felt a thrill of fear, of fear and pleasure. But we did not show it; we froze and listened, like her. The house was quiet, the clock began to strike nine, and as soon as the last note sounded, Nicole cast aside all restraint and shouted in a high and excited voice, "So what do you want me to tell you tonight?" and Dan shot back, "Tell us about when you were in New York." "Why not," said Nicole, as if braving some mysterious taboo; but she was a poor storyteller and the taboo we might otherwise have been able to track down was drowned in her stock descriptions. When all was said and done, her story bored us. What we really liked was having her in our room, and when she left we forgot the secret, its existence, its content, and all the excitement that emanated from it, *that was how it was, madame; sometimes I think we were unwitting hosts to a diabolical mechanism implanted in us by the manipulator of our fate. Believing in that would mean at least believing in something, it would mean having someone to talk to, madame, I have only you . . .*

It was not New York's sights that flowed straight from my eyes to my pen, it was Nicole's descriptions that flowed straight from my memory to my pen. The sights my eyes could not help noticing merely functioned as a trigger.

Sometimes I would reread those terse missives, out of mere inertia, as I waited for the next sentence to come, and I was astonished: it invariably seemed to me that someone else was writing what was set down there in my handwriting.

I read and read again and fell into a kind of torpor and the letter did not go out until the next day, sometimes a week later, and some I forgot to mail altogether.

At the time I did not realize that those descriptions came to me from our childhood, from Nicole, that in fact all I was doing was copying down her dictation, in that somnambulant trancelike state in which I lived throughout my stay in New York. But did Nicole recognize those sights and words of hers? I doubt it.

She would have recognized "her" landscapes, but not the way in which she had described them to us. And recognizing in my letters what she herself had already seen in New York must have relieved her, given her the feeling that we were in a familiar place, close by. Perhaps that is why she never perceived the emptiness of my letters, why she did not come over right away, why she waited six months, six long months — and even then her departure took place in a mood of violent revulsion, the way you throw yourself from the top of a cliff to shorten the journey down, to cancel the distance you have allowed to pile up.

TWENTY-EIGHT

Lazy Kids

RETURNING from one of my exhausting walks in the city one afternoon, I found my brother waiting at the top of the stairs.

He was holding two big brown canvas sacks that sagged heavily, one in each hand. He watched me climb the stairs.

Fatigue blurred my vision. The figure standing on the prow of the upper landing, beneath a glassed-in roof that admitted a harsh, almost tangible light, looked like a dispenser of justice, with the countenance of one who in some other world weighs merits against transgressions according to criteria that for centuries have remained beyond our understanding. Was it the dizzying spectacle of so many centuries bent beneath the yoke of those enigmatic scales, or was it merely a kind of regression to chronic vaypigo (but it could not have been that; it would never again be that; we had never experienced our childhood vaypigo any other way but together, and we had ministered to it together, whereas the weakness that overcame me on that stairway affected me alone and I had to face it alone)? Whatever the answer, I stumbled and barked my shin most cruelly against the hard steps.

"You're not at the studio?" I stammered.

"I went to pick these up," he said, hefting the two sacks one by one and at some distance from his body, as if devils were locked inside them and he feared their claws.

"You went to get those?"

"I went to the post office."

"The post office?"

I remained in the middle of the stairway, still held in bondage to the step on which I had stumbled by the pain in my shin. His words seemed in some curious way to be the cause of that pain, striking my sore leg like thrown stones.

"For you."

"For me?"

"Yes," he said, dropping the two sacks. They sagged and spread out, revealing unexpected angles, as if this time they contained skeletons.

"What do you mean, for me?"

Words in those days hardly served as useful and welcome bridges between the two of us. Mounted upon them, we would instead hail each other before passing each other by or quite simply losing sight of each other.

We conversed mainly by parroting what the other had just said.

It was as if a remark could not be considered trustworthy unless repeated several times over by one or the other. Only after several such repetitions was it possible to grope for another remark, which was then in its turn subjected to the same process.

Oh, I see all that now because every detail of that scene on the stairs, harmless though it was, is before me. *And harmless as it is, how is it connected to Tiresia's story, toward which I am directing all my efforts? It will not leave me, it steps unbidden before me, but why, madame? And it is the same with many other scenes, perhaps all of them. What does it want from me . . . to defer Tiresia's story . . . to hasten its telling . . . ? Perhaps I am wrong about everything . . . Madame, I have no yardstick to go by . . . no power . . .*

"What is it?" said Dan.

"I don't know," I said.

And how I meant it. How could I answer when I did not even know what the question was about?

Unbelievable though it may seem, one moment I saw the two brown post office sacks at the top of the stairs and the next the whole picture had been swallowed up in the hard light under the glass roof. "What is it?" my brother said, and his question echoed as if in ocean shoals. Suddenly adrift, I answered, "I don't know," and my brother too was adrift. For a moment we drifted together over the shoals and then it was over: the two sacks that had collapsed into such strange shapes at the top of the stairs became distinct again, and my brother told me to keep climbing.

And we returned to the makeshift world we had distractedly built on the brittle stilts of our wobbly exchanges. A world bristling with those hellish repetitions we had painfully to negotiate, as if traversing roadblocks.

"But you must know what's in them."

"I must know what's in them?"

"They're addressed to you."

"What?"

"To you."

"To me?"

"Helleur."

"Helleur?"

"Isn't your name Helleur?"

"It must be for *Dan* Helleur."

"Oh," said my brother, suddenly intrigued and studying the slip of paper. "It just says Helleur."

"Then it could be for you."

"Or for you."

*   *   *

It went on and on. I no longer recall the exact sequence, but the sentences kept coming, one linked to the next chain gang–style, yes, that was it, as if we were dragged along by a chain of absurd but solidly linked phrases. And how tight that chain, that hellish articulated serpent, held us!

No way of breaking loose until it was ready, of its own volition, to let this or that link give way, after perhaps ten minutes of chilly feverish discussion, of feverish chill, and then the chain of our exasperated exchanges snapped and I climbed the stairs. We opened the sacks and found books.

They were the brown canvas bags of the French post office — the lettering was faded, but how had Dan missed seeing it? — and inside were the law manuals and reviews I had asked my husband Yves to send me. The notice had arrived during one of my abominable walks, and Dan had gone to the post office in my stead.

I had requested the books, sure enough, but I had pictured them arriving in neatly tied packages with double knots like the ones Tiresia tied when she sent presents to our cousins. Not these nautical kit bags.

"They're my law books."

"They're your law books," Dan repeated absently, suddenly miles away and anxious to get back to the studio.

But that evening he returned and the first words he said, before the door was even closed, were the very same ones.

"They're your law books?"

His voice was full of challenge and pain and rage.

"I have an exam," I said.

"What do you need with an exam?" he said.

Which meant "What do you need with an exam that you'll take in France with a view to working in France, far from me and nothing to do with dancing?"

But I could not yet hear that; the dreadful manipulator of our destiny did not permit it, and I retorted nastily that although he might intend to spend his whole life developing his back muscles for Alwin's benefit, I intended to earn my living.

Hardly had I said it before the floor seemed literally to heave and vomit something out between us. And then, blindly, with all the fire of our youth, we sprang together astride that something, which was rage.

*   *   *

Dan said:

"All those books! You need all those?"

And I said that "all those" were not much for someone who intended to use her brain.

Or else:

"All those books! So you're planning to stay?"

"Do you want me to leave?"

And my leaving was the thing Dan feared most in the world. Malice had hit the bull's-eye, and Dan screamed:

"Well, you've accomplished your mission, haven't you?"

"What mission?"

And we were off at a gallop again astride our rage, the same rage but each of us astride our own, side by side, as the hounds of our minds had once coursed side by side.

Night fell, sirens wailed in the distance over the roar of traffic, we had forgotten dinner, forgotten to do anything, even watch TV, we were too disheartened and agitated to sleep, and we would be exhausted the next day.

I had meant to start studying for those exams, scheduled for September, but I ran into an apparently simple and yet insurmountable obstacle: I could not lift my manuals.

Neither lift them nor in consequence carry them to a table to open them.

Yves had sent them, and I had removed them from the two big brown canvas post office sacks and stacked them on the floor next to the platform, which was where I spent most of my time.

Most of the manuals were red, and piled up like bricks that might as well have been concrete. Bending to pick one up, to raise it, exhausted me in advance. A rope of my nerves seemed to tug at the top of my head, my forearms ached, my neck ached and grew stiff.

Those manuals were too heavy: it was as simple as that. My mind had approached them and lifted them, and at once their weight had been transferred to my muscles, and now my whole being ached.

A chain reaction then set in.

The ache was unbearable. Any activity that lay beyond its perimeters was out of the question. It forced you to give it all your attention. It forced you to focus on escaping that stiffness in the neck, that heaviness in the forearms, and that pain in the head which was like a distant storm rumbling under low skies and which was not vaypigo but something quite new, against which I had no weapons.

A new affliction taking root in the body is like an unknown epidemic bursting upon the world: you cannot grasp what is happening, you think it must be a mistake, something on the order of a meteorite blown off course and whose debris the highway department will quickly clear away.

And you go on not grasping what is happening. You turn to forms of exorcism, you try to go back to when the affliction did not exist, to when you were a child.

Or else you try to go beyond the affliction's reach, to another body, for instance.

You twist and turn in all directions as in a nightmare.

I attempted a few exercises on the bar, reaching back to the things Nicole had taught me.

I could learn nothing more from Dan. His dancing was now beyond my reach: I could no longer distinguish its component elements. My thoughts were most often on Nicole; it was so hard to picture her in this city and yet it was from her that I sought help.

At that bar in Dan's loft I realized how gentle and patient Nicole had been with me and with my ungifted efforts.

"Listen to the music, Estelle, listen and let yourself go," she said in the blue garage.

I listened but it did no good. The music entered my mind and, quite unable to let go, took hold of it; my mind followed the progress of the notes across spaces that disclosed themselves the further I delved, spaces both unfamiliar and enchanting to me. "Estelle, you're not listening to the music," said Nicole, almost in despair. Yes, I was listening to the music, I was even absorbed in it, but my focus was fragmented and I was not hearing "the whole music." Launching itself upon those fragments it had captured, my mind soared, my mind tested its wings.

My body remained earthbound.

"Move, Estelle, move," said Nicole.

But moving meant tearing myself away from this inner exploration. Moving meant throwing a ponderous stone, the stone of my body, through the gossamer web of the music which was all I wanted.

A picture suddenly returns to me.

A black shape standing in light. It must be summer; the garage doors are open and that black motionless upright form outside is Tiresia. But Tiresia never came to the garage. In her wanderings about the garden, she must have found herself near my father's study and therefore close to the garage, which was next door to it. She must have stopped when the erratic pattern of her wandering brought her face-to-face with the blaring din of the record player outside the garage doors. Almost at breaking point, her golden curls unraveling in sweat, Nicole was saying "Listen to the music, Estelle," when suddenly something astonishing happened — so astonishing that Nicole and I stopped in mid-exercise.

Tiresia was in the garage, a black shape in that sky-blue setting that never saw anything but our pink-clad bodies (Nicole insisted that we wear very pale pink for dancing, the shade of pink that is not flesh-colored despite its name but the color of an idealized flesh). That black shape against the blue did such violence that deep inside its wood-and-metal heart the record player heard it and at once stopped too. And in the silence we heard, "But that's all Estelle is doing — listening."

Oh, if Tiresia had been my mother I would have flung myself into her lap. My heart was beating violently, for it was "truth" in person I had just heard, and truth heard in person for the first time causes a strange commotion in those unused to it. But the one who was my mother was Nicole and I dared not move.

Nicole was deathly pale. "If it's music that stops her dancing, then make her play, make her make music." I cannot recall their words and am even uncertain of those I have quoted, but I know that Tiresia had come into our garage and that then I had heard the truth in person.

Then I was in the living room in front of the piano, Nicole frenziedly twirling the stool to bring it down to my height, clumsily and cruelly pinching her fingers in the process. A trembling Tiresia attempted to shut the keyboard, but Nicole with unabated frenzy interposed her bruised hand. Tiresia too was pale, a terrifying pallor — but that cannot be, *I can't be remembering it, madame, you could not see Tiresia's face beneath her veil, yet I know inside myself that she was pale. Oh, madame, you see what I am offering you — "inner memories." Madame, unless you too have an inner sense to guide you I am very much afraid that you will be lost. And then, madame, I too will be lost . . .* Anyway, I was at the piano, and my hands were shaking so hard that they fell upon the keys as if severed at the wrists, and the piano wept.

Our grand piano's pitiful weeping rang through the house, and suddenly my father was there, and my memory too breaks off.

*   *   *

Often in the blue garage I had felt like saying "Shh!" to Nicole, but she would not have understood and I would have been unable to explain.

I felt like saying "Shh, you're bothering me!" and what would our little mother Nicole have made of that, Nicole who so badly wanted her children to be little dancing prodigies? She wouldn't even have known how to slap me or scold me.

Ah, if Nicole had been able to slap or scold, perhaps I would have had the courage to say "Shh, you're bothering me, Nicole" or, like Adrien, to say "Shit! You're bothering me." I would have said it nastily the way real children do and Nicole would have flown at me like an ogress, her features contorted. The slap would have landed, I would have screamed, and perhaps at one stroke, under the pressure of rebellion, the solution would have materialized, the solution that might have saved me, that might have saved us both, Dan.

Nicole could see I was not getting there. "First you have to relax," she said, "let me show you."

And those exercises I loved, because they were slow and there was no music to follow. "Unwind vertebra by vertebra," said Nicole. "Spread your legs, let your head drop suddenly as if it's very heavy, let everything go at once." And I liked to remain in that position, head down and floating between my legs. Set free, the notes that were inside it fell upward and floated in their turn; I heard them literally falling upward and then floating free, then I shook my head, and the notes rolled from one side to the other.

In Paris, when I lived with Dan and everything we tried became possible, I attempted to produce those sounds. It was at the conservatory, when I was preparing for the Marguerite Long Prize competition. I wanted "upside down" notes, which would float free in unstructured patterns. The results made Dan and me collapse with laughter. "Watch out for the faucet effect," said Dan, and in fact my notes trickled out crassly like water from a narrow pipe. "But I like the faucet effect," said Dan, ready at once to dance it. "Stop it, stop it," I spluttered, "that's not what I'm after." "Well, what are you after?" And I told him about Nicole's lesson, "Let everything go at once and just float." "Oh," said Dan, "what you need is a container, a vanishing container." And I finally did manage it, producing the musical equivalent of a head in which liberated notes turned upside down and floated, with the head then disappearing . . . Of course I did not play that piece in the contest, but thanks to it I was able to play the one that earned me the prize. *I have tried to recover the piece, madame, but it eludes my memory, slips through my fingers; the gift I possessed died with my brother. Are such things possible: for three years I possessed a gift and now it is gone . . .*

And then Nicole would make me start the same exercise over again, but this time at the bar. I liked the support it gave. You had less need to think of your limbs because the bar took them in hand. In a way the bar took care of my body; I entrusted my body to it and was free to pursue the notes that pleased me, the notes I detached from the rest of the music, or rather that detached themselves, and I followed them . . .

It was those exercises I tried to repeat in Dan's loft. But they were not enough.

One look at the manuals, the law manuals sent by Yves and stacked below the platform, and at once the same discomfort assailed me, the same despair at ever lifting them.

I told myself, "I'll get over it." And to get over it I told myself I must go out, walk, walk the length and breadth of Manhattan, look at the river, the sky, the planes in the sky.

And go on walking.

Since I could not manage a return to childhood, I had to try to go elsewhere, to push into new territory, and to do that I resolved to walk to the limits of physical pain, to walk until I crossed a threshold beyond which my body could not but become another: that must be my goal.

Let fatigue inexorably soak into my muscles, let my muscles begin to metamorphose, to cling to the bones of the leg, first in ponderous clumps and then like stolid mutant animals pursuing their own private goals beyond human understanding, and then soon the shoulders too would be invaded, and the arms. Another life would take possession, seize the baton, and what was "myself" would be driven back into an ever-shrinking space. I would watch my ankles swell, and ropes appear under the skin of my hands, my shoes would tighten painfully and I would begin to groan. But I had to walk, and soon pain itself would cross a threshold, and beyond that threshold I would no longer be the same.

My body sagged forward, my legs dragged, my neck drooped, tension took brazen command of my features and I moaned aloud.

Walk! Keep walking! I reached the great bridge, miles from home, and the Hudson flowed by far below. Ready-made thoughts raced along the few paths of my mind still unoccupied by the invader, *an unknown disease, madame, which attacks the body like an invader,* schoolgirl thoughts about the great river that flows down from Canada, about the island where Indians once galloped. But soon the invader was already advancing along these pathways as well and my thoughts, never very bold, flattened themselves against the sides to let it pass, and I walked on, heading toward old age, decrepitude, abandonment . . .

Then I headed back down Broadway.

Those I had come close to resembling lay slumped on benches along the central dividing strip, sprawled on subway grilles between the two opposing traffic flows amid greasy windblown waste. Through stinging reddened eyes I stared at them and was drawn to them. How I envied them the benches on which they lay . . . Oh, to escape one's invader once and for all, to become unrecognizable to everyone and to oneself, at the dusty intersection of two streets, sunk in the moment, aware only of the traffic roar and siren's howl, a small whirlwind of soiled paper, of indistinct cries, of chance words . . .

"Hey, lady?"

I looked up. A policeman was looking curiously at me.

"Anything wrong?"

"No, no. It's the heat."

"Need some help?"

"No, I'll get a taxi."

"I'll call one," said this policeman.

And suddenly, because of those simple words, a small measure of good sense returned. I straightened up, pushed back my soaked hair, and unleashed the old hunt of my mind in pursuit of the tedious convulsing of my features. The invader had decamped; I had managed to shake him off by changing bodies. The field was clear for me to return to myself.

And right away I felt swept by a beneficent flood, the flood set in motion by our own powers, the flood that thrusts us out into the great swirling commerce of desires, and for the woman restored to me the instant she rose from that vagrant's bench the flood meant a desire to return to the loft, to cook for Dan, to have a shower, to write to our father.

How kind that policeman was.

Stationed at the curb like a big bumblebee, he whistled. I loved his whistle, and at once a yellow taxi slowed down with a squealing of brakes, and I loved that yellow taxi that looked like a big butterfly.

Right there on hot, sticky, dusty Broadway I rediscovered the garden of our childhood suddenly descending at my feet as if on a fairy's command. Happiness flooded me. I loved everything about this city.

There were so many butterflies when we were children. We used to chase them, particularly the big yellow ones with downy wings.

"There are hardly any butterflies this summer," my father had written to me. *"Yesterday when I was walking on the lawn I saw one, a small yellow one, and suddenly I saw you and Dan, hand in hand, your two small faces bobbing behind the insect as if it were pulling you along with its magic wings. And your cry of horror when I told you that people collected them by pinning them to a corkboard in a case. Dan shouted, 'Papa, let's make our garden a sanctuary for all the butterflies in the world.' I said yes, of course, without really giving it a thought. I never really gave you a thought, Estelle; how I regret it now. I believed you were from a different world, flying free — I too thought you were magic.*

"We all need to believe in something, and at that time I no longer believed in anything, either God or men or politics. I did not really believe even in justice; I dedicated myself to it because I saw no alternative, but Estelle, surely it can't be human not to believe in anything — and you know what I think now? I think I believed in you.

"You were always together, you and Dan, and you seemed to possess a strange wisdom, the innocence of those who know everything in advance. And you were so beautiful, Estelle, I have never seen such beautiful children. And always together. I can't speak to you of my life with Nicole. She has not always been happy; it's neither my fault nor hers, poor girl, but whenever I saw you and Dan, I believe it was the picture of the total couple I saw, brother and sister indissoluble.

"How strange these things are; I am only just starting to understand them. I thought you too were invulnerable. The need to believe and to hope that had survived in me without my knowing shifted toward you two and I did not know that either. That is why I saw you without seeing you.

"What a father I have been, Estelle! A father in a dream, I see it now; if I were not so old, I believe I would go and see a psychiatrist. It's becoming fashionable, you know, even in our little town. I suspect your old school-teacher of taking the plunge — I've seen her on the Paris train every day at the same hour, looking mysterious and absorbed.

"*That's why I'm so anxious now, Estelle. My feet are returning to earth, and I'm afraid for you. I had set you in an iridescent bubble that floated ceaselessly before me — to my great joy. But now that bubble has burst: you are people with a past, and we ourselves, Tiresia, Nicole, and I, are that past, as is the great world around us, which I fear has only changed superficially. You remember what your Doctor Minor said when people complimented him on his talents as a doctor: 'Bah! I know my Major!' Well, I too have my giant Hydra, for the toil of thousands like me never manages to destroy it and the lawyer that I am seems to shrink day after day. I'm afraid I'll end up a dwarf, like your doctor, who finds himself more and more 'minor,' not to say 'minus,' when contemplating his 'Major.' But I'm afraid I'm worrying you. Minor and I are both very well and we still quarrel over our favorite war; the other day he called me a 'repressed Englishman,' and I replied that he was a 'Romanov man-qué' . . . as you see we're both still full of fight.*

"*Estelle, why aren't you coming back? I'm afraid you won't be able to take your exams in September. Tell me about Dan. Do you believe in what he's doing over there? My Estelle, sometimes I feel like warning you against being lured too far from yourself. You and Dan inevitably will take different paths. Don't try to follow him too far down his path, even if he wanders too far from yours.*

"*I sent you over there, and now here I am trying to bring you back. What an inconsistent father, you must be thinking.*

"*That little yellow butterfly on the lawn. Adrien's father claims that nuclear testing has transformed the atmosphere and made the butterflies disappear. Mrs. Neighbor shrugs; they've bought a television set and she's oblivious to anything else. She speaks of distant countries as if she lived there, but she is blind to what goes on in her own garden. We still talk of repairing the hole in the wall under the lilac, but can you believe it, hornets have built their nest there, a sort of big Venetian lantern that hums night and day. Nobody dares go near. We should call the fire department, and I'm afraid the products they use will also destroy the little butterfly I saw.*"

The yellow taxi hummed through the city traffic and my father's letter sang inside my head like a forgotten choir. I gently massaged my legs, my energy returned, a feeling of confidence, then suddenly a surge of joy. I was in New York, on a visit to my brother. This evening I would go and see him dance and afterward he had promised to take me somewhere: "This is something you've never seen, Estelle!" We would phone our father and invite them to come over, we would repaint the loft for them, we would take Nicole to a rehearsal and she would see how magnificent Dan was, oh, the joy to see Nicole's face transfigured, and I would show my father my manuals, I would tell him I had enrolled at Columbia, which was almost true (I had asked for an application form and spoken on the phone with the course counselor, and now it only remained to hurry home and hammer out the fine points of these plans with Dan and make an appointment for an interview at Columbia Law School).

When the taxi dropped me in front of the old building at 100 Greene Street everything was simple and beautiful.

My "eyesight" was scarcely clearer than before, but at least I was alive to our neighborhood. Something of the magnificent harmony of its cast-iron facades reached me, and the twin presence of 72 and 28 Greene Street warmed my heart ("They're a couple," David, another dancer, had told us, "seventy-two is bigger and has a kind of virile panache, twenty-eight is female and more discreet, but both are of almost identical conception"). And for once, as if it were the companion of that big pair of buildings, I savored the trompe l'oeil cat on the trompe l'oeil facade of the corner of Spring Street.

I flung myself into the staircase, a strange staircase that looked like a succession of tall ladders, one set up on each landing and all rearing upward as if to storm fortress walls, with the light from the glass roof dropping straight and solid like a plumb line in a mine shaft.

I remembered the curving sweep of the staircase at home, its burnished wooden steps gracefully changing shape at the bend and its banister turning with equal grace, so smooth to the touch, as if walls and staircase had jointly agreed to find the supplest arrangement, the arrangement best adapted to the feeble inhabitants of the house, so as to help them — but discreetly — in their incessant climbs and descents.

Still thinking of those tender stairs at home, I launched myself too fast up these New York stairs, each indistinguishable from the one below as they marched upward to storm the blinding whiteness of the glass roof. Unaccustomed to this near-vertical ascent, my shins bumped painfully into the risers, the staircase cut my legs from under me, and I fell to my knees, sliding one or two steps farther down.

"Here she comes," said a surly, mocking voice. Alwin had come out onto the landing. I could see his form outlined in the dazzling light from above.

* * *

The small fallen puppet stood up: the staircase made it rise, the staircase made it fall.

"Estelle, do you think you could . . . ," said my brother Dan.

Morning, noon, and night: "Do you think you could . . . ," said my brother Dan.

"Could you wash this shirt, go to the deli, go to the bank, get me the paper, there's a story, something I need to read, could you . . . " Morning, noon, and night, and up and down the stairs the little puppet ran.

"Alwin says I'm nowhere near getting this, I don't have the time, could you go to the pharmacy, I need some aspirin." It was the middle of the night and Dan had wakened me; he had been in the loft across the landing and I could see how pale he was. "I went to bed late, Estelle, I can't sleep, could you go get me some aspirin?" "It's just our vaypigo, Dan, it'll pass," I said with a laugh or an attempt at a laugh, but he wanted me to move, he kept me constantly busy. And if I turned toward my law manuals:

"Estelle, you're not here to do law."

"But I have exams in September, Dan."

"Poison Ivy will take them for you," he said.

I began to yell:

"Don't call him Poison Ivy!"

It was Dan's turn to yell:

"Why wouldn't I call him Poison Ivy, why not, tell me, why not?"

He spoke in English, the language he always used when in the grip of uncontrollable emotion; the alien tongue for the most intimate thoughts, only now do I understand that.

"Why, tell me!"

"Because he's my husband, that's why!"

I knew exactly how heavy and sharp that arrow was, exactly how much pain it would cause, and what would ensue. But I did not know what the arrow was made of or why I loosed it. Such, alas, was the madness that gripped us.

"A husband! Well, Ay-drien would have been better," he shouted.

"Ay-drien, Ay-drien," I shouted back, repeating the name English-style the way he had pronounced it. "Can you tell me what Ay-drien has to do with this?"

What Adrien had to do with it I now understand much better. Our neighbor Adrien, the boy from next door who knew about our attic, the gap in the wall beneath the lilac, the ditch at the far end of the meadow, and our silvery pond — Adrien our almost-brother.

And suddenly we were fighting like wildcats about Adrien.

"Ay-drien has balls, that's what!" shouted my brother — again in English, so that I had no idea what he said.

"What, what?"

I was shrieking so loud my eardrums hurt, I was gripping my brother's arm. We were close to blows.

"He says that a certain Adrien, a native of your precious little French town, I presume, has balls."

"Alwin!"

There he was, the inevitable Alwin, brought here by our yelling, his eternal sarong around his waist.

"And what do you want her to do with this Adrien's balls?" he asked Dan.

"Oh, damn it all," said Dan, suddenly deflated.

"Dan doesn't like me talking that way," Alwin said placidly, addressing himself to an invisible breath of air. "He has ideas about sisters, old-fashioned ideas. I don't blame him. But he should realize that sisters and dancing don't mix."

"What?"

I was outraged.

"What? I run his errands, I wash his shirts, I get his papers and his aspirin and all the rest, what is it, what do you want —"

"He never needed a sister for that before. Ever since his sister arrived here he's been acting like a baby, that's what I think, and his dancing —"

And Dan suddenly turned against Alwin.

"What about my dancing? It's gone downhill, that's what you mean, isn't it, Alwin? But you're wrong, I'm dancing better, only you don't want to see it, you're afraid of seeing it, because I'm going farther than you, farther than you can even see —"

And abruptly he stopped. That often happened with my brother Dan: he would break off in mid-tirade as if his mind had gone blank, as if a cloud had enveloped him, a cloud that in reality was time — thousands of droplets of seconds condensed around him into an unknowable number of years. When he emerged from it, he was different.

"You want to know something, Alwin? I don't care if I don't dance half as well. I don't care. Just leave me alone, will you? And leave her alone. I'll dance the way I want to."

"Fine," said Alwin, leaving. "Fine."

On the landing he turned and delivered his poisoned shaft:

"Like your mother Nicole, think about it, Dan, like your mother Nicole."

Then Alwin was gone, and Dan and I were alone like two mad lost dogs in the big darkened loft.

Police sirens howled in the night, police lights briefly kindled the ceiling, then vanished, and the sound of night returned like an ocean surging against the foot of the cliff, breaking against the foot of stairs so steep you could not imagine climbing them on nights like this without being at once pitched into outer darkness with limbs shattered and contorted.

We could not go out on such nights.

The poisoned shaft with which Alwin had closed the door on us locked it more surely than a real iron bolt could have done. He had sealed us in as if inside a seashell, and inside that seashell we collapsed onto the raft of the platform mattress, far apart from each other, dead tired. The stabbing howls of sirens seemed to wander in the deepest-buried reaches of our awareness; we collapsed and those horrible cries roamed our hidden reaches, dragging our defenseless souls behind them like the bodies of the vanquished tied to horses' tails and being bumped about on cruel wayside stones before being tossed into a dungeon's dark depths . . . Sometimes one of those howls cut straight into us and came back up out of our throats as if through a deserted gun slit. I would hear my brother groan painfully and sit up in sudden terror, no longer knowing where we were, what had happened, and why we were so unhappy.

Graying cloud bellies hung low at the windows and our raft drifted lost in a dead mist. We were ugly in that colorless hour, neither day nor night, with neither memories nor future plans. Each had aroused the other with his moans, and now we were like two dying fish. Of the day gone by nothing supported us from below, and of the day to come not a plank was lowered to us.

How did humans manage to get up every morning, to throw themselves into their day with a shark's lust for the heady blood taste of the hours ahead?

We were stiff all over, as stiff as if we had spent the night crammed inside a roomless airless oyster shell.

We let this dawn hour pass and then other hours. This inertia was new to us, since neither one nor the other got up first, since it created expectancy in us, an expectancy that we kept well under control, well stifled, and that in return stifled us.

We lay quite still, not even turning to face each other, and took shallow breaths, content to have just enough air and anxious not to draw attention to ourselves out of an unreasonable fear that this small quantity of air might be withheld.

"Just lazy kids," Alwin said contemptuously.

Perhaps we had indeed become lazy, I because for the first time I was far from my studies, and Dan because my presence had taken him back to the capricious vein of childhood.

"Just lazy kids," said Alwin.

And I derived pleasure from it exactly as I would from a sugared almond, malice-coated on the outside and hiding secret sweetness within.

If I could, I would have kept Dan even longer under his sheet on the platform mattress, supine, arms outspread, through the sweltering heat of day and the humidity of evening, if just to see that expression of Alwin's, his contempt, his disgust, yes, his disgust.

Just to hear him say "lazy" again.

It was a snake he set down to slither over us. "Lazy." Even today, if I want to feel a wave of hatred I have only to think of that word.

It meant "Dan is not an artist, capricious but capable of discipline, Dan is not a child, savage but possessing genius, Dan when all is said and done is just lazy, and his sister too is lazy, from the same mold, both of them — one of them on his own might fool you, but taken together painfully obvious, lazy kids, children of the same mother, soft and sentimental like her, no willpower, just lazy . . ."

And then I could have relegated Alwin to a world where he was nothing and understood nothing, where his standards were no sharper-edged than cheap fairground penknives, a world where he no longer counted. I heard our father's voice at night in the Helleur house when he opened the door of our child's bedroom and found us sitting close together, with me reading a book aloud. Dan would be asking astonishing eager questions, and I would be devoting all my energies to the search for replies. And when our father arrived my worried frown would suddenly vanish, for he would give Dan an answer, more profound and weightier than the one I had struggled so hard to produce.

"*My poor Estelle,*" wrote our father, "*you were such a serious child. Sometimes I think we have given you too heavy a responsibility with Dan.*

Now that I am so worried I have to say it. You're the one who raised him, Estelle, not because we didn't love him, I don't need to tell you that, but because you seemed to do it so much better than we could.

"But what tortures me now is this: was it we who with love and gratitude allowed Estelle to take her little brother in hand, or was it our weakness that handed Dan over to Estelle? I believe that none of us three was capable of raising a child.

"You, Estelle, raised yourself, thank God. But what of Dan? I confined myself to appreciating his verbal agility and his resourcefulness; Nicole doted on his beauty and his grace; and Tiresia kept an eye on you both from a distance, in her own way, you know, silently . . . but it was you, Estelle, who rowed the family boat. Why didn't I see that before? Why is it obvious to me only now?

"As if the worry I am now experiencing had finally stripped away a kind of concealing veil . . . a layer not of unconcern — I have never been unconcerned — but of dull-witted inertia. Luckily you were always such a serious worker and Dan was always so lively . . ."

I was "a serious worker" and Dan was "lively," but Alwin wasn't interested in any of that.

He was indifferent to what Dan had been.

Dan for him began on Long Island, at Kennedy Airport, where his plane had landed, and to Alwin that already seemed a long journey, for he had gone to pick up the newcomer himself, losing an afternoon in traffic jams and then several more days watching him dance and persuading him to stay, for Dan had intended to see several companies before deciding.

I sometimes think that if Alwin had been able to look beyond that airport, to go back in time to that silvery lawn where Dan had really danced for the first time around the sister he loved, beneath the balustrade that like a marble balcony in a dream opera bore our father and Nicole, in that house in which the shrouded wordless woman of our childhood waited somewhere, attentive and silent, if Alwin had been able to hear Dan say in his grown-up voice what he said to me as a child that first time, "The earth is calling us, the earth is why I dance," if Alwin had been able to do all that, then the dancer of genius inside my brother would have blossomed fully, then our destiny would have followed that blossoming, and neither my father nor Dan nor Nicole nor Tiresia would have died . . . Often in my pain I thought Alwin was a murderer.

TWENTY-NINE

More Loft

W E EACH TOOK a long shower. Dan ordered a pizza from Mulberry Street, in Little Italy. It arrived barely a quarter hour later, round and enormous in its square cardboard box; we drank Cokes with crushed ice, calm and sated. We said little between large mouthfuls of crusty pizza dripping with sauce and thick with melted cheese.

But below the even surface of Dan's voice, as if below the taut square covering of a pond, I heard the distant bubbling of a spring.

These images do not arise by accident.

Small, almost square, that pond was at the upper corner of our meadow; you could see its motionless reflection from afar, like a handkerchief spread out on the grass. But Dan and I knew its secret.

We would lie on the ground, heads very close to the water but not touching it, for we respected that small discreet pond and had no wish to disturb it in its meditation among the pond grasses. And there in the great silence of the meadow, after lying for a moment among the small sounds of insects and lazy water bubbles, we heard the distant keening of the spring.

"When a spring suddenly dries up," Tiresia told us one day, "it means some great change is about to happen in the earth, a tremor, a disaster of some kind . . ."

Every afternoon after school we went to the pond to listen for the sound of the spring, to make sure that the ground our house stood on was still at peace, that no disaster was brewing.

We were the guardians of the spring. As long as we could hear it, peace would remain among us. But beware: we must not forget even for a single day. If we failed to visit it just once, we thought, the spring would forget to flow. It was like a heart whose continued beating depended on us.

Because of it we refused to travel.

"This is ridiculous, Estelle," said our father. "We're going to the seashore for three days and you don't want to come?"

I lowered my eyes, embarrassed but stubborn. "No, Father . . ."

"Dan?" asked our father.

Dan shook his head gravely. "No, Father."

"What's got into these kids, do you know, Nicole?"

"Oh, come on, Dan, Estelle," said Nicole in her childish, passionate voice, "we'll be bored without you, come on, we'll dance on the beach . . ."

And we were so ashamed for not yielding to her.

Standing up to our father was easier: you were standing up to authority, a reaction we had learned at school. Naturally the comparison applied only remotely to our situation at home with our father, but at least we could convince ourselves and act accordingly, at the expense of a little guilt.

But Nicole! That meant standing up to charm, which to us was true sin. Our unhappiness reached its peak when Nicole talked about dancing on the sand by the sea ("On the in-between sand," she explained — neither the wet, which was on the ocean side, nor the dry, which was on the land side, but the strip between the two, neither gold nor brown, hard but not too hard, responsive to the feet, letting them sink in just a little before propelling them forward, oh, it was special and wonderful to dance on that sand, said Nicole, it was as if you had no more willpower, no more head giving orders, just feet on the sand, feet talking to the sand, come on, come on, you'll see . . .).

Terribly ashamed, we turned to Tiresia. I have no idea what she read in our eyes, nor do I recall what she said, nor whether she even spoke at all, but our father and Nicole eventually left for the seashore while Tiresia stayed behind and so did we. So we were able to go down to the spring the way we did every day, around six o'clock as the light began to wane and the pond cast that indescribable reflection up from the grass as if in meditation. We were able to go on accomplishing our solemn task down there, ensuring that the earth would continue to hold together and hold our house up and that no disaster would erupt from the inflamed and inscrutable bowels of matter.

We must have performed this rite for years. Tiresia, who was always there when we called her, must have known. But our father and Nicole neither saw nor suspected the existence of the ritual.

Did Tiresia ever tell them why we refused to go to the seashore? I do not know why, but I doubt it. I imagine Tiresia forever silent.

*   *   *

Then our cousins came, and the separation of our teens, and we forgot the spring.

And years later came the disaster that swept away our little island, killing those who dwelt there and leaving me the only survivor. So I would like to believe at least in fate, I would like to see a sign in the mute eye of that little pond we loved. It has probably dried up by now, since they are going to build apartments in what used to be our meadow.

But I remember something else: Adrien, in the little glassed-in box they had added onto the side of their house and in which they had installed a bathroom ("For guests," they said proudly, even though they never had guests). I remember Adrien perched on the toilet bowl there, standing upright at the bull's-eye window, which was as narrow as an archery slit, firing arrows at our pond . . .

On one occasion, deprived (perhaps by the cunning and greed of his brothers) of his usual weapons, he resorted to more primitive methods. We watched from behind our apple tree as he pivoted on his heel with uplifted arm and hurled a stone into the pond.

"How disgusting," I said to Dan, "how truly disgusting."

I have no idea why an onslaught with bare hands and stones struck me as more outrageous than a bow-and-arrow attack. But when I try to re-create that moment my sense of outrage and injury is most powerful, and beyond that is a sense of injury visited upon something far bigger than ourselves. I feel the same rage all over again, a rage that — for reasons I cannot recall — was also stimulating and sweet-tasting.

Perhaps the reasons lay not in the act but in something else that happened that day, something I have now forgotten.

"Shh," my brother said, "watch this, Estelle, you're going to see something you've never seen before."

Adrien took one last roundhouse swing with his arm, but he had too little room and his arm sharply bumped the window. It swung open, causing him to slip, and when he tried to regain his balance his foot caught the base of the bathroom window frame. It crashed to earth below, just a foot from the deck chair in which Mrs. Neighbor was having her siesta.

The irascible Mr. Neighbor returned home like thunder that night, his rage clearly audible from our house: "Wait till I get my hands on

you, you little . . ." Adrien, fleeing the storm, limped to the gap in
the wall and took refuge in the garden on our side, while Mr. Neighbor, restrained by his wife, abandoned the pursuit.

Dan and I took Adrien something to drink, for he was wincing
with what seemed genuine pain.

How had that window frame come unhinged? The mystery set
my father and Nicole and even Tiresia laughing.

Each of us had a theory. Our father believed that after adding that
hideous blister onto the side of their house, Adrien's parents had
run out of funds for building a real window. The fallen window was
therefore only a makeshift covering, and to prove his point he drew
it for us. Nicole argued that Adrien's younger brothers, knowing his
habits, had sabotaged the window to punish him for bossing them
around. I no longer recall Tiresia's interpretation.

In addition to the wrath visited on him by Mr. Neighbor, Adrien
suffered a sprained ankle, which kept him bedridden for several
weeks, and peace returned to our pond.

We waylaid our Doctor Minor in the street to ask him not to
make Adrien better too soon. He put his bag down and looked at
us with concern.

"You realize what you are asking me?"

"Yes, not to make Adrien better too soon," we repeated, speaking
very clearly for we suspected that he was already a little deaf.

"Never ask that, never ask such a thing."

"Why not, Doctor Minor?"

"It's bad luck, that's why."

"But it's Adrien who brings us bad luck."

"What do you mean?" our doctor asked, looking deep into our
eyes.

"Adrien hurts our pond."

With his arrows Adrien pierced the delicate skin of the pond, at
whose bottom dwelt the spring that held our world together.

His arrows pierced the opaque bright-glinting surface, snaked
down into the forbidden depths, and stung the secret spring. The
arrows disappeared into the wounds; they never came up.

Each time our pond was wounded, and each time it absorbed the
weapon. And then we forgot about it, and nobody came to listen for
the murmur of its spring or to attack its unspeaking surface. And
then they all died, the meadow was sold, the spring dried up, and
apartments will rise in their place.

*   *   *

They all died, but Adrien merely sprained his ankle.

My brother is rotting in his coffin, but Adrien shuttles between Hong Kong and Canton, returning each time more tanned and more dynamic, and to keep up his tan and his dynamism he frequents health clubs and expensive restaurants. Adrien prospers while my brother rots.

I see no sign anywhere, madame, what am I to do?

I met Adrien again a few days ago. For the first time since Tiresia's death.

His parents were worried about me. "She hasn't been here for so long . . . does she know the meadow has been sold?" To please his mother, Adrien invited me out to dinner. As in the past.

And because of those things that have been stirring constantly inside me ever since I first spoke to you, madame, I accepted.

He was in good spirits. His lightweight suit, of Italian cut, flattered him. In fact, had it not been for a kind of peasant doggedness in his features he could have been a magazine playboy rather than the prickly childhood companion who had long ago sprained his ankle slipping into the toilet bowl because he wanted to irritate his two small neighbors, Dan and Estelle.

"My cat has four feet, a tail, and whiskers . . ."

"My family had five people, three grown-ups and two children, and four of them are dead . . ."

"Do you still like the opera, Adrien?"

"Of course. My wife and I have a subscription to the Paris Opera, and we go every year to the Bayreuth Festival; it's German, you may recall."

His cheerful, prosperous appearance, the festive mood he is so good at creating (but which can so quickly become a wife-swapping mood — oh Adrien, with you a person has to be permanently on guard), impressed me. So did the glittering restaurant, and the wine.

When a spring disappears it is because a disaster is brewing, Tiresia had told us. The spring had been riddled with arrows and stones, and had disappeared. Its guardians forgot it. My brother Dan is rotting in his grave and Adrien prospers.

"I'm thinking of writing an opera, Adrien."

"Oh yes? What kind?"

"I already have a story, I'm having a writer do the libretto, and I'm composing the music."

"Estelle, you amaze me."

He was ready to be enthusiastic. Yes, the plan pleased him: I was coming to meet him, I was entering his world, in which opera through some mysterious social chemistry had an important place. Adrien poured me a glass of pink champagne, the kind that always makes me drunk (and I believe he knows it).

And because of his enthusiasm and the pink champagne and a pain that had returned to gnaw at my heart, I reminded him of the pond incident, of the arrows, of the dislodged window, of his sprained ankle. And his old rage flared fiercely all over again. Oh, we were in the nouvelle cuisine restaurant so loudly celebrated by the high priests of gastronomy, and the waiters stood in array like the footmen in the fairy tales, and the place was packed with elegant ladies and svelte gentlemen — but Adrien was once again the furious little boy standing at his archery slit and sending arrows and stones into the pond next door. And from behind an apple tree the children named Dan and Estelle still kept stealthy watch, the children he loved and loathed more than anything in the world, his feelings an inextricable welter that he would never attempt to disentangle because he despised feelings and books and intellectuals and unpaid effort and suffering and deliberateness and everything that did not ring with the echo of an enormous tip slammed down on the table of a luxury restaurant.

I know. I know that Adrien has credit cards and that the tips he and everyone else leave are crisp flat bills. Because that is how things are today. But if all we had was enormous coins, fat and glittering, he would roll the fattest and the most glittering onto the table to hear it ring, to hear it ring forever in praise of the life he has dedicated himself to, the life he worships.

"Your opera sounds like a good idea. Much too good for you; you'll never manage it."

And my own anger flared up too, my old anger at Adrien, who was not my brother and whom I might have loved and married and had done with, but who was not my brother . . . oh, Adrien, how I still loathe you because you're alive and you'll never be my brother.

"Why shouldn't I manage it? I won the Marguerite Long Prize, and a record I helped make won the top French record award."

That was how I talked with Adrien.

"First, that was a long time ago. And then your Marguerite What's-her-name and your Grand Prix or whatever it was for the record, that's just like high school prizes, in other words, nothing at all, rewards for teachers' pets. Opera isn't that."

"What is it, then?"

"Have you looked at the opera, at the Opera House on the Place de l'Opéra in Paris, have you taken a look at it? Opera is people."

"Opera is music."

"It's people who come to listen to music. And what they want is feelings, simple, strong feelings. But what you want is to blur everything with subtleties, you want to crank out your modern music, which pisses everyone off and which doesn't have a single tune worth remembering."

"You're wrong, Adrien, I want a real show, with gorgeous sets, dance, singing, wonderful characters, tunes everyone can recognize and love," *everyone, madame, the nameless beings I encounter in the street, in the subway, those whose faces are mournful, who no longer know they are alive; I want to give them my love, the love of the Helleurs, so that they may know how strongly and vibrantly love lived in that family. Father, you remember what you used to say, a sack of shit onstage, and a dancer has to move that sack of shit, but the auditorium is crowded with exactly the same kind of people, and some in the streets, the subway. This show is for them too — the living, my contemporaries — they too have to drag this sack of shit around every day. My mother Nicole wanted to break free and soar into the sky, my brother Dan wanted to rip it from the earth which calls us, my mother Tiresia sank into it and was lost, and my father Andrew Helleur kept all three of them afloat because his compassion encompassed their striving. It's my turn now, madame. For those who are no longer anything but excrement in the gloom of their coffins, I want settings from the underworld, I want lights, supple dancers' bodies, singers' voices, music, the breathing of the living, I want the applauding hands of the living; let them alight on those hands, let them enter the awareness of the living, let that awareness be safe haven from them, madame . . . This is the opera libretto I want you to write for me.* "My family had five people, three grown-ups and two children, and four of them are dead." *Will all that suffice for love, madame, for an opera libretto, because I hate their death . . .*

"First of all, what's the subject of your opera?" Adrien said to me.

It was only a few days ago, in the restaurant he took me to on one of his returns from Hong Kong or Canton.

"No, it was the Philippines. God, Estelle, your geography's pretty skimpy. I guess you haven't traveled much."

I must have made a gesture of protest.

"Oh, New York, spare me! You didn't see a thing there, not one damned thing. And if by chance you did happen to see something you sure as hell forgot it in that stupid convent of yours."

"You can't see anything, Estelle," he went on. "Apart from you and that goddamned brother of yours, you've never seen a thing."

I could not believe it: there he sat telling me these things as if all that time had not elapsed. And what he said was true and at the same time utterly false.

"I bet you've already forgotten what I do. Import-export. It won't mean a thing to you. I could go on telling you for the rest of my life, you wouldn't remember. You don't even know what I buy and what I sell. I'm sure you haven't even heard of the boutique — the topflight boutique — which bears my name, Adrien N., on the rue du Bac. Tell me, Estelle, what do I do when I go to the Philippines?"

I do not know what came over me. Adrien drove me wild, as only he could, and he knew it. I thought my years in the convent would have changed all that, but Adrien still drove me wild. I began to sing, quite loud, louder than just humming: "Adrien grabs his sickle and flies to the Philippines, to go and cut wicker. On the way he meets a girl, all on her own but trouble, all on her own but trouble . . ."

"Shut your mouth, Estelle, or I'll smash this bottle on the table."

And I shut my mouth, because Adrien would have done it.

"Listen, of course I know you sell wicker furniture."

"Okay, okay, tell me what your opera's about."

And I realized it was impossible. Tell Adrien my opera?

Already it had fled, evaporated on the spot under his mocking stare, but I did not want to be at a loss with Adrien. I groped for words, for a sentence so simple and direct it would not have a single flaw through which he could intrude with his sneering sarcasm . . . "*My cat has four feet, a tail, and whiskers . . .*" I did not want him secreting his corrosive toxins in my still embryonic opera. Ah, if Adrien were to enter my opera today there would be no hope for it. Later perhaps, later . . .

"It's a love story, Adrien."

"Of course, they're always love stories. What else?"

And suddenly I saw him blush, that dark flush that swept the skin around his eyes and raced up his forehead; I had so often seen that somber conflagration race toward his hairline, which seemed to shrink back as if from a burning blast, to waver like the scorched edge of a forest. I was frightened.

"I know," Adrien hissed between his teeth, "it's your story you want to tell, your goddamned story, and I'll be in it, won't I be in it, Estelle, the bad guy, the villain, and your precious brother will be the pure one, the beautiful one, the leading tenor, and I'll be the bass, and you'll have me sing the great rape scene under the lilac beside the dead brother's body, oh, I hate you, Estelle, if only you knew how much I hate you, you and all your fucking bullshit . . ."

The pink champagne bottle leapt from the bucket and Adrien broke it clean on the table between us. This was just a few days ago.

And this is what I said to Adrien as the champagne slowly spread in golden bubbles on the tablecloth, bubbles that dripped slowly to the floor and I heard every tiny splash they made, I heard it with delight and horror, the crystalline sound of champagne cascading from the table, and above that sound my voice said:

"If you didn't exist, Adrien, I'd have to invent you."

I also said:

"Not much point in going to athletic clubs and doing so much karate if you can't even control yourself . . ."

"That's it, Estelle, go on, stab, stab, it does you good . . ."

And then, yes, I did stab, I was drunk with that champagne I had not drunk, drunk with that forest fire climbing on Adrien's forehead, and I hurled my brother's death at his head. "It was your fault, Adrien." "How do you figure that?" "Because you should have known, you should have told me." "Told you what, I knew nothing." "You didn't want to, you were jealous." "Jealous of Dan? Give me a break!" "You were older than he was." "So were you, you were also older than he was." "And you're still jealous of him, jealous of a dead man." And we went on exchanging nonsensical charges and suddenly Adrien dipped his hand into the puddle of champagne and then slowly stroked my face.

And I knew why he was doing it: to make me bite him, because I hated that caress, and as he expected I did bite him, and with my teeth closed tight on the fleshy part of his hand he leaned across and said:

"Come down to the john with me, Estelle, it's what you want, isn't it, and I don't give a fuck why but it's what I want too."

The whole time we were in that toilet cubicle, the water in the nearby urinals flowing with the same crystalline cascading sound, my head whirling, "No sign, no meaning," the little pool winked and beckoned in my head, uncoupled memories raced about and collided head-on with great spurting flashes that arched aloft, tracing disjointed geometrical figures. "I've drunk too much," I said to Adrien. "Too bad," he said. The toilet smell was awful. I gulped it down in great gasps. Was it possible for time to cancel itself out in this way, for everything to begin all over again, with the same pain, the same horror? I was hurtling back into the past with nothing to hold me, as if down a deep narrow well, all the way down with Adrien, who thrust at me with all his strength, who hammered me down into that funnel-shaped crater from whose depths the terrible smell of matter arose, the smell of my brother's putrefying body, and then we had reached the bottom and were brought up with a bump. There was nothing more.

Adrien closed his fly, his expression mulish. I tugged my skirt down.

We went back upstairs, with me following a few minute behind him. The champagne had been replaced; I swallowed an aspirin. Adrien had watched me cross the room, his features relaxing. Suddenly there was no more rage between us, no more anything.

"You've turned into a good-looker, Estelle," said Adrien. "As a girl you were a bit awkward, but now . . ."

He said it sincerely, in the boastful, cynical-seeming way in which his sincerity expressed itself. I laughed, suddenly feeling a flood of gratitude toward him, for my opera had returned to take up residence inside me.

For that is what I was feeling: my opera, like a tame bird I had briefly lost in the woods. It had heard the hunter's black voice, and at that voice had burst from its leafy hiding place and come winging straight to my bosom for protection. Now it sat there, its song momentarily stilled, *but you will help me, madame . . .*

Suddenly, as I thought of you, madame, of the help you can be to me, a dancer came into my mind, C. La Liane. She is starring at the Théâtre de la Ville at this very moment, and I remembered that Michael knew her. She is the dancer I want for Nicole, and I promised myself I would write to Michael and ask him to be my intermediary. Oh, madame, your libretto will be so beautiful she will have to accept, she will dance Nicole's part, and once we have her we will find all the other dancers we need, and my poor pale beings will shine . . .

My discomfort disappeared as the meal progressed, the flood of gratitude submerged the arid wastes between Adrien and me and then was gently absorbed into those arid expanses. And soon, by a process well known to me, aridity and flood fell into perfect balance, the ground became neutral, boredom held sway. Adrien and I were bored stiff together.

I was eager to leave.

As the meal drew to a close there was a return of artificial high spirits precisely because the end was near. In a few moments we would be out in the cool of the street, each restored to freedom. Adrien too must have felt it, for his spirits bubbled so high that I began to fear a new crisis. But now it was a simple fear, easy to resolve: you just had to focus on finding a taxi.

Adrien would be going home on foot. "Are you sure . . . ?" I said. "It's my own business!" he answered. Since his accident he walked with a slight limp, but he did not like it to show. Walking alone had always calmed him, and in any case what happened next was not my business; he always landed on his feet. Adrien was a businessman, after all.

THIRTY

The Staircase Dance

*A*ND NOW I was telling Dan the story of our childhood.

When he came home late at night I woke up at once; he was always tired and hungry. I asked him, "Do you remember the meals you used to cook when you were a kid?" He looked at me with that handsome face on which fatigue had settled like a sensual veil, and his eyes questioned me. "You mean that time in the kitchen after Tiresia left?" "Yes," I said, "yes, do you remember the things you invented?"

That voice of one back from the grave . . .

"What things, Estelle? I don't remember. It all seems long ago."

"You invented a dish you said was magic because although it had very ordinary ingredients, nobody had ever thought of mixing them together. You said people mixed them with other ingredients, flour, eggs, milk, a million things, but never the two on their own."

"Estelle," my brother said uneasily. "The things you're talking about. They seem very close, I can feel them in the air. I really said those things, Estelle?"

And suddenly I too was troubled. I heard Dan's child's voice: "These two, see, people never mix only the two of them together. So let's do that, Estelle."

"What was it?" said my brother's grown-up voice. "Tell me, please."

And, vaguely resentful, I said:

"Work it out yourself."

And to get under my skin because we were not entirely friends, he listed everything he ate in this country when Alwin was not keeping an eye on him — pizza, hamburgers, Kentucky Fried Chicken, French fries, heroes, tuna sandwiches, and hot dogs.

"Two ingredients people never put together, Dan."

"Estelle, I'm tired, I want to sleep, you tell me."

But I knew that his tiredness was in another person, not the one I was with.

Tiredness was in the one who had disciplined his back muscles all afternoon in Alwin's unheated, unventilated studio, in the one who had then roamed the stifling dusty New York night to return with shadows under his eyes and hoarse voice (and from its hoarseness I guessed he had ducked out of the baking heat of the streets into the ice-cold caves of many bars; some things I guessed, but so little, hardly anything at all). Tiredness was not in the one I was with, for at this very moment, aroused by my question, he was literally changing before my eyes.

The heavy, sleepy look receded, giving place to the sparkle I knew so well, and all his features came alive as if lit by a campfire, and a procession of little feelings danced in a ring around his face.

"Think, Dan, domestic and exotic, animal and vegetable, yellow and very dark brown . . ."

Suddenly he leapt up, pulled on his T-shirt, hunted feverishly for money, and raced to the door.

How avidly I absorbed every one of his movements, dancer's movements, mobilized for an errand dedicated to me alone.

I heard his body's descent of the stairs, not the heavy clumping descent of most of our neighbors, nor the succession of near-falls and barked shins that was so often my lot, but a sprightly flirtation with the steps, those sheer steps so disinclined for diplomacy but with which my brother negotiated artfully, subtly, and always victoriously — oh, I have no idea how to express it.

Not a gesture of my brother Dan's, not a move, was dull and

mechanical and soulless. His every gesture at every moment contained his whole life; his every movement was a pas de deux danced with the world.

The door slammed behind him, my heart raced, and I hurried out onto the landing so as not to miss some new phrase of his dance. I opened the door noiselessly and came out under the glass-paned roof and I watched.

No more than that. And I did not know that I was watching my love.

And then he returned, the same whirlwind of life as he used to be.

I felt him at the foot of the stairs even before I heard him. A cloud of energy billowed upward, forewarning each stair in turn, making it feel, making it anticipate, like piano keys bracing for the player's next move. I knew that my brother Dan was back, that he was at the bottom of the building inches from the first step, because my perception underwent a change — and the staircase, which had been empty and narrow, swelled with presence, thrust back its walls. The whole staircase became a huge piano lying submissively athwart the building, and suddenly my brother's feet were running up its keys, and the sound filled the whole space of the building that had been so empty and narrow, filled it with music and dance.

Out of the question to go back under the skylight, for he would have seen me too, and that I could not stand. But I stayed close to the door and listened all the way to the last note, to the final bouquet as he sprang onto the landing. The door opened.

"Estelle," he shouted, as if I were far away . . .

Sometimes these days a strange thing happens: I am in the street when I hear my name. I stop with pounding heart. Someone was calling me. I turn and look around.

It can happen several times in quick succession, it can stop happening for long periods.

Estelle . . .

There is nobody left to call me by that name.

Only Adrien. But he says it with such contempt, it is a name he considers provincial and absurd: "It sounds like the priest's housekeeper," he says, managing in the same breath to pour scorn on my stay in the convent. I know the book in which the village priest's housekeeper is named Estelle, but Adrien does not read books. How did he find out?

If I told him it came from a book, he would not believe me. Yet he must somehow have encountered the passage, or else someone mentioned it to him. He has forgotten novel and plot and the person who mentioned it to him, retaining only my name and the association that qualifies him to despise me.

"Estelle," shouted my brother.

I turned slowly, as if I had not heard him coming, as if my concerns had been elsewhere, and he stepped forward like a dancer crossing the stage, hands held out in offering.

"Look," he said.

"Your hand," he said, and he put a small brown paper bag in my hand.

"Your other hand," and he put another small brown paper bag in my other hand.

Then he stepped behind me, stretched out my arm and gently undid the bag. Eggs appeared, sitting as if in a nest.

"Don't move," he whispered, "they'll break."

And suddenly it was just the way it had been that day on the lawn when Dan danced for my parents.

Obedient, absorbed, my body positioned itself as my brother asked. I did not move, I was but the center for his dance. Perhaps from timidity, my arm trembled a little: since leaving home I had attended no more dance classes, and Nicole was no longer there to correct my posture. I could no longer hold my arms outstretched without trembling. Yet I felt old lessons return to my body; my shoulders settled into place of their own volition, low and straight; my neck swiveled slightly and I even felt a surge of pride stiffen my back.

It was my love seeking its path, my unknown love seeking through this muscular activity to emerge into the light, to live.

Dan remained behind me, his hand supporting the arm that bore the little brown nest of eggs. Neither one of us moved, but it was still a dance, as if we both heard the music that held our bodies thus suspended. Then that music we heard must have broken off: Dan removed the nest, my arm dropped, and I held the second brown paper bag out to him. It contained a package of grated chocolate, spangled with tiny flakes of multicolored sugar. And our dance was over.

"You see, I haven't forgotten," said Dan.

*   *   *

And all over again we prepared our absurd childhood dish, eggs fried and sprinkled with chocolate. At the last moment I said, "All the same, Dan, it would taste better with Swiss cheese and ketchup," but he laughed. "No way, Estelle, this is what I really want — you too!"

And I remember what happened in me, a furtive and total reordering of my being, which I no longer recognized, which took me by surprise, and which I finally recognized: our old happiness.

I had been without it for so long.

Satisfactions had in the interim come my way, under the general heading of happiness, and in my passive way I had accepted them as such. But they had been nothing more than satisfactions, things that happened, things that pleased others, and something of the pleasure felt by those others bounced back onto me. So it had been with my small undergraduate successes, and my marriage to Yves, but what point is there in listing them, for all that had come my way since Dan had been small events, pleasant or unpleasant, the stream of small events flowing past me, and me standing there, nothing more.

Dan got ready to break the eggs. Standing beside him, I held the chocolate package, already opened. Dan stopped.

"No, you do the eggs and I pour on the chocolate."

"But what does it matter, Dan?"

"You always broke the eggs."

"Because I was the bigger one, but now you're bigger so it's your turn."

We bickered over that tiny point exactly the way we did as children, totally absorbed by the discussion, digging up the strangest of arguments and solemnly reviewing them. And finally:

"The eggs are your job and the chocolate's mine, it just feels right," said Dan. "It's as if I'm hearing an order."

And there the argument ended, for that had been our old understanding, when one of us said he or she heard an order, the other had to give in.

Very gently I tapped the first egg against the wooden table edge. Tap, tap, tap.

It must have been around the middle of the night, the hour when in monasteries they hasten to the chapel for a service that resembles the midnight watch over starless ocean, the hour when in hospitals they die, when silence falls over every city in the world, a car faintly heard in the distance, the sky abandoned to its own vastness, solitary footsteps wandering the lost pathways of a dream.

An empty space formed in the bosom of time, and we were inside it, hemmed in by its ill-defined eggshell-brittle walls.

Tap, tap, tap, how gently I tapped.

"Scared you'll wake someone?" whispered Dan.

"Yes," I nodded in reply.

Our shoulders touched. For the first time we were close. I recall his question with violence: "Scared you'll wake someone?" Yes, I was scared I would wake "someone." But whose slumber was threatened by the tiny tapping of the egg against the table?

At the foot of the sheer cliff of our staircase, the world's greatest metropolis sprawled like a black sleeping lake. But it slumbered only on the surface. Here and there in the silence bubbles burst as if a sleeper sunk many fathoms down were gulping for air, heaving with the spasms of his secret gestations, wave-borne from metropolis to metropolis beneath the immense human mass of our planet. Was that the sleeper we were afraid of awakening?

Sometimes it seems to me (if that is possible, and I do not think anyone can prove it is not) that my brother and I were slipping across time, that we possessed what might (however contradictory it may seem) be called foreknowledge of the past. Something within us knew what catastrophe our destiny was carrying us to, and what in the past had thrown us off course. But that knowledge was closed to us.

The sleeper sunk deep beneath the vast human mass of the planet had already been awakened, he had already devastated our Old World, and he would return, leapfrogging decades, in a different form, miniaturized now to invisibility, the form of a virus, to visit random devastation on much smaller areas. And in the meantime we had appeared on the surface, two tiny fragments of the human mass, and were living out our lives aboard the vessel of the present, our eyes too weak to pick out the horizon ahead, and the horizon behind, and to see how they ultimately merged.

"Go ahead, Estelle!"

I at once broke that egg on the sharpest edge of the stove.

*   *   *

The white spread tentatively, now in one direction and now in another, gingerly bearing its yellow heart. Then it came to a hesitant halt, and seemed in its turn to look at us and to wait.

We had forgotten to light the stove.

At the window hung the smoky red-tinged light of the city, held at bay by a grimy glass screen. The appliances lined up against the wall looked like an irregular row of monoliths. Our burner flickered timidly on one of them, and our twin silhouettes bent over the blue flame. At the other end of the loft the door was lost in darkness.

We were absorbed and wholly ourselves, absorbed in something that concerned us alone.

Do such things belong to opera? I can hear Adrien's sneer: "What you want is to blur everything with subtleties." No, of course they did not belong to opera: "Have you looked at the Opera, at the Opera House on the Place de l'Opéra in Paris?" Get away from me, Adrien, what do you know of what is at the core of every work of art? You enter the glittering theater and you leave three or four hours later, and you're still the same, nothing has changed, and off you go to dinner. To one of your nice expensive restaurants, Adrien, go on, off you go. Maybe I know nothing, but you know even less, *madame, I need you so desperately . . .*

Then Dan, at once solemn and intimate (that was exactly what we were enacting: an intimate ritual), sparingly sprinkled the chocolate on the eggs, and they, already trembling with the heat from the gas, trembled anew as they received this shower of brown shavings strewn with bright-colored spangles; they trembled and then absorbed the shower. Their flesh changed: even as it turned from clear to opaque white it was slowly streaked with the brown-black of melting chocolate. The sight mesmerized us.

It was a most capacious skillet. Having observed that first egg on its cautious tentative journey of exploration, we wanted to (no, we did not "want to," we felt obliged to) watch another and another. Soon we had utterly lost the capacity either to plan or to call a halt, and it was the same with the chocolate.

It was certainly a large omelette with a large quantity of chocolate. We ate all of it.

And got sick.

*   *   *

We soiled our sheets and changed them, and later we soiled them again. "I don't have any more sheets, Estelle," said Dan, chalk-white as he leaned against the dresser. "Use towels," I told him. "There are no more towels," said Dan. "Then paper towels." "Yes, paper towels," said Dan, but he could not find them, and suddenly his eyes swam with vertigo. I recognized it because it also swam in mine. "Never mind," I said, and we lay down on the floor. "Do you make love to your husband?" Dan asked bizarrely, then a fresh wave of nausea cut off speech. Afterward we splashed ourselves with cold water in the shower, too weak to draw the plastic curtain, or to dry ourselves (but in any case, there were neither towels nor paper). Then we returned to the bed, to the bare mattress. "We won't be sick again, will we?" I mumbled. "What did you say?" mumbled Dan. "Seems to me we threw up more than we ate," I heard, or something on those lines, and finally we fell asleep.

And in the morning Alwin came in.

He stood in the open door and sniffed the air in the loft. We had piled our dirty linen in a corner.

"Lazy and dirty," he said and left, without a word to Dan.

At that anxiety returned, along with the hostility of our teens. I jumped over to the heap of dirty linen.

"Where are you going?" said Dan.

"To wash all these."

It was not my voice, nor was it his. They were voices we had drained of their blood, voices we had drained like chickens with cut throats, voices we sent forth to speak in our stead on a stage neither of us was willing to revisit.

But we stood guard in the wings; oh, how vigilantly we stood guard!

"You don't even know where to look for a launderette," said Dan.

"I'll find one."

"You don't have a bag."

"I'll wrap it up in one of the sheets."

"And walk around with that stench under your arm?"

"Dan, what do you want me to do?"

I was close to tears, and Dan heard those tears in the pallid ghost of my voice. He got up, white, with plastered hair, and when he came close his mouth smelled sour.

"Brush your teeth, you stink."

"So do you."

We brushed our teeth together in the little washbasin and then we washed our faces and then our hair.

They were gestures from our childhood, the unconscious unceasing joint gestures of our childhood, and we returned unhesitatingly to our allotted places. Under our new grown-up covering the children of yesteryear returned, called back by those gestures and unable ever again to separate. And although we had no idea what it was, we felt this presence inside us, impelling us to prolong those gestures, impelling us to seek solutions.

We finally decided to take care of the laundry together, then to wait together until it was ready for the dryer, and when it was dry to have a coffee in the corner coffee shop.

We sat on stools, hunched over our paper coffee cups and doughnuts. In five minutes the coffee would be drunk and the doughnuts chewed down, and the man at the counter would clear the cups, and that would be the signal for us to slide from our stools. That was how things were in this city.

I said sulkily:

"I don't like the cafés here."

"Why not?" said Dan.

Dan should have been at the studio, and already we were getting into a pointless quarrel, insignificant and nasty but no doubt important, since we remained sitting there, and then we went to another coffee shop, then we stood on the sidewalk, we even stood at the foot of our staircase just to continue that pointless, nasty quarrel instead of going to the dance studio or to the law manuals.

Yes, it seemed more important to keep our quarrel going.

"Why don't you like coffee shops?" said Dan threateningly.

"Because, because . . ."

What I wanted to say was this: "Because you can't sit around in them," and just below that was another remark: "Because around here they don't let you just hang out," and another remark hovered lower still: "Because they don't let you hang out together," and lowest of all was "Because two people can't just sit around together in them." That was what had made me sulky, but I did not know it, I only knew that something was there, black under my tongue, and that I could not bring it out into the light.

"You don't like anything here," said Dan, "you're like all the little French kids who come over here with their closed minds and criticize everything . . ."

"And you're not a little French kid?"

"I want to see things, not just criticize."

"But that's all I ever do is see things. I walk around the city, I go to see you at the studio . . ."

"You come to see me at the studio?"

"I don't come to the studio?"

"You're there for one minute and then you're gone!"

"I'm there for one minute . . . !"

"You don't like the studio either, and you don't understand anything Alwin does, and you don't understand Alwin or anything in this city."

My brother Dan was in a bad temper too, and now I know very well that there were other remarks below his own remarks as well, just as black, like poison mushrooms, remarks that said, "You don't love the city I love, because you don't love me, that's what hurts me, because you don't love me, my sister . . ."

All through all those New York days, whenever we spoke, there were those poison mushrooms under our tongues. We had no idea what they were; we just moved from moment to moment, stupefied by their venom, sliding down the slope of time in that black intoxication with occasional brief remissions, nighttime remissions. And then it was as if those mushrooms, finally letting their poison settle back down inside them, began to glow phosphorescent in the dark, their magic light illuminating the narrow circle formed by the mattress where we lay, the ghostly window, the ceiling where bright lights played, the reflections of fleeting blazes in the city or in its sky. And I recalled for Dan the stories of our childhood in the Old World, and all around, as if to escort or protect them, the air conditioners hummed in the heat-saturated air.

But now it was not yet night, and sooner or later we would have to go about our business.

We separated with rage in our hearts. Dan returned to the studio. I wanted to follow him, but I had to take the laundry back upstairs, there were the manuals to study, and I was scared of Alwin's look.

Then evening returned. We were so weary, from the previous night, from the day. I had not opened my law books, I had wandered about the city, more of those too-long, too-painful walks. Dan had worked, and came back with empty head and bruised body. We scarcely had the strength for a few words of greeting, then our bodies spontaneously collapsed. There was nothing to think about, nothing to say. Our bodies dragged themselves to bed.

"Haven't got the energy to go to Alwin's," said Dan, throwing himself fully dressed on the platform mattress.

Going to Alwin's was a way of acting, of talking, of dining, a way of continuing to be for dancing, the way Alwin was. From that moment (it must have been halfway through my stay) Dan never went back to sleep at Alwin's.

We dozed for a moment, then, as if despite myself, I heard myself say, "Dan, do you remember . . . ?"

"What?" said Dan's sleepy voice, and from our supine bodies, side by side on that huge bare mattress, our children's voices arose.

They emerged from the limp chrysalises of our grown-up voices like bright butterflies. Our bodies remained motionless, lying well apart from each other, the abandoned sloughs from which Dan's and Estelle's children's voices had escaped and reached us as we listened, half-somnolent.

"When you danced on the lawn . . ."

"Tell me, Estelle . . ."

"The earth is calling us . . ."

"Go on . . ."

THIRTY-ONE

Snow

ONE MORNING the phone rang, very early, it seemed to us. The silence was profound. The noises from the street were sporadic and sounded muffled. We were still sleeping. It was Michael.

"Have you seen it, have you seen it?"

"Seen what?"

"I can't believe it!"

"What, what?"

"No cab for me today!"

Michael's warm voice seemed to erupt in spasms from the phone.

For him a day off from work was extremely rare. Dan listened, but as soon as he hung up he went back to sleep.

A few moments later the phone rang again.

"Hi, it's Kenny, have you seen . . ."

"Yes," said Dan, to cut him short; all he wanted was to go back to sleep.

"No airport for me today so . . ."

"That was Kenny," Dan said to me as he settled back into slumber, "they've sent half their employees home."

Then it was David, the one whose father was an architect and wanted him to be an architect too, and did not at all approve of his studying dance in a derelict studio under the guidance of an eccentric teacher with no immediate likelihood of earning his living.

"So, no dancing for us today, huh, Dan!"

"You bet," said Dan.

Then Djuma (nobody knew exactly what language he spoke or how he lived, nor even whether he was a girl or a boy, but he never missed a lesson, never missed a second of Alwin's presence).

"Okay, Djuma," answered my brother with a wink at me that meant "As usual, didn't understand a thing."

And then Michael again.

By now we were awake. And in a condition to understand that a snowstorm had swooped down during the night, and that the city and a good part of the state were at a standstill.

Winter had been here for weeks already.

In Alwin's studio ice coated the insides of the windows.

Every morning the boiling water bubbling through the studio stove struggled with its hostile sister, the icy water of condensation. It asked and besought her through the intermediary of sopping paper towels to leave, but the icy water held her ground and held the towels in her freezing grip. "Damn it," yelled the disciples of Dance, ready to smash the windows in their just but less than judicious anger. Then wily Alwin spoke: "Leave her alone," he said, and you could not tell exactly what that feminine being he referred to as "her" could be.

I was convinced he meant me, Estelle. For these past months my brother's dancing had made huge strides; it was now better than it had ever been, despite our sleepless nights and outlandish quarrels, as if that sleeplessness and those quarrels had spurred Dan to a great leap forward, as if with that same leap and without even trying he had crossed a barrier that should have withstood him for long months.

"Leave her alone," said Alwin, without raising his voice. The dancers protested, but wily Alwin, diplomatic Alwin knew what he was talking about, for the icy water, once approached and then left alone, always melted of its own volition.

The building no longer had electricity, but once the gray pretwilight hours had passed, candles and storm lanterns offered the color and notion of warmth, the color and notion only, but that was enough. What was more, Alwin made his dancers walk up and down the stairs on tiptoe several times, very lightly so as not to go through the flimsy floorboards, each one with a candlestick in his hand to control body and breathing. Flickering along in the half-light, it made a strange and captivating procession, disappearing at the turns in a fading whisper of dance slippers, then reemerging almost at once, its return preceded in the darkness by the same swelling whisper, a silent bobbing procession with great billows of steam haloing each head and the candlelight flashing capriciously off the dark peeling walls.

The chains that once hoisted the elevator were going through their death throes; they would no longer heave themselves rattling and creaking from floor to floor. Frozen forever in the black mine shaft of a cage, they now had a certain dignity, the dignity of relics, cold, untouchable.

While the group warmed itself by going up and down stairs, I went to study those chains.

"Lazy, dirty kids," Alwin had said. "And selfish too," the chains told me. How long was it since I had written home? I scarcely read my father's letters anymore. They intimidated me, even though my father never reproached me. *"Well, it seems you have decided to take a sabbatical year, as they say over there,"* he wrote. *"You probably needed it and I'm sure you will put it to good use, my dear Estelle. Only don't forget to make your long-term arrangements in advance, whether for here or over there. You know how it is with these things, you mustn't miss the deadline; the doors of the law never change, you can't just stand outside and hope they'll open on their own. I understand that it's too late for this semester at Columbia, but perhaps not for the next one — and then of course there's all the extramural knowledge you're absorbing. After all, young Americans have been doing the European tour for years and years; it's time young Frenchmen and -women did the American version.*

"On the other hand it worries me that you never ask for money. I'm

*sending you this money order on Minor's express instructions; he accuses
me of negligence. He has heard that New York is going through an
unprecedented cold spell and asked me if you even possess such a thing as
a winter coat. 'A coat,' I said, 'well, I imagine she does.' 'Mr. Helleur, do
you know what season this is, and what season it was when your daughter
left?' I dare not choose a coat for you myself, although I had a look in the
stores when I was in Paris the other day; but what is appropriate in one
city is not necessarily appropriate in another. Anyway, dear Estelle, don't
catch pneumonia, and if Dan is lost body and soul to dancing as he seems
to be (and since you probably have to be that way in order to achieve
anything in that field), would you yet again be his big sister and buy
him a garment as per Minor's instructions — but one that meets his, your,
and the city's approval."* He never mentioned my husband Yves, but
he gave me news of home and said he hoped we would come back
for Christmas, particularly for Tiresia's and Nicole's sakes.

In one of the wild stores that proliferated along Canal Street, Dan
and I bought two extravagant but very warm coats, his yellow and
mine purple, padded from top to bottom, and making us look like
Muppets.

We spread them over our bedclothes at night. Between sessions
at the studio Dan wrapped himself in his. And whether idling in the
loft or tramping the streets, I was hardly ever out of mine.

I truly think that without those coats Dan and I would have fallen
ill that winter.

For something was wrong.

Despite Dan's enormous progress, something was wrong.

He had started to disappear for whole nights. When he came back,
he seemed not to know me, not to know Alwin, not to know dancing.
For days on end he refused to go to the studio, remaining supine on
the platform and staring at the TV set we had found in the street
and that for want of an antenna hardly worked. Once the screen
showed a blurred couple making indistinct movements, and Dan said
something. Thinking I had heard a question, I said, "Well, yes." "Yes
what?" said Dan. "Yes, I make love with my husband." "I didn't ask
you anything," he replied. Then Alwin was back with his "Lazy, dirty
kids," but Dan never stirred. When he finally returned to the studio
he seemed to remember nothing, to be starting again from scratch.

With aching heart I watched him drag his body around like a
foreign, almost repugnant object. And Alwin's look at such times,
his scathing, icy look.

Curiously, Alwin resembled Dan at such times. I had seen that look in my brother's eyes several times, whenever we fell into one of our ugly quarrels. Yes, there was a definite resemblance, but it emerged only in their demonic moments: the same demon must have seized hold of them at different moments, and a strange demon it must have been, for it gave them both the look of an untamable Indian, the same arrogant toss of the head to shake aside the same lock that fell across their temples.

But to see it you needed a particular angle, a split second seized on the wing, for Alwin was always cold and reserved, while even when he fell Dan emitted an aura of dazzlement, a halo, I do not know how to express it, a golden light radiating from within, a light that dazzled even him, giving his face the surprised and questioning look it had always had, a light that dazzled — in the most ordinary sense of the word — all those looking at him.

Dan was extraordinarily beautiful and he was in the fullest flower of his youth.

And then his hair was soft with bronze highlights, while Alwin's was stiff and utterly black, like those of the distant Indian ancestor he must stem from. But we knew nothing of Alwin's life, and his resemblance to Dan went unnoticed.

I was learning English and continuing as best I could with the law, attending classes at Columbia Law School. But I merely skimmed our father's letters; I had almost stopped writing; and Poison Ivy's phone calls seemed to drop into the ocean as soon as I received them, to be forgotten almost at once.

In the old ice-fraught building I went to look at the elevator chains.

There was a cathedral hush there, unmarred by the whispering procession of dance slippers in the central stairwell. I stood there, spellbound for reasons mysterious to me, perhaps simply because I did not know where else to go while Alwin marched his company up and down that way.

The studio, abandoned to ghostly, motionless stalactites and stalagmites that vanished sometimes without warning as if at the crack of a suddenly opened grave, frightened me. I could not stay alone in that desert moonscape where all my nerves seemed to dance; I preferred the recess at the end of the entry hall where the black empty mouth of the elevator shaft yawned wide.

I gazed upon it as if on a niche in a chapel, on an altar in church, as if perhaps on something else that did not quite reach the surface of my consciousness, but of course there was nothing inside but the blackened chains rimed here and there with frost. When the dancers' candles went by in the hall, or the well-aimed headlights of a snow-plow pierced the depths of the building, the chains gleamed with swift glints, silver eels that seemed to slide along the links, silver threads on black . . . Was it that which held me, was it my dreadful foreknowledge?

Sometimes things were right.

On the evening of the great snowstorm, my brother burst into the loft, not bothering to shake his big yellow garment, his face radiant.

Mind you, he often wore a radiant expression; on its own it meant nothing — despite the cold we were young and healthy, and the slightest thing could make us radiant. I would not even mention it if the look on his face had been just that. But he was different. Normally, high spirits overlay our distress, settled upon it, so to speak, but the distress stayed buried there and the high spirits, hovering over it as if on stilts, had a distinctly drunken air. But now there were no shakily piled layers of distress on his face, just joy sitting directly on his skin. I saw it at once, and even before he could speak I shouted:

"What is it, Dan?"

"Now you can write to Tiresia," he said in a voice that carried the same simple joy as his face.

"What do you mean?"

Dan never spoke of our past during the day, never mentioned our father or Nicole or Tiresia. It was only at night, after we had dozed a little and then wakened, that we summoned the denizens of our old home: "Do you remember, Dan . . . ?" "No, tell me, Estelle . . ." Every night we spent together the same thing happened on that platform: we fell asleep, then, unfailingly, one of us would wake with a start; if it was me I murmured, "Do you remember, Dan?" and if it was Dan he babbled as if in a dream, "No, tell me, Estelle." And that was enough to wake the other one, and our childhood stole back to lie down between us, seemed literally to lie down between us, taking each of us in its arms, rocking us, soothing us, until we finally fell asleep again . . . to awake the next morning disappointed and sulky at finding only the empty expanse of mattress between us and a great weariness in our limbs, as if after a fall.

*   *   *

"Now you can write to Tiresia, Estelle, and I'll add my own message to Tiresia, and that way Tiresia can give our news to Father and Nicole."

And just the way I did when we were children, understanding nothing of the mysterious negotiations that had led to this assertion, I followed Dan blindly.

You can understand nothing and still be in the light. And I know the reverse of that strange truth: assertions can bear one another up as if in a transparent wave yet nevertheless leave you in the dark. For years with Dan I had known light at the heart of incomprehensible phrases, and for too many months now I had known only darkness in the tight-knit sequence of our exchanges, but now it was light again.

"I have a piano, Estelle, a magnificent grand piano."

Dan was breathless, hardly able to speak.

"But how did you pay — ? What have you done, this is crazy!"

"Come on, Estelle, hurry," he said, already outside and halfway down the first flight of stairs.

"Where to?" I shouted.

His voice came from far below. "Come on!" "Where to, Dan?" I hesitated: should I go back up to get my purple coat and risk losing Dan? He was already at street level, I heard the door opening and getting ready to close. "Dan, wait for me!" and I dived into the stairwell.

Outside, as if it were crouching on the thick snow that covered the sidewalk, stood a huge glossy black piano, its sphinx feet set delicately in the snow, and down the whole length of the street, right down the middle of that inescapable whiteness, were deep, wide tracks like those of a large animal.

It was still snowing, and around the piano four of the company's dancers were breathing hard.

It was they who had called that morning; I knew them all: Michael the cabdriver, Kenny the airport employee, David the professional architecture student, and Djuma. They were not the best dancers, except for Djuma, but the ones I liked best and the ones who often spoke to me.

Dan assiduously brushed away the snowflakes as they settled on the piano; to do so he had to keep moving from one side to the other, stooping and rising (that famous flexibility of the spine), and suddenly we realized he was dancing.

He danced in the white whirlwind fluttering about the black piano, his hair flying wild and bright around his face, and alerted to his beauty the snow rushed in from every quarter of the heavens, and now it was with the snow that he waltzed, with its clouds of downy butterflies that seemed to draw him in some undisclosed direction . . . The four boys instinctively pulled back, I went to stand in their midst, and they clustered around me, their arms like heavy scarves around my shoulders (for in the end I had not gone back upstairs for my purple coat) and our small mesmerized group was as motionless as the cat in the mural or the stately columns on the cast-iron facades.

The snow drew my brother steadily closer to the street lamp. And while flight after flight of lilliputian dancers arose on sparkling wings in its beams, surrounding him, absorbing him into the yellow halo that seemed to absorb our gaze as well, a languorous pelt was spreading, deepening, swelling on the motionless piano.

"Dan, where's the piano?" one of our group suddenly shouted.

His shout of real fright sobered us all.

Indeed, the piano had disappeared. The street already lay under a fresh layer of virgin snow, and the piano was no longer distinguishable from the other soft humped forms barely visible in the vast white darkness.

Had it not been for its black legs still to be seen above the sidewalk, the piano's ghostly mask might just as well have veiled a car, a cluster of garbage cans, or a mound of the miscellaneous odds and ends you find in all the old streets of SoHo.

(A memory crossed my mind: a bunch of black flowers we thought we had seen in Alwin's hands one day, but he had immediately turned his back on us and stuffed them into the trash can.)

We shook ourselves awake and set to work, because now we had to get this preposterous object upstairs. My brother and his friends had already lugged it down several streets by brute force and with the help of cunning stratagems they tried to describe to me as they puffed up the stairs, but I was not listening because I was assailed by the memory of a scene that was familiar yet different, its poles reversed. I had no idea what it was, and was concerned for Dan, who bore up the rear leg in such a posture that I felt he was carrying the whole enormous weight of the piano.

"Are you okay, Dan?" I asked, stooping to catch a glimpse of him beneath the piano carcass.

"Yes, fine, keep on guiding us," he said, sticking his face out a little to let me see his delighted expression.

Luckily for the piano and unluckily for its bearers, there was no bend to negotiate: the flights succeeded each other at rigid 180-degree angles at each floor, which made it a steep but straight climb.

"Keep on guiding us, Estelle," my brother called out delightedly.

For my task was to show the more or less blind porters the way. I moved up ahead of them, trying to protect the stair rail and the paint in the stairwell, and watching where people were putting their feet. Dan was at the lower end, bent double, one hand supporting the piano's rear leg . . . And suddenly I recognized the memory that burdened my forehead and caused me to stoop every two or three steps to look at Dan bent beneath that excessive weight (yet a weight he bore without apparent effort, as if in a trance, with that smile edged with the merest hint of strain) . . .

It had been years ago, in the meadow of the Helleur house. I climbed the grassy bank with a massive wooden ladder on my back and Dan hopped around me, guiding me ("Like a pilot fish, Estelle"), adjusting the ladder's trajectory, calling out the number of yards still to go.

We had to take the ladder from the apple tree in the middle of the meadow to the foot of the lean-to behind the house; our objective was the little door Dan had spotted above the lean-to's tin roof, and that little door opened into the secluded attic that would be our refuge for years. It was I, a little girl of nine or ten, who bore the ladder. It cut into my shoulder; carrying it was beyond a child's power; but by the grace of my little brother, bobbing about before my eyes, I had carried it.

And now I was the one guiding him, and he was carrying the massive cumbersome thing we needed, and carrying it as if by some mysterious grace.

At the end of that unforgiving climb the dancers set the piano down on the landing under the skylight with triumphant grunts and gathered around Dan, who was the last to straighten up. He took off his big yellow coat and his sweaters, which had made him hot but had served as padding against the hard wood of the piano. The others, likewise divesting themselves, all oohed and aahed at Dan's physique, walked around him, laughingly feeling his biceps and following the rivulets of sweat down the long slender muscles beneath the matte skin. "Say, Dan, I didn't think you were this strong, you should go in for kick boxing," said one. "Or karate," said another. And they pushed him around playfully, assuming attack postures, and my brother responded. Then they were all prowling around him again, feeling his muscles, and finally my brother leapt in a barefoot half-split onto the piano, arms spread wide aloft. "Okay," he said, "admire me! And hold me up too," he added, "this piano is slippery." At once he was borne up from all sides, one dancer for each foot and the two others behind him holding his waist and the base of his arms, as if he were a statue held up for public admiration, although I was the only public there, since I was the only one not taking part in the work. My brother rose up, like a statue borne aloft only for me, and although I had known my brother's body since birth I lowered my eyes, for this time too I was unable to look at him. I see it clearly now: throughout that stay in New York, when Dan's almost naked body was constantly before my eyes — a body in which everything existed but to extol that nakedness, to embellish and strengthen it, to achieve the full power and grace of its maleness — I had not seen it.

Suddenly Djuma spoke. The blurred sounds he made conveyed a most equivocal message (which was why Alwin called him the oracle). But we were struck.

"We're making Estelle uncomfortable, I think," one of the dancers, Michael, translated. Michael loved me in his fashion, I believe.

Every now and then I find myself thinking that one day this story will come out, and that it will in part be thanks to you. I believe that you are standing ready somewhere, in the street outside, perhaps, that you are waiting patiently for this beast to emerge from me, that when it does emerge for you in the street outside it will be just an ordinary animal, one of those thousands of dogs you see following their noses along the sidewalks, an animal you can tame in short order. And then my apartment will be empty, and peaceful, and I will be able to settle into it to read or to watch those television programs that look so interesting and that sometimes tempt me so strongly.

(Or travel with Phil. He is away for a few weeks, madame, on a site where they plan to build a bridge. If he had been here, I might not have accepted Adrien's invitation . . .)

I am opening my heart and soul to you, madame. You must be well aware how naive and coarse and ill-bred that "heart and soul" is. Oh, how surprised people would be to find just how naive and coarse and ill-bred the hearts and souls of even the greatest of us can be! Yet that is what they build on. You too, I am sure, otherwise . . . But I know very well what kind of ground one builds on, dirty mud and a yearning as old as the world itself, formless and muddy, twisting and wriggling in its depths like a beautiful devil . . .

If I could not talk to you from time to time, madame, I could not survive . . .

"We're making Estelle uncomfortable," Michael said.

"Well, no wonder," said Kenny, as if it were his discovery.

"I would be too, in her place," said David, ever ready to put himself in someone else's place.

"We must look pretty stupid," Djuma may have added.

As I said, those four were my friends.

The group at once broke up, the piano was manhandled into the loft, and a little later that evening a friend of Michael's came in to tune it, a friend of his or his stepbrother or his stepfather.

One of my major difficulties in the alien tongue was the vocabulary of family relationships. The words were simply unrecognizable to me. Perhaps the fault lay in American pronunciation.

I found it impossible to establish a safe bridge between American "daughter" and French *fille*. Sometimes I heard "water," sometimes *auteur*, sometimes even "doughnut" (we consumed quantities of them, to us they served as food and consolation). Outlandish transferals could occur at any time and in unpredictable ways, there was the rub. Once I even heard "not for her" or "not her" instead of "daughter," and there was at once such a violent upheaval within me that I had one of those spectacular attacks of dizziness, *impossible to describe to you, madame,* except that everything went black and white together and I had to get off a bus between stops. I remember the concern and kindness of the driver, but who was the one who was talking to me about a "daughter"? For the moment I cannot tell; could it be that I said the word to myself in my own head, with the deliberate aim of mishearing, *oh, how I need your help . . .*

I was equally helpless with the English word "brother," in which I never managed to hear the real meaning but all sorts of other things, in particular "other."

For a long time I thought that people speaking to me about Dan were saying "your other," and I found that normal. *I found it normal, madame, you see what a state I was in . . .*

Once someone (it was Alwin, surely) said to me, "Your brother called," and I heard "Your other cold," and it seemed quite reasonable for Alwin to be saying this strange thing to me. It effortlessly entered my soul, which was at once burning hot and cold; that was how I explained such strange misunderstandings to myself, for I was a student, I had already earned degrees, I had learned a lot of Russian without the slightest difficulty from Doctor Minor, our father knew Latin and at table liked to play "veni vidi vici" with us, as we called it, and worse than all the rest, our father was English . . . But language is not an inherited given, and apart from the one word "awe" he had taught us (we had retained it with no trouble because we thought it was the exclamation "oh," pronounced differently, of course, given the language difference, and that "oh" seemed to us to be in perfect harmony with his explanation), apart from that "awe," our father never spoke English to us. "Too close to German," he once said to us; it had sounded like just one more enigmatic remark among all the other remarks that seemed almost to escort him, like an invisible guard brigade.

And although like most children we were greedy for explanations, we never sought them for these enigmatic remarks. They were his personal bodyguard and they held us at bay. We did not even want to question our father, never considered it. I believe we would have thought it ill-mannered.

And yet, madame, we should have. ". . . English . . . too close . . . German . . ." We needed to hear those words as if we had read them, we needed to read them as if they had been written on an SOS message, and to imagine great spaces between the words eaten away by salt, erased by time. We needed to imagine that the salt was the salt of ancient tears, and in that all-erasing time lay our father's fear, his anguish, his pathos, his heartbreaking striving, and also his hope. And then we needed to start deciphering.

But we were not up to it, madame, and fate made us pay dearly.

THIRTY-TWO

Parish Piano

THE PIANO sat in the loft, tuned by Michael's friend . . . or by his stepbrother or stepfather.

The sound was not so full and rich as the notes of Tiresia's piano, but it served its purpose, and we were enormously pleased. Nor did we really try to understand what the "purpose" it served so well might be.

"Well, now, what will you do with it?" said Michael, who seemed not to believe we really wanted to play it.

Michael drove a taxi part of the day and at night, but he attended the studio regularly in the evenings and was certainly Alwin's most malleable student.

He was utterly devoted to Alwin's cause. But he was just as loyal to the company (which sometimes caused conflicts that tormented him and amused us), to the building (which he would willingly have rebuilt with his own hands), and to the elevator (which he wanted to show to another friend or stepfather or stepbrother, this one an automobile mechanic, who he believed was sure to make the necessary repairs).

Michael reminded me a little of Alex Bonneville back home.

"So what's it for?" he said, as if we were discussing a decorative object or a household appliance.

"It's so we can write to Tiresia," my brother answered, without malice, I believe.

"And who's Tiresia?"

"Somebody back home."

Michael nodded, perhaps deciding that we needed a big writing desk and that the piano's smooth surface seemed to answer our needs.

Everyone knows that in the Old World they love the art of letter writing; perhaps the new computer paper has revived their liking for parchment scrolls that have to be unrolled; and of course everyone knows that SoHo-dwellers have certain peculiar customs, one of them being to use objects for purposes other than those originally intended. Someone had recently transformed several refrigerators into bar stools (painted and upholstered but still uncomfortable), had arranged them around a fine wide deep-pile carpet, the idea being to dramatize the icy incarceration of the individual when isolated, and then await the moment when the guests — the individuals in question — abandoned their glacial seats to slide down to the warmth of the carpet and be with the others. "To get stoned, of course," said Michael with a certain contempt, for you had to be rich to realize such fantasies, and he was just a cabdriver. Someone else had converted a vintage Duesenberg into a small private living room with all the conveniences: television, leather armchairs, rug, and even curtains to shut out the rest of the room in which the sleek antique held pride of place. An aquarium could serve as a bathtub and a bathtub serve as a bed. Why shouldn't a piano serve as a writing desk?

So Michael had spent a whole evening struggling to shift a heavy wooden carcass for a pair of eccentric friends who needed only its flat smooth top. And yet, even though a store in nearby Canal Street sold perfectly good boards and trestles, he had not objected. He trusted us, he was wholly devoted to our cause as well — whatever it might be.

In any case, he accepted our explanation: thanks to the piano, we would be able to write to this "Tiresia back home." He had no need to understand why; the important thing was that this incongruous explanation be right for us, and we looked so happy that it had to be right.

So he too was happy, and had no wish to ask questions.

"Now, since weather conditions have temporarily immobilized my cab — ," he said to us.

As soon as he started to talk about his taxi he fell unconsciously into formal jargon shot through with expressions that seemed weighty or important to him; we believed it was to scare away devils. Alex did the same thing when he talked soccer; he too must have feared certain devils, the kind that look with jaundiced eye on the muscles and joints of athletes and lurk in stadiums for the chance to pounce on their prey.

So with his cab immobilized, Michael was not working that evening. Long after the others had left, and after many beers, he left on foot with his friend or stepfather or stepbrother the piano tuner, the two of them singing the Doors song "The End" at the top of their voices.

Michael's words winged up through the snow-laden air, and the snow penetrated and transformed them so that what reached us was something different, the confused words of a ghostly voice that had found its way back to this world through the flaky turbulence of the snowfall . . . And then the ghostly echo was lost forever, and Dan in three strides was at the piano.

"So what do you think of my find, Estelle?"

His find was a very middling sort of piano, and only a baby grand at that, despite what my brother had yelled in his excitement. Its tone was accurate, but tight and a little metallic. My brother had learned that the little church near Alwin's studio wanted to get rid of its piano because it had received a gift of another, a real grand, and brand-new.

The priest wanted nothing for the old one. He simply wanted it taken away. He did not want to be saddled with moving expenses. But he was anxious to find a satisfactory owner for the old piano, of which he must have been very fond. Many people did the same sort of thing with their old car, not wanting to "dump" it on just anyone, said Michael, whose only source of references and guidelines was the world of cars, a world so rich and so seemingly inexhaustible that he had turned it into a vast parable of man's destiny. We often told him that he should become a preacher, that he would be the ideal preacher of the automobile civilization, that sermons built around a badly inflated tire would be more effective than those built around an ear of wheat or a fish, that since the age of priests and fishers of souls was dead he should put God's word on wheels in order to become the first person in history to give rides to hitchhiking souls.

And Michael, simple but shrewd, would question us sadly: "You think I'm wasting my time trying to dance?" We at once answered, "No, Michael, it was a joke," but Michael did not understand joking; joking must have been another kind of devil for him, and he had a superstitious fear of devils, to which he always referred in the plural. "I had devils in my oil filter this morning," he might say on arriving at the studio.

Indeed, he believed the whole world was prey to devils. With one exception: devils stopped at the studio door, scared off beyond a doubt by Alwin, which probably accounted for Michael's consubstantial gratitude for him.

Michael had gone off in the snow, and we had no thought either of Alwin or of devils or of death.

"The priest was so glad it was for us, Estelle! He thought we wanted the piano for Alwin's studio, as a musical accompaniment (the poor old guy had no idea what Alwin thinks about that!), and he gave me a long sermon about art going hand in hand with religion or vice versa, and how happy he would be to think his piano was serving beauty. And then he suggested that perhaps we could come around and put on a 'little dance number' for his charity fete; he said it would be much better than the cakes his parishioners always baked and how ill they made him . . . I couldn't make out whether he meant the cakes or the parishioners."

"Alwin would never —"

"You're wrong, Estelle, I'm sure Alwin would dance for his charity do. Alwin believes you can dance anywhere and for anyone."

"So that's why he practices the world's most uncommercial brand of dancing!"

Dan was too excited to be deflated by sarcasm.

"He thinks it's the others who do complicated things, you know, what he calls reference elephants."

In fact, I had already heard that expression, reference elephants, without even wondering what it meant. But I did not want to be sidetracked onto Alwin.

"So you're going to dance in the Baptist Church?"

"Michael said yes at once, as if the minister were doing him a personal favor. Jabbing him in the back did no good, he didn't get it: 'Careful, careful, Michael,' but he went on, 'Sure, Mr. Clergyman, how nice, Mr. Clergyman,' there was no stopping him. He must have rhinoceros hide; he didn't feel a thing even though I was jabbing like mad."

"But Dan, you know Michael has only one convoy for transporting his ideas; if he dispatches it out to his lips there's no way he can send it to his back."

"How did you think that one up?" said Dan, with the surprise of one who has sought long and unavailingly for the solution to a problem, who is suddenly presented with it, and who finds it to be very simple.

"Michael is like Alex Bonneville, that's all."

"Right," said Dan, more impressed than ever. "I wouldn't have thought of that."

"Oh, come on, it's the analogy, the old Miss Marple trick. You remember, in the mysteries I used to read you in the attic. Anyway, what happened, did you disabuse the minister?"

"That wasn't the point, Estelle."

"Well, do you want to dance for him or don't you?"

"It was the piano's destination we had to lie about, the rest will follow naturally. I mean that if the piano is not going to Alwin's studio the minister no longer has a real reason for asking us to put on a dance number, as he calls it, for his fete. Mind you, perhaps it will come off, certainly even, but let's say that he will no longer have any means of psychological pressure and that he'll be under an obligation to us."

"What difference does that make?"

"A big difference, Estelle. It means we'll dance exactly what we want to dance, as we want to. He won't be able to force anything on us."

"In any case, that's how Alwin always operates, isn't it? What he wants and only what he wants. I can't imagine him modifying a single step to please a minister or anyone else . . . apart from his precious composers."

"Yes, but now it'll be a foregone conclusion, no need to fight, and for us it will be all profit because it'll put Alwin in a good mood."

And we collapsed into laughter. Whether icy or scalding, Alwin's bad moods terrorized us. But right now, with the two of us here together and Alwin with his musician friends upstate, waiting for the studio's stalactites and stalagmites to disappear, the thought of those moods set us howling.

I cannot tear myself away from that conversation. I wish I could report it in its every detail. I wish I could replay it indefinitely, be in it still — not for its content, which was trivial enough, the small change of our short life in New York, but precisely because of that triviality, for it would mean there was still someone with me to carry that triviality, to give it the inner flame that it possessed and that gave every word such a brilliant glow.

At that time, because of Poison Ivy and because of my own stupidity and lack of experience, I held only serious conversations in high regard. In fact it was through Yves that I had had the opportunity of undergoing ("taking part in" would be too strong a term) such exchanges, at social gatherings with one of his law professors, who later joined the government. And of course through Alwin and his followers.

But if I had to choose now from among all the conversations that have found a foothold in my memory, I would choose the trivial a thousand times over, for the others stand up alone, but the trivial ones need the support of love.

But without you, madame, it would amount to nothing, for conveying the leaps, the burning questions, the passionate voices that we brought to it all is beyond me. Oh, how I loved that disinterested yet just a shade wily minister, and trusting Michael, and the parishioners with their baked charitable offerings, and that orphaned piano, and that other, newer piano in the church, which might one day accompany "this little number by our dear neighbors, the dance company down the street, come to offer their art to God and to you good people, just as you have offered to God these excellent cakes for our charities and for the development of our church . . ." And in that moment I still did not know it was love that fed our joy in exchanging every detail and every variation of detail in everything that happened around us.

I was happy about the piano, worried that agility was slow in returning to my fingers, haunted by Djuma's oracular voice, and stirred by the statuary that in the space of a few moments had flowered and faded beneath the skylight on our landing. I was reassured by Michael's kindness, excited by the scale of the snowfall, and stirred all over again by Dan's dance with those white downy butterflies under the milky light of the street lamp. And also tired by the hour, already late, and too agitated to think of rest: at one moment the phone rang repeatedly, and in the midst of this whirlwind we had no intention of picking it up; it rang and rang, and we paid it no more heed than we would a siren in the street, but I did not know that all this and even that extraordinary negligence was love. And Dan did not know either.

Had someone at once explained it to us, within seconds of its happening, we would still have denied it. But we would know one day, in the long run we would know . . .

And now Dan and I were alone in the loft. The piano served its purpose, that was certain, for we went on being joyful, and we believed this whole business was indeed what we had told Michael it was. The business of this piano was to make us write to Tiresia. But we did not write to Tiresia.

We drank piping-hot coffee while outside it went on snowing. We heard on TV that flights had been delayed or forced to land in Washington; that upstate New York was still stricken, that helicopters were overflying the highways to pick up people in distress; we were spellbound, and we talked and talked.

"Well, Alwin's not about to return soon," said Dan.

"You remember Sara . . ."

"Sara, the girl from Canada?"

"Yes, that story she told about being snowbound on the highway and rescued by a helicopter . . ."

"Taken to spend the night in a church . . ."

"We thought it was to impress us . . ."

"But apparently it was true . . ."

"We should write and apologize . . ."

"Dear Cousin Sara, a few years ago in the Helleur home a fallacious charge was leveled at you. You were convicted of advanced mythomania. Blah blah blah, with our deepest apologies."

"Better not."

"Why not?"

"No apologies for her."

"Why?"

"Don't you remember what she used to say?"

"What?"

"That we were all crazy, starting with you and me."

"When did she say that?"

"When we kissed the garden under the full moon."

"We kissed the garden . . ."

"We were covered with dirt and scratches."

"We were a bit crazy, though, weren't we?"

"And also when you danced on the lawn."

"Estelle?"

"What?"

"Play me that tune."

"Which tune?"

"Nicole's."

"But why?"

"I want to dance."

"To Nicole's music?"

"Yes, don't look so scared, Alwin's not here."

"I'm not scared of Alwin."

"Go on, then."

I could no longer play. I fumbled at the old piano, and Dan fumbled about the loft, stopping every time I played a false note. Then little by little the sixteen famous bars of Ravel's *Bolero* took shape again, Dan rediscovered his movements, and there came a series of false notes like eddies in a stream. Dan waited patiently; a few bars took shape and as if I were going back in time I followed them . . . playing the passages for piano from a piece of music we had so often heard when Dan was tiny, with Tiresia at the piano, our father on the violin and Minor on the cello, Schubert's Trio in B-flat Major, op. 100.

Suddenly my brother came behind me, took me by the shoulders, and kissed me: "Oh, Estelle, I feel something beneath my feet, it's been so long, so long since I felt it, play, Estelle, play."

In the whole of my time in New York it was the first time he had kissed me. I began to improvise, and suddenly we were indeed writing our letter to Tiresia. And I swear that it was not my fingers playing, that would have been impossible: I had not played for years, not since I had left the Helleur house, not since my marriage, yet my fingers raced over the keys, left behind them the hackneyed *Bolero* we had heard churned out in the blue garage on Nicole's record player so often that it had become something else, turned into Nicole's music . . . They left behind them the Schubert fragments so intimately linked in my mind to the three familiar figures in our living room that they too had changed into something other than themselves (and I even reproduced the mistakes Minor used to make on his cello, mistakes that over time had to my mind become more or less integral parts of the piece).

My hands left behind them the worn-out music of the Helleur home, and sought other, unknown pieces that belonged more intimately to my brother and to me, series of notes that were our own private places at home, the attic, the meadow, the ditch, the cave, the pond, the lawn, Dan's dance on the lawn. I played unhesitatingly, miraculously. It was my love but it could not have been my fingers; they were Tiresia's, ask not how, I know such things can happen but not how they happen.

They were the fingers of a woman who before presiding over our childhood with veiled face in our provincial Helleur home had been a young pianist celebrated and in demand everywhere. And this was her way of thanking us for the idea we had hit on, thanking us for this old piano Dan had brought so that I might write to her. She was responding from the other side of the ocean by making it miraculously vibrate, addressing us with a kind of presentiment, in a last burst of strength, in an irresistible explosion of her talent. And Dan too must have sensed this unexpected power in my music, for he was dancing as he never danced for Alwin. Oh, I know very well that Alwin's technique lay behind his movements, Alwin's genius; the technique endured. But that genius had melted away before a more powerful genius, the genius of my brother Dan, who was dancing our love for the very last time.

THIRTY-THREE

Poison Ivy

I PLAYED; I played and Dan danced. There was a noise at the door. We failed to hear it.

It bothered us; it was a noise that belonged neither to the night nor the snow. Those old hounds of our minds, without our knowledge, sniffed at the crack under the door, emitting rumbling growls to drive it off, while I went on playing and Dan went on dancing.

On nights when I cannot sleep, madame, and in daytime too on the street, when fear foundering with all hands in the depths of the crowd overcomes me, I try to describe that night's dance to myself so that I will be ready when my brother's day of celebration comes, so that I will always keep that day of celebration in view.

But there is no picture in my memory.

All I have is an abstract and imperious urge, if such a thing is possible, an urge that is all in my head . . . not something I am yet ready to hang words or music on. But madame, on the day I have a stage and dancers and a choreographer before me, I will need only to follow that urge for the choreographer spontaneously to perceive it and to see the figures moving; and the dancer too will feel it; it will flow like sap through his muscles, and then I will recognize my brother Dan.

The piano had ended up in the center of the loft, on that great empty bare floor, almost out of reach of the light from the lamp that stood at platform height by the windows.

We were in a half-light, made gentle and intimate by the velvety silence outside and the scalloped snow heaped on the windowsills.

I experimented with sounds, my eyes wandering from the keys to my brother.

He stood there, listening, positioning his body, his eyes on me, expectant. I saw how he had placed his body and at once my eyes returned to the keys and my fingers set a sequence in motion. I raised my eyes again; my brother had stretched out an arm; I had guessed right; my heart leapt. My fingers flung the melody in another direction and my brother had already moved in that same direction, his body poised to leap. My fingers paused briefly on the last chord, then repeated it strongly, as if to offer a springboard, as if to galvanize the dancer, and suddenly we plunged together into the unknown and a waterfall of notes and movements bubbled forth . . .

I played on the light bank of the keyboard, sensing rather than seeing the supple form in the quiet gloom.

We slowed, hesitated. I watched for his every move and he for mine. Dance and music brushed each other and separated and then drifted together again. Gently, slowly, almost fitfully, we established a cautious understanding, mutually attentive, utterly serious, utterly focused, prolonging lengthy movements that led nowhere, just to rest, just for tranquillity, then we branched anew into exploratory movement and suddenly a rhythm was born, a rhythm we were helpless to resist, bubbling up like uncontrollable laughter: a tornado of sounds whirled Dan away, and I felt the precise moment when that tornado blew itself out, the moment when my brother's lungs were ready to burst.

But there are other ways I could say all this, for instance, that my brother's body sensed the precise moment when the tornado blew itself out, the precise moment when my own strength came to an end.

And the two of us moved inshore to a quieter sound — isolated sounds for isolated movements, the dying echo of the tornado — and at last Dan collapsed beside me, laying his head on my knees while I let my fingers wander over the piano's keys.

"Oh, Estelle," he gasped. "Oh!"

In response, but softly, as if I were merely quoting, I repeated a few of the pieces we had just improvised. They came back to me unbidden.

"Yes," said Dan, "that was so good, that one, no, not that one, that was too fast."

I am not sure he really spoke; his arms were around my waist; he communicated with me through physical pressure, and I fully understood him. It was as if we were retracing the path we had earlier followed, minutely dissecting things only we could understand; and on the morrow, when we began again, the work of our minds and bodies would be stronger and richer. In that moment it seemed obvious: it was for that morrow, for all the morrows to come, that

we returned to the dance we had enacted, for the first time, for the
last time, in wonderment and discovery, together.

We finally took note of the noise at the door. We took note of it
because of the changing light.

From the glass roof of the landing, which extended over that end
of the loft, a wan light bathed us, banishing the cocooned glow of
the snow, the gentle and intimate half-light in which we had created
our dance.

"Got to change that bulb," muttered Dan, thinking no doubt of
the naked bulb that so harshly lit the landing and stairwell.

Someone was knocking; we heard it clearly now.

"Alwin," I said.

"The exterminator," said Dan.

But we did not get up. And at that very moment, the black rectangle of the doorway turned to livid light and we saw a human being
outlined in the threshold.

Despite the fears of New Yorkers and the warnings we endlessly
received, my brother and I never locked the loft door.

"Real *provinciaux*," said Alwin contemptuously.

He always said *provinciaux* in French. It was a word he never tired
of using, apparently the only word of our language he knew, and
when he uttered it he did so with very particular spitefulness. I never
wondered how he came to know the word or why it was the only
one he used, why he always injected it with the same emotional
charge, or what pleasure he derived from that bitter emotion that
seemed to make his stomach writhe.

Once we heard him chewing over a succession of unintelligible
sounds. We registered that succession of sounds, we chewed it over,
and as so often happened, we were able after the event to decipher
the litany.

It was: *une provinciale des provinciales, un provincial des provinciaux*
(a provincial woman among provincial women, a provincial man
among provincial men).

Alwin appeared to know nothing else of our language, apart from
a few technical dance terms he pronounced in exaggeratedly American fashion. There too I never wondered why. Most of the dancers
in the company pronounced them better than he did; they at least
made an effort in the direction of the original tongue, a sort of
acknowledgment embodied in the muscles of their vocal apparatus,

but Alwin made an effort in the opposite direction. It was as if he sought to leach every last French sound away from those linguistic tools. I felt that he was ripping the nerves out of living words and turning them into puppets pliant to his will. Oh, it angered me; I felt that anger rise in me, but I did not wonder where it came from. I wondered about nothing — why should I have wondered about that?

The demon who held us did his job well: the threads we might have followed trailed in all directions, yet we did not pick up a single one.

And now I clearly see what I am doing. I move aside, turn away from that dark outline in the livid frame of the doorway, my stomach tightens and I am afraid. I could easily start to mutter like Alwin, I could say *un parisien des parisiens, une parisienne des parisiennes* (a Parisian among Parisians, a Parisienne among Parisiennes), yes, you, Mr. Parisian, go back to your neighborhoods coiled tight as snail shells, hide under them, go crawling wherever you want in your own country — but not here, with your Austrian loden and your Scottish muffler and your English shoes and your suitcase with brass fittings (all of them fake, incidentally) . . . yes, poor young Yves, beware, for we are going to drag you down into that most poisonous ivy, into the venom-laden sumac, and it will consume us all; go back, go quickly, leave us.

Our visitor entered, and our beautiful moment of respite shut in upon itself with a metallic click, the click of the door Yves shut behind him when we failed to make a move.

The time switch went off in the stairwell, darkening the loft skylight, and a second metallic sound attached itself like a link to the first: the brass corners of the suitcase coming into contact with the floor and its handle toppling to one side with a click.

My fingers were still on the keys. Dan's arms were still on my knees. We stared at the door. I think we were unable to believe in such treachery from a door we always left unlocked. So Alwin was right, you could trust nothing in New York; yes, I believe that is what we were thinking: we were irritated. Our minds were slow, dull.

The snow fell thickly, pattering against the windows. No, it was quite impossible for anyone to have reached here in such weather. I believe we were ready to fall asleep on our feet, our heads were

full of snow, and in that cocooned drowsiness there was no place for
a wayfarer.

My brother was in dance tights, bare-chested, still gleaming with
sweat. I wore the floppy outsize T-shirt he used between exercises,
with the outlandish purple coat thrown across it.

I had been hot from helping move the piano and had undressed.
Then we had launched together into our ballet and I had gotten cold
sitting on the piano stool, and from habit I had simply grabbed that
garment that was always so eager to help, to do service as blanket,
tent, and stole . . .

Why am I passing on all this foolishness and all these details, madame?
There must be a reason, and if I do not believe in that reason, then
everything I tell you is foolishness and details. I must learn to believe . . .

I sometimes think of that husband I so briefly possessed, madame.
Perhaps because of Phil. I am starting to see him in his own light,
as a hardworking and perhaps stubborn young man. His parents
worked at the Les Halles market, his studies were financed by schol-
arships, and he took the civil service entrance exam to the Ecole
Nationale d'Administration — unsuccessfully. "Too many rough
edges," he said without bitterness, then passed the entrance exam
to the civil service school in Lille — "a notch lower on the scale,"
he said, "but give me time." Then he joined the public health faculty
in Rouen, aiming to become part of the social services inspectorate.
After that I lost sight of him. Adrien told me he was working as an
adviser to a member of the government, that he had appeared on
television. I never watch television and listen to little of what Adrien
says, but on that occasion I must have listened.

I had been touched by Yves' simplicity, the modest way his ambition expressed itself. He went exactly where his intelligence led
him, without commotion, without a single superfluous step: it moved
swift and straight. He helped me through the thickets of my law
manuals, almost harshly, never making allowances, but once our work
session was over he wanted to talk to me of my father's work, and
also about Schubert, which bothered me. What Yves wanted was
specific references; he wanted to create for himself a kind of ceremonial uniform for the world toward which his intelligence and hard
work were leading him. Only it did not fit him, and I withdrew.

He would have liked me to play the piano for him, liked us to
have a piano in our home, but I could not play for him and the idea
of a piano in our student roost revolted me.

We had scarcely had time to know each other, but to put our marriage in a nutshell for you, madame, I could say that Yves prowled around me as if around a shell in which he thought he had glimpsed a bright light, something he coveted. But the shell remained sealed, becoming more and more impregnable at each of his attempts, we did not even have time to begin to fight.

Perhaps we might never have fought, perhaps there was more to him than I sensed. He was young, halfway between Dan and me in age; I had been a slow student and he a fast one; he was still happy, and making love gave him wings, whereas it exhausted me. I lay in bed afterward as if stupefied. "Estelle, I'll have to earn a lot of money so you can hang around in bed," he used to say, quite without bitterness. I found it nice. As I have said, my thoughts in those days went nowhere; they slumbered inside me.

On the phone I had told him that I was studying English, that it would be useful, that the classes at Columbia were interesting. It reassured him: there was no need to be cunning, my mind hit on the exact words he needed to hear and my voice uttered them; I had no part in it.

And now there he stood in the doorway of our loft. Madame, I am telling you all this even though it cannot be part of an opera, for I finally saw through Yves' eyes something I had not seen earlier, and I want you too to see it, madame. For what Yves saw must assuredly go into the opera. Here is what I saw through Yves' eyes, and here is how our destiny lurched from one step to the next in its hellish downward fall.

What Yves saw was a half-light enclosed in a soft glow, nestling in the silence in the snow, and at the heart of that half-light he saw a big gleaming piano, and Estelle in a white T-shirt with her hands on the keys, still playing, perhaps, as she had never agreed to play for him . . . And at Estelle's feet a young man he did not know, of heart-rending beauty, torso bare, sweat and exhaustion further enhancing the beauty of his face and body, his arms on Estelle's knees, and both of them turning to stare in his direction, not moving, not looking at him, against the purple backcloth of a fabric that seemed to isolate and protect them.

Such must have been the sight that met Yves' eyes.

He had flown in on an angry impulse and had landed in Washington, where he must have taken a train. No one had answered his phone calls, nor had anyone answered the door even though he could hear a piano playing. At last he had turned the door handle, and that was the sight that had met his eyes: the sight that was to hasten our fall and awaken death, which had awaited us so long.

Almost at once, it seems, I see us walking through snow already turning dirty, it was late evening, the wind blew down the icy canyons of the streets, huge gouts of steam billowed up from the underground pipes.

"What's that?" asked Yves. "It's hell," answered Dan. "Where are we going?" said Yves. "Ask Estelle," said Dan. "Where are we going, Estelle?" "I don't know, Yves" —

I did not know where we were going, at times we walked abreast, at times in single file, I sweated and shivered in my thick purple tent, Dan moved forward in his yellow carapace like a submarine through the black air, Yves pulled his loden coat around him against the ceaseless tugging of the wind, his face screwed up against the cold, wrinkled as a mummy's —

Then we were walking down by the Hudson, with big ice floes jostling one another on its surface, the ice meeting with a jarring crunch that set your teeth on edge, on the sidewalk invisible strips of frozen earth had escaped the salt, Yves slipped in his leather-soled English shoes, steadying himself against the low wall, his woolen gloves sticking to the ice, the wind still tugging tirelessly at his coat —

The wind raced like a madman down the street, I had no idea why we had come so far uptown, we were already at West 116th Street, perhaps Yves had asked to see Columbia University, to make sure I really was taking classes there, I do not recall —

"Let's take the bus, Dan." "Not a chance," said Dan. "Why on earth not?" "Yves wants to sightsee so we'll sightsee." He was no longer my brother Dan, he was the other, the one I had met at the airport six months earlier, the one at whose side I had waited for a nonexistent suitcase in the wasteland of the baggage-claim area, the one who looked so dreadfully like my brother, we were right back where we had started —

"Enough sightseeing for one day," said Yves, essaying a smile at once obliterated by the wind. "You haven't seen anything yet," said Dan. "Well, show me, then," said Yves. "I'll show you," said Dan, and my rage fed on theirs, I felt that it was too late now, too late for a bus or subway or taxi, the wind buffeted us along on legs that walked by themselves, we fell into step like three soldiers forging straight ahead toward their obscure and precise soldier's goal —

We had walked back down a goodly stretch of the city when we came to a vacant lot. Dan straddled the sagging fence and we followed him along a pier, with water slapping a few yards away, there was less ice on the river here, probably because of the proximity of a fairly big ship, rusted and lifeless-looking, but this was probably misleading, for a red light flickered at water level, my brother pointed it out, the pier was deserted, black and creaking —

"It's an abandoned port," said Yves, as if his thin lips were chiseling the words from a block of ice. "Abandoned by God, not men," said Dan, he laughed foolishly, here was my brother, pure intelligence when he danced, laughing foolishly. "Are we going to board this ship?" I said. "Is it a nightclub?" said Yves. "It is the lower depths," said my brother. "The lower depths, interesting," said Yves.

The closer we got to the end of the jetty, the more distorted and the stupider our speech became, I was suddenly afraid I was in a nightmare with our mother, was this what awakened Nicole night after night, this progress in a cloud of stupid remarks toward the black water? "It's a nightmare," I shouted. "No," said Yves, "we're going to dance," that word stung me like a slap, I saw the shape of a skull behind Yves' cold-distorted features, he tried to touch my shoulder, I shook him off with a nervous start, to regain his balance he clutched at Dan and the two of them tottered for a second on the frozen edge of the pier, they did not fall, but I knew, I knew beyond any shadow of doubt that death was waiting, whether here or a little bit farther on, I knew that all three of us knew it, but our knowledge was shut up tight inside each one of us.

We were in a dreadful state, we felt hunted without the consolation of being able to acknowledge it to each other, my bones rattled together in terror, Yves too was terrified, I read panic in his body, he had been told that in New York crime was everywhere, motiveless crime, he was prepared for it and unafraid of it, but here something else was attacking him, he felt cornered, with his back held flat against the wall, but he had no idea by whom or where the wall was, my brother too was afraid, my brother was so perceptive, he sensed that we were falling faster and faster into a deep cauldron, but he had nothing to grab to slow our fall, and worse, he felt that the weight dragging us down was inside him, but he did not understand why, his eyes were hopeless, oh, how unbearable that look in my brother's eyes was to me.

"Well, let's go down there, Dan," I said. "You want to?" he said. "Yes, yes," I shouted at him through the wind. "You can't go in, Estelle," he said. "Why?" shouted Yves. "Because she's a girl," said my brother flatly, and the squall too suddenly flattened, and the three of us stood there looking at one another.

For a second it seemed we would be able to turn right around and head toward the streets, toward subway stations, buses, and taxis, but the weight dragging us down was now inside me, I had felt no impact, merely an abrupt awareness of ponderous, gigantic oppressiveness.

I shouted, "I want to go." "No," said Dan, and that no literally pushed me back, I was in icy water, no, not river water, I was on a gangway, yet I was drenched, my purple garment was like a sodden rag recovered from a drowned body.

The wind howled again, mingled with melted snow and sleet, now we were in some kind of entryway, its floor slightly heaving, no, I do not see us in an entryway, we were in some toilets, I hear the sound of water flowing against zinc walls, they were men's toilets, the only kind they had, Dan kept the door closed, I soon got dry, we knocked back a stiff shot of spirits, Yves handed me clothes my brother had gone to get, jeans with a front zipper my fingers were unable to fasten, they were a man's pants, a man's jacket too. "Put this on," said my brother, he tugged a close-fitting black cap onto my head, then he went out again and came back with another drink and finally we left with Dan leading, me following, and Yves bringing up the rear —

We left as if we were roped together, the three of us tied closer than we would ever be, we walked along a dark corridor but my brother moved without hesitation, oh, how well my brother knew this place —

Later still we were outside, at the intersection of Christopher Street and Eleventh Avenue, and very young boys skipped around a bench kissing and laughing hysterically, one of them was snorting a plastic bag he held tight against his face, it was already dawn —

"You're crazy," Yves yelled —

"Nobody's harmed you," I said —

He vomited several times, fatigue had devoured the flesh on his face, he said again, "You're crazy." Dan answered nastily, "You wanted to sightsee." "I'm leaving," said Yves. "You haven't seen Alwin or the studio," said my brother. Yves turned his back on him. "Come with me," he said to me. "When?" "Right now." We stumbled along exhaustedly, Yves kept saying "Come with me" and talking about the morning flight, standby seats, sleeping at the airport —

We went to get his case, a line of snowplows returning to base silenced us for a moment, and there stood a taxi. "You're both crazy," said Yves, he was sobbing, we stood on the curb watching the taxi, which skidded, then moved slowly away. We waved, I would never again see the boy Yves.

"Poison Ivy," my brother muttered, almost sadly.

That was all he said all the way home. We bought coffee and doughnuts in a coffee shop.

"Poison Ivy," muttered Dan and I nodded, poison ivy indeed, it amounted to a long, weighty exchange, and then we had nothing more to say, the snow began to thaw, Alwin would soon be back, I knew now what my brother did at night, the studio would soon resume work, the university would open its doors again, anyway we had to sleep.

At G.

THIRTY-FOUR

The Little Stream

THE NEXT DAY I found three letters from my father in the mailbox, one quite long, the second short, and a third shorter still.

"My dear Estelle,

"We too are snowed under, and Mr. Neighbor is upset because his trucks are stuck at the warehouse. What he tried to convey to me this morning as we strolled together — each on his own side of the dividing wall — was the fact that his livelihood is subject to all kinds of capricious variables. 'Isn't it unfair, Mr. Helleur,' he said to me, 'that a man like me — a man of regular, stable habits, at home only with what is predictable, one day just like the day before and the day after — has to put up with constant unbearable unforeseeable accidents. All kinds of uncontrollable events can break out anywhere on the whole length of the chain I oversee and operate. A truck, for instance. Maybe for some reason (and believe me, there can be a million reasons!) it won't run. Or if it does run, the driver might feel ill or the weather cancel operations. And if there's nothing wrong with the weather, the driver, or the truck, there can always be an accident, my truck can end up in a ditch — driver, cargo, and all, and we won't necessarily be able to locate the cause, or it won't be sufficient cause, a smokescreen cause, you might say. That's what is intolerable, Mr. Helleur, not knowing why you're on the losing end . . .'

"I told him we were in the same boat. No matter how good a lawyer one may be (and let's have no illusions on that score), the time inevitably comes when one doesn't understand why such and such a criminal act was committed. 'You have no idea how that can haunt you,' I said. 'Yes, Mr. Helleur,' Mr. Neighbor broke in, 'I hear what you're saying, but it's not really the same, for you don't have to understand your client to defend him. And even if you do understand him it won't prevent the same criminal acts from being committed all over again, so you shouldn't lose any sleep over it.' (Please note this prime example of Mr. Neighbor's logical progression, Estelle, I'm sure you'll have no trouble recognizing it.) 'Whereas *with me,' he went on, 'no truck, no work, and if I don't understand why it ended up in the ditch I always keep on worrying that the mystery may trigger another accident, and that's what keeps me awake at night, Mr. Helleur . . .'*

"Mr. Neighbor also treated me to a lecture about moles, claiming that molehills are merely the tops of ventilator shafts designed to aerate their tunnels. 'Or else how would they breathe, tell me that, how else do you think they would breathe, Mr. Helleur?' he said triumphantly, as if he were the one who designed mole runs.

"There lies the great difference between Mr. Neighbor and me. He takes everything in nature as if he himself had created it (which of course doesn't prevent him from grumbling and grousing and doing everything he can to counter it). Whereas I experience creation as something profoundly alien to me. But there it is, I'm paralyzed with respect for it.

"Moles put up those unsightly mounds so that they can breathe, so be it, but your cherished lawn is a scene of devastation, which I find intolerable. Nothing new there, you know my problems with the animal kingdom, Estelle, as well as with instinct in general and the whole of nature!

"It is comforting to think that all this is a powerful urge attempting to transcend matter. If I see moles and wasps and thrushes and worms and the whole cruel bloodthirsty bunch (luckily we have no wild beasts in our area!) as experiments, not as thought-out creations, I feel better. What's more, I can see a role for myself — administering all this blind experimentation until something better comes along. Yes, then I feel better.

"Do you know what Minor says when I talk of these things to him? He tells me I need to try one of his remedies: 'A harmless little sedative which will help you discuss the weather with your neighbor without obliging you to question the whole of creation, my dear Helleur . . .' I told him my philosophy was worth more than his sedatives. But he doesn't agree. 'That might just be so,' he says, 'if you carried your philosophy to its logical conclusion, if it brought you to Christ and faith, but you give up halfway . . .'

"Minor's insight is astounding. For he is absolutely right: I do stop halfway, Estelle. I understand this second source of morality and religion, yes, but it's not going to push me into a church to swallow a piece of baked flour!

"I mention these things because at this very moment Nicole is down at the Church of Sainte-Marie-du-Marché. She goes a lot these days. It's as if for her the church has replaced the blue garage. She must have great powers of self-suggestion; for years now she has made do with that garage with its faded blue wallcovering and practically the same piece of music.

(Bolero *suited her so badly, but the more I told her so, the more she clung to it.) And now she makes do with this small, rather plain church. It hurts me to think of her sitting all alone in a pew in that damp building between unadorned walls — not even one stained-glass window! — and I'm sorry we don't have some great cathedral to better feed the yearning in her soul.*

"She goes to church, yet you know how ignorant she is and is determined to remain. When I ask what she does there, she says 'I pray.' 'What for, Nicole?' 'For Dan to come back' or else 'For Dan to stay there and become a star,' anyway, the usual things. Sometimes she says she goes to church to see the angels.

"Tiresia, who knows the Bible so well, can't stand this kind of little-girl talk. You never knew about their quarrel, Estelle: they loved you children too much to drag you into the swamp they thrashed about in. And by now they have got over the worst of it; at least I think so. Nicole wants to believe, so she believes in Christ and the angels, in my opinion because they are what is most immediate to her: after all, our neighbors go to Sainte-Marie-du-Marché and put on their best clothes to go there! If we were in India she'd worship Shiva, who would suit her better with his multiple arms and his dance (yes, I realize we are woefully deprived in the matter of dancing deities!). She says she believes in Christ but her belief simply blanks out the crucifixion. She looks at that terrible cross above the altar, and sees only angels dancing in heaven . . . Perhaps I'm the one who understands nothing, perhaps the souls of those closest to you are the hardest to look into . . .

"And this of course hurts Tiresia, this belief in a savior who had not stooped to save her. 'But He will save you in the next world, Tiresia,' Nicole would say. I did not like that quarrel of theirs, Estelle. I was not convinced of Nicole's innocence. Sometimes I thought I read an unbearable gloating in her eyes . . .

"So while Nicole was in church I would read Tiresia passages from the Old Testament, the ones she liked. But she can no longer stand the Bible either. Once upon a time Job's lamentations consoled her, but now they irritate her, I realize.

"That's more or less how things are here, in the depths of our own harsh winter . . ."

He had written his second letter during a sleepless night, and this is what it said:

"Estelle,

"I fear I have made a bad mistake.

"I've been working at my desk tonight because the snow kept me awake: it suggests a kind of presence, almost as if someone were waiting outside. Anyway, I came downstairs to my study, turned on the little electric heater, and opened the window to have a view of your lawn. It's most beautiful in the snow and moonlight (you can hardly make out the molehills). Then I settled down to work — my duty cases, all routine, really — but suddenly the words of my favorite philosopher came back to me, a passage I once read to you when you came to ask me a question in that little voice of yours, at once childish and serious . . .

"You were such a serious child. So was Dan. I used to marvel at your extraordinary seriousness. But I realize now that I profited from it, that it suited me. I told myself that if you possessed inner wisdom (from whatever source), wisdom that generated such seriousness in you, then my task would be easier . . .

"But to return to that passage. I can still see you: you had opened my study door without knocking, you held yourself very straight, and you said in that serious voice, 'Father, what do you do for a living?' I knew that Dan was hidden somewhere behind you; the two of you must have consulted together and decided you had to have an answer at once, even if it meant disturbing me in my study. And you, the elder one, had been dispatched to find out.

"So I rose and went to my personal bookshelves, the ones with revolving compartments. With your intense gaze on me, I pulled out a volume and read you the passage in question. And I said: 'There, my daughter, that is what I do for a living: I work to make sure that this man is not forgotten . . .'

"It was a little pompous; forgive me, Estelle. But I sensed that you required nothing less, I sensed that you two were at one of those turning points in life when complete answers are required. You made me repeat the words, then repeated them after me; I guessed it was so that you could pass them on to Dan. You were so endearing, Estelle, in your little creased skirt with your big rubber boots caked as usual with mud, memorizing the declarations of my favorite philosopher as painstakingly as if they were one of La Fontaine's fables.

"And then you left, still mouthing the words, and you didn't know this but I followed you, and Dan was indeed waiting in the corridor. You were so afraid of forgetting that you told him the whole thing right away, the whole passage, practically without a mistake. The two of you sat there in that dark corridor whispering together, and then in his excitement Dan forgot to whisper and said out loud: 'So Father's job is to make sure this man is never forgotten, is that it, Estelle?'

"I was moved to tears. I returned to my study feeling at once humbled and magnified. Humbled because my work does not often soar to such heights, magnified because however low it may rank on the scale of human activities, it does nevertheless strive to attain those heights.

"And this very night that passage has returned to me. It was extraordinary, Estelle. It spoke within me like a voice (if I told Minor about this he would give that sidelong look and say: 'What voice, my dear Helleur?' and I'd look like a fool, but I know you understand, dear Estelle). I can more or less reproduce the passage without consulting the book it comes from:

" 'What would we do if we learned that for the safety of the people, for the very existence of humankind, there was somewhere a man, an innocent man, condemned to undergo everlasting torment? We would perhaps consent to it, if it was agreed that a magic potion made us forget it . . . but if we had to know it, to think about it, to tell ourselves that this man was subjected to atrocious torture in order that we might exist, that this was a fundamental condition of existence in general — ah no! it would be better to accept that nothing exists, to let the planet disintegrate.'

"Do you recognize it?

"I felt that there was something to be learned in it for me, something unrelated to what the philosopher put into it. And unrelated also to the self-interested interpretation of it that I gave to you.

"It's that magic potion that bothers me, Estelle, that continues to bother me so deeply even as I write these lines to you, not knowing what either one of you is doing at this moment.

"I believe I am guilty of a most serious lapse.

"I believe that for us three, for Tiresia, Nicole, and me, your childhood was the magic potion we sought to drink, and sought to have you both drink as well. Your childhood: a magic potion to wipe out all the evil in the world, to let us begin all over again.

"But tonight I am swept by anxious presentiments: what if I was wrong from start to finish, what if Minor was right?

"And now you talk to me about the Vietnam War, Estelle, in every letter, you talk of your fears for your friend Michael, of that boy Kenny who is a conscientious objector and wants to get to Canada, of the architect's son, David, I believe, who actually wants to enlist, of that demonstration you took part in. We saw some of it on the neighbors' TV. You told me that one of the dancers, Djuma, I think, dressed up as a skeleton; we saw that skeleton in close-up for just a second, but perhaps it wasn't Djuma . . . I daren't discuss these things with Tiresia, still less Nicole; in fact, I skip those passages when I read your letters out at the table . . ."

* * *

"Estelle, those quarrels Minor and I used to have in my car outside the garden gate were over something concerning us all, concerning you and your brother . . .

"I have just reached for the phone, Estelle, but then I imagined it ringing in your apartment, in what you call your 'loft.' No, I'll just call in a few days' time to wish you a happy new year . . ."

Unsigned.

The third letter said:

"Dear Dan and Estelle,

"Well, talk about wasted effort! I meant to send you a photo of the house under snow and of its lawn dwellers, a photo taken by Adrien, who came to visit his parents over the holiday, and instead I sent you an incoherent scrap of letter I thought I had consigned to the wastebasket.

"I suppose the truth is that I wanted a little pity, and there's no doubt that I miss you, my dear children . . .

"In any case I'd like you to be able to have some fun after a tiring semester, so I'm enclosing a money order . . . Adrien took this photo with a newfangled camera that develops its film on the spot — maybe that explains our odd expressions. Now I must leave you, my dear ones, for the neighbors are coming over for a drink and I must make sure we are well supplied. I send you a big hug (and if you send Minor a New Year's card don't say a word to him about my nocturnal ruminations: I want to keep the upper hand over that old sickbed scarecrow!). Affectionately, your father."

I held the three letters in my hand and reread them fragment by fragment, unable to find a logical sequence if I read them in normal order, and hoping perhaps to find one in disorder. Then I walked slowly up the stairs. Dan was on the landing, abnormally pale under the skylight; he was saying something to me.

"What?"

"Adrien . . ."

For a second I thought he was reading the letters from a distance. There was something terrifying in the idea: I felt an electric shock, my father's letters jerked convulsively in my fingers — but already I had rejected that possibility. I climbed the remaining stairs at top speed, painfully barking my shins. Our neighbor Adrien was on the phone.

"What is it?"

I was screaming, as if the very mention of Adrien's name made my voice rise higher.

"Are you deaf, you two?" Adrien bellowed over the transatlantic line. "Come back right now, that's all!"

Behind his fury I heard his mother, probably trying to calm him.

"I want to speak to Minor," I said.

"Minor has enough on his plate as it is. Christ Almighty, Estelle, don't you understand what you're told?"

"But what on earth are you telling us?"

"Come back, come back immediately!"

And suddenly the line went dead. Even that distant sound so like the ocean that lay between us had gone. Nothing.

"What did he say?" asked my brother.

Unbelievable though it must seem, my brother and I had not heard the message.

We had both heard Adrien furiously telling us we were deaf. Was that why we had been unable to hear what followed?

Our phone line was dead; we spent a few feverish minutes trying to call a series of numbers. But in vain: neither men nor machines seemed to understand what we wanted. We suffered the agonies of the deaf, for whom nothing trustworthy resides in words. Then we found ourselves packing — yes, that seemed right, all those small movements, all that activity — and then we were at the airport, scanning the departure schedules, looking at the aircraft parked outside, and here too people seemed deaf: they steered us to Icelandic Airlines. "Reykjavik-Brussels," said the girl in uniform. "Reykjavik-Brussels," my brother desperately parroted, and I read rather than heard the words on his lips and the same despair invaded me, no, no, it would take too long — "Let's call Kenny," we said, but we did not know his extension; even looking for that would take too long.

Suddenly we spied a kind of bubble nodding from side to side atop an enormous mass, a big furry black head we recognized at once as if the six months that had gone by since my arrival had been just one sideways swing of his head. And he recognized us. His head stood still on his neck, he seemed to understand our uncontrolled gestures, he wriggled out from under his desk and started walking, and we followed, falling all over each other's feet in order not to be left behind. I do not know by what act of legerdemain it happened, but we found ourselves in the first-class section of a TWA plane, with a red rose on the cloth covering our table-tray, champagne, and the attentive ministrations of a stewardess whose chief concern seemed to be our well-being.

Every now and then she moved away to perform a few tasks for other passengers, but she at once returned to us. Dan and I drank a lot, accepting the glasses this stewardess handed us exactly as if they had been medication, and we had the strange conviction that if we asked her a question she would know the answer.

"Beautiful stewardess with the golden hair and compassionate smile, tell us please what our neighbor and childhood friend Adrien said to us, Adrien who loves us so little and who cannot do without us just as we cannot do without him . . ." And this airborne fairy godmother would stoop over us, just as she was doing now, and she would pour her answer into our glass in a sparkling froth of champagne bubbles . . . But the roar of the engines or perhaps the altitude made us deaf and at the same time perhaps mute. We asked no question, we just drank, hoping that the answer would "anyway" be in our glasses, that it would be within us, swallowed and digested, without our needing to ask or understand.

Oh, I am trying to come up with explanations, but perhaps it would be enough to say we were mad, my brother and I must have been mad as we winged our way toward the cemetery in our native town and drank champagne, deaf and dumb, side by side, neither friends nor enemies, merely waiting. Since Adrien's call we had been transported into a kind of parenthesis. Our fate hung unsettled in the balance; and even if we knew nothing else we knew in a sense that we were headed toward a final settlement of accounts with fate. And in the meantime, so as not to mar the consummation of that settlement, we drank.

And in the train too we sat in the bar, alternating espressos and drinks after our long diet of American Cokes and Styrofoam cups of weak coffee. The drinks helped everything flash by at top speed — time, the landscape, people, Adrien at the station, our neighbors at home with Minor, the latter with his face curiously scarred. Someone, Adrien's mother, I believe, tried to make us take off our garish Canal Street garments. "Let them be," said the doctor in strangely masterful tones, "Tiresia's purple and Nicole's yellow, just right, just right," and we too felt it was just right. We staggered along the same old road leading to the cemetery with the strange feeling that we had no business there leading that long long procession . . . Every now and then we turned back to survey the humped undulating line of hats: shouldn't we have been on our stool in the attic beneath the raised fanlight? At one point Dan whispered, "Do you think that this time we'll get to see the burial?" and I felt the old helpless laughter well up, I knew exactly what he meant.

At our attic window we had always been denied the climactic moment, the moment when they lowered the coffin into the ground, because of the distance or our too-narrow field of vision or the procession blocking our view, but this time we were going to be in the stalls and the idea kept triggering spasms of laughter we had great difficulty forcing back down our throats.

I am sure people thought we were sobbing, or holding back our sobs. In the vicinity of death it is always easy to fool anybody, and in any case we were pale, we looked ill and numbed.

"Ill with sorrow, numb with sorrow . . ." "Drunk with sorrow" as well, but it was all right, nobody was likely to find us out.

The coffins danced before our eyes, and so did the faces of the people leaning toward us, we kissed every face that came within reach, people were moved by our spontaneity, "Poor kids," they murmured.

My brother kissed, then I kissed, and if people approached us from the other side — for a certain confusion reigned — I kissed first and then my brother unflinchingly followed suit. Adrien filed past; I kissed him with the same eagerness and heard him mutter savagely, "Stop playing the goddamned fool."

For a second it disconcerted me, but his mother was right behind him and leaned forward and kissed me, her cheeks wet with tears, all was well. I held my cheek against hers long enough for it to get wet, it did me good to appropriate tears I myself was unable to produce. And when Adrien's father bent to kiss me my cheek was appropriately wet for his kiss, but he was not simply content to kiss me, he was saying something through his tears: "I loved him, you know, I loved Mr. Helleur, don't think that because we quarreled . . . I'm going to miss him, I loved him, my sweet one." I stared in amazement at Mr. Neighbor; I would have loved to be able to comfort him, but how did you put yourself on an intimate footing with a grown-up you regarded as a kind of ogre all through your childhood, harmless, perhaps, but prickly if you touched him . . . I passed Mr. Neighbor to my brother, and to my brother he said the same thing or much the same: "I have no one to talk to anymore, no one" — sniffing most vehemently on that "no one" — "He was a man, a man of the old school, you know what I mean, Dan, someone you can talk to about life." Clearly, Mr. Neighbor's sorrows weighed heavily on him.

I believe I began to sober up thinking of Nicole: nobody said anything about Nicole. I leaned over to my brother. "It's not fair, they're not saying anything about Nicole." I saw my brother agree; we were still standing at the main cemetery gate, angry by now, would nobody speak to us of Nicole?

The storekeeper who sold dance slippers and inflatable mattresses appeared, all gloom beneath his hat and accompanied by his wife.

"Miss Helleur, Mr. Dan, your father meant a lot to our town . . . ," he said, raising his hat.

"Did he, and what about Nicole?"

"Nicole?"

"Their mother," his wife whispered.

"She bought all her dance slippers from you and you don't even know her name . . ."

Anger was rumbling in me like a river in spate, as if hitherto-frozen blood had begun to flow again, flinging up echoes of my voice along caverns lined with blood-swollen mucous membrane, I was wallowing in anger.

"And you don't even know her name . . ."

My brother was pale, he had me by the shoulders, holding me tight against him, our two angers united and flowed forth together.

"She bought dozens of slippers from you, do you even know what color she liked?"

"Blue," said the storekeeper, keeping his voice low so as to bring our voices down, our choleric drunken voices.

"Then why did you always give her pink ones?" said my brother.

"I gave her what the suppliers delivered. There just weren't any blue ones, Mr. Dan . . ."

"But she wanted blue, sky blue, and not flesh pink, didn't you understand that? not the pink of flesh that rots but the blue of sky you dance in . . ."

It seemed to us that we had just understood Nicole, that we had just pierced through to the roots of her fragile sublime soul and wanted all our listeners to know it.

"I'll try to do better in the future," the storekeeper said absurdly, but it calmed us down.

Calmed us only for a moment. We remained standing close to-gether. "What about Nicole?" we said as each person came forward to offer condolences, "What about Nicole?" we barked even before the person opened his mouth.

There were a lot of people.

People we had seen making their way through the garden to our father's study, people we had never seen, people who thanked us for what our father had done for them. A man stopped in front of us, steeped in distress. "Dan, Estelle, your father was a better philosopher than I am. What I taught was just formula, but he had philosophy in his blood." "What about Nicole?" It was our old high school philosophy teacher, we had not recognized the face transformed by sorrow. "What about Nicole?" But he did not answer. Oh, how angry we were. "That's right, just formula. Leave, please leave . . ."

By now we were saying "What about Nicole?" almost mechanically; we were tired. And every time we said it Adrien growled threateningly behind us.

"That's it, keep it up, you'll never change, go on, say it to him too, say it to the whole town, they really didn't deserve this, neither Mr. Helleur nor Nicole . . . Nor Nicole . . ."

And suddenly we saw him vanish behind the wall. We heard a car door slam, then Adrien returned bearing before him a wreath of light blue irises, a blue so pure and so beautiful that Dan and I stopped short. We gazed at Adrien, who held the wreath out to us with a solemn gesture that would have made us laugh if it had not also been so threatening. On the wreath was a white sash bearing in gold letters the words "To the most beautiful woman in G., to Nicole, A.N."

We stared at those strange words: "To the most beautiful woman in G., to Nicole" and the two following initials we had at first read as "amen."

A.N., Adrien Neighbor, of course. We longed to leap for his throat, to claw away the muscles that held his features hard and taut, but the wreath was of great beauty, it was the perfect wreath for Nicole, the one we should have ordered for her, and our anger flowed down another channel. The whole procession had filed past. We set off down the path leading to the grave, staggering, arms still tight around each other, and at last we had an objective.

Alex and his father were blubbering, one on each side of the grave. They were waiting for everyone to leave before finishing their work.

"Alex," I said, "please put the iris wreath all alone in the center, on the gravestone."

"And the others . . . miss?"

"Why do you call me miss? Just put the others around them, sort of framing them."

"If you want," said Alex with a nervous glance at his father.

But his father had been drinking; wine and grief combined had drawn his fangs. For a second I wondered how Alex's father, the man who buried the whole town, could feel such grief for these two deceased persons. "What on earth can Father have done for them? We must ask him when we get home," I said in my diminished state to Dan, and Dan nodded his approval, he too was wondering what favor the sexton could have owed our father, he too wanted to put the question to our father when we got home, to our father, whom we would find in his study as we always did whenever we had an important question to ask . . .

"Perhaps that's not right," said Adrien's mother, who had followed us anxiously.

"What?" said Adrien.

"That wreath all on its own, why did you do that? We presented a wreath in all our names, in the name of our whole family, you know, Dan . . ."

"Oh, let them horse around if they want to," said Adrien. "Alex knows what to do."

"Adrien, don't speak like that in Mr. Helleur's presence," said Adrien's father, and we did not know which Mr. Helleur he was talking about.

"In any case we must leave," said Adrien, "they're out on their feet." And I heard with perfect clarity: "Because the bastards are falling-down drunk, that's why . . ."

"I want to walk home with Estelle," said Dan.

"Sure, but you can't stand up, and neither can she," said Adrien, shoving us into his car.

But suddenly I was resisting.

"Wait, wait . . ."

"What is it now?"

"I want to see something . . ."

I went back to the cemetery gate. I stared at the glowing heap of flowers around Alex and his father, who still faced us, who still stood motionless.

"What are you looking for?" murmured Dan.

"I don't know, I don't know . . ."

In my head was a task that made me narrow my eyes, a task that struggled to burst out in the midst of the flowers. I studied the mound of flowers surrounding the coffins: how would I recognize what I was looking for even if it was there? I would have to beat a path for myself, thrust obstacles aside to the left and right, stoop . . . But no, if the thing had been there, it would have been visible at once amid the gaily colored petals, a sumptuous monstrous stain; I was making a fearful effort to remember, a bunch of black flowers floated in my memory, but what meaning could it have? The effort was too great, the vision that had brought me back here faltered, and the black stain faded among the colors like a creation of my tired mind.

"I don't know . . . ," I said to Dan, returning with him to Adrien's car.

In the car, uncontrollable laughter returned.

"So you loved Nicole?" I said to Adrien.

"If there was anyone worth loving in that house . . . ," growled Adrien.

"The whole time he came over to our house it was to see Nicole, what do you think of that, Dan?"

It seemed unbelievably funny to me. Dan and I spluttered with helpless mirth, the laughter mingling with the nausea that had begun to sweep over us.

"If I could," said Adrien, "I'd smash both your faces against the cemetery wall."

He drove with somber concentration. At our house something seemed out of place. The house looked empty.

"The house looks empty," I said to Dan in questioning tones.

Dan frowned.

"Father's car isn't here," he said, pronouncing his words with great care.

"Where is our father's car, Adrien, why do we have to be with you, where's the car?"

"You're out of your minds, both of you," said Adrien. "You scare me, I'm leaving, get out."

"I'm not getting out until you tell us where our father's car is and why we have to sit here and listen to your crap."

Adrien made a wrenching U-turn outside our house, turning so violently that he hit the fence, and twisted in his seat to face us.

"You want to know where Mr. Helleur's car is? Is that what you said, Estelle?"

"That's what she said, yes," answered Dan, imitating Adrien's voice.

"Okay, I'll show you, since you don't seem able to understand what anyone tells you."

He roared away at top speed, not even glancing at Alex's car bearing his father and mother back from the cemetery.

We took the little road that ran behind our meadow, the shortcut leading to the highway. At the foot of the hill, Adrien shifted into first and began the slow climb. At the top he stopped. The far slope was thick with ice. Protective barriers closed off the whole of that segment of road. Below, a few hundred yards before the crossroads, in a hollow under big oaks that kept it in permanent shade, was the little stream, or rather brook, that occasionally overflowed and deposited puddles on top of the bridge, which was the same height as the road.

Our father's car was there, planted in one of the oaks.

"Take a look," said Adrien.

Adrien took a cigar from his pocket.

"Go on, go and look."

His voice was beginning to frighten me.

Dan and I slithered and stumbled down the slope. Now all we felt was great weariness, and a sense of imminent disaster. We splashed through icy mud. It was already getting dark. Suddenly the stage was harshly lit: Adrien had switched on his headlights.

From the stream rose a white mist that seemed to waver in the glaring light. We approached the car.

"Father," Dan murmured.

He held the door that hung open, curiously mutilated. The windshield was smashed out, the steering wheel buckled, but what attracted our attention was an object on the car floor by the gas pedal. Dan bent down.

He set the object delicately in the palm of his left hand.

"Estelle?" said my brother, his voice hardly recognizable.

That object should not have been there. Drunk though we were, we realized that it was not in the right place.

It was a woman's shoe with a stiletto heel, one of Nicole's shoes. It was full of blood.

"Give it to me."

Dan handed me the shoe. The congealed liquid inside it was dull and unwinking in the headlights, which Adrien was now flicking on and off to call us back. We moved from darkness into light and it was as if we were traversing strata of time. Dan did what I would have done, or perhaps it was I who did it. Then we placed the emptied shoe on the car seat, patting the seat to create a hollow in which the shoe toppled over like an exhausted bird in a nest. Then we gently pushed the shattered door to; it refused to remain closed and Dan ripped off his belt and lashed the door shut.

We climbed back up the hill. The engine came to life, Adrien's car backed and turned, and its beams no longer glared into our eyes but he went on switching the lights on and off and on until we looked and saw another car on the other side of the road. It was upside down.

"Minor's car!"

We stopped dead, turned to stone. Here too the fog throbbed in the glare of the lights, and you could hear the uncertain trickle of the little stream. Dan suddenly knelt and scratched at the earth. At this spot the bank was covered with sawdust, but beneath the shavings the surface was icy, biting.

"Feel, Estelle," said Dan.

He placed my hand on that surface.

"Do you feel it, do you feel it?" he said.

Oh, how I felt the bite of that black ice, its greedy teeth that seemed still to tremble with the passion they had consummated.

"The earth is calling us," Dan softly said.

Above, Adrien made a careful turn. We scrambled up the slope to rejoin him, half-upright and half on all fours, straightening up finally with the help of the barriers.

"What happened?" said Dan in the car.

We were utterly sober.

"Yves called," said Adrien.

"Yves?"

"Your husband, Estelle, don't start acting the asshole again. He called as soon as he got back to Paris. Apparently he went over to get you in New York. Anyway, he called from the airport; he must have been going crazy. Your father wasn't at home. Nicole took the call. I don't know what Yves told her, but she raced across the garden, just as she was, in high heels, coatless, and she jumped in your father's car and left."

"Left?"

"For Paris, to take the plane."

"She can't drive."

"She could drive well enough to leave, anyway. When your father came back, Tiresia was out on the front steps. Your father rushed into our garden yelling like a crazy man, wanting to borrow my father's car. But one of the truckers had taken it. Your father ran over to Minor's and they left together. We heard them from our house as they took the turn by the little meadow, skidding all over the ice. The road was like a skating rink, Estelle. It was crazy. Nicole must have realized it, anyway, had turned back. They reached the stream — you know how narrow the bridge is there — and they saw a car coming from the opposite direction in the fog, driving at an insane speed. Your father recognized his car and tried to let it pass by turning off into the ditch . . ."

"And Minor?"

"Unhurt. My parents found him a little later, dazed but safe."

"Your parents?"

"They were worried, they came with a police car."

We turned all this over slowly in our minds. After a moment, when the car had been standing outside our house for some time, Dan asked:

"The sawdust on the bridge?"

There was such tension in his voice.

I knew what was happening inside him. That sawdust would have saved our parents. If it had been there before they went by, then they would not have been dead, they would still be in the house, the accident would have taken place in another dimension of time, a mere possibility, a warning, and we would be leaping happily from this car, we would be racing along the garden path to the steps . . .

"My father came along afterward . . . with his bucket of sawdust . . . He had already spread some before, but the stream had risen again and washed it away," said Adrien. "With his little bucket of sawdust, my father, yes . . . ," he said malevolently.

And that malevolence brought us right back to the point it had started from, to its ultimate point of origin.

"Who made the phone call?" said Dan.

"Yves, your asshole of a husband, Estelle."

"Poison Ivy," Dan shouted. "Poison Ivy, I knew it, Estelle!"

And suddenly Adrien was yelling:

"Fuck off, fuck off, both of you!"

THIRTY-FIVE

Dr. Minor's Major

ADRIEN yelled, "Fuck off!"

He jumped out, wrenching the door wide and howling like a dog, "Fuck off!", unable to stop.

It seemed to us that his voice rent the cold air like a flint spearhead, and flew on to the end of the road and all the way to the cemetery. It was that which finally induced us to get out: our parents must not hear that coarse noise, must not be dragged into our sordid screaming match with Adrien.

Our parents must know nothing, worry about nothing. Ever. On this as on every other occasion.

He had hold of the door, shaking it as if he were rattling on prison bars. "Fuck off . . ." The pallid light from the car crawled all over his features and advanced toward the fire that seemed to blaze black at the roots of his hair.

We struggled out of the backseats, moving past him with a kind of respect. "Take it easy, Adrien," my brother said gently, and I believe that at that moment he would willingly have put his hand on Adrien's shoulder, and Adrien, who was always alive to every one of our slightest impulses, must actually have felt that light touch on his skin. What was in us at once traveled into him, and was there distorted. We saw his shoulder recoil convulsively. If I had been able to leave that car ahead of him, I would have pulverized my brother's friendly impulse in the very cell, in the neuron where it took shape; I would have dragged Dan straight to the house, I would have forbidden him to see the face of our almost-brother, of our false brother.

I knew the gesture Dan had wanted to make, and with the same certainty I knew how Adrien would respond.

"Don't touch me," he said, his voice suddenly low again, low and black.

"I didn't touch you, Adrien," said Dan as if struck to the quick.

But my brother did not move; he stayed there on the far side of

the door. I was still inside the car, and I felt his compassion shrink
and turn into a questioning, then a kind of expectation, and suddenly
that expectation spilled over into a ground made ready for war, and
Adrien leapt onto that ground.

"You're the one who killed them," he growled, already upon Dan
and grabbing him by the throat.

And Dan my brother, my brother I had never seen do anything
but dance, Dan was a fighting fury.

The house and road swam in fog, but the glow from the still open
car revealed the gritty and glittering gravel of the sidewalk, the shining cement of the curb, and a patch of strangely shiny road. In a
second I saw all that and a hideous fear seized me.

I felt that if we remained there those things would at once swallow
us, we would smash into them and they would clamp their jaws shut
upon us and hurl us into that ghostly car that glowed so palely, we
would fall into it unconscious and bereft of will, the wheels would
start stealthily to roll, and the vehicle would vanish in the darkness
and fog.

The smell of the grave suffocated me; I think my nerves were
about to give out. I tugged Dan and Adrien inside the garden gate,
the smell of the grave pursuing me and giving me superhuman
strength, for locked in combat as they were, they moved forward
with me, Adrien repeating, "You killed them," and Dan replying,
"Don't say that or I'll kill you." I was hitting out too, but my blows
were simply to keep us all moving.

I wanted to get to our lawn; I had the dim strong notion that there
we would all be saved, my brother and I and Adrien as well. And at
last we were there, my brother and Adrien rolling on the frozen
grass in a struggle full of gasps and heavy thuds, and myself entangled
with them to separate them or to hit them — it seemed to be the
same thing — and to hear the breathless savage words, scarcely audible, that spurted from their steaming lips: "You killed them," "I'll
kill you, Adrien." At the heart of our tangled group I strained to
catch their words before they could slither off into the darkness like
lithe and malevolent slugs; I hugged them to me to prevent them
reaching the ground, to prevent them penetrating the earth. That
insensate notion multiplied my strength tenfold; I remember feeling
astonishment as all that strength rushed in.

Dense humidity hung in the air like black sheets; it was as if we
were also fighting those sheets as they flapped clingingly all about
us, it was as if all three of us were congealed in their folds. We no

longer felt pain, we were anesthetized by cold and fatigue, but with intense zones of pain about the lips and eyes, as if we had become nightmare beings, vampirelike, and that knowledge made us all the more insane, all the more ferocious. I believe if we had stayed on the asphalt surface of the road we would have literally killed one another.

Suddenly the fog turned yellow, yellow tinged with red.

We stopped, deathly pale; the light seemed to well up from our hellish brawl, from the braziers of our battered bodies; we no longer knew who we were, we had gone too far, we were afraid.

From the doorway a figure moved out onto the steps.

"Father," Dan murmured passionately.

That appeal, at once swallowed in fog . . .

With one jerk Adrien wrenched himself free and fled into the darkness, a fleeting, already invisible shadow, but the frozen earth, the earth that was our enemy, sent back the echo of his footsteps exactly as if it held him captive in one of its underground passageways. And we followed that sound of footsteps. As he had done when we were children, he ran toward the wall, the wall between our gardens, where there was a gap beneath the lilac, and there we heard the scrape of a stone or a bough. Spurred by a kind of terror, he must have hesitated before finding the spot.

Then nothing more.

"They still haven't fixed that gap."

It was my brother's voice.

He formed his words slowly, gropingly, questioningly, but what struck me was that he uttered them in a loud clear voice. As if he were trying out a voice, perhaps his old voice, recalling it in order to test it.

We were standing now, making no attempt to adjust our disheveled clothes. We were wholly in that voice of Dan's, in that change taking place inside him.

"They never fixed that gap," he said again, louder.

Now it was a statement.

My brother Dan was finally back, and retaking possession of our old house. And those simple words dispelled our father's ghost, which had appeared on the steps; they drove our parents back into the past. With a shudder I felt for the first time their physical presence over there in the cemetery. It was not their bodies I sensed, it was merely their absence from here and their transferal to there, and after that, in the wake of that absence, a change that was slowly coming about.

On the fog-shrouded lawn the "presence" penetrated my brother and swelled up inside him, and soon that presence would penetrate the hallways and begin to fill the whole house. To what exact extent I could not guess, but I sensed subtle and powerful shifts of energy, and into my heart, free so far of pain, free so far of sorrow, came that feeling for which there is no word in French, that feeling our father had described to us, which was the first and only word of his mother tongue he had ever taught us: "awe." And now for the first time there was room inside me for what that word was, and I felt it uncoil in all its power. "Father," I said inside my head, "this is awe."

"No," Minor answered from the steps, "they never did repair that gap."

His voice did not come out to us, it went in the direction of Adrien's vanished footsteps.

In our neighbors' house, a light on the second-floor landing went on and then off. Everything was quiet. The door of our own house had swung shut. But we could hear Minor breathing. He was still out on the steps. We stood motionless in fog that was once more dark.

"Are you alone, Dan?" said Minor.

"I'm with Estelle."

"Oh," he said with a kind of relief. "Then come in. I was expecting you."

We joined him.

In the dim hallway he studied us.

Did we even ask him how he felt, whether he would suffer any ill effects from the accident into which our parents had dragged him, whether he had been injured, whether he was at that moment in pain? I think not. Yet he had not been at the funeral. We had given it no thought.

And now it was he who was looking after us, he who had been in that car upended in ice and mud, whose crazily spinning wheels must finally have creaked to a halt, their noise giving place to the low and insistent prattle of the little stream beneath the frozen reeds in fog-invaded night, beside a shape that had been his best friend and was now a corpse . . .

*   *   *

I still cannot leave that scene. For years now I have prowled around it, sometimes hearing the strange spinning of the wheels, and then my heart starts beating and my mind flees, but a moment later it is back at that scene I am condemned forever to haunt, attracted this time by the prattle of the stream, and again my heart beats madly.

How appalling that small insignificant sound must have been. Sometimes I think I know exactly how it must have sounded: it must have sounded like a color, exactly like the color black. And I am unable to express in words what horror that idea then caused me, the color black embodied in the lonely prattling of an icy stream stealing along beneath ice-stiffened reeds, at first very faint in the wreckage of that night, then clearer and clearer, the sound of a horror . . .

He studied us, the two of us side by side before him, just as we had stood so often before. And the subtle shifts I had felt at work continued, were going on at that very moment. I now perceived a modification of size relationships: I was now the small one compared with Dan; and Minor, who had always seemed so robust to us, had become frail; and the house all about us, unaccustomed to these changes, itself seemed prey to a process that made its former surroundings uncertain. Beyond the entranceway familiar lines briefly emerged from the gloom, then sank back into it, caught in a sphere that was like fog upon water, and we did not yet know when it would lift . . .

On the side wall behind Minor a slender vertical shape swam into sight; my eyes locked onto it and it rounded itself out into a reflecting oval. It was Nicole's big looking glass, the one I had caught her studying one day, swathed in flowing taffeta, seeking some fairy-tale reflection, and my heart began to beat again.

I felt that we should go to that mirror and in its depths interrogate the picture Minor had before him: Dan tall and Estelle short now, one yellow, the other purple, and those broad streaks of blood on us and our hands torn and our faces lacerated, split lips, burning eyes . . . From the depths of Nicole's looking glass that picture was finding its way to me, but from far away, much too far. Minor was in the way, and it was not his strength that prevented us from approaching the mirror and interrogating the picture of this couple that had just entered our old house.

On the contrary, I felt strangely certain that at another time he would have urged us toward it with all his massive and benevolent authority. But now he was weak, and it was his weakness that stood between us and the mirror.

Minor studied us and his gaze stopped at the surface of ourselves. Oh, he saw us, he saw the blood and the dirt and those bruises we bore, but he left them where they were; he lacked the strength to banish them back below the surface. Yet a little later, in a few minutes, he would make one last attempt.

"My Major has come," he said at last in a changed voice.

As if one person, my brother and I stiffened. Silence.

"There was nothing I could do," he went on in the same broken voice. Still silence.

"My Major . . . he came just like lightning."

And suddenly we perceived another absence, a limited absence this time, circumscribed within a small rectangle of such density that it seemed there really was a hole in our blurred vision of the house, a hole from which Minor in that one instant stood apart.

He did not have his doctor's bag.

We had never seen him without that bag, either in his hand or sitting beside him, but invariably reinforcing the power of his presence. And now he stood before us, hands bare and empty, as if cut off from their source, and incongruously taking their place in the lit space that seemed to glow between us and him.

And now our eyes left Nicole's looking glass behind and groped their way up the stairs to the second floor. I believe we confusedly expected to hear the cries familiar from our childhood nights. But all was still. The nightmares that dwelt there were silent. And our eyes came back to Minor's empty hands: the nightmares were not keeping silent, they had left. Nicole had taken them with her, and Minor no longer needed his bag with its faithful syringes, ever ready to speed to the rescue of the Helleur household with their magical contents that forced monsters from the past to submit.

Our good doctor had not come running to treat our mother Nicole, our young mother Nicole who screamed at night when the labyrinth of her nightmares encircled her and she could find no exit. Our doctor had not come racing from his house, had not made the gravel of the garden path crunch beneath his wheels, he had not bounded up the stairs still wearing his coat, snapping orders to our father and solace to the two terrified children standing hand in hand at the end of the corridor.

Then why was he here at this hour of the night?

The absence of that bag shocked us, and so did Minor's empty hands.

" 'She' is in there," he said.

His voice was lower, but was once again strong.

I tried to speak, but my swollen lips would not let me. I felt that my brother was trying to do the same, and perhaps a few sounds did emerge from our immobilized lips, sounds Minor understood, or perhaps he relied on the expression on our ravaged faces.

Who, who, Doctor Minor, who was there?

Could we have been mistaken, could it be the young woman with the red shoe, the blood-filled shoe, could it have been Nicole the golden-haired, Nicole our mother? Well, then, yes, that must be why no one had mentioned her to us at the cemetery, that was why her doctor was in the house . . . drunkenness was again upsetting our minds. Doctor, is pain like certain drugs, drugs you cannot take with alcohol because alcohol has a potentiating action, that is the right word, isn't it, good old doctor of ours who isn't our doctor anymore, does alcohol potentiate pain?

"Tiresia," he said.

We stood petrified, as if caught committing a crime.

Tiresia! She had not been at the cemetery either. At one stroke we realized that we had forgotten her and yet that it was she we had been waiting for, she who would tell us what we needed, who would explain all that tomfoolery at the cemetery to us, who would talk to us about Nicole. Oh, Tiresia, how we needed her! But why was Minor keeping us out in the hallway?

We wanted to see her at once; our wits were returning to us and we thought that the doctor was delaying our approach because of our frightening appearance. And if that was so, then no doubt he was right; the glimmer of good sense that remained to us told us that. We had to clean up, to change.

"We'll go and change," I said.

But Minor stopped us with a gesture.

"I have been keeping her company," he said by way of explanation.

Then:

"I'm afraid of making a mistake."

The same words our father used.

And he looked at us, oh, how our old Doctor Minor looked at

us. We could never have deciphered that look; we perceived it, that was all. It was a look that on some mysterious scales was the equivalent of Nicole's nightmares, the equivalent of Alwin's looks at my brother, and the concern in our father's letter and Poison Ivy's sobs on the hard-packed snow of the New York sidewalks and Adrien's fury on the telephone and our black rage on the lawn.

"Yet we must," he went on, as if to himself.

"There," he said, pointing to the little room beyond the living room.

He led the way.

That little room behind the living room must in more ambitious days have been planned as a clearing room. We had never used it as anything but a utility room. Our few toys and our boots were kept there, between cases our father would come and stretch out on the cast-off sofa that sat there, Nicole came there to try out new slippers, and Tiresia would retire there for short spells when we had guests and their commotion tired her.

At that moment she was seated on the sofa, quite still, her veil drawn across her face.

She did not raise her head, she did not move, yet we knew that her whole being was alive to our presence; we had been able to read Tiresia's body for so long!

She did not see us and perhaps she did not hear us, but she knew we were there and it was almost more than her strength could bear. That was why she sat so still, her head bent beneath her veil, Tiresia who had always held herself so straight. All that we understood perfectly; we needed no explanations from Minor or anyone else.

We were back at the focal point of our household. We wanted to run to her, yet we remained uncertain, for that body of Tiresia's, although so alive with our presence, gave us no idea of our own place. The focal point of our household was there, blind as it had always been, but it no longer gave out any kind of signal. So we looked at its hands, resting as always on her lap, and it was to those hands that Dan and I went, kneeling down on either side, each of us squeezing one of her hands in ours, each with his head resting on that hand.

"Tiresia," said Minor, his voice much too loud, "Estelle and Dan are here."

That voice of Minor's hurt me. It was attempting to rediscover its old professional firmness, but it was too lame. It was a voice out of order.

"Tiresia, Estelle and Dan came back for the funeral.

". . . Estelle and Dan are with you, here in the house.

". . . You must speak to them.

". . . I don't believe they have had dinner.

". . . Did you think to get their room ready?

". . . Tiresia?"

She did not reply, but in her hands we felt the shock waves the doctor's words sent through her, and because of those hands vibrating inside ours, like the infinitely sensitive instruments of a secret, lost, imperiled, hugely imperiled focal point of life, we decided that he was speaking too loud, that his voice was too harsh, his words too brutal, and we huddled closer around Tiresia to protect her.

"Very well," sighed Minor.

From then on everything became very strange. I literally felt something akin to a wind from elsewhere enter the room, and my brother felt it too (forgive me for telling you such senseless things, but I have no other way of describing what happened next and it all happened so quickly), that wind blew in, black as coal and laden with moans the like of which we had never heard, with screams, tumult and bloody silences adding to the tumult, it seemed to tear us from where we knelt and we found ourselves a yard away from Tiresia, on either side of her, standing, afraid. Minor's voice spoke on through that torment, a voice that was his but was changed by something we could not fathom.

"I have made up my mind," he said. "I'm going to tell them, Tiresia, I'm going to tell Dan and Estelle Helleur . . ."

His voice was lost in the violence of the wind that had swooped down on us. Tiresia at once shrank; I have never seen anything like that shrinking and hope never again to do so. As if solidified, her body became like a projectile, and that motionless projectile, of dreadful compactness, was aimed at Minor.

In a second we were between her and Minor, each of us holding one of her arms. They were hard as marble; it was impossible to straighten them. We seized her bodily, we seized Tiresia whom we had never, never once, touched on the body, and that body was utterly rigid, as if bereft of articulations, and it seemed to go on compacting for an instant that seemed like an eternity, oh, how clearly

I understood that old cliché, and that black whirlwind full of unspeakable torments went on whistling in our ears.

Icy fear sat on Minor's face, a fear it had never worn for our
mother's nightmares. He drew back. "I don't have my bag," he said
to us like a lost man, and right after it we thought we heard a laugh.

"Tiresia," Minor shouted so loud it seemed his throat was bursting.

And in the soundless pause that followed:

"Tiresia," said Minor in a supernaturally tense voice, "I will respect
your wish, I swear it by Helleur and by Nicole."

The body we held in our arms seemed to break apart, and the wind
violently veered; it carried away our doctor, it carried Tiresia away;
an ambulance came for her; she had not regained consciousness.
Long after he was gone and we were alone we still heard Minor's
words. "It's my fault, I am taking her to the clinic, you stay here,
you can come later, it's my fault." We sat on alone in that big, utterly
still, quiet house, the Helleur house, henceforth our house alone.

It was the heart of the night.

We had not slept for more than twenty-four hours.

THIRTY-SIX

The Sheet in the Night

Dᴵᴅ ᴛʜᴇʏ lock the front door at night?" Dan said serenely.

"I don't know."

"Then I'll leave it open, shall I?"

"Wide open?"

"Yes."

The door was wide open to the night fog, a black gulf.

We watched it for a moment.

We felt for the switch in the kitchen. Dan filled a pitcher. I put
glasses on the table.

"No, let's take it all upstairs."

Where was the old tray? In the same place, in the dresser. I took the tray with the pitcher and glasses. Dan turned off the faucet and closed the dresser door.

"I want to turn on the garden light," he said, ferreting around in the entranceway.

"On the other side, Dan, they changed it."

The curve of the balustrade jumped into focus on the outside steps. Balustrade and steps were solid, reliable-looking landmarks. Surely they could be seen from a distance, standing out from the fog like that.

"Is that okay?"

"Yes, that's okay."

I was in the hallway, the tray in my hand.

How cold the night was.

The forces of corpse-devouring cold were massed across the landscape. For the moment they remained outside the house, kept at a distance by the garden light and the ramparts of the balustrade, but we felt their basilisk breath.

"We should turn up the heat, Estelle."

We had no idea how to go about it. At length we remembered the thermostat our parents had installed in the living room.

We listened to the sudden growl of the boiler. Heat leapt into the hall. Oh, let our house burn, let its heat and its light carry into the coldest of outer darknesses, let it guide lost travelers, let it proclaim its existence . . .

We went up, the banister showing us the way. The stairs were gentle and turned gently.

"Want me to take the tray?"

"No, I'm fine."

Switching on the staircase light, switching on the landing light. Switching off the staircase light, switching off the landing light. Dan's movements were unhurried. At each pause I waited, my eyes on him.

In my little-girl bedroom the bed was made. The same narrow bed with the same acanthus leaf carved on the wooden headboard.

We set the tray on the floor. We sat down on the edge of the bed. My brother bent, poured water into each glass. We drank.

"Do you want more, Estelle?"

"Yes."

My brother rose. He refilled the pitcher in the little bathroom between my bedroom and his. He returned and I drank a glass and then another.

"I was thirsty, Dan."

"Want some more?"

"No."

"Come on, then."

We went to the old bathroom at the end of the corridor.

"We left our things downstairs."

"I'll get them."

"I'll go with you."

"Yes, you come too."

We spoke and moved like sleepwalkers. Our bags stood in a corner of the hall. When we returned to the bathroom we realized that there was nothing in them. In New York we had simply picked them up from the platform in the loft, too perturbed to pack them.

We looked at the small articles on the bathroom shelf.

"We'll buy toothbrushes tomorrow," said Dan.

I was seated on the edge of the bathtub, my head as if in a dream, unable to make the smallest move.

"Yet I don't seem sleepy, Dan."

My brother was helping me to undress.

"You need water on your skin as well," he said.

I stood naked in the shower. My brother undressed in his turn. He fumbled with the shower fittings; they also seemed to have been changed.

"Turn the handle toward red, Dan."

Hot water came out. We stood under the beneficent stream for a long time, seeking to direct it to where there was most of ourselves. Our bodies were disintegrating pyramids; we let them melt into each other.

Dan was no longer beside me; water rushed around my feet like steaming vapor. Then he was back and steering me out of the shower.

"Turn around, now this way."

"What is it?"

"The sheet from your bedroom."

The touch of the sheet was soft. My brother held part of it in one hand and with the other slowly dried me. The rest of the sheet trailed on the floor. My eyes closed.

"Now your turn," I said, scarcely able to hear my own voice.

And I dried him, leaning against him to reach his shoulders.

"Your back isn't dry yet."

"Doesn't matter."

The sheet was damp. We looked for somewhere to hang it, but it was too big. We shook it out, opened the window, and let it hang outside. My body suddenly slumped down with the sheet onto the windowsill. Night rolled in like great waves converging on the whiteness of the sheet. My brother grasped my shoulders and lifted me. We left, shutting the door behind us.

We walked slowly down the long corridor, naked, arms around each other, our limbs at once leaden and feather light. Halfway down the corridor, my brother picked me up.

"You're out on your feet."

He stretched me out on the little bed.

"So are you."

I moved over to make room for him. He toppled onto the narrow strip of bed.

"I won't get my mattress, Estelle."

"No, stay here, Dan."

I turned to face him, he pulled me to him and then I pulled him toward me, his face on my breast. We shifted a little more and then slept. My brother was inside me; he had slipped inside me very gently with sleep.

Often since then I have had this fantasy of love, of sleeping with the sex of your lover inside you and waking up dug out like a warm nest and feeling inside that nest the weight of your lover's sex. But inevitably the flesh of both parties gives up, and the bodies return to their original frontiers, for the fabulous union cannot hold. No matter how strong the love, the bodies separate.

But on that night of our fullest exhaustion it happened. My brother's sex was in mine and did not move for what remained to us of night. And we slept.

We slept deeply.

We burrowed deep deep down into the heart of sleep, beyond sleeplessness and beyond dreams, down to where sleep is no longer sleep but its very wellspring, a vigil so intense that no living thing can bear it, can approach it only in the very deepest sleeping state.

*   *   *

Dawn came, then morning; the fog was gone. Someone had seen the white sheet at the window, had seen the light on our front steps, the door wide open onto the cold garden.

Someone had come to that door, had wandered about in the chilled rooms below, then had climbed the stairs, toward the heat.

Someone now observed us.

Then the footsteps went back down and stopped on the ground floor.

Someone was waiting below.

"Did you hear that?" I murmured.

"Someone saw us, Estelle."

He gently touched my shoulder, my arm.

"Do you hurt?"

"A little."

"There?"

"We have to get up."

"Let me warm you first."

And my dancer brother, who knew so well what a body needs in order to move, my brother rubbed my stiff sore limbs.

"What should we wear, Dan?"

That was easy: there was nothing we could wear. Our parents were not there for us to go and borrow their clothes, and our own clothes were soiled with a dead woman's blood and the grime of a fight on sodden ground.

There was nothing we could wear, and someone was waiting below.

"Feel better, Estelle?" my brother said softly.

"Yes."

"Then let's go down."

"But someone is there."

"Let's ask that someone for clothes."

"Like this, naked?"

"They've already seen us!"

We were still whispering, but I followed Dan into the corridor.

We went downstairs like that, just as we were, naked and disheveled, covered with swollen bruises, and only halfway back from our great sleep.

Adrien was leaning against the steps outside, smoking a cigarette, watching us descend. On his face too were swollen bruises.

"I'm going to shut the door," said Dan peacefully. "Please come in."

Adrien threw away his cigarette and came in.

"Now listen, Adrien," said Dan. "We have absolutely no clothes. I want you to go and buy the things I'm going to put down on a list, you know where to go, sneakers at the sporting goods store, sweaters at Monoprix, a skirt at Dames de France, pants at —"

"You want me to go get you some clothes?" said Adrien.

"We'll get coats ourselves once you've brought the rest."

"Are you serious?" said Adrien.

"We need clothes," said Dan.

"You fuck your sister and then you want me to go buy you clothes?"

Adrien swung around on his heel and left, slamming the door.

"Estelle," said Dan.

And in the same second I said "Dan." Suddenly we laughed.

We were in each other's arms, shaking with our old uncontrollable laughter, our faces too sore to touch. Dan was stroking my hair and I was stroking his. "Well, well," he kept saying, and I knew the whole of the long speech that lay behind that "well," and I replied in my own way with another long speech contained in a tiny noise I heard in my throat.

"Now that it's done," said Dan (which meant "Now that Adrien has well and truly seen us"), "let's get dressed anyway."

It turned out to be quite easy. We reverted to our childhood habits of disguise, a sheet wound about the waist, a blanket draped over head and shoulders, here and there safety pins (found in the usual place in Nicole's chest of drawers on the landing). Then we made coffee in the kitchen.

We moved without haste, weighing every article with our eyes before taking hold of it, and the things in the house obeyed.

There is nothing stranger than what is familiar. When you expect the strange, you are ready for anything, ready for surprises: the strange fits automatically into a labeled, ready-made slot, and when it comes to pass you may be deeply disconcerted, but at least you recognize the astonishment you had been expecting.

With the familiar you are not ready to be surprised. And experiencing such surprise engenders a sense of strangeness all the stranger for being indefinable.

The tray we had found the day before in its accustomed place in the dresser, the pitcher we had filled with water from the same old faucet that leaked at the joint, the Venetian glasses with which Nicole had filled the house and which by now were all mismatched, the safety pins in her mahogany chest of drawers on the landing . . . Those things were there, in place, but how strange it was to be their new owners.

It absorbed all our attention. We drank our coffee, eyes glued to the discolored patches on the ceiling that we had probably been looking at for years. But until now they had not addressed themselves particularly to us.

Everything in the house now spoke to us, and it was strange to be thus solicited. How insistent the solicitation felt: from within every object a strange power tugged at us, and responding required our combined forces.

At the table we sat elbow to elbow. On our feet too we steered one toward the other, ceaselessly skirting things in order to come together. I remember it as irresolution, obstacles to be overcome, furniture or even small articles, Dan's arm pushing aside a cup to settle against my arm . . .

Nicole. All her short life she had done that, skirting obstacles to reach what she aspired so mightily to attain. We children among other things were the obstacles, forcing her to accomplish tattered gestures she wanted no part of; what she aspired to was not other living beings but a dream, an ideal garland of movements to array herself with, the flawless dance of glorious bodies no living being ever knows.

We were back in the kitchen looking for lightbulbs when the window glass suddenly shattered with a sound like an explosion and something flew across the room, thudding into my hip before falling to our feet.

It was a package. It had fallen apart in its flight.

All the clothes we had asked Adrien for were there, absolutely right as to size, not a single item missing, with even some accessories we had not thought of . . . but black, all black, skirt, sweaters, pants, socks, belt, even the sneakers.

Dan was studying the sneakers in amazement.

"He's blackened them with shoe polish, Estelle!"

The glass had shattered all over the kitchen tiles. To sweep up the sharp splinters we had to put on the black sneakers. Stains came off on our hands and ankles; when we tried later to remove them with soap they were reluctant to go. Adrien had not just used shoe polish. He has told me since then what product he added, but its name always escapes me.

We cleaned up the glass splinters, then arranged the clothes on the table and sat down to look at them.

We could not tear our eyes from those clothes. There was something about them we could not understand. Dan picked them up and weighed them in his hands.

"No," he said.

"I agree," I said.

"The sneakers?" asked Dan.

"Not them either," I said.

We removed the sneakers and carefully placed them on the heap of black clothes.

The ground was frozen and the air biting, but I do not think we felt anything.

We walked barefoot on the backyard gravel in our blanket-and-sheet getups, pierced by every tongue the cold possessed, and we felt neither the cold nor the sharp edges of the gravel.

"Money?' I said suddenly.

We had nothing, apart from a handful of dollars and cents. My French checkbook had stayed in Paris with Yves. Dan stopped for a second, then shrugged.

"They'll give us credit," he said, "until —"

"Of course," I said.

We resumed our walk.

"You're cutting your feet, Estelle, I'll carry you."

"Oh no you won't, it would be too heavy on this gravel."

"You forget I'm a dancer."

"And you forget that for six months I've been looking at a dancer."

"Let me see your feet."

Dan delicately raised my heel. My soles were unbroken. He smiled. We were absurdly proud.

We rounded the corner of the house.

Before us the garden stretched with its wide central pathway, and at the end of the pathway the railing with its old-fashioned spear points, and beyond it the street.

The street was lifeless.

Our house was the last one. If you turned right you headed for the cemetery, and if you turned left you walked along two or three hundred yards of deserted wisteria-hung sidewalks before coming to small, almost equally dull streets and just beyond them the not very tall church beside the market square, which led into the shopping center.

For a moment we contemplated the big garden, the pathway crossing it, and the gate opening out onto the street. We thought we heard — borne in by our memories — the sounds of the square and its adjoining streets, the streets where the sporting goods store, Monoprix, and Dames de France all did business . . .

My brother looked at me. He looked at the sheet twisted around my waist with twine (Mr. Neighbor had left us a big spool one day, of the kind he used for smaller freight items in his work), the quilted blanket worn like a cape above it and already ripped by the safety pins tugging at the fabric, my bare feet streaked with black by the sneakers. I caught his look, I sensed the hesitation forming behind it.

"Dan," I said firmly, "I will not wear those black things . . ."

How is it that I saw and still see my own getup and not my brother's? I think the shifts I had perceived the day before on first entering the house were still going on, and now they had reached a most secret zone within us, the zone we communicated through.

Normally Dan and I had no need to look at each other. Indeed, I believe that we looked very rarely at each other: we had a direct view "from inside."

But my brother was looking at me. And caught body and soul, I plunged into his eyes and in those eyes I straddled his look; that look went straight to me, and for the first time perhaps it traveled to me, as it were, "from the outside." Through his eyes I saw myself from the outside.

That look was new.

In that moment, as we gazed at the garden spread out before us (and, beyond the garden, the street and the town), my brother had moved more swiftly than I: he was already able to direct that outside look at me. And in that external trajectory, his look had harvested something of the invisible secretions ceaselessly produced by agglomerations of human souls, secretions that then float in moving clouds about cities.

Two people in our town had a peculiar appearance: Mr. Raymond and an old drunkard known for lack both of information and interest as the Idiot. Probably our appearance was even more peculiar.

Dan slowed down. Our undertaking worried him; he was afraid for me.

But I saw nothing very special in his getup. I still saw Dan from inside, as I always had.

"Listen," I said to him, "let's at least go as far as the novelty store."

Its windows also offered a few garments, shapeless enough to fit any body. It was the very closest store. My idea was to make a first stop there before going farther into the town.

I pulled my brother toward the garden pathway, toward the road.

"We'll never wear Adrien's black clothes."

My voice surprised me. It rang high and clear in the icy air.

Almost at once a car that must have been waiting a little way along drew up outside the gate, its engine turning softly. The back door opened.

We reached the end of the path, pushed through the gate, got in the car, shut the door.

"I did what you asked," said Adrien stubbornly.

"We're not going to wear those clothes."

"You have to wear black," he said.

"No," I said, "no, no, no."

Adrien turned to look at me. He must have heard sobs in my voice.

"As you like," he said, his voice suddenly unembellished.

He changed gear and the car moved off.

So Adrien drove us into town, he sitting in his dark suit at the wheel while we sat in the back in our disguise of sheets and blankets.

He stopped and looked for what we asked for and came out. He went back in to ask for a different color, the color we specified, and came out again to confer with us, and if that particular color was not to be had, we left, and Adrien drove us. He drove us for the rest of the morning, then he dropped us in front of our house.

"Good-bye," he said.

"Thank you," we said.

We took out our packages.

Adrien hesitated.

"Need a hand?"

"No, that's okay," we said.

Then the door slammed and the car shot away, skidding out into the middle of the road.

We waited for it to straighten out and vanish into our neighbors' garage, then we went into the house, arms full of our new clothes.

THIRTY-SEVEN

White Yellow Purple

WHAT WE had been so stubbornly set on was brightly colored clothes.

Perhaps in our confused minds a phrase from the day before had bobbed to the surface, the words Minor muttered when he saw us in our thick quilted gaudy Canal Street clothes: "Let them be, let them be, Nicole's yellow and Tiresia's purple, just right."

Yellow, purple . . . Those colors were not common in our town, and less so in winter, and even less for clothes.

"I could swear you were doing it deliberately," Adrien had said. "You couldn't look worse if you were going to a carnival." He was wrong. We were indeed buying our mourning clothes, but we did not know it. And he did not know that for us Nicole lived in perpetual glory in her yellow tulip dress and Tiresia in the long purple sheath that fell open at the legs in siren folds.

Yet those dresses must have existed somewhere in his memory; he had seen them one long-gone day, one distant afternoon . . .

Our parents had been expecting a visit from our neighbors and their eldest child, Adrien. The living room windows were wide open, it

was summer, someone had made a joke about the wilted potted plant
Mr. Neighbor would surely present to us, and suddenly, as if wafted
in on a warm breeze blowing in from nowhere, heady joy took
possession of our living room, weaving garlands of laughter and
sending the rustle of dresses up the stairs and around the room, and
in the glow that our austere old living room consented to, the sulky
countenances of our parents faded away and gave place to yellow
pink and purple pink, camellia white, butterfly, prince and queen of
legend, just as our neighbor's bald skull suddenly went by under the
window, and soon the bell rang and the inevitable potted plant came
in through the garden door, looking like the bovine face of some
stray ruminant.

I recently asked Adrien about that summer afternoon.

He readily admits to seeing our father in a white suit one day. "It
made me really uneasy! White on a man, as if for a bride!" Poor
Adrien! For the whole of that visit his eyes had been glued on Nicole,
and when by the nature of things he was obliged to tear his gaze
away it was just to stick out his tongue at me from behind his mother's
back.

As for the dresses: "Oh, come on! Do you think everything re-
volved around you goddamned Helleurs? I had other fish to fry, and
anyway you were all crazy, how do you expect me to remember one
thing rather than another!"

Adrien, Adrien, if you had balls, you would think, and remember!

But Adrien does not want to think or remember.

Yet that old picture, buried in his weed-choked labyrinthine mind,
must have quickened to life, announcing itself like a distant glimmer,
and it was because of it that Adrien now did the senseless things we
asked of him.

For he obeyed us on all points.

He offered us gray garments, then dark green, then brown. "This
one?" Adrien asked hopefully. No, it was not right. "Well, what is
it you do want? We've ransacked every store in this damned town,
we can't go rummaging through people's drawers . . ."

We did not really know what we were after either, but it was not
gray or bronze-green or brown. But when we reached the Pronuptia
bridal store Dan suddenly exclaimed "There!" and pointed at the
window.

I believe that at that moment, possibly for the only time in his
life, Adrien felt himself weaken.

He could not stand us but he could not extricate himself from
our madness; if we had asked him, he would have carried out the
mannequin seated in splendor in the window, seized it bodily with
its veils, its bouquets, and its gown stiff with lace. For us he would
have brought back that enormous white matrimonial hot-air balloon. But what Dan was pointing at was a corsage, a small-town-
bridesmaid's corsage, somewhat mawkish but of a brilliant yellow.

"That?" said Adrien, flabbergasted.

"Yes, yes."

We were most eager.

Nearby, close by, tall elegant roses swaying on their stems, air like
balm, on a slender sun-warmed bare shoulder a strap slipped and a
man's hand pulled it back up, lingered tenderly, buttercups and daf-
fodils in the meadow, and the gorse glowing on the encircling hills;
sitting there in the backseat of Adrien's car we swam in the color
yellow like blissful drugged birds.

"Cheesy and expensive," said Adrien after investigating the store.

"Get it," Dan replied, and Adrien returned to the store, too weak
to protest further.

We watched him go through the door like a bent weary traveling
salesman, diminished in dark clothes that did not suit him. And he
came back: "There's a skirt to match," he said, so exactly repeating
a saleslady's toneless articulation that we laughed.

"Get it," and he went back and returned with the package.

"It looks stupid," he said.

"We'll worry about that," Dan replied.

"It's in your name, Helleur, they'll send you the bill."

"Fine!" said Dan.

And now as if on the wings of a phantom another color invaded
our mind — the air grew purple: plush chairs, brocade curtains, tall
haughty roses standing on a gleaming piano, the piano open, a man
standing attentively by the piano; as the first notes rose the tall roses
shed their leaves and fused with the music, the silent music of purple
petals saturating our heads.

Oh, that purple had entered us. And snared in it, as we had been
snared in the yellow, both snared in identical fascination, we had no
need to explain our quest to Adrien, to reveal the reasons for it.

"I don't understand you," Adrien grumbled. So much the worse
for him, and anyway it was his nature to complain. "Whining Adrien"
we called him when we were children.

What could we have told him? We knew what we did not want. And what we wanted we chanced upon as we went along. Why complicate everything, Adrien?

Sweaters purple enough to suit us were to be found only in the women's department, but Dan rejected the skimpy offerings, sending Adrien back twice and three times for a larger size. He finally returned empty-handed.

"We don't have red in that size," said the saleslady.

"Hold on there," said Adrien, "I said purple, not red."

"It's all the same," said the saleslady.

"I'll have to check," said Adrien.

"Okay, take what she has, but big, big," said Dan.

Adrien was off again.

"We don't have red in the large sizes," the saleslady repeated, "you see, sir, red is one of the wilder colors, for young people . . ."

"The saleslady says she only has red in small."

"I don't want a tight sweater," said Dan.

"I don't get it," said Adrien, "you used to be skin and bone."

"I was a kid," said Dan.

"I suppose so," said Adrien, and his sulky gaze traveled over Dan's splendid frame, the muscles outlined by the badly fastened blanket he wore.

We drove up and down streets. "I'm going myself," cried my brother, preparing to jump from the car, barefoot as a monk beneath his blanket. "No, no," Adrien implored, and we kept driving.

Like some splendid stage set, the color purple filled our heads, and we, ensconced in the car, waited for costumes worthy of that set to appear onstage.

But perhaps I should explain, madame. This all took place in a small provincial town in France, at the end of the sixties, a little town, somewhat sleepy, nestled among hills. Postwar prosperity was slow to reach us — and no, there was not a very wide range of clothes to choose from.

Dan had to make do with a shirt with narrow maroon stripes.

"Looks old on you," said Adrien.

"None of your business," said my brother.

"I charged it to Helleur —," said Adrien.

"And we'll get the bill!" said my brother.

"What?"

"Nothing."

But a necktie found by chance brought us great contentment: it was almost the color purple. "You in a tie!" Adrien exclaimed. And since there was no such thing as pants in shades of yellow and red, Dan made us go back to the sporting goods store, where they still had a pair of white canvas pants left over from summer. White too pleased us.

We sent Adrien into several more stores in search of everyday items we needed. But this time he went unprotesting. We had the essentials. Yellow, purple, white. Those colors warmed our hearts, they seemed exactly right. We felt we had done a good deed.

Thus the hounds of our minds were off and running along their obscure trail, flank to flank and tenacious, along their obscure trail in hot pursuit of incandescent colors that even before their birth had already dazzled them.

At home we dressed carefully. I had never seen Dan tackle a necktie.

"Wear it like a scarf," I suggested.

"No," he answered firmly.

Strangely enough, he tied the knot as if he had been doing it all his life.

I could not take my eyes from his fingers moving deftly around that knot . . .

Our father . . . How many times had I watched him knotting his tie in Nicole's mirror in the hall? Why in the hall? I think now that our father had a little weakness; I think that every now and then this man, who never stopped worrying about the members of his family, needed us to notice him. His ties hung in the little cloakroom beneath the stairs. When he stood before the mirror, right in the center of the hall, and began this painstaking and absorbing operation, he was guaranteed spectators, young or old . . .

And now, fascinated, strangely absorbed, I followed my brother's nimble fingers as they knotted the purple tie without realizing that the oft-observed gestures of our father had come to life again in that nimbleness.

At one point Dan turned toward me and our eyes met.

In his look were our whole house, our childhood, the previous day, our night, the present moment. All of that passed from him to me and then returned reinforced through my eyes to him: our whole house, our childhood, the previous day, our night, the present moment.

And we were unaware of that broad movement that carried along so much time and place and feeling. Even today I can scarcely give expression to these things. All I find is this verb "to look." *You, madame, my writer, is there in our language another, richer, more complete verb than this "to look"? Find it, I beg you, please find it.*

I had some trouble getting my new clothes to go together. The color was indeed the same as Nicole's tulip dress, but the style was not hers at all: the skirt was narrow, not large and billowing, not a lady's skirt. Now it was Dan's turn to observe me. There was something intrigued in his expression; he seemed to have run aground on a problem whose constituent elements escaped him.

High-heeled shoes with thin stiletto heels, the ones we had pointed out to Adrien in the store window. They fastened with a strap. I stood up. In those heels I was tall, much taller than Nicole, who was in any case inches shorter than me. I took a few steps to test my balance. In those heels my gait was not a dancer's.

"You don't look like Nicole," said Dan.

"Oh," I said.

Nothing more.

Madame, the dread manipulator of our destiny led us by the nose; we did not even hear our own words. "You don't look like Nicole." "Oh," I said, nothing more. Fettered thoughts, massive stone slabs, fog, I could still howl, so many years later.

The next moment was already there. We were clothed.

"What now?" said my brother.

"The garage."

We went down to Nicole's garage, her blue garage, her studio, her paradise.

What a small room it was! It would not have been big enough for a single one of Dan's splits . . . or Michael's, or Kenny's, or David's, or Djuma's. And thinking of Alwin in this place gave me an unspeakable pang, a sense of irreparable desolation.

The blue hangings were faded. Along the whole length of the bar the blue was grimy.

"So this was Nicole's sky," Dan muttered.

We were sitting on the carpet. It was cold in that room, which had been added on to the side of the house and whose walls were probably made of cinder blocks. The old familiar smell of jasmine, skin, and dust had gone. There was now only a smell of cold. We shivered.

"You couldn't dance here."

"No, of course not."

We were whispering.

"Maybe we should turn it back into a garage?" I went on, a little louder.

"There's no more car."

"We could buy one."

"Put a car here?" said Dan helplessly.

"Come on," I said, getting up first.

We went up to Tiresia's room. On the landing we hesitated for a second. Dan put his hand on the doorknob.

"Wait," I said.

The balance of forces in constant play between us had shifted yet again.

"Wait."

My old vaypigo was stirring within me. I was sweating. The horror that had carried off Tiresia whistled in my ears, distorted words writhed about me, too charred to be deciphered . . . Perhaps I am mistaken. Perhaps, affected by what I later learned, interpretations have insinuated themselves, injecting run-of-the-mill sensations with exalted meaning. *But what does that kind of truth matter to me, madame? Mine burns within me and is my only reason for telling this story. It seemed to me that if we opened the door, a damped-down furnace would burst forth with a roar.*

"It's hot," I said.

"It always gets hotter the higher you climb," said Dan.

His hand dropped from the knob.

"Another time?" he said.

I nodded.

As we went back down to the first floor my uneasiness began to fade. We had left the front door open, and although we had been shivering in Nicole's garage a few moments earlier, the cold now did me good, dispelling the vaypigo.

We went into our father's study. I knew that study better than Dan did. At the end of my high school years and the beginning of my law studies, I had often come here to question my father on one point or another. I walked eagerly in, then turned. Dan stood on the threshold, looking almost jammed in the doorway.

"Come in!"

But he made no move.

"Tell me what you see on that shelf," he said.

"Which one?"

"The one right in front of you."

I read out the titles to him.

"And the next one?"

I began to move down the glass-fronted bookshelves, telling my brother what books were there.

"Remember what Father used to say?"

"What about, Dan?"

"About his work."

"His cases?"

"No, about the man being tortured."

I was struck. Dan had been very small when our father quoted that passage of his favorite philosopher to me.

"You remember that?"

"Yes, but not very well. I wanted to know the exact words."

I did not understand.

"Find me the words he told you."

"Now, Dan?"

"Yes, now."

His voice had an edge that seemed to bite into my flesh.

"But I no longer know which book it was in."

"His philosopher's, the one he was always reading."

"Bergson?"

"Yes."

A peculiar anguish came to me with his words. How did Dan know what our father read? On the other hand, how could he not have known? I realized that I had made my brother a stranger in our house, because it had suited me, perhaps . . .

"Look, Estelle," he said in the same hard voice.

"But where, where do you want me to look?"

"The Bergsons are there."

My head swam. My anguish intensified. The Bergsons were in the little revolving bookshelf my brother was pointing to. I should have known, yet it seemed like the first time I had ever seen that shelf.

"There are a lot of them, Dan."

"You've studied a lot, Estelle, you ought to know."

I took a volume at random. The lines ran together and I could not read. I tried to replace it, but my hands were shaking and the

book's neighbor slid sideways, upsetting the whole row, which collapsed in a sharp-cornered cascade onto my feet. I retrieved one of
the volumes, but this one too I was unable to read. Then I examined
them all one by one, trying at least to get an idea from their titles.
I could not.

"You really don't know, Estelle?"

I had replaced every book, probably in the wrong order.

My two hands went on clinging to the shelf, and I went on clinging
to my two hands, staring at them as if I possessed nothing else in
the world; then my head fell forward onto them.

"My God, it's physical," I said.

Those words came unbidden, crossing my lips like autonomous
beings, those words that had sealed our separation more than seven
years before. I have no words to describe the sensation, words passing
through your body, being uttered by your voice and thereafter laying
claim to their own existence.

All the time that had piled up during those seven years, seemingly
so well formed, so rock solid with meaning, collapsed before them
like a defeated army, quite simply canceled itself out. It was the same
quartet of words, everyday and for that very reason frightening
words, stubbornly present, spurning all negotiation.

"My God, it's physical." So those few absurd words had been
there all along, tucked away in oblivion but enduring in all their
monstrous imbecilic vitality, and now they had sprung forth intact
and complacent. I was stunned, and suddenly drained of strength to
fight.

How old my pain was; it flowed back up in bitter floods, in tumultuous floods, breasting the past's sheer cliffs as it reached up to me.

"My God, it's physical."

The stupid words cried out, louder and louder, the flood boiled
about my head, I screamed, "It's physical, Dan."

"Estelle, I love you," my brother cried.

On the edge of a cliff, my vision brutally clear, I saw two shapes in
pale light, two children. They were walking to meet each other when
a sudden convulsion threw them together. That same convulsion was
about to separate them, to make them fall. "Dan," I shouted . . .

We were those children, and we did collide, but we did not fall.
We hugged and we pulled each other away from that cliff edge where
ferocious pain was howling. "My love, my love," said my brother,

we kissed hard, and walls and doors floated past us; then we were in the entranceway, tottering, and kissing desperately for fear of letting go, even for a second.

"It was here, here," I sobbed, pointing to the spot where we had recognized our love only to lose it at once.

A few floor tiles in the entranceway between the kitchen and the stairs, harmless and without mystery in the light of day, and that very harmlessness making me sob even harder. I saw them, Dan in shorts, bare-chested, Estelle in her shirt of embroidered cotton, long and white, so provincial, "You were wearing shorts, I was in my night-shirt, here, right here."

"I love you, I love you," said my brother, and we moved toward my bedroom, shaking off the ferocious pain that now howled from afar. Our kisses drove it to flight, our kisses like burning brands drove off the beast that had for so long slaked its thirst at our hearts. It was falling from the cliff, falling.

And the smaller it became, the greater grew the strength returning to us, wave upon wave, inexhaustible.

In the same bedroom where we slept throughout our childhood, where we had slept the previous night exhausted, one inside the other, we finally became lovers, and that love was a clear powerful stream, free of the beast that had nourished itself for so many years on our strength.

THIRTY-EIGHT

The Exchange

Madame, *I fear you will forsake my brother and me.*
The moment draws on, and the horizon of the past constantly recedes. But it does not grow faint — on the contrary, madame, it grows wider, presenting more and ever-wider space, and this space is ever more densely, ever more irresistibly populated.

Such growth of the past never stops; it reaches forward, right up to the present, while the present itself goes its merry way, and I attempt to bridge the two of them with this flimsy edifice.

I do not know whether such language even begins to reflect the truth, whether our father's philosopher would have approved. It is so long since I read him; I no longer read, madame, not even the paper; what I learn of the world comes to me through Phil and I pretend, just pretend, to know what is going on. I have time only for speaking to you. I must surely be getting stupid: I tell you whatever comes to me, raw and unprocessed; only my confidence in you sustains me. So quickly, here is this flimsy edifice to bring you here, you who are not me, so that you can turn it into a palace in which to play the music I still hear inside me.

At this precise moment a melody for flute, so light it must be swimming through and around heavy cells of matter to reach the kingdom of death, and then those beings at last delivered begin to move, I hear them draw near. Do not forsake us, madame, they seek a palace in which to live forever.

I have to speak to you of Tiresia, of our Doctor Minor, of my husband Yves, of that attorney who came into our lives; I have to give you explanations that make sense, but anxiety unsettles me. What I want to tell you now is what happened that night, which must have been the third night we spent alone in our house.

I heard Nicole's clock chime on the landing, and my brother was not by my side. It was 3:00 A.M. Our bodies had been together virtually every second since our return to the town of our birth.

"Dan?"

I looked into the corridor, toward the faint glow of the clock's pendulum. The house was dark.

I felt the air displaced by his passage: he had walked down this corridor, he had walked down the stairs, but then, then what? I leaned over the banister for a second.

Madame, that house like all other houses was made of walls, of stones, of cement and wood, and I know that those things do not speak; but I also know that as I leaned over the gently sloping bend in the stairs I perceived traces of light, a displacement of the air, in that dark motionless space. Our house told me that Dan had gone down, had sought a specific spot on the first floor, and then had moved on.

Our house told me all that, and if you cannot believe me then forsake me now, you are not for me . . . no, do not forsake me: my brother had left the house, madame, and it was his wake of light and displaced air that troubled my mind, like a current of particles. Perhaps there are physical theories for this kind of phenomenon. I am simply telling you what I felt. That current was strong, and it drew me.

Yet I was not afraid; this was not fear.

I dressed very quickly. The yellow silk blouse, the yellow silk skirt, high-heeled shoes. We had not yet had time to buy coats.

I stumbled downstairs.

On a coat peg in the kitchen I found a crocheted shawl that was neither Nicole's nor Tiresia's; it probably belonged to our neighbor's maid. When the shawl refused to detach itself from the peg, I tugged, and with a strange soft ripping it finally came loose. I threw it around my shoulders and it hit me with an unpleasant thud on the shoulder blade, the impact bringing tears to my eyes. But I had no time to give it thought: all I felt was the urge to leave the house, to make haste, and if I wept it was because I was not moving fast enough.

Something was happening; my only fear was that I would not be equal to it.

The night was cold and clear, the shadows in the garden stood out clearly, but it was outdoors and I no longer felt my brother's presence.

Skirting the house, I went and stood below our old attic; the little door above the tin-roofed lean-to was black, so black in the whiteness of the moon that it left a dark blur in the center of my eye.

"Dan isn't here," the door's invisibility said. "If he were, you would be able to see me," the little door's intensity said. "I do not know where he is, but keep looking for him, don't stay here," it said. "That's why I'm keeping out of your sight, so that you won't linger here, go on, go away . . . ," it said.

There was no one up there; the door had not been opened.

I went out to the apple tree in the meadow.

What hard going the meadow was in the frost! In places my heels broke through the surface between clumps of earth, as if the earth were seizing me by those slender spikes. "Nicole," a voice sobbed, and I stopped, stunned by my distress, in the middle of that black field flecked with glittering points of white, and again I heard that sob, "Nicole, Nicole." It was nearby, it was inside me, it was my own voice weeping.

Oh, my dancing Nicole on your too-flat slippers or your too-high heels, so that was what you were building, a relationship with the earth. The whole time we thought of you as frivolous or distracted, you too maintained a relationship with the earth.

An obscure and ugly fight waged at the bottom of your frail soul: dance slippers for conciliation or for cunning, stiletto heels for attack or perhaps for flight, for escape to the sky, I know not what . . . Nicole, leave me, I'm looking for Dan. "Nicole, leave me," I cried out, and the frail, gentle young woman withdrew, and my eyes rose to the apple tree.

With my gaze still caught in the branches, I reached the middle of the meadow.

Our fine leafy tree, the object of Mr. Raymond's envy, the witness of our patient waiting, was now frozen and skeletal, as if it had died with the old man who talked to it. But there was an almost muscular tension in its stiffened boughs; its absence of movement informed rather than repulsed me.

"Dan didn't come this way; if he had, you would see something, a broken twig, an out-of-place glittering, but he didn't come, so I'm playing dead," said the apple tree of the long stations of our childhood. "But I don't know where he is," it said with hard twisted features in the moon-white light. "Look for him, go on, go away . . . ," it said.

I went down to the ditch into which Dan had dropped like a stone onto one of our cousins, who was himself like a stone in our life, stone upon stone, the first disturbance registered in our childhood . . . But our rich deep ditch was no longer there; nothing was left but a slight unevenness in the ground. "Dan is not in me," said our childhood's ditch. "If he were, I would be here too, you would see me," it said from that unevenness which was like the saddened surface of the regret that had filled it in. "Don't stay here," it said, "look for him, go on, go away . . ."

I left the meadow by the hedge at its far end and climbed the side of the hill to the crevice where our cave lay. The bushes had grown thicker since our departure, no one had been by recently. The cold smell at the opening was that of absence.

I was in the defensive screen of small alleyways guarding the approaches to the marketplace. All the shutters were closed, the housefronts had their backs turned to me. I walked out in front of the church; its double doors were shut tight. I knelt and pressed my ear to the ground, the way we did when we were children. Not a sound. The few streets fanning out from the square were silent and deserted.

A strange idea occurred to me. I went to the bridal store; the spot the yellow blouse had occupied in its window was well and truly empty. Then I went to the sporting goods store in the next street and glued my face to the window, which in those days had neither grille nor iron blinds: the white pants that had been pinned there on a poster of a yacht and the sea were no longer there. This did not relieve me, it simply confirmed something for me, but what?

I was outside the cemetery. The gate was locked. I shook it but it refused to move. Thrusting my head between the railings, I studied the pathways inside. The graves were perfectly aligned, and I could have read the names on the stones almost to the end of the central pathway, even in the neighboring paths. And suddenly that ordered perfection worried me more than anything else. "Alex," I called in a low voice. The caretaker's little house stood right beside the gate. "Alex, Alex . . ."

I was afraid of shouting, afraid of disturbing our father and Nicole.

The upstairs shutters opened.

"Estelle?"

"Is Dan there?"

Alex leaned right out, clinging to his shutter like a bird about to fall. At the top of his voice he whispered:

"No, why, what's up?"

"I don't know where Dan is."

"Wait, I'll be down, wait, okay?" Alex whispered energetically.

I was standing in front of the door of the little house. A few icy moments went by, then someone was running in the cemetery. I hurried to the fence; it was Alex, face jammed between two railings, features twitching with frustration.

"My father has locked all the keys away, I can't come out."

"Alex, go and see."

"What?"

"In the cemetery, take a look."

"I promise you there's nothing there."

"Please, go and look."

A long, long interlude. Alex went, go on, Alex, faithful friend, not for a second did I lose sight of his figure, he was running now, a quiet unhurried small-town-athlete's run. I could see him among the crosses and monuments, among the graves, I could hear the soft hiss of air expelled from his lungs, quiet, unhurried. Today he is the cemetery caretaker and runs the local soccer team. He has married Adrien's cousin twice or thrice removed, the girl in the revealing blouse with the stains under her arms. And over there in New York Michael now owns his cab and runs a small dance school in his native Bronx. DeNoDe (Dance Not Drugs) he calls it, where neighborhood kids come after school, free or for a nominal fee, and every evening Michael is there, attentive and passionate. Dear Michael, dear Alex, if you had only been with us in the days that lay ahead . . .

"Not a soul," said Alex, who was not even breathing hard.

He touched my hands as he clutched the railings.

"Wait there, Estelle, don't leave, okay?"

He came back with something hanging from his arm.

"Put that on, you're frozen."

"What is it?"

"A coat of my mother's."

"Your mother's?"

"Yes, why not, you can put it on, we're in the same boat now, anyway."

His mother had died when he was born. She too was in the cemetery. That at least was how I understood his meaning; it seemed utterly right to me. I took that other dead woman's coat but could not get it on.

"I'm not doing it deliberately, I swear, Alex," I said between chattering teeth.

He tried to help me through the railings. He could not get it on me either.

"But what's that on your back, Estelle?"

"Where?"

"Turn around, there, on your shoulder."

Tugging at the shawl I had slipped on before leaving the house, he extracted the round end of a piece of wood from its loose-knit links.

"What is that?" he asked, mesmerized.

"It looks like a coat peg; throw it away."

The other end of the peg was embedded in a clump of hard white material.

"It's plaster! Plaster, can you believe it!"

Of course it was plaster, why was Alex making such a big thing of this? The coat peg and a chunk of plaster had come away when I pulled the shawl off the wall, nothing more.

"But you were carrying it on your back, Estelle. On your back!"

It bothered him horribly. I was hurt.

I finally managed to wriggle the coat on, but one end of the shawl remained trapped under the shoulder of that garment, which was tight and narrow, the way the fashions of that time dictated. Alex had hold of the other end of the shawl, in which the coat peg was still enmeshed.

He held it as if he had a poisonous toadstool in his hand. I pulled back sharply. The shawl was ripped from Alex's grasp and the peg seemed to leap back through the railings.

We stared at each other, white-faced.

"What's going on with you and your brother?" said Alex.

"Go back to bed, please."

"I don't understand you."

"Go back to bed, Alex, I'm going home now."

"I try to understand, I'd like to understand you, Estelle."

"I'm going home now, thanks for the coat."

"Yet you two are my best friends. Even Adrien —"

"I'm not cold anymore, thanks for everything."

"It's not the same with Adrien. He's like me, except of course he'll go much farther."

"Alex, I beg you . . ."

"But you and your brother!"

He was almost sobbing.

"It's not right, what you're doing."

"No, Alex, it's not right."

"And with Mr. Helleur and Nicole right here in my cemetery, it isn't right . . ."

I saw how moved he was. I understood that, stable though he was, something was pushing him over the edge, but my main concern was to have him return to his little house. "Later, later, Alex," that was what I thought with a heartlessness that staggers me today.

I do not know whether I loved him at the time. I believe Adrien was right: I could not see past my brother. I saw neither my father nor my mother nor Tiresia, still less our neighbors, still less Alex.

Only now do I see them all clearly — oh, madame, they are in my head night and day. And what does "in my head" mean? They are in my heart,

*in my blood, in the spasms of my bowels, in the storms of my blood vessels,
in my brain where the pictures I constantly seek arise, so intense is my
yearning for them, madame. It is my whole body I offer them, an ardent
happy offering that I myself do not comprehend.*

Phil, perhaps only a few days ago, said to me:

"Claire, I'd like you to feel good; I'd like to help you be happy."

He blushed after such declarations.

Probably it was one of those nights when Nicole torments me the
way her nightmares used to, when I get up from bed ("Claire, what
are you doing?" "I'm just getting a drink" and in my head as if in
insidious warning I hear his words from the early days of our acquaintance: "*This woman who wanders about at night*," "Just getting
a drink, Phil . . .").

Or perhaps it was the day after one of those nights when Nicole
torments me and which are like the day after her nightmares, full of
fantasy and of high spirits, of too-high spirits, to make up for the
time swallowed by torment . . .

Phil had noticed these changes of mood. Despite all my attempts
to hide them, he had noticed. If he knew they are but tiny symptoms
of what floods and scalds and freezes me inside, unendingly . . .

"Little Clarinette, I'd like to help you," he said, blushing as if
already anxious to take back his words.

And I sniggered to myself. It was not "being happy" I wanted, it
was finding Dan and our father and Tiresia and our whole Helleur
household, and now Alex . . .

What can a being like Phil, a being from today on this planet
where my brother died, what can he understand of what "being
happy" means to me?

Phil's skin when he blushes . . . I thought the skin of real people
was flat and smooth and glowing. Phil's skin is pitted, and his eyes
do not light it up. And those blushes, like those of Adrien's girl
cousin when she promenaded down the road on Sundays . . . My
brother never blushed, his skin simply took on greater depth, and
when he smiled his skin lit up as if from within.

Yet this is what astonishes me, Phil is a real being. Living. I am
close to him. I want to be close to him.

"Forget it," he said abruptly, turning his head in that brusque
manner he occasionally, very occasionally, has, when something in-
timidates him and he decides all at once to wash his hands of it.

That too, madame. A dancer's movements, the smallest of his
gestures, are beauty. Phil's movements are simply lunges, attempts,

misses. I was going to say "are simply part of life." But I have promised myself that henceforth I will love what is here . . . life.

Now Alex was really sobbing, slumped against the railing.

He wore his sports windbreaker, but in his haste had put it on inside out, and the black fabric square that served as the inside backing for the badge outside looked like an emblem of grief on his robust chest.

"A good-looking lad," Minor used to say. "Alex has something Slavic in his appearance" was our father's comment, "that must be what catches your attention, Minor. Those high cheekbones and blue eyes, it's strange, isn't it, you could swear Mr. Raymond was his father . . . Yes, very strange," our father went on in a faraway voice. "Well, well, Helleur," said Minor, the two men looked at each other, our father seemed to make an effort. "Alex Bonneville, yes, a well set up young man," he said. "Yes, that's it," said Minor, "a well set up young man, and a good lad too."

Tears spilled from Alex's blue eyes and ran down his high cheekbones. But I saw none of that. Ashamed of his weeping, he rubbed away the tears as they fell.

"You and your brother . . ."

"Alex!"

"You and your brother, I'll never understand you."

I had managed to rid myself of the peg and shawl.

"Take these to your house, please, Alex, I'll come get them tomorrow. And I'll bring back the coat."

The idea that I would be returning on the morrow, indeed in a few hours, calmed him.

He was out of his depth. Our parents were still alive for him, yet now they dwelt in his cemetery, in premises where he was master, in his own playground, his personal garden. It intimidated him, made him lose sight of his bearings. But his body was solid. And my promise to return early the next day put his feet back onto familiar ground. He stopped sobbing, and mumbled apologies.

"Here I am crying, and you . . . I don't know what's wrong with me . . . I'm okay now, you can go home . . ."

"No, you go first," I said firmly.

Alex never resisted a firm order. He kissed me through the railings and left in the direction of his house. He had recovered his unhurried elastic step.

"And I'll wait till you close your shutters, okay, Alex?"

"Okay, Estelle."

A few moments later he was at his window waving me a last good-bye and pulling the shutters closed without further ado.

I stood alone outside the cemetery.

I stared at the mound of flowers glittering under moon and frost.

I stared and stared.

I do not know how long I stayed with my forehead pressed to the railing, eyes locked on those flowers. The night was clear and cold, time cast off from eternity.

There was a shrill piping and a bird flew up from the yew that stood just inside the gate. Then I felt that what had been moving within me all night long had found its place. It was simple and obvious, and its obviousness released me. I could finally have wept.

The rectangles of the graves stood out a little less clearly in this predawn hour, but they had acquired a somber, forbidding density that promised they would be returning to duty on the morrow, and in the same instant the flowers heaped behind them, so brilliant in the moonlight only a moment ago, grew pale and lost their sharpness. I was at last weeping inside me.

Father, this is what I wanted to tell you:

I will not resume my studies, the law can do nothing for me, cannot help me look at your graves, please understand me, Father, I need something to help me look at your graves, to help me come here tomorrow or the day after that and kneel by your graves. We haven't done that yet, we were too weak, but soon we will come. I will not study law anymore. And if that's hard for you to understand, Father, ask Nicole, she'll explain.

And now I knew where Dan was.

I left for the little stream.

I saw our car from the top of the slope. It was no longer tangled with the tree that had demolished it. It sat on the shoulder, just like any car whose driver had for instance gone looking for mushrooms. The barriers still stood on either side of the lethal slope, but Minor's car had been removed.

It all seemed routine to me. It was only later that I learned about the maneuverings and even the illegalities that had taken place so that the two cars could await our return, each on its own side of the little stream, and so that our father's car could remain there a few days longer as we had requested.

Dan was sitting asleep at the wheel.

I sat down next to him and put my head on his shoulder.

"Oh, Estelle!"

He drew me close to him; his face, hollowed by fatigue, had changed during the night.

But it was not fatigue that had changed him.

"I got the car clear but I couldn't get the engine started, Estelle. But since the door has almost come off . . ."

Understood, Dan!

We undid the belt of Dan's, which had been holding it together, and the door came away in our hands practically on its own. I put Nicole's shoe in my coat pocket, Alex's mother's coat.

We knew exactly where we wanted to go.

We cut across the road a little farther on, avoiding the slope that was still slippery despite all Mr. Neighbor's sawdust. As we walked Dan talked to me. "I went to his study, Estelle . . . I found that passage of his philosopher's . . . I also looked at his files." And I told Dan that I would not be going on with my law studies, that they were not enough, that I would be going back to the piano. "Yes, Estelle," he said, and he would not be returning to New York. He would study law, like our father, in order to carry on with his cases. "Dancing isn't enough, Estelle. The things I saw in his dossiers . . ."

No need to explain why law, which was not enough for me, was enough for him, why this or why that . . . We would discuss it all, of course, later on, and even for the rest of our lives — but it would be for the pleasure of speaking to each other, not in order to explain anything.

Holding the car door between us, we walked over frozen fields, then up the little path over the hill, and finally through rocks and bushes. The door only just fit the cave mouth, scraping against the walls.

"Think the matches are still there?" I said. "Here they are," said Dan, quicker than I: he was always the one in charge of fires when we were children . . . They were in their usual place, a small tin box in a cleft, and we set fire to a branch and raised it blazing to the wall. The cave had not changed; the strange red drawing was there still, as enigmatic as ever. We set the wounded door before it.

"There," said Dan, "we entrust their car to your keeping."

And since some kind of explanation seemed necessary:

"We didn't want it sent for scrap, but this was all we could do."

We waited for the small fire to die out, then we left, taking

Nicole's shoe with us, and replaced the brush outside the cave mouth.

In the house we put Nicole's shoe in the closet on the landing with our Canal Street clothing, stained with her blood, and with all the black clothes Adrien had brought us. Then we locked the closet and put the key at the top of the grandfather clock.

It would soon be morning. Our new clothes were ruined. We were totally exhausted, but calm and happy.

"Estelle, you take your bedroom, I'll sleep in mine on my mattress. Tomorrow —"

Tomorrow our life together would begin. It meant projects, visits, decisions. We wanted to be ready for it all; we were in deadly earnest.

But we could not leave each other. On the landing we moved back and forth from his room to mine; finally we left our doors open, and fatigue pushed us both into the real normal sleep we needed. We slept nearly twenty-four hours.

THIRTY-NINE

Those Duty Cases

*W*HAT Dan had found in our father's study was a series of black folders piled on the lowest shelf of one of his bookcases.

Even today, the thought of those black folders affects me so strongly that I cannot mention them without first making a detour.

Our father's bookcases were in fact a series of shelves set along the length of the wall. But to conceal the bare planks a carpenter had lovingly fashioned doors designed to open in pairs, like a sequence of individual display cases.

For a third of the height of each case, the carpenter had used a solid wood panel on which he had chiseled out straight slender horizontal lines, one above the other, along three sides. Above, he had carved out two large rectangles in which he had set blue and red stained-glass panes with a very slender, half-open yellow rose undulating convolvulus-fashion between the blue and orange. To see the details on the colored panes you had to hold a light behind the glass. But the close-set horizontal lines at the base of the doors were visible from the study entrance.

Those lines were intended to represent the pages of an open book, but the workmanship was so discreet that the designer's intention could be muted or bold, depending on the mood of the onlooker. I myself must once have known the meaning of the lines, but by dint of seeing them I had forgotten.

My brother had found out that night.

"I woke up, Estelle, and I heard Father's voice asking me to come down to his study. It wasn't his voice the way we knew it, it was a different voice because it had crossed through my own sleep to come and wake me, but I recognized it and it was like a magnet. I went downstairs . . ."

"You didn't call me?"

"My love, it was something I had to do myself. My heart was beating fast and yet I was calm. I got to the study and turned on the light . . ."

"Yes?"

"No one was there," my brother went on with a great effort.

"What did you think you'd find, Dan?"

He spoke slowly, choosing his words with care. He was usually so animated that sometimes I think that this must have been his first incursion into the kingdom of death, that something inside him knew it, was already girding to face it.

"Not that emptiness . . . not that physical absence of a person . . . There was such a feeling of density . . . I think it would have surprised me less if I had found Adrien there."

"Adrien!"

"Hiding in a corner, the way he used to when he wanted to scare us, or Minor, or anyone, as long as he scared someone. I was completely at a loss, more than I have ever been . . . I've always known what I have to do . . . you know, one foot after the other. Even when I didn't have the energy or the wherewithal I have never hesitated. But down there . . . I literally didn't know where to turn."

"You didn't call me?"

"You couldn't have helped me, Estelle."

"Yet I found you tonight."

"Yes, my love, but you had only to guess *my* intention. In Father's study I had to guess . . . to guess fate's intention; I don't know how to say it, Estelle."

At the cemetery gate that night I too had needed to be alone, to see the heap of flowers pale and glowing on the grave, to guess . . . fate's intention.

But I had merely wondered in passing. For my brother was the one who had gotten up first, and all I had done was look for him.

"Does it make any difference, Estelle?"

"I don't know."

I know now that it did make a difference and I know where that difference lay; I am even beginning to understand how today it reaches around me and alters the course I take.

My brother got up first, and all I did was look for him.

Madame, I do not know what you do in a life where you do not swim amid the wake of another's flesh. For months and years I have sought the answer. I was in the wake of my brother's flesh, swimming strongly, steadily, arms buffeting the swell . . . All gone now, everything the same; my body stopped short at its own frontiers — oh, this pain, madame.

"I don't know, Dan."

And at the time I was not interested in knowing. What distressed me was the thought of Dan alone in our father's study, feeling lost, not knowing where to put himself.

"I took out one of his Bergsons from the little revolving bookcase and found the passage at once."

"The part about the man being tortured?"

"About the man being tortured, the man we mustn't forget. Listen to this, Estelle: I opened the book and my eyes fell directly on that sentence. It jumped out from the rest of the page; I didn't have to look, I recognized it. The words came to me exactly as you repeated them to me all that time ago in the little corridor where I was waiting for you."

"You even remember that?"

"Remember what, Estelle?"

"The little corridor . . ."

The little dark corridor connecting the other downstairs rooms and our father's study. A door at the very end opened onto a short concrete stairway leading to Nicole's garage. There was another way into our father's study, through the hallway and the living room, which also served when need be as a waiting room. But it was the little back corridor that drew us.

There we listened, deafened, to our mother's unending *Bolero* and the patter of her slippers, and sometimes also to heavier sounds, indefinable sounds, the sounds of Nicole hard at work in the blue garage, and then it was as if we were hearing the blind rooting of a lost animal. And when silence followed, it felt as if our hearts had literally been unhooked as we huddled in the unlit corridor. And then the indefinable sounds resumed, heavy, sporadic.

"That music is so wrong for her," our father muttered, "that cold-blooded reptile Ravel," and seeing our alarm he laughed: "It's just a quotation." A quotation it might have been, but we saw our mother caught in ice-cold coils . . . "And yet perhaps it's the music best suited to her," he added on another occasion, addressing us as if in another dimension of life we had been blessed with infinite understanding.

And we accepted his enigmatic words with a grave nod, as if we understood.

What we liked best was the patter of dance slippers. It was a cause of such joy — the slippers our mother bought in the sporting goods store, the cakes at the pastry shop afterward, the cake box that we would use to keep our collections, the ribbons, Nicole's enthusiasm . . .

From the study itself little sound emerged, except when our father had a client. But we felt his presence: we sometimes heard his chair creak, or the window open, and we knew then that he was looking at the garden in order to unwind. And even when everything was quiet we convinced ourselves that we could hear him reading. And I do not mean the rustle of turning pages.

One day when we were sitting there as usual, utterly still in the darkness and barely breathing, he suddenly emerged.

"Dan and Estelle, what are you doing here?"

"We're listening to you read, Papa."

"Is that true, Estelle?"

"Yes, Papa."

"But I'm reading to myself, silently!"

"We're listening to you read to yourself, that's what Dan meant, Papa."

Our father did not laugh or reprove us. He leaned against the wall and looked at us. And Dan the supernatural little rogue said:

"And why did you come out, Papa?"

Silence, then:

"I heard you listening to me."

His voice was calm, thoughtful.

Nobody else in our town had such a calm, thoughtful voice, not even Doctor Minor or the philosophy teacher, although they came closest. But Minor's voice masked turmoil and the teacher's irritation. As for other grown-up men we knew, Adrien's father, for instance ("Adrien! Little brat! Come here right now!"), their voices were mere tools, more or less rough-hewn.

"I heard you listening to me."

If he had told us he could see us through the wall we would have believed him.

He reached out both hands, one to each of us, to help us rise, and we both walked off down the little corridor holding each other tight.

At the end we turned. He was still leaning against the wall by his open door. He gave us a little wave. We too gave him a little wave. He was our father.

"The little corridor where we listened. You were worried, Estelle, I forced you to come . . ."

Dan had drawn me by the hand toward that little corridor, and I followed, my heat beating, what abundance of life in my heart. We sat for hours on the floor, and finally we were afraid even to get up to leave!

"And that day I was the one who made you knock at the study door . . . How could I have forgotten it all these years? Yet it was a great revelation, those words about the man we must not forget, about what our father did for a living . . . I had to know what he did . . . Maybe the other kids at school asked me. Yes, that's it . . . the first day at elementary school . . . 'Dan, what does your dad do?' I said, 'He helps Mr. Raymond pick apples' — it must have been the season for it — and the other kids laughed at me. So I decided to stick to my guns: 'He picks apples,' I told them again. You remember what Father used to say sometimes — 'These poor folks get themselves squashed like apples' — but the kids went on laughing and suddenly there was a kind of whirlpool in my head; it was because of Father, you understand, those kids like a pack of dogs and me drowning in that whirlpool inside me. It had never happened before . . . God, how I loved him, Estelle . . ."

My brother's voice faded away. At the back of his throat, as if captive in the bottom of some pit, I heard his frightened moans, "Father, Father," and I pressed my lips hard against his. I could no more weep than he could, but we held on to each other with straining sinews. And then my brother's voice crossed the barrier and we sat back down against the wall, eyes still unseeing, in a kind of astonishment: it was so strange to be alone in silence, amid disembodied sounds, like being in an unknown land in which pieces of our former universe had taken root, and we had to move forward . . .

"Dan?"

"I think I had made three discoveries at once. First, that grown-ups had 'jobs,' second, that grown-up jobs were all-important, more important than anything I had so far encountered, and third, that I did not know what that all-important thing was as far as our father was concerned . . . So I begged you to go and ask him."

"Estelle, go and ask him, go on, please," he said. I answered, "Dan, I've already explained," but I was unable to assuage him. His small face was stiff with passion. "No," he said, "what you say doesn't mean anything." No doubt the explanations I had given him were not clear enough.

"They were clear, Estelle, but they didn't give me the key, they were like a front, while I wanted to know about inside . . . I was sure there was something behind the words you so painstakingly strung together for me. You said 'He defends people' but that seemed just like my 'He picks apples.' I was sure Father's job could not just be a facade, and it was driving me crazy . . . I had to know, and you, my love, you went, and when you came back you had the key . . . The words were at once chiseled into my mind . . . Only the plaque bearing the words came loose and fell to the foot of my memory's wall, you understand, fell to the foot of my memory's wall, and all those years I passed back and forth without noticing it."

"Now listen, Estelle, this is strangest of all. I put Bergson's book down and looked up at the row of doors along Father's bookshelves. And suddenly I saw those lines. You know, the carved lines. Estelle, I had never seen them before! Can you believe it? We went into Father's study hundreds of times when we were little, but I never noticed those lines. And they weren't really lines I was seeing, they were the pages of a book. What's wrong, my love?"

In the second my brother said "the pages of a book" I suddenly saw those "pages."

I literally saw the pages of that wooden book delicately lift as my brother stepped forward, eyes fixed on their faintly undulating lines. At his passage the wooden pages trembled, then subsided.

He walked on past the bookcases. The night was deep and utterly still. Outside, frost on the lawn, the garden railings, glittering and black, and the empty road, and the white regal moon.

He walked, full of that presence that had come seeking him in his slumber, and now the trembling pages no longer subsided at his passage; the light of the moon fell directly upon them . . .

"Had you switched off the light, Dan?" I murmured.

"I had always seen that study in daylight, or at night with the light on, so I decided that . . . if there was anything to see . . . that I had not yet seen . . . it had to be with different lighting . . . No, that's not true . . ."

"Dan?"

"I decided that Father couldn't stand electric light anymore, oh, Estelle!"

I hugged my brother tight, his face on my breasts as I stroked his hair.

Don't reproach yourself, darling brother; our parents are dead, but it is not you who thrust them down into their grave. They are dead, darling brother, don't tremble so, you are not hurting them, not rejecting them. They will never again be in this house: neither bright light nor any light is any longer for them, and my darling, if you give them the light of the moon it is only to feed your own stubborn hope. A ghost gliding in the pale cold light of the moon, oh, my brother, even that — which is already so little — even that does not exist, don't tremble, Dan.

My brother came to a halt before one of the bookcase doors, which had opened as if of its own accord.

". . . as if someone had pulled on it, Estelle, a hand or a backdraft. I spun around to the window; nothing was moving, but I could see the main gate beyond the black-and-white lawn, and it seemed to me that it was the cemetery gate, oh, Estelle, something was happening . . . It was the cemetery gate and I saw it open . . . What was really opening was the bookcase door, and it was me opening it. But —"

"Yes, Dan."

We were in my bedroom, close-locked, naked and shivering despite the blankets we had collected (mine and those from Dan's bedroom and the little downstairs room), a mountain of blankets and the heat of the radiators turned on full blast.

Throughout our stay we kept the boiler going full force, and at night we left the front door open and the garden light turned on. Every morning the door would be shut and the lights extinguished. "It isn't me," Adrien said, "I don't give a fuck what you do up there." "Yes, it's me," Mr. Neighbor said reproachfully, and we did not mind, we just went on leaving the front door open and the garden light burning in the icy fog-shrouded night, and Mr. Neighbor always came over to put things back in proper order, the order he believed to have been that of his neighbor Helleur. We never exchanged a word on the subject, and that suited us.

In those days we were naked almost all the time. Only our bodies had the power to set our minds at ease; we could not absent ourselves from looking at them. Even a bathrobe was too much, a bathrobe could set off a rage of anxiety — "Take that off, oh, take that off, I can't see your body anymore." My brother pressed his face against my clitoris, "You're a girl, my love, you're a girl," and we laughed and cried at once, endlessly overcome. "My visits to that boat moored on the Hudson, they weren't for me, Estelle, and I knew it, but I couldn't see any way out." And I took my brother's penis in my hands and said, "It's the first time" and Dan said, "What's the first time, my love?" Silly things, we dived into silliness as if into very sweet honey, and we laughed and we cried all over again because my brother was already inside me and our words sped away like tiny paper boats being stripped of their rigging in the mounting flood . . .

Then we were close-locked again, momentarily reassured, able to speak again, full of seriousness . . .

"There were these black folders . . . And I knew that they were what Father wanted me to look at. They looked like graves, Estelle . . . I don't know why I say that; they were just folders piled on top of each other, lots of folders — but I saw graves, not like the graves in our cemetery, clean and lined up neatly and covered with flowers. No, something I had never seen before, and now I can hardly describe it, a fleeting impression, heaps of dead pressed between black pages, and you had to pry those pages apart — that was what Father was telling me, they mustn't be left lying between those black pages . . .

"I dumped a pile of those folders on Father's desk, turned on his lamp, and began to read . . .

"I read until the middle of the night . . .

"How little I knew, Estelle . . ."

Madame, we had no idea how very little we knew. From the files on "Resistance Deportees," a folder was missing, and another from the "War-

time Deportees" file. So was a third that had consisted mainly of photos and was listed in the index as "Franco-German Agreement of July 15, 1960," and finally a folder from a different batch was missing, entitled "Civil Registry" . . .

My brother pulled me convulsively to him.

"All that time in New York and even before that, I had only myself, my body. Only my body, you understand, Estelle. I fought with my muscles, just my muscles, against the earth that is calling us. One blind thing pitted against another, even blinder thing. And my mind . . . lost in that confusion of raw materials . . . and trying to outmaneuver them . . . it too was blind . . ."

Lying against him, I caressed his splendid body, and I did not see a confusion of raw materials under his dark-honey skin, skin the color of autumn leaves in the season Americans call Indian summer in that part of a very old continent that one day became New England. "That's the color of your skin," Alwin had said, with a broad gesture encompassing the vast North American woodland. Dan, Michael, and I had looked at one another in bewilderment, and Alwin reverted to his habitual taciturnity. It was a Sunday; Michael had taken us all in his cab for a ride along the old Indian trails. The following Sunday we took the same trip, but Alwin had refused to come. "Silly, all this," he had said, and once again we stared at one another in bewilderment.

No, I saw no confusion of raw materials . . . and later, I would think back to that moment when my brother's skin seemed to me as rich and strong as a continent, oh, my poor love.

"What was in the folders, Dan?"

"Medical reports, addresses, statistics . . . And letters, and photos, horrible photos, all from the war, Estelle, the last war . . . Our father worked like a whole beehive, Estelle, he fought for people, specific cases, specific goals . . . I can't let those cases just drop. That's what I've decided, Estelle."

"You're a dancer, Dan."

"We'll live in Paris, Estelle, I'm going to enroll in law school — I'll go very fast. I started tonight; you have to help me."

My brother's only qualification was his baccalaureate, earned by the skin of his teeth, and then only because my father went to root him out at the conservatory, where he had hidden on the very morning of the first orals. I heard all about it much later.

At 5:00 A.M., the morning of the exam, our father went to Dan's room and saw that he was not there. He went to the neighbors': Adrien knew nothing, nor did Alex out at his little house in the cemetery. As for my brother's new friends, our father knew neither their names nor their addresses.

Nicole did not want Dan to take that exam, for fear he might forget about dancing. She had had her nightmares during the night and was now resting, sedated by Minor.

Returning overwhelmed from his vain quest, exhausted by his sleepless night and the conflict with Nicole, our father bumped into Tiresia. Tiresia had been seeking our father all over the house, while he had been looking for Dan all over town. And our father, running into Tiresia's dark shape halfway up the stairs, knew at once where Dan was.

"He has to take that exam" was all he said.

Tiresia made coffee for him. Then he drove straight to the conservatory, which was located virtually under the eaves of city hall. The caretaker was of course still in bed. Not a chink of light was showing in the large gray mass of city hall on the main square of our town, not an open door. But our father was sure Dan was there. He strained his ears and thought he heard a distant sound . . .

He managed to rouse the concierge, who first listened expressionlessly to his story and then at once played the part required of him — army greatcoat over pajamas, flashlight, skeleton key.

"Mr. Helleur, this reminds me of my Resistance days," he said as they mounted the main staircase with their shoes in their hands and the flashlight trained ahead.

But the concierge was disappointed. My brother gave him no chance to relive his Resistance glory days. When they reached the landing they heard music coming from one of the rooms at the end of the corridor, the record room.

"*The Ride of the Valkyrie,*" said our father, suddenly white with anger.

"He's trying to keep his spirits up, Mr. Helleur," said the caretaker, once recovered from his disappointment.

"His spirits?"

"He's scared, poor kid, all alone in this big empty place!"

My brother was not frightened of the big empty building — "Well, not very frightened, Estelle" — but of our father's anger, and more so of our father's disappointment at not finding him in his bedroom on the morning of the exam. So he was deadening his feelings by dancing along in the Valkyries' wake. "And you know, Estelle, I think that's just what Papa couldn't swallow — the ride of the Valkyries . . ."

He did not hear his two pursuers approach. They found him leaping back and forth across the whole length of the big room in simultaneous imitation of a galloping horse and rider of that galloping horse, clippety-clop across the room, horse snorting and rider spurring, and both mount and rider wheeling around in one single wide movement for another ride across the room, lance at the ready, great warlike leaps over the tables . . .

"I'd never seen anything like it, and I've seen a lot," said the caretaker. "Mr. Helleur and I stopped dead in our tracks. Mr. Helleur was so pale I decided I had to do something, and finally it occurred to me to disconnect the record player — the outlet was just beside the door. The music stopped and thanks to the surprise, Mr. Helleur was able to take his boy away."

Poor Father, he was obliged to drive off with him at top speed, for the oral was being held in the next town, a good two or three hours' drive from ours. Luckily Dan had lied when he told our parents he was listed for eight-thirty that morning: in fact, he was supposed to be there that afternoon, and our father had to wait for him. "Father looked so unhappy at having to watch over me, Estelle. I think he believed I would try to escape at any moment. But for me it was over. He had won, and all I wanted was for him to get some rest. I went to see the examiner and she let me go through a bit earlier, so I gave it all I had . . . for Father, right? At least I could give him that, because after that I was determined to get right away."

My brother and I had so many things to tell each other in the three years we lived together.

We talked without stopping as if we knew our time was short. I made him tell me over and over again about small escapades like that exam, with our father and the city hall caretaker catching him hurdling across the tables at six in the morning with the appalling racket of the Valkyries ringing in their ears.

I could go back to it day after day. One day I would need to know the color of the tables and whether they came with chairs or benches; and if the benches were bolted to the tables, how he had managed to vault both tables and benches at once; and if he had recognized the caretaker in his army greatcoat; and how he had managed to get into a building as tight shut as a bank ("Up the drainpipe, Estelle, and through the skylight in the attic; I never miss a badly closed skylight, and rooftops as you know don't scare me . . ."). Yes, brother cat, no obstacle to you.

Once in the middle of the night when we were in our Paris apartment (the second one, during the time we were rich), I asked my brother to tell me once again about his city hall break-in. "My dearest one, why don't I just show you?" he said. "Show me? How?" "Get dressed and we'll go to G.!" "What, now, in the middle of the night?" "Absolutely," he said, pulling me out of bed and feeding me into my skirt while I was still struggling to understand his meaning.

A little later we were in the car and speeding toward our native town. We reached it at five in the morning, almost the hour at which our father had found Dan. I watched as my brother the cat, not weary even after our long drive, climbed the fence, dropped down on the other side, and squirmed up the gutter onto the roof. He pushed at the skylight and vanished inside . . . Dan, come back, how gray and gloomy this building is and I am alone in this empty square, in this town from which all those we loved have vanished, Father, Nicole, Minor, Tiresia . . . Dan, where are you?

Suddenly he was behind me. "I came out through the back, but you're crying, Estelle, I'm here, I'm here, my love." And we made love in the car in that deserted square outside the gray and gloomy facade of the city hall building, suddenly terrified, with that terror that occasionally came over us and that could be appeased only by love, our bodies mixed, sweat, grunting, smells.

And we went back immediately afterward without stopping at our old house, which was slowly succumbing to mildew.

"It's a disgrace," Adrien told us, "huge patches of mildew on the uprights of the doors, like wheels. You could at least come by every now and then. My father no longer has the heart to go in, it makes him cry every time, and my mother doesn't want him to go there. You must have stones for hearts; all you think about is fucking, you bastards, you think only of yourselves, you have no respect for the dead . . ."

We did not hear him. My brother was magic and his magic shielded us.

FORTY

The Attorney

WE STAYED on a few more weeks in our town of G.

We were very tired and at the same time full of an astonishingly abundant energy. That tiredness and that mysterious energy worked their purpose in us, and we waited.

Our father's lawyer called us in. By telegram. For we had disconnected the phone. "We'll reconnect it soon," Dan said, and I wholly approved. "We'll read the mail later too," and indeed that seemed the only course open to us. "Yes, no time just now," I said, carefully stacking the mail on our father's desk.

Time was like a person, a common brother we had just discovered. He had to live inside the house, close by us around the clock; we could not send him out to meet other people on trivial errands that might have taken him from us.

That time of ours, so like a real person, was very dear to us, and we could not bear to be parted from it. We literally felt it by our side; it absorbed us utterly in a way that had nothing to do with the everyday things we did, such as going up and down stairs, deciding where to sit, snuggling together, trekking to the cellar for canned food, eating, tidying up . . .

None of those activities distracted us from our new and much dearer companion, time; on the contrary, they kept him by us, and this presence of his in turn kept us together and protected my brother and me.

We did nothing and the days went by.

Until finally, a resolute knocking made itself heard at the front door.

Nobody could have used that door knocker since the arrival of electricity. Perhaps that was what impelled us to respond — curiosity, surprise.

"I didn't like to ring," said the young post office messenger.

He probably knew that the house was in mourning. "That house is in mourning," they had told him. *What words, madame, so commonplace, so quietly confident. Oh, no need to stress such words: "That house is in mourning." It was our house, the commonplace words had arrived, they gave orders, and we obeyed.*

The messenger brought us an injunction to call on the attorney.

Once the messenger was gone we realized that our companion time had left as well. Dan and I looked at each other.

"You have shadows under your eyes, Estelle."

"And you need to shave."

No more time for anything. We set busily to work: shave, makeup, haircut with kitchen scissors, sheets changed, deodorant, general tidying up. Then we went to see the attorney.

He was our old philosophy teacher's brother.

"My brother and your father were very fond of each other. My brother said that of the two of them, your father was the true philosopher. We often got together for one reason or another, quite often in this very office. Mr. Helleur used to sit there."

We looked at the chair where our father used to sit.

"The conversation always began the same way. 'My neighbor has pointed out to me,' your father would say. Your neighbor, the one with the small freight business. That man was a source of continual astonishment and reflection for your father. I don't know him personally. I was often tempted to drop in at his house, to take a look, to try to understand what your father found in him. But I never did; it would have seemed indiscreet . . . and now even more so."

The attorney sighed.

"I didn't carry my weight in those conversations between my brother and Mr. Helleur. I have little time for reading. But strange as it may seem, even though they were Greek to me, those conversations meant more to me than anything else. I don't really understand why . . . but now I'm bored . . ."

We looked steadily at him. He looked as if he might cry. But he did not. It was our own unshed tears floating about the room that we imagined on the point of welling from his eyes.

"I don't understand it, Mr. Helleur, Miss Helleur, I'm bored now."

We listened attentively to him, more attentively than we had ever listened to his brother the philosophy teacher.

"And things aren't the same with my brother anymore. We're very fond of each other but we have little in common. You know my brother, he's a teacher. And I . . . I'm an attorney. Your father was the link between us. We still see each other, but we're uncomfortable and have nothing to say."

We nodded as if well acquainted with such situations.

"One day your father arrived looking very excited. He told us a story involving a mole and a dressing-down by his neighbor. He and my brother got their teeth into the story, dragging the whole history of philosophy into it, and I didn't miss a single crumb of what they said. But if I tried to repeat it to you I wouldn't know how, not a hope . . .

"Ah well, ah well," he went on, "I've gone back to being myself, and my brother to being himself. An attorney and a teacher.

"If your father were here I'd have no trouble digging up that story for you; you'd laugh yourselves silly. But without him, nothing doing. I'm helpless."

He took the glasses back to the kitchen and put away the sherry ("The sherry I kept for your father") and returned to sit behind his desk. His voice changed: it seemed to have returned to its true dwelling place on the massive desk, among several pairs of glasses, a heap of directories, a bronze inkpot holder with the statuette of a horse. That was where his real voice lurked. And this is what the voice told us.

The house had been purchased by our father and it was in our names, Dan Helleur and Estelle Helleur, but Tiresia had the lifetime use of it.

"So you cannot sell it as long as Tiresia is alive," said the attorney, looking inquiringly at us.

"We have no intention of selling the house," we said.

But, the attorney's voice went on — and now we distinctly felt that it came from a raptor's nest built into a cleft in a cliff face — although we could not sell the house we were the possessors of a small fortune that came to us from Tiresia . . . and Nicole.

"That money was set aside for you from 1949 onward, and further sums were added after 1964," said the attorney, and his voice swooped down upon us. "Nothing stands in the way of your using it now if you wish."

We did not reply, having heard no question in his remark and having no question ourselves.

"I suppose," said the attorney after a short pause — and now it seemed to us that the raptor, whose questing beak had failed to seize us, had alighted nearby with a clatter of wings — "I suppose you are thinking of Tiresia and of the clinic costs. I believe you need have no concern on that score. Tiresia has a pension as well as a personal income, money invested in the days when she gave concerts."

No, we had felt no concern on Tiresia's behalf. This man's remarks seemed curious to us, agitated and full of detours, but we listened to him politely.

"When you go to see her, will you tell her that everything has been done according to her and Mr. Helleur's wishes?"

The attorney's voice gave up its objectives and flew back to its lair on the massive desk, among the three pairs of glasses, the heap of directories, and the horse statuette. But our armor had abruptly been pierced.

Go to see Tiresia? We had not thought of that.

Tiresia belonged to our home, was our home. Tiresia was walls, rooms, staircase, stair rail, staircase landing. She could not be anywhere but in our house. I believe, yes, I am certain that we had at no point even considered her absence. Perhaps we had imagined that she was temporarily away, looking after our parents in the cemetery . . .

But Tiresia was not peacefully communing with our parents' grave. She was in a clinic.

That was what finally emerged from this exchange we had consented to. Suddenly we were on our feet, anxious to leave.

"Then you must come back," said the attorney, "there are many details to be settled."

We agreed to come back later.

As we were leaving the attorney said in sudden anxiety:

"You will tell her that everything has been done according to her and Mr. Helleur's wishes, won't you? Exactly those words? Her wishes, Mr. Helleur's wishes."

We said "Yes, yes, of course" with all the sincerity we could muster. We were afraid that this attorney would never let us go; he even came out into his front garden with us, still fussing about those wishes.

But we were no longer listening.

As soon as we were out in the street we began to run.

We reached home breathless, and at once phoned Minor.

"Ah," he said, "I was wondering when you would decide to call me."

"What's wrong with her?" we said, both crouched over the phone.

"Shock. A state of shock."

"We have to see her right now."

"Oh," said the doctor.

"Can you take us?"

"No," said the doctor.

"Dr. Minor!" exclaimed two very small children, Dan and Estelle.

The phone was not working well; voices seemed to be sobbing on the line, there were screams, as if from the end of a dark corridor, as if from behind the locked doors of a room at the end of a dark corridor.

"Dr. Minor!" begged two very small children.

"Be quiet, stop, stop!" said the doctor, and suddenly his voice was once again warm with rich Russian intonations.

The voice we had not heard for so many years. The voice he used when he was moved, when he patted our heads in the corridor after our mother's nightmares, *"Malchiki, malchiki."* Or the voice when he approached boiling point in his talks with my father. The good Russian voice of our good Doctor Minor. It stopped us dead. Oh, our Doctor Minor, are there still candies hidden in the jungle of your bag, are there still syringes for fighting off the enemies of the Helleur household?

"Listen to me, Dan and Estelle! Are you listening?"

"Yes, yes," said the children.

"You know very well that I would take you —"

"Doctor, Doctor Minor?"

"— but Tiresia doesn't want you to visit her."

Tiresia did not want us to visit?

"We must try to understand, we must respect her wishes . . . I visit her every day, I'll give you her news . . ."

"Then we'll come over to your house right away," said the little boy Dan.

"Don't come."

Doctor? Our Doctor Minor? What was he saying? We stood there close together. The receiver had moved away from us as if of its own accord and it was hanging from Dan's hand, and the voice coming from it seemed far away, already so far away. It already reached us from the depths of the past, whispering inside that earpiece. And it seemed to us that the earpiece had picked up that whisper by accident, that the whisper had insinuated itself into its small perforations but that the wire had been severed, had long since been severed.

"I have grown suddenly old, my Major has been to see me. You remember my Major, Dan and Estelle. He has called, and I am old. I cannot see you just now but I'll send my replacement, Dan and Estelle, my dear children, my dear children . . ."

My dear children.

We hung up very softly.

III

Paris

FORTY-ONE

Under the Eaves

*P*ARIS.

Our garret apartment under the eaves.

With my elbows on the windowsill, I watched my brother turn the corner and race down the sidewalk, the flaps of his raincoat taking wing, so intent on speed that his brows knitted, his eyes riveted to the ground. He was racing to be with me.

Forget the subway, forget the sidewalks, forget the courtyard of our building: all he wanted was to get back to me.

I clattered down the stairs, all six flights, and reached him just as he swung the street door open, and suddenly everything leapt to life — the crowded subway he had taken, the sidewalks behind him, the courtyard of our building where the concierge and her little boy weeded a flower bed.

He seized me in his arms and whirled me high in the air with a laugh: "If you only knew, if you only knew." And I laughed in advance, and the concierge laughed too. So many things had happened, in the subway, in the street; so many things were happening now in the courtyard with the concierge's little boy . . . As we talked to her a whole clandestine exchange took place between us, full of twists and turns. And as we went upstairs my brother described them to me, for as soon as we were together what had been empty was repopulated — stories leapt forth, epics, dreadful tragedies, comedies that made us sob with mirth. Later we would literally fall into sleep, as if life had pitched a shovelful of stones at our heads. The stones would settle down into our inner depths and we would awaken, astonished by this brief sleep and once again invigorated.

I sometimes had painful headaches. I curled up in a corner of the bed and Dan gently rubbed my scalp. "There," I said. "Yes, I can feel it," he said, "it's hot." He pressed an ice cube against the spot where the pain lay. He could stay there without moving, pressing hard, until the cube melted, then would go get another and resume his solemn unmoving stance. "I'd like you to bore a little hole," I said, "to let the heat escape like steam." "Or else we could go around with a watering can inside," he said.

We did not laugh. The sealed container of the skull seemed to us a serious problem indeed. We simply tried to transpose the problem to a parallel space where we might be more at ease, where a human being might be given a little more latitude to walk around inside his body to check and effect repairs. The mere notion of such a space finally did both of us good.

We were very good at manufacturing parallel spaces.

If ice cube, drilling, and watering proved ineffective, we tried another method: Dan attempted to attract the headache elsewhere, to distract it, to make it emerge through my skin and to catch it with his hands. His stroking started at the head and then drew the pain elsewhere. I tried to follow the path of his hands. Most of the time it worked.

And my brother often had nightmares. The ones that disturbed him most were the geometrical nightmares. "I was never very good at geometry, but you should see the shapes that come into my head: symmetrical figures, designs and diagrams of bewildering complexity." I remembered Alwin's scraps of paper and his random sketches. I told Dan he needed to dance.

It was three or four in the morning in our little one-room garret apartment, where there was scarcely room for two people to move at the same time. But Dan agreed with me. I perched on the table, carefully, because it wobbled. On the mattress that stayed on the floor, Dan stretched his limbs, executed leaps, invented sequences of movements: "Movement for Solo Mattress," "Arabesque for Eighty Square Feet," or "Foam Rubber Fandango" (the mattress was of foam rubber, the cheapest material we could find). He danced until the geometrical figures disengaged from his head.

The grumpy old crone who occupied another one-room apartment down the hall, right next door to the communal toilets, would tell the concierge that we were disgusting animals to be at it like that so late at night, that the creaking of the floorboards woke her. The concierge, who was very young and full-breasted, relayed it all to us with a happy laugh.

The old biddy's swollen legs could barely carry her. We never actually saw her going out early in the morning to do her shopping. We sensed everything, but we saw nothing.

I believe now that the world was merely a colossal stage for Dan and Estelle's love.

My brother had another kind of nightmare. He was being chased (or he did the chasing; it was never clear which). The chase went through many unexpected twists and turns; nothing seemed able to stop it. I heard my brother moaning and woke him. It was again three or four in the morning. This time he described every detail of the chase, and I tried to suggest solutions, to find means of escape he might not have seen: "If you were running past a fence of rotting wood, why didn't you kick one of the planks so as to get to the other side?" "Hmmm," he mused, "but what was on the other side?" "A calm green meadow covered with daisies and buttercups." We lingered awhile in that heavenly meadow that looked like the Helleur meadow in its glory days (although I do not believe we realized this). It gave us new strength to change the course of Dan's disastrous nightmare journey, and he did indeed discover all kinds of possible escapes, many of them comical. We finally ended up in a Laurel and Hardy movie and laughed like lunatics, lurching into the walls, which, it must be said, were never more than a few inches away!

Our neighbor in the apartment on our left hammered on the wall; we could almost see his meaty fist with its short, thick fingers. "They must be drunkards, those two," he would say to the concierge. "They start up in the middle of the night, they talk drivel and laugh boozily — it can't go on!" The concierge warned us to be careful because that lodger was a policeman, and you never know. "Well, what about him with his TV? Every evening, as soon as he gets home, he rushes to his set. He keeps it at full blast all night long, and does he worry about anyone else?" "The TV isn't the same," said the concierge. Nevertheless we too hammered on the wall. The policeman came out and said my brother "needs to be taught a lesson." My brother did a Charlie Chaplin shadowboxing routine, and the policeman gaped. "I think he's feebleminded," the policeman told the concierge, but he no longer turned the TV up so loud.

"These headaches and nightmares, they're just our ordinary vaypigo," Dan said one day.

We had forgotten that term from our childhood. It put us into transports of delirious laughter; we were crazy with joy, we hugged as if our hold on life had almost been prized loose, we made love, we kissed, we made love again, we were exhausted, we were happy.

The concierge believed us to be young marrieds. It was easy; we had the same name. We liked her a lot because her husband always had his hands on her bottom or around her waist, and she would coo and melt against him. "Mr. Dan is so handsome," she said. "Ah, if only I were younger . . . but he loves only you!" The concierge was about my age. The day she found she was pregnant, she asked: "What about you? What are you waiting for?" Then she saw the sadness on our faces, and suddenly I believed she suspected: they are both named Helleur; they could be cousins, or brother and sister.

But then she was even more on my side. She made me a dress, for she was also a seamstress. "Mr. Dan should see how beautiful you are." It is true that the dress made me beautiful. "Do you think he doesn't see it?" I asked the concierge. "He loves you so much he doesn't see you," she answered enigmatically, and just as enigmatically that phrase made me happy. I went to wait for Dan at the metro. His hug almost suffocated me, and since he had not yet seen the dress, that made me happy. Later I showed him the dress. "It's quite true you're beautiful, Estelle," he said with a nod, meaning "It's true that people in the street who see you must think that you're beautiful," but in any case that didn't concern us.

It concerned us sometimes when dealing with Adrien. But we were used to Adrien.

One night we were awakened by strange noises from the apartment on the right. It sounded like someone groaning in pain. "They're making love," said Dan, amazed. We were almost indignant that others made love, made those sounds, others who did not love each other, who were not brother and sister. We lay there listening, rigid and distressed, until the sighs came to an end. Then we nestled close together, but we did not make love. There were three of us on our mattress on the floor: Dan, I, and our astonishment. And when there were three of us this way, we entertained our guest, this third character, and could do nothing else.

A few weeks or months earlier, in our old Helleur house, we had had a guest of this type. Our guest had been time, our own special time, and we had been preoccupied with him exclusively.

Often we had to deal with an unexpected guest. Sometimes he was called astonishment, sometimes fear, sometimes stupefaction — which is not the same as astonishment. There is also sorrow, and of course love.

I must speak of these guests. They hampered our so-called professional life, and our social life as well. "Have you taken a good look at yourselves?" grumbled Adrien. "I'm sick and tired of hanging around with a pair of ghosts." But when our secret guests left, we made fantastic recoveries. "Take it easy," said Adrien, "you're wearing me out," although Adrien is particularly hard to wear out.

"It's repulsive to be glued together like that all the time," said Adrien with disgust. True disgust, for Adrien never pretends.

Dan and I did not realize that human beings tend to remain in their own personal space; certainly that is tidier. Whereas, there sat the two of us, in a booth opposite Adrien at the Café Wepler, sitting like snails under Adrien's disgusted stare, our slimy antennae out, trying to squeeze ourselves into the same shell. Poor Adrien, it must indeed have repelled him. He hated snails when he was small and only took part in our races on the dividing wall by proxy, sending one of his younger brothers or a cousin to represent him.

He could not bear my brother's hand on my shoulder, my hand on my brother's waist, his lips on my neck, my eyes always upon him: "Estelle, you'll wear his face out." He could not bear our clothes: "You always look as if you just got out of bed or just ran a marathon in the jungle." He could not bear our conversations: "Can't you ever talk about normal things?" "What kind of things, Adrien?" "I don't know, cars, TV anchorwomen, skiing." He could not stand our apartment: "I'm obliged to go to the café for a piss before I visit your place, with its Turkish-style water hole on the landing. I can see the old girl's buttocks hanging over it and the cop's; there's always streaks of shit . . ." "And our buttocks, can you see them as well?" inquired Dan. "No need of that, you've shown them to me often enough!" "When was that?" Dan wanted to know, starting to get angry. "In your house, in your family house, damn it! When I found you like a couple of dogs the day after — " "Shut your mouth!" "And then you came down the stairs stark naked, taking your time, stark naked, to give me a front view as well!" "So what? You liked it, didn't you?" "And what if I told people, huh? What if I told everyone, my parents, the attorney, the two Bonnevilles, your dear Minor, the whole damned town?" "You won't, Adrien," I said. "And why won't I?" "Because you always loved Nicole . . ." This answer satisfied Adrien, and I knew it. It calmed us down; the mention of Nicole calmed us down.

"When are we going to see you with a girl?" we asked him.

"One thing's for sure, I'd never bring a girl to your place."

"Why is that?"

"Why?" echoed Adrien, giving us a cynical look.

"Yes, why?" demanded Dan, looking him up and down. That gesture was calculated to enrage Adrien, for Adrien might be muscular but he is scarcely taller than I am and a good head shorter than Dan.

"Because I happen to be normal and plan to marry one day."

"So?"

"So I don't want my wife to see —"

"See what?"

We were ready to go for his throat, to fight as we fought the night of our parents' burial on the frost-hard lawn.

"All your filth."

"Our filth?"

"Homosexuality, incest, murder, abandonment of family. Isn't that enough?"

Homosexuality, incest, murder, and what was that last thing? Oh yes, abandonment of family. He was probably thinking of Tiresia, whom we never visit.

Oh, Doctor Minor, how could Adrien understand Tiresia?

And suddenly we burst into crazed laughter. "Homosexuality, incest, murder, abandonment. Adrien, Adrien, if you did not exist, we would have to invent you" was all we managed to say through our howls of laughter. The black conflagration at his hairline blazed and blazed.

As he left he slammed the door, which immediately sprang back open again, as was its peculiarity. Simultaneously, the noise brought forth the old woman from her lair beside the toilets. As she passed our open doorway, she saw us writhing in mirth and spluttering out "Homosexuality, incest, murder, abandonment." Whereupon she, too, slammed the wretched door, and at once it swung back into her face. She shuffled backward in her old slippers. "Savages," she said, "animals, savages." We eventually apologized and gave her a pot of flowers.

We tried diligently, and tenderly and painfully, my brother and I, not to shut out the other world, the world just next to ours. We worked at it earnestly, albeit clumsily. Adrien may have helped us in this regard. Of all that we knew nothing, and Adrien still less.

Sometimes it seemed we might very easily slip back toward our childhood, toward Estelle's bed, at whose foot the young boy Dan laid his mattress, and even further back, to the meadow where the warbling baby Dan shook a rain of blossoms down on his sister's dazzled eyes, and still further, to the room where the scarce-born infant wept alone in his crib, back to that first day when his sister clutched him to her flat little-girl chest, the day when it seemed to them both that the first living being had just arrived on earth. Sometimes it seemed we might slip irrevocably and never budge from that hypnotic memory, coiled forever around us.

*   *   *

And sometimes it seemed we might slip in the other direction, every-thing went so fast. My brother read night and day; his overcharged mind could no longer call a halt. I helped him reach the point where I stopped my law studies. He reached it much quicker than I had, doubling and tripling the normal workload, running from one library to the next, making me run too. If I had been enrolled, I could have taken all these exams at the same time he did, but I no longer wanted to do law. I only wanted to help Dan get started, but he took the lead, drawing me along in his wake. I thought he wanted to swallow the whole university library; for just one assignment he cleared the shelves of knowledge for miles around. Sometimes I was scared. "Acting upon the world, Estelle, you understand, not just entertain-ing it, not just making it think, but acting, you understand, my love."

As a teenager he had made a pact with his muscles, counting heavily on them in his struggle against the earth's attraction. He had felt that force pulling on his legs one day on our front lawn, so powerful, the force of that earth that called him, that called us all.

And now as a young man he counted on his mind in the struggle against forces on the surface of the earth that sought to destroy us. "Because the earth will get us in any case, Estelle. Can you believe I never realized that? Nicole never realized it either, or if she did . . . oh, my poor Nicole."

Tears were in his eyes, and my heart swelled with grief. Nicole in her garage with its faded hangings and the same sixteen bars of Ravel's *Bolero,* for years and years, with no other weapons than those sky-blue hangings and those sixteen bars and her pretty slippers she so carefully renewed. Little Nicole with the curls on her nape, our little mother Nicole. "Who cares if the earth will get us? It took Father and Nicole and all who have been and will be. We will all end in it. But until then . . . What matters, Estelle, is what we can do *until then* . . ."

If my brother Dan had known who our parents were and what had happened to them "on the surface of the earth," if my brother Dan had heard Tiresia's story, I believe he would not have slept one single hour . . .

Up until . . . I don't know . . . He wanted to know the right answer to counter all forms of dishonesty, error, hypocrisy, deception. He wanted to be able to block all the exits for criminals, to know all the possible loopholes in order to seal them forever. Elsewhere he wanted to blast open stone walls . . .

I believe that is how he spoke, madame, but his words were beautiful.

He wanted to know all the meanings ever found in the world. "I want to know them all, Estelle, everything that men have dreamed up, since that first drawing, you remember, on the wall of our cave. It too was looking for a meaning; it had just begun. And I too have just begun."

Our tiny lodging groaned beneath the books; I was afraid the floor would collapse onto the floor below. The concierge stared at us. "Miss Estelle, Mr. Dan, you work too hard; you must stop for a moment . . ."

Surprised, we did stop, on the three steps leading to her apartment, in the shaft of sunlight that dropped down between the buildings. She talked about her house in Portugal, how she met her husband as she shot down a rocky path on her bicycle and crashed into him — "straight into his balls at our very first meeting." She made us coffee and we sat contentedly on her steps, looking adoringly up at her. She was so full of joy. "You are really like two kids," she said to us, and I had the feeling she would willingly have breast-fed us.

"Look, here comes your friend Adrien," she said. "Now there's a man who doesn't look as if he has money worries," and she continued in a low voice: "Never the same shirt twice running and never a wrinkle; I'm an expert. Not like you, eh? You should bring me your laundry from time to time, not often, my husband would be jealous, but every now and then, eh, Mr. Dan!"

Adrien's shirt was perfectly ironed, never the same in the evening as in the morning, and when we asked him how he managed to iron so many shirts, the roots of his hair burst into flame at his forehead and he told us to wipe our bottoms with our books. That was his supreme insult, since it combined the two things he genuinely loathed: school latrines and textbooks. In childhood, when Dan and I spent hours reading in our attic or in the meadow, he would prowl around us, baleful, frustrated, looking for a quarrel and often finding it.

We knew perfectly well what he did with his shirts. Every two weeks he took them home, stuffed in a big canvas bag, to his mother in G. He obstinately refused to let us open the bag when we asked him. And this was not just because of a kind of schoolboy shame; it was also out of pity. For we had nobody to take our laundry to. His mother had surely suggested to him that he take our shirts too. I could almost hear Mrs. Neighbor: "Poor motherless lambs, I'd willingly do it for them, Adrien, and your father would agree, in memory of Mr. Helleur." And Adrien most likely replied: "Ironed shirts are much too normal for them. If I suggested it to them they'd probably send you books to iron." And Mrs. Neighbor, who had always taken us seriously, probably looked at her son somewhat anxiously. "But sweetheart, I don't know how to iron books!"

Adrien could not stand us but he could not stay away from us. He visited us in our attic apartment under the eaves, which he contemptuously referred to as our "suite" (for in fact we were privileged to have *two* tiny rooms with an adjoining door). But no sooner was Adrien seated on a chair than he was fidgeting restlessly, and invariably after a few moments he suggested taking us somewhere.

"But we're fine here," said Dan.

"It's stifling here," said Adrien in summer (it was true; we were just under the roof).

"Take your jacket off."

But Adriens hate taking their coats off.

Or else in winter:

"It's freezing here" (which was true, for the same reason).

"Put a sweater on, Adrien."

But Adriens do not put sweaters on, just their precious shirts under their suits.

Then he said:

"I'm taking you out . . ."

He got on our nerves; he wasted our time, preventing us from studying our law books, our philosophy texts, our music books, our scores, for our exams. He kept us from earning our units of credit.

"Your units of debit," he said.

Or else:

"Nullities of credit" or "Units of nullity."

At the peak of his fury:

"Fucking units of fucking bullshit."

At his sweetest:

"You and your units of pallor. Get some fresh air like normal people do. Are you coming or not? I'll take you . . ."

He stopped us from studying, but we went with him; we could not help ourselves. After all, he was our only link to the Helleur house.

"Where are we going, Adrien?"

"For a ride."

"Adrien, we're on the highway."

"So?"

"We have to get back."

"To your units of nullity?"

"Take us back."

Adrien cackled. He had a big Citroën-Maserati, and he drove it fast. In midafternoon we reached a town called Vienne and stopped outside a hotel called Hotel Central.

"I've booked three rooms," said Adrien, "because tonight we'll be too drunk to leave."

"Three rooms?"

"Sure," he said, "one for me, one for Dan, one for Estelle. You surely don't expect me to share with Dan?" he added in a voice heavy with crude innuendo.

Oh, he had not forgotten Poison Ivy's phone call; he had stored its venom and would draw it out whenever an opportunity arose. Once again we were ready to smash his face in.

Adrien really had reserved three rooms. It was incredibly hot. Tired from the drive, we squabbled like dogs, and trapped in our quarrel we were unable to separate.

All three of us found ourselves in one of the rooms. The bed was enormous. Adrien and Dan each dropped into a chair. Unfortunately, the sun blazed through the windows. Even with closed drapes we were sweating. Even if we were to shut up, we would sweat. I left Dan and Adrien to their bitter squabbling and found a big thick soft towel (Adrien had chosen a fine hotel). I soaked it thoroughly in the shower, wrung it out, and returned to spread it on the bed. Then I lay down on it in my panties and bra.

Its coolness penetrated me, and little by little my rage ebbed. I drifted on Dan's voice; I was happy. Dan and Adrien had enough of being angry and sweating. Suddenly I heard them no more. When they saw my nice cool towel on the bed, they each got a big thick soft wet towel like mine and stretched out in their shorts, one on either side of me. My brother held my hand, Adrien stopped complaining, and we dozed in coolness on that stifling afternoon in Vienne, France.

FORTY-TWO

The Pyramid

THERE the three of us lay on that monumental bed in the Hotel Central, all in the same bedroom, with those white wet towels cooling our backs and isolating us in our private oases, while outside the heat worked its will, the noisy heat of Vienne: vehicles ceaselessly growling at the crossroads, the breezy voices of passersby, the roar of buses, the buzzing of flies at the curtains, and the kind of noise heat itself produces in a town in late afternoon, a kind of noise I am unable to describe.

But you will be able to, madame, and you will also be able to guess what those three supine bodies on white towels mean, two of them holding hands, all three gazing drowsily at the ceiling.

Details, drifting fragments, madame. I cannot linger, I cannot wait for answers; I must move quickly. Fear, you know how hard fear rides me . . .

A little later, Adrien went down to his car. He returned bearing a suitcase, oh, not like Poison Ivy's, which made such a disastrous sound with its old metal fittings in the doorway of our loft. It was a designer case, of the kind intended for air travel, even though Adrien had as yet never taken a plane, but he very soon would, and he knew it.

From the case he removed two men's suits, white suits. He savored our surprise.

"I'm taking you to the Pyramid," he said.

We were still on the bed, Dan in shorts, I in bra and panties, both alone now on a kind of boat drifting across waters of uncertain configuration, and because of that sudden uncertainty (uncertainty too was one of our guests), we were no longer sure where we were.

We were together. Shoulder to shoulder, warm arms side by side, hand in hand. Our two hands had such power together, they demanded all our strength. Nothing remained in our wrung-out brains;

our brains flapped like two sails over the moistness of the towels.
They were so white, those towels, their whiteness enveloping us like
a mist, absorbing our last shreds of coherent thought.

We were together, but where?
    "The Pyramid, in Egypt?" I said tentatively.
    "Mind you, there are several of them," said Dan, making a marked
effort to get back to dry land.
    "The Pyramid in Vienne," said Adrien, "the best food in France!
But of course you've never heard of it, you're such ignorant assholes."
    "You brought us all this way to go to a restaurant, Adrien? I don't
believe you!"

The Pyramid in Egypt, the Pyramid in Vienne. We exchanged monster's stares, each in his own camp, certain of the other's madness,
we recovered our certainty of the other's madness as if jolted into
it by a thunderclap, with shocked, shattered stares.

And now it occurs to me that it was for this precise reason that we
never broke irreparably from Adrien. Intimately convinced of the
other's error, each was comforted in the sense of his personal proximity to . . . to what? To the being itself, of course.
    But we were only children, filled with fear. We needed to check,
to keep striking the spark that comforted us by rubbing our incompatible personalities against each other.
    *An explanation, another one, does it matter, madame? Your libretto
will need no explanations.*

"A restaurant where Albert Lebrun ordered a banquet of eight dishes
including the great *délices de Saint Antoine en feuilleté,* but you're such
rubes we'd better say it was pig's knuckles, so pig's knuckles it is . . ."
    "Pig's knuckles it is," Dan murmured almost despite himself.
    I gently pinched his hand. Adrien did not hear. He went on with
his monologue.
    "— but they made him weep, can you imagine, making a president
of France weep just with a dish. He was late for the opera, and you
know what he said? 'I prefer to be damned right here; Faust can
wait!' And he might have added Cocteau, Colette, and Sacha Guitry
to the list."
    He was really wearing us down. We let our attention wander,
relaxing our shoreward push. We went back to our white boats and
our guest, the great uncertainty.

"So obviously we couldn't go looking like that," he said, pointing to where our clothes lay on the rug.

He had a suit for himself — his own — and another he had borrowed for Dan. But what about me?

"Oh," Adrien said carelessly, "women don't count."

Careless or insolent? Or something else?

Suddenly I heard a window shatter, I felt a thud against my hip, I saw a table and on the table clothes, exactly the right size, obsessively right — but the clothes were black. I saw sneakers; I heard Dan's voice: "He's blackened them with shoe polish, Estelle!"

Mischief was in me, teeming inside me, holding me fast; I heard my father's voice: "Look out, they have the devil in them," and suddenly I no longer feared anything. The crawling sensation squeezed tight under my tongue and my voice rang firm.

"Listen, both of you," I said, "I'm going to have a bath and wash my hair. I want you to get me a dress, any old dress, white if possible, you know what suits me."

Adrien thought he had defeated me. My brother gave me a look that said "You don't want me with you in the game you're playing, whatever it is, but I think I know what it is," but my look replied, "Of course, but what I want you to do is take him away, so go with him and get a white dress, not the first you look at but the fourth or fifth." They left. I watched through the window as they vanished down a side street; they would be away for a good half hour.

I needed only five minutes, plus another ten.

Five to go down to the desk and ask for black shoe polish, ten to blacken the smaller of the two jackets.

When Adrien and Dan returned I was working on the pants.

Adrien stood in the doorway, unable either to advance or retreat.

Tears streamed down my face. "Bastard, bastard!" I cried. "There was no need to make the dead deader than they already were." My syntax collapsed, my words tumbled out, "Not the dead only for dying, the living for shoe polish too."

I still hear our father's gently mocking voice, "Look out, they have the devil in them today . . ."

It happened so rarely to us (we were extraordinarily well behaved children) that perhaps he was relieved that we sometimes had the devil in us. But this time I'll get him, Father, and get him good, oh, Father, Father . . .

* * *

Dan took me in his arms, rolled with me on the rug. He too wept, our faces and arms black with polish. Adrien mumbled indistinct things as he shut the door and peered at the chaos around us.

Soon afterward we were in the tub with Adrien scrubbing us energetically.

"Shit everywhere," said Adrien, "wherever you go you leave shit behind you. Thank God we have two other rooms."

Finally, at 10:00 P.M., calm and collected, we were ready for the Pyramid.

Adrien was in his everyday clothes, which smelled of the long hot drive, Dan wore the white suit, and I had on a white dress.

"Great," said Adrien, "now I look like the best man!"

I was tired now; I wanted to make Adrien happy, so I had let them wash my hair and put on my makeup. "The tragic look suits you," Adrien said without sarcasm, and Dan kissed my neck. The kiss meant "Don't listen, my dear one, I know that the happy look suits you very well, and the loving look, oh, my loving one, that too suits you very very well." "Stop crawling all over her," Adrien snapped. "Okay," said Dan, "since you're paying."

We went on foot down rather gloomy streets, like those of G. at night. Could such a famous restaurant really be at the end of such a gloomy street?

And suddenly we were among masses of parked cars, a terrace garden, dinner-jacketed waiters, flowers.

A lady approached, past her first youth, pleasant, swathed in a broad shawl. I noticed her fingers, painted a flawless red. She greeted us, guided us, seated us. As she withdrew Adrien whispered:

"The owner's wife, Mrs. Point."

Probably the lady had no need of a name. For the person who welcomed you into this small kingdom, "Mrs." probably sufficed, it was a word like *porter, headwaiter, sommelier, knight,* and please don't ask stupid questions, Dan and Estelle . . .

Adrien was looking pleased. I still felt the sting of tears at my eyelids; I glanced at Dan, and he narrowed his eyes as if he too felt that sting. Suddenly he leaned across to kiss me, I rose abruptly to reach for him — and jerked tablecloth, flowers, glasses, silverware, and bread rolls from the table.

Adrien maintained his composure. We moved to another table and they brought us a menu, on a single sheet, rectangular and very tall. "My goodness," I cried, "so many choices!" A passing waiter gave a small smile.

"Shut up, Estelle, for God's sake!"

"Why?"

"They serve us the lot, everything on the menu."

"What are you talking about?"

"It's their special thing here. You only get a very small serving with each dish, but that way you get to taste everything."

"Oh."

A moment later something else occurred to me.

"There's no price, it must be very expensive, gosh, thanks, Adrien."

"There's no price on *your* menu," said Adrien, looking pleased with himself.

Dan burst out laughing.

"No prices on Estelle's menu! Adrien, I could never have believed you were that protective of the ladies."

"Idiot," said Adrien, red-faced, "it's the same with all the women's menus."

Suddenly we were weary; none of this interested us anymore. We thought of our little "suite" under the eaves, anxiety seized us, and we wanted to go home at once.

At that time it was always happening.

Whenever we left home, anxiety sooner or later grabbed us, as if we had been away too long, as if we had forgotten something most important.

Then we had to get home quickly, hurrying past our darling concierge's lodge. She saw us and smiled. "Any messages for us?" She shook her head and went on sewing or washing dishes or sorting mail. There was a phone in the lodge, but none under the eaves.

But who could call us?

Minor wrote regularly, always with the same news: that Tiresia was holding her own, that she asked after us, that she did not want us to visit. Michael at long intervals sent telegrams, always ending with the same words: "Love, Michael." Alex sent postcards from G. with "Wish you were here" written in the message space. He must have used up the whole series, doubtless a brief one, of cards depicting our little town, so for a time he had been sending cards from other little towns in the vicinity, towns where his soccer team's tours took him. But there was never anything but "Wish you were here" written on the back.

Our concierge knew our three correspondents. "From the doctor," she would say as soon as she saw us. Or "From the American," or "From the soccer player."

But when we asked "Any messages?" she knew we were not thinking of them.

She knew the message we mentioned would not be from the doctor, or the American, or the soccer player, but she did not know whom it would be from.

Neither did we.

Sometimes because of something our concierge said we were made vaguely aware that we were repeating ourselves. So for variety we said, "Any massages for us?" when we were in good spirits, and when we were not so merry, "Any massacres for us?" And the concierge answered with one of her own quirky little jokes, or by being facetious, which is of course a way of saying no.

Adrien was talking:

"She's a widow. When they got married she built the terrace and garden, and when Mr. Point died . . . In fact, an hour or two before he died, you know what he said? He said, 'With all the care I've been getting I'm sure to die cured.' I really admire him. He built all this up himself. And afterward she carried on exactly the way he began, I really admire her, she's a great lady. Yes, yes," he said, "I really admire her."

But we were not listening.

Since this place and this red-nailed woman in a shawl and that thickset man in the photo in the entryway and that *poularde de Bresse truffée en si* (but once again we got it wrong, it was *truffée en vessie,* in other words, truffles inside a pig's bladder, one of the owner's celebrated discoveries), since none of that interested us, and since the big beautiful plates and the tiny decorative details on the big beautiful plates did not interest us, and since the silverware and flowers did not interest us, since nothing interested us, we just wanted to go home. We wanted to see our concierge, to be home, within range of her strong bold voice with its Portuguese roll . . .

The streets of Vienne between our hotel and the restaurant . . . Long, gray, closed faces. On the restaurant terrace the apex of the pyramid, gray, like the monuments on the graves in our town cemetery.

Where was Alex on a Sunday like this? Certainly not at the cemetery. Probably at a soccer match, an away game.

Who would warn us if —

If what, Dan and Estelle?

Beneath their gray gravestones, inside the coffins you saw being lowered on ropes — what if they needed you? Who knows what the dead get up to? In the whole vast landscape of books Dan raced through in his dancer's stride we found nothing concerning our father and Nicole, although (however wrongheaded the undertaking) that was what my brother sought, a reply to that one question. I knew it, and because of it I ran for him from one bookstore to the next, I waited in libraries, I read for him . . .

We were in Vienne, tense, apprehensive, with Adrien.

"What are you thinking about?" asked Adrien.

"About our concierge."

And it was true.

"You must think I'm a fool," said Adrien.

"Our concierge would love to have these recipes," said Dan, making a huge effort.

"Oh," said Adrien, mollified.

And he was off again.

"Point's idea . . . a chicken has to taste of chicken. It mustn't lose any of its essential flavor. And the same for all ingredients . . . With the complicated recipes of the past you could mask the difference between a top-notch chicken and just any old hen . . . the quality of the ingredients . . . focus on the taste of a product and then enhance it . . . never use a sauce to conceal a defect, but only as a supreme complement . . . Prince Curnonsky . . . *Demi-deuil* . . .

"Of course you have no idea what that is?"

"What?"

"*Poularde demi-deuil.*"

Adrien, we hate you, we could cut you up into little pieces, stuff you into a pig's bladder . . .

"Don't make that face. It won't be on your plate tonight, it's not one of Point's dishes. Mère Filliou invented it. A fatted chicken with black truffles slipped under the skin, but on one side only, hence *demi-deuil,* half-mourning. What? You don't like truffles?"

"We don't mind them," we said.

He spoke of crayfish tails in toasted cheese shells, of game pâté in pastry, of a fantastic Burgundy, Romanée Conti.

We arrived at the raspberries and wild strawberries. Adrien took out a cigar and brought a rambling sentence to a close.

". . . and that's what I like, you see, not crap like that maid's room of yours."

"Yes, Adrien," we said.

"I'm going to start a business of my own."

"Why not, Adrien?"

"You think I can?"

"Certainly you can."

We meant it.

"I've already started . . . Want me to tell you?"

"Of course."

"Wicker from the Philippines."

"Wicker?"

"I buy wicker furniture there, for next to nothing, then I transform it, I paint it, I lacquer it, I upholster it, it'll catch on, mark my words, it'll catch on . . ."

Wicker furniture, lacquered, upholstered . . .

Our faces had resumed their unconcerned expressions, and Adrien decided we were envious. He leaned forward in a cloud of cigar smoke:

"But you —"

"What about us?"

"You too —"

"You want us as partners?"

"No, you're too crazy. But you could live differently, you could live as well as I do."

"What do you mean?"

"Instead of staying in those two miserable rooms where it's always too cold or too hot."

"We like it there."

"Perhaps it's okay for fucking —"

"Adrien!"

"But Estelle has no piano. I don't understand you, she's given up her studies, she says she wants to play the piano like Tiresia, and she doesn't even have a piano. But Tiresia definitely did have a piano, even if she had stopped playing."

We stared at Adrien, astounded. Dan was agitated:

"It's true, Estelle, you don't have a piano. I have to find you a piano, I have to find . . . Do people find pianos in churches here?"

"In churches, have you lost your mind?"

"No, no, but —"

"But first you have to move."

"Impossible," I said.

"Why?"

"Because of the concierge."

I saw that Adrien was about to explode. I tried to catch myself.

"You know how much I earn, Adrien, with that lady executive who has me type all her documents in sextuplicate. Sextuplicate — just imagine when you have to correct an error! I earn enough in one hour to buy one and a half sandwiches. And Dan with his dance lessons in that nice school on rue Legendre? The same."

Adrien leaned back in his chair. A waiter took it for a signal and came running.

"Sir?"

"Champagne," said Adrien.

And as the tiny bubbles popped in our noses, Adrien said to us:

"Then why do you do it?"

"To pay for our studies."

"You're crazy, you're the craziest people I've ever come across! What the hell is stopping you from going to the attorney and getting your money from him?"

"What attorney?" said Dan.

"What money?" I said.

"The philosophy teacher's brother, he's rolling in money."

"What's that have to do with us?"

Once again we had misheard.

Adrien began again.

"There's huge amounts of money waiting for you with the attorney. Everyone knows that, except you, apparently."

And at one stroke we did indeed know it.

A voice in its burrow among its victims and their remains, pairs of glasses, piled-up directories, a voice that came and went in its lair on the vast surface of a massive desk.

Then suddenly the nature of the air changed, the nest of a raptor wedged into a cleft in a rock face. That was where the voice was coming from. It swooped down on us. The raptor whose questing bill had not managed to rip us apart was again beating its wings beside us.

And the noise of those great beating wings prevented us from hearing what the voice had said.

                                *   *   *

An agitated, urgent, feathered rustling, filling the head, making every membrane in the head throb, a thrashing of wings, an agitation like that of rain beating against a windshield and put to flight by the wipers but returning to beat hard as we drove, rain that blinded us to the road ahead, just as the clatter of the raptor's wings prevented us hearing, a thrashing of wings . . .

"You remember, Dan, crows on the dark meadow, that year it rained all winter long; Father said there had never been so many crows, Nicole yelled, 'Make them go away, oh, please make them go away,' Tiresia put her hands over Nicole's eyes but Nicole went on looking and yelling, Father ran into the meadow and the crows flew away. We were with him, do you remember, Dan, that great beating of wings? On the way back to the house, Father took us each by the hand, and suddenly he said, 'This house will be yours, what do crows matter?' "

"That's not what he said. He said: 'This house will be yours so to you crows don't matter!' "

"After that he said . . . it was in English, I don't recall . . ."

"I do. It was a strange word: *nevermore.* He repeated it several times, then he said, 'None of this is for you.' I recall it very clearly because I was thinking of the box of lollipops we got from Canada and I thought he meant those lollipops. And I said, 'The lollipops aren't for us, Papa?' "

"And he put an arm around each of us, laughing, and he said, 'Oh, yes, they are for you, all the lollipops in the world, and so is that rainbow, oh, my darlings, how beautiful you look under that rainbow . . .' "

"He said, 'Everything has been washed clean, everything is in its place.' "

"And we thought he meant the veranda, where we had stacked all our toys and painted and made a huge mess that he had asked us to clean up."

"We thought the veranda had washed itself by magic."

"We thought reindeer had done it; we heard 'reindeer' instead of 'rainbow.' "

"Then we went off meekly to our rooms . . ."

"And later when Nicole came to remind us that we hadn't straightened up our rooms, we cried out, 'But Papa said everything had been washed and put in its place.' "

"And Nicole said, 'How could that be? All your toys and the

paints are still outside.' I can still hear her: 'How could that be?' Not for a second did she imagine we would lie to her . . ."

"And we told her, 'It's the reindeer, Papa said they washed everything clean and put it in its place . . .' "

"And Nicole laughed, she laughed, she never yelled at us, oh, Nicole, Nicole . . ."

"Don't cry my love, my little love . . ."

The wipers thrashed back and forth at high speed over the glass. The heat had finally broken, the heavens had opened, it was the middle of the night, and we were fleeing Vienne in Adrien's Citroën-Maserati. We were racing toward our apartment, to our dear concierge, who would tell us if there were any messages for us, toward the only place where we should be, where those in need of us might find us, call us.

We were fairly drunk when we left the Pyramid. Adrien was furious because the waiter had brought Dan the check.

"Don't get mad, Adrien, it was because of the suit," I said.

It had not been because of that damned suit that the waiter had come to Dan, but because of his beauty and bearing.

Yet he knew very well that Dan was the guest, that I was simply the guest's consort; he knew full well who the leader of our little group was, no waiter could make such a mistake, let alone a waiter at the Pyramid. The signs had been clear. Adrien had led the way in. Adrien had ordered the meal. Adrien had ordered the champagne. It was Adrien who had tipped his chair back and smoked a fat cigar. Even if White Suit sat in the other chair and White Dress in the companion to the other chair, it was clearly the short stocky one in the business suit who would pull out his credit card.

But it was my brother who drew all the looks.

Drawing people's looks.

The expression is unexceptional, but if you reflect that the drawn look originates in people's eyes, that those eyes are twins set in one head, that the head itself is like the body's summit, that the body projecting the look can move and change direction, then you will understand the power that this attraction exerted upon looks can reveal: the power to move mountains.

The waiter had approached our table with the salver bearing the check, and walked toward Adrien.

The course he was navigating, the orientation of his upper body, all indicated he was headed with that high-held salver toward Adrien, the leader of our group. But suddenly something went awry in that perfect-waiter machinery, a slight modification perhaps of his angle of approach, and now he was looking at Dan, heading straight for Dan, and it was at Dan's place, as if hypnotized, that he deposited the chased silver dish, like a glittering offering to a god.

And then to wipe out this hideous misunderstanding we drank yet another bottle of champagne, still Dom Pérignon, before leaving more or less steady on our feet.

But in that gray street, grayer still now that night had pushed with crushing weight into shaded corners and the pallid street lamps had finally asserted their mastery of the gloom, out in that street, so like all the streets of our town of G. at night, we began to pitch and toss, Adrien leading, the drunkest but the most resolute, and Dan and myself less drunk but once more weighed down by our guest un-certainty, who hung about our necks like the fatal albatross in the poem. Letting Adrien take us in tow, we followed as he staggered from side to side, our eyes stinging as if from salt spray in the foggy glare of the lights above our heads.

"The Pyramid, the Pyramid," Adrien shouted with the eagerness of a sailor sighting land, and the Pyramid stood before us, gray and mute on the outer reaches of our dripping vision.

"That's strange," said Adrien, "I thought we had left it behind." A hundred yards later he again chanted, "The Pyramid, the Pyramid"; our eyes still stung but now it was sand, we were swaying across a waste of sand and shingle, and once again the Pyramid rose before us, gray and mute.

"Shit, full circle again," Adrien belched. He had fallen at the foot of the structure. "It reminds me of something," he gurgled with effort. "Come on, Adrien," we begged, but he did not want to go. "It reminds me of something," he said again. "What is it, you know what it is, tell me and I'll get up." We picked him up by his arms, but he fell back heavily.

Adrien became threatening: "Even assholes like you know things, you must know what it reminds me of." He brushed his hand along his hairline and at once removed it as though something there were aflame. "Adrien, it's the cemetery," my brother Dan said harshly, but we resumed our walk, with us in front this time, and Adrien behind, with us getting sober and Adrien muttering things, "No fun, assholes and no fun."

Dan and I were no longer drunk at all, the uncertain had retreated, we wanted to go home, and Adrien finally followed us, concentrating on not losing us, keeping the white banner of our clothes before him in the gray night of Vienne.

We tried to take him to one of the two other rooms we had reserved, but nothing doing, he crawled along the corridor, determined to return to the first, "the one where you made that goddamned mess, that's the one for me," and that finally was where we put him.

"Adrien, we're leaving," we told him.

But he made no reply.

"Adrien, we're taking your car."

Reply, whether of acquiescence or refusal, unintelligible.

"You can take the train tomorrow, we'll phone you, we'll pick you up at the station."

Snores.

And we left.

We reached Paris at dawn; the garbage collectors had not yet made their rounds, we had trouble parking Adrien's big car, then we reached our concierge's lodge. Its shutters were closed. Dan hurried up to the seventh floor in case there was a sheet of paper stuck to it with "So-and-so called . . . call back at such-and-such" in her large untidy hand, or under the door, or on our table since she had a key. But there was nothing, Dan's expression told me, and we no longer had the courage to go back up to the seventh floor. We sat down on the three steps outside the lodge where we had so often enjoyed sunlight and piping-hot coffee, listening to the approaching roar of the garbage truck. It went past and still we waited. Suddenly a bell rang in the lodge. White-faced, we rose, and a few seconds later the concierge fumbled with the lock, opened the door, saw us seemingly rising up before her, and jumped back with a scream. Her husband shouted something in Portuguese from the bedroom as she recovered her wits:

"Well, you two certainly timed it well, it's for you . . ."

And we bundled into her lodge and took the phone:

"Fuck, are you crazy?" yelled Adrien in slurred but highly audible tones. "You leave me just lying here, my head hurts, my car has vanished, where did we leave it . . ."

We dropped the receiver and our concierge took it:

"Ah, Mr. Adrien, it's you. Yes, don't worry, they're here. How did they get here?" She looked at us. "In your car, they say . . . They say they will come and get you at the station . . . The next train . . . You are very welcome, Mr. Adrien . . . Take some aspirin . . . Yes, thank you, you're welcome, yes, I will, until then . . ."

She hung up and looked at us, a little alarmed but already laughing:

"Well, you certainly scared me. But what is it you're always waiting for? Will you tell me one day?"

She was dressed curiously, with red socks that came up to her knees, a green quilted nightgown (she had not yet put on her bra and you sensed the swell of her soft, ample bosom beneath), and a big floppy sweater, stained pink in the wash, a whole get-up sadly eloquent of an unheated basement dwelling. But her little turned-up nose and laughing eyes and dimples transformed her into a goblin, a small mischievous fairy living in a house in an enchanted forest.

"I'll make coffee, we'll have breakfast with my husband, up you get, Mario . . ."

We sat around the table with its yellowed oilcloth top, with some of yesterday's mail still unsorted . . . "Junk mail, no hurry for that" — she boiled water behind the folding door of the cubbyhole-kitchen, and soon we were buttering our bread with her and her husband, finally relaxed, happy once more.

And suddenly my brother said:

"But she's the rainbow, look at her clothes!"

And I said:

"Yes, that's you. You're the rainbow."

And her husband Mario said:

"A rebow, ma Dlourès, oh oh!"

FORTY-THREE

Happiness

OUR BODIES collided in the depths of the night.

My brother quickly turned on the lamp: raw blindness on my face, my brother cupping it in his hands, "Estelle, Estelle," our hearts beat violently, I screwed my eyes up, his firm hands still holding my face under the lamp, our hair tousled, our features swollen, and the smells of the night in our mouths, but it was truly us, us alone together in our new apartment.

*   *   *

We scrutinized every detail of our faces in the light of the lamp, softer now, allowing our eyes to relax; we had to touch those circles beneath the eyes, run fingers through those wild masses of hair. I lightly brushed the tiny whiskers on my brother's cheeks, he followed the line etched on my face by a fold in the sheets, we sniffed the odors of mouths, armpits, sex; it was us.

Around us was the silent space of our apartment, whose door and windows would open only if we wished it, which was ours, vast, new, and we were in that space.

We were still dazed, as if a happiness whose existence we had forgotten, a happiness we had not hoped for ourselves, had arrived.

Our stay in the tiny suite under the eaves seemed merely to have been a passage, a nest for the frightened children to rebuild their strength. I believe we then understood for the first time that we were grown-up . . . and free.

And in the room with five windows ("Almost a cathedral nave," our friend Vlad said when he first saw it) our happiness slid along the bar, slipped across the floor with its long brown planks, luxuriated in the piano's bulk. The bar with the stark shadow it threw on the wall would be for our hands, that floor gleaming mysteriously in the gloom would be for our feet, and the piano . . . oh, the piano, we scarcely dared let our eyes rest on it, so strongly did it represent the essence of our happiness. Its curves asserted themselves majestically in that space, it proclaimed that Dan and Estelle lived here, that it was their representative, the representative of their happiness in this place. And it was an imposing piano. Luster burst from its lines, emerged from the depths of its frame, like the manifestation of a spirit keeping watch within. It was strong, it was our protector.

We went back into the corridor to return to our bedroom. We were almost awed; we had seen our happiness at work in space, and now we needed to be together in our bed.

Our bed was still no more than a jumbled mountain of blankets. Soon there would be a thick rug, then an Oriental carpet, then a comfortable mattress, but we would never reach the point of a complete bed — we did not have the time. And yet we wanted to be grown-up and far away from the old bedroom in the Helleur house where two children still slept in each other's arms on the floor, at the foot of a little girl's bed too small for the two of them . . . But we never found a bed to suit us and would return from our vain searching with only an extra blanket, each one more appealing, more beautiful, irresistible. *Do you know, madame, that there are blankets more precious than furs, blankets that are like the skins of creatures that do not exist but that should exist, ideal creatures that in their goodness have plucked out their own fur and feathers to help us who are so naked? That was our bed, a heap of sumptuous covers.*

The phone rang. It was Adrien.

"What the hell were you doing? The phone's been ringing for hours."

"Do you realize what time it is?"

"I've just arrived, I'm at the airport."

We recalled guiltily that Adrien had just practically circled the globe.

Luckily he was so excited that he rattled on: "New York, Chicago, Brasília, Rio de Janeiro, Tokyo, Hong Kong, made contacts everywhere, just wait, one of these days I'll be listed on the stock exchange." "Fantastic, Adrien." "Much more than you can imagine, and Hong Kong, what a place, that bay . . . Chinese rich as Croesus . . ."

We stopped listening, left the receiver dangling, we simply listened to the ups and downs of his voice, which sounded like a merry-go-round of roller coasters — but careful! he had stopped, and we dived for the receiver.

"So how is it?"

"What, how is what, Adrien?"

"The new apartment."

"Wonderful."

And Adrien exulted:

"I was right, eh, better to be rich and on track than broke in a shack, huh, huh?"

This was the latest avatar of his favorite saying; he must have worked hard at it and was clearly proud of the rhyme. "Huh," he said again, "better to be rich and on track than broke in a shack." He wanted to pull us along with him, and we were so numbed — sometimes Adrien literally stunned us — that we went along with him. "Sure, Adrien," we said, then caught ourselves and added, "All this is thanks to you, Adrien," and "Thanks for reminding us about the attorney," but our voice was slurred, and if our old childhood enemy sometimes lacked perspicacity, his moods made up for it.

"Never mind," he said, "don't bother."

His voice was once again grumpy, mulish.

"You were fucking, and I'm disturbing you. Doesn't anything besides fucking interest you?"

And he hung up.

*   *   *

Madame, if I said to you, "We fucked," would that be enough? "My cat has four feet, a tail, and whiskers," could that be enough? If so, then I might as well toss all my descriptions in the wastebasket, for what I tell you will mean nothing to anybody.

You must be my translator, madame. You must find what in the language of now can translate what I have described to you. I want to keep my feet in the now, glue myself to the mass of others, of the living, of my contemporaries, you must translate, but madame, without traducing, is that possible, do you think . . .

Love is intimidating.

We learn that and it surprises us.

On the stove with its control panel set with cosmic fluorescences, we set a small plank; and on the plank our portable gas burner from the garret apartment.

That poor three-burner camp stove had also been intimidated. We realized that right away, and took it down to the inner courtyard of our new building, where there was a fountain. It could never have borne being washed in the superb Bauhaus bathtub, there were so many black trickle marks down its sides. It took us two or three scouring pads and sponges to clean it; what a scrubbing and currying. A neighbor walking past in suit and tie conspicuously drew away from the trickle of grimy water. We returned to the huge kitchen with the portable cooker, as modest as ever but now a healthy blue color, and now it held its own atop the haughty stove, a little like a child's drawing displayed among paintings by the masters.

The refrigerator was too tall for us to put anything whatsoever on it. We did not even consider it. As in our garret apartment we left our yogurt tubs every night on the windowsill, which was as broad as a balcony. They were no longer the same kind of yogurt: these were a creamy white and came in glass pots, and beside them was the caviar brought by our new friend Vladimir; and always a magnum or two of champagne. We were rich.

We were rich and had bought furniture, of all kinds as long as it seemed expensive; we lacked discernment. But it remained in its packaging, swelling the haphazard mountain of boxes in the two back rooms. In the evening we would go and look at them, hoping they would have become tame enough for us to be able finally to bring them out. But where to put them? In the big living room there was already the bar, the piano, and a floor so meditative it would be doing it an injury to weigh it down with even one piece of furniture. "I am not a beast of burden," it would surely say, and we did not want to turn it into a beast of burden. We satisfied ourselves with putting our trestle table in a corner by the window. It too had been scoured in the courtyard fountain, and repainted by Mario. Utterly discreet, melting into the wall, it was now Dan's desk.

He had set out his books on the cardboard containers of the new furniture (with the new furniture still in its containers) in the two rear rooms, and whenever he needed one he rose from the table, walked along the wall by the bar, and returned by the same route.

I did the same thing with my scores. I walked along by the bar and returned by the bar. When I was at the piano I could see my brother seated at his trestle table at the far end of the room. My exercises did not disturb him; his concentration was total. But I often glanced up and looked at his back, upright as a young tree, his neck, his hair, bronzed as Indian-summer foliage in New England. I thought nothing. Why should I have thoughts? Everything was in place in the world and we were in that world.

We had put two plastic basins in the bathroom, brought from our garret apartment and cleaned in the fountain. Under the basins we put our old bath mat, laundered in our old concierge's washing machine.

The two basins on their mat stood before the big Bauhaus washbasin. (Contemplating our bathroom, Adrien had used the term "Bauhaus," along with others, such as Art Deco, but we understood nothing of all that, and we had chosen the two syllables of Bauhaus because the way we pronounced it the word evoked the French word *beau,* and less obviously because of the German accent Adrien had ostentatiously assumed when pronouncing the word. Doubtless in us a long-unrecognized desire had begun to tremble, but so far it trembled only at the sonorities emitted by Adrien, whose accent was distinctly iffy. And at that exact point the story of Kafka's insect, Gregor Samsa, came back to me, "Samsa could be a part for a dancer, yes, it could, those little feet filling up the whole space." Our father had frowned, Nicole had cried, our father and Tiresia had exchanged a few brief words in German, oh, madame, so many lost opportunities!)

We each stepped into a basin, turned on the faucet in the fine Bauhaus washstand, and carefully reached out to wet a facecloth. Then we rubbed each other, taking care not to splash; it took time and effort, but in a way that suited us.

"You're so alone in a bathroom," said my brother. "Estelle, can you imagine the number of actions you perform alone . . ." That idea worried us: so many actions, can you imagine, combing your hair, brushing your teeth, dressing, walking in the street, so many actions, almost all of life. At least with our two basins we were together, we could be washed there only by each other, otherwise there would be splashing and we did not want to splash, we did not want to mar the magnificent bathtub, the magnificent washstand, and their irreproachable whiteness.

Adrien paid us a call. He strode rapidly through the apartment. "Not bad," he said of the living room with its five windows. This apartment was in a sense his doing. "Without me you'd never have called the attorney, you wouldn't have found this apartment, you wouldn't have seen that real estate agent, you'd still be rotting miserably in your poky little garret apartment!"

Our concierge also felt that this apartment was somewhat her doing. It was located almost opposite our old building and it was she who found that it was for sale. "So we won't lose sight of each other, isn't that so, Mr. Dan . . ."

"Yes, but if I hadn't asked her, she'd never have dreamed of mentioning it to you," Adrien was thinking. "How powerful I am now, how kind to the weak, of course I've done all this in memory of Mr. Helleur, who was a good man, better than you two scum, anyway. And in memory of Nicole, who was an angel, so beautiful that I still haven't found a woman to equal her . . . If they were still alive it's them I'd be inviting to the famous restaurants I go to these days, and I'd give Nicole Guerlain perfume and Trismégite scarves, she at least would appreciate that kind of thing, but I no longer have anyone to show what I've accomplished, no one but these two idiots. Well, maybe they'll get better in the long run, they've already managed to buy a decent apartment, let's see the other rooms . . ."

But, struck suddenly with anxiety, we did not show him the two back rooms. "What's behind those doors?" said Adrien. "Two rooms, but for the moment we're using them as junk rooms, come and see the bathroom and kitchen." The bathroom and kitchen saved us; and thanks to them a tour of our bedroom was also forgotten. Steamship, launchpad, heavenly bodies, ecstasy (we whisked the basins and camp stove out of sight). "All the right appliances," said Adrien, looking knowledgeable. "But you need furniture," he said as he left.

We concurred, we agreed most heartily with him, exaggerating our agreement to please him, for we wanted most earnestly to please him; we understood that we might have shown him much more appreciation, and we realized that our new guest happiness was the most complex of all who had taken up residence with us.

We did not want our new guest happiness to turn now and hurt our friend Adrien, Adrien who was not two as we were, who had strayed so far from the being . . . "You're quite right, old pal, we need furniture, you're so very right."

It was wasted effort.

A truck blocked the street below. In fluted letters on its brown sides were the words:

ADRIEN N.
RUE DU BAC

And the label on the four fat packages read "Helleur."

"So they're for you!" exclaimed our excited former concierge. "No, no," we said fearfully to the deliveryman when he asked us to sign. "Bah, give it to me," said the concierge, "that truck belongs to Mr. Adrien, so I'll sign!"

There was a wicker sofa, two wicker armchairs, and a wicker coffee table. The first three articles were upholstered with a sumptuous leaf-pattern fabric, while the base of the table was of intersecting strips of reed, its wicker lacquered bright green.

There was also a note:

"Better to be rich and sitting in Adrien's chairs than broke and sleeping under the stairs. You can have them at cost, pay me when you like. And no black this time!"

We were flabbergasted.

"How lucky he didn't see the heap of furniture in the back rooms!" was what we immediately thought.

We were flabbergasted and touched.

"How could we have forgotten that he makes furniture!"

We were flabbergasted, touched, and very soon angry.

For it was no good moving those four wicker numbers around the big room, facing them this way and that, shifting their spatial arrangement. They were a nuisance.

But to whom?

To our guest happiness, who needed all that empty space between the piano, the bar, and the trestle table in order to stretch out and take his ease.

"I was fighting with my body," said Dan. "To rip it apart from matter. From matter that wanted to take it back . . .

"The earth and my body were on the same shore . . .

"My body could be an ally, but it would only let itself be taken by main force, and was capable at all times of reverting to its earlier allegiance . . .

"A certainty cried out in me: that there was not much time for ripping my body apart from matter, for bringing it over to my side . . .

"There were the other dancers, of course, and Alwin, but the battlefield was my body, fighting my muscles with my muscles, my bones with my bones, my whole weight with my whole weight . . .

"When I heard myself and let myself go, it seemed to me that my muscles abandoned me, I literally heard the call of matter deep down within them, my flesh spread horizontally, and an appeal rose toward it, my muscles turned soft, they no longer belonged to me, and I sprang up with one leap . . .

"I had to be on my feet at all times, upright, you understand, to recover control of my muscles so that they would recover control of my body . . .

"I danced asleep on my feet. It drove Alwin crazy, he yelled: 'Dan, if you don't learn to rest you'll never amount to anything . . .'

"Alwin knew everything about dancing, but that he didn't know. Sleep for him was nothing but a hiatus between two light spaces. Sleep for him was like backstage for an audience. He slept little, no more than five hours, but deep unbroken sleep . . .

"I tried to explain to him. He looked at me with those black eyes of his: 'That's your female side, Dan.' He didn't like women, you know, Estelle. 'Blind flesh' was what he called them . . .

"It was such a lonely task. Just my body against my body . . .

"The spectators watched us, Estelle, and remained seated. And then they went back home, and nothing had changed. The dancer wins a small victory over matter on the narrow battlefield of his body, but it makes no difference to all the flesh around him, the unending flesh of the world . . .

"We serve no purpose but to stir up the digestive systems of people who can afford a ticket to the ballet . . .

"And I had had enough. I could not do without dancing, but it was no longer enough for me . . ."

"And law, Dan, is that enough for you?"

We had been talking for ages; dawn could not be far off. We lay close together in the middle of the pile of blankets in our bedroom. Sometimes we dozed a little. In that half sleep my brother grew restless, spoke incoherently.

"What are you saying?"

I heard Dan say "Nicole," then:

"What did I say?"

"You were speaking of . . . of them, of Nicole."

He leaned back against the wall, looking frightened.

"I don't want what happened to Nicole to happen to me."

And suddenly I too was frightened.

"What do you mean?"

We were whispering.

"I don't quite know, Estelle. It seems to me that Nicole was trying to right a wrong."

And I discovered that I had always known it.

"A huge, enormous wrong. But she didn't have the means, you see . . . Just that frail body of hers — not even all that talented — and that garage. Nothing else."

Before leaving our old house we had looked into the drawers in our father's study and found a bundle of papers kept in a folder like the others. But those papers had no letterhead, no official stamp. They bore only our father's writing, his slender sloping hand, sometimes just a few lines in mid-page. There was no date.

We took one out at random.

"*Mrs. Neighbor in her deck chair . . . Swelling calves, thick neck, common sense, rooted in the now, no sense of responsibility for the world, the perfect accountant . . . The children call her Mrs. Mother . . . 'Without my wife, my business would collapse,' says Mr. Neighbor . . . Hint of commiseration for me in his tone . . . 'A man needs a reliable woman, Mr. Helleur,' says Mrs. Mother, stretched out all cozy on her deck chair . . . She talks of her son Adrien and his romantic exploits . . . 'Just now he needs to have a good time, later he'll find a reliable woman, I trust him . . .' She's my neighbor's wife, we talk across the garden wall . . . A reliable woman . . .*

"*Yet how much better I like these other two women: my poor Nicole, whom I can hear at this instant through the wall, pitter-patter in her little dance slippers, and Tiresia, whom I saw just now with both hands on the piano lid, as if she were listening to a piece of music being played inside and transmitted to her through her fingertips . . .*

"How much better I like these two women . . ."

And on another sheet stapled to the first:

"Tiresia's white fingers on the black piano lid. You would swear she was listening through her fingers. Sometimes they move, delicately, as if the music had changed place; then they are still again . . ."

On another:

"I am absentminded today, I realize I am reading a case inattentively, I feel uneasy . . . For I can no longer hear Nicole in her garage. No more of her endless Boléro, *which suits her so badly, no more pitter-patter, no more confused sounds of striving . . . I feel as if a little flame had gone out, I perceive a darkening, that's why I'm not reading so well . . ."*

These words all alone on another sheet in the same set:

"I so much prefer these two women . . ."

As we read that phrase for the third time, we were suddenly aware that these notes were in English. Our father never spoke to us in English.

The bundle of papers slipped from our hands. We closed the folder and carefully tied the black ribbons.

We did not touch it again . . .

If only we had read it! But once again we pushed away the ladder fate offered to us, the ladder hanging from the blindly careering train of our destiny. Our father's clashes with Minor, their long quarrel that was always on the same subject, if only we had taken those papers out . . .

In any case it was already too late. We would have had to find them years earlier, before my brother left for New York, before his fatal visits to that boat moored behind the empty space of an abandoned Hudson River pontoon. But we had been in our attic at the back of the house, or under the apple tree, or by the pond, or in the ditch at the end of the meadow, or in our cave among the undergrowth in the hills. We were excessively dreamy children; we would have had to be less dreamy children, curious children.

Our parents would have had to be different, what happened to them should never have happened, the sequence was endless, it went right back to the first man on earth and even before him, before this earth.

So was it written that there was no chance for us? Or was there somewhere another branch we might have taken, a small lateral branch we might without prejudice have detached from the world's main growth, a branch to bear my brother and me on its tip, just for this one life? Surely the tree of the world could have spared one tiny branch broken off at the right spot?

"I so much prefer these two women . . ."
We stopped there, and shut the folder on our father's private papers.

"The most magnificent theater in the world will never be anything but Nicole's garage. And I want to do something, Estelle, to control levers that can lift, transform, prevent . . .

"I will guard Nicole's flame but keep it hidden at the heart of my strength like a little candle that you and I alone can see . . ."

What did he want to do? My brother wanted to study international law, to concern himself with the rights of refugees and political prisoners and prisoners of war, monitor the implementation of human rights legislation, above all to fight torture . . .

He was twenty. Three years later he was dead.

And we also talked of me.

"You can be as famous as Tiresia," said Dan.

"And I'll give concerts for the causes you defend."

"Yeah, do that, my friends," a well-loved voice seemed to encourage us. In New York, spurred on by Michael, we went to every demonstration against the Vietnam War. Once, dressed in rags painted blood red, we staged a macabre scene in Grand Central Station, dancing and carrying on and raising a ruckus. The police arrived, we were roughed up, Alwin said nothing. That night the dancers were exultant but Michael's mood was grim. "Kid stuff, all that," he said. "What we really need — " Like all the others, Michael dreaded having his name drawn for the draft. Djuma's had been, but he had managed — no one understood how — not to go. Michael, who was poor and black, knew he would have no chance. "What we really need —" Well, well, Michael, we found what we really needed.

It was another night and we were speaking of him again.

"We should send him some money so he can get rid of that taxi."

"So he can follow Alwin's courses right through."

"So he can open that little dance school in the Bronx."

"He'll never get rid of the taxi."

"Then so he can drive it a bit less."

"And dance a bit more."

"But he'll spend it on the kids' school."

"So what, if that's what he wants."

"What he wants is fantastic."

"He's found his way."

"We must help him."

"Then let's do it."

We did it. And Michael was able to open his little dance school.

"But I still have that cab," he wrote to us, "just in case you decide to come back, so I can pick you up at the airport."

And we realized that as we had predicted, he was still driving his taxi through New York's streets during the day, only perhaps a little less. Dancing was his pleasure, and the dance school was sharing his pleasure, but that car in the city was his metaphysical universe, the nurturing environment of his thought and speech . . .

We no longer confined ourselves to reconstructing our childhood, the way we had during our sleepless New York nights.

We talked now of our recent past, of Michael, who was so dear to us, of dancing and piano, of the Vietnam War, which we believed to be our war. But we talked too of everything else that occurred to us from day to day, and the flow was rich or else we were wading powerfully through it; we explored more and more widely the piece of the universe that was ours.

And what I did not know of Dan's life he told me. And what he did not know of my life I told him, and gradually those territories too were annexed to our piece of shared universe, and it truly seemed as if by progressing in this way we could annex the whole universe.

Afternoon. I left the conservatory on the rue de Madrid and turned up the rue de Rome, my usual itinerary.

Behind the railings on the bridge over the rue de la Condamine I saw a silhouette, distant, slipping from bar to bar, and something struck me. Usually pedestrians up there gave the impression that they were caged. But with that figure it was exactly the opposite:

that figure gave the impression that the whole city was in a cage and that the person up there was walking in unconfined space. Suddenly I felt imprisoned, my heart began to pound, I ran to the railings of the bridge, toward that dancing silhouette, toward my freedom. The street was long, and the bars confining me flowed endlessly by.

I reached the bridge opening, and shouted "Dan!" At the other end the walker turned: it was my brother. He had returned from Nanterre University via the Pont Cardinet station. We ran to meet and my brother hoisted me aloft and whirled me in his arms, and as I whirled around in the middle of the bridge I saw a "Danger" sign waltz around us. Then my brother set me back down, we hugged each other, breathless, almost dazed, as we always were whenever we met after being separated.

Below the bridge, coming in from the opposite direction, trains crisscrossed with a thunderous din, and it seemed to us that these trains were literally issuing forth from our clasped bodies. Brief silence. Another train came in, alone. In the growing din our bodies grew closer, in the diminishing din the train drew away; there we were one against the other, astonished and delighted by that swift conjurer's trick. We repeated the experiment with two or three other trains, then, reassured, we walked peacefully off, hand in hand.

On the brown cliff face of a building's back wall we saw the traces of an ancient advertisement that must once have been of gigantic size. Patches of blue seemed to stand out from the wall and blossom in the pink late-afternoon light, and suddenly we read "Dubonnet."

The letters, swallowed for years in the grime on the wall, had resurfaced. We stopped, surprised by this new magic trick, shut our eyes, then opened them. The priceless blue still stood out from the wall, "Dubonnet," and we reeled along together to the end of the bridge, drunk with happiness.

One morning we went down the stairs into the metro, concerned like everyone else with the tasks of the day ahead, when something caused us to stumble. We clutched at each other to keep our balance and suddenly stopped, appalled.

Everywhere there was a shuddering, along the lines of buildings, around the contours of every object, and behind it crackled invisible lines of sparks that threw every atom of the city directly into our eyes.

In that second an immense thing had its being, everywhere around us. We had almost walked right past it. How could that be?

An immense thing had reared up ahead of us, touching our skin, lying along our nerve paths, oh, you astonished passersby, forgive us for turning so suddenly on our heels, for thrusting back upstairs against the flow, irradiating you with smiles, you passersby too weary to protest. We opened our wings amid the throng, we took wing, we glided through the air above the streets, scanning facades, sky, trees, people. We turned our eyes toward you and our eyes licked you, embraced you. We were possessed, dazzled, as we floated onward, locked together.

We reached the zoo in the Bois de Vincennes. The lions were out, lying side by side on their cement parapet. "Remember the cave?" said my brother. We watched the lions and elephants, through our bodies' quickened cells rubbed our flanks against immemorial ages all the way back to the beginnings of humankind. We went from enclosure to enclosure and no animal was foreign to us. We belonged to time; time belonged to us.

We walked in the nearby woods with the white plume of an airplane flowing in the very pale sky above. We watched it for a long time. We were not *in* that plane, we *were* that plane, and all its passengers and its trajectory and its destination; we belonged to the planet and the planet belonged to us.

Shining cars raced along the beltway. We were the ribbon of the roadway and the ribbon of cars, we were the stillness of the roadway and the movement of the cars, all at the same time, in the unending succession of flashing light.

We saw a cluster of very tall buildings, close-huddled with long empty verticals separating them. Nothing frightened us, neither their size nor the whole vast space against which they stood out, we were their root systems and their soaring, we were their compactness and their emptiness.

We took the Eiffel Tower elevator and gazed out at the tablecloth of buildings that stretched to the round horizon. We felt no fear: we were the ones who had built them, the ones who were in them, and the ones who would destroy them.

We walked and walked. Night fell and we were in a cab, leaning against each other in the unbelievable comfort of a cab, worn out, scarcely conscious enough to realize that we had crossed the city from end to end. But our weariness was merely the opposite face of energy; we felt happiness flowing powerfully through us.

And that same energy wafted us from day to day and we feared nothing of the outside world. My brother had applied to take several exams at once, each of them easy for him. And I played the piano, I studied, I entered competitions, the last of them for the Marguerite Long Prize; of course I won it. That powerful inner flow swept aside all obstacles, swirling us along and swirling along all those we encountered.

FORTY-FOUR

Lettuce-Leaf Dance

*T*HAT YEAR my brother needed to chalk up seventeen accumulated credits, as they called exams in those days.

We had come to live in Paris, as Dan had decided to do on the third night of our mourning, standing in our father's study, where the carved doors had opened up for him like the pages of a book, revealing thick folders like tombstones, and in those folders the dead who must never be forgotten.

Seventeen exams, twelve in law and five in philosophy (for he was taking philosophy too). From Bergson he had worked his way back up the long chain of philosophers to the very beginning, and returning later to Bergson he took the chain in the opposite direction, the direction leading to our present. He read ceaselessly; prodigious energies had torn loose within him and he was hungry to make up for what he called "time lost in confused substances" (*confused substances, how those two words still hurt me, oh, madame, the body of my love, the earth . . .*). He gulped down double helpings, quadruple ones, since he had sworn to go twice as fast as the normal degree course, and in both disciplines at once.

He chalked up his accumulated credits ("Your granulated birdshit," Adrien still sneered, but we paid him no heed) in exactly the way I imagined him hurdling the conservatory tables the night of *The Ride of the Valkyrie.* His memory was faultless, and with that memory as an ally he vaulted all obstacles . . .

He no longer danced. Yet my brother Dan remained a dancer.

One evening when he had been working late and I had gone to sleep without waiting for him, he woke me up.

"Estelle, come look."

His eyes shone with excitement. I followed him into the big room, where he usually worked. The furniture was pushed back against the walls. Dan was barefoot and in a tracksuit.

"What's going on?"

"Do you remember the article Father mentioned to you in a letter?"

"On wasps?"

"Yes. Well, I'm going to give you a few paragraphs on the subject."

I looked blank.

"I'm going to dance the granting of custody and the withdrawal of custody rights."

"Without music?" I asked automatically.

"You're going to play the music."

"On the piano?"

"No, all you do is read the score."

"What score?"

"Here we are."

All bustle, Dan went to his worktable, and came back with a familiar green soft-backed volume:

Civil Law
Civil Liability
Legal Studies Publications
158 rue Saint-Jacques
Paris V

"There's your score. Read from here."

Nothing he did seemed strange or impossible to me. I took the old law manual. Dan set me down on the piano and I started to read the following words:

" 'Consequently, the granting of custody is annulled, and therefore liability under article 1383 or article 1385, for things without owners, for *res nullius,* and for things of which neither owner nor guardian can be identified.' "

I read slowly, stressing each syllable.

From time to time Dan gave me a brief direction:

"Heavier," and the words became stone, and Dan moved with ponderous leaps, swallowing a deep lungful after each leap, as if those few movements had cost lungs and muscles an enormous effort.

"Repeat *res nullius,*" and I repeated *res nullius* with every variation in tone I could think of, and Dan moved in tune with each variation.

"Now go to the snow," he said.

I knew where that snow was; it was on the following page. " 'In fact, if we consider that the proprietor of the building is not the guardian of snow accumulated on the roof, it is because the snow would itself constitute *res nullius*. Only in that sense could liability based on the proprietor's fault be admitted, on condition, of course, that the victim be able to prove such fault. Thus there may be fault in allowing the snow to stagnate on the roof before a probable thaw date. The Supreme Court has expressly admitted liability based on the fault of the building's proprietor . . .' "

Dan moved ponderously about the room, the drumming of my voice directly imprinting itself in the motion of his body, and the reciprocal drumming of his body imprinting itself in my voice, both of us imprisoned in a kind of trance. "That's right, that's right, Estelle," Dan murmured. How heavy the words in that law manual were, syllables like bricks, and with every breath I expelled those bricks into the air and they fell. And their fall was Dan's leap and his fall to the earth. I baked each new word with my breath and Dan shaped it with his body.

This strange exercise held us spellbound.

"Now the chorus," whispered Dan.

And I took up the word "snow" again and modulated it, carefully following Dan's movements. My body snowed, the air in the room snowed, so did the piano I sat on and the furniture pushed back against the walls; everything snowed around Dan, who was the very snow itself, light, dancing. And as if called forth by that word, a vision wandered about us . . .

Cast-iron pillars etched against the milky gloom, Greene Street obliterated along with its facades (number 72, the big one, and its companion, 28) looking like white swans with their heads tucked beneath their wings, and even our own 100, ghostlike behind us, the street furred over, snowflakes cavorting in the street lamp's glow, long gaudy bright flights in the street lamp's glow, downy wings overlapping, and the small knot of dancers around Estelle, and the big piano crouching on its black paws in the snow, and Dan dancing . . .

Dan felt the emotion in my voice.

"Your snow's melting, Estelle, go on to the stone throwing."

Dance of the thrown bottles:

"Is the railway liable for damage caused by bottles thrown from its trains?"

My voice whispered: " 'Is the railway liable for damage, liable for damage, liable for damage . . .' "

Dan limbered up with a couple of discreet jetés at the back of the room; then when I felt he was ready I yelled "Bottles thrown" and from a crouch Dan suddenly leapt the whole room to land in a split at my feet, as if his limbs were dislocated, while I ended in tragic tones, "From its trains, from its trains . . ."

Lettuce-leaf dance:

"On page 225 of the manual, the decree of the Court of Rennes of November 21, 1972 (D. 1973, 640), based on article 1384, refused to recognize liability on the part of a store operator on whose premises a customer slipped on a lettuce leaf and fell."

"Lettuce leaf in a law manual," Dan solemnly announced.

In a brief respite between figures we threw the five windows open.

Our street in Paris was small and little used. At that hour of the night it was utterly still. No window showed a light. The night was huge, calm. All that disturbed it was the streetlight hanging from the wall outside, within reach of our window. So as not to have its light between us and the vastness of the night, we draped a blanket over that streetlight. Inside the apartment the lights were out. You could see the stars in the sky.

Amid law manuals:

"Turn the lettuce over," said Dan.

I sat down at the piano.

"Toss the lettuce," chanted Dan.

I played emphatically.

"Scatter the lettuce," shouted Dan.

His voice was strong, it must have filled the street, and my fingers too came down hard on the keys, and the dancer's body made the whole room shake. How full of joy my brother Dan was as he played the lettuce leaf! We had no thought for our neighbors, nor for the policemen in the station house in the next street a few yards from our own.

We were kicking up a din in this peaceful neighborhood in the middle of the night, and we were quite unaware of it.

"You and your brother, I'll never understand you," Alex would have said sadly. "You think only of yourselves, you bastards," Adrien would have said.

"The lettuce goes around and around," Dan yelled, his voice a kind of roar that seemed to want to cover the city and perhaps fly across to the far side of the ocean to summon our friends the dancers, Kenny at airport customs going to get his umpteenth cup of coffee, David dozing through an architecture lecture, Djuma lost in dreams of glory, and especially Michael, Michael perhaps even now slumped in his cab in dense late-afternoon traffic, unable to identify this nostalgia that had suddenly swamped him . . .

"The lettuce . . . ," roared my brother, whirling around the room.

And I roared at my piano, striking chords in rich delirium.

"The lettuce is airborne."

With one leap Dan perched on the windowsill, where he sang at the top of his voice, arms stretched heavenward, to the accompaniment of what seemed to me the music most appropriate to record the savage joy of a lettuce leaf that had escaped both store operator and customer, had broken free of every article in the civil code, and was now reaching with boundless pinions toward boundless space, and I thumped my piano furiously to help waft that leaf upward to join the great cloud convoys sailing high above the Atlantic to America, to our lost friends the dancers, to Michael, who always signed his telegrams "Love . . ."

"What was that?" Dan was saying at the window, no longer spreading heaven-bound wings but bent double on the sill, as if trying to listen through the noise of the piano to words spoken by someone in the street below.

His tone sobered me at once.

It was his flattest tone, the one he used with envoys from the everyday. "Estelle, my darling," he often warned me, half-seriously, half-laughing, "with envoys from the everyday, always be careful and polite." I dashed over to join him at the window.

In the street two uniformed policemen were looking upward at the blanket draped over the streetlight.

"Did you put that there?" said the younger one.

"Absolutely, Officer," said Dan.

"You're going to have to take it off," said the elder.

"No problem," said Dan, "we've finished anyway."

Holding on to me and leaning sideways and out, he pulled at the blanket, but it slipped and fell at the officers' feet. They stooped, picked the article up, turned it over and over as we watched, fascinated. Finally the younger one slung it over his shoulder while the elder one looked up at us.

"And now you have to come to the station with us."

"To the station?" exclaimed my brother.

He seemed delighted.

"The young lady too," said the younger one.

"Well, certainly," said my brother, "certainly my sister will come along. The station, that's not something that happens every day!"

He had already forgotten the first requirement of our code of conduct: With envoys from the everyday, be careful.

But I had not.

I was shaking with cold and fear. "Dan," I muttered. Was it my old anxiety, snatches of conversation overheard between our father and Minor, certain of the words that erupted from Nicole's nightmares? Whatever it was, wariness sat rigid within me. I feared the police, I did not understand Dan's enthusiasm.

Then everything suddenly changed.

There I was with my brother, voyaging together in the middle of life's stream when suddenly (the way it always happens when you voyage thus together) all kinds of disparate objects bumped up against us, these two policemen, also in life's stream, who had bumped into our building's shins, oh, how I understood my brother's hilarity; I was madly happy. In a few short seconds we were out in the street.

"You see," I said to the officers, "we wanted to dance."

"And dancing," my brother added, "when you haven't danced for a long time, it drives you crazy."

"When my wife dances," said the elder of the two policemen, "she goes right out of her mind."

"With women it's natural," the younger one said a little more circumspectly, "but with men —"

"I don't know about that," said the elder, "when my nephew's listening to rock there's no reasoning with him."

"Now if it was soccer," said the younger, "I might be the same . . ."

"That's it, that's it," said Dan, "soccer is exactly the same, the feeling you get when you have to take a penalty kick . . ."

"And you score!" added the younger.

"Yeah!"

"Yeah!" said the younger one, and he imitated the roar of a crowd gone mad.

The two uniforms walked down the street with us, side by side, and I saw that extraordinary thing and I thought, "He is casting a spell on the police of this town." I thought it in English, as if we were in a movie with French subtitles, and my spirits lifted even higher. The four of us were making quite a din in this quiet street where the smallest sound made echoes ring. Our nameless denouncers lurking behind their windows must have been closing their shutters in disappointment. My brother had my arm; I felt as if I were slipping in a kayak over the deliciously smooth back of a rolling stream.

We had never been inside a station house. It was just a big room with two other policemen behind a long counter on the left, looking up with the heavy eyes of surprised nocturnal animals when they saw us come in.

I do not remember what happened immediately afterward, but next I see us sitting on chairs like harmless anglers picnicking on their camp stools. My brother talked and talked, his words bobbing like a cork on the surface, and I followed those words. One of the officers had a son who had gone to try his luck in a French restaurant in San Francisco; this son sent letters that spoke extensively of baseball; my brother assumed the posture of a hitter, they lent him a carbine to serve as a bat, he was incredibly funny with that carbine, and we laughed helplessly, my sides hurt. I wondered what was going to happen to us but my brother was there; I trusted in him . . . my brother was magic and his magic shielded us.

And when we returned we stumbled across Vlad, asleep on the sidewalk, head pillowed on his case of caviar.

FORTY-FIVE

Not Married?

HERE NOW is why we had so many new articles piled up and unused in the two rooms at the back of our new apartment.

Mario, husband of our old concierge, came to help us install the bar in the big living room.

"I no understand."

"What, Mario?"

"Is too big."

"No it's not."

"Yes."

"Why?"

"For the *miudos,* like this," he said, lowering his outstretched palm to knee level.

We had trouble understanding him; his French was much less distinct than his wife's, but thinking about his wife we suddenly guessed where his thoughts lay. Dlourès was pregnant, and what did he know of us? Nothing, except that we were about the same age as they were, and that we had just moved into a bigger apartment. No doubt he saw chubby babies clinging to the bar as they took their first shaky steps. Through his eyes that vision also entered ours, and we felt strangely troubled. Dlourès was our rainbow, but Mario was nothing to us, and we fell silent and focused our attention on mixing the plaster, and the noise of the electric drill covered the silence.

Then Mario left and we looked at the bar.

After a moment my brother said:

"You understand, Estelle, if I want to do two degree courses at once, I have to be able to unwind from time to time. Not that I want to start dancing again, I just want to use it, to refocus, because for two courses I need twice the energy, understand?"

I burst out laughing.

That term "degree course" was strange on my brother's lips.

"You're not taking me seriously," he said.

He abruptly removed his hand from the bar, which he had been idly caressing for some moments.

I made no reply, waiting for him to finish his sentence.

But he did not go on, he remained silent; the hand that had been stroking the honey-colored bar hung by his side like a long-handled shovel.

Yes, that was the image that came to me, perhaps because of our concierge's husband, who had just left, Mario, who was a construction worker.

That subtly caressing hand hanging like a long-handled shovel, the defeated body leaning on it, for my brother seemed to lean on his arm as if on the long slender handle of a shovel, but the arm was not rooted in any ground, and my brother was leaning on emptiness.

I became aware of the void beneath that hanging arm of his.

"What do you mean, Dan?"

"You don't take me seriously."

I was petrified, I could think of nothing to say.

"Poison Ivy you took seriously."

"Yves, Yves?"

"Yes, he was real lawyer material, I'm just short pants and a beanie, right?"

Eeney-meeney-miney-moe, catch a tiger by the toe, if he hollers, let him go, eeney-meeney-miney-moe.

The childish syllables swirled dizzily around me. I fell at his feet and hugged his knees . . .

Madame, I was hugging his knees. In an instant, fear like an imperishable scourge lashing down through the centuries had driven my body to its knees the way so many other bodies had been forced down, the ancient posture rediscovered in a hairsbreadth, and my teeth chattered and I shook and in my tight-folded arms I felt my brother's legs shaking too.

"Why haven't you divorced him yet?"

What, what did you ask me, my brother, my love?

"You haven't divorced Poison Ivy, you haven't even written to him, you haven't even called . . ."

"But Dan . . ."

Surprise ballooned huge inside my head.

"What?"

"But Dan, I don't need a divorce."

"Why not?"

"Because we weren't ever married!"

And the words I uttered were almost as shattering for me as they were for Dan.

Yves and I had held a reception, sent invitations to friends, had those friends with us the day of our "wedding." Yves referred to me as "my wife" and I to him as "my husband."

But here was my brother Dan pronouncing the word "divorce," as strange on his lips as "degree course," and I heard myself responding to that strange word . . .

And my voice was dull, my voice was merely an aerial bridge for another voice, the voice I heard in the words of a letter written in a slender slanting hand:

"My dear Estelle,

"This request may appear strange to you, may appear strange both to you and to Yves, whom I consider already your husband, since as you know I am happy with your choice.

"*Yet I make this request.*

"*If it does not cause dissension between you, and if you see in it no major drawback, I would prefer you not to marry within the letter of the law.*

"*There, I've said it.*

"*I want you to understand, Estelle (and I want your husband to believe it), that this has nothing to do with him. We are happy that you are getting married and that you are marrying this young man of whom you have spoken to us for so long, and with whom I had the pleasure of talking when you came to the house.*

"*But if you agree, the three of us here would prefer it if you could wait a little, and, I repeat, for reasons concerning us and in no way concerning you.*"

Another letter followed, reaching me that same day.

"*My little girl,*

"*I wish I could retrieve the letter I wrote and mailed last night.*

"*My feelings about all of you, the people I love most in the world, are so strong that they confuse my judgment and unhinge my common sense, which otherwise function very satisfactorily: as you know, my dear, I am not a bad lawyer — 'neither confused nor unhinged,' as even Minor admits.*

"*Yet my letters to you might seem to suggest the opposite.*

"*If I seemed terse, Estelle, it was because I know how misplaced my request must seem. I say again, I am happy with this marriage; in fact, you can have no idea how happy; and we like everything about Yves.*

"*Are you eager, are both of you very eager to get married legally, to fill out papers at city hall and the lawyer's office?*

"*My dear, if that is the case I shall of course withdraw my request.*

"*I wish I could explain, my dear, dear little girl.*

"*I am at least at liberty to tell you that I do not have Minor's blessing. He believes I am in error and has long thought so. But I am so worried about our home, 'the Helleur home,' as you used to call it (grant me the use of your expression, since our home is in fact what is at issue here).*

"*Tiresia scarcely ever plays the piano anymore. I fear your and Dan's departure may have removed the main reason she had to go on playing. Teaching you was one of her great joys.*

"*Nicole is always in her garage or at church. But she danced better when you were both here, and went to church less often.*

"*So a marriage, my little girl, so to speak an 'official' end to the childhood chapter . . .*

"*I fear emotional aftereffects, squalls . . .*

"If Dan at least were here. But turning to him is even harder for me than appealing to you. You've always been so reasonable.

"Estelle, I fear I'm tying myself up in knots. My explanations are worthless. They fill me with shame, they smack too much of blackmail.

"It would be better if you considered my request, just as it is, naked, without poor excuses.

"Estelle, my darling, don't get married officially, not right away, there are contractual problems, you have no idea how irritating they can be.

"But if you agree, have a fine reception just the same, and let me pay for it, with lots of champagne and salmon (my own favorite, as you know, but order whatever you want). Go to Bernstein's on Place de la Madeleine, they know us very well, tell them to send me the bill, and don't hold back. You have always asked for so little. Just this once — for what will be your wedding when all is said and done — I want you to ask a lot. I want you to splurge.

"And flowers, Nicole wants you to have heaps of flowers (including Nicole roses). Next door to Bernstein's is Au Bouquet de la Madeleine. I've had professional dealings with them; tell them your name and you'll get the finest flowers in the world. And if you need clothes I don't want to impose on you (I'll send a check if you prefer), but if it suits, you can go to Meyer Frères on the rue Saint-Honoré; one brother there does men's clothes and the other women's, high fashion, I mean, and I repeat, don't skimp, Estelle, for my sake if not for yours. Don't let me down in front of all those people, let's this once take your friend Adrien's advice, let's rise to the occasion, let the provinces outshine Paris, do it for us since we're too doddering to do it ourselves, it pleases us even to think about it. Yes, all three of us are excited at the thought — I because I have my pride and this would be a most acceptable way of feeding it, Tiresia because she thinks she is reliving her youth (she liked fine things, you know, and could afford them), and Nicole because it helps flesh out her dreams a little."

My father went on to give me several more addresses: furniture stores, rug dealers, cutlers and glassware merchants, mirror stores and jewelers, even an upholsterer and a knifesmith: a regular catalog, as if he hoped it would atone for some misdeed that saddened and tormented him.

That list, and his accompanying comments and stories, had wiped out my initial stupefaction, had made me first smile and then laugh out loud. They had in them all my father's humor, all his love for people and his storyteller talents, all his tenderness toward me, and in the end his strange opening request had seemed just a little un-important favor I could easily grant him.

And there is no doubt that his list of stores with their renowned names played no small part in my change of attitude. In my blindness.

A blindness that persisted, whose persistence nothing seemed able to prevent.

And those fairyland establishments glittered before my eyes. "Can you imagine, Yves, going to Bernstein's, to Meyer Frères, ordering whatever we like at Bernstein's and Meyer Frères?"

We lived modestly in our town (my brother and I, that is, for as far as external appearances went we seemed very different from our parents). "For God's sake," Adrien used to say to me, "you're rigged out like a bag lady. You'd never see Nicole in clothes like those!"

Nicole's dresses, her "dance studio," our father's car, and Tiresia's piano probably made us a cut above the others in our little town. But probably even more than such things, it was the mere existence of our parents that made them so much a cut above in the eyes of our little neighbor Adrien: our father's elegance and style, Nicole's beauty, and Tiresia's presence, never quite hidden by her veil and her reserve.

Yes, we had lived modestly, but my father's dazzling catalog worked its will on me. Perhaps not so much the effect of desire as of fondness.

And on Yves the effect was literally anesthetic.

Resentment sat in residence in the frown with which he first received my father's bizarre request. I felt that resentment taking shape, and to distract him from it (even though I never showed my father's letters to anyone), I let him read the section with the list of stores. As I have said, Yves came from a poor family; he started to read and as he moved from paragraph to paragraph I saw his re-sentment anesthetize itself. He read with memory alert, as he did when working on one of his textbooks, and by the time he finished reading he knew all the names and addresses by heart. "Well, Estelle, let's take a look, why not?" And we spent a week going from store to store (although skipping the upholsterer and the knifesmith, whose addresses had disoriented us) and window-shopping, but not feeling the need to go in and introduce ourselves. And as the week wore on our plan to get married in due form at city hall faded.

We decided to confine ourselves to the simple act of fusion, accompanied by invitations, reception, a shared apartment, and sundry other activities.

The city hall ceremony was quite simply dropped, without either of us at any point arriving at a decision. Perhaps this suited us in a way. We knew that kind of formality took time, and we were in the midst of exams. That is what we told Yves' parents, who to our astonishment raised no objection. *I seek for a reason, madame, I seek one everywhere, this deadlock on the official aspects of marriage must seem strange in a pair of law students, in fact it still seems strange to me. The other day, talking to Phil, I told him the story as if it had happened to old friends of mine. "Highly unlikely" was his comment. "Or else law degrees aren't worth a cent and the universities need reforming. There must have been something else beneath, something they weren't about to tell you, Claire!" And in that instant I was so sure he was right that I agreed with him, sincerely: yes, highly unlikely. So now I wonder, have I finally changed, have I finally succeeded in becoming a being of today, a being in the now? If what seems unlikely nevertheless did take place, what should you do — dash your head against the walls, shout "I am unlikely but I am!"? We just went to the movies, nothing more . . .*

I believe Yves and I lived in the conviction that we were wholly and normally married.

We threw a reception, and had we wished, that reception might have been lavish, but we had very few people to invite and we made do with Mr. Bernstein's champagne bottles, paid for with Yves' brand-new checkbook.

"Oh," said Dan, passionately following all this, his hands on my shoulders, as I told him all this, still kneeling and hugging his knees, my face lifted to his, his face bent to mine . . .

In the building across the street, on the same floor as ours, a man leaning from a window was watching us. Our windows too, all five of them, were open. We turned toward him for a second.

"I see," said Dan, "so that's how it happened."

Suddenly he seized me by the waist, hoisted me in the air, and began to whirl around the big empty room. How light I was in my brother's arms, my legs wrapped tight around his waist, my whole upper body thrown back, the five windows spinning toward me like deep whirling wells of light. "We're going to vanish down one of those wells of light," I thought, and it was a thought without fear.

The windows receded and returned and we whirled and whirled . . .

Softly my brother slowed his mad dance, and we returned to our point of departure and were finally still, Dan recovering his breath, still holding me in his arms. Dizzy, I put my head on his shoulder; the dizziness persisted but I was happy at the center of all that whirling, my whole being a Catherine wheel perched like a galaxy upon his shoulder.

The man across the street was still watching us. He smoked thoughtfully.

I set my feet back on the ground. We had things to do, we had to settle in . . .

"By the way," Dan said distractedly, "what about your passport?"

"My passport?"

"Where was it issued?"

"At G., Father took care of it, I didn't have time . . ."

Dan frowned, as if trying to retrieve an idea that had already fled. I watched him frown. And then a second later we had forgotten all about it.

We were trying out the bar. Dan wanted me to list the stores our father had mentioned again, where they were, which ones Yves and I had actually gone to see, what they were like . . . And as we worked on our pliés and jetés, I went through Father's list window by window for him and took him down the itinerary Yves had chosen.

"We'll go back together, okay, Estelle?"

There was no need to reply, Dan could read my yeses and noes on my face.

"But this time we'll go in and we'll buy what Father wanted you to buy. You'll remember what he wanted, Estelle?"

"I still have his letter, Dan."

And suddenly my brother looked as if he had been struck by lightning.

"You have his letter?"

"I have all his letters."

"All of them?"

A veil of mist had floated before his eyes, but behind it his gaze glittered piercingly, like a ray breaking through the rain, thrusting it suddenly aside, and rain started to fall down either side of that ray in big slow drops. I drank the tears on my brother's cheek.

"Don't cry, Dan, I have them all."

"He wrote to me as well, but I barely noticed. I read the letter at top speed and then I threw it away. I was out of my mind that whole time . . . Father's letters. In New York garbage cans, oh, Estelle, I can't stand it . . ."

The man at the window opposite had finished smoking. He straightened up and drew the two wings of the shutters in toward him. The movement caught our eye. For a second our eyes and his met, then he shut the window and we saw his reflection vanish in the pane. There were no curtains on that floor.

"The only floor without curtains," said Dan, as if to steady his voice.

"No, it has curtains," I said. "But apparently he never closes them. Can you see the edges, Dan, inside the frame?"

"Yes, I see."

We were now entirely taken up with studying the floor across from ours. We knew it took our minds off our grief. We knew it was good for us to focus on a piece of reality, to dismantle it right down to its smallest component. Our grief eventually retreated, disgusted by such stubborn obsessive interest.

FORTY-SIX

The Philosopher, Dlourès, the Philosopher

NEXT MORNING we decided to call on the man smoking so thoughtfully at the window of the apartment opposite ours. He turned out to be a philosopher — a famous and fascinating philosopher. Vlad never stopped marveling at the coincidence that had made us neighbors. "You can have no idea," he said, "when I was back there, behind the Curtain, I used to dream of attending his lectures." Vlad would have loved to be invited, "but he finds you more fun," he said with a shrug. "More fun?" "Yes," said Vlad, "he likes strange animals." We were hurt: "Now you're talking to us like

Adrien," and he kissed the tops of our heads, "No, no, my dear ones, it's just that despite my adventures I'm very run-of-the-mill. Besides," he added, suddenly serious, "I may no longer be a writer or a dissident or anything interesting at all, but I'll gladly accept his wasp and his orchid!" "What?" "You'll see," he said, "you'll see!"

After we left the philosopher's, I whirled around and around on the stairs outside, like a water sprite bathed in my brother's laughter, free, weightless, afraid of nothing, my body a silvery flash, my mind glittering in the water like a miraculous fish. My hair cascaded over my brother's shoulders, and his long bronze forelock swept my forehead, each one's hair tickling the other, arousing little ripples of laughter that had been sleeping just under the skin, and those ripples set in leaping motion the giant laugh that slumbered in our depths.

And the huge helpless mirth of our childhood was upon us. It rolled us around, shook us: Mr. Raymond's apple tree shook like a possessed person brandishing Mr. Raymond at us, a Mr. Raymond who scowled more fiercely than ever as he himself brandished his fork, the trees, oh, oh, the trees, oh, the trees planted in our head . . . And was wicker a tree? we wondered. "We have a friend who makes cane furniture," Adrien, are you a tree? and if you are a tree then we will be the grass, oh, oh, to tickle your feet, our ticklish friend . . .

"Don't come on the lawn, Adrien, you're not allowed." "And why aren't I allowed?" "Because you hurt it when you walk on it." "And how do I hurt it when I walk on it?" "Because you can't dance . . ." And next morning there was a turd on the lawn. "What on earth is that?" our father wondered. "It must be that dog you took in," Mr. Neighbor said uneasily. "Not a chance," said Mr. Raymond, "that's not dog shit." "We'll clean it up," Dan and I said, all contrition.

After that we tried to teach Adrien how to dance, under the lilac so as not to be seen, using the dividing wall as a bar. "Shit, I can't do it," said Adrien, and you know, you know what, Dan, now he's taking dance lessons, tango and rock, is that true, Estelle, yes, yes, I swear . . .

Arm in arm we staggered around the courtyard of the philosopher's building; arm in arm we approached the outer door. The sky was a deep velvet blue shot with stars: we were intoxicated by that heavenly liquor swirling down over us through the myriad perforations of the stars, and the street swam in velvet-smooth liquor. Every street in Paris swam in a deep velvety sky-blue liquor. My God, were we

really here on this precise point on the planet, bathing in the liquor
that came to us from the flowing sky? We stopped, and we literally
felt the whole universe flood us, at this precise spot on the globe
where we were standing, and yet it was such a tiny spot, no bigger
than a courtyard, what a miracle . . .

"You'll unscrew your heads," cried a voice that tried hard to whisper.

It was our concierge, in a nightgown, her head thrust out above
it, her bosom squeezed into its neckline like a plump mouse caught
between shutters.

"I heard a little noise, and wanted to see if it was the people who
steal my flowerpots at night, but it was just you!"

The stars climbed hastily back up to where they had been hanging,
the sky stretched itself out again on its frame of rooftops, we
stretched our necks a little to the left and right to relax our vertebrae,
and at once all our ideas came back down to earth, particularly one . . .

"Dlourès, Dlourès, we have to talk."

"Talk about what?"

"About Adrien."

"Mr. Adrien?"

"Yes, yes . . ."

And Dlourès, who was much more impressed than she realized
by Adrien (and who, if she had to choose, would certainly have
chosen him over Dan, who was too tall and too handsome, and too
laughing or too serious, but it came more or less to the same, too
much either way, precisely what Adrien was not, and our concierge,
who was intelligent, knew all that very well), Dlourès softly shut her
window so as not to wake her husband Mario. Soon we heard her
door creak and out she came, a plump little mouse that had wriggled
free and was now shaking itself, and the three of us sat down on the
little steps between the rows of flowerpots, a pot on each step, the
very pots envious hands had been stealing. "And only a few steps
from the police station," she said, "if I were them I'd be ashamed."
"The thieves?" "No, the police, of course." But we did not want to
discuss flowerpots, thieves, and police, we had a deal to suggest, a
bargain, a contract.

"So that's it, do you agree?"

"That beautiful new furniture?"

"Yes, all four pieces."

"But what will Mr. Adrien say?"

"That's the point, he won't."

"How will that be?"

"When he comes to see us we'll take them back, just for as long as he's here."

"The sofa, the armchairs, and the table?"

"They're light, Dlourès, they're made of wicker."

"And what will Mario say?"

"Tell him they're a present from Adrien."

"A present from Mr. Adrien!"

"Well, yes, Adrien is very fond of you."

"But Mario would break them over my head!"

A problem.

Most certainly Mario, to whom our bar represented the foresight of a young couple concerned about the first unsteady steps of their chubby babes, Mario, who each summer worked with his own hands on a house he was building in Portugal for his wife, and whose sleep at that very moment was untroubled by potential thieves or by our excited whispers . . . no, out of the question, Mario would never swallow a present from Mr. Adrien, lightweight wicker or not.

"Then tell him the truth."

"What's that?"

"That you were given them because we had other furniture."

"And that it's Mr. Adrien's furniture?"

Palaver.

No, no point in specifying its origin, in any case Mario never went down the rue du Bac and did not read *International Decorating.*

After an hour's discussion (animated but muffled because of the disturbance of the peace it was a part of Dlourès's duties to prevent), we ceded ownership of the four pieces of wicker furniture signed Adrien N. to Dlourès dos Reyes, as well as the immediate and future enjoyment thereof, with one reservation, viz., that in the event of an announced visit to the residence of the former owners by the aforementioned Adrien N., the former owners would themselves ferry the four pieces back across the street and replace them in their apartment, the foregoing for the duration of the visit by the said Adrien N., the said visit not to exceed a maximum of two hours, for the attested reason that beyond two hours no visit was bearable. "But," said Dlourès, "what if Mr. Adrien doesn't let us know he's coming?"

"He always warns us ahead of time," we said.

"He calls before he leaves?"

"Yes."

"But what if your phone's busy?"

"He calls again from Place Clichy."

"And if it's still busy?"

"He has a drink at the Wepler and calls again."

"He's scared of catching you," said Dlourès.

"Doing what?"

"Making love."

We all three nodded our different nods. We seemed absorbed in gloomy meditation. Silence on the steps. Through the half-closed door we heard Mario's light snoring.

And in any case, Adrien called less and less often.

Even his gift, his semi-gift of wicker furniture, might have been intended to mark the parting of the ways. Unconsciously on his part, of course, and we only vaguely suspected it (thus do human relationships communicate along buried channels).

For the moment we were simply infatuated with our solution. We had been most convincing, and Dlourès was no longer putting up a fight. If we had not been afraid of waking Mario we would have brought the furniture over then and there.

We were so eager to have the vast space between bar and piano restored to us. My brother had said he would not dance again, that he would dance only to clear his thoughts, but he danced every day and on this night, on our return from the philosopher's, my brother danced.

The wicker numbers were piled up in the entryway. They looked as if they were making ready to leave, and already we no longer gave them a thought.

In the brilliantly lit room my brother danced. There were no curtains on our windows, and the faces of the buildings were somber. Night seemed to crouch listening in the street.

Grass dance, tree dance.

"Oh, Estelle, how I miss Michael!"

I looked up from the piano.

"I need him to help me dance. Look, I'm doing the grass and the tree, and I like both, but if he were here we could take turns doing the grass and the tree and then something else would come up, it might be the wind, for example . . ."

And suddenly there were tears in my brother's eyes.

"I'd like to see Michael dance, just one last time."

"Why are you talking like that, Dan?"

"I don't know, Estelle, I don't know."

And we stood stock-still in the middle of the room, very close together, not knowing what had settled upon us.

A creak out in the street made us look up. We saw a dim figure in the window opposite, quickly swallowed up by unfolding iron shutters. It was perhaps the philosopher, perhaps sending us a small signal. We did not move, so sunk were we in our pain-racked trance.

But we went to his apartment.

We orbited about him like two small and powerfully attracted satellites. Everything he said gripped us. My brother greedily read everything he had written and everything written about him, and I read as well. My intelligence fell at the foot of his sentences, gasping for air, but my dreams coiled up in them as if in their natural habitat. I understood nothing but was illuminated: it was like forging into dark undergrowth sporadically shot through with long shafts of light, and perhaps our progress was like that of hounds following a scent through the murk.

"Listen to this sentence, Estelle: *Lightning is distinct from black sky yet must draw it along in its wake as if it were distinct from what will not be distinct from it.* Do you hear that, Estelle?" And I saw the great black cloth of the sky climbing like a bridal train behind the lightning. I did not hear the rest of the page; I saw and submerged myself in that vision; and then my brother danced and I played, both of us strangely transported, it was as if we were winging our way back up into the heart of the universe, to the well-kept secret of the universe, moving in a whirl of phrases, each of which glittered like an electrical discharge. Our philosopher's sentences laid themselves on us scale by scale; they throbbed and glowed through the night, they became our skin. We could countenance no other combination of words; in fact, any other combination would have damaged our new skin, led us down dismal blind alleys, delayed our climb back into the heart of the universe. "I don't understand your gobbledygook," Adrien grumbled at first. And later, "What a pity to waste your talent on intellectuals who give you nothing in return," he said in a fit of disillusioned benevolence. "Who wouldn't we waste our talent on?" we said to him, and he shrugged.

His New York store had opened a few days earlier. He had not had time to visit our old building on 100 Greene Street. He had just bought himself a Jaguar.

*   *   *

"It's the far shore, isn't it?" the philosopher said to us. We were standing at the window in his apartment, looking across at our own apartment and its windows.

All five windows were open, you could see the bar and the reflection of the piano. And suddenly something happened.

There was a baby by the wall, trying to reach up to the bar, but of course it was too high, just as Mario had warned, and the baby fell back out of sight.

My brother and I were shattered. It was as if we had dreamed a terrible dream: had we really seen that infant lost in a space that was ours away over there on the other side of the street?

"Look, Dlourès is in your place," said the philosopher.

It was indeed Dlourès. Her baby of a few months was bawling, and she quickly picked it up; she had come to get her sewing machine, which I had borrowed (I was making curtains, for we spent too much time naked and the mutterings of the old lady on the seventh floor had worried us). Just then she saw us and waved. Oh, Dlourès, stay in our apartment, don't go, stay there whenever we are away, don't forsake us, don't leave our space empty, exposed to the dreams roaming there, to the gathering nightmares. Be our lightning rod, you and your chubby baby who is crying so lustily, nightmares have no power over you . . .

"The little secret, is that it?" said the philosopher when we were seated around his dining room table (and Dlourès, who knew us well, had left a light on in our place opposite), "the dirty little secret . . ."

"Yes," we said, "the dirty little secret."

"Which fills scavengers' bellies and is hostile to life."

"Yes," we said, "which is hostile to life."

"Which hinges on Mama and Papa, and makes us play at being mysterious and important, and makes us bow under the burden, and makes us shout to the world, look how I accept my burden, look at the secret weighing me down."

"Bah," we said, "ridiculous secrets people keep wrapped in cocoons."

"And in whose name we endlessly devise new robes so that priests may enact their dead play on that dead stage, spreading over it interpretation after interpretation, like so many shrouds piled on a reliquary empty of secrets."

"Too horrible to think of," we said.

"And we dwell in the black hole of our Me, dearer than all else to us, with our lovely little secrets and our need to strut under their banner, and all around is the white wall on which our dear little hole has been pinned up and which is constantly swept by great encoding beams . . ."

"Dancing was a way of decocooning the secret," said Dan.

"So we must generate flows . . ."

"Every movement tears away part of the mummy's swaddling bands and hurls them in the air and sets them to dancing . . ."

"We must plan a line of retreat . . ."

"I threw the bandages all around me on the lawn and they shone in the moon and became scarves of wind and light, and our parents sitting on the stairs looked on and they were like two dark clouds with a glow spreading from their center, and I whirled faster and faster and Estelle was in the middle of the lawn . . ."

"Absolute speed, measured not between two points but in differences of intensity . . ."

"And I don't know what Estelle was doing in the middle of the lawn, I didn't see her, I didn't look at her, but without her there wouldn't have been anything — neither the lawn nor my dance nor our parents like two dark clouds on the stairs and that bright glow spreading all around them . . ."

"Do you have parents?" said the philosopher suddenly.

"They're dead," we answered.

"Oh," said the philosopher.

"A car wreck," we said.

We went home with our arms around each other. In the courtyard we listened for a moment by Dlourès's window. The baby was crying softly; Dlourès would not be coming out. We went wordlessly into the street; we would not go home at once. "What was he talking about?" I said. "Freedom, my love, just freedom," said my brother. "But he's so imperious." "He's like Alwin," said my brother, but my thoughts did not wish to turn to the philosopher or to Alwin; they returned to their private refrain. "Couldn't you really see me on the lawn?" I said. "No, I couldn't," said my brother, "and I can't explain why."

And I cannot see you either, my brother, you who are my life's medium, I come and go through you and everywhere in you doors open. The universe tilts and turns around us, we are a satellite full

of portholes, held perfectly stable by its immense speed . . . Who
were you, brother of mine, my door to the universe, the window
that never stopped opening, my satellite with blue portholes, lightning *and* the black cloth of the sky.

    *I cannot describe my brother to you, madame, and I do not even have
any photos.*

FORTY-SEVEN

Domination of Black

> *At night, by the fire,*
> *The colors of the bushes*
> *And of the fallen leaves,*
> *Repeating themselves,*
> *Turned in the room,*
> *Like the leaves themselves*
> *Turning in the wind.*
> *Yes: but the color of the heavy hemlocks*
> *Came striding*
> *And I remembered the cry of the peacocks.*

S TRIDING, Michael, or *striding in?*"

    Michael's eyes were all tears. He turned briefly away and wiped
them with his shirtsleeve.

    "Michael?"

    "*Striding,* Dan, just *striding.*"

Michael's shirt might itself be the peacock plumage of the poem: it
was silver shot through with shimme ing colors. He had brought Dan
a shirt identical to his, except that its fabric was gold.

    Michael had put his on as soon as he reached the airport, as a
mark of celebration and to cheer and dazzle us. But I was not at the
airport to pick him up. The silver shirt dazzled only the nurses; the
golden shirt had to be disinfected before it could be brought into
the sterile chamber. Now it lay spread on the bed, and Dan held its

sleeve in his emaciated hand as if he feared it might escape him.

I came out of the chamber when Michael appeared at the glass window. If the shirt fell I would need to go back through the disinfectant lock, which would take long minutes.

Yes: but the color of the heavy hemlocks
Came striding
And I remembered the cry of the peacocks.

We scarcely recognized the voice that filled the corridor. I must have turned the communication mike up to maximum volume, and the feeble broken whisper that would not have been heard unaided through the glass screen resounded in the visitors' corridor with distorted power. The sick man could scarcely speak, but the voice of his sickness was triumphant; it flaunted its fissures and its cracks with hideous immodesty. From a distance Bosch's ailing beggars are pitiful, but enlarged by a magnifying glass his people disappear and nothing remains but the disease, the radiant, exuberant disease. My brother's throat was overrun by parasitic mycoses that his exhausted body was powerless to repulse. He lay on his cot behind the glass porthole of his sterile room, his lips scarcely able to move, yet in the white corridor on the other side of the window the invincible choir of fungi, avid for dominion, swelled and subsided and swelled and crackled.

Michael looked at me, terrified. Turning my back to the glass, I whispered:

"The mike's broken, either it's too loud or you don't hear anything."

Until then we had not needed the mike. Since he had been in his sterile environment my brother had not wanted visitors: "Time, too short, Estelle."

I stayed in the room with him all day; only the masked nurse came in. I too wore a mask. "Take it off, Estelle, I want to taste your mouth." "No, Dan." "Then kiss me with the mask." I pressed my lips behind their double layer of fluffy white paper against Dan's mouth for three or four seconds. "Kiss me some more." "You'll suffocate, Dan." "I don't care, kiss me, Estelle." Outside the summer air was hot and heavy with live smells, but in that room the air was dead. "Go outside for a while, Estelle, you need to breathe." "I don't want to go outside, Dan." The TV stayed on at all times: footage of the Tour de France came and went, bikes pumping their way through our nightmare, and I kept my eye on the white-corpuscle count, the bike-race statistics rode piggyback on the corpuscle statistics; one day I realized that I was looking at the screen with its crude carnival colors and praying, I was praying to the man in the yellow jersey, begging him to haul the white corpuscles in his wake; their progress was so slow, so horribly slow, and the relapses were even more horrible.

Then I turned to my brother, and he was sleeping. No, he was not sleeping; when I looked at him he knew, and at once his eyes opened and he looked at me and I drowned in his look, I sank slowly into his look. Our whole life was there and I bathed deeply in the waters of our life, I reached deep down to the most distant springs of our childhood. "You'll wear your eyes out," the nurse told us cheerfully. It was the same expression that Adrien used, but no, our eyes did not wear themselves out in those deep waters, they revived. Mysteriously we felt better and I was able to read to my brother the poems he loved, and he was able to listen.

But the one he always came back to was Wallace Stevens's poem "Domination of Black," to which Alwin had once created a ballet for four dancers.

My brother in a dark red leotard was the flame in the poem, Michael in black was the hemlocks, Djuma in brown danced the whirling leaves, and Alwin in gray was the poet. His musician had written a score striated by the peacock's strange cry. The ballet was very sober and strangely moving. I had always felt sure that Alwin composed it for my brother; he did not normally base his choreographies on poems. But one evening Dan had returned from a poetry reading in the Village moved and trembling. "What are you so worked up about?" Alwin said in his cold sarcastic manner. "It's that poem I heard," said Dan, and he staggered us by reciting it from memory. "Nice," Alwin said with the same remarkable lack of enthusiasm he showed for everything that did not come directly from him, and we thought he had already forgotten; but a few weeks later he took the three dancers apart and put them "on this little odd piece." This was the dance the group put on at the minister's parish fete. And later the minister congratulated these young people, who "so vividly evoked the pain of the human being calling on his Creator." At least that was what he kept saying as he sought someone to congratulate — but Djuma had already disappeared, Michael and Dan were busy massaging their muscles, and Alwin, features set and impassive, looked like a tree unwilling to move even a single branch.

So the minister turned to me, squeezing my hands effusively, "The pain of the human being calling on his Creator, wasn't that it?" while Alwin looked at me with his unfathomable look, and I stammered, "It was just peacocks and leaves . . ."

Once again the mike was thronged with sounds, sighs passing over coral, shreds of sighs, swarms of shreds breathed out over corals; it was like the cry of a bodiless soul dragging itself over an inhuman planet. Michael looked at me: "Can this be happening, Estelle, where are we, surely we've lost our way, let's leave, let's leave . . ." And my look begged his: "We're in hell, Michael, but it is us, it really is us, don't leave, don't leave us . . ." He turned toward the window; from his bed Dan watched us intently, and his lips moved. I went to the mike.

"Dan, I can say the poem instead of you."

But the strange strength of death was already in my brother. Nothing could stop that breathlessness; it breathed the words more than it uttered them.

> *The colors of their tails*
> *Were like the leaves themselves*
> *Turning in the wind*
> *In the twilight wind.*
> *They swept over the room,*
> *Just as they flew from the boughs of the hemlocks*
> *Down to the ground.*

When the line was too long the voice faltered, seeming to sink down into some fathomless cavern. It hurled all its strength into the *h* of hemlocks but flagged again on the *s,* it sank and did not rise again. Michael stared at me with stricken eyes, and at that very moment, borne on a gasp that barely left the body emitting it, we heard "down to the ground," and in the same movement Michael and I both whirled to the chamber window as if Dan himself had just slid to the ground.

Head thrown back, he closed his eyes. The echo of his words hovered facedown over his body: "down to the ground." I felt this echo might collapse onto him, spread over him — "down to the ground" like a shroud.

"Stay here," I said abruptly to Michael.

He understood at once.

"Run," he said.

Air lock: several long, long minutes.

When I entered the room, Dan had recovered somewhat. From the corridor, starred against the window, Michael smiled in at him, his vigorous smile over splendid teeth, "A muscular smile," Dan had said in New York, and we noticed that there were no real smiles around us, occasional fleeting contractions, as if sinews had atrophied and skin lost its glow. "Your sunshine smile" was another thing Dan said, and in a burst of sudden enthusiasm (Dan could hoist enthusiasm from a vacuum) the other dancers offered their own contributions to this description, adding "seaside" and "seashell" and many others until they had transformed the original expression into a regular exercise for developing the muscles of the tongue, an exercise that Michael, serious even in fun, made them repeat painstakingly in order to teach them how to smile — "seaside seashell sunshine smile," and it worked, for the exercise invariably ended in explosions of laughter.

Aloof, unbending, Alwin would wait for what he called our "antics" to die down. And my brother and I believed that he willingly saw very ancient pagan rites in our caperings around Michael's smile, worship of the waters, of shells and the sun, and we felt a surge of gratitude at his generous interpretation of our friendship for Michael. One day later on, quite by chance, we discovered our error concerning the meaning of that word "antics" (in French *antique* means ancient). When we realized its true meaning, my brother was furious. "Oh, damn Alwin, damn him!" he cried, in a whirlwind of fury that carried him along despite himself, and in the midst of that whirlwind he suddenly said a surprising thing. "It's his being Indian and Michael black, oh, goddamn him!" "What, how do you mean, Dan?" But already his anger had ebbed and he no longer recalled what he meant.

Michael's smile held my brother's eyes open as if by a transferal of muscular force. The silver shirt shone in the waning sun. "Yes," said Michael's smile, "yes, Dan." I sat at the head of the bed and pillowed my brother's head in my arms, both of us facing the window, where the silver shirt with its constellation of colors seemed to throb in the light, and my brother's voice took the poem up again from the beginning, and Michael danced for us. Not just his hemlock role — he was also the turning leaves and the wind and the flames and the poet.

He re-created a dance full of darkness and conflagration and violent entreaty. Michael did not want to stint.

> *I heard them cry — the peacocks.*
> *Was it a cry against the twilight*
> *Or against the leaves themselves*
> *Turning in the wind,*
> *Turning as the flames*
> *Turned in the fire,*
> *Turning as the tails of the peacocks*
> *Turned in the loud fire,*
> *Loud as the hemlocks*
> *Full of the cry of the peacocks?*
> *Or was it a cry against the hemlocks?*

My eyes were dry. In the darkened room only the golden shirt in my brother's fingers glittered. We lay still, staring at the figure with its silver highlights moving against the transparency of the sky.

> *Or was it a cry against the hemlocks?*
> *Or was it a cry against the hemlocks?*

My brother's voice repeated the lines, low, unrebellious, barely questioning, but it ravaged my mind like a sob, and on the other side of the glass it must have filled the air, drenched it with leaden dampness, a deathbed saturation. But Michael did not falter. Facing my brother, he repeated the same movement, one lonely arm rising from his motionless body like a tree. Then he waited. All you could hear was my brother's obstructed breathing, the wind struggling through that lush jungle of mycoses, and Michael's arm, melting now into the fluid dark, seemed to be saying farewell.

The nurses came, they turned on the light, they illuminated the visitors' corridor. Michael was no longer there and my brother lay with closed eyes on his bed. In the night he died.

I will believe forever that in his head my brother had made his way all alone to the end of the poem:

> *Out of the window*
> *I saw how the planets gathered*

Like the leaves themselves
Turning in the wind.
I saw how the night came,
Came striding like the color of the heavy hemlocks
I felt afraid.
And I remembered the cry of the peacocks.

At G.

FORTY-EIGHT

"We Are Eternal"

A VAN drove my brother's body to our native town.

"Sit beside me, madame," said the driver.

"No."

I climbed in behind. The second the vehicle lurched forward I stretched out on top of the coffin.

Crucifixion-fashion, hands hooking on in front, feet behind.

One thing bothered me. My brother had been taller than I, so how was this position possible? "It's natural," I told myself, "his illness shrank him." Then another idea suggested itself: my own limbs had stretched; someone had granted this dispensation, the master of the length of bodies and coffins, perhaps. I was certain in that moment that he existed. For such a master to exist had to be good, since he would establish relations between the dead and the living. "Yes," I thought, "he did a good job of measuring: my limbs exactly fit this coffin."

I was forgetting that my brother's arms were by his side.

There was this perception within me of my brother's body stretched out beneath my own body in the same position as mine, arms raised above his head, my hands pressing down upon his hands the way they sometimes did when we made love.

The pole of my thoughts had disappeared. But my thoughts continued to mill about it, directionless, twisting and turning under the impact of storm-rocked perceptions.

I fell asleep.

There, lying on the coffin in the mortuary van taking my brother back to our town, I slept.

For years and years afterward I yearned after that sleep. It was the deepest sleep of my life. It was the sleep that led me to my dead brother.

I sank down through stratum after stratum, dropping from wakefulness to a half consciousness in which I still heard the traffic on the road, and then dropping deeper still, sinking ever deeper toward the place where Dan was. I knew he was tarrying there on death's threshold, that he had not yet left for the fathomless abyss where I could not join him.

He was right there, just beneath my body, yet I had to sink down through all those strata.

For the first time he could not come to meet me halfway. No more leaping or bounding for my brother the dancer. The weight of the earth held him fast. He could only await me.

The power of his waiting was my guide. I let myself drop like a stone, my whole body a heavy stone that fell without thought. The deeper it fell toward the place where Dan waited for it, the murkier thoughts became, the more they mingled with the body's fibers, and the body's fibers themselves packed tighter together, and soon all I was aware of was this sense of a stone tumbling ever deeper; and then all awareness was gone.

A stabbing pain woke me. My joints were stiff, my pelvis painfully bruised by the coffin. We must have been halfway to our destination.

Waking from a sleep in which I had been with Dan, my body was battered as it sometimes had been after love. I felt sated, grateful for an absence of pain. Pain had moved a little way off.

I was in a mist-shrouded field on the outskirts of death, and luxuriating in a rest. The silence was around me, shielding me, shielding the memory of my sleep with my brother.

Was I really awake? The van driver later told me that there was heavy traffic going both ways on the road, mainly trucks that he had had trouble overtaking, but I heard nothing. After that deep sleep with my brother at death's frontier (my brother had been there, alone, waiting for me), our bodies separated and I found myself on the other side of that frontier, in silence, without pain, without thought.

That place I have never forgotten. It was the thing I sought to recapture, later, at the convent. The dark silent field of mists where even thoughts never entered, whose password no living being had ever known . . . and then the outskirts, where somewhere, like immaterial gossamer, there would be marks of my brother's passage.

Next I heard the sound of the van. I sat up, keeping just one hand on the coffin, the way we did when we made love on top of each other.

I fell asleep for a second time. Because of this second sleep I know that the first had been of another kind, had been what I have described. This was but a brief, superficial spell; my hand slid from the coffin and at once I awoke to put it back, the way we did when during the night one of our hands slipped from the other's body.

All the time my brother was living (the long wasteland of our separation excepted) not a single night went by in which we were not bound one to the other. Not for one night did I lose contact with my brother.

Oh yes — one night.

My brother was weeping beside me. He wept soundlessly, in a way that chilled me. By that time he had stopped sleeping in his child's cot. Perhaps it was just a little before our cousins; that period of our childhood does not divide itself into years but discrete sections ordained according to their own inner hierarchy. "Dan, what's wrong?" I shook him but he went on, as if weeping inside himself. I lay on top of him, covering his body, my arms encircling his head and my feet holding his feet fast, and I went on calling, "Dan, Dan," and little by little he came bobbing up, returned to his own surface. And suddenly he flung both his arms around me: "I couldn't find you, my hand slipped and I couldn't find you, Estelle. I was in black water and the ship was drifting away, and then I couldn't see the ship's side anymore, oh, Estelle . . ." I listened to him in terror. And I swore to myself that henceforth I would keep vigil to ensure that this thing, this break in the contact of our two bodies, would never happen again. To ensure that sleep would never again lure me into those lethal zones where there was no one to command arms and hands.

When my hand slipped from the coffin in the mortuary van I at once awoke and replaced it. What I need, I thought, is a handhold on it, something to grip, and that thought gave me an idea. I removed my panty hose and tied my wrist to the handle on the side of the coffin. I thought that my brother would not feel me so easily there, but I was afraid of what fatigue might do to us.

In the house we had no idea where to put the coffin. The funeral-home people put it on the dining room table. But that did not seem right to me. I was anxious and nervous, and so was Tiresia.

Dan, what can we do not to abandon you?

"Tiresia, he's too far away now. Even if I lie on the coffin he won't feel me. You understand, Tiresia? In the van he could still feel me. But now he's already too far away. Look, look, Tiresia, I'm putting my hand here but I can't feel anything. Oh, what can I do? We mustn't leave him alone. I am afraid of hearing him weep, Tiresia, you remember, Tiresia, like that night he woke up crying because he didn't know where I was?"

Tiresia was turned toward me. It seemed to me she understood.

"Yes, Tiresia?"

She never talked anymore, but I read her body. Behind the somber glasses her gaze was fixed on me. And when I said "Tiresia, yes, yes?" I felt at one stroke the power of her attention. There existed of her no more than that attention trained on me; and to my question, to any question of mine, there could be only the immediate gift of her whole body.

And I understood that she had found a solution and was answering me.

Tiresia and I slid the coffin off the top of the table, and carried it across the room. All she did was follow my lead, but I had no trouble moving.

Just as I had carried a long wooden ladder when I was a little girl, supported only by the faith of an even littler boy, Dan, my dainty pilot fish wriggling ahead. The coffin was terribly heavy, but I had rediscovered that sense of a task not only possible but easy because it was inspired by my brother.

I hoisted the coffin onto the piano, scratching the black varnished wood, gouging out splinters, but it was unimportant now. Tiresia and I looked at the piano's mutilated curve, the flayed wood protruding like bone. Never had we been closer. Contentment fell upon us.

Then Tiresia returned to her chair by the window. The effort had exhausted her, and I knew she was in pain. I went to get her usual medication. It was night. Dan would be buried the next day.

The piano was closed, its music stand empty. Again I looked at Tiresia.

"I can't remember anything by heart. Tiresia?"

Again her attention, trained on me. She rose.

"Tiresia?"

She went to the door, and I followed her as far as the hallway. She went up toward her bedroom, but I did not want to follow her farther: we never went into her room. I waited at the foot of the stairs. Tiresia did not climb fast and I was impatient. Each step she negotiated resulted from an effort of my will, and I felt that effort in my heart. I gripped the banister: quickly, Tiresia, quickly, fear is at the gates and I cannot linger. Her room was so high up and she moved so slowly. At last I knew she had reached her goal; without seeing her, without even hearing her, I knew what she was doing.

The first score came fluttering down.

It too obeyed the laws of gravity. It went at the exact speed the earth permitted, oh, this submission of objects to the earth's desire, it was unbearable to me. But what else could I have wanted? For it to flutter directly down onto my head, probably.

I picked it up and put it on the step, with the second already on its way.

"Drop them all at once, Tiresia, please."

Silence at the top of the stairs, a focusing of attention.

And the whole pile of scores fell at my feet. I picked them up in no particular order. No matter if they were damaged; they would never again be used.

When Tiresia returned I spread them out on the coffin.

I sat on the stool and uncovered the keys. How intensely white they glowed! I took a score at random, and suddenly paralysis overcame me.

"Can I do it? Can I do it?"

Tiresia pulled a chair in beside the stool.

"No, not you, Tiresia, I'm the one who must play and I can't anymore."

I was weeping. Not for my brother's death but because I could no longer read the score. The notes were very black.

Tiresia removed that score and brought another.

It was a very simple melody, one of the first Dan and I ever learned to play. Yet I would have been unable to find the notes without the score.

Tiresia was of that night as if of me, giving her body to my errant mind and her mind to my anesthetized body. She put that child's score on the piano stand before my eyes and my fingers rediscovered their marks along the long white skeleton of the keys. And little by little that skeleton came to life. No one had played that piano for months; I could feel it in the imperceptible stiffness of the keys, in the chill of their touch, in the curiously empty resonance of their sound. But it had been tuned; as soon as I started to play I knew it had been tuned, that someone had taken care of it the whole time the house had been empty. It was as if the piano had been waiting for this moment, with my brother's body resting on its back, with my hands fingering its keys.

The sounds began to come. Tiresia turned the pages of the score, I brushed the white skeleton, and it disintegrated beneath my fingers, dissolved into sounds; the sounds never stopped coming, and I played as perhaps I never had played. Sometimes I hesitated over a chord; then at once Tiresia's patient hand rested on mine, guiding it, and I caught myself and the obstacle disappeared, my momentum was restored.

Tiresia's attention supported me, never relaxing, focusing totally on my playing.

I felt that within her a door she had kept closed for years was opening: she was opening that door for me one last time, and from it came the Tiresia of yore, the renowned, brilliant pianist, and at her side was another Tiresia, this one too coming onstage through another door, the mother I had never had, strong and sheltering.

I felt these two Tiresias I had never known: I felt them on the left and the right of the woman in the black veil who stooped over the piano at my side. I felt that if I had raised my eyes I could have seen them.

I played pieces I thought myself unable to play. I was so weary that sometimes my head nodded, but my hands worked tirelessly and Tiresia's mind drove them on. I abandoned myself to her. A cup of coffee steamed on the little round table beside me, and later there was another cup; I have no idea how they got there, except that when Tiresia came back from the kitchen there were cakes too, slices of the gingerbread Dan and I so loved when we were little. I played and played and one score replaced another on the rest. Did I even hear the music? I do not think so.

I played for my dead brother: on no account must the sounds tarry with me. I dispatched them directly to my brother; they had stratum after stratum to cross, so great a distance that now I could no longer hope to cover it, but I committed all my strength to the task of winging the notes to him; not a single one remained with me, I did not hear them, I saw them wing away like messenger birds.

The piano vibrated. As long as it vibrated, as long as those flights of sounds burst from it, I still held my brother.

His presence was tenuous and shaky. All that held him was this vibration. He must have been able to perceive it through the field of mist on the outskirts of death where he lingered.

*   *   *

It was daytime. Standing behind me, Tiresia was massaging my shoulders, and I went on playing. She massaged my shoulders, the nape of my neck, my back, and it was as if she were controlling the mesmerized keys through my exhausted body.

The funeral-parlor people were at the door. I was still playing. Then I felt Tiresia's hands slide down my arms, settle on my hands, hold them still.

"Is it now?" I said.

Tiresia's hands answered "It's now." I shut the keyboard.

"Don't you wish to change, madame?" the director said to me.

I knew him well; he was the man who had taken care of our father and our mother, of our doctor. I had settled everything with him by phone, and now I looked uncomprehendingly at him.

"Madame," he said, "people will be there. At your father's vault —"

Change? I thought he wanted me to change places with my brother, I thought he was telling me this could be done, that we could make such a last-minute change . . .

I was with Tiresia in my bedroom. She dressed me in a black dress, a dress of hers that was exactly my size, and even at this point I still believed we were preparing to change, that she was getting me ready to take my brother's place in the coffin.

And then I was in the black car following the coffin, alone with the funeral-parlor director.

"Mrs. Helleur is not coming," he said. "The funeral service and all these people, it would be too much for her. She has not really left the house since —"

Mrs. Helleur? After a moment I realized he meant Tiresia. I would be saying good-bye to my brother alone.

My mind cleared. Henceforth I was alone, I would always be alone. But there were things to be done. I had made a promise to my brother.

I started to pay attention. The director was telling me that in accordance with my instructions no invitations had been sent out, but nevertheless there would inevitably be many people. "This is a small town," he said. Dissemble now, Estelle, think of your promise. "Of course," I said. At the cemetery gate I saw people. There were only couples, it seemed to me, and beside Alex and Adrien's cousin there was even a child, whom I kissed.

Then what had taken place at our parents' burial happened all over again. The only difference was that Dan was not with me. But I told myself, "Dissemble, Estelle, dissemble, do what you did last time you came here for death," and I found the right words to say.

I saw the two coffins again, one on the right, the other on the left, our father's and our mother's coffins. Then something happened that surprised me. Two men dropped into the vault, took one coffin, and placed it on the next shelf down. In a flash they did the same with the other. There were three shelves, and there were now two available places at the top and two at the bottom. I was able to make the calculation, but it seemed empty of meaning to me. Since in any case Dan would not be staying in that place.

Adrien came and stood beside me, looking somber and angry. The same look as when he drove us through the streets of our town in search of purple and yellow and white mourning garb, when he watched us walking downstairs in our house hand in hand and naked, when he found his white suit smeared with black shoe polish at the Hotel Central in Vienne. Oh, Dan, if you could see Adrien!

His look cheered me up.

"Why are you making that face, Adrien?"

"What?"

"After all, you should be pleased."

"What are you babbling about now?"

"Homosexuality, incest, parricide, isn't that what you said?"

"Shove it, Estelle!"

"All those horrors shut away all at once in one small box!"

Adrien grabbed my arm, his hairline flaming, and he whispered explosively:

"D'you want my help tonight?"

"Yes."

"Then shut the hell up, now and forever, okay?"

"Yes, Adrien."

Mrs. Mother was behind us. I turned to her and gave voice sincerely to what I was thinking at that moment:

"I do not know what we would do without your son."

"Yes, yes," said Mrs. Mother, "and he also went to get Tiresia from the clinic . . ."

How hard it was to listen to these people. Estelle, be careful, think of your promise.

"Yes, Dan, I haven't forgotten, that's why I'm here."

"Sister of mine, do you remember the cave we used to visit when we were kids?"

"You led me by the hand, I was scared but I followed you."

"You had to stoop to get in, the tunnel was low, when I turned I could see your white ankle socks."

"I cried out: 'Dan, where are we going?' and you answered: 'Back to the beginning of time.'"

"I was proud to be leading you, your hand trembled in mine like a bird."

"The tunnel made a right-angle turn and the light disappeared. I had nothing but you."

"I was taking my big sister back to the beginning of time, and I was leading the way."

"Places changed shape to accommodate you, I'd have followed you anywhere."

"In the cave I said to you: 'Look, Estelle, oh, sister of mine, look at the red drawing on the wall.'"

"The cave was dry and round, you pointed the light straight ahead, you said: 'It's you, Estelle, it's you.'"

" 'Of course it's me, little brother, but where are you?' "

" 'I'm in the same place exactly, the same lines for me, that's why you can't see me.' "

" 'Does that mean we were the same, Dan brother of mine, at the beginning of time?' "

" 'If you look from here you see Estelle, and if you look from there you see Dan.' "

"You moved the light and I saw my long legs and awkward body, and you moved the light and I saw all your energy and your little-boy's neck."

"You shouted: 'It's your neck, Dan!' and I put the light down to get a better look."

"We went closer to the wall but our shadows grew, covering the rock and hiding the drawing."

"Then we held hands and sat down in front of the rock."

"You said: 'We are the beginning of time, and at the beginning of time we were already here.'"

" 'So we're very old, Dan?' "

" 'We are eternal, Estelle.' "

FORTY-NINE

In the Cave

*T*IRESIA was waiting for me in the garden. I helped her climb the steps to the front door. We went in and shut the door and were in the hall.

Those words . . . how commonplace they sound. They could be part of any story, be uttered by any lips; they say nothing beyond the acts they describe.

Yet for me they have meant the omnipotence of death, a new form of that omnipotence, but merely one more in a sequence that would unendingly renew itself, with all the wealth of invention and all the fecund proliferation of mildew. A fanatical, perverse wealth, making use of the smallest object, the slightest niche in time.

Death is the most constant of familiars; I felt it penetrating my inner being, penetrating deeper than Dan or even I would have been able to go. It knew everything, it spared nothing, it was meticulousness itself, and its presence like an escorting shadow threw the smallest accident of reality into high relief. You could not overlook it: much more than life itself, it possessed the meaning of reality.

Life was like a dream you could not grasp, but death coming up on it from behind gave that dream a fearful power of intrusion. And death you could not escape. Life had never been obsessively demanding in this way; life drew you gently along, the way dreams do. But death awaited me at every turn, like a schoolmaster standing at the side of a narrow corridor with his stick, not striking me but striking the surrounding landscape, charging it with bringing the message of death without delay. And I had to accept that message and accept the pain it bore me.

I had known this moment would come: the moment of my return to a house eternally bereft of Dan's presence. I knew that in this horrible return, every second that elapsed would seem sweeter than the present moment.

The second the funeral-home car left the cemetery gates I was thinking of that house whose embrace would be beggared even of Dan's body.

The road seemed cruelly long: a mile, perhaps less? The sound of the piano would never reach Dan beneath his tombstone up in the cemetery. My fingers twitched at this nervous computing of distance. I thought I felt Tiresia's hand brush mine as it used to when I was unable to play.

"I won't even be able to play the piano!" I cried out.

The driver's eyes in the rearview mirror: a sharp knife edge.

Throughout that short ride I said over and over, "I won't even be able to play the piano." I was repeating it for Tiresia's benefit, so that my words and their cargo of pain might fly to her and take up residence in her, prepare me for the moment when we would be in that living room bereft of Dan's presence, the moment when my pain would not be able to dash headlong through the keyboard's white teeth.

And we accomplished those acts: we climbed the few steps to the front door; we went inside; we shut the door.

Death crouched in the house but made no noise. It let me move into that still unfamiliar space, that private place forever Dan's.

And I did not yet know where death lurked. It no longer sat on yesterday's throne in the coffin on the black platform of the piano between the two living room windows. Its lawless prowling presence was everywhere. Steel yourself, Estelle, sooner or later it will pounce, there is no defense against it in the whole wide world, it is in your house and is boundlessly cunning.

We did not turn the lights on. It was already getting dark. Or perhaps it was just later in that day, which was swelling and contracting like an irritated bowel. It got dark and we wandered about without lights, Tiresia somewhere upstairs while I stayed in the downstairs rooms.

Suddenly, in mid-hallway near the kitchen door, a pool of moonlight spilled onto the floor. A white halo rose from it, and in that halo were a boy and girl.

They were children still, but Dan was already the taller one. He held Estelle in his arms. Suddenly he thrust her away and I heard his cracked thirteen-year-old voice, "My God, it's physical." I saw them in those two precise moments — the moment when their two bodies came together and the moment they pulled apart, and the two moments seemed mingled, seemed but one, the tightening of the knot that would throttle their life away.

I saw them so clearly. There was no feeling in me, just that vision, filling me utterly. I was but the receptacle of that vision, and the vision endured . . .

I feel how impossible it is to convey such things, madame; all I can do is say them. At that moment, that was what death meant: it was still so much of a stranger to me, I could only watch what it was doing to me.

I heard a moan. At once Dan and Estelle disappeared. I must have flipped the switch, for the hall light came on. Tiresia had her hand on the banister and her body was bent, it was sending out an appeal to me. In me there was supernatural energy, the energy of death. Supporting Tiresia with my shoulder, I helped her climb, step by slow step, to the upstairs floor. I set her down in front of her doorway, the doorway we had never crossed.

Next I was in the garden, by the wall that separated us from the neighbors' garden. It was nearly night. I recall that I looked for the gap we used for going from one garden to the other. I could no longer find the place, and thought I must be at the wrong wall. I went over to the other side, skirting the lawn where Dan had danced around me, watched by our parents from the front steps. Hardly had I reached the other wall when I abruptly turned. Something tugged at me. I had to go back to the lawn.

But I paused there for a moment, waiting for death to show me Dan and Estelle as it already had done once that day. Death of my brother, bring the moon out from behind the clouds, let its light fall on the grass, let the grass be edged with silver, and in that nimbus let a form appear, on its knees, its head in its hands, and dancing all around it another form, dancing its grotesque sublime dance. Oh, I beseech you, show them to me.

Fainthearted Estelle, how little you know if you still hope for kindness from death!

But nothing materialized on the lawn. It lay there, dull, flat, dry, and small too. Gone was the lush vigor of the grass, gone the lawn's slow undulation, like the rolling gait of a great cat bearing Dan and me on its back, bearing us away.

It was dry, with small exposed patches of earth. I gazed at them.

How obscure and threatening those little patches were! They devoured my gaze. Yes, there it was, the prowler I awaited, it had come, but only to show me this, this deserted lawn, and beneath it the earth . . .

"Sand, some sand for the lawn!"

Everything was still: the chestnuts, the tulip tree, the rhododendron bushes — massed motionless shapes from which no help could come.

Tiresia, far away in her bedroom at the other side of the house, exhausted by these days away from the clinic, was probably sleeping her drugged sleep, yet it was to her that I cried out, because I knew that come what might, she would hear me.

Her soul had long ago been ripped from her body, and ever since torn fragments had floated about her, unable to fit together again properly, to rediscover their safe inviolate place in her body, and one of those floating fragments heard me. *Please understand these things, madame, I do not understand them, but they were real.*

"Tiresia, sand for the lawn!"

And at once I felt my words break free of me, I felt them snatched up and carried off by a fragment of Tiresia's soul: in a few days this devastated space would disappear and I would no longer see the bare earth there. In a few days sand brought in from the sea by a truck belonging to our neighbor would be spread thick over the lawn. I had found a way out in this one brief skirmish with death.

My limbs were shot through with electrical impulses. Even if I defeated death every time, I could not afford a second's delay, for death was at my heels. I reached the dividing wall at a run. The ruined gap lay before me, and a breath like that of a yawning rotting mouth rose from the ground. Death was dogging every step I took. I clutched at the branches of the tree so as to weigh less heavily on the earth, and at once they gave off a choking smell of fermented lilac. "Dan," I said, and I saw his face again as it was when he concentrated before starting to dance. Then I let myself slide to the ground and set both hands on the earth, pressing hard until that choking exhalation retreated back beneath the surface, until my palms had tamed the violent texture of the earth. Then I kneaded a crumbling handful of loam and rested my face upon it.

Again the shocks coursing through my limbs. Act, act!

With my elbows resting on the lips of the gap in the wall, I split a holly leaf down the middle, held it to my mouth, and blew. No sound emerged. My chest was empty, and soon my mouth was full of blood. "Not blood, air!" you cowardly leaf, shake free of roots and clinging earth and become the wind's ally, whistle, whistle!

"Dan," I said again. And I saw a girl's tense hands pressing the folded sharp-thorned leaf to her lips. "Not like that," the boy laughingly scolded. "Hold the leaf a little farther away; and don't blow too hard."

The whistle finally rose above the dividing wall, crossed the garden and flew toward the windows of the house next door: the whistle Dan had taught me, the whistle with which we hailed our little neighbors at night. We had always been fearful of waking their parents — and tonight was the same. I did not want the parents, I wanted one of the children, one only. But I knew that if anyone heard the holly leaf whistle after all these years it would be Adrien, the roughest and toughest of our neighbors, the one I needed.

"Stop that goddamned whistling!"

And there he was!

"I was hoping you'd changed your mind."

"I haven't."

A flashlight beam played over my face.

When he spoke again, his voice had changed. It was his old voice, a sullen child's voice.

"Fine, Estelle."

Without raising a finger Adrien my eternal enemy had understood me. That was how things were in this new kingdom of death.

"I want —"

"I know what you want," he broke in with the old brutality I remembered so well.

For the first time in days I felt relief.

"What about you, what do you want?" I said with a kind of laugh.

"What we said."

"Now?"

"Of course."

"I'm having my period."

"Estelle, don't start all your shit."

He jumped over the little wall. He still had on the dark suit he had worn to the funeral, the one he had worn when our parents were buried.

That too relieved me. It was right. I knew where I was, there was none of the doubt that might lead to misunderstanding; I was in death's kingdom now, no holds barred, and I pushed ahead as I had to.

I too wore dark clothes, but not my own. The skirt was tight and I had trouble pulling it up. Adrien did not help me. That too was a relief. Yes, all was well. I had managed not to wander off course in these dark places where I ventured alone.

I noticed that under the skirt were stockings and a sort of girdle with garters. Why was I dressed in this way? Then I remembered Tiresia: she must have given me this underwear because I had nothing to wear for the funeral. The girdle bothered me, I could not feel my flesh under it, my hands groped at the unfamiliar object and were unable to remove it.

"Stop," said Adrien.

I stopped.

"Stop laughing like that, it's driving me crazy."

I put my hands on the two ledges of the wall and let myself fall back, my head lolling to and fro in the gap, momentarily exhausted.

"And don't do that with your head," said Adrien. "Estelle, stop playing the fool or I won't do what you want."

I heard the click of his flashlight, but I saw no light, I just felt warmth on my skin because he was holding the light close. His hands spread my thighs and fumbled to withdraw the tampon.

"Not much blood there, Estelle."

"It's been that way for five months," I said.

I knew the words would be a slap in the face to him, that that was how he would take them, that that was good.

"Oh," he said. Meaning message received.

I heard his thoughts buzzing about my parted thighs, black and bitter thoughts that exactly matched my own sense of disintegration. He hated the part of himself that had believed it desired this love, that had lived for years on unrequited desire and obsession with revenge, and now he saw it had all been nothing, nothing but this, something he did not even want, and his thoughts — deprived of direction like wasps unable to find their nest — were now swarming aimlessly, metamorphosing into scorpions, which turned their stings on themselves. For that was how love was in death's kingdom.

I realized that my heels were sinking deep, small crumbs of earth spilled into my shoes to be crushed in disgust by my feet.

Bowel noises. In a flash of horror-filled insight I realized that seen in the glare of a flashlight, that part of my body must have looked

like livestock hindquarters in some carnival peep show. Down, down
I went into death's domains, and the greater the horror between us
grew, the tighter it bound us. The only love that could exist here
was my enemy's love.

And that flashlight he refused to relinquish, gripping it with one
hand, pulling it back up each time it started to slip, while his other
hand clutched at my buttocks! That infernal light like a leprous patch
on my skin. The smell of lilac poured into my mouth and nostrils
like poisoned chloroform, and from the ground the smell of earth
rose into my opened vagina, journeying up through my body to
accumulate in my mouth like mud.

"Estelle," Adrien said.

He pulled me against him, his head dropping into the hollow of
my neck, oh, I heard what was at work in his voice — he was not in
hell like me, he wanted to return to unconfined air, to take a gulp
of pure air, that was why he had called out to me, that was what he
wanted from me.

"I can't," he muttered.

What was needed from me was tender encouragement, the amorous code words in use among the living, anything, Adrien was not
particular, even in the madness of that night he stayed the same,
hard, mistrustful.

Today I think I was mistaken. I think I was the one who had wanted
Adrien in this way, ever since my brother's birth.

One day in the course of my fifth year I must have charged him,
secretly but once and for all, with the burden of my own violence
and with all there was of fury and distress in our child's world, so
that only beauty would be left over for my brother.

I could give Adrien no tender encouragement; all I could give was
the horror that was in me. I whirled and slapped him hard. It was a
stinging slap, and his old rage returned and with it his vigor and
vitality: how well we understood each other, my enemy and I. He
gripped my arms and twisted them, throwing me back against the
gap. Stones ground into my pelvis, and the chips of soil that had
invaded my shoes bit into my feet, boring into them, and my feet
fought back — a distant battlefront, peripheral but bloody.

Our lovemaking was brutal, joyless, deliberately bruising, and that
was how it had to be if I were to retain the supernatural strength of
death, which despite my exhaustion I possessed.

Not for a second did I doubt Adrien.

*   *   *

Yet I knew exactly what he had become — a man avid for money and respectability and hoarding both commodities more and more greedily, inviting us on increasingly costly outings but never letting us invite him.

"Dan, it's Adrien on the phone." "What for?" "To go to a restaurant." "What restaurant?" "I don't know, a new chef . . ." "Another new chef!" "Well, what should I tell him?" "Tell him yes, of course, Estelle." I removed my hand from the mouthpiece and at once heard his irritated voice, "So you asked permission?" and I said "We're on, Adrien."

He had not come to our place since telling us about his furniture business. But he needed to talk to us about his new stores, his travels, his cars. At such times he treated us to what was virtually a caricature of himself, so hateful to him were we; it both repelled and fascinated us. It never occurred to us to refuse these dinner invitations. "We mustn't ever forget that the Adriens exist!" said Dan as he got dressed, and his face glowed. I told him: "You look like a bullfighter preparing for the corrida!" And his face glowed brighter.

"Adrien, I'll bury you and everyone like you," my brother said once as we staggered drunkenly from a restaurant hung with flowers, flowers everywhere, on the wallpaper, on the plates, in the vases, in the middle of that improbable street on the other side of the Place Clichy cemetery, where Adrien had explained to us how he ran his wicker furniture business in the Philippines. We had drained a last bottle of champagne; Dan was trying to explain how far he had gone in his studies and was describing an essay he had written on certain aspects of labor legislation. "That's typical of you," Adrien said contemptuously, "you write about things like workmen's compensation and you've never employed a single worker. Do you know how many people I employ?"

He had slapped several high-denomination bills onto the tray in which the check had been brought to us. To Adrien such sums were no more than small change, and he never paid by check. We sat on for a while amid this abundance of blazing color as if in the middle of a canvas, the three of us with flaming cheeks. Then we left, arm in arm. "I'll bury you and everyone like you," my brother chanted. "Sure you will," grunted Adrien. "Stay nice and safe at home with your books and you'll be okay," and suddenly there we were at the cemetery gate at the bottom of the hill, not at all sure how we had gotten there.

Adrien clung to the gate. There was a hotel behind it, he said, with fine soft towels . . . "But not white, God knows why . . ." Then he stretched out on the sidewalk just under the bridge. Dan said we would keep watch over him, and then he began to dance, while Adrien, still recumbent, applauded him. "Dance, kid, dance," he said, and the slurred syllables set us off into waves of helpless laughter. "Dance, Dan, dance," said Adrien, "you're better-looking but I'm stronger than you, I'm stronger because I'm already dead, and you think you're alive!" and he clapped his hands from his supine position, shoes at three o'clock, to speed up the rhythm. My head began to swim. Suddenly Dan stopped. He held my forehead as waves of nausea swept me; his own drunkenness had vanished. "My love, could you be pregnant?" he whispered in my ear. "Dan, you know perfectly well —" "Estelle, Estelle, what the hell does anyone know?"

And the little sponges I put in my vagina to kill our children, my love (since brother and sister may not have offspring), were perhaps monstrous, and so were contraceptives and all the rest . . . "Dan, you know perfectly well —" and he said, "Estelle, my love, what does anyone know?"

"There they go again, back in their private bubble," said Adrien, who hated these asides of ours. And every time he said it the transparent bubble in Hieronymus Bosch's picture floated before our eyes. "What bubble?" my brother once asked slyly. "I don't know," Adrien said irritably, "a bubble, everyone knows what a bubble is, for God's sake!"

He was back on his feet and waiting for us a little farther on, leaning against a street lamp and looking glum. I was crying in Dan's arms, and he was holding me tight as usual; then I felt better, and we went into a few bars to please Adrien. He was becoming lewd. We went past a gay bar. "Let's go in and demand a blow job," he grunted, "what do you say, Dan? Get a blow job apiece." Then he wrenched open the door of a taxi waiting at a red light. Furious, the driver erupted from his vehicle. "Nobody opens my door like that!" "Oh no? How do they open it, then?" said Adrien. "They behave themselves," said the cabbie. "I'll show you how to behave," said Adrien, leaping into karate-fighting posture. "A little prick like you?" yelled the driver, whose rage was starting to surprise us. He had a knife in his hand. Dan pulled Adrien away while I tried to calm the man with the knife. Adrien suddenly rounded on Dan: "You can paw that asshole if you want to, but keep your hands off me, you goddamned thieving dancing boy." So we changed places: Adrien abruptly calmed down, he took my arm, and we walked away a few steps. The two of us looked like peaceable strollers. With the cabbie too all was now well. He was back in his vehicle and Dan leaned against the door, chatting quietly. And the whole thing was summed up with the usual little dictum, this time it was "Better to be rich and kicking ass than poor and kissing ass," or something in that vein.

Such were our outings with Adrien.

Afterward Dan and I were so happy to be back again in our apartment, to bathe together, to lie down in clean sheets, to talk softly.

Yes, Adrien was rich and respected, but his outward show had never worked with me: I had a direct line to his childhood, and I knew he would not fail me. For this one night he belonged to me; he would follow me into the appalling adventure I was embarking on. For that reason, and also because he was my enemy and all of this was happening in death's kingdom.

"Stand under the street lamp," he said, resuming what I called his professional voice.

"You look hideous," he said coldly, "you have blood and dirt all over you, and your face is twitching like a lunatic's. You need to get washed."

I would not. I was afraid of warm water and everyday acts. I was afraid they would take away my strength.

Adrien did not insist. He himself had a vigorous cleanup, scrubbing at his clothes, tightening his necktie. He cleaned his shoes with his handkerchief. Then he took a small comb from his pocket and, examining himself in my eyes, combed his hair. I let him do it. To each his own source of strength.

The cemetery gate was unlocked. Alex had not failed me either. The heavy portal creaked in the night, and in the distance a dog howled. A figure detached itself from the wall.

"Estelle, I don't know what you have in mind . . ."

"Alex!"

"But you be careful, you take care of yourself."

"Alex!"

He was weeping as he looked at me.

"Poor Estelle, poor, poor Estelle . . . There's a water faucet by the gate, I can turn it on for you."

He too wanted me to wash. But I was just as afraid of the cold water from the cemetery faucet, the faucet on which they screwed the long sinewy hose they used to water the flowers on the graves.

"Go to bed, Alex, you should be in bed."

He stayed there, hesitant, looking imploringly at Adrien.

"Get out of here," I said suddenly, advancing on him.

"Estelle, Miss Estelle, you, you —"

He backed away, almost choking in his distress.

"You can go, Alex, everything's fine," Adrien said quietly.

Alex wanted nothing more. All he wanted was someone else taking charge of the situation, another man, especially if that man were wearing a suit and demonstrating authority. Alex yielded. Sadness did not suit him; as he left with bent head and limply dangling arms he wore it like a badly cut suit.

"Okay. Well, good night, then . . . sir."

We waited for him to pass out through the gate; we listened to the sound of his motorcycle swell up the hill and then fade.

"To think I played soccer with that guy and he was better than me," muttered Adrien.

"Why did he call you sir?"

"Because that's how I want it."

"And he called me miss, why, why?"

"Take a look at your face! You scared him."

"Alex isn't afraid of me, he's afraid *for* me."

"Did you sleep with him too for this favor?"

"He didn't ask for anything."

All this while we were straining to lift the stone, heaving, shoving. How heavy that coffin was! Yet it was not an onerous task: with my brother Dan guiding me what was impossible became possible.

"You're as strong as a bull, Estelle, I always thought so, but if I'd known earlier I'd have feared for my life under the lilac back there."

"And I'd like to kill you, Adrien, but later, when we finish."

Adrien laughed.

"Come on, Estelle, breaking the law one time is enough! You don't have your mighty protector anymore, remember!"

We carried the coffin to the van.

I had no time to think of my brother, to speak to him, but it did not matter. When all this is over, when Adrien is gone, then Dan, my love, I shall be all yours, be patient, I will keep every word of my promise.

"Shit, Estelle, this is killing me, I need a drink."

We set the coffin down and I sat on it while Adrien drank. He offered me water too and I accepted unreservedly, cars need gasoline, after all. What I did not like was the noise he made as he gulped down the water, the sound ringing out obscenely in the silence of the cemetery. Poor helpless mouths of the dead, unable to rise but perhaps yearning for that terrible noise of suction on the surface, for air, for water . . .

Adrien came and sat next to me on the coffin. We were briefly exhausted.

"Dan, I can't go on."

"Me neither, Dan," said Adrien. "I don't like this business."

He tapped the coffin.

"If you like, I'll take you back to your home, over there," and he nodded in the direction of the grave.

At once my strength returned.

"Dan, don't listen to him."

"Dan, old pal, I advise you to get back home."

"I have a contract with Adrien."

"She's going to bring you trouble, you can bet on that."

Once again I slapped Adrien, savagely. Again he gripped my arms, and we slid down beside the coffin. Adrien held my two wrists tight against the lid.

"Let him decide, you little bitch. At least give him a choice."

We stopped moving, turned suddenly to stone by the silence, by the place. The graves glowed faintly; most were granite, and the specks of mica in them sporadically picked up glints of light, tiny glitterings that seemed to send a message, instantly effaced, from grave to grave.

There was a stealthy rustling in the bushes along the wall. Adrien and I stared unblinkingly into each other's eyes, as if determined to see nothing and thus be unprovoking. Suddenly a cat jumped from the wall, walked cautiously toward us, its pupils dilated in the pale darkness, then fled.

"You scared it too," sighed Adrien.

We rose and went on. The gate, the van, the road, the crossroads just this side of our houses.

The crossroads before our houses. My last fight with Adrien.

"Turn here," I said suddenly.

"What?"

"Go down to the little stream."

"That's not the way."

"And then the hillside."

"I don't get it."

"Do as I say."

"This isn't what we —"

"Do as I say."

The van had stopped at the center of the crossroads. From down on the left came the gurgle of the little stream, swollen by recent rains. The undergrowth was silent. Farther on, up the slope, loomed the outline of our house with its little belvedere and weather vane, and beside it our neighbors' house. The effect of perspective made them look like the same house, a mass of curious proportions, ghostly against the dark backcloth of the sky.

"Adrien, there's a place on the hillside."

"No way."

"Why?"

"In your garden, the lilac will hide him."

"And you'll spy on us through the gap."

"I'll get that wall repaired, at my expense," Adrien said furiously. "I'll build a steel wall if I can."

I began to weep. I could not weep for my brother's death, but I wept for that detail.

I felt that I was spinning down in free fall through the superimposed layers of my lives, traversing all the years of my life when I had not wept because Dan was there and I was his elder, the one standing between him and harm, or standing behind him to catch him if harm had raised a threatening paw.

I hurtled headlong toward an obscure age before Dan's birth, when I must have sobbed for loneliness and stamped with an impatience that was still nameless. I had no memory of it, but at that moment I knew that was the period I was rediscovering, and it was like a vast fog made up of a million bitter saline droplets.

"Estelle, stop these games."

"You don't understand."

"Maybe I don't, but let me tell you something. I'm going to take your coffin, alone if need be, and I'm taking it right back to your vault in the cemetery."

"It's a place nobody knows about."

"But it's in the hills, everyone goes there, and of course you'll be there the whole time whimpering like a dog. I give you about a week before the whole town knows what we've done."

"And then?"

"Shit, Estelle, the law doesn't allow you to bury people just anywhere."

"I don't give a damn for the law. The law didn't take care of my brother."

"But I do give a damn about it. I don't mind helping you move your damned coffin and digging a hole for it, but nothing more, do you hear?"

"There's no hole to dig."

"What do you mean?"

"It's a special place Dan found. We went there all the time."

"You went there all the time and I didn't know it?"

"We wanted it to be just for us. We watched out for you, Adrien. One of us kept watch at the wall, the other from across the road, and when we were sure you were really in your house we got away very fast. You never caught us, Adrien, you never suspected a thing."

Adrien listened, astonished. He knew everything about us. That this thing had escaped him, that we had managed to have a secret, was a blow.

He started the van.

"Show me," he said.

In the little chamber at the end of the tunnel Adrien swung his flashlight around. Suddenly the red elk appeared.

"But this is a prehistoric cave!" he exclaimed. "I didn't know there were any around here."

He examined the ground, stooping low. A cookie tin, a pack of cigarettes, a piece of cloth. This last article intrigued him for a moment. "Ah, ribbons, for your braids!" A drawing book and colored crayons. "What were you doing?" "We were trying to copy the red elk." "Why do you call it an elk?" "Because we didn't know what it was and we had never seen an elk." "And that?" "That's the car door." "Mr. Helleur's car, you're both crazy!"

"This is where I want to put him, Adrien."

"Too dangerous."

"For thousands of years nobody found this cave."

No answer.

"For thousands of years, Adrien, so why is anyone going to find it now?"

No reply.

*   *   *

A shift occurred in me, mud slides, ancient eddies of tiny feelings, fragmented sights, fleeing legs, scowls, a face with its tongue stuck out, arrows in the pond, a falling window frame, crushed toys. I laughed.

"Now you know the secret, you're caught."

"And what does that mean?"

"You've seen the red elk: it'll bring you bad luck if you don't obey it."

"Shut the hell up, Estelle."

It was his old voice, aggressive, surly. As a child he had been terribly, shamefully superstitious.

He turned the light back on the wall. The elk seemed to stare at him.

We did not utter a word the whole time we were carrying Dan's coffin through the undergrowth. And not another word after we had set him down at the mouth of the tunnel and returned to the roadway leading from the hills over the little stream to the crossroads.

Adrien drove tight-lipped, not looking at me. We sat apart from each other.

The van stopped between our two houses.

The night grew pale, and as if disfigured we were pallid too. A bird began to sing somewhere in the bushes, a tiny song, but so near-seeming that it gripped me. It was the first manifestation of the world to enter me since Dan's death.

The bird sang, a series of small, quite personal chirrupings, and dawn brightened. I raised my eyes to the sky, a delicate gray with great white clouds that moved. That moved!

I knew that death had given me yet another little tap on the shoulder. Look, listen, it said. It is the first day since the death of your soul, a bird is singing, the clouds are pursuing their course.

"Estelle?" said Adrien.

I looked at him.

I was so alone now. Oh, how I regretted the tramplings of the night, our wickedness, the slaps, the quarrel that had cut me off from time's flow.

There was no more space outside of time. Henceforth there would no longer be anything more for me than this same moment, indefinitely extended yet always the same through all its transformations.

I saw Adrien, rings beneath his eyes, skin sagging, whisker-darkened, all marks that wiped away his truculent look and the arrogant set of his features.

"You're tired, Adrien."

"I'd like to have finished, but it's dawn."

"I'll finish tomorrow."

"Just the way I said, the entrance filled in and closed, with bushes over it."

"You can check if you like."

"I won't be here."

"When do you leave?"

"On the first train, just time to change."

"Thank you for what you did."

"Don't ever mention it to me. I did nothing, it didn't happen."

"I'll never mention it."

"And two things, Estelle."

"Yes."

"Be careful of Tiresia."

"She won't say anything."

"Not deliberately."

"What do you mean?"

"Tiresia is sick."

"I know. She's always been sick."

"She's sick in a way you don't see."

"What was the other thing?"

"I never want anything more to do with this business, you, your brother, the whole Helleur household."

"Very well, Adrien."

I was answering mechanically.

Already Adrien had ceased to belong in my life. All his words applied to the future, and for me the future stopped on the following night, when I would fulfill my promise. After that came nothing, but that did not concern Adrien; and I wanted to be fair and reasonable with him.

He had been enormously helpful to us, to my brother and me.

I went to the front steps, where a morning of calamity threw strange shadows. I climbed them.

My body alone acted now, my thoughts had foundered. They lay flat on the bottom of what people call the mind, flat and motionless.

And so did I: I lay on my bed, flat and motionless, my eyes riveted to the ceiling. I believe I did not change position throughout that day, nor did I sleep or once look elsewhere, but perhaps that is impossible.

I lay dead still on the gravestone of my thoughts, and did not move.

FIFTY

"Once, Only Once, Estelle"

THAT evening the electric shocks revisited me.

My promise, how long it was all taking, two days already! Dan, I haven't forgotten. Is it already night?

My eyes were by turns cruelly sharp and dim with a dimness that was no less distressing.

For a moment or two the lines of the furniture crowded one another in the bedroom, like a mighty throng that seemed to be bellowing something, the lines and details of the furniture thrusting powerfully forward and mutely bellowing. And yet a moment later they seemed distant, reduced to the nothingness of mere objects.

"I am weakening" — that is what came to my mind. I was afraid. I did not remember when I had last slept and eaten. Perhaps I had waited too long, perhaps I would be too weak.

Oh, Doctor Minor, why did you abandon us?

For you truly abandoned my brother and me, didn't you? The only one you truly loved was our father, isn't that so, Doctor, and when your Major got him in its sights you gave not a damn for the others — no interest at all, you hung around awhile, out of politeness, then you called your great nemesis and let yourself be plucked like a flower. You said to him, "I'm just a Band-Aid dispenser, just a little minor, a minus even, and you're the great Major, so I give up." But what about us, the children?

Oh Doctor, Doctor Minor, please please come.

The door opened and someone came in, wearing a heavy overcoat. I could not see his face properly. "Who are you?" "Sh!" he said. In his hand was a bag, which he set on the bed. "There," he said, "if you're good I'll let you look inside." "Are you sure the microbes are locked in?" whispered a small excited voice. "Shut tight, Dan." "And the viruses?" "Double tight." "And the syringe?" "I told it not to try to ambush you. In any case, it's tired, it's already been working hard with your mama and wants to rest." "Is Nicole asleep?" "Yes." "Then everything's all right?" "Everything's all right." "So we can look in the bag?" "Yes, but you, the tall one, first I'm going to give you a little syrup, you look really peaky." "If Estelle's having some, I want some too!" "Why's that?" "Because I do whatever Estelle does." "Well, my boy, your eyes seem to be glittering, a little syrup won't do you any harm either." "Can we look in your bag now?" "Yes, my little *malchiki*." "Oh, Estelle, come and look, there are lozenges!" "Thank you, Doctor Minor, thank you."

My heart was steadier. I rose.

Tiresia stood in the kitchen.

She had made a cake: it was partly burned. I can still see it, curiously swollen, in places yellow, in others blackened.

"You've always burned cakes, Tiresia."

At once, her attention was trained on me.

"But you know that's how we like them."

There was nothing else on the table. I ate some cake. There was wine, and I had some of that too. Sometimes I smiled at Tiresia. I said again, "We like burned cakes, you know." I noticed traces of flour on her black dress and I got up to dust her off.

The clock on the second floor began to strike. The din was enormous, a battering ram thudding into the frail vessel we sailed in. Then I began to laugh, for this was simply the shape of time in death's kingdom. "Tiresia, time is pounding!" I laughed at my familiarity with death. This time it had not taken me long to recognize it.

The chiming stopped and I laughed again. For now death delegated silence to me.

And then the phone rang. And once again it was death's doing.

For I knew that the phone would never again mean my brother's voice. Never again would I have before me that wide spectrum of possibilities to sift through as I approached the instrument, as I raised the receiver, that spectrum on which I had once been able to train the searchlight of my assumptions. What good was the spectrum, no matter how wide? For the possibilities no longer included my brother's voice. It was because his voice had once dwelt among those possibilities that I had been able to rise, to approach the device, to raise the receiver. With his voice now eliminated, no further action was possible: the whole rainbow-hued spectrum had abruptly shrunk into one thin white line that said nothing to me. I did not answer.

Tiresia was in her bedroom. Lying out in the meadow, I stared steadily at her light. When that light went out I would rise and fulfill my promise.

I did not think of anything. I noticed only the electrical spasms here and there in my body.

I was preparing to do something that summons up horror, something the law forbids. Not because someone might be harmed by it, but because of that horror for which no justification is needed.

Perhaps you will turn me down when we meet, madame, precisely because of the thing about to happen here. But remember, madame, this is also why I have sought you out . . .

The thing was a horror and yet it was nothing. And that is the truth.

There I lay supine in my childhood meadow, watching the light in a window of our parents' house. I was who I had always been. And I was about to do the only thing I could possibly do: it was natural and straightforward, the fulfillment of a promise, and my body's natural urge.

Yet if I spoke of this thing today — to Phil, to our handful of acquaintances, to the students in my piano classes, to the other renters in my building — Claire would disappear as if by magic and in her place there would be a monster.

What I did is not of the here and now.

Yesterday on a walk in the city I looked at the big advertisements plastered on every wall. Ever since the law has allowed advertising on the facades of residential buildings, bare walls have vanished. You never knew this new city, Dan. It created itself while I was in a convent cell and while you were in your coffin.

It is such a cheerful city, nothing but fleet figures, smiles, sunlit idylls. Out on the street, from a certain angle and at a certain time of day, the windows reflect the colors of the posters, and it is as if the building interiors had been invaded in their turn by these fleet figures, these smiles, these sunlit idylls.

No more peeling walls, no more big bare surfaces to be flooded by harsh winter light, no more dull shades of gray. Death is nowhere to be seen, Dan.

The stores in our neighborhood have changed. The jeweler, the tailor, the lingerie store owner, all those small storekeepers so proud of their wares, who thought they would be eternally respected and prosperous, all have disappeared.

Oh, Dan, at night we used to tell each other about our little skirmishes with them, we gave them nicknames that threw us into irresistible gales of laughter. They acted out an endless comedy for us; we invented whole lives for them.

The jeweler, so well set up in his little jewelry store, was a reincarnation of Mr. Préfleuri: we pictured him trotting upstairs in his shop at night pursued by two leaping diamonds. I remember, Dan, that you even danced the dance of the leaping diamonds. My eyes started from my head: I could actually see two of you! "How do you do it?" I yelled. "I just throw myself around, Estelle!"

The dresser and his acolyte we called Taylor & Cutter. The lingerie lady crept furtively around among her piles of cardboard boxes, throwing anxious looks at the doorway to her lair. She feared dark skins, all skins, in fact; what she really needed was moonlight customers. Do you remember the trick we played on her, Dan? You dressed up as an African, with an enormous frizzy wig, huge dark glasses, a tropical shirt. I was in the store pretending to buy stockings, and you came in with our radio on your shoulder belting out an earsplitting din. Oh, that wretched little she-rat, her eyes shot in every direction, terrified, malevolent. I asked her the price of her stockings, and she stuttered and floundered . . . "What do you want, sir?" she asked you. "Panties for my girlfriend." "What size?" You pulled down all the advertising shots she had carefully set out to look like photographs in her little store. You picked the plumpest one of them all and you said: "This, only three times bigger." "I don't have that size, sir." "What's that? You specialize in midget backsides?" Oh, Dan, how could we have laughed so much? I still see the wart on her lip, a blemish that must have filled her youth with despair, and the acute distress on her face. In the end we bought a whole bunch of her frilly little numbers, some of the most expensive ones, to calm her down. She's gone, Dan. This isn't a world for her anymore.

Our little stores and our little storekeepers have all gone. The piece of the century that bore us, our raft, our own dear raft, has foundered in the vast depths of time.

On the avenue are big windowless warehouses, and inside on tables are goods piled up in ill-defined heaps, goods brought in from every corner of the planet, from all those places we meant to visit when we were through studying: they aren't worth much and don't cost much and are changed every week. Between those warehouses new boutiques are constantly sprouting, following no kind of pattern, all glittering chrome and bristling antennas, full of screens of all sizes, of cheap gadgets. Loudspeakers on the street play deafening music; you can no longer cross from one sidewalk to the next: linked chains crisscross the street, braying music, neon lights, jostling . . .

Sometimes I think the world too fears death. Our parents tried not to attract its attention, but nowadays we attack it, we try to overpower it with racket and glare. And people too have changed, Dan. They have color all over them — in their hair, on their clothes, their shoes, their skin; and accessories that glisten and click; and they have earphones on their heads, huge glasses on their eyes (glasses that no longer even follow the shapes of their eyes), and they have portable phones in their pockets. They don't have a single sense not working overtime.

I'm that way too, Dan, I've bought all that stuff; I don't use it all at once, but I try. And as a result death retreats, because then you are in the very heart of his kingdom and can no longer see it, since by damming and sealing up all the breaches of the senses you have become incapable of feeling.

There are no more cemeteries. Cemeteries take up too much room, are too visible. The living don't want them anymore: they're being bought up, Dan, by means of small statutes and big compensation, and building on them in glass and steel.

To bury anyone you need a special permit, and the price is exorbitant. No one buries anymore in the world I live in, Dan. They burn and throw away. The living want the space, they don't want to let the dead have it. Sometimes I fear that death will seek revenge and at one stroke turn our whole planet into one huge cemetery.

Our parents' vault has disappeared. I was glad it happened, Dan, because your real grave was in the hills. But the greed of the living is unending. They have invaded the cemetery and spilled over into the hills.

Your secret grave is no longer anything but a tiny vacant lot hanging on (thanks to my stubbornness and our money) among towering high-rises, colored like clouds and striped with great steel spears that flame at night. A catwalk runs over the vacant lot, connecting two external elevators. So nobody needs to walk through this place where the earth shows through the concrete, where there are no more pathways, where ivy has overgrown the grave.

The last time I went to see you I was unable to enter the vacant lot. The doorway of the building leading to it had been condemned. I was unable to find out why. I had to go out on the catwalk and look down on you from up there, look down on the ivy drying in the sun. People went past, they glanced down to see what I was looking at. You know what they said, Dan? They said, "That place mars the buildings." And I wanted to plow them up with a sharp knife and turn over every smallest furrow of their flesh to remind them of what they so arrogantly ignore — the fact that their own bodies could in a few seconds be exactly like that earth, that repulsive earth that mars their precious goddamned buildings.

But that is only a bad dream: our town cemetery is intact and our cave inviolate. But I often have that dream, and I always mix up the two grave sites.

The light in Tiresia's room never went out. I stopped watching. What did it matter if Tiresia came down and caught me! It occurred to me that Tiresia had long been a part of death. I need not worry about her.

Then all the emotion of those past months swept down on me like a hurricane. I could no longer think, so strong was my desire, my desire to see my brother again. It had been so long, an eternity since I had left him, since I had spoken to him; it was monstrous, unbearable. It was a nightmare that I had until now accepted, but now it had to stop: my stomach heaved, I bent double and held myself around the waist, and my heart galloped far ahead of me. I could not keep up with it. I ran out of breath in my mad rush to catch up with it.

I crossed the road, climbed the hillside, and was outside the cave. "Dan, I can't go on, put an end to this game, come and help me, come and speak to me."

Oh, how I yearned to see him! I was certain now that something was about to happen, that a bout of madness was coming to an end, that I had only to raise the coffin lid, to raise his eyelids, and our eyes would meet, I would take his hand and help him rise (he would be weakened, of course, he would lean on me), and we would swiftly leave this lost path we had somehow been lulled into following. "A moment's inattention, that's all it was, Dan." I pulled gently on the canvas, folded it in four like a sheet, and set it on the ground. Then I pulled the coffin outside, to be in the moonlight. I caressed the lid, for it would not do to frighten my brother, who had been so ill and suffered so much. "Oh, how we've suffered, Dan, I'll be very careful." I pushed gently on the screws, then slowly turned, a mere caress. I lifted the lid and laid it delicately on the ground like a bedcover no longer needed. I lingeringly caressed the body that was there, then I lay down on top of it.

"Dan, I am here."

It began to rain. I felt myself urinate.

Later, rage shook me. "So you mean to leave me alone? You're playing their game, you're on their side now?"

Confusion burgeoned in me. It was as if a needle were planted in my heart, with pain radiating out from its point. I recognized it: it was the needle that had embedded itself there when Dan left for New York, when I went to see him over there, when he had become a stranger. That thorn I thought had disappeared was in the same place, exactly the same. And now I confused this pain with the pain of his death.

I grabbed Dan's head and banged it against the bottom of the coffin. "Stop it, stop hurting me." I lost consciousness. When I opened my eyes the sun was up. I was stiff and cold. And suddenly I saw Dan's face. My poor, poor love! And I started to weep. The smell of his mouth! And there was another smell mingled with it, that of my own body, which had lost control. "Dan, my little brother, it is over, I've done what you wanted, I won't come back, it's over, Dan, over, over . . ." I hugged him as tight as I could, his clothes were wet from the rain, I kissed him on his awful face, and then I tore away from him and replaced the lid, without the screws, pushed the coffin into the cave, and cleaned up all around. I pulled bushes across the entrance and scattered a few stones in front of them.

For some time someone had been helping me. "Oh, Tiresia," I said, suddenly surprised.

And somewhere, in some inadmissible depths of my mind, I knew I had just taken my first leap away from Dan. "Please, let me do it alone." I was thinking of her, of her broken body, and I was afraid she would hurt herself. I took the shovel from her hands. The sound of traffic rose from the horizon. We were the survivors — taking care of life's business, handling tools, helping pat the dust from each other's clothes, watching over those close to us, thinking of our neighbors. "He always needed room, for dancing, that's what it's for, you see, Tiresia."

I wanted her to see things clearly; I knew she must have understood, as she usually did, through scraps of her torn soul, through her body, but in the supernatural brightness of that sun-filled morning I had a new anxiety. I saw how her hands trembled, how jerkily she moved, like something old and broken. What if her body began to misfire, to respond to the wrong commands?

"Do you understand, Tiresia?" She indicated yes, and I realized something else. Tiresia was not speaking. Then I banished that care as well.

Later she washed me.

I was naked in the tub on the second floor and she was washing me. She was a little taller than I; it was easy to let her take care of me. I thought of Nicole. So fragile and small, she would not have been able to wash me in this way. In fact, had Nicole ever performed such motherly acts with me? I tried to remember who had looked after me when I was a child. Before Dan, I recalled nothing. After, I saw us both together in the big tub with four feet, washing each other in our rambunctious way.

Tiresia passed the washcloth between my buttocks and the folds of my vagina. I spread my legs and in astonishment watched her work. She was washing me as if I were a little girl, a nursling. And with astonishment I saw happiness come over me, a childish aimless happiness, like a kitten's. I turned over, I bent, raised my arms, stretched my neck. The water gurgled away a first time; I watched the soapy surface sink as if it were the back of that kitten slinking away. But it was not over. Tiresia drew another bath; I must have been very dirty, must have smelled most foul. She washed me in all the same places again, and then came a shower. Then Tiresia dried me, her moves still those of a mother with her nursling. I found myself on my bed as Tiresia rummaged through my chest of drawers. She returned with several tubes and vials, and I saw her carefully reading the directions. Then she took my feet and began to massage them with that mint- and camphor-scented cream I had forgotten all about.

It was so gentle, so soothing. I thought of Dan's feet and began to cry. Tiresia stopped, thinking she had hurt me. "I was thinking of Dan's feet, Tiresia, his dancer's feet, and now all stiff." Tiresia inclined her head. "At right angles to each other, at three o'clock, just the way Adrien's feet were one day when he was drunk. He lay down in the street outside a restaurant with his feet spread just like that, was it a spell, Tiresia?" She gently took my feet; at first they resisted, but they finally yielded. Then she was massaging my legs. She let oil trickle over my sex, and then I saw her again looking through the creams and pots. "At our place in Paris I have a cream for the breasts, Tiresia. I had creams for everything, I wanted to keep in condition because of Dan, you know, because he was so beautiful. So would you believe it, I also had a cream for my breasts!" I laughed through my tears and Tiresia listened. "And you know what he did one day, Tiresia? He switched the contents of my pots, and for a month I used the breast cream on my face and vice versa, and I didn't notice a thing! And when he told me about his trick he said, 'I just wanted to check on one small thing, Estelle, my tiny sister.' I said 'What?' and he said, 'I wanted to see whether these beauty products really interested you or whether you were doing it just for me.' I said 'So?' And he said, 'Well, now I know you're doing it just for me,' and I said again, 'So?' And he said, 'So you still love me,' and he added, 'In which case I'm quite willing for you to spend our nest egg on pots of cream if that's your way of loving me, you poor goose,' and I said, 'Goose yourself, you don't think I see what you do every morning in the bathroom?' He said, 'What?' with an innocent look, oh, so innocent, Tiresia! I said, 'You work out, Dan!' Working out, not dancing, you understand, Tiresia? If it had been dancing, I would not have seen it as being for me. But it was plain old working out, like any old office worker, and it was for me, just to keep his fine youthful body. 'So what?' he said, and I told him, 'So I'm quite willing for you to splurge on an exercise bike with gold pedals and electronic chronometer if you like!' "

Every time I started to speak, Tiresia's hands stopped moving. They remained on my skin, the very embodiment of listening. And when my delivery speeded up, her hands seemed to try to slow it down. I spoke very quickly sometimes; perhaps she could not follow me; perhaps that speed worried her. Evening came again. That night Tiresia slept on my bed, fully dressed, with my head resting in the hollow of her arm. I sensed that with her other arm she was putting out the light, then removing her glasses and veil. I fell asleep, and the needle of pain briefly shrank back into a small, more or less motionless spike in my breast.

It was the third night.

I woke up. Moonlight bathed the room. Beside me Tiresia breathed the rather hoarse breathing we remembered. I saw her glasses on the night table. Her veil must have slipped to the floor. I wanted to go back to sleep, but the glasses dogged my every step into the sleep I was seeking to rediscover, humping along on their earpieces like some clumsy insect, their large inscrutable eyes fixed on me. I emerged once and for all from sleep. The glasses were still on the night table and had lost their insect look. They were ordinary glasses — but were still capable of coming after me in halting pursuit if I did not do as they wished.

Of course I would do as they wished. Resisting was no longer important.

Gently I pulled myself free and raised myself on an elbow. And looked.

Poor, poor Tiresia. That was what she had been hiding all those years. I went back to sleep.

I woke up again. The little spike of pain had opened again like the spokes of an umbrella, returning to its full size — a big needle stuck fast in the center of my chest. "But what hurts so badly?" For a brief moment I could not remember.

Oh, if one could only remain forever in such a moment, or at least be able to return to it to rest, but already the next moment was at hand, the moment when I remembered everything, and that moment was just like the one in which I had risen to my feet in the meadow with that unbearable desire to see my brother again.

I wanted to climb back again to the cave, to lie down on him again; it seemed to me that I had not truly fulfilled my promise, that it was now he was calling for me and needing my help, perhaps because he could feel decomposition gnawing at him . . . Oh, my brother, what did he feel, how could it be that I was unable to help him! I was about to get up and in that very moment I heard his voice in the hospital: "Once, only once, Estelle, after I'm buried, so that you see me really dead."

I had thought he feared being buried alive and wanted me to make sure. It had seemed natural: to a dancer, the idea of forced immobility was horror.

And now, only too well, I understood something else. What he feared was that I might be unable to escape the memory of him. He wanted to imprint his death likeness in me so that it would forever expunge his living likeness and let me resume living. And I was divided. Which voice should I obey, the hospital voice, which was so urgent and loving? Or that other voice I thought I heard, distorted, pain-racked, rising from the bottom of the meadow? "Once, only once, Estelle," whispered the loving voice.

*   *   *

It was dawn. Tiresia was no longer there. Everything was gray and faded. What would I be doing from now on? Now? In an hour? Tomorrow?

I could hear time literally moving, gently pulling the world from under my feet. My parents were dead, Dan was dead, Tiresia no longer spoke, our house was empty. I had no foothold against that inexorable slipping away.

And something was perturbing me, a curious detail that must have struck me at one moment or another in that fearful chaos of sensations. Two words — but which words? It seemed to me they had been spoken by the funeral-parlor director.

Tiresia came in. She bore a tray with coffee. Moved, I sat up. Tiresia had never done that before. It had happened a few times with Nicole, during one of her fits of enthusiasm when she had managed to believe in her dreams. She would come in on the points of her dance slippers with a tray absurdly overloaded with foods of all kinds. "Up you get, my darlings," she said, and she seemed to take wing, her soaring movements evoking for us both the extravagance and the excitement of a world tour. "You'll be in all my photos," she told us, and we gazed at her, not really awake, half-alarmed, half-delighted. We found her absurd, of course, but we loved her and her charm unfailingly drew us in. How pretty and pathetic Nicole must have been, with the little round bun on that fragile head, with that little-girl face, my Nicole. Had I ever called her Mama? Dan called her Mama, but not me. I had always called her Nicole, and sometimes to myself when my heart overflowed, my Nicole. Never Mama, or Mother.

And by an association of subterranean thoughts, a question occurred to me.

"Tiresia, did you know? About Dan and me? That we loved each other? That we were lovers? That we wanted to live together forever?"

I looked at Tiresia, and the words rang in my head, but I could not say them. Dan and I had sworn to each other that we would say nothing to our parents. They seemed so fragile to us . . .

My head swam; I felt myself turn white. A second later my head was bent over the cup Tiresia held, and I was breathing in the steaming coffee.

At that moment I knew I could not think of all those things. They were too much for me. I could not even think of Tiresia's face, which

I had seen that night in the moon-bathed bedroom. I was no longer anything more than a defeated body. The energy of horror had forsaken me, and I let myself sink.

FIFTY-ONE

Nicole's Invisible Ones

THEY SAY "forsaking the world" and "entering a convent" as if the world were everything and the convent a tiny box for shutting yourself off from everything. But for the person in search of the invisible, it was exactly the opposite. For her the world was nothing, and the convent a sort of antechamber, admittedly small but one that allowed her to leave the nothing and enter into the unknown, the place that she left in search of her brother, without knowing what tools to use, the path, the way. The convent opened onto an otherworld — and that was all she wanted.

Here below: a tiny box of matches, used, blackened matches, among them her brother, just one small wooden stick stretched out for eternity. The convent: a passage to the dizzying elsewhere, to where what was dead went on living, to where the light from cold fires flickered on, to a sky where extinguished planets could still be seen, and thither with all her strength she hurled her soul so that it might whirl away, numb and unknowing, into those immensities, since they were the elsewheres of the otherworld.

The convent was on an isolated spur in the mountains of V. An avenue of plane trees led to the main gate, which stayed wide open (the nuns had a tiny Citroën that chugged up and down the steep narrow road at all hours). Getting into the courtyard was no problem, and a simple bellpull opened the parlor door for me.

Before going in I glanced into the courtyard: a big eyeless building loomed all down one side of it.

I knew you had to go through the parlor first, but that mass of masonry was why I was here. I longed to hear the creak of a closing door; I had thought there would be an actual gate; I wanted an enclosure that would cut me palpably off from a world that contained my dead brother, an enclosure that the world containing my dead brother could not penetrate. Once cut off from that world, once inside that enclosure, I would be delivered from the place that contained death and would finally be able to seek my brother.

All my faculties had collapsed and their debris had rearranged itself most strangely in an amorphous agglutination around one single idea: seeing my brother again.

That monstrous agglutination had at first remained supine, in the hollow shell of our house in G., and then a wan glow had passed over it, a glow that was perhaps only in its mind, that was perhaps only a memory, or the memory of a mention made by someone else, and now under the influence of that glow, this thing moved, emerged from a cab, walked up the avenue of plane trees, and rang the parlor bell.

From the outside, she was a girl of twenty-nine, Estelle Helleur. She was me.

When we were children only our mother spoke of an otherworld, of invisible beings you perceived through the power of faith, in the secret of your heart. These invisible ones revealed themselves in privileged places like churches or monasteries, or else in gratitude to certain disciplines such as dancing. This was more or less what I remembered of Nicole's words.

Dancing was not for me, but I had those other things she spoke of. Faith, yes, I had that: my faith in Dan. It was powerful; I did not even know how powerful, for it was the only growth that had emerged from the monstrous agglutination of my crumbled faculties, and it dwelt in the secret of my heart. Now all it needed was for me to carry all these things into one of those privileged places Nicole spoke of, and through the power of my faith, in the secret of my heart, the invisible would become visible, and I would see my brother again.

That is what must have been happening inside my benighted head.

My father never spoke of another world; he spoke of this one, where there were killers and torturers to be unmasked; it was into this world that he poured all his faith and strength. I had thought I could do as he did, and with that in mind I had forged through my law studies, intending to become a lawyer, judge, magistrate, righter of this world's wrongs. But it never occurred to me that there are things which cannot be righted.

Dan was dead, and not all the knowledge or effort of any jurist could ever repeal that death. Nothing more in my father's world could hold me back. My father, to whom I had been so close, who had been the pillar of my childhood and my youth, I at once forgot. In all those years in the convent he never entered my mind. His picture was faint, a small flickering thing on the brink of disappearance, to which I never turned my face. He could not help me.

As for Tiresia, she was almost wholly in another world. That Dan and I had instinctively known. Tiresia did not really belong to our town, our little provincial town, the seat of our Helleur home, its garden and its meadow, the cave in the hills, the elementary school, our two high schools, the small church square, the doorway opposite the church, the witch above the doorway, our neighbors and the neighbors' cousins, and all that made up our children's lives. Probably Tiresia spoke to us when we were small, but her words did not stick to all those town matters. As soon as she spoke to us it was as if our town suddenly retreated, oh, only a little, less than an inch, but it was enough.

"Did you pass your math test?" said Tiresia, and at once the test that had been blood of our blood the whole week, and in any case the thorn in our side, became a somewhat curious matter, taking its place in a long line, just one more item in a long faceless line, to which you assuredly could not devote body or soul. It was a little disappointing: we felt suddenly deflated, toppled from our high horse in a way, but almost simultaneously a wave of warmth swept us along with that toppling and that disappointment, a wave like a flow of warm water inside us, and we were back in our warm-water bath, the one that belonged only to us, where we soaked together. Because she was "from another world," Tiresia drew us out of this world, the only one we knew, the world of our little town.

Of course she did not take us to that other world where she dwelt, wandered, rambled perhaps. She drew us and she left us where we were. But where we were was Dan and me. Tiresia brought us back to ourselves, to the place that belonged to us alone.

She was strange, Tiresia, in her black dresses, and that veil, and those dark glasses, and that otherworldly voice, and that whole body that shouted a presence, that could not be overlooked, that accepted looks and never returned them. Certainly our mother Nicole was beautiful; people looked at her, and we too looked at her. But from her your look could skip onward, intact and fickle. Nicole was like the other people of the town, simply much more beautiful, a specimen of humankind, superior but nothing more than a specimen. Tiresia was humankind itself.

I realize how clumsy and pretentious my words must seem. Nothing ever taught me how to name that thing which was in our house and which revealed itself in Tiresia's body, yet all my life I had been groping for it as if I had guessed that it was the mark of our destiny, and even today it is toward it that I reach, to elucidate it, Madame Writer, so that you may see order in what I am putting together for you, Madame Writer, my writer, if only I can.

Tiresia had no face, barely an outline. We found that natural; she had always seemed that way. Or almost always, at least as far as I was concerned. We never dreamed of asking questions, of removing those glasses or raising that veil. We could not have done so, even in play or in a moment of clumsiness. But in Tiresia's presence, play and clumsiness were out of the question. Between her and the rest of the world stood an invisible border, which we clearly felt, which did not permit crossing. Even when we pressed against her, clutched at a corner of her dress or at her hand, which often happened (for Tiresia was the center of our home, close by or far — but close by as soon as we needed her — she was always there), even at such moments there was that narrow space we never crossed. Nicole we devoured with kisses, we tumbled all over her, rubbed her skin, grasped her waist, licked her cheeks, her neck with the tiny ringlets that drove us crazy, there was no wall between Nicole and us. And yet . . . she was less essential to us.

The look that fell upon Tiresia sank as if into a dark and compact substance. And that substance never returned looks. I cannot express it otherwise. Looking at Tiresia was not looking at a body but looking at "the body." Our mother Nicole could be half-naked in those summer dresses that were held at the shoulder by one simple thread, and that suited her so well, but she was only her own body. Tiresia, always veiled from head to foot, was "the body," and it was a strange, painful, stunning thing. That is really what I am trying to say, something that stunned us and prevented us asking questions or exploring. Tiresia was beyond question. She neutralized all our usual faculties for thought and reaction.

Yet she spoke only of trivialities, of the small things of our everyday life. She never spoke of that other world, the world to which we sensed she belonged. Tiresia confined herself to the most ordinary and material matters of our life.

As soon as Nicole launched into metaphysical questions, Tiresia withdrew; she seemed to retreat into the fastnesses of her veil.

"Are you going to church today?" Tiresia would ask.

It was a practical question, to find out whether she should get us ready to go out.

"I don't know," Nicole would begin, drawing out her words. "Truly I don't know. But these children have nothing in their lives, I really must give them something, a belief of some kind. You can't live without a belief."

We did not like such speeches from Nicole. They seemed to rise into the air like poisoned exhalations belching from some fearsome pit that had been there since long before we were born, a pit we did not know, where paths were obscure and perhaps even impossible to find.

And at once we perceived Tiresia's withdrawal.

There was a kind of radiation around Tiresia, a dark radiation to which we were accustomed, in which we lived, and that radiation would suddenly disappear.

And we would find ourselves fleetingly in the ordinary light of a Sunday morning. It had the strangest effect on us, almost indescribable to anyone who has not known these abrupt passages. The ordinary light of a Sunday morning, a little cold and boring, and everything distinct from everything else, and time creeping about behind us.

It did not last.

"Very well, I'll go to church and take them with me," said Nicole. "If you wouldn't mind dressing them . . ."

And it was over.

The dark radiation that was our familiar element was back again. Things were once more connected to one another, and time stood looking us in the eye.

Sometimes at the table, Nicole suddenly set down her fork and stopped eating. We looked at her. "What am I dong here?" she said.

It was not a question intended to elicit a response, intended to walk arm in arm with that response into a conversation. Nicole's question sought no partner: it was intended to travel alone and to arouse sleeping fears.

"What am I doing here?" Oh, at such moments how we hated Nicole. Tiresia disappeared into her absence; our father assumed his physician voice, which we also hated. "You should go for a walk with the children this afternoon, Nicole, instead of locking yourself away in the garage . . ." How absurd that voice was in our father's throat. It did not suit him. Only our old doctor had the right to it, because he made good, effective use of it, because he had acquired it the hard way. Minor's voice had been fashioned, refashioned, transformed, and had finally been brought to perfection in the mold of a profession to which he had given himself body and soul. In and of itself it had become a potion, a sort of unendingly beneficent premedication.

We hated Nicole for summoning into our father's throat a voice that was not his, that rang false, that gave us goose bumps.

And of course a few minutes later we were sorry for her, we were angry with our father for not giving her an answer, even a token answer, for the smallest thing made Nicole happy.

And we understood her.

In fact, Dan and I had no need to ask ourselves such questions, for there were two of us. But Nicole was all alone, and it could not have been any fun to be all alone; it made you look lost and anxious, it made you ask silly questions. All that we sensed!

Oh, madame, if we had possessed a capacity for analysis on a par with our capacity for intuition, how fast we would have traveled. How quickly we would have disentangled the threads in which we were enmeshed!

IV

At the Convent

FIFTY-TWO

The Convent Moons

NICOLE took us to church several times. To the Catholic Church. Our father, born a Protestant, had become a full-fledged atheist, but he looked on these visits without animosity.

"What Nicole likes in the Catholic Church is the music, the vestments, the ritual," he smiled. "If this country possessed a church whose priests danced, that would be her church. Perhaps I should take her to Africa, or to black American churches." Nicole turned red with anger but never answered, because it was true.

There were few pictures in our church, but Nicole loved them. "You see," she whispered, "they're trying to make us see Someone. At least they try. The Protestants and Jews don't even try. I need to see Someone." There was one picture in particular she kept going back to, of Jesus walking on the choppy waters of Lake Tiberias. "Look, Estelle and Dan, he's walking on water, only a dancer could do that, the greatest dancer in the world." And we agreed. "But no point telling them at home, they wouldn't understand," and there too we agreed.

At the Elevation, her body seemed to take off from the pew, her proud little golden head with its high-flying bun stretched upward, and for a moment there was no point speaking to her; she heard nothing.

On the Sunday when she showed us "the greatest dancer in the world," Nicole went down to her garage earlier than usual, leaving Tiresia to do the dishes. Dan had at once offered to help, and normally I would have stayed with Dan, but something urged me to follow Nicole. I took a plate to the kitchen, then without letting anyone know I went off down the small corridor. The door of the blue garage was ajar, and I took up my post behind it. "What are you doing there, sweetheart?" whispered my father, who had emerged noiselessly from his study; perhaps he too had seen the half-open door. "I'm watching Nicole," I answered; he put his hand on my shoulder and we watched together.

At first Nicole stood folded in upon herself, head and arms hidden by her shoulders, and her torso curled down over the rest of her body. Then slowly she unfolded, her limbs groping upward like antennae: there was something terribly moving in that blind seeking by a sightless foot or sightless hand, such intensity did Nicole put into it. Then her body seemed to find its axis and straightened up, and her limbs too found a common orientation. Her head softly moved into upright position, with her whole body following, her hands rising heavenward, and then Nicole stood arrow straight on her points, upright as a trembling shaft. And her face, the face of one of Fra Angelico's child madonnas, was of inhuman seriousness.

My heart thudded.

"Look, Estelle," whispered my father, who knew that dance of our mother's well. "Nicole is rebuilding the cathedrals in her very own way."

"If only, if only there were dancing in church, Nicole would be saved," he said another time.

"That dance company is not for her," he said on yet another occasion, looking worried. "She will never find her place in it. They are too worldly, do you understand, Estelle?"

No, I did not really understand.

We went to watch Nicole dance with her company. The show was sponsored by a nondenominational cultural organization, influential in our town, and was held in the ballroom of city hall, converted for the occasion into a theater. The ballet was a success, judging by the small salvos of applause that repeatedly erupted from the audience. But I took none of that in, being much too preoccupied with watching Nicole. I was afraid she might stumble or make a mistake, and I could feel our father's anxiety. Many of his acquaintances were there, people who would come and speak to him during the intermission, ask him if that were not his wife and our mother whose name appeared on the program.

"Perhaps I should have taken you all to live in a big city," he muttered. "Oh, Estelle, how can a man know what to do? Perhaps I was wrong, quite wrong."

Nicole had a small part. She never danced alone but in the middle of a group. I sensed that she was subtly out of tune with the others; it was a disharmony that had nothing to do with rhythm, and I was unable to identify it.

"Nicole seeks connectedness and all the others are disconnected, that's what's wrong," my father said. "You see, Estelle, the whole reason she dances is to escape disconnectedness."

"Poor little thing," he said a moment later, tears in his eyes, "she dances like an angel in heaven, or at least the way she imagines an angel dancing in heaven."

His remarks bothered me; I did not want to hear all those things. My father always said "you understand, Estelle," and I believed I did understand. And that little phrase, acting on me like a narcotic, prevented me from asking questions, from thinking, from realizing that in fact I understood nothing.

And I was also afraid that the people around us might hear, might be induced to see what my father saw, and then Nicole's career might be ruined — for at that time I wanted to believe in a career for our mother. She had carried us in fantasy to so many countries, decked with so many bouquets and gifts, shown us so many renowned opera houses in so many capital cities, that in her dreams we were the miraculous children of a revered artist, of a great star. Dan let himself be wholly drawn in, and because he believed, I believed.

"I'm afraid she could turn Dan's head, you understand, Estelle," my father told me, and I was angry that he should be afraid, angry that he would not leave us in peace inside the gilded dream that harmed no one.

"Just look at him!" he said with a nudge.

I turned toward Dan. His expression! He sat there with arms hanging limp as if they did not belong to him, features frozen, eyes staring.

"Dan!" I whispered.

He did not stir.

"Do you like it, Dan?"

He turned his head and looked at us without moving a muscle of his face, as if the question meant nothing at all. Then his head turned back to the stage and he reverted to that strange posture, arms limp, eyes staring.

"He almost looks like a simpleton," my father said into my ear.

Several times during the performance he turned to Dan. I could not help noticing, for I was sitting between them and he had to lean across me.

"I believe he too sees invisible things," he said to me.

Oh, Father, stop making me your confidant, stop letting those enigmatic remarks of yours fall on me, remarks you deny me the means of deciphering, remarks that fill me with this mortal dread.

I sometimes think that the way we were positioned that night —

my father sitting next to me, and me sitting next to Dan, and Nicole
up on the stage — brought our life to a vital turning point, a turning
point it would take Dan and me years to bend back in the other
direction. And Tiresia was not there.

*I could think absolutely anything, madame. I am looking for stages in
our destiny, for a sequence that might hold these people and their story
together, even though it must float alone like a cloud in the immensity of
space, a cloud formed by my stubbornness alone, with nothing before and
nothing after, as I know very well. But I have to have that sequence in
order for you to come, madame, and in order to go from one point to another,
and out of solid sentences I weave this cloud, which threatens unendingly
to dissolve, and that would be unbearable to me, madame.*

*My pale beings are adrift, madame, please bring them down to solid
ground; give them outlines, colors, voices, not just to give them life (that
madness has left me) but so that my vision may have an object, and so
that this object may be visible to everyone. If ever a desire existed on earth
it is this, madame. I cannot explain it, but there is no other desire in me,
and it feeds on the devastation of desires. For all the rest, madame — my
determination to live in the now, my love for Phil, my wanderings in the
city — they are all simply oars feathering the surface.*

Our father watched Nicole and spoke to me. I watched Nicole and
listened to our father. Fear crept into me. Yes, Father, Nicole seeks
the impossible, and it is madness.

Estelle would not dance; Estelle would not enter the body's arabesque. She would stand to one side at a table, weighing in the scales
of reason the follies others brought her so that she should reconsti-
tute the components of those follies and bring them back within legal
norms. Estelle would never soar aloft on the tail of a helium balloon;
she would lay enough ballast in for herself and stay close to earth to
watch the others with a spyglass. Good, Father: Estelle will not dance;
in any case she does not want to. She is too heavy and too big-boned.
Dancing is not Estelle's style, she is well behaved, she is the elder
child, her father's support and confidant, since his wife plays both
the angel and the child, conceding only the pitter-patter of her points
to the household, audible through the walls on certain evenings when
storm winds are not shaking the big chestnut trees in the garden.

All the same, Father, Estelle would play the piano. Yes, she would
play the piano, but that was because Tiresia wished it so, since Tiresia
herself could no longer play.

Teaching Estelle was good for Tiresia.
Did Estelle play well?
Did anyone know or care?

Nicole wanted the piano to come to the garage, she wanted her daughter to play so that she herself could dance. But the piano stayed in the living room: it was too big for the garage, and Tiresia could not play for Nicole. And Tiresia needed the piano a little longer, just a little longer.

"For heaven's sake, Nicole, Tiresia still needs the piano," my father said one evening, suddenly irritated, his forehead somber.

"Then let's put an upright in the garage," Nicole said stubbornly.

"And who will play it?"

"Tiresia, Estelle, I don't know, you . . . yes, what about you?"

"Nicole, if I played the piano for you to dance by I would have no more clients, there would be no house, and therefore no piano, and therefore no dancing. I thought at least you knew all that," said our father bitterly.

"Then Estelle —"

"Estelle goes to school! Don't you even realize that? She goes to school and soon she'll be going to university!"

"And Nicole never went to university, Nicole knows nothing, just dancing, which is no good to anyone, that's what you mean. But you don't explain why Nicole never went to university, why she doesn't know anything and can only put her hopes in dancing, you don't mention any of that . . ."

White and upright and trembling, oh, Nicole how I wished I could help you. You were the little girl in that house. I wanted to take you in my arms and smooth the little curls framing your face and give you a piano and new slippers and a taffeta dress and tell you that all was well and that you could dance if you wished. I wanted to tell you that we would look after the house and taxes and Dan's studies and take care of the chestnut tree that the lightning uprooted and sprawled across the lawn, as well as car repairs, Father's clients, Tiresia's medicine . . . Dance, Nicole, dance if it pleases you! It doesn't bother me at all; I love to hear the patter of your points and Ravel's *Bolero* and your laughter when you tell us you will be a star and we will be the children of a star.

I turned to my father to tell him these things; he was white and upright, and he too was trembling; and on his features, almost invariably composed, there was a painful contraction I had never seen. Then my heart turned over and it was to him I wanted to run, to stand beside him, take his hand, tell him, "Father, don't worry, she talks like a baby, I've seen the light on at night in your study, I've hauled myself up at the window and seen your worried face bent over those folders that put food on our table, I've seen you with your arms around Nicole when she has her nightmares, stroking her and comforting her, I've seen you lead Tiresia to the big piano you bought for her, I've seen you encourage her and listen to her, and now I hear what you're saying for Estelle, your daughter, oh, Father, don't worry."

"Be quiet, Nicole, not in front of Estelle."

"Estelle, always Estelle or Tiresia. Never Nicole. Hasn't Nicole paid her debt yet? No, she hasn't, because now there's Dan and she has to pay all over again. Is that what you mean?"

I looked at my mother. Nicole, whom I never called Mama, but who was my mother. In any case I was on her side; she was beautiful and in pain; I would have gone on all fours to wipe up the unpleasantnesses she splashed all around her.

"If you wish," sighed my father. "If you wish to say such things."

"Then give me a piano and give me Tiresia to play for me," said Nicole with wicked obstinacy, as if she no longer expected anything. As if she sought only to vex the adversary in order to make the rejection last a little longer, the rejection that was nonetheless part of a dialogue and allowed you to speak of what interested you, which was in any case better than silence — and better too than ordinary conversations, all of which seemed to emanate from a dead planet.

"Tiresia has already played for you," my father said harshly.

"I know, I know," yelled Nicole.

"Try to persuade her."

"She won't, she won't."

"Dance hurts her."

"I'm not asking her to dance. I'm the one who dances. All she has to do is accompany me. She's a pianist, isn't she, a famous pianist? She was very willing to play to make herself famous, but not for Nicole . . . Never for Nicole."

My father stepped forward, his hand raised. He was about to slap Nicole, to slap her hard. I would see it, I saw it already; her frail body would crash into the table, she would break a limb, she would be unable to dance again; no one in that house would ever laugh again, for Nicole was the only one who laughed. But Tiresia stood suddenly in the doorway. My father and Nicole saw her, my father began to cry, oh, only a little, a sigh rather than a sob, and Nicole was in his arms. They held each other tight, hugging without touching. That I noticed: they were in each other's arms but at a slight distance from each other. And Tiresia came to pull me to her, and she too hugged me in that same way, at a slight remove, and then Dan came. "Oh, a play," he said. "Where do you want me to stand?"

He was so funny and graceful, with his forelock and his impudent look. But perhaps my memory is lying to me, is hurrying in to spare me pain. Perhaps my father did strike Nicole, or else Nicole struck my father. Perhaps dreadful things did happen; I cannot quite remember; all at once Dan was there and the whole horror subsided.

"I am looking for someone," I said to the nun who greeted me. My lips were white, the light was white, her veil was white.

Speaking was such an effort. "I am not a believer," I muttered. I did not want to deceive them.

"You are in pain," the nun said placidly.

I nodded. If I had said yes, I would have wept and told my whole story. I did not want to cry, I did not want to tell my story. I wanted to enter this place, enter silence and find Dan. I had to lie and tell the truth. Those two things did not seem incompatible to me, just difficult. I had to leash myself in, keeping special watch on my tears and the risk of a rush of confidences.

It was important not to let myself spill out through any kind of leak, for I knew what would then await me: a hideous decomposition of my being, or perhaps a long and patient form of consolation — but in either case I should lose Dan, and losing my desire to see him would mean my own end. It would be worse than death, since I would be present at that end, at my own death. The very idea was unbearable to me.

I looked up at the nun. On her depended my entry. My stubbornness returned.

("Estelle, you'll be on your own, without me to help you: you'll have to outwit death and outwit the living . . .")

"I have nothing else to tell you. My life is empty, the world is empty. I seek the one who has left it."

Through the parlor window I saw a big garden. There were broad flower beds and warm pools of sunlight and rosebushes everywhere. Beyond them a small stand of lime trees shading three benches. On the benches sat three old women stripping blossoms from the branches into big baskets set on the ground before them.

("I believe that I have been a father in a dream, Estelle, and now I regret that there were no grandmothers in your growing up, but you and Dan did not seem to want a family at all . . .")

"Oh no," I murmured to myself. The sight had reopened a wound. I turned sharply away to look at the blank wall on the other side.

And through that wall I saw what I was yearning to see: a big building with massive outer walls. Within them was a square empty courtyard, surrounded by a covered walk with low vaulted arcades whose columns threw regular shadows on its flagstones. The court-yard too was paved. Held at bay by stone and shade, the sun remained austere and upright. There was no one to be seen.

I saw all that through the wall.

"That's a cloister for the silent just behind there, isn't it?" I said to the nun, indicating the wall.

She looked at me with a hint of surprise.

"Yes. We have a garden for recreation in front, where you see some of our older sisters picking lime blossoms, and on the other side, facing south, we have some fields, which are an important part of our work. But yes, inside the building is the garden, anyway, what we call the garden, the part we have designated for silence. How did you know?"

"I saw it."

"But . . . it's inside."

"I saw it. Sister, I want to go to that garden."

The nun suggested instead that I go to the hostelry.

"I cannot."

"Why can't you? I shall see you every day, we will have time to know each other. If it's a question of money . . ."

"I ask if I can go to the garden and you suggest the hostelry."

I looked straight at her. There was so much sureness in me, it was not my voice speaking, not my sundered heart, not my ravaged person. I have no idea where those words came from. At times it seemed to me that Nicole was close by and prompting me. At times that feeling faded and there was just this voice coming from my wearied body. Strong, authoritarian, with words unknown to me as late as the day before.

The nun turned red. I saw the flush spread to her neck and pale cheeks. Something violent and intoxicating entered me. My own flesh had been reduced to nothing, humiliated, destroyed, deprived of life, and now I saw in me that same power over another's flesh. From the inferno of pain I had brought back a power and now realized it for the first time.

In me at that moment was scalding ice. How old was that nun? Not much older than I. I knew with certainty that I was the stronger. She had not traveled through the night on an endless journey stretched out on the planks that covered her dead brother, her elbows and knees on fire, her face thudding into the wood at every bump. She had not wrested a coffin from the cemetery earth for the price of a black and hateful transaction of passion. She had not lain face-down on her dead brother's stinking corpse, losing her urine and her feces, and banging that unrecognizable head against an abject coffin plank. And the earth, the struggle with the earth . . . She had not known even the whiteness of a spring morning, the pure sky parted by an aircraft, the sounds of a city, the first sun, nor understood that all this was vertigo, refined and cruel torture, an unbearable thing that made those who had held out day by day all winter suddenly commit suicide, that made sick people who were still fighting suddenly die.

"I don't want to be separated anymore, even for a day."

"There are rules here," she said. "First I must speak to the community."

"I will wait for you."

"It is the hour for services now, and after that our meal."

"I will wait."

"You must eat too."

"I hunger for one thing only."

"I cannot leave you alone in the parlor."

"But you cannot make me leave."

"This is madness."

("Estelle, my love, you have to outwit the living.")

"What is madness in men's eyes is wisdom in God's eyes."

That is exactly what I said: "What is madness in men's eyes is wisdom in God's eyes."

I was no longer myself; I was someone else who had been living inside me without my knowing her. I heard her speak and act, as if my very body itself were undergoing metamorphosis. In a flash I saw my skin blister in several places: with a light tug you could have pulled it clear, but what lay underneath? That flash had not given me time to see. All I felt was a body I did not know growing inside me, all I felt was this metamorphosis.

Perhaps it was a kind of premonition. For later I had what must have been a kind of giant eczema. My skin peeled off in strips and I believed it was the onset of the plague, of the disease that had carried Dan off, and later on another skin appeared beneath it and I was cured. My body had already foreseen it, although I myself still knew nothing.

But I regresssed. My confidence faltered, and the nun saw.

"My sisters will not like that," she said.

And I understood the warning. I was going too fast: here life had order; you had to conform, to bend. The inner division that would soon be so familiar was already taking over. I heard my voice speaking inside: "Careful, Estelle."

"We believe that when people are determined, they know how to wait."

"Forgive me," I said.

"Go to your room in the hostelry, and the novice mother will see you this afternoon."

Again vertigo. Going to a room and waiting. Whiteness. The pure sky parted by an aircraft. The sounds of a city. The first sun. Again that torture.

"Take me to your garden, only for a moment, then I'll leave and wait."

Again she turned red. But she was powerless before my despair. She shrugged, in that graceful impulsive way I was to see so much of. Then she gave me her assent, adding some words I did not understand.

"What must I do?" I said.

"Just hop over that low wall."

"This wall?"

"Well, yes, you're wearing trousers, aren't you?"

I was suddenly intimidated. In my obsession, I had been so focused on myself that I had failed to see this low wall, symbolic of enclosure, between us. Plaster, eighteen inches high. Suddenly I could no longer stir. My muscles were lifeless. Laughing, the nun gave me her hand.

"You're a strange one all right!"

I stammered something: "How can you be so cheerful?" or else "How can you be so young?" and she said something in return — "You'll be cheerful too," or else "You'll be young too." But that little wall was such an obstacle to me, I was lost, I could not hear.

"I don't know what's the matter," I said, "my legs won't move."

My whole being was turned toward that garden, oh, I had to get there, if only for a few seconds, I had to get into that place, and then I could leave it and wait, and set myself upon a road again. But there was this wall.

Was it the memory of another wall, of the wall where I had started to struggle against death? They did not look alike; in the first one there had been that gap beneath the lilac where Adrien came through, the gap I had buttressed my arms against as Adrien pounded his body into mine; and there had been the smell of earth and the smell of lilac and prefigured by both smells the putrefying odor of a corpse.

The wall here was low, neat, white-painted; there was no smell (only that particular smell that lingers when you have removed every smell that can be removed), the ground was cement, there were no memories in the air. All memories too had been removed, and the air was neutral and calm.

And I realized that it was the crumbling garden wall that I missed, that this scrubbed plaster was unbearable to me, that I longed for the smells and the darkness of death, and Adrien's body, which was still part of Dan's death, and the lilac drooping to the ground. That white wall paralyzed me, stopped me dead.

"Wait," said the nun.

She sat astride it and was across.

"There," she said.

Then she took my arm and opened a door to what looked like a closet, with a narrow winding corridor beyond. "Well," she said kindly, "your legs seem to be working now. It sometimes happens, you know: the idea of being enclosed can frighten people, we don't even think of it anymore, and as you see we forget all about it when the need arises. In fact we want to get rid of that low wall around the parlor, but some of the older sisters are still attached to it, so we're waiting to let them get accustomed to the idea. Perhaps we'll start with a little gate, we don't want to ruffle anyone's feathers . . . The changes since Vatican Two have been hard for some of them . . . we have to be understanding . . . Now just lean on me, we're nearly there . . ." Her chatter entered me although I was not really listening. What I did register, on the other hand, was that my momentary weakness had opened the garden to me.

She was all goodness, offering me her arm to lean on, a river of words, complicity. Reaching the end of the corridor, she cocked an ear.

"Services have begun, so no one will see us," she said with a little gurgling laugh. "We're in luck."

And she led me under the arches of the walkway.

"Helping the weak and the sick, that is their strength," I said to myself. And I knew I would enter that convent and exactly how I would enter it. I knew what I would tell the novice mother that afternoon. I had just understood one thing about this place, a petty, shallow kind of understanding, but it would get me in — of that I was sure.

"You see, you're walking better now," said the nun.

"It's because I'm here," I murmured.

And that too was true.

That I would like to understand and also make clear to others. That duplicity which was not dishonesty. To a certain degree in the depths of pain it is impossible to lie. But this too: at a certain point in hell, it is impossible to tell the truth.

I did not really see the garden. We were in the walkway and it lay behind the stained glass spanning the cloister arches. The walkway: austere light, the firmness of stone, regular shadows on the floor, the hem of the nun's robe. It was quite enough. It suited me perfectly. I felt sorrow at the idea of leaving this place to go to the hostelry.

"I feel sorrow," I said.

"Yes," said the nun.

"Sorrow at having to leave this place."

"But we've had our walk here now," said the nun. "It's over and we must go."

My room in the hostelry had flowered wallpaper, a crucifix on the wall, an earthenware bowl on the table. It all disturbed me. I could no longer absorb things. I found those wreaths of colored flowers exhausting. Wreaths! All I wanted was straight lines in the dark. They penetrated me like thorns, those flowers gibbering like troops of monkeys. "But who on earth comes here?" Was it meant to look cheerful, was this their idea of consolation? And that piece of pottery, had the nuns made it? Was I too going to have to make that sort of thing, ask myself questions about objects, worry about a tower, a shape? The idea of touching wet clay with your hands!

And the crucifix?

Nicole, did you really believe in all this?

I rose suddenly and seized the object, it had some kind of dried vegetation sticking to it and irritating me. I tore it off and threw it under the bed, then I turned the cross this way and that. "What am I going to do with this?" I said to myself. I began to feel an itch on my scalp, an itch that would very shortly devour my whole body. I scratched myself with a branch of the crucifix. The itching stopped. "Not bad for a start," I thought.

I put it on the table and told it, "Dance, dance for me." I thought of Nicole, I could almost see her slipping into the wood, the branches beginning to rise like arms, the upright beam delicately splitting. Soon, I thought, its apex would come to life, would show me Nicole's head with high-piled hair, the way she used to wear it to dance. "Do it," I said to the crucifix, but I said it without conviction; I did not want to spend my strength in that room, for I was not there to call on Nicole.

It was already thanks to her that I had gotten this far, because of the church she took us to as children, because of her angel dance and the invisible ones she told us about. She had given me what she could, and I sensed that my exhausted memory could ask no more of her from where she now was.

I set the crucifix back down on the table. "It can't be so bad," I thought, "if it brought me a picture, just a picture, of Nicole dancing. Perhaps once I'm here I'll be able to get a lot more out of this piece of wood, once my strength is focused. For two thousand years this has helped so many people to see things," I thought. "I'll try it too."

Someone was in the room.

"I knocked, but you didn't answer. I took the liberty of coming in. I see I'm disturbing you . . . the crucifix . . ."

It seemed to me that these women were talkative, which would suit me very well. I had taken hold of myself again as she spoke. It was now or never. My only chance.

"I brought you your red bag that you left in the parlor. It's so pretty, it's —"

"Sister, I want to enter. Now. Not in a month, not tomorrow. I waited for you through the service, through the meal. It was torture. These flowers here tortured my head."

"Speak to me," said the nun.

I had the words all ready: the adversity that had struck our house, our family decimated, the plague that was in me, my own inevitable death within a few days, at most a year, our mother who took us to church (I invented these last words for our mother) to "seek comfort in God's house."

"I can no longer stand on my feet. One step in the street and I fall. I expended my last strength getting here."

How easy to lie, since it was the truth. I felt that I was slipping out of that chair, that I was about to fall at that woman's feet.

She was my first doorway. I was down on the ground, on my knees before her, and since I did not know how to pray my body prayed for me. And how well it prayed! I could rely on it, and the doorway moved softly, opened a little.

That long bout of vertigo. Chaos of sensations. I was lying down. My skin burned, blistered, flaked. The itch occupied my whole being. I lost hope. I had not had time even to begin my quest, and I was going to die, to end up far from Dan. I had to find him but I had not even begun to seek, and I was terrified. I wanted to return home: "At least Tiresia will put me in our cave with Dan." In fact, though, I realized that Tiresia would not be able to fight the civil institutions governing disposal of the dead.

I would die here, I would be buried here. If I asked for more, the best I could expect would be burial in the cemetery of our town. They would open the vault and find that Dan's coffin was no longer there, and Tiresia would face the questioning alone. I could not bear the idea of Tiresia tramping up the hills, forced to look for the place, to explain. Then they would have to bring the coffin back to the vault. How — with Adrien's help? I was not equal to talking with Adrien. Like insatiable crows, all these questions hopped and flapped inside my head, and it seemed to me that they pecked at my body and carried off strips of my flesh.

But it was only the nuns delicately lifting away the skin that was coming loose. I stood up to leave.

"I shall not see him before I die."

"Have faith."

And I shouted:

"He is why I came here! Why do you think I came? To see you, to see your moon faces? You're not beautiful, you can't dance, you don't have bodies. I came here to see him, him, and if I can't see him I'll leave again, do you hear, I'll leave again."

I shouted and shouted. The nuns saw my lips moving, but never a sound emerged. "Have faith," they said.

I was mesmerized by those moon faces. In the first part of my stay, while I was sick and then while I was recovering, I could not tell them apart. Those veil-framed faces seemed written in, like the moon against the backcloth of the sky, and as with the moon I did not really see features on those faces. They were ovals of absence, framed voids, and I remembered all those evenings when Dan and I had gazed at the moon from the garden lawn.

I must have been wrong, of course, but it seemed to me that in no other part of the world did the moon seem as big as from our little town.

So broad was it that it seemed to be nearing the earth. We looked about us in fear, but the street and its houses remained peaceable, so perhaps everything was normal? Yet when we looked up again the disk seemed to have grown still broader. Directly over our garden it waited, like some enigmatic envoy from space, and we did not understand its message. We held on tight to the chestnut tree.

The sun had never affected us in this way: it carried out its solar duties through all the vagaries of the weather, which in our part of the world was a difficult partner. It had never occurred to us to wonder what its message was; it was simply a hard worker. But the moon clearly had no job to do. It just opened up — and on earth everything immediately and subtly changed, the scent of the lilac impregnated every layer of air, the murky outlines of secrecy gathered around the mass of the chestnut trees and rhododendrons, and the light-flooded lawn seemed the stuff of revelation. Then moon and garden remained in that state, and nothing further happened.

"This thing is here and tells us nothing, how can that be?" said Dan. I can still hear his exclamation of wounded surprise; I recall how I took him by the shoulders, and later around the waist, how I wished I could give him the reply that refused to come. I did not care at all myself if the moon showed us nothing, nothing beyond that enormous indiscreet disk above our heads. The only answer I needed was in Dan, and I feared his look of hunger, the wounded look he directed at the moon.

"It's because it looks like an eye, Dan, you think it's looking at you, but it's just dead matter." "Dead matter," he murmured.

"He's like a little puppy wanting to howl at the moon," said our father, watching Dan as the full moon bathed the lawn. And I did not like him saying that, I was afraid those words might unleash a howling of terrifying, unsuspected power in Dan. "He's like his mother," said our father. Nor did I like that sentence. "The moon doesn't do anything to me, yet I'm his sister," I snapped back at him. "Always defending him," my father sighed. "Well, that's fine, it's all I could have asked for."

And now it was my turn to look for something in those white black-bordered moons.

I sat in the chapel during yet another service on which I was unable to focus. I still did not know the words of the Psalms, and there was just one prayer in me: "Let me see you." Sometimes, when out of weariness I let myself be drawn along by the nuns' words and addressed myself to their own invisible being ("Let me see YOU"), I raised my eyes and looked around me a little. For the evening service they lit only the two clusters of candles on either side of the altar, and the chapel aisles were dark. Standing with slightly bent heads, the nuns were chanting. I was in a state of icy lucidity. Suddenly they all raised their heads toward the glow of the altar, and against a black moorland I saw those rows of moons rise beside me, within reach of me. "Dan," I said. It seemed to me that the whole chapel rang with my cry. How could they not have heard? And if I had shouted inside my head, was it possible that they had not heard in their midst this head that contained a cry so different from theirs?

Was that the power that had attracted me down this road to the convent? Dan's moon? I had brought it close, that moon he hunted like a dog, I had as it were pulled it down to earth, and here it had even multiplied: there were fifteen, twenty moons in that chapel, with features scarcely clearer than Dan's moon up in the sky.

It was a stupid revelation, and had I been able I would have laughed or wept. It had no sense yet it was tremendous. I let myself slide down onto the prie-dieu and for a moment forgot the service and the presence of the nuns. That small fragment of our childhood was there, and it was linked to the time after Dan's death by a grotesque link, but one that belonged so profoundly to my brother and me that it could be understood only by the two of us. And since it was understood, it meant that both of us had been there for the duration of that act of understanding.

That, more or less, madame, was the train of thought whose light so powerfully illuminated my ailing brain.

I see no other explanation for that brief moment of relief, or rather of release. In the chapel that evening I was granted a pause. I saw my hands, bright white on my knees, and recognized them as my hands. It was really me. Estelle was here, in a convent, seeking her brother through a moon's pale disk. Who but Estelle and Dan could understand that? So Dan was there, and most certainly Estelle was there. Returning in this way to self, after so many days' absence, was truly falling from the moon. How far I was from all this convent nonsense! If at that moment someone had called me out of the building for one reason or another, I would have headed quite naturally for the exit, I would have gone on walking and would not even have thought any more of turning back.

When the service ended the erratic construction that had briefly sheltered me dissolved, gone like a shaft of moonlight.

In silence outside the chapel the nuns dispersed. Beneath cloisters dimly lit by guttering candle ends, each of them alone beneath her veil, some hugging the walls, some gliding from column to column, the black robes fled across the flagstones and were one by one swallowed by the dark orifice of the stairway.

Night. Sleeping or not sleeping, it was the same. The same waiting, taut as a bowstring.

FIFTY-THREE

You That Still Live, Disturb Her Not

I REMAINED for a few days at the hostelry. After the novice mother, another convent officer came to see me, the Mother Superior. She led me down long corridors.

"The community is willing to take you into its bosom," she said. "You will go on a retreat . . ."

She broke off.

"You will be an observer for as long as you need, then you can decide . . ."

We moved into a gallery with a paved floor, open on one side through arcades overlooking the inner courtyard, which was also paved. Flat stones, that was what I wanted . . .

"It's our garden of silence," said the Superior.

Something struck me. I reflected, laboriously. Then I had it.

"I've been here before," I murmured.

"I know, the novice mother brought you here the day you arrived. We've opened the cloister doors to show you the pretty lawn in the center."

Something in those words also struck me, something concerning this garden. It worried me; why was she talking about a lawn? But I had not the strength to think any further.

Later, later.

We climbed a stone staircase, dark, wide, winding. On the second-floor landing we brushed past an enormous black shape standing before a glass cage containing a sort of clock. The shape did not turn around.

On the third floor we turned right and were suddenly in a spacious corridor with a dark, glowing wooden floor. We turned left, and the corridor came to an end at a window flooded with light. It seemed to me that if we went on walking we would tumble into that light and be swallowed up at one gulp.

The Superior walked with rapid but measured steps; in fact her gait was restrained, even slow; oh, if only she could continue to walk like that on that dark gleaming floor toward that blinding glare at the end. Relief flowed into my body from that measured walk of hers, from that vast dark-glowing floor, from the length of the corridor down which we were walking and walking, and from that possibility at its far end.

To pass on into the light, your body suddenly transformed into light, diffused in that blinding incandescence . . . for a second I truly believed that a gift had been offered me and that I had found the place where that gift was waiting.

The Superior stopped at a door. Above was written "Our Lady of Joy." The Superior watched me decipher the words. She smiled.

They had a store of smiles in their cheeks (and I really thought "store," or rather "stock" — well-trained smiles, standing guard just behind their faces and leaping forward at the first summons to spread their wings, gracious, implacable smiles).

She rummaged through her keys, then suddenly shrugged and pushed the door. It was not locked. "We had a bishop here last week," she said. "He smoked a pipe, that's why there's this smell . . ." She busied herself with a curious little object; later on I realized it was a can of deodorant. Then she threw the window open. It worked by means of a long horizontal wooden bar, which you tilted up into a vertical position from its latch in the center. With the windows freed, the wooden bar fell into place next to the adjacent closet.

"An antiquated gadget," said the Superior with a little laugh. "We are poor. But it works. Be careful not to get hit on the head when it comes down or when you push against the window."

She showed me the view.

"It's a wonderful view. It's better when there are fewer clouds. Those are the V. Mountains. Lower down is our town and over there in the gap is the county town."

She waved at the table:

"You're a student, so we've given you the room with a desk. You can go on working."

We went back across the corridor and she showed me the toilets. Three glass-paned doors side by side, then another one, and squeezed in between them a small washbasin with a water heater. The glass doors gave me a strange feeling, as if someone were crouching behind them.

"We put all this in recently," said the Superior. "Our founder was not a great believer in mortification. So we took advantage of Vatican Two."

Absorbed all of a sudden, she studied something in the water heater. I did not understand why she was fussing with it, why she was keeping me waiting. I had already waited a long time in the hostelry, and now I wanted to go on moving forward. Above all, no stopping.

"It works," she said, "but sometimes the pilot light goes out. Call the nursing sister if that happens. She takes care of it."

Impatience was giving me cramps. I could not remain focused on the same object.

"I don't need hot water," I said.

She looked at me in surprise.

"You'll need to shower."

Shower? I did not even understand the word, I heard "share," and it seemed to me that a fault of locution had given it another sound that wiped away its meaning.

I was impatient to see that long gleaming wood floor again, the dim corridors, the dark and winding stair. Those images did me good; my mind longed for them.

Today I know I was seeking some equivalent of the grave.

A place of close confinement, of cellars, of low vaults, of paved damp earth, a hard and bitter hold on the body, a hold intended to break the body, to deny it to itself. And in the sequence of hours not a single crack for the past to creep up to the surface, to come up to breathe and spread its poisonous exhalations. Fighting poison with a stronger poison, no doubt that was the demented idea to which my doomed body clung.

The corridors I had seen were the closest I had so far come.

And now I was delivered to this light, almost spacious room, with several lamps, one on the vast desk, one on the night table, and another one, just a bulb (but why so many lights?), in the ceiling.

Before leaving, the Superior put a typewritten house schedule on the table. It was in a plastic sleeve and dog-eared at one corner.

I see all those details clearly. I thought I had forgotten them. I had thought they would disappear with the madness that had called them into being around me; I had thought they would settle like dust upon my brother's coffin; I had thought it would all sink gently and inexorably into the earth like a slowly cooling heart in fusion.

But I did not forget them.

Weekday Schedule

6:30 A.M.	Prayers
7:30	Service, lessons
8:00	Breakfast
8:30	Lauds
11:00	Mass
Noon	Lunch
1:45 P.M.	Median hour
3:45	Tea
5:30	Vespers, prayers
6:45	Supper
8:45	Compline

I looked at three words on that list. Why were they underlined?

Under this schedule were the following words:

"The timetable for services is for your information only, to let you know when you can join us or, on the contrary, be more or less certain of enjoying solitude in our chapel. On the other hand, we do ask you to respect the mealtime schedule!"

That exclamation point at the end of the paragraph stuck in me like an arrow.

There was more.

Sunday Schedule

8:00 A.M.	Breakfast
8:30	Lauds
9:00	Mass
9:30	Matins, lessons
Noon	Lunch
2:00 P.M.	Quiet hour

Then nothing. A blank under this column.

What? A break in the routine? This dreadful blank on Sunday afternoon . . .

Later the Superior would explain to me that since Sunday afternoon followed the same schedule as on weekdays the nuns had not considered it necessary to copy the same information again.

"Not considered it necessary, what do you mean?"

"I beg your pardon," said the Superior, "you're slurring a little, I didn't understand."

Her voice was lively and crisp. She did not understand what I meant. She had no idea what I was talking about. She was like Adrien's mother.

I put the paper down on the table, the desk at which the bishop had worked as he smoked his pipe, where there was now a small object that was a deodorant spray, oh, why did I have to experience these details, these hideous everyday details? and I turned to the window.

I was hoping for the same white glare as the one at the end of the corridor so that, if only for a moment, I might find rest. Instead, there was a green mountain crowned with a statue, a town nestled at the foot of the mountain, on its right a rocky tableland, and far away at the end of the valley another, bigger city shimmering through the heat. All very picturesque, like a postcard I felt I had already seen. But where? Here, of course, just a few seconds earlier: the Superior herself had called me to the window to show me this landscape. The enthusiasm in her voice, her eager anticipation of my admiration . . . It was too much, memories already, people, words, I had to arrest this tidal wave, I had not come to the right place, too many things were happening here, superabundant life, a torrent.

Someone knocked. I started forward, not to open the door but to leave.

A nun stood there, her upper body bent almost at right angles, her veil spread over that upper body like a black cloth on a table. Hidden beneath was her face.

"It is vespers, let me show you to the chapel," whispered a scarcely audible voice.

The black figure began to walk, and I followed a few steps behind. It moved slowly, methodically swaying from one foot to the other. A black, hypnotic pendulum. The corridor, the stairs, the gallery, the chapel.

The black figure disappeared and another, equally stooped, drew near. "Sit there," it said to me.

I sat down in the pew that would thenceforth be mine. The sisters were there in two rows. A high subdued chant rose heavenward.

"God succor us, Lord sustain us . . ."

Tomorrow, I knew, I would also be singing to that melody, I would melt into those chants, the hot red flow of my pain would find riverbanks there. I would no longer need to struggle with it; a vast network of canals stood open to it and it had only to follow, leaving me to the black torpor I yearned for, to motionlessness, to silence, to nothingness.

Every day I would come to this place. I would stand very straight in front of my chapel stall, and my pain would flow out from me to those waiting channels, and I would be able to float down inside myself toward that empty crypt from which I never wanted to be separated.

"Even as measureless as Your immensity, O Lord, is our need of You. Your place is marked in the depths of our hearts like a great emptiness, like a wound."

How easy it would be to repeat those words.

They were the first I heard. Because of them and a few similar ones, I would also be able to recite all those which had no other meaning than that conveyed by their syntax.

Psalms, canticles, hymns: a great maze of words in which I would henceforth walk, like one with bound eyes, and it was what I wanted.

I wanted those chants to serve as gangplanks, to gain me entry into that unknown building, if only it really were unknown, self-sufficient, demanding nothing of me, reminding me of nothing.

With Sister Theologian (I called her that because I did not wish to know her name) I walked along a pathway overrun by wild grass and shaded by poplars. It was in a secluded corner of the convent gardens, below the slope crowned by the little rustic convent cemetery. The pathway led to a big wooden gate, and beyond it were fields, one of them belonging to the convent, others to local farmers.

"We always open this gate, of course," said Sister Theologian. "There are two huge cherry trees in this field." "Two cherry trees?" I repeated uncomprehendingly. "Yes indeed," she said with a little chuckle, "we can't give up our cherries just because they're outside the grounds, can we?"

Do not talk to me about cherry trees or farmers, Sister Theologian, or about your life's small reverses and victories. Do not talk to me of the now, of the present time, and of the people in it. I wish to know nothing of a time that contains my brother's death.

I lowered my head, my expression blank; never would I respond to her laughter and provocation.

"In the Bible you lent me," I said to Sister Theologian, "there are these footnotes pointing out, pointing out, oh, plays on words —"

"The ecumenical translation of the Bible," Sister Theologian at once replied, "the range of possible meanings . . ."

And we were back at the doors of that abstract edifice I had come here to shut myself up in, the edifice I never wanted to leave.

Sister Theologian was mistress of novices. I had to be wary of her.

Floor and stalls in the little chapel were of dark gleaming wood, like the corridors; my gaze rested on that wood, reclined on it, stretched out on it. Let nothing distract me from it. As long as I could see that dark surface my fears were still; I knew I was where I was supposed to be.

The gentle lament of the nuns' chant rose from it, each voice like a feebly bubbling spring. I kept unflagging watch (let nothing distract me from it!). I lay stretched out on a long wooden plank. It was restful to my eyes, dark and marbled with darker veins, it was the very inside of my soul, but it was not dead; it reflected the light as if from deep within it some other light called back to it; it was the dim light of my vigil, and that light merged with the thin chant that rose, the voice of my vigil over the vigilant darkness of the wood (oh, let nothing at all distract me from it!).

I waited impatiently for services. When the crystalline tinkle rang through the convent (it was timed automatically by the clock I had seen in its glass cage on the second floor) something leapt fluttering inside me and I at once dropped what I was doing. I longed for those services: time to return to chapel, the hieratic postures of the nuns, the sound of the zither, the thin, tremulous chants, the muted lighting, and the long wooden boards, dark and gleaming.

At last I saw the communicating gate into the cloister.

Through an archway by the choir stalls the chapel communicated with the small convent church. The grille was there, small regular squares formed by intersecting crosspieces, a black and solid grille, the top half of which could be slid down beside the other; then the portress would take out a huge key and plant it in the lock.

Let the cloister remain tight shut, let the two halves of the grille remain solidly bracketed, let nothing of the world that contained my dead brother be allowed to come into this place where I was killing his death.

But after the first service every morning, the grille was left open. Close by, where the bellpulls hung down into the chapel, stood a dark figure, hands folded, waiting. All the nuns waited too.

From outside came pandemonium, a noise of engines dying and voices taking over from them; danger assumed solid shape; beyond the archway you almost felt the nave of the church swell with expectation; and then suddenly you felt footsteps. Someone was walking about out there in that place that opened onto the outside world. My heart began to beat threateningly. Behind those footsteps were more steps.

The sound of those steps, clattering noisily on the church flagstones, was not a monastic sound; it was not the sound of creatures of silence; I was afraid, and suddenly there they were.

Human beings, two, a couple.

A fat woman with bare legs, a bald-headed man, both of them squeezed into suits too small for them, how could you avoid seeing such details, seeing these creatures who came from the world where they said my brother was dead, these creatures who brought the unbearable vitality of death into this place where I held it in leash, where I stifled it? . . . Go back, go back! Oh, my sisters, drive them away, lock the gate, lock the big church door, let no more flesh of the outside world bring its contagion here, its contamination, all that swarming maggotry of details dragging my brother's death behind it.

How I hated these intruders, this horrible couple. They walked on tiptoe: did they think it made them less intrusive, did they think they melted into the darkness of the wood, into the gleaming highlights of the wood, into the silence? They stopped for a moment by the entrance to pick up sheets of plainsong music, exchanging a few embarrassed words in low tones, their clothing ugly, the bare skin of their legs and skull ugly. Then they were walking in that absurd way again, on tiptoe, which caused them to waddle, oh, how could you avoid looking at them, hearing them, yet still they advanced, hugging the wall, my sisters, are you going to let them penetrate so deep into the heart of your chapel?

The nuns stood, each one motionless before her stall, faces lowered, hands in the wide sleeves of their scapulars, and the couple came forward from the rear. There were more of them now, coming forward with the same clumsy gait that clattered unpleasantly on the church flagstones. They would be back tomorrow and the next day and the next. I would have to see their faces, the features of human beings from the outside world, the world surviving obscenely in the wasteland of my brother's death. Their features wounded me, I could neither keep vigil nor chant nor hear my soul on the long wooden boards.

The nuns knelt before their stalls, heads turned to the cross before the open archway of the enclosing wall. I still stood, unaware that the end of the service was at hand, my eyes still riveted on those beings brought in from the outside to disturb my work in this place, this place I wanted to resemble a crypt. But the nuns remained on their knees and, in an unbelieving stupor, I saw the visitors stir and turn around, lumpish, ill at ease, and troop out in single file.

When they reached the dividing line between the chapel and the public area of the church, they briefly turned their heads. I saw the image of ourselves that they were stealing from us — the gloom of the chapel, the kneeling figures sunk in meditation — and I hated them for absconding to the outside world with that image. For it was an image of which I was a part — that figure on the left there, not kneeling, not wearing a veil. Did you think she was praying for you, that she too was a devout woman, as you would put it, interceding for you, dispensing you of the need to suffer and to think?

Stupid vile creatures, the woman standing there is thinking neither of God nor of you, she is thinking of the brother she seeks, and of her own body, which she must keep safe for that purpose — and only for that purpose. And she hates you for bringing into her presence your reek of the living, which is merely the opposite of the stench of death.

You that still live, disturb her not as she keeps vigil on the brink of death.

FIFTY-FOUR

"He Looked Like Dan"

WHAT I wanted was to hurl myself into those days that had led other women like me toward what they sought, toward a person. To hurl myself bodily, as they say, into those days. I knew nothing of the way time was organized in the lives of those women, nor what they gave of themselves, nor what was expected of them.

This may seem strange, but the idea of religion, the word, even, had not so much as touched me. I had gone to the convent because I knew it might be a place of vision, a place where it occasionally happened that you saw what was no longer there to see.

There had been nothing else in my head; my mind was sick, could only act upon one idea, a poor and simple idea, and because that idea was poor and simple my mind could take hold of it, and because my mind was too weak to grasp any other idea, it followed the one that had managed to penetrate it.

My mind had only that idea to follow, and it followed it animal-fashion.

And it was Nicole's poor words — tossed into the air as a provocation because dancing was not enough for her, because she did not know what tormented her, because she did not know what to devote herself to — it was those few unhealthy words, thrown out at random, falling like fast-fading plants, that had launched me on this mad course.

Oh, Nicole, if you could know how your fragile words haunted me, how desperately I sought them. No mixture of words could be useful to me; my body rejected them all except for those that you in your ignorance had fashioned. I pursued them deep into my memory, thrusting aside everything that interfered, the voices of the denizens of our houses, and my head constantly hurt me. But it seemed to me that inside that pain in my head there was a sharp clean point that dug and dug and suddenly drew out Nicole's words, like designated quarry, bright against dim ground.

"You know, Estelle, sometimes I see him," she would whisper.

I was a child at the time. "Who," I whispered back, "the one they trucified?"

Nicole had never corrected that childish mistake. Possibly the Crucifixion did not interest her; indeed, it must have been horrifying to a person who danced to efface the distress of bodies.

("from the stiffness of death the human frame will rise,
like a shuddering sail it will catch the wind,
and the wind will lift it skyward, and the arabesque unfold,
the angelic arabesque with neither break nor interruption . . .")

Probably Nicole did not even see that body, twisted into angular horror, nailed motionless.

"Who?" I whispered to Nicole in the pew of our little empty church. "Who, the one they trucified?" and she looked at me in surprise.

"No," she whispered after a second, "the one who dances in heaven."

"Who dances in heaven, Nicole?"

"He dances through veils of air, Estelle. He dances to set right what we do to our bodies down here on earth."

"What do we do to our bodies, Nicole?"

"Sweet Estelle, you couldn't know, you'll never know, horrible things . . . But he dances for us, he straightens twisted arms and bent legs, oh, if only you could see him dance, he wipes away all ugliness and all pain."

"Could I see him, Nicole? I'd like to see him."

"You can't, Estelle, you don't know what pain and ugliness are."

"Yes I do, Nicole, I do."

And Nicole looked at me with her child's eyes and whispered:

"What do you know, Estelle?"

"It's because of Tiresia. He dances for Tiresia's body, and so do you, but you can't do it right, that's why you come here . . ."

Nicole's eyes opened wide, and in them rose the hugely astonished frightened look she sometimes wore. Softer than ever, she whispered:

"Oh, Estelle, where do you get such ideas, who's been talking to you?"

And suddenly her alarm troubled me and I no longer clearly understood what I had meant; I felt ashamed. Nicole and I fell silent in the silent church and sat without stirring a muscle, sat long enough for our finger joints to stiffen, for it was cold in the church. I was not surprised that Nicole should come to this place where nothing happened, where nobody stirred, where we were numb with cold. I probably believed that it was a place where you were supposed to whisper, and that was why we went there: to tell each other things that could only be whispered.

I liked going to church with Nicole because it was the only place where she spoke to me alone, in a whisper so low it could belong either to speech or to silence, depending on infinitesimal shifts in the breezes that blew in upon us from unknown lands. And that whisper that might or might not have existed fit our lives, fit something in our lives, something I perceived without knowing what it was.

"Nicole, have you seen him?"

"Listen, my sweet Estelle, you remember the sky on summer nights when it's so pure it really doesn't have any more color, it's just transparency, you remember that?"

"Yes, Nicole."

"You're sure?"

"I'm sure, Nicole. When the bats come out they seem to be slicing that transparency to pieces."

Those summertime bats in our garden, flitting so swiftly in the evening air, stitching erratic angles at once swallowed by the sky . . .

"Yes, that's it," said Nicole. "Well, that's him, the sky — that's him dancing, all of him."

And I heard a few more snatches:

". . . nothing damaged . . . nothing broken . . . fluid . . ."

In the garage built onto our house, Nicole had hung a pale blue fabric on the walls, sky blue, and to that sky in our garage she offered herself, all of herself, a small sacrificial bat longing to wear angel's wings.

One day we went into the church while Dan was with us. I was carrying him as I always did. Nicole allowed us to caress her, but she sought no contact with our bodies.

We all three sat down in the same pew, one of the rear pews, perhaps the rearmost one; there were not many of them, in any case. Dan was contented, handsome. Nicole and I resumed our whispering.

"I'd like to see him, Nicole, the invisible one."

I was insistent that day, my voice whining and sulky. I believe that the girls at school had spoken of the church; they said they had seen things there that I knew nothing of, in splendid raiment — the Virgin, the saints. I wanted Nicole to show them to me, I heard the stupidity in my voice, but I was a child, just a little girl, after all, and that day I was unable to nestle into Nicole's confidence, that intimacy with her that only really established itself in church (my dancing in the garage was never satisfactory) and that I so badly wanted, intimacy with my mother.

"Nicole, I'd like to see him, have you seen him?"

I did not want to hear about the transparency of the sky on summer evenings!

She gave me a strange look, oh, I knew that look too, and suddenly she leaned toward me and said, still very low but it seemed to me she shouted:

"Yes, Estelle, I most certainly have."

"Where?"

"In New York, that's where, Estelle, he was tall and slender and brown, he danced as I have never seen anyone dance . . ."

"What did he look like, Nicole?"

She directed that strange look at me, a look that invited secrecy between her and me, secrecy of which I had no knowledge. That "other" look of Nicole's bound me terribly to her, and at the same time established a painful distance between us.

I could not untangle all these things. I sought to drink of Nicole, of weak Nicole, who did not herself know whereof to drink. Only today do I truly think of her, truly see her.

Last night (Phil came to get me, and we slept at his place) I woke up shouting "Nicole!" I wanted so much to see her, to lend her my life and strength now that I have enough and to spare.

How I must have weighed on her, following her everywhere, spying on her, trying to touch her hair and her skin. Nicole was so supple and silky, and I was an avid and disturbed little girl. Now she is dead, and last night I felt her pass like a spark close by me. I woke, violently longing to take her in my arms, to rock her, to tell her all I knew and to tell her that none of it mattered, that I loved her, I adored her, that I would devote all the time I could to her, that her old age would be as spoiled as the most wonderful of childhoods.

I shouted "Nicole!" Phil turned over. "What?" he mumbled.

My heart beating violently, I braced myself against this flood of regrets. It was quite out of the question for Phil to dive after me into that abyss, or even to notice it, out of the question for the word "nightmare" to be uttered. I did not reply and he went back to sleep. That is how Phil is. The hurricane howls past just by him, but he hears only a slight rustle; and ignored, despised, the hurricane itself becomes that slight rustle.

I listened to him breathing for a long time. Then I relaxed. The sounds of night traffic came in from the street. How city noise has changed for me. For ages, the smallest engine purr, the sound of a passing motorbike, the distant rumble of traffic on a main road, would pitch me into wakefulness. Phil lives on a boulevard by one of the city gates: trucks run up and down it day and night; his apartment windows are not double glazed. My first times with him I felt that trucks were coming right into our bedroom. I could not believe in a life led in such uproar. "You're right," Phil said placidly, "it's noisy," and I felt as if I had landed on a planet inhabited by beings of another species. I averted my gaze so that he would not see the fixity of my stare.

Now the roar of trucks lulls me. It is part of the city I live in and sleep in, sprawled at my ease on one of the numberless cliff ledges that perch over its pumping arteries, sprawled next to the man with whom I make love, listening to the river flow by with its familiar fits and starts, and I grow quiet.

That sound, and Phil's breathing, little by little drew me out of my dream, drew me along like a strong steady current; I found my footing again in this life of today. Oh, Nicole, my little Nicole, my little mother, go back to your grave, I am not forgetting you. Sometimes it seems to me that I am at last becoming your real daughter, and on days when Dan pulls back from me a little, I feel that it is for you I want to write this opera — to celebrate you, Nicole, small innocent mad mother.

I will seek out a dancer for you, the very best. I will persuade her, and her dance will be yours, the one that you sought all your short life and that I will finally have found for you. Return to your grave, Nicole. I will bring you the dancer you wanted to become, I will give her to you, sleep soundly, Nicole, soon I will come and call you in our little municipal cemetery slumbering at the end of its empty small-town road; you will be able to leave limbo and spread yourself out in the body of a world-famous dancer brought here specially for you from the greatest city in the world, the city that rejected and humiliated you. You shall be yourself at long last; you will have your revenge, my pretty little mother, our little mother with the sky-blue slippers.

It was almost dawn when I awoke aching to see you, and then I could not go back to sleep. I tingled all over with the need to leap out of bed, to return to these pages of notes I am scribbling, notes that at this moment are Nicole's story. She called to me in my post-coital sleep and I was revisited by this burning urge to give Nicole the dance she had never been able to create herself, to give her the wings she dreamed of so that she might finally soar aloft.

This is not how it would happen if I were a writer, madame. My story would follow a clear plan, my characters would be ready and filed neatly away in their folders until needed, and I would not have to pour words into the chapter frames, all pegged out and cordoned off. But I have no characters, just the creatures of my love, so the growth taking place is beyond my control. Sometimes for days on end it is dormant, and then, in the middle of the night or at dawn, I feel it move again, then memories take shape and I harvest what I can of these short-lived fruit.

But where to record them once harvested? Your lover's bed is scarcely the place. And when at last I can try to set the harvest on paper, madame, in words, it has evaporated. Or turned into something else. I am not a writer — oh, how I need you, madame.

Dawn glowed dimly through the bedroom curtains. It was a Sunday morning. "At last we can sleep without that goddamn alarm going off, a morning in bed with you, Claire, how about the whole day?" Phil had said over the phone. For one reason or another we had been obliged to skip several Sunday mornings running. "It's weird, I never used to look forward to my day off like this, I must be getting old, what about you?" He laughed, but I could not answer.

It was Sunday morning and he got up; strong back, strong voice. "Don't you move, Claire, I'm going to get croissants, no, please, don't move, then I'll make breakfast and bring it to you in bed." He was back, already dressed. "Then I'll play with you." He came back again from the door: "Wait for me, okay?"

I waited, forcing myself to fix in my head that scene in the church that had returned to me. And later, when we made love again, after breakfast in bed, I was unable to take my leave of you, Nicole.

I did what I had never done with Dan: without drawing attention to it, I kept my distance from my own body. I manage very well to do such things these days, that is how it is, no doubt Phil does it too, unwittingly perhaps. I shall not try to ask him; it is enough for our bodies to be close, and for me to hear his calm voice say as we separate: "I'll call you this evening." "Yes, call me," I say; it is enough, and I manage.

I too am becoming one of those beings of another species on this unknown planet.

In the church I said to Nicole:

"What did he look like?"

She still wore that "other" look. Her eyes had fallen on Dan, who lay in my arms, contented and handsome like the son of a Madonna, and suddenly she said:

"He looked like Dan."

And she pushed herself against the back of her pew as if she had just shed a heavy burden.

I heard her breathe out noisily, then take a long inward breath. Suddenly she turned toward us with her laughing face and that rare, merry spontaneity that used to drive us mad with joy:

"My little darlings, it's so boring here, let's go and eat pastries at the bakery."

FIFTY-FIVE

Setting a Trap for Death

I WENT to find the Superior. "Look, my room is too big," I said to her, "the view is too beautiful, there's too much light, give me another room."

"You don't like your room?"

"You don't understand, it's too big, the view's too beautiful, there's too much light."

I had learned those three points by heart, so fearful was I of being unable to find the right words when I spoke to the Superior.

"It is the one we give our visitors. There are two others, but they are right next to it, I don't see the difference . . ."

"I want to obey, I want to do as you wish in everything, just make the conditions right . . ."

"The conditions?"

"I have to be able to pray, all the time . . . If I can pray all will be well, you'll hear no more from me, I'll do everything you do."

"Very well," said the Mother in that placid practical voice that hurt me because it led toward life, "where do you think you could pray?"

"I saw windows looking out onto the little garden of silence. Give me a room there, I don't want to see anything more of the outside, oh, Sister, I have so little time left for praying, you know it, so little time . . ."

Those words, those words coming to me . . .

"But," said the Superior, "there are no rooms over the square garden."

"I saw them."

"I know you can see through walls," said the Superior, "but there are no rooms over the square garden."

Something in my face then. About to rise, the Superior sat back down. Then she began to laugh:

"You mean the troglodyte cells?"

"I don't know."

"We call them that because they are in the part of the building that was dug out of the hillside, how on earth did you stumble onto them? But you know, they're terrible, we no longer use them."

"Give me one, I'll fix it up myself, and once I've prayed a little, just for a few days, I'll go back with the others."

"Very well," said the Superior.

Laughter lingered in her voice, the memory of those troglodyte cells.

"Very well," she said.

Problem solved. Problem to one side, solution to the other, the two together (despite the incongruity) equaled problem solved. Therefore no more incongruity.

I had intercepted her on her return from a series of expeditions into town in the Citroën. She still had her flat shoes on and her raincoat, plain, no frills. It reminded me of the clothes worn by the mothers in our town, the mothers who were not Nicole.

"What is it?"

"Your raincoat . . ."

"What?" said the Superior in surprise.

"It looks like those the women wore . . . in the town."

"How else am I going to drive our little car? In a habit? I bought it at Dames de France, and I'm very pleased with it."

And she laughed again, patting the raincoat proudly. How old could the Superior have been? Not much older than myself and there was not a shadow on her face. Surely the sisters had elected her for her cheerful and practical nature.

"But I'm glad that you talk to me a little of trivial things, clothes, perhaps you miss yours; you were wearing a very fine suit when you arrived here . . . I saw it, you know!"

Sister Theologian was dangerous because she wanted my soul. But Mother Superior was even more dangerous because it was equilibrium, not the soul, that interested her: "We need balanced women in the community . . ."

With a last laugh she added, "And don't forget, we're not Trappists here," waving me away with one hand and rearranging her veil with the other.

Still concerned for my equilibrium, no doubt, the Superior one day sent me to the kitchens to wash the dishes. I lost my way and came out in a corridor different from the others. It reminded me of an old attic.

The floorboards were unpolished and dust-colored; the walls too seemed dust-colored, and so did the regularly spaced doors, doors you guessed led into deserted, forgotten rooms. The convent must once have known more opulent days when all its cells were occupied. Then it had lost its older nuns, who had gone one by one to the little cemetery on the grassy slope along the outer wall. There had been no replacements for them, and now this corridor served as a lumber area. On one windowsill were empty jam jars with faded labels. There were baskets piled up in a corner, and a broom that had lost its bristles.

But I had been wrong on one point: it was not the cells that overlooked the garden of silence, but the corridor. And I had been wrong on another point: there were no flagstones in that garden, as I thought I had seen that first day, but a lawn, a lawn! The cells themselves looked out onto the rear of the estate. The ground, sloping sharply at this spot, cut off the view from the rooms, but slope or no slope, there was a real farmyard out there, with chickens scraping around, with a barn where the nuns stored their harvest and put sheets out to dry, a fishpond full of vigorously swimming fish, the gardener's toolshed . . .

And all that was more frightening than the postcard view from my first room. They were far from being troglodytic, those cells! There were cats too. Cats can't be kept out. I was amazed.

"Our founder did not believe in excessive mortification . . ." Was there not one real cell in this vast mass of buildings? No, there would be no such thing. "Our founder" would not have held with one nun differing in any way from the others. That would have been the sin of pride. The sin of pride! What were my own sins? Dissembling was the least of them. And the worst was sin against God's order. On his right the living, on his left the dead, and never the twain shall meet. Look at each other, yes, some will be permitted to do that, rarely, in specific circumstances, but no mixing, never any crisscrossing between the two groups. But I knew that if I managed to look I would also cross that line. I had already managed to cross over into this convent. From there I would certainly be able to push even deeper. Perhaps I should have chosen a stricter religious order. But it would never have accepted me, would have seen through my dissembling at once. "Our founder" had been willing to accept sick or handicapped women. I had been taken in as one of that category, clinging hidden beneath the bellies of these enfeebled sheep. So "no excessive mortification." And therefore no cell. But where there were cells — real, mortifying cells — I would not have been accepted.

I wept with bitterness as one by one I opened the doors of those excessively bright rooms.

But one of them, the fifth, looked gloomier. Its window seemed to be sealed shut. I went in, and saw that the window merely looked out on a wall of the barn. This was something "our founder" had not foreseen!

You could see neither chickens nor laundry nor harvest nor any of the sisters whose chores took them out there. You could not see the mountains or the sky above, the sky that reflects every living human mood, so much so that you cannot look at it without thinking of those manifold moods of the living, without being seized by regrets, fears, hopes, dreams, exultation — oh, there are too many things in the sky. It has clouds in strange shapes, and in those shapes can be seen every shape on earth, as well as all the once elusive shapes that wander in the mind. It has the sun, the moon, every shade of color and, worse, every degree of shade and light, as variegated as the soul's fluctuating intensities. It has wind, lightning, airplanes, smoke, and on top of all that it reflects all the memories of all the living scurrying along the tangled pathways of their fates beneath its gaze. Who can raise eyes to heaven without seeing one moment or another of his life? And so it goes, ad nauseam, for all the living who have ever existed. But those who are dead are in the ground, and the sky no longer sees them.

I would find only memories in the sky and I wanted no memories. I wanted my brother, I wanted no cell open to the sky, I wanted a cell without light, without a view. Neither would I find my brother in equilibrium ("We need balanced women in the community," the Superior said again, looking placidly at me, yes, Mother, but your community can go hang itself). It was not through equilibrium that I would bring my brother back but through the sharpest possible concentration of my being, it was down that narrow path that I would seek him. It would require enormous concentration, funneled into the narrowest of tunnels, to find him in the kingdom of the dead and draw him back in to me. A racing lightning bolt, then the sucking force of a tornado. There were no other possibilities open to me, and for that to happen I had to eliminate heaven and earth and the living, I had to erect about me that barrier of white words, of lunar faces, of shapes in scapulars, and of walls and walls.

To reach the kitchen I hugged the refectory wall. Once there I began to pluck the nuns' humble dinnerware from the big scalding sink.

But my fingers were still too sensitive and the water blistered them, so I was given a skimmer. With it I fished out the plates that lay at the bottom like strange flatfish; I drew them to the surface and as soon as their round backs appeared I caught them and set them down after a couple of wipes with a cloth. Then I rubbed them and rubbed them before piling them one on top of the other.

Steam formed on the old leaded panes, quickly shutting off the outside world — farmyard, chickens, laundry, the cat perched on the sill. Then they were gone, and my eyes rested on the misted panes.

*   *   *

If I kept my eyes lowered I sooner or later saw the nuns' feet.

Some were in sandals, bare, and those had a shape: they were the feet of the living, and I had no wish to see them. Some were in street shoes, with little heels, even, and those shoes too had a shape: they had been chosen in stores, stores in the town; so the nuns went into town, they chose shoes, they were alive, all too alive.

It was better to direct your gaze a little higher. They wore uniforms, the scapular, of course, but they also wore aprons for dishwashing, nylon aprons, denim aprons with a zip fastener in front, waffled plastic aprons, printed aprons. Who had stitched them, chosen them, provided them? Living people, more living people. Do not look at the shoes, Estelle, do not look at the aprons, direct your gaze still higher . . . But higher up were the faces.

In the kitchen the faces were too near.

And higher still, the veils.

The veils at least were all the same but not all were pinned to the head in the same way. Some exposed hair, brown or graying hair, with an implantation on the forehead. What was it like underneath? Clipped? The same style for everyone? Neck length or shorter?

Too many questions, and the sight of the hair of the living was unbearable to me.

The days went by and I saw that the veils themselves dissembled. There were long ones, such as I would have liked, long and black and voluminous; but there were also browns and beiges and whites. Some were short, very short, mere knotted kerchiefs. And they did not have identical folds. The veils too bore the mark of the living.

One morning I saw a young nun stooping over the bowed back of an old nun, arranging the folds of her veil with hands more talkative even than lips, attentive, expert hands, their movements no doubt bored and repetitive yet performing their task and taking interest in it, the undying interest you must have in order to carry a task to its conclusion, and which in any case is always present whenever the living are involved.

I averted my gaze, but hands were everywhere, how could I avoid seeing them?

In chapel hands came into their own. They were little domestic animals that carried psalters and turned pages, turned the pages of prayer books according to the hour, to the day, to the year. They were birds charged with bearing the pain and the praise of humans;

they rose swiftly, then abruptly checked their flight, falling back palms up, offering themselves like cats' bellies, and I watched intently to see whether the Great Manipulator's finger would come down and tickle them in the hollows of their little bellies, but they fell back and huddled tight together . . . What could they be holding so tight? The elusive fly of our nursery games? If I sneezed or spat or made a loud noise in this quiet chapel, would those hands open and each release a fly, release a cloud of flies to billow upward in the middle of the chapel? But there was no fly in my hands. I must not look at those hands!

But there would be worse, much worse, there would be Sister Theologian's hands, and after that, eyes, voices, no, please, no . . .

The dishes, yes, that was my job after every meal. In one of their books I read, "Offer up the humblest of tasks, offer up your vexations and your pain." Was it thus that things worked for them? They made an offering and they received, but what did they receive and what must I do to receive my brother? I had to watch them, follow their example; if they were there it was because they had found what they were seeking. One of the nuns turned suddenly to me, a warm smile on her face. "We can speak now," she said, pointing to the misted-over clock above us. "Our founder" had not wanted excessive mortification; the nuns had taken a vow of silence but there were moments of recreation. I lowered my eyes, what could I say?

"That was a lot of dishes!"

"Yes," said the nun delightedly, wiping her hands on her apron, "a real community-size dishwashing."

Another nun appeared, bearing on a tray the dirty dishes of nuns too old or too sick to come down to the refectory. After the main washing up the second washing up invariably followed. I took up skimmer and cloth again, and the nun did something unusual: she broke off her bustling activity and leaned against the edge of the sink.

"Washing thirty people's dishes, all these big dishes all week long!" she sighed. "You need great virtue to do it all week long."

Then her voice grew light and cheerful again:

"Not all week long, really! Since Vatican Two we get a day off, one day a week when we don't have to be in the kitchen."

I kept my eyes on the wall, where a forest of ladles, draining racks, knives, everything that had a handle and a hook, hung from a horizontal wooden bar. I too hung from that bar.

That long speech by the nun . . . all those words, all those things belonging to the living: "virtue, Vatican Two, one day a week . . ." I did not want to know of such things, enormous, weighty speech, few words but each word like a yoke of oxen dragging an endless string of wagons all loaded to the brim, the world's tumbrels, war and resistance, strikes, hunger strikes, demands, prisons, feminism, Muslim fundamentalism, racism, war, my face puckered . . . And now another nun poured a bucket of clean water over the big flat stone, hollowed in the center, where we washed the biggest receptacles. I wanted to redirect the nun's speech toward that broad stone, so that her words could be sluiced clean by the torrent of fresh water falling from the bucket, so that they could be washed down the drain and be gobbled up and digested in the gizzards and stomachs of the chickens rooting about outside.

Let silence come back to surround me like a wall, oh, my sisters, do not disturb me for I must think of the one who is dead. In the corridor outside your cells I saw these words written on a piece of paper you have carefully framed:

"In order to respect everyone's prayers, please keep absolute silence in the corridor and the rooms."

Could you not see that I prayed everywhere, that I must not be disturbed, that for me there was no "recreation," no "community moment," as you call that hour when you chatter like magpies to one another in the big reception room looking onto the recreation garden? No time and no place not set aside for prayer, since I have not yet found the one I seek.

My sisters, give me your silence, give me your clothes that are all the same and your faces like moons, and your words like bricks all from the same wall and your movements like cement from that wall. Let life not enter, let all openings be sealed, let life not enter so that death may draw near. Oh, my sisters, make not the smallest of life's sounds, for death is ferocious and I must tame it. I must catch it one day in one of these dusty corridors, I must trap it here, in this place it will have mistaken for a grave. Once it lets itself be lured here I will leap on it and never let go until it shows me what it has taken from me.

Others have done so, oh, my sisters. I have read it in your book, the priceless book you read from every day. And that is why I am here. Let me build a tomb here in order to spring my trap on death.

FIFTY-SIX

Who's Walking
Around Up There?

THE night hours.

There were no night services here. "Our founder did not want them," the Superior told me. "He wanted the weak and the sick to be able to enter this order."

How sorely I missed those night prayers. The hours were empty and worrying. What could be done with that reclining body? I was bereft of ideas for its employment. One reason I had come to this convent was so that someone other than me would find this body something to do, drive it hour by hour to perform tasks that did not require my participation, tasks unlike anything I had ever known. I had brought my body here to have it subjected to a schedule, to be deprived of time for memory and pain. But the night hours?

I could not seek my brother at night.

The convent was utterly still. What were the nuns doing? Once or twice I got up to go to the toilets the Superior had shown me that first day. There were no toilets near the troglodyte cells ("They were built before Vatican Two," they reminded me): in other words, they were prehistoric caves, but I must not think of caves either. I rose, the floorboards creaked, and in my clumsiness I let go of the door, which worked with a small bolt. To prevent it slamming noisily shut, I caught it and slid the bolt into its hole, but it squeaked. Then came the glass-paned doors, three on the left for the showers, one on the right for the toilet, a dripping sound there, most immodest in this silence, and again creaking floorboards. I looked down the long corridor; a small night-light glowed halfway down, then the end of the corridor was swallowed in darkness.

All the cell doors were closed, and the sisters inside were asleep. They did not seek the invisible being during the night, for they had already found him.

Found him once at least, and were now sleeping, sure they would find him again.

> *"Without seeing we love you,*
> *Without seeing we believe*
> *And we exult, o Lord.*
> *Sure that you will redeem us,*
> *We believe in you."*

I could not seek my brother alone at night in this convent. When the nuns slept, when I no longer saw their habits, their gait, their mannerisms, when services planted like stout sturdy columns in the succession of hours did not make of the day a kind of cathedral to serve as a foundation for our actions, I no longer believed in their world.

Around me there was nothing more than a silent convent delivered up to the anarchy of time, and in that convent I did not know what to do.

A sudden creaking in the ceiling of my cell. Who was walking around up there? Walking with agitated steps, in profound torment? Uneven steps, rapid, then slow, then once again hurried — and then suddenly nothing, silence.

It was not the first time I had heard those steps.

Night. Do not think. Lie rigid. And with rigid thoughts.

Then I was up, drenched in icy sweat, sweat welling everywhere, cold rivulets, all this cold welling terrifyingly from me. I had waited too long, I thought. I was wasting time, nothing was happening here, I had come to the wrong place. My idea had been a mistake, and all this time my brother was getting farther away. What would his body be like now? Soon everything about him would be irretrievable. I had to find another way, move faster. I had to cut him off at one bend or another in his long march into the depths of death's kingdom.

I stood there in that room. Outside were corridors and black stairways and a door locked every evening after vespers by the extern sister, and beyond were the high outer walls of the convent. I was trapped, I had put myself in this trap. The sweat continued to roll off me.

On the ceiling the sound of footsteps resumed, just above my cell. I climbed onto the table, I was almost high enough. "Please, come and help me!" I rapped gently on the ceiling and the noise stopped: someone was listening.

"My brother is dead, I have to leave!"

I was convinced that the man or woman walking up there had heard me, was kneeling.

"I thought I might find him here, but I was wrong."

I was whispering, I was not even sure the words emerged from my mouth, but the person was listening; the creaking had resumed but more discreetly, and as soon as I spoke it stopped.

"You, the one not sleeping up there, come and help me!

"Help, help!"

I strained my ears. The creaking faded rapidly away.

They were coming to get me. I lay down to wait.

I must have fallen asleep.

That was toward the middle of my stay at the convent. The nuns told me there were swallows nesting in the attic.

Soon I would stop hearing swallows.

I would sleep, exhausted by the long days. If I could not sleep I would go to the oratory or chapel and recite the prayers I had learned. Or rather I would read them in a small soft voice, read them and reread them, for I never managed to commit any of them to memory. Repeating them pushed back the fearful horror of time. Repetition was a sort of tapestry that you had to weave every day, and as soon as you stopped this tapestry at once unraveled. But the moment you resumed your weaving it was around you once again, solid and protective. It kept the demons at bay and allowed the mind to keep vigil for the one it sought.

FIFTY-SEVEN

Meeting in the Corridor

THERE are beings who have seen the unseeable.

I forgot all I read, all I was given to read, prayers passed my lips and at once evaporated, and my body retained nothing. It sought emptiness; it even thrust away memories of my brother. Memories would bring lamentation, and then consolation.

No lamentation. No consolation.

What my body wanted was to wander the corridors, mulish, stupid, stiff, head down, gaze fixed. I followed on its heels, trying to be as unobtrusive as possible.

Deep inside it were a few images, concealed, dark; it never touched them, but they were what kept it moving, in them it found the strength it needed to live this leaden existence.

The hay stood high in the field and the two trees were heavy with cherries. The farmers picked them, leaving a quarter of the harvest to the convent. The gooseberries too were ripe. Nuns judged to be of medium strength went out to them every day, while the feebler nuns took care of the limes. The gardener would pull branches down, and three bent old nuns, sitting in the shade on the benches, stripped the branches onto their carefully spread black aprons, tossing the fragrant leaves into big baskets.

I knew two of the three, the one who knocked at my door when it was time for services (even after I had stopped needing the reminder), and the one who ushered me to my place in chapel (even though I no longer needed her either). I recognized one by her slurred speech and the other by her shaky but authoritative gestures. But I never even saw their faces; to do so I would have had to stoop, and I never did. The third nun came from another convent that must have been shut down for want of nuns. "All dead," someone told me. I approached her, but she wanted nothing to do with me; and I recognized her only from her way of moving her neck to bring the veil even lower over her face. "Get away, get away from me," the veil said to me.

Nuns who had reached the end of their physical powers remained upstairs, some never leaving their beds. I did not know how many of them there were. "They are preparing for death," said the Superior, "they are brave." I saw their dirty dishes come down after the main dishwashing in the kitchen, and I washed and dried them. But something prevented me visiting them. My stubborn body held me back. Sister Beatrice went up there every morning, and every afternoon she went into town in the little rattling Citroën to visit those who were hospitalized. She gave me their news during our walks together. She would give me a sidelong look. No doubt she thought I was selfish, not a good addition to the community. But my stubbornness put her on her mettle. I was a tough bone for her young novice-mother teeth to handle.

I did not want to think about Sister Beatrice's feelings. I wished I had not noticed that prematurely-old-mouse look on her face and the smile that could at any moment restore childhood to it. Too withered and suddenly too childlike, her lightning-swift swings unsettled me, unseated the fixity of my gaze — and then it was too late, her face had entered me and I was obliged to see her. It was the same with her hands: they had a life of their own; they were mobile, tactile, erectile, constantly on the move, reeling off whole speeches all the more voluble for their utter soundlessness. While Beatrice's mouth expressed itself moderately and confidently, her hands went on a far-ranging walkabout, darting to her temples and her robe, lunging skyward, pointing fanatically in a direction no one looked in, her index finger curling and uncurling like a creature from some other domain, her middle finger outstretched with the imperiousness of a master of empire, and her wrist sometimes trembling, all the fingers crumpling shut like pitiful little leaves. Full of murdered passions, those hands had a voice — and since that voice did not speak, it reached me; I was forced to look. As for the whole woman — the small sly convent dweller, the artful dodger of this community — for me she had first of all been the novice mother, then Sister Theologian, and now she was Beatrice. I wished I did not know her name and did not have to utter it.

Luckily a new postulant arrived, a girl of twenty, active in face and body, a trained athlete, and beautiful. But this girl threw herself into the religious life with the same concrete fervor she had apparently brought to top-level competition. Soon Sister Beatrice resumed her daily walks with me in the avenue under the poplars. What did it matter, my body was still farther gone in dull indifference; and with its help I would yield up to Sister Beatrice only what I wanted to.

The cherries were picked by the farmers, the gooseberries by the moderately strong nuns, and the lime leaves by the weaker ones. But there was still the hay to be gotten in.

There were still scythes to be swung under the sun, fences to be rebuilt, posts dug up and replanted, stones removed. Only the young postulant and Sister Marie-Marthe and I were strong enough. The postulant had to study a lot. So Sister Marie-Marthe and I met every day in the shed, where we kept our work clothes.

She pulled on old jeans under her robe, took off the robe, and put on an old gardening jacket. A short veil for her hair, big boots for her feet. I did the same. We were both strong. "No more eczema," said Marie-Marthe, glancing at my bare arms as she pushed out into mid-field with her scythe on her shoulder.

It was hot. We dripped sweat. Marie-Marthe removed the veil from her hair and took off her gardener's jacket. She wore a T-shirt and her breasts wobbled under it, firm and round.

Sister Marie-Marthe had a story too, and she would tell it to me: ten brothers and sisters, computer studies — "And to think that here I'm in charge of gardening, I've sent away for books, I'm crazy about gardening, I swear it, I'm crazy about it." "More than computers?" "No comparison, that was death, this is life." Not a tremor on her hale features, her strong arms vigorously scything. How lucky I was that Sister Marie-Marthe was not Sister Beatrice. Her eyes never sought me out. "Ridiculous to go haying in a gown and veil," she said, "I don't give a damn what the Curia says, they're a bunch of old woman haters." But she was not looking for my opinion. And the second the bell rang for services she picked up her veil and hurried over to the shed to change. Even her tan seemed to disappear, and in the chapel her face, like all the other faces, would look like a pale moon against a black moorland.

"Sister Beatrice has the faith of growing grass, and Sister Marie-Marthe the faith of stones," the Superior told me one day in her placid voice, but I thought I detected a proposal behind her cordial manner. Here are two possible paths, she was saying, which one would suit you? And I grew fearful at the thought of grass that sows its seed without anyone knowing, of stones that can hit you full force in the temple. Luckily I rarely saw the Superior; she was always busy with something.

After Mass, during what they called the community hour — the recreation period that saw them all foregather in the big reception room, where there was a piano, a cassette player, checkers, embroidery, armchairs — I would go back to the orchard shed.

Amid smells of earth, of dust, of fruit turned sour, I came to find the only nun who could help me.

This nun was no longer there. She died in 1923, and must have been a shy and backward woman. Her life was painful — but she had seen what she wanted to see. Her name was Sister Josepha.

I did not find the book that told of her visions in the community library, or in Sister Beatrice's library, or in the Superior's office, or on the oratory shelves.

I found it while cleaning out the shed, behind a heap of desk drawers. It was dirty and partly torn: perhaps the pages had been used to paper the bottom of a fruit basket, a gooseberry basket, because gooseberries stain. And there were red stains on the remaining pages.

It was the only book I read for myself. I read everything Sister Beatrice gave me, but I did it for her, out of cunning. And of all those books of hers I kept only the pulp, spitting out the juice so that it should neither enter nor nourish me.

But Sister Josepha's book was not really a book. It was only a word, just one. Its sentences existed only to bear that one word, and that word was "seeing."

Through that jumble of pious images and naive statuary and imbecilic commentary, through masses of gossipy and bigoted nonsense, I was seeking one single word, "seeing." And I was glad that the language of the book was stupid, its scenery rudimentary, its characters unlikable, and Josepha herself bent and shriveled — for they were merely undergrowth to be pushed aside. Working in the fields had hardened me to this kind of task: a clean sweep of the scythe, whole armfuls of grass at a time, roots, one step after the other, back bent, harsh sun . . . My stubborn mind moved effortlessly in the crudely daubed spaces of that pathetic book, with no worthwhile obstacle between it and the word it sought: "seeing."

If they had asked me: "What do you know of beings who have seen the unseeable?" I would have had nothing to say. The mystics, no, I had never been able to read them. Underhandedly, perhaps, just to test me, Sister Beatrice had given me Saint Teresa of Avila and Saint John of the Cross and Catherine Emmerich to read, and one day there was a book lying about in the oratory, a paperback, you couldn't miss it. It was *Portrait of Marthe Robin*.

Teresa wearied me: there were too many people around her, too much busyness. John's metaphors I slid over; the book on Catherine first discussed her childhood and was too long, and the problems arising from Marthe's simple existence did not interest me. Was it true that she could neither drink nor eat nor receive light nor move her legs and yet lived and counseled people in a voice that was gentle and enthralling?

My brother neither drank nor ate nor saw the light, but he did not live and I did not hear his voice.

"What do you know of beings who have seen the unseeable?" Perhaps I would have uttered (with a slow and heavy tongue) the following words: "The meeting in the corridor." And if I had been asked, "What do you mean by that?" my tongue would have cloven to my palate.

Truly I could only see: the picture of a black corridor and somewhere halfway down its length a radiance.

And this is how it happened to one of those beings who saw the unseeable, to Sister Josepha, a humble novice of the Feuillant Convent at Poitiers in the first half of the twentieth century.

She was at work in the laundry room when suddenly He appeared to her. But her work was urgent, and she asked Him to allow her to persevere at her task, at the same time asking His pardon for this liberty . . .

That night, as she went up to the fourth floor to close the windows, which were her responsibility, she continued to reiterate her love for Him on whom her thoughts were forever fixed.

"Suddenly, reaching the upstairs corridor" — she wrote — *"I saw Him approaching me from the other end."*

He was haloed in radiant light that bathed the long dark corridor; He walked swiftly, as if impatient to meet her.

"Where have you been?" He asked her.

"I have been closing the downstairs windows, Lord!"

"And where are you going?"

"To finish my task up here, Lord Jesus."

"Those are the wrong answers," He said to her.

"I did not understand what He meant. He went on:

" 'I come from Love and I go to Love. For whether you come up here or go downstairs, you are always in my Heart, which is the Fount of Love. I am with thee.'

"He disappeared, but He left me with a joy I cannot express."

This woman who had seen the unseeable saw it in a place like the one I had found. In convents the unseeable is sometimes seen. That was why I had come to a convent.

A convent is made of unmoving walls that enclose a space. Inside that space, if I were attentive, if my concentration were total, if I managed to master time, if my mind were empty enough, I would be able to summon up the unseeable.

I threaded my way through a forest of thorns, of hearts, of wounds, of arms, of little feet, of flowing blood and tears, swinging the scythe with great swinging swipes, Josepha, where do you see the one you see?

"As I climb to the fourth floor to close the windows . . ."
When, Josepha?
"As I sweep the stairs . . ."
As she sweeps the primitive flagstones of the ancient cloister of the
Feuillants . . .
And after that when, Josepha?
Later . . .
Where, later?
As she goes to get coal from the garden . . .
And where else?
". . . in the laundry, where I worked . . ."
". . . in the dormitory, where my cot was . . ."
In the dormitory, Josepha?
"I was in the dormitory making the children's beds . . ."

And in the oratory, at Mass, in the cell of some sainted woman or
other, in contemplation. But those places I avoided; she saw too
many things there that tired me, things that glittered, burned, kindled, spurted forth, too much hullabaloo for the one inexorably
sinking into death's dust.

Encountering Josepha on the stairs, in the garden, the laundry, at
her sweeping or darning or dishwashing, I stopped. They were like
clearings for me, places where my atrophied mind could rest. Josepha, what's happening in the attic? For that morning she was in the
attic, *"getting the laundry ready for the wash,"* she said, *"and since my
only wish is to be an instrument of repair, I simply asked Our Lord to
save as many souls as I had handkerchiefs to count . . ."*

What was Josepha talking about, why was she sometimes unwilling
to see Him, why did she pull back? She had told Him she was afraid,
she wanted to live an ordinary life; these visits of the One she so
loved frightened her, she felt unworthy, she feared the devil's tricks,
she was afraid of her community's disbelief. She struggled and then
gave up. And then once again she grew fearful: how had she been
able to doubt Him, who was she to refuse Him? Her body trembled,
her mind chastised itself; she longed to make good, and she offered
Him souls for the saving. As many souls as handkerchiefs. Handkerchiefs for souls. At the cost of her poor mortal suffering.

That was what I pieced together — with great effort and only after
several readings, for I did not understand and my head hurt.

I was no longer following Josepha; she spoke like everyone else
here, like Marie-Marthe or Beatrice or Madeleine. She was no longer
my sister and my brother's sister and I wanted to weep.

Josepha Menendez, modest Spanish seamstress, of modest origins, coadjutrix of the Society of the Sacred Heart, humble and self-effacing, believed herself the instrument of the salvation of souls, offered herself up in sacrifice, suffered terribly in her flesh, died in Poitiers at the age of thirty-three, still unknown today, still not canonized . . .

None of that mattered to me.

And neither did the transaction between Josepha and her love, the sufferings of the one compared with the sufferings of the other, with her carrying His cross to allow Him to rest, giving Him her own soul that He might save other souls, for *love is not loved*, that is what your lover said, *love is not loved*, yes, but the lover most certainly is loved. Poor Josepha, how I wish I could tear her from this book, poor sickly child with her fragile head, have her looked after, our Doctor Minor could have done it, let her see and let her love without sorrow among the daisies and buttercups of our meadow in the sun, yes, Minor could have done it, "Lies!" he had yelled, out there on the road. But Minor was dead; he could not help me or anyone else. Josepha had been offered love but no lover, and then that bitter transaction, with Him asking of her and with her agreeing, with Him saving souls and her helping Him, and the rebuffs, the bargaining, the hemming and hawing, all so complicated . . . I could not follow the tortuous course of their affair, I wanted to weep once again, I was alone.

"What on earth are you doing in the shed?" said Marie-Marthe in her big hearty voice.

Silhouetted against the light, she almost filled the doorway. So she could not make me out very well.

"I'm praying."

"But it stinks here — old dust and rats. Phew! How can you pray in here?"

"I'm coming."

Luckily Marie-Marthe was impatient. "We've had trouble with her," the Superior told me. "She's like a runaway horse." She did not wait for me; she was already on her way.

That's enough for today, Josepha, just one more sentence, though, no matter what page, chosen at random. " '*What consoled me today,'* He said, '*was that you did not leave me alone.*' "

I left to join Marie-Marthe, already in the upper field. I ran, scaring the chickens and making Madeleine-Marie with her basket of washing turn right around and stare. I climbed the mound and went past the fishpond with its darkly glowing scales, I was breathless and dripping but momentarily relieved, and in any case Sister Marie-Marthe was a volcano of activity, with grass and clods flying about her. There was a hole under the fence, she said, and something (but what?) was getting in. I did not listen.

I was here so that you would not be alone, my brother, and so that I could comfort you once I found you.

The one who had seen the unseeable saw it in a place like the one I had come to. In convents the unseeable is sometimes seen. So I stayed in the convent.

"Suddenly, reaching the upstairs corridor, I saw Him approaching me from the other end."

Here there were many corridors: the cloistered walkway around the garden of silence, spacious rectangular corridors on the upper floors, small obscure passageways connecting the main rooms.

I walked down those corridors where time did not exist, where nothing happened to stifle my resolve and the idea that my brother might be seen. I would walk for as many years as were needed, outside time, focused, empty.

Convent corridors. It was there I awaited my brother.

I needed the nuns to hold time around me, the way I wanted it.

At night, in their absence, I could do nothing. Memories came, pain and uncertainty attacked me. I heard the world all around going on its way — trains, planes, the sounds of distant cars, rain or storm. Time bogged me down, buried my resolve, and the idea that my brother might be seen grew wan: the rumble of trains, planes, and cars crushed the idea, tearing it apart, and it was as if I were being hacked to pieces, oh, how easily I could have gone mad during those nights. Time lunged snarling and tugging at me, and I fought back, determined not to be trapped in its machinery, for if it carried me away it would mean that I had forgotten my brother. I would have been dead. I needed the nuns so that I could believe in what held me here.

The nuns never spoke of the unseeable. Never in their own words. When they did, it was in coded speech. They drove before them a flock of docile sentences about what could not be seen. I liked to feel their discourse about me; it comforted me in my obstinacy but left me free to seek the one I wanted.

The nuns never spoke of what happens when you pray, whether alone or in concert. To each her own quest. I knew full well that they sought a man called Jesus. It did not bother me. What I knew above all else was that this man had been dead much longer than my brother. He died hundreds of years ago, yet people had seen him and went on seeing him.

Nicole said to me one day (I was a very young child and the three of us were sitting in the rear pew in the Church of Sainte-Marie-du-Marché, huddled close because it was cold), Nicole told me with a blush that she had seen that man. She had seen him in New York and he looked like Dan. Dan was in my arms and his face shone with beauty.

If Nicole had seen that unseeable being who died so long ago, and if that unseeable one looked like Dan, then I — so much more focused and determined than Nicole — should certainly manage to see Dan, who looked like that unseeable being but who had the advantage over him of being only very recently dead.

Such was the logic of my madness.

I see now that it was not madness. That my body had its wisdom, which it did not reveal to me. It had not brought me to this convent to show me a poor dead person, but to snuff out the last embers of my pain with the extinguisher of a long-dead time. That my mind could not know.

I sought my brother. Just to see him. Nothing else.

I needed the nuns to go on living in that madness.

But they had to go on being pieces of the building, rooms in the convent. I had to go on seeing their long robes and their veils in front of me like a wall — moving, of course, but a wall, the convent's mobile superstructure.

I wanted them in their nuns' habits, with their encrypted speech and their silence. I wanted their shuffling, discreet steps, I wanted their bent heads, the ritual of their hands, their genuflections, their chants, I wanted the uniforms hastening silently down the corridors, one behind the other, and the bowed veils, and the ritual of meals and services and schedules and seasons. And to cement all that I wanted the lines of the great book from which they read every day in their slow steady voices, that thread running through our time and holding it together, oh, how ready I was to perch upon it, to read it, recite it, chant it, anything, and immediately afterward I forgot.

And I was very willing to discuss it all with Sister Marie-Christophe — the dates, the translations, events, meanings, whatever . . . All that knowledge draping itself over me but never entering. I forgot or recalled it all at will. All that I wanted.

But the nuns could not come too close, not close enough for me to see their faces or know their past or learn their tastes, their whims, their characters. No individual history must be granted ingress to the magic place I strove to maintain for my brother's coming, no individual history with its own miasma, the working of time, life's decomposition and reconstitution. I did not want to hear them speak. I hated Vatican II for introducing something of life into this place, which I wanted to keep outside time.

Throughout my stay at the convent there would be this struggle to keep the nuns about me and to prevent them from drawing near.

My old intelligence had died with my brother, but from its corpse a seed of cunning had sprouted, bringing forth a tendril as lean, twisted, tough, as a weed. I had become cunning.

It was not my intelligence that spoke with Beatrice (I now knew that name, irreversibly) when we strolled through the grounds or in the cloisters around the silent garden, or sat in the novice common room or the little library-oratory that was her favorite place. It was not my intelligence that spoke with her, but my cunning.

Beatrice had taught philosophy in a private school. She was the one the nuns had delegated to sound me out, to help me, with the ultimate end either of keeping or rejecting me. I had known it at once; I had known she would be my worst enemy and my hardest fight.

If the Superior had taken me under her wing I would have been unable to struggle. She was too practical, too straightforward. But Beatrice was my age, and it was her first year as mistress of novices. I was her first quarry, and her mind was more on the hunt than on me. That was my great stroke of luck.

Her at least I would have to look in the face, to detach from the moving wall of uniformed nuns; I would have to watch her every shift of expression, and hear the special tones of her voice when she was not singing.

*   *   *

Beatrice was in the choir and also a soloist. All the beauty of the services came from her — but it was not there that she was my enemy.

When she sang she was my sister and helped me in my search. Her voice put me at the very center, where I wanted to be, and as I listened to her all my tension and concentration took shape again. Thanks to her pure steady haunting song, my tattered soul regrouped: tatters floated back to me from all sides and I hugged them tight about the tiny place from which I meant to call my brother, from which I meant to wrest him from death's kingdom.

Beatrice helped me and I revered her. She knew it. She had noticed my gaze directed steadily at her during services; she knew that I was her servant, that I followed her devotedly, abjectly, that I clung to her singing and waited to receive the flame of my faith from her.

But outside services I was her enemy, for she was mine. She did not know that my faith was not hers, that I sought to use her faith to make mine live, that I had come like a vampire to mantle their love with mine. All that I had to hide from her.

If Beatrice saw through me, they would sooner or later drive me away. I trembled simply at the thought. My work here was not over; I had a task to fulfill, and I would carry it through to the end, no matter where he was. I myself had no idea where, but my will was fierce and my cunning indomitable.

Beatrice was intelligent. She had not long worn the teaching veil, which had once been black but which since Vatican II was dark brown in this order. Her novitiate and provisional vows had been brief. Before that, she had taught "outside," as they put it — and she knew how people thought on the outside.

She came to meet me on what she thought was my own ground, on what would indeed have been my ground if I had come just to visit, to scout the territory, as she believed to be the case.

She would say "People often think that . . ." or "People on the outside imagine that . . ." And she would laugh at the people on the outside with their naive fears . . . but we know better, don't we, Estelle?

What was Beatrice saying? I walked beside her, not answering right away, for my thoughts were slow-moving, and I feared her. I feared having her on my territory, where I hid the brother I wanted to see again. I kept hidden behind me a tall young man with bronze-black hair. If Beatrice had asked, "Who is that behind you?" I would have said, "There's no one behind me, that's just my shadow." I was eternally afraid she would unmask me. *"Estelle, you are here for a broken heart, you don't enter a convent for a broken heart, you enter a convent because you are seeking . . ." "But I am seeking, Beatrice." "Yes, but you seek a man of flesh and blood with a firm and supple member to rub your flesh and hands to cup your breasts and shining gaze to make you believe in love's everlasting nature."* My knees knocked, I dreaded hearing those words, what could I have said? *"You too seek a man of flesh and blood, a man with a wound in his left side and a wound in each hand and drops of sweat on his forehead." "But that man is God, and we seek him for the rest of humankind."* I sweated with distress, what answer could I have made? *"It was your God who took him from me, if I can see my brother again then I will seek yours as well."*

"— To cut a long story short," concluded Beatrice, "we do not want the papal enclosure, we want the monastic enclosure. Which in fact is what we do have, as you have seen."

I nodded. And that was the end of that day's conversation. The sun dropped down toward the high enclosure wall. I had escaped the danger, and now I hastened back to chapel to hear Beatrice's pure soprano. Then I would go back down that darkened corridor on whose flagstones veiled shapes silently glided, to be swallowed one by one in the dark orifice of the stairs.

"Suddenly, reaching the upstairs corridor, I saw Him approaching me from the other end."

I walked and walked down those corridors.

It was daytime, and I approached the big window at the end. Beyond the panes a curtain of rain fell; I stared at it steadily, wearily, staring in hope and oblivion. Perhaps the curtain would part and my brother would give me a hurried sign and I would go and speak with him through the glass. He would tell me where he dwelt, what was happening with him, and when we would be able to talk again. It would be short, like a phone call all the way across the world with hissing rain in the background and the static of glass molecules, but I would know how things were with him and I would tell him what I was doing in this world of the living. I would tell him, oh, very, very quickly, about the gooseberries and the limes and it would make him smile, and he would tell me how to bring him back again. I would take careful note, and then it would be over, with the curtain of rain outside the window and its deafening patter, and I would return to my convent chores.

*   *   *

"He was haloed in radiant light that bathed the long dark corridor."

I walked down the corridor, the window at the end flaming in the setting sun. I had to shut my dazzled eyes, and suddenly my brother was there, the whole of him on my retina, smiling amid the dancing colored dots. "Keep your eyes shut, keep walking, say nothing, I managed to get away, listen quickly to what I have to tell you . . ."

"He walked swiftly, as if impatient to meet her."

I walked down the corridor. Someone approached from the far end and my heart began to pound. He walked swiftly, as if impatient to meet me; no nun walked like that. "Dan!" "Yes, Estelle, yes, you managed it, it's me . . ." His voice was rich and hot with excitement, and I kissed him madly. "Show me your room, Estelle." I led him to my cell, to my bed, and we pushed it against the wall. "Is it really you, Dan?" "You'll see if it's me, Estelle," his hand was between my thighs and he was making that very gentle rolling motion with his thumb, "First one side, then the other, remember, Estelle?" that delicate motion which reawakened my sleeping flesh, dispatching its small amorous emissaries . . . and later it was the same small motion, but with his tongue, and my flesh leapt and advanced on all fronts. "So, is it me or isn't it, Estelle?" And now I believed him and we were there on that bed, one inside the other, exchanging the thousand small things of our intimacy. "I no longer wash down there, Dan, and I don't wear perfume anymore." And he told me how it was where he came from, and I teased him about his glorious body, and he teased me about my religious body. All night long we exchanged these thousand small things of our intimacy, and I knew when and how we would meet again. I had not been wrong, I had come to the right place.

"Suddenly, reaching the upstairs corridor . . ."

I walked down the corridor, my head bowed. I had to go and close the windows, for it was night and winter was coming. I had been here so long I walked like the nuns. I no longer thought about anything except the windows to be closed, about dinner in a few minutes, and suddenly there was a gentle tug on my robe. I turned, and my brother was there, barely visible in the gloom. I took him in my arms to separate him completely from the shadows. He said nothing, I heard his heart beating hard, hard because his ribs were brittle and his flesh too sparse. "Carry me to your bed," he murmured, and I took him in my arms and carried him to my bed. Nobody saw us, and on my bed his strength returned. "It was the effort of getting here," he murmured. "You had stopped thinking of me; at that very moment I had found out how to reach you, but you were no longer thinking of me. What an effort it was, you remember what you used to say, it takes two to make a couple, but there was just me for the two of us." I wept, my body dissolving in my weeping, and my brother was horrified. "Don't weep, Estelle, my love," but the tears flowed despite me, my brother turned to shadow and I became a puddle of water.

I walked and walked down those corridors, and the seasons went by. I waited everywhere, all the time, but I still did not see my brother.

FIFTY-EIGHT

"They Were Planning to Kill Me"

SOMETHING happened.

Some time earlier I had returned to my old cell. The Superior had decided this. She gave no explanation and I asked for none.

There was no sound at night in the big central corridor. Yet I heard a soft hooting. You had to hear it with your head, for the silence was deep — but I heard it.

The nuns too must have heard it, for they sat up in their beds and were waiting. The hooting passed by outside their doors, and one by one they rose and slipped their feet onto the floor. They had not undressed the night before, and were still wearing their scapulars; only their feet were bare. They waited a little longer, then slipped out to their doors, their bare feet moving almost soundlessly. The doors all opened at once, with not a single creak, onto the dim-lit gallery, and then they formed ranks, with the Mother Superior directing them.

They were coming to kill me.

And for the first time I became aware of the isolation of this huge building, of the acres and acres of grounds around us, of the perimeter wall shutting those acres off from the highway. The town lay far below, and the only living things here were the fish with their thrusting fins in the pond and the numberless prowling cats and the chickens. Not an opening in the walls, except for the great portal, which the extern sister closed every night, and the gate at the back, which opened onto the fields.

Now they were quite close; I could feel them crowding a few feet from my cell. How could I have thought myself one of them, one of theirs? They had made mock of me from the start. They were tall, the Mother Superior the tallest of them all, and now they moved forward in one concerted gliding movement.

They were coming to kill me — why not? — no one would ever know, my body would go to the fish, the cats, the chickens, why not? . . . The Mother Superior had a knife, and I was frightened, horribly frightened.

"What is it?"

Phil had turned the light on.

"Claire, wake up."

He handed me a glass of water and pushed back my sweat-soaked hair.

"Well, now, well, now," he said.

I had had that nightmare toward the end of my stay at the convent; I thought I had forgotten it. The nuns had been huge, taller than the corridor they were walking in, but the ceiling had risen to accommodate them . . .

"Claire, don't go back to sleep!"

I said:

"They were planning to kill me. I couldn't find the door."

"Who was planning to kill you?"

"Women . . ."

"And the door?"

"What door?"

"Claire," said Phil, "there's something wrong here."

He rose and paced the bedroom. Underwear strewed the floor, delicate red lace articles and a few black ones, all items he had bought for me.

He walked about naked, worried-looking, without a glance at the underwear he liked so much yet taking care not to trample it. Deprived of its habitual resolve, his member, so often swollen, swung limply from thigh to thigh.

Despite myself I smiled, and my nightmare receded somewhat. How I loved Phil.

"What's the matter, Phil?"

"Just a second, Claire."

"It was only a nightmare."

"You have a lot of them; d'you think I haven't noticed?"

"Not all that many . . ."

"And something's just occurred to me, Claire. I'm a fool not to have thought of it earlier."

"Thought of what?"

On the contrary, it seemed to me that Phil thought of everything — shopping, fixing my bike, tickets for when we went out, even medication for the nausea that still sometimes swept over me (Alka-Seltzer, aspirin — dear sweet Phil, perhaps he was vaguely aware that there were other kinds of medicine and that there were people who took those other kinds of medicine, but I never showed him the medicine I kept in the inner pocket of my bag), and now here he was making coffee in the kitchen to comfort me.

We drank the coffee.

What did a cup of coffee matter in the middle of the night? I would take one of my secret pills, unobtrusively, and go back to sleep. Yes, what did it matter? As long as I finally reach you, madame.

"Now come and take a look, Claire."

He handed me one of his shirts and I slipped it on.

"There, look, that's the door I put back on its hinges because you asked me to. There's no one in the living room. There's the kitchen, the door's open, no one in there, no one in the bathroom either. And there, Claire?"

He pointed to the door I had never seen open.

"It's a closet," I said.

"No," said Phil.

He opened the door with a key.

Before us was a very cheerful little room, painted pink with wallpaper of long jungle vines on which little monkeys of all colors were swinging. A narrow bed of unpainted wood, and beside it a crib overflowing with dolls. A few tiny dresses on hangers below a white shelf from which the leaves of an enormous fern cascaded down (but it was not a fern, oh, my father, how alike we still are!), green, bursting with health, exuberant.

"I have a daughter. Her name is Liliane. She's six."
I was fascinated by the plant.
"How did you manage it?"
"Manage what?"
"This fern."
"The chlorophytum? I water it when you're not here."

Phil looked sulky. But his irritations did not worry me, had never worried me, were not directed at me. Oh, Phil, don't distress yourself, *"It all goes so much deeper, so much deeper,"* now the group of nuns had stopped dead in the dim convent corridor and in a delayed reaction I repeated "Liliane," and only then remembered that this vision of the nuns was but a memory, the memory of an old, absurd nightmare.

The nuns did not kill me. The next morning they were toiling away at their usual chores.

And at the convent I saw them more and more, saw them clearly.

Madeleine in the steaming kitchen, hands on hips, and her kindly smile as she said, "Now we can talk" —

Her twin sister Madeleine-Marie, who spread our coarse sheets on the beds as if they were priceless stoles and said delightedly, whatever the weather, "Another great big beautiful day" —

Marie-Marthe, an energetic worker in the fields and an ardent worshiper in chapel and who because of that energy and ardor could not help singing too loud . . . Appalled, the nuns all turned toward her, but she did not notice and picked up the refrain at the top of her voice . . . "A runaway horse," the Superior had said, indulgence stronger in her voice than irritation —

The Superior herself, chatting with her deputy in a low voice but with such animation that sometimes a hint of that beautiful voice echoed out alone in the silence of the refectory . . . And in any case she was always ready to break that silence: "My sisters, it gives me pleasure to tell you that today we received a letter from our dear sister who has left to celebrate her parents' golden wedding, she says she is well, that her grandnieces already attend catechism, that she misses us . . . My sisters, it gives me pleasure to tell you that today we receive a newcomer among us, her name is Estelle, I ask you to keep her in your thoughts during our prayers, even though, ahem, today is fruit-preserve day . . ."

(The novices were very familiar with their Superior's irrepressible gaiety, but they never took advantage of it, they laughed modestly and returned quickly to their silence) —

The Superior and her devotion to Beatrice: in a missal the latter lent me I found a sacred picture with the words "To the most angelic, the one who helped me through my dark hours, may you continue to show me the way, forever the most affectionate of your sisters," and signed with the Superior's first name, I was certain that Beatrice had deliberately left the picture for me to see, so that I who gave neither joy nor affection to the community should read its message of love —

And also the three bent-backed old women who had finally lowered their barriers after I broke the upper branches of the lime tree for them . . . One had been married, another almost, and the third had lost a child at an early age: those were the things they discussed under the lime tree, just like any old ladies in a tea shop — but with serenity and much humor, humor for which they always ended by asking forgiveness . . . my adorable old women to whom I listened as I sat perched in the lime tree —

And then Beatrice again, my sister and enemy, the one I loved and loathed in equal measure: her voice on the paths as we walked together, calculating, persuasive, and that same voice in chapel, so strange it made you shudder, a voice of heaven and earth at once, so moving it could convert a devil (but not being a devil, I could not be converted), my Sister Theologian with her small prematurely aged yet sometimes so wonderfully childlike face.

I saw them all, I saw them clearly; I had come here to see my brother, but they were the ones I saw.

Each in her own way caught my attention.

I wanted a brother, just one brother, and I had found sisters, a score of sisters. I did not know what that meant, whether I should laugh, whether that was how life went, whether that was the kind of thing that happened to survivors.

I have not written to them, madame. Through all my years of half life since leaving the convent I have never written to them. I have thought of it nearly every day but I could not, and finally it was they who wrote to me, by the hand of Beatrice . . .

"I could kick myself," said Phil. "How could I have imagined that you wouldn't see that door!"

"But . . ."

"That it wouldn't bother you!"

"But Phil . . ."

"There it is, I have a little girl."

"Yes, Phil."

"Her mother took her when she left. We weren't married. And the law says I have neither rights nor responsibilities concerning the child."

"Yes, Phil."

"She bears my name, I saw her being born, really being born, I mean, I raised her as a baby but I have neither rights nor responsibilities!"

"Yes, Phil."

"I kept it all hidden from you."

" . . ."

"God knows why."

" . . ."

"And caused you all these nightmares."

" . . ."

"She's only a small child, Claire, she wouldn't try to kill you."

" . . ."

"Maybe I wanted virgin territory for you, a pure intact space to offer you."

" . . ."

"I sensed you were from another world, I was scared."

" . . ."

"I have a child."

" . . ."

"So what do you say now, Claire?"

Somewhere in a dim-lit corridor at night the nuns were still tight-massed and jostling, and now this child Liliane had come forward in her little dress with its pale-flower pattern amid vines on which small colored monkeys swung, beneath the fronds of a large, very green plant full of vitality and exuberance, for years I have fought to find some thread in destiny, oh, Dan my brother, will it never end . . .

"Perhaps I made a mistake, a bad mistake," Phil said. *"I thought you were magic . . . but tonight I am invaded by troubled premonitions, what if I had been mistaken from start to finish, what if Minor were right . . ."* "Lies!" shouted Minor, bursting from the car . . . Oh, Father . . . *"I fear I have made a bad mistake . . ."* Father, do not distress yourself!

"You've been simple and straight," Phil said anxiously.
"Don't distress yourself, Phil."
"It goes so much deeper, so much deeper . . ."
"There's something else," he said.
"Let's sleep," I said.
"But there's something else."
"Later."
"Promise?"
"I promise, Phil."

I would meet the child Liliane a little later. She lived with her mother for three years; then her mother had gone off with a diplomat. The child became a nuisance and her father was allowed to take her back. That was what Phil wanted so desperately to tell me: that the child was coming back to his house, that he could no longer belong entirely to me; those were his words, madame. We went to get the child at the airport.

It was a Sunday. There was heavy traffic and a constant shifting from lane to lane on the beltway.

Phil was a good driver, without that excitability of Adrien's that used to scare me so much. Nor his aggressiveness. He gave way when you had to give way, he was no businessman, my Phil; he was happy when he began building a bridge and he was happy when he completed it, no matter whether the bridge was long or short. "Joining one shore to the other gives me a kick, that's all." He did not dream of plastering his name across the world, of soaring heavenward in glittering towers with his name blazoned in giant letters at the top, like the giant "Adrien N." sign, fluted gold letters on a brown background, fast approaching us on the highway (I turned around for a second look, but the child Liliane's curly head blocked my view). The beltway was our great causeway, the lion causeway to the fabled city; those illuminated billboards were the lions, and Adrien was among them, farewell, farewell again, Adrien, false brother, my sex trembled inside me.

What did it matter, tonight Phil and I would make love, we would caress, our hands would plot a bridge between two foreign bodies.

"I stand on one shore," Phil said one night, "and I look across, and then I feel something, an urge, the same as in love, to go looking for that opposite shore, as far away as if it were at the other end of time."

And my desire for him would start to travel across that bridge our hands had plotted, and our bodies would slowly feel their way to their marks, perhaps it was like driving piles between two shores.

"When a bridge is finished I go back there alone at night, I cross the barriers and go out to the middle, and the wind blows and the wetlands below glint dully, and I unzip my pants . . . Claire, you wouldn't believe how hard my penis springs out and then I ejaculate into space. They're my own private orgasms, I've never known anything calmer or more powerful, and when it's over I slump against the guardrail and that's it . . . My ambition stops with that bridge: it climbs, it crosses the gulf, and it comes down again on the other side. I'll never be rich, my little Clarinette, not like your friend Adrien N."

Phil liked underwear and we played for hours on end with those small frilly things, and little by little the two shores of our bodies drew near, unhurriedly, for the bridge was solid and would soon join the two shores. Our pleasure would travel at its ease, travel as far as it pleased, from one body to the other, and the only thing that could distract us now was the small noise of the child Liliane's footsteps. "I'm glad you got me to replace that door," Phil said with a blush, and with the brusque diffidence that had astonished me at the beginning of our encounter. "Now I'm going to put in a lock."

So went our love: no shattered bottles, no biting, no threats, none of the violent gestures that were the marks of your rage, Adrien, doubtless the same rage that splattered your name in giant letters along the beltway, the glittering causeway leading to the capital, the lion causeway.

On the lion causeway I thought of the men I had known. I have not described lovemaking with my brother to you, madame; it was a world you entered all in one piece and left all in one piece, a world that would not be broken down and itemized. Like beauty, it dazzled and overwhelmed and left no memory.

Phil liked panties that rode high on the hips, stockings that clung leechlike and unaided to the thighs; he also liked garter belts, which made a triangle on the belly and rectangles on the thighs, he liked the crescents bras dug into breasts, he liked the slight puckering of compressed flesh.

If beauty was what entered you in one piece and refused to be itemized, then beauty did not enter Phil. He could approach it only through flesh cutouts. The flesh of the living could not go to him naked in all its horror and splendor, for then he would have seen only a confused mass where his desire lost its way and consumed itself. No, he had to mark flesh out in squares, trace shorelines there, and from one shore to another he could throw bridges . . . From bridge to bridge his desire found its path, and I walked unhesitatingly with him down those paths, happy, always happy, for we were not brother and sister, we were not Dan and Estelle.

"Tell me a story," Liliane said suddenly.

It was late, the traffic was hardly moving, and the child was imperious, almost nasty. For a second I saw the glass case in the parlor where the nuns exhibited their shoddy needlework, the dusty little children's garments, permanently shut away from the fresh air.

"A story I don't know," said Liliane.

My heart was beating angrily.

I stole a look at Phil. He seemed absorbed by the traffic.

"Yes . . ."

"Well?"

"Once upon a time there was a girl . . ."

"And?"

"A very beautiful, very good girl. The fairies had given her good fingers and she played the piano very well. Echoes of her fame reached a young man who lived in a far country, and from then on, more than anything else in the world, he wanted to meet this girl whose music so charmed him. One day the girl gave a concert. The young man bought a seat in the front row and when the girl came onstage the young man knew that he not only loved her music but he loved the musician as well."

"Yes," the child broke in, "because he could see her clearly from his seat. But how could she see him?"

"Because he wore a uniform."

"A prince's uniform?"

"An air force pilot's uniform. The girl saw this young man watching her from the front row of the stalls and she played better than she had ever played. They got married and had a little daughter. They called the little girl Estelle. Estelle means star. They thought fate had set a star in heaven above them to protect them. People who love each other very much sometimes believe that, and that was why they gave their little girl that name."

"But what if it had been a boy?" said Liliane.

"Then they'd have picked another name, just as nice, but wait, there's a little boy in this story too."

"Estelle's so lucky," the child sighed. "She has a little brother."

"How do you know it's her brother?" said Phil, who had been listening for some time.

"Because I want one."

"One what?"

"A brother."

This did not happen the day she arrived, of course, but on one of the weekends we spent in the country, for we spent weekends in the country because of the child. She wanted to go on trips, she wanted a dog, or a cat or fish, she wanted a bike, she wanted a brother — it went on and on, Dan, she never stopped, and I had come back to everyday life just to find you, the way people seek and find the departed in life. I wanted to be in life, Dan, in order to be able in my turn to sift through the departed, and I had hoped somehow that Phil would make life stand still around me, would hold it at bay while I pondered what to do. And now here was the child Liliane, who wanted stories, who liked trips and fun; soon she stopped being spiteful the way she had been at the beginning, *I must hurry, I must find you very soon, madame, for the child Liliane is infinitely resourceful . . .*

A few days ago I found her sitting on the floor by the little tape recorder I gave her the day she arrived. Madame, do you know what she was playing? She was playing the cassette Phil dropped in my mailbox early in our encounter. "A con job," I had called it — Phil had made copies of songs and I did not mind listening to them; I was ready to take whatever the now had to offer. I say "the now," madame, two ordinary little words, it took me so long to say them, the now, a time when there would be only me, when there would not be my brother . . . But I bowed my head and took what it offered, because my plan was to bring my brother into it, into the now, I needed just a little more time and knowledge to proceed and I would bring my brother into the now.

My plan has not changed, Dan, but I must move fast. I had listened once to Phil's cassette, then put it in Vlad's red wallet, and I put the red wallet in my big bag, the one I carry everywhere with my scores and my papers and the little articles of makeup the child Liliane likes to take out to play with and I let her. But she had been after more than that, more than the powder compact she tirelessly snaps open and shut, although it is always exactly the same little click, and the lipstick she likes sliding back into its tube (but again it is the same little click when the stick reaches the end of the tube), and the two little clicking sounds make her laugh and she shakes her pretty red head, but they are not enough, even to a child's heart. And the child Liliane also seeks what would be enough for her heart.

She was a more tenacious seeker than I realized. She had secretly unearthed my cassette from the red wallet, and now, sitting all alone in the middle of the room, she watched me come in from under her beautiful child's hair, the wavy, glossy hair of the Madonnas, her features motionless, her eyes fixed on me and empty of expression. She was at once Madonna and Child from those countless old pictures, and for a second I felt I had within me the people who painted them and I heard a kind of noise, *it goes so much deeper, so much deeper, my God* — but at the very same time I saw that small hand on the volume knob, turning it up, turning it up to maximum volume, while those two small eyes continued to stare at me from beneath the red-gold waves, little tight waves frozen as still as the lashes over the eyes, as the breath caught behind the small pale lips.

> *The earth's a vacuum cleaner and it wants our bodies,*
> *   sucks them in, wills them in,*
> *And it wants you too, so don't give in but jump in the air,*
> *   jump in the air,*
> *We're all headed down for the dusty grave, little brother,*
> *   so jump in the air,*
> *If you're scared give me your hand,*
> *Little kangaroo, little sister, and jump in the air,*
> *Give it everything you have*
> *To escape that hungry grave,*
> *Jump in the air.*

Not long before I would have sought a meaning there, a coincidence, but I no longer have time. And now I have to hear that song every day, for the child Liliane has appropriated the cassette and also the red leather wallet, Vlad's pride, still almost new. Its gilt rings jingle when the child dances, for sometimes she forgets to spy on me from beneath the motionless tent of her hair. She leaps about and dances and yells, with the red wallet whirling at the end of its slender strap and her strong-calved little legs (Phil's legs) leaping with faith, with passion, around the tape recorder: "Give it everything you have / To escape that hungry grave, / Jump in the air . . ."

Driving home from the country along the beltway, she would fall asleep standing between the two front seats. I tried to stretch her out on the backseat, but she always straightened up again, half-asleep, and came back to stand upright in front. Oh, Dan, my love, how lost I was, we never had little children around us, you never had any and I had only you, and you were my love, what do you do with little children who are not your love, *"You and Dan seemed so little in need of a family — you always poked fun at our neighbors, at Adrien's brothers and cousins. . . . Strangely, it's only now that I wish for grandparents, cousins, what have you . . ."* Another story, said Liliane.

"Once upon a time there were three parents, three good and very loving parents, and they had two very beautiful children. The two children truly loved each other, but since they were brother and sister they could not get married."

"Couldn't have a baby," she gurgled, her thumb in her mouth.

"The brother died and the sister nearly died of despair."

"She's asleep," said Phil.

Miraculously there was a parking spot right in front of the building, between an overturned wastebasket and some empty florist's boxes. Phil got the child out and upstairs with a thousand precautions, laying her down in the bedroom with the little multicolored monkeys. The green plant seemed to have grown even taller, but it sat upon the shelf as if in a crouch, its long leaves looking like claws semi-sheathed in the green mass that hid the earthenware sides of the pot. I would really have to get used to plants, I told myself.

Suddenly the child called out. She had sat straight up in bed and was looking around like a little lost ghost.

"The story . . ."

"But it's late."

"The story."

I sat beside her in the semi-darkness.

"Once upon a time there were two children who truly loved each other . . ."

"The story."

"But they had an enemy called the Major, it was because of him."

"The story."

"Once upon a time there were two children who loved each other . . . Liliane, my sweet, are you asleep?"

Eyes closed, the child murmured:

"Two children who loved each other . . ."

The curtains in the half-open window stirred. The big city's dark sky glowed a delicate red, and it seemed to me that the child's breath flew to the window opening, gently stirring the curtain, flew heavenward, carrying with it the last words of my love, mingling them with all the other breaths exhaled by the city, and swirling them all together up there in that deep darkness delicately tinged with blood and shot through with the ill-defined glow of the stars.

The child slept. A light went on in the building next door, picking up red highlights in her hair. The little white face had that same ill-defined glow. I bent over her for a second. I was looking for something.

"You must be careful, my love, you will have to outwit death, outwit the living . . ."

FIFTY-NINE

"I Won't Ask You to My Wedding"

BEYOND the outer wall a horn was blaring.

Then it stopped.

Sister Beatrice had let go and handed me over to Sister Marie-Marthe. I was now Marie-Marthe's appointed assistant for farm duties.

I no longer went to oratory, and sometimes even skipped services. I had no idea what the other nuns thought. I had still not seen anything. And they never told me what they saw. Everyone for herself; no loose talk.

I no longer roamed the corridors.

I preferred the shed, even though Sister Josepha's book had long since disappeared. I preferred the washhouse, through which spring water gushed, and the little nuns' cemetery, where I uprooted crabgrass, and the gooseberry bushes, which were wholly under my care.

What all those places had in common was their proximity to the enclosure wall. That was where I now spent most of my time; that was where I felt comfortable.

And it was there that I heard the horn again blare from the other side of the wall.

The sound moved, as if it were hugging the wall. The car must have been moving along slowly, engine idling, for the only sound was that persistent, strident horn. I walked in its wake and we moved along together, each on his own side of the wall. Then suddenly it surged forward and overtook me and I began to run beside the wall. Soon the horn was far ahead, at the upper end of the grounds, and all I heard was the blood pounding against my eardrums. I retraced my steps, cutting across the fields to the gooseberry beds, to the triangular patch where we piled the cut lime branches and gooseberry roots and barrowloads of weeds. They had sat there turning into compost for so long that they almost topped the enclosure wall, and if you climbed onto the mound you could see a stretch of the narrow road leading down to the town. I had often watched the nuns' Citroën go rattling down that track.

And there sat a gray car, rakish, powerful, glittering in the sun. There was no one inside. "Adrien!" I screamed.

"Adrien, Adrien!"

"In the parlor," said Marie-Marthe, who had followed me.

Of course, the parlor.

In the parlor, where the low wall symbolic of enclosure had been removed, the Superior sat in a chair chatting pleasantly to a gentleman whose back was turned to me. She smiled; she looked serious, but she smiled and her voice was musical.

"Your friend —"

"Madame, let me do this," said Adrien.

"Of course . . ."

A moment of hesitation, but the Superior did not rise from her chair.

"Estelle," said Adrien, "Tiresia is dying; I've come to get you."

"You must go to her side," said the Superior.

"Yes," said my voice.

"I'll wait for you," said Adrien.

"Here," said the Superior.

"In my car," said Adrien.

"Very well," said the Superior.

"Let's go," my voice said.

"Your things," said the Superior.

"Your clothes," said Adrien.

"No, no, I need nothing, let's go at once," my voice begged.

"Here," said someone from behind the parlor doorway.

Dangling at medium height in the doorway was a red, rectangular, quite small object.

It was a leather wallet embossed with the logo of a famous Italian leather maker, a luxurious object that even the Superior must have recognized, for over the years advertisements for it had covered the walls of every city.

Hung with gilt rings, glittering, supple, the slender strap swung in the void.

"What is — ?" said the Superior, arching her eyebrows.

Marie-Marthe stepped forward.

"A runaway horse," the Superior had once said. Marie-Marthe seemed embarrassed by her burden, which was light, the strap dancing and the gilt rings on the strap jingling with each step she took.

The wallet came in twelve shades, always shown together in the ads that Vlad dreamed up. The beauty of the ads lay in their permanently renewable multicolor arrangement, with the target item never shown per se but always, as it were, inserted into an encompassing scheme, an overarching fantasy item. There had been a fan, a butterfly, a rainbow, a sunset, a bird of paradise, a naughty weather vane, iridescent soap bubbles, and many others. The idea was for the target item and the fantasy item to blur just enough to form a third object, a true work of art, a seductive snare for the mind — although each element had to remain independently recognizable. "Otherwise," Vlad said eagerly, "it wouldn't work." For after his flow of caviar dried up he had plunged heart and soul into this new flow — "Much bubblinger than caviar," he said, and we paid no heed to his neologism, being too wrought up over our own interpretation, naturally gleaned at our philosopher's feet. "It's the orchid capturing the wasp,"

we said to Vladimir, as if nothing were more obvious. And he, impressed and trusting in his own ignorance, unquestioningly allowed
the splendid idea to effervesce within him. And one day he came
over to see us with a big cardboard box; in it was a lithograph, his
way of thanking us for the most beautiful of all his handbag ads. The
twelve wallets were of course well in evidence, but so were wasp
and orchid — an "upmarket" composition, said Vladimir, who caught
new words like the flu (and we, pathetic cowardly betrayers of friendship, thought only of the philosopher's anger). Vladimir was too
excited to notice our anxiety, and we were too upset to notice that
he did not notice it, and next day, full of remorse, we took the
lithograph to a frame shop on the Faubourg Saint-Honoré and selected an enormous, horribly expensive frame. It had to be transported in a van, and once we got it home we could not decide where
to hang it, for our philosopher had a direct horizontal view into our
apartment. The monstrous object therefore joined the growing co-
hort of articles we exiled and summoned back (depending on their
donor's visit) in times of catastrophe. The lithograph in its prisonlike
frame went to our grocer at the bottom of the street, a Vietnamese
boat person. He was quite willing to have his store so decorated,
and meanwhile our philosopher frequented the grocer at the top of
the street, a Cambodian camp survivor. We felt there was little risk
that the twain would meet . . .

We bought all twelve wallets plus the red one. Then I gave away the
twelve and kept the red.

"I was . . . I went . . . into your . . . in her room," said Marie-Marthe.
  "Those are my papers," said my voice.
  "So, shall we go?" said Adrien.
  "Thank you . . . Marie-Marthe."
  "Good-bye, sir."
  "Good-bye, Sister."
  "Estelle?"

We were already outside, in the courtyard I had first entered, then
we were leaving through the wide-open gate (where the little
Citroën stood with its nose against the church wall), going down the
avenue of plane trees, going down the little road. The bend, then
the car.
  "It's a Jaguar; I just bought it," said Adrien.

His hands rested on the wheel, lingered a little.

"A hot-blooded animal," he said.

Then his hand was turning the key. He looked down, his face absorbed.

I noticed the engine sound: a Gregorian chant, sober, full-throated.

"It's different," I said.

"About Tiresia . . . I'm sorry," said Adrien.

"Different from the Citroën," I said.

"I was afraid you'd refuse to come," he explained.

I immersed myself in the rumbling of the engine, I flowed into valves, rods, and piston, my limbs wedding their motion, oil seeping into my joints; the rumbling filled my head like a choir singing in a cathedral nave.

"Are you listening?"

"Yes."

"She wanted to go back to your house, so the clinic sent her with a day nurse. My mother went round at night, are you listening?"

"Yes."

"It's a matter of days, and she's asking for you."

"Me?"

"You, yes, who do you think?"

Silence.

"And my mother can't spend every night there."

"Yes."

We drove through town and took the highway, the one that wound its gray way up the side of a green and brown mountain range, the one I had seen in the life-size postcard the Mother Superior showed me when she opened the window of my first cell. "It's a wonderful view," she had said. And then: "Be careful not to get hit on the head when it comes down." And just then the latch had slipped the wrong way and the Superior's face briefly wore an ugly grimace, followed immediately by her smile — one of those smiles the nuns could call up from behind their cheeks, smiles that at the first summons rushed forward to spread their wings before the nuns' faces.

The latch had fallen sideways, abruptly bisecting the landscape with a great diagonal stroke. The memory returned to me with devastating clarity. It was already memory.

*   *   *

"I might as well tell you that Alex and I put the coffin back in its grave."

"Thank you, Adrien."

"Your prehistoric cave . . ."

"Yes?"

"I asked around. There are no prehistoric caves in the area."

"No?"

"It was just one of old Raymond's hiding places. He must have lived up there for a while."

"Lived there?"

"You know they found him dead up on the hillside, apparently in just such a hole."

"Mr. Raymond . . ."

"And that drawing, that kind of red animal on the wall . . . in my opinion he did it. It looked a bit like you . . ."

"Yes."

"I mean you and your brother."

"Yes."

"Apparently he drew pictures, chromos of the same kind, when he was young."

Even though the road sloped steeply, the engine barely made a sound. We were still not far from the town and there was a lot of traffic in both directions — horns, noisy overtakings, small troops of motor-assisted bikes going as fast as they could.

It was this noise that had filled my first cell, as if the cell had really been the cell of a honeycomb and the whole convent an immense cake, both of them made to receive the honey of life, as if the wind carried that honey, heedless of the souls in residence there, thrusting them against the walls like black lichen, and the lively noise penetrated and filled everything. "We raised the enclosure wall," the Superior said, "but it did no good . . ." "Once the whole hill belonged to us, but our property was confiscated and the town keeps on growing . . ."

"You do understand, don't you, Tiresia doesn't have long . . ."

"Yes."

"The vault is to be opened and we needed . . ."

"Yes, thank you both so much."

*   *   *

The traffic thinned and I had time to watch the cars we overtook. Behind their windows I saw the flesh of the living, like that of the couple who came into the chapel . . . How I had hated those horrible tubs of flesh, tiptoeing in to contain the noise of their passage, and how vain their effort had been. For the sound of the living was deafening; the sound had come in through the enclosure fence and at once cracks raced through the silence, great cracks that seemed to run out all the way up to the vault where I sought refuge, until the whole world seemed fissured, delivered up defenseless to the threat of collapse, and if I had been able I would have torn the grille off the enclosure with my arms so that the flesh of the living could never again enter. All that had been so long ago, at the beginning of my stay at the convent.

Very few people from the outside ever came to our chapel: barely a dozen, most of them old. I had grown used to them, in any case, they were approaching the end; from year to year their flesh seemed less virulent; they were moving toward a vanishing point; they no longer bothered me.

On the road the flesh of the living teemed. Every car bore a full cargo, flesh cheek by jowl with steel, flesh and meat bowling along the road, the road welcoming these good companions with open arms . . .

Many people, fully functional, well cared for.

Particularly their haircuts, but of course that is what I had time to notice.

We had reached the highway. We needed gas and Adrien wanted to eat. In the end, since it could not be a first-class restaurant, we settled for a sandwich. "If you can't have the best champagne, get the best wine; if you can't have the best wine, get the best beer; if you can't have the best beer, get the best water" was another of his favorite sayings. We parked by the side of the road and he came back with a big packet of sandwiches and several beers.

"Just what the doctor ordered," he exulted, arranging paper napkins on our laps.

And suddenly I realized that his passion for fashionable restaurants and fine cuisine was all surface ("Better be well fed and rich than . . ."), was merely his ambition's angry desire. His body had always preferred simpler, more plebeian fare. He was grateful for those humble sandwiches and that quite unremarkable beer, he was glad that my nun's habit had prevented him from looking for something better, and the only area in which ambition could still command him was his clothing.

He was maniacally careful not to stain his shirt cuffs, his trousers, the seat leather. And he was happy with me because my ample robe received all unwanted crumbs and droplets.

I was starting to see Adrien, and it was a strange feeling.

There was a line at the self-service gas pump. And a line at the self-service cafeteria. But the gasoline had been extracted in distant countries; the foodstuffs selected by the slow-moving line came from unknown farms. It had all been produced by others, and those who were here were merely a link in the great chain of human exchanges.

In the convent we had eaten only our own vegetables and fruit, our poultry and our fish.

Now I was stepping back into the ranks, into the anonymous lines of earth beings, everyone dependent on everyone. I had no designs on anyone, and no one had designs on me. Cars came, stopped, left, the ribbon of highway that extended to cover the earth awaited them, and we too would slip into the anonymous files of cars running across this earth in search of a life that was lived on the horizontal.

"I'm getting married," said Adrien.

"Yes."

"To the daughter of a German industrialist."

"Yes."

"She does some singing, you know, she's highly talented, she's a member of a working group at the opera."

"Is she beautiful?"

"She's an angel. Golden hair, skin like milk, and elegant, I mean naturally elegant, like Nicole, if you know what I mean."

Adrien gave a happy little laugh:

"I had to fight to land her. I wasn't the only one after her."

There was a new cheerfulness in his voice, something candidly relaxed and merry.

"How did you manage?"

"I like opera, you know, and then I hit it off with her father. He was born in a small town too. And I think she loves me, what can I say, it happens."

"Better to be rich and wed than jerking off and underfed" had been another of Adrien's slogans from the old days, and because of it we had found it easy to despise him. We despised him and he turned aggressive — everything was in order! "Better to be rich and wed than . . ." Haunting, Adrien's sayings.

"What's that you're mumbling?"

"Oh, something from long ago."

But he did not follow up; things from long ago did not interest him.

"So what do you think?"

"What about?"

"Me getting married."

"I think it's splendid."

A bit thin: I would have to find something better than that.

"Your mother must be pleased."

"Not so sure about that," said Adrien.

"Why not?"

"She's German . . . you know, they have old prejudices because of the war, my father was a prisoner for three years, and —"

"And what?"

"I think she'd have preferred someone from G., someone who would keep me close to home."

"Yet it seems to be a good marriage."

"Yes, but we'll be far away. And they don't think any amount of money can buy the comfortable life well-heeled people live in our town. They would have preferred me to be like Alex: safe little job, local girl, a little house a stone's throw from them . . . In fact, they see a lot more of Alex than of me; my mother's crazy about his kid."

"You'll have kids too."

"I hope so, but they'll be half German, they'll spend half their vacations in Germany, they won't belong only to my parents . . ."

"I suppose that's true . . ."

"You want to know what?"

"What?"

"You're the one my mother wanted me to marry."

Mrs. Mother! Can it be true!

"Mrs. Neighbor in her deck chair . . . Swelling calves, thick neck . . . no sense of responsibility for the world, the perfect accountant . . . 'Without my wife, my business would collapse,' says Mr. Neighbor . . . 'A man needs a reliable woman, Mr. Helleur,' says Mrs. Mother . . . She talks of her son Adrien and his romantic exploits . . . 'Just now he needs to have a

good time, later he'll find a reliable woman, I trust him . . .' A reliable woman . . .

"*How much better I like these two women . . .*"

"A penny for your thoughts."

"I was thinking of your mother."

"You find it strange?"

"Yes."

"I never told her anything about your . . . well, you know. I'm not an informer, whatever you may have thought."

"We didn't think that, Adrien."

"Anyway, I never ratted on you. She adored your father and she thought you were the perfect daughter, hardworking and serious, not like my cousin."

"And now."

"Oh, still. Don't forget, she sent me to get you. I'm not here for kicks; I have urgent business right now."

"I know, Adrien, thanks."

We were already reaching the slopes: winding roads, granite rocks, violet heather in the ditches, wind, vast clouds sailing aloft.

Adrien drove faster.

"I'd like to be able to make the next plane."

"The plane?"

"There's an airport here now, didn't you know?"

"What about your car?"

"I have to be back here soon anyway."

I was beginning to feel nauseated.

We were at the big crossroads, the narrow road that dropped down to the little stream, crossed it and climbed back up. The crossroads, then our road with the cemetery on the right, and huddled together by a trick of perspective on the left our two houses, looking like just one, strange and ghostly against the lowering sky.

As usual, Adrien stopped between the two houses.

"Estelle . . . ," he said.

"Yes?"

"I won't ask you to my wedding."

"No problem, Adrien."

"But I'll come . . . for Tiresia."

"Thank you, Adrien."

"My parents want it."

"Thanks for all you've done already, Adrien."

Mrs. Mother appeared at her window; she must have been watching for some time.

"Scram," said Adrien, "otherwise you'll have to talk to my mother."

Such was my return, madame.

At G.

SIXTY

"My Daughter, My Own Little Daughter"

FOR FIVE DAYS Tiresia talked.

Then her story was done. She stopped taking nourishment and she spoke only to say these words: "My daughter, my own little daughter."

For me that was enough. I wanted no other life, coming and going in our house, being in the living room, near the piano with Tiresia lying beside it, tranquil in our father's big bed.

There was much to do, for despite the clinic's advice I had dismissed the day nurse. I changed Tiresia's IV bag, gave her all her shots, sponged the face on which flesh crushed so long ago awoke in one last protest, replaced her catheter, and washed her pudendum. And it was then I saw her stomach and upper thighs, the deep scars, the atrophy, the loss of muscle mass, the ribbed sutures, all those stigmata of absolute evil imprinted on flesh that had once seemed so tender to me. I caressed the pathways of the pillage and she let me do so. I said to her, "They did this to you here?" and — brushing the tops of her thighs — "This is why you couldn't make love?" Her skin responded and I laid my head on her stomach, and it felt as if I were lying on ground that had been plowed up by shells and that years later exhaled the same unbearable distress.

A New York friend of Dan's, a photographer, once went to view the old Verdun battlefields. He came back possessed. The Verdun mud had stuck to his soul and he had taken hundreds of photos, just of the mud. "The mud speaks," he said, "it's a hell that's extinct but still radioactive." He had gone back again and again in all seasons, stumbling into shell holes full of muddy water and stagnant earth, into trenches, into pillboxes, tripping over iron spikes called corkscrews and galleries choked with dead branches. Everywhere beneath

moss and pine needles were double-necked French canteens, fragments of mess kits, helmets, moldy iron-studded boots, machine-gun
loaders, stick grenades. But there were also bones, sometimes dug
up by wild boars — femurs, ribs, tibias, jaws — horse bones, mule
bones, human bones, all mixed up. Once he had almost trod on the
intact fuse of a 210-millimeter shell still protruding from the ground.
He had taken hundreds more photos; he had met the last survivors
on both sides of the frontier; he had plumbed the official archives.

He wanted to do a book. "Five hundred thousand shells a day,
terribly young people torn to pieces by shrapnel, turned into living
torches by flamethrowers, buried alive in the liquid-mud explosions
of mortar shells, or eaten by gas-inflicted gangrene, or disemboweled
with their intestines exposed to the air — and do you know what
they called out? 'Mama,' that was the word, from one end to the
other of those fields of slaughter, 'Mama' . . . We can't let people
forget it."

As an epigraph to the book, he had selected a sentence of San-
tayana's: "Those who cannot remember the past are condemned to
repeat it," and another, of Yevtushenko's: "Whoever forgets yesterday's victims will himself be the victim tomorrow." We found that
beautiful but enigmatic. Later on after his night with our father's
folders, my brother would recall those two phrases. They utterly
changed the course of his life: they became the one central truth for
him, as they must have for our friend in the forests of Verdun.

The book had required an enormous amount of research. And
after that, to become a book in the accepted sense, it had required
massive condensation. Many promises were made to the author-
photographer, both by the Defense Ministry and the French Vet-
erans' Association; publishers pledged their support; but the book
would not come. He went back to Verdun to take more pictures,
and we began to lose hope for him. We urged him to move on to a
different, less macabre subject.

He would answer, "I lie flat on the earth for hours on end, sometimes a whole night"; he would say, "I don't take a single photo
without first lying on the ground"; and we would have no idea what
to say in reply. He was older than we, and we thought he took things
too hard.

How well I now understand our friend. It was his soul he sought
to affix to the mud of Verdun, so that like a vast din the desperate
cries of the dead could flow into him, all humankind's appalling
inexplicable suffering.

And I could not leave the ravaged earth of my mother's body.

*   *   *

I realize, madame, that I am speaking to you of an earlier war, the twentieth century's first world war, in order not to speak to you of my mother's war, of my own war, since I was born in a backwater of that second conflict.

I recall our friend's photographs, the memories he brought back with him, all those concrete things that moved him and the precise labels he gave them. I recall his words, and I have used them: it was "his" war. But the war that gave birth to me — the most imperceptible of sighs from the enormous continent-straddling monster, a handful of pathetic individuals thrown up against one another, an obscure collision on the shoulder of a provincial road by a little backcountry stream, a rape, madame: that was my war — and about that war, silence, suppression.

Apart from a handful of bombers flying black across the sky, I experienced nothing of it, and I cannot speak of what I learned of it.

How could I blame my mother and the denizens of our home for being killed right at the start and then keeping silent year after year, all through our infancy and our youth?

I went outside: into the garden to see the trees, to the fence to pick up the mail, to the lilac at the wall to chat with Mrs. Neighbor. But suddenly I stopped, and then I ran, abandoning the letters, Mrs. Neighbor, the small garden chores, and I ran to the living room, where the curtains, although drawn to protect Tiresia's eyes, allowed shafts of sunlight timid as visitors at a deathbed to filter in. There I threw myself down on the bed, sobbing "Mama, Mama."

That word, which I had never used as a child, bored down to undreamed-of depths, summoning up ungovernable emotion. "Mama" — even today when I hear that word uttered in the street at school doors, the same emotion rolls in, something linked to our gloomy childhood, to the light that Tiresia's story had kindled behind the gloom, light and gloom not interpenetrating but simply embracing, *I do not know what it can be, madame — a rush of emotion, perhaps, at the absurd and magnificent pathos of life — but my whole body was invaded, and when the wave ebbed I felt immense fatigue and the need to sleep.*

Perhaps that is how it is for people who never said "Mama" in their childhood, who say it for the first time when they are grown and their mother is already gone.

"My daughter, my own little daughter," said Tiresia, groping about to set her hand on mine, her voice full of enormous compassion. I say "enormous" because it was the only feeling still in her, occupying the entire extent of her being (and who can say to what mysterious distances a being can extend?). It seemed to me that from behind that ruined, hideously emaciated body, that body on the verge of disintegration, an almost limitless aura radiated out, reaching centuries back into the past, branching out through the linked chain of the living, bearing its fading light unimaginable distances.

At first Tiresia had but one idea: to tell her story, the story that had loomed in the background of all our lives. To tell it she mustered all her energies; and because she had been speechless for so long it was a strange performance. But she was determined to leave nothing out: she wanted me, her daughter, to know all. In her exhausted voice, barely capable of variation in tone or expression, she told me all the most intimate details — her meeting with my father, her affection for her young pupil Nicole — as well as the most hideous ones — her first arrest, the rape, her second arrest and deportation to the camp — and the murkiest — the arrangement the three of them worked out, Nicole's regrets, Nicole's flight to join an American dance troupe, my brother's birth, more about their arrangement, jealousy, conflict, their love for us . . .

Every one of her words, reaching the ancient desert of her speech, struck intense sparks the way I imagine mirages do across the arid expanse of the sands, and like the whole desert I vibrated under the onslaught of those elusive flashes.

Then she took fright.

The whole time she was talking, she seemed hardly able to see me. She was stern. Once her story was told she turned away and did not look at me again.

I did not understand her fear; all I wanted was to hear those words again — "My daughter, my own little daughter." But she had stopped saying them, and I wept beside her, noiselessly; the tears flowed of themselves, I could not hold them back. "Why are you crying?" Tiresia said almost roughly. "Because you've stopped calling me your daughter, your own little daughter," I told her — and at once perceived the joy that entered her. For a moment I even thought she might recover. I smothered her with kisses, I devoured her; then I resumed my position beside her, my head beside her body on the bed, my hand resting lightly on the form molded by the bedcovers, and a little relief came over her. She had brought to fruition everything that life had so carelessly tossed into her path, and her task was done. She was bequeathing to me a solidly rebuilt past, one that would no longer lead me into confusing mists and treacherous quicksands. I was now alone, but I could set out on my path.

All that her body expressed. All that, and also regret at not having done it earlier. Oh, Doctor Minor, so that was the subject of your eternal quarrel with our father! Shut up with him in his car outside the gate, away from indiscreet ears, you told him, "You have to tell the children." And we children, hidden behind the rhododendrons, we used to see your blazing quarrel — but the windows were rolled up and we heard nothing. "Speak," you told him, "speak, Helleur — in any case, the children already know in their hearts." And you told him: "The truth will free Tiresia from her silence and Nicole from her childish dreams" and also: "You yourself will lose this rapid heartbeat of yours." And finally, as a last resort, you probably said, "And the kids' little ailments, their vaypigo, where do you think that comes from!" Our father must have resisted. "We want them to grow up innocent and at peace," he probably told you, and it was at that point that we saw you burst from the car, cramming your hat on your head and banging your bag against your thigh ("Like an angry gorilla," Dan said). Our father would stay in the car and the doctor would stride off down the road; and one day, beside himself with rage, he yelled "Lies!" so loud that the empty street seemed to shake, and off he went bareheaded, hair flapping in the breeze, forgetting his bag in the car; and our father ran after him, proffering that bag in his outstretched arm . . .

Through my hand that rested on her body and my gaze held in hers, I understood all that my mother said. And through the same channels I was able to reassure her: she had been forced to live this long silence and I to withdraw into a cloister; time had had its way with us; but this moment redeemed everything. Now she had found peace and I was happy.

"My daughter, my own little daughter . . ."

I did not stir, I let her words unfold in me, gave them all the time they needed to unfold. And when they had found their resting place I could rise and resume the household chores.

Not for long. I had to return to my mother, to hear again the words that soon no one would be able to say to me.

At one point I laughed. "Well, Mama, what am I? German, English,

French? And Dan, Indian, American, English, French? All that! And Mr. Raymond, Polish and French and God knows what, and Alex, French and something else, isn't he, Mama — Slav, in any case? And Minor, Russian and French and Jewish, and our concierge, Portuguese and French! All that just for us, Mama, and there's more I've probably overlooked." Yes, there were certainly some I had overlooked; I saw it in my mother's eyes. But I bubbled over with happiness as if all those mingled nationalities and races brought with them a superabundance of life, a superabundance we so sorely needed, oh, Mama.

Something happened. Half-lying beside Tiresia, I dozed. All around was night, cold and hard, and a child who was me tried to float in that night. But every movement threw her against barriers, I was surrounded by dense emptiness, my arms struck out in it and turned to ice, distant sounds flitted across like bursting planets out of all proportion to the child in its crib; in the past there had been a soft pulsating night; now there was this black, icy void.

Two tiny glittering points appeared in the depths of the night, drew near, and hovered over my crib. From them came the warmth and smell of my night of yesteryear, and I reached up toward those two points, toward the round gentle halo between them, the halo framed by their glittering, the halo that was everything that was good in the world — "Mama!"

"Mama, the little diamond earrings, I saw them on you, I saw them on you when you were my mother!"

Tiresia gently shook her head.

"That's impossible, that's impossible, you were only a few months old . . ."

But you wore them, Mama, and I saw them, I saw those earrings framing your face! Terrible pain took hold of me: I had possessed my mother for a few months after my birth, and now I was finding her again just a few hours before her death. My whole being was pegged between those two poles of time. The child perceiving her mother inside that soft jeweled glow in the midst of the mortal night shouted out inside me, shouted out inside the grown-up who was going to lose her again for ever and ever that very same night. Oh, those earrings, how they burned my head. They had gone to Nicole at the time of their first "arrangement," and it was then I lost my mother.

A baby's memory. A memory that should have been crushed

beneath the mass of subsequent memories — yet it had bored its way intact through all the strata of my life, tiny and brilliant. And that thought suddenly assuaged me. My pain went away — my mother glittered at the depth of my being, and nothing could make her leave it.

She got weaker. To cheer her a little, to cheer our reunion, I told her stories about the convent; they amused her because at the clinic she had been looked after by nuns. I picked the least offensive stories.

"Mama, in the parlor there were glass display cases with stuff they made — bibs, children's pullovers, rompers, place mats (lots of place mats!), everything very ugly, coarse crochet work and crude colors, so ugly it was weird. You felt that they had done it all for monster babies, hybrids of humans and supernatural beings, and I wondered what strange things had gone on in their minds . . . But no doubt I was wrong: Dan and I had spent too much time in expensive stores after we got rich (thanks to you, Mama). The nuns said all this stuff was for sale, but it was hard to believe. The wares were dusty and the cases looked as if they had never been opened; what's more, they were in the part of the parlor most remote from visitors. One day near the end I wanted to buy a bib; our town had come back into my thoughts, and perhaps I wanted to send a present to Alex's child. Mama, I could never find the nun who kept the key to those cases. With one impregnable excuse after another they sent me from nun to nun until I gave up. Not one of them ever betrayed the secret. Can you understand that, Mama?"

My mother smiled. How beautiful it made her in my eyes. That disfigured face was dearer to me than everything in the world: beauty rose from those craters and ravines, hovered above them like a luminous mist, and I did not find her disfigured, much less so than so many faces everywhere in the streets, with features plucked and pulled in every direction as if by battalions of malevolent lilliputians. No luminous mist on those faces!

And in that mist I rested: "I pity the nuns," I said, "they do not have their mother's body." I was staggered by my good fortune.

At one point Tiresia became agitated. Something was tormenting her, and I knew at once what it was. "The coffin is back in its place, Mama," I told her. "Adrien and Alex put it back."

Her face relaxed. I gave her her last medication, and we remained there together, my head against her body, my hand in her hand, watched over first by the soft rays of the sun, then by the little piano lamp, in a state of happiness that seemed the most absolute of my life, even though it was but a mirage. But I was not the eager traveler, I was the desert itself. And the mirage was more intimate to me than anything in the world.

SIXTY-ONE

Adrien

ON THE STONE were three names: Andrew Helleur, Nicole Helleur, Dan Helleur. Now there was this fourth: Thérèse Helleur.

As his mother had requested, Adrien came back. He drove me.

Ahead was the hearse. During the short ride a thought came to me: "Adrien is driving me to my mother's funeral, he drove me to my father and Nicole's funeral . . . Is this thing with Adrien a kind of marriage? Is that what marriages are?"

He took me home. We went into the living room.

"Better move this bed," he said.

"Yes."

His somber energy did me good. I was ready to receive him.

Tiresia's words had separated me from myself. Estelle's past was complete, whole. My mother had gathered in the long ill-defined vines that had trailed through my mind like maidenhair; she had drawn them back one after another to the past, where they belonged. With her dying voice she had rewoven the fabric of my past and I had no more seeking to do. I had only to leave. To leave death's domain, where the creatures of my past had vanished.

I was still too close, too weak and vulnerable. Adrien was the only one who could venture into these zones, and he would stride in, noisy, utterly ignorant of his surroundings. In fact he was already there, clomping up and down the living room floor with those shoes that made the planks creak.

"You're wearing the same shoes you did at my parents' funeral."

"Idiot!" said Adrien. "Same style, but obviously not the same shoes!"

Adrien would be the guide who smuggled me out of death's domain, but he would never know it.

"What are you laughing at?"

"Do you always buy the same style, Adrien?"

"Yes, what's funny about that?"

What a guide you will be, Adrien!

Your shoes were sturdy and your footsteps loud. They would frighten the dead. And I didn't love you, which was precisely why I could follow you. I was betraying no one. One left death's domain any way one could. What one needed was a guide who did not know he was a guide, a guide with resonant footwear and pulverizing tread. One was hauled free of death's dominion by ugliness — otherwise there was no leaving it. There was no other way. I could not explain it but I knew.

Beauty was vanishing into far places along with my dead, and floating in its wake like a veil of gossamer were those pallid threads that had held me back so long. My mother freed me from them and now I was moving away.

But the ground where I found my footing would always be foreign ground.

The bell. Alex was at the door.

"Just in time," said Adrien, "you can help me move this bed upstairs."

"I came to see Estelle, to see if she needed anything," said Alex.

"She needs you to help me take this bed upstairs, pal."

"That's . . . that's the deceased's bed," Alex managed to say. "Is it okay with you, Estelle?"

I would not call myself Estelle anymore. My mother had taken her child with her, the child called Estelle, a child meant for a stellar destiny. Now that star too was vanishing in the dark far places of death. I would need another name.

"If you don't mind, Alex."

We had a hard time. We had to take the bed apart.

"Did you dismantle it to bring it down?" I asked.

"He did," said Adrien.

"I've built coffins," stammered Alex, almost apologetically.

"I didn't want my mother to climb all those stairs," said Adrien.

Later Adrien, Alex, and I sat in the living room. It looked almost the way it used to. Adrien's mother came over. She was worried because it was so late, and Adrien told her he would stay with me that first night. "Come to our house," Mrs. Mother said to me. "No, she might as well get used to it," said Adrien. "I'll bring you a tray, then," she said. "Alex can get the tray," said Adrien. "He can eat something with us . . . before he leaves."

I listened to all this. That's right, Adrien, my trusty guide: I heard your rough words in the squelching swamp, I wallowed behind you, you splashed with every step, but it was because your shoes found firm ground under the mud of death's dominion.

"Shit," said Adrien, "Alex sticks around like glue."

We drank something strong.

"What are you going to do?" said Adrien.

"Same as before."

"You're crazy," he said. "You can't go back to live with the nuns. First of all, take that off. I can't stand it. The veil, maybe, but not the robe, no thanks!"

Very well.

Adrien, my guide, I followed you. I put on the old overalls and sweater I used to wear when we went to the cave or the ditch or to pick up the arrows that had fallen near the pond. Poor Adrien, he probably imagined that the good sisters, as he called them, would be shocked to see me dressed this way. I thought of Marie-Marthe in her T-shirt, her round breasts swinging beneath the cotton, sweating and slashing with her scythe under the sun.

"Why are you laughing?"

"Stop asking me why I'm laughing, it annoys me."

"It annoys me too! It's as if you're talking to somebody else all the time!"

Alex returned with the tray and the three of us ate in my living room. Alex talked about building coffins; every now and then he broke off to look hopelessly at me.

He was wondering whether he should be discussing such things with someone who had just lost a relative. But it was his work; it was what he knew. Adrien answered in monosyllables. From time to time he looked at me. I knew what he was wondering. He was wondering why I did not show both of them the door, whether I was being polite or had something in the back of my mind. That was how my neighbor and enemy was. He thought people always had something in the back of their mind. I do not believe he ever thought you could have something *in* your mind.

And at that moment he was right. I had nothing in my mind, but I did have something in the back of it.

My head was strangely empty and light. Everything slid by: Tiresia's burial, the return, the living room now delivered of her bed, Mrs. Mother's sandwiches, Alex and Adrien in armchairs, each looking uncertainly at me, and me with this emptiness.

Time dragged on. Alex rose. He looked like a lost dog. He turned to Adrien, his whole posture a question: "Are you coming with me?"

"Don't worry about me, pal, I'm staying," said Adrien, without getting up from his chair.

Thus did Alex depart.

"So . . . ," said Adrien.

I said nothing.

"That's it, then," he went on, "they've all left you. Your father, Nicole, your brother, Tiresia . . . Your house is empty, Estelle . . . I'm the only one left."

"My cat has four feet, a tail, and whiskers," good, well done, Adrien, "My family had three grown-ups and two children and four are dead." Stay with me, Adrien, you're not disappointing me, you've never disappointed me . . . That is what I think now, madame, and perhaps it is what I thought then, but I was in such a state, so cold, with centers of burning that I could not feel, and I still had a task to fulfill. Always after death a task . . . and after that?

Still I said nothing.

"In fact it requires a certain courage to stay here," he said. "Your house is bad luck."

"Alex would have stayed."

"Alex!" Adrien began to laugh. "That's why he loves you — your house is like a cemetery and he feels at home here."

"And why are you staying?"

"Hmmm . . ."

"Why?"

"I want to see how you're going to react after all these shocks. What are you going to dream up now? Once it was digging up a corpse . . ."

"Adrien!"

"And after that fucking on a coffin . . ."

"Not true!"

"Well, not too far wrong either. Another time it was becoming a nun. I've been watching you for years, Estelle, you and your precious brother, I know you by heart and yet you surprise me every time. So what are you going to do now, Estelle, tell me."

Oh, how clearly I saw what I had to do.

Adrien, my guide, you were the one I would burden with Tiresia's story. I would set it *in* your head. You would carry the secret of the gods; I would give it to you because it was dark and sinister and absurd. And you would carry it without even realizing it, because the secret of the gods did not matter a damn to you. Tossing it into you would be exactly like tossing it to the winds, and that was what I wanted.

Oh, Adrien, how dear to me you were; how closely bound; how unimportant!

"It's cold," he said.

We lit a fire, we pulled the couch up to the fireplace and tucked blankets around us.

I do not know how to speak of such things, the things you do when everything is dead and you go on existing. My words are just that, words that you utter when everything is dead and you go on existing.

We made a fire, we pulled the couch close, we tucked blankets around us.

There was no longer anyone in whom to cry out, in whom to scream. No longer anyone bearing within himself enough space for you to plunge into. From now on words: cabs, you got into one, then into another; you did not remember the driver's face; he did not remember yours; he went here, then there. Words: segments without a posterity.

"I'll get wood," said Adrien. "I'll get a blanket," said Estelle. "Get several," said Adrien. "Pull the couch closer," said Estelle. "Your end," said Adrien.

They were not building a house for themselves, not a shelter. Just a place on the carpet in front of a fire.

No longer anyone in whom to scream, or begin to scream, or begin to form the beginnings of a scream . . . No one.

Naturally I could direct that scream, turn it toward the person now with me, toward Adrien.

The scream leapt out all right, but halfway there it changed, it could not find the space it sought. Finding only a recipient, it shriveled and curled up.

Unable to find its space, my scream turned into a flight of small spiteful darts. And spiteful darts can always find a destination, a wall.

Which was not so bad. With Adrien, I was spiteful.

Could spitefulness be the vessel that brought you back from the land of death?

My brother: kid-words that found a meadow to gambol in, tide-words that found a sea to roll in, flake-words that found a carpet of snow to settle on, butterfly-words that found a flowering field to sip nectar in, star-words that found a sky to twinkle in, faltering words that found a nest to huddle in, deformed monstrous misbegotten words that found their den of thieves . . . Whatever form those words assumed, the stroke of a wand changed the space that opened to receive them . . .

My brother was my space.

Adrien was merely a destination.

You do not see space; space is in you and around you.

I see Adrien's features, separate and distinct: his slightly hooked nose, just a nose, his too-high forehead, so much forehead for so few thoughts, just a forehead, and his neck, strong and broad, just a neck. And to him I am just a nose, a forehead, a neck, all to be considered one at a time. Adrien most assuredly did not find me beautiful. Most assuredly I repelled him, and that repulsion exuded from him. It was his most personal attribute.

"So then, Estelle?"

We were in front of the fire now, with our backs to the couch. Might as well finish undressing. But I was afraid to see my body, which I had not seen for some years. I perceived this modesty, this anxiety . . . for Adrien: how could that be?

"If you laugh once more, Estelle, I'll hit you!"

I undressed at one stroke.

"Well, now," said Adrien, "well, now . . ."

Tiresia's voice keened inside my head: "My daughter, my little daughter." For a moment I listened. Henceforth there would be no more modesty, no more anxiety. "My daughter, my little daughter . . ."

Not only was I naked, but I too was looking at that flesh: it had grown pale and the skin on the legs was rough and coarse. I touched that skin; I raised both hands to my head, and my hair, cropped thick and short, felt strange under my palms. I touched my belly, and the fleece there recalled nothing except, fleetingly, the patches of moss we sometimes felt on the nuns' tombstones before we raised them. I looked up at Adrien and for a moment we stared at each other.

"No period this time?"

"I no longer have periods, Adrien."

He had his old sullen look. His features were motionless, and so were mine, and our childhood memories marched forth as we gazed — but they were strange memories, you would have sworn that they were emerging from a place dark and choked with undergrowth, that they had been twisted and fractured, that they were a tangle of blackened thorns. I did not recognize them, yet they were our memories . . . What had happened to us, what had happened to our childhood, Adrien?

"Your turn now."

Adrien undressed.

The garments of the one you do not love. Never have they constituted a whole: they stand separate, freshly purchased. You can see them being picked off a row, a shelf, or a pile; then being ironed in order to eliminate folds or sharpen creases; then into cellophane in order to transform the whole into a gift package. Adrien's body was well cared for; it had been exposed to exercise, to the sun, to caresses. But I saw only disparate pieces, athlete's legs with swelling calves . . . A calf . . . The remains of the dance.

And by the remains of the dance I lay.

"Okay, Estelle, what now?"

"I'll tell you a story."

"Put your hand here."

"Later, Adrien."

"Give me your hand, there. Can you feel . . ."

"Yes, Adrien."

"Feel my prick, Estelle?"

"Yes . . ."

"This time it's for you."

"I don't ask anything of you."

"What we did under the lilac a long time ago, that wasn't for you."

"I don't regret it, Adrien."

"It wasn't for you or me, it was for him."

"I don't regret what we did."

"Stroke me."

"Later."

"Stroke me . . . just for me."

"Adrien."

"It's the last time, don't forget."

"I know, Adrien."

"After that I'll be married . . ."

"I don't ask anything of you."

"Look at me. It's been a long time since you saw a man — don't you feel like it?"

"I want to talk to you."

"Well, talk about my prick, Estelle. Don't you like it? God, your hand's cold."

"You know you have a beautiful body . . ."

"Your hand's cold, it's on my prick and it isn't moving, and it feels good, there's only you, you know . . ."

"I want to talk to you."

"I'm scared when you talk, Estelle. Every time you ever talked you came out on top."

"I don't want to be on top in anything, Adrien — I've lost it all."

"For God's sake, I know my body's in shape, Estelle, I work out, you've laughed at me enough . . ."

"If you could only accept apologies . . ."

"I don't want apologies, I want to have your hand there, and I want you to look at me."

"Adrien, there are so many others . . ."

"I want to be naked here just once, in your house. My prick is straight and hard, and it's shorter than your brother's but thicker, isn't that so, Estelle?"

"That's right, Adrien."

"And brown, almost black, his was more golden, right?"

"How well you know us, Adrien."

"And I just work out, I don't dance or fool with music. People who don't dance or play music don't know how to make love, that's what everyone in your house thought, didn't they, Estelle?"

"Adrien?"

"Or maybe you didn't think anything? Did you even think I had a dick?"

"What are you trying —"

"I'm not angry, Estelle. Do you think I'm angry?"

"No."

"So answer. Did you ever even think I had a dick?"

"I don't know."

"You acted as if I wasn't there."

"You never told us you were coming over, you never asked permission."

"Don't think I didn't see you . . ."

"Who?"

"You, her, you two, him, I don't know, all of you . . ."

"Adrien, that's what I want to talk to you about."

"Talk to me with your lips and hands."

"You have everything, Adrien, you've had lots of women . . ."

"I know, I know . . ."

"Look at me, I'm all chapped and my skin is rough, and I don't even know how I smell down there."

"That's not what this is about . . ."

"I don't know anything anymore, what can I do?"

"I'd like to give you something."

"You're going to be married, and I want nothing from you."

"Your heart is as hard as stone, Estelle, the convent hasn't changed you . . . but leave your hand on my dick. For a while."

"I'm going to tell you a story."

"Why can't you let yourself go and make love like everyone else, once, just once, Estelle?"

"This story begins during a war . . ."

"I didn't come here to hear a story."

"Wait, this was our war, the one your parents got married in . . ."

"Estelle . . ."

"The one I was born in, the second world war of the twentieth century . . ."

Mysteriously my hold had returned, my old hold over our neighbor Adrien, whom I did not love and who did not love me. His stare was somber and steady. He stopped interrupting.

Later we got dressed again, a little. The moon had risen, the hellish white moon, and hovered just outside the window. The road was utterly silent. Adrien went to the window and looked across at his house.

"My parents did mention all that, I believe, a long, long time ago.

Your father did parachute jumps and Tiresia was a Resistance courier. My father was one of her mail drops. I imagine that's why your father chose this area to settle in . . ."

The logs had gradually burned down. Adrien took more off the pile we had made and we spent some time rebuilding the fire.

"That part too I must have heard, but it's so far back in my memory. She came over on a bike by a deserted side road, from over by the little stream . . . It was late, no one ever really knew who it was — the Germans, our own militia? Maybe local people, roaring drunk, Alex's father, quite possibly, he drank like a madman after his wife died . . . Militiamen, Germans. At least I think that's what people said . . . but as soon as I came in everyone would stop talking and my father gave me that dirty look he put on when he was going to clout me, you know, and I would get out quick."

Adrien came back to lie beside me.

"Well, nothing we can do about all that now."

"Wait, that's not all . . ."

The moon hid behind one of the big chestnut trees in the garden, leaving the room in a half darkness in which the logs glowed a fiercer red.

"What, both of them?"

"Both of them."

"And the younger girl was Nicole! So that's why they were so . . . so . . ."

"Yes, so cracked."

"In Paris, while she was having a piano lesson! Poor Nicole!"

"And Tiresia, what they did to her . . ."

"But Nicole was so young, she had nothing to do with it."

"Tiresia wasn't much older and she had risked her whole life."

"Why did they take her away?"

"Whom?"

"Nicole."

"They made no distinctions. If I hadn't been at the neighbors' at the time they would have taken me too, and I was just a baby."

"Good, you're still here."

"Wait, you don't know everything. About Dan and me."

*   *   *

The moon had come out on the other side of the chestnut tree. Whiteness had piled up at the far end of the living room, and in the fireplace the embers we had scraped together among the ashes seemed to be hatching an immemorial furnace.

Adrien abruptly rose. I had never seen him and would never again see him so shattered.

He paced up and down the room, at times passing the fireplace, where his dark form seemed to loom immoderately large against the glowing embers behind, at other times fading like a ghost into the lunar zone at the far end. I think he was fighting back tears.

"So. Neither you nor Dan. And there I was bursting with envy, envious of how he held both of you by the hand and spoke to you and looked at you the whole time, and never told you that you couldn't do things; how I wished he could have been my father, I bet you never knew that! You wouldn't believe how long I spent making up convoluted stories in my head — mistaken identity, child substitution, desertion, adoption — I'd forgotten it all, Estelle, but now it's coming back. I used to dream about it all the time: that Mr. Helleur was my father and not yours, that your real father was my father, or Alex's father, or Mr. Raymond, yes, it was Mr. Raymond I usually saddled you with, I almost ended up believing it . . . Mr. Helleur never drove me away, even when I dropped by without warning, no matter what the hour. I needed to see him . . . I even needed to see him at night. I used to come over and watch through your windows, I wedged myself up on the sill to be able to hear what he was telling you, but all I ever heard was the sound of his voice, never one word louder than the other, and his sense of humor, which put everything in its place . . . He never gave anyone a hard time . . . And you weren't even his children.

"Mr. Helleur," Adrien said as he paced up and down, "the only person I ever admired, Estelle, I wanted to be like him, but you and your brother didn't even realize I was there . . . Mr. Helleur, Mr. Helleur," he said again and again.

And suddenly I realized that he was uttering those words just as I had that very morning been saying "Mama." The words with which you try to reach the pain deep inside you, or the words with which your pain lures you on, and you move in, repeating the magic word to make the hatches swing open, you advance upon your pain because it alone can lead you so far, can open up those hitherto-unknown depths, which open in their turn upon the limitless somber magma in which all humankind's roots are embedded.

*   *   *

Adrien said:

"I'm going, I'm going."

But he went on prowling around, muttering "Mr. Helleur."

"Adrien, it's not over yet."

He returned unprotesting, still overwhelmed. I do not think he even heard me, it was just that he could not leave a place where the only being he had admired still, in a sense, lived on.

I went on talking. We slept a little. We woke up. We ate the rest of the sandwiches. Adrien reached a hand toward me.

"It's not over . . ."

The last log snapped in two in a shower of sparks, and the two ends fell to the outward side. We poked them back onto the embers.

"That isn't all . . ."

The moon grew pale. We had moved closer to the fire. A damp furtive cold began to creep in from doors and windows. My father had softly withdrawn with the shadows of night, just as he used to withdraw into his study, leaving neither conflict nor bitterness behind him, just a kind of melancholy peace colored by a smile. But what occupied us now was something terribly different. My story now moved in a series of jolts and Adrien kept interrupting; his questions threw me off track; he had drunk another glass.

"But why did she agree?" he said angrily, slamming the glass so hard on the mantelpiece that it broke.

"She owed her life to them . . . and she loved them."

"Bullshit!"

There he stood, Adrien, the whole Adrien, the way he had always been. Seeing him in that old light helped me, for I had been thrown off course by his grief for my father. But his violence did me good, and something started to crack in the hard shell the convent had built around me. I loved Adrien's rages. I realized I had always loved them. And in that moment, despite all my years in the convent, despite my mother's death and the cemetery and the terrible loneliness even now biding its time, I loved them still. Like fingers inching toward a nagging itch, I slid toward Adrien's rage.

"Bullshit! God, this house must have been gloomy for her! And this town! And pretending to be your mother as well, God, what a job! Why didn't she stay with that choreographer of hers, what was his name again?"

"Alwin . . . But that still isn't all."

Adrien would never accept that Nicole could have loved my father, loved Tiresia, loved me, passionately, in spite of everything . . .

And as if I had said nothing, he was off again: "Why did she agree?"

Now you listen, Adrien, because so far I've told you nothing, Adrien, listen. You loved Nicole, so you have to know everything, right to the bitter end . . .

Do you think love can be a smile, the rustle of a dress, a milky shoulder, a pretty naked body seen by you? Most certainly by you, Adrien: you were always in our house. And perhaps touched by you, Nicole was so soft, putting a rose in her hair and patting the curls at the nape of her neck, I saw it all — but who could have helped it, I didn't hold it against you . . . Did you really believe that love would be grace and beauty for you alone, and that all the death, torture, endless pain of love, would be reserved for me? You loved her, Adrien, and you most certainly told her so. And perhaps she smiled at you and kissed you. She was gentle, and you thought that one day you would conquer her with your money, because of course she refused you, laughed sweetly and refused you. But for your first love you had beauty, you had Nicole: have you any idea how lucky you were, Adrien? So now you have to know everything down to the bitter end, you have to know what she endured, what our winged beauty endured, our Venus rising from the waves. And you have to know what my mother Tiresia endured. Otherwise it would be unjust, Adrien, too unjust.

"Why did she agree, why did she keep it up?"

"Because of what happened in the camp."

"You've already told me that."

"I haven't described it to you."

"I don't want to hear."

"Yes."

"It's in the past."

"It's not in the past, it keeps on."

"No one ever talks about it anymore, not even my parents."

"You have to know . . ."

"It has nothing to do with me, it doesn't interest me, do you hear, Estelle?"

"The past keeps on, it kept on when we were kids, it kept on yesterday, it's keeping on right now."

"You're crazy."

"The past is going on right now, Adrien."

"Shut your mouth!"

"At this very moment, Adrien, between you and me. You're shouting because of this past — and you don't even know what it is."

"You're the one who's making me yell, you've always made me yell."

"No: it's the unknown past."

"It's you, Estelle, you bring out the devil in me, you've driven me crazy for years and years."

"I didn't realize, I realized nothing."

"I could have killed, Estelle, I want to kill now. I could wring your neck, like that, right now, and watch your eyes bulge out of your head, and your tongue stick out of your mouth, and your face swell and turn black, God, how good it would make me feel, Estelle, if your head burst like a puffball . . ."

"That's because you don't want to know anything, Adrien, you don't want to know anything about life — just how much money you can extract from it, for your own satisfaction, and nothing else . . ."

"And you talk and talk and you look at me with those big eyes I hate that go through me without seeing me . . ."

"You can squeeze, but you won't squeeze quite hard enough: you want to listen, you can't help yourself . . ."

"Your hands are cold on mine, you might as well be dead already, God, can you feel how badly I want to squeeze, how much I want to kill you . . ."

"It isn't you, Adrien, it's the past . . ."

"That hurt, didn't it?"

"Yes."

"What about that?"

"Yes."

"And that? What's the matter, cat got your tongue? I like it when you stop talking, Estelle. Listen to that silence. Do you hear it? Answer me!"

"Yes."

"See, I've let go a little, but I don't know if I'll let go of you altogether. Talk, go on. Talk, Estelle!"

But it was not I who spoke; madame, if it had been, I could tell you now what I said then. It was someone else inside me, it was my mother and all the other women who died before her, who were tortured to death before her. It was their screams, their death throes, they were indescribable . . . I am approaching the end, madame, look what is happening to me . . . I could not, I cannot tell you my mother's story.

But I clearly see the two of them, Estelle and Adrien, upright, face-to-face, his hands around her neck, her hands on his. Anyone going past the window would take them for lovers, two shadowy forms in the firelight, facing each other, embracing. For the rest of that night they remained standing there. Later Adrien relaxed his grip. Sometimes he spoke, in rapid bursts, his features moving as if a bolt were being unscrewed, his face moving and taking on the shape of all the other faces he might have had. One by one all his possible faces came to the surface and vanished, and at one point he suddenly released Estelle's throat and sprang back as if a monster had bitten him. She moved toward him, her demeanor gentle and soothing, but he stood rigid and then shrugged. Then she folded her arms back across her breast. It was cold, and he did not move again, nor did he again stretch out his hand toward her, either to threaten her or to touch her body. And now I am looking straight at her, madame. I am looking at her but her back is to me and I cannot hear what she says nor can I see her face. Now it is no longer anything but a picture — moonlight, dead embers, empty house, nothing but a picture, and I want to scream, madame, I too could kill. But there is no one to kill, and I call out for help to you, madame, to you . . .

The fire was out. We shivered in the cold, we shivered and talked.

"Stop stammering, Estelle."

"You're the one who's stammering."

"It's cold, and shit, you don't have any more logs."

"I'll get some."

"Where?"

"At the back, under the lean-to."

"No, no, I'm leaving."

We flapped our arms in the air, we poked at the ashes, we walked nervously up and down.

"Listen, I'll get logs."

"Forget it."

"Why are you staying?"

"I'll stay if I feel like it."

"Well, if you're staying I'll go and . . ."

"Can't you stop talking for even one second?"

We were still shivering with cold, and bickering. We were back at our marks; they were still there; we would never have any others. But although we did not yet know it, we were different. The new being proceeds with the words and gestures of the old one. We always trail one or two steps behind ourselves — and so for a little time still we would go on talking like the Estelle and Adrien of old. But neither one meant anything to the other anymore. A few years later on, in a sudden recrudescence of their old selves, they would rediscover forgotten cries and gestures, they would have one last and most ugly coupling — not beneath a lilac tree in a garden but in the basement of a famous restaurant, in the toilets, in a narrow cubicle, amid gurgling water and plumbing noises. A swift and unsatisfactory coupling, just to set the old horror in motion once again between them, and on your part, Adrien, from a kind of curiosity, like scratching an old itch. And afterward champagne, and then you would forget and go back to your prosperous affairs and the wife you had found and who had managed to make you happy and likable. For you are now a likable man, rather better even than many others, I acknowledge it, but our paths will never cross again . . .

"Aha," Adrien said suddenly and unexpectedly.

He started to laugh. His laugh seemed to convulse him inwardly. But it was as if he were unwilling to let it out, as if the last thing he wanted was for others to enjoy it. For a second I thought he had lost his mind. But no, it was the old Adrien cackling away.

"Aha!" he said. "He wasn't your brother! Poor Estelle, all of a sudden you lose a lot of your attraction, yes, a lot!"

Dawn was breaking behind the big chestnuts. Small bird sounds came from the garden. Another day. Tiresia was dead.

"Now go, Adrien . . ."

He rubbed his cheeks and chin as if wiping the emotion from his face with his hands. His features seemed carved in wood, hard lichen-coated wood. He stretched his arms, flexed them a few times. "You're going to have to replace that boiler," he said. There was no more hesitation in him. He was in a hurry to shower, shave, change his shirt.

"I'll go home and then leave. And you can go to hell, Estelle, all the way to hell, you and your family, and don't come back to torment me."

I took his arm and kised him, bizarrely, on his elbow.

"Thank you."

He pushed me roughly away.

"I don't thank you. What do you want me to do with all the horrors you've told me?"

"It wasn't just horrors . . ."

"Who cares. All I know is we didn't even fuck, and now I'm too beat, go to hell, Estelle."

No, Adrien and I were not exactly model lovers.

From the threshold I watched him reach the gap in the wall in swift, long strides. Every inch a businessman, Adrien was. I ran out to the front steps. I wanted to call him. I wanted him to look back from the gap in the wall and then I would call him; his name was on my lips — "Turn around, turn around." My eyes misted over and I could not see if he turned. I went back into the house.

"Mama." "My daughter, my little daughter . . ."

SIXTY-TWO

"*Don't Have Your Revenge on Us*"

THEN ONE DAY the door in the house across the way swung open and we saw a man we didn't know and a woman in black who at that time couldn't walk unaided. And there was a baby and a fair-haired girl, so fair-haired she couldn't have been a local girl, and pretty, so pretty. My husband came to get me, he said, 'Could that possibly be . . . ,' but he didn't dare finish his sentence. That broken woman in black, you wouldn't have recognized her, your mother had been a beautiful woman, proud, stately, but truly beautiful. She couldn't have been more than twenty-six or twenty-seven. And then there was this girl with them . . . We clearly remembered the story of the young piano student the Germans picked up along with your mother — but it made no sense, we could see the way she looked at your father, she was in love, like a teenager. 'It can't be,' I told my husband. Even thinking such things felt like blasphemy. When the piano arrived a few days later, though, our suspicions returned. But in those days we were just getting our freight business on its feet, and I had just found out I was pregnant — with Adrien — and now perhaps he's going to die, my Adrien, oh, Estelle . . ."

Tears flowed down the rather coarse face, and my gaze moved to the hairline, where the hair grew bushy and dark, just like Adrien's; there was no following the thoughts hiding in those thickets, I would never be able to seize the thoughts rising up in supplication like mourners of old.

"And now poor Mr. Neighbor's worried sick . . . Do you remember how he used to be, the ogre who scared you so? 'There's nothing to discuss,' he told Adrien, he's so unbending, there are some things you can't talk to him about, things that make him see red. And of course that just eggs Adrien on — it's always been that way between them, everything seems fine and then out of the blue they're quarreling. It's not that they don't love each other, but they're so alike . . . And now he's in pain. 'Go on,' he told me, 'you go, go and see her, talk to her . . .' "

Do you honestly believe, Mrs. Neighbor, that I hold fate in my hands? Do you believe that those who have had dealings with death possess secret links to it? Is that what you think — that I have returned to the land of the living in search of dark revenge, and that Adrien is the sacrifice I require?

"I have to explain to you, Estelle, you have to understand me . . . One evening — I remember it as if it were yesterday — my husband came home early from work, it was still light out. A man rang our doorbell and introduced himself: 'Mr. Helleur,' he said. It was our new neighbor, and he wanted to speak to both of us —

"We certainly weren't expecting what he was about to tell us. I thought he was just being polite, but he said right away, 'Could I speak to you, to both of you?' We all sat down, and by the time he left it was pitch-dark, with a big moon. My husband and I didn't even have the strength to speak. We went straight to bed and that's where it all began for us —

"It all seems like yesterday; our generation doesn't keep jumping around the way yours does. All those years seem like a long smooth carpet, and all you have to do is turn around and you glide straight back to the day that stuck in your memory —

"Anyway, in the middle of the night I woke up feeling very strange, I felt as if the moon were shining straight into my face. I got up, and realized we hadn't had the strength to close the shutters when we went to bed —

"I said to my husband, 'Aren't we making a mistake?' but he didn't answer right away. I thought he was annoyed, and perhaps I dozed off, because suddenly he was saying, 'It's a secret that belongs to the gods.' I tell you, it gave me goose bumps; Mr. Neighbor is not a man who talks about the gods. Then we lay there not daring to move, I won't forget that night —

"We were young, there were all kinds of things we hadn't ever thought about, and that night it was as if we were thinking every thought you ever think in your whole life, all at once —

"You can talk about one thought — but every thought at once, there's no way you can talk through that, so we said nothing, and in any case Mr. Neighbor's mind was made up: once he's decided something he won't turn back. It's his way of being loyal —

"For him Tiresia was like the Resistance. She had asked us for something, so we agreed. 'It's the least we can do for her,' he said. Perhaps he saw it as repaying a war debt —

"But I didn't agree, my little Estelle, I thought it could only bring us trouble, and your Doctor Minor didn't agree either, that was obvious to me; but my husband is stubborn; he did what he saw as his duty, and in those days it did seem that he was right . . . If you could have seen the state Tiresia was in, she was actually a few inches shorter than before, we didn't want to become her executioners —

"So I finally gave way even though I didn't like it. 'There are things you don't understand,' my husband said, I think he was trying to convince himself, in any case he had given his word, that's why, Estelle — and now all these deaths, oh, it wrings my heart . . ."

Do you imagine that on some secret pair of scales Adrien might balance out all my dead ones? That now, to appease my wrath, I could cause the jagged sheet of metal to sink even deeper into his body, could cause his veins to burst and flood his brain with blood? And that soon I would be the one escorting you up that familiar, that so familiar road, the road to our cemetery?

"For you see, Estelle, we had never laid eyes on her husband, but after Tiresia's arrest we wrote to him, we offered to keep the baby, we were almost in the countryside out here. He answered that he could not be parted from you . . . He already loved you so much, you see, and of course life here too was getting difficult — the Reich Division was moving north through our area and the air was thick with talk of reprisals —

"Long afterward we received another letter from your father, he said Tiresia was back and he asked whether there might not be a house for sale in the area —

"There was the house next door, deserted by its owner, yes, the one who dug that big ditch at the bottom of your meadow, he thought it was still the Great War and he wanted trenches everywhere, I believed he ended up in the rest home —

"We sent your father the real estate agent's address and then we forgot about it, after all, we scarcely knew them . . ."

Adrien had stumbled, as if beneath a too-heavy burden. He was not so strong after all. He had let me down for the very first time: oh, Adrien, your fine squeaky shoes and your gleaming car were not proof enough! Just one moment of weakness, just one word of love —"What we did under the lilac wasn't for you, but this time it is, Estelle"— and death had drawn near.

Adrien had not been light as the wind. He had stumbled, and now our neighbor's thoughts rose up to confront me, she had come running through the graves looking stricken, and I had risen to meet her.

"That child Nicole, it was so obvious she wasn't your mother. Sometimes I looked in to see how things were going with all of you; she did her best; she put all her strength into it; it's just that she was inefficient. That's why Mr. Neighbor and I sent Adrien's Nanou across to help out a little —

"Luckily you weren't a difficult child, it was very strange, in fact, yes, Estelle, it was strange, it was as if, I don't know how to say this, it was as if you understood the whole situation and were trying to make things easier for her —

"You were so calm, and you had that steady way of looking at people, I never saw a child with eyes like yours. 'That kid would die if she thought it would help the others,' I used to tell my husband, and he said, 'She's a girl, that's all, girls are more sensible,' but I think he was just as impressed as I was —

"Compared with Adrien, anyway — we had to cuff him into line! I admit I had a few unworthy thoughts, 'It's not fair,' I thought, but that wasn't often, believe me, it was when I was tired. I had started

looking after the company's books and it made life difficult for
me . . ."

One day, suddenly thrusting the branches apart, Mr. Raymond leaned
down to where my brother and I sat under the tree. But he was not
looking at us: something else had caught his attention — three
women coming down the meadow, Nicole as usual barely dressed,
her blouse slipping off her shoulder, Tiresia veiled, and our neighbor's wife in an apron dress too tight for her (Dan and I were convinced that she cut her clothes from the company's packing canvas).
"There they are," Mr. Raymond rumbled, "there they are" —
  "Yes, yes, the crazy one in black and the blond prickteaser, we
know all about them, but what about the third one, tell us about her,
Mr. Raymond," and he cackled, "That one's pure crabgrass; there's
a lot more like that around here, and she'll still be around long after
the other two have gone under . . . She's the one you should have
for a mother, you stupid little vermin . . ."
  And now our mother had gone under, like the yellow rose. And
Tiresia, like the purple rose. And our father, like the white camellia.
And the crabgrass was still there, stifling me.
  "She was barely seventeen at the time, maybe less. She had huge
eyes and she was always anxious and utterly lost if your father moved
away or Tiresia or you, Estelle. She trembled the moment anyone
raised his voice: even my husband got into the habit of speaking
softly in her presence, although you know that loud voice of his, it's
scared you enough times —
  "And that clock she put on the landing later on, do you know
why? It was because it chimed the hours. That way, she thought,
nobody would ever be able to leave altogether in his sleep! That's
what she told me: 'They won't go altogether away in their sleep, Mrs.
Neighbor.' And I wanted to tell her that we wouldn't be able to
sneak off either because of those chimes of hers. We could hear
them all the way over in our house but we got used to them. It gave
us a shock when the clock stopped, as if Nicole had died all over
again. Mr. Neighbor used to go over to fix it — yes, while you
were away — and now I'm worried that ours too will stop, the one
outside Adrien's room, oh, Estelle, I'm afraid we're going to be
punished . . ."

Her voice assailed me, hoarse with weeping, and it was as if all the
sounds of the town were entering me through that voice, as if that

alien sound were taking over our story, the story of the house of Helleur, appropriating it, blending other stories into it, grinding them up and mingling them with our own. It seemed to me that my mother's story was already being smothered beneath words not of her choosing — oh, at least leave me our story! It's all too soon, Mrs. Neighbor, and I am too weak . . .

"Minor gave her injections and she got better day by day. She started to laugh and cut capers on the lawn to make you laugh (well, we called it cutting capers but of course it was really dancing), and she started to sing . . . So you see, it was impossible to turn back —

"We didn't think about it every day, we had our own lives to live, but we sensed things. Nicole was afraid nobody loved her, she was afraid of finishing up alone, without the love of the only people who remained to her, but she thought that if she did what Tiresia wanted, if she became your mother and Mr. Helleur's wife, then she would be bonded to you all and nothing could ever separate you . . . That was what we felt, without ever really thinking about it —

"Yes, yes, in her way she was an angel, your little mother Nicole, even when she ran away —

"I don't know which of you she loved most: Tiresia first, then your father, and after that you, and later on Dan. And by the end all the same, you were indistinguishable to her: it must sometimes have felt like a safety net around her heart, I think that's why she ran off, but of course it wasn't our place to judge —

"As well as what she went through, what she experienced in place of a normal growing up —

"She hadn't even been Tiresia's student, really. That was her older sister, whose name was also Thérèse . . . This older sister was very gifted; Nicole admired her passionately — and one day little Nicole turned up at your house in Paris. She no longer had an older sister, or parents, or any family at all — they were all dead, blown to bits in air raids, and she was in a way deranged, and obsessed with taking piano lessons —

"And Tiresia saw that she wanted to emulate her sister, that it was very important to her, so the younger sister had her lessons; she was not very gifted, but it calmed her down, in fact, she herself told us shortly after your arrival, 'Tiresia has stabilized and restructured me' — she was so proud of those big words, but to us it sounded weird. Oh yes, sometimes Nicole seemed very weird to us, but we told ourselves we had not gone through what she had had to face . . ."

*   *   *

Daylight reached out over the graves in the cemetery, and I stared at this woman who carried the images of my own departed ones in her head, who could make them walk and talk at will. There had been a time when I could have hurled myself upon that head that contained my dead, but now I just looked at it. The features stood out starkly on the face like the pathways through the graves, like Alex's father's little house, like the hosepipe coiled beneath the wall faucet, like the wrought iron gate and the road and the aircraft streaking over the pines that clothed the hills, the morning plane that had just taken off from our new airfield.

"I don't suffer from nerves, Estelle, I eat well, I sleep, nothing much gets me down, but let me tell you, the only nightmares I ever had in my life were because of that torturer —

"We certainly had our share of executions around here, and there was that village where they burned everyone alive in the church, but what your father told us we couldn't bring ourselves to believe, scientific experiments they called them —

"Do you know why Adrien's little brothers were born so long after he was? It was because I couldn't stop thinking about it, thinking about the torturer. He had his hooks in my ovaries, he lived inside my belly, sometimes it really wasn't funny for us —

"You might think, Estelle, that we deliberately hid all those things from you, but that wasn't how it was, my sweet. First came the shock and then silence, and then life coming in on top of it. And whenever we were able to see things clearly we still hesitated — because of Tiresia and Nicole, because of what they had suffered —

"But those brief moments of clear-sightedness hurt. Mr. Neighbor used to take off in his truck, and I would go over the books for the day . . . Your family was a source of worry, joy as well, but lots of worry —

"You mustn't think of us as cowards or criminals, that's what Adrien yelled at us this morning, perhaps you believed it too or perhaps you might believe it one of these days, but things like that aren't for everyone, you can't control them . . . That's why you must listen to me, why I beg you to listen to me, Estelle . . ."

On the convent's land there had been an isolated overgrown plot. Marie-Marthe never included it in her planting plans, never took me there to clear it with our scythes. A shed, a scarcely recognizable statue, and three disemboweled armchairs guarded its approaches. Draped with bindweed, they made a tattered, whimsical rampart that glittered in rain and sunshine like a gigantic spider. Standing there facing Mrs. Neighbor, I thought longingly back to those ramparts.

The grass behind them was tall, high-tossing stems with nodding, waving heads. The whole field rustled with conversation . . . What a place that field was to make gentle mock of the rule of silence! And how everything in me now yearned for that soft murmur passing from head to feathered head, a wordless pictureless murmur . . .

"You have to understand us, Estelle. In prison camp Nicole went slowly crazy waiting for it to be her turn. But Tiresia saved her life. She possessed extraordinary magnetism, your mother. Magnetism and endurance, a kind of faith, wisdom . . . I don't know how to put it, but she saved a lot of girls in that camp, although I don't know how long it could have gone on — she was dying when the camp was liberated —

"Later both of them received official compensation — for 'special assistance to victims of pseudomedical experiments' — that was in 1964, I think —

"Tiresia recovered, but she never wanted to be seen again. She didn't want her child to have a mother who 'bore horror in her person.' Your father repeated those words to us many times on the night of that first visit. They made our blood run cold —

"He would not desert her . . . 'You don't leave a woman like that, you agree, don't you, Mr. Neighbor,' and my husband had tears in his eyes —

"That's how Tiresia had her idea. It soon became an obsession: that Nicole should become your mother, you know how pretty Nicole was, she looked like a rose, that's what your father used to say and he was right, and she was yellow, after a few months' rest and good care she was as fresh as a newly opened rose —

"He wanted to bequeath a clean past to you, I don't quite know how to put it, but your father could talk, it still sends shivers through me the way he explained it to us —

"And there you are: he asked us to act as if Nicole were your mother, because we were their closest neighbors, and had known Tiresia in the Resistance. I immediately thought of what would come up later on, when you would need official papers and things, but my husband said, 'He's a lawyer, he knows about that kind of thing.' I think Mr. Neighbor understood your father, and he too wanted to forget the war —

"And of course things didn't always go well with all of you. Your parents never showed it, but we couldn't help worrying that Tiresia never spoke to anyone and Nicole shut herself away in her garage —

"My husband sometimes spoke to her: 'Have you ever thought of taking a job?' he asked her. 'It would get you out of the house.' But she just looked at him: 'I can't, Mr. Neighbor, if I stop dancing everything will stop, everything will stop' —

"And then he got to like your father, even though they were not very much alike, my husband was always fuming about one thing or another, and Mr. Helleur used to address him in that humorous way of his, that was how they communicated, and believe me, Estelle, they got on well —

"And of course we didn't think about all of you all the time, we gradually got used to things — and then one fine day Nicole was gone . . . she had run away, vanished, and I said to my husband, 'It was bound to happen.' And he said, 'She'll be back' —

"She did come back, and then Dan was born, and that was all a total mystery to us, Estelle, I swear it, Nicole never spoke about what happened over there in America, she just told my husband she wouldn't dance anymore, that it was over for her, but you know we don't know a thing about dancing, that whole dancing business seemed weird to us, especially when Dan took it up —

"Adrien's business also seems strange to us: in my day it was usually women who looked after furniture and decoration, and in any case it wasn't something people like us did . . . And then all that travel abroad, yes, I know, Estelle, you understand that kind of thing better —

"And now this German girl, you're the one I wanted him to marry, I would have liked you as my daughter-in-law, I'll never be able to speak to his German girl the way I speak to you —

"Kerstin, yes, I shouldn't call her 'the German girl,' I wouldn't like them to treat my son that way over in Düsseldorf, but they probably do, we're all the same, I imagine, no one better than anyone else —

"And now who knows if there'll even be a wedding, oh, Estelle, my little Estelle, don't have your revenge on us . . ."

One day a nun placed a radio on the pulpit that looked down over our long refectory tables. From then on, we heard the news summary at every meal: "In return play at the head of the national soccer league, Alex beat Nice by three goals to . . ." Pitter-patter, rustle-rustle, up rushed the duty nun to turn the volume down. But despite the marked drop in the din, the voice of the sports commentator was still perfectly audible in our big refectory. The announcer spoke with the intense, exuberant accents of southwestern France; no one could have taken his voice for a nun's; and did the nuns in any case listen to soccer commentary? They behaved exactly as usual, eyes demurely on their plates. Impossible to tell whether flags were raised or celebratory drums thundered in those ears. From the outside they looked like sleeping ears, tucked away beneath their veils. I too had a veil; it was the Auxerre-Nice match; but I had distinctly heard "Alex."

A time comes when you can no longer go on not hearing, and then what you do hear blends monstrously with what remains silent within you. I hugged the outer wall of the property, I stood still among the grasses . . .

"Here I am blubbering away, Estelle, and you standing there listening to me with all those bereavements you've had! Your eyes look just the way they did when you were little, they wrung my heart, you know, those eyes of yours, my Lord, when I think of your troubles, when I think of your troubles, Estelle —

"Just thinking of them all under the ground makes me weep —

"Before her baby was born Nicole used to say, 'It's over for me,' she meant dancing, but we felt that she was talking about her death; perhaps she had had a premonition: she didn't look as if she belonged in this world —

"But then after the baby came she pulled herself together, and then she had Dan, and he was really somebody, much livelier than you, it was a circus wherever he went, but he was as nervous as his mother and that worried me. 'That child's like a flame,' I said to my husband, and I said to myself, 'Better not blow on him too hard' —

"Nicole started dancing again, and you and your brother were inseparable, it was touching to see you together. In my whole life, in my whole life, Estelle, I've never seen a pair of children like you two, and I don't know why but sometimes that wrung my heart as well —

"Sometimes, especially when you had grown, it was a little strange to see you together like that the whole time. But for us you were brother and sister, that's right, Estelle, brother and sister, we never saw it differently —

"Adrien was already giving us quite enough trouble, he was getting moody, just like his father, and always squabbling with you two, yet he was always at your place. 'Where is he?' 'At the Helleur house.' Never a day went by without my husband and me saying those words —

"I sometimes wondered what went on with the three of you, but you always patched up your quarrels. When we asked Adrien, he told us, 'That's our business,' that's the way he used to speak to us —

"And Mr. Helleur helped him with his homework, Adrien didn't like school, you know, and Mr. Helleur helped him too when he pulled that stupid trick on the café owner, that collaborator who hated us. It could have ended badly, but your father went to enormous lengths, and I think it changed Adrien, at least he stopped doing stupid things . . .

"Never, never would I have dreamed . . . How could I, Estelle? You were children, brother and sister, we had always known you that way, oh, how blind we were . . ."

The child Liliane did not want stories from her books; she wanted a story from me. That first day on our way back from the airport she had managed to get her fingers around a thread of my life, and that thread she set about unwinding, trying to reel off my heart and my flesh, roll them around her little finger and suck them into dissolution. But her stratagem was merely the stratagem of a very small child, anxious and forlorn, and I was stronger, madame. Seeing that little white face under that too-luxuriant hair, seeing that little hand stealthily turning up the volume of the song, the song that sang louder and louder "Jump in the air," I realized how great my strength was. It was a strength I had not even guessed at, and in that moment it revealed itself in all its simplicity and its obviousness —

I did not abandon my opera to the innocent stratagem of a child, I did not deliver my opera up to her for her to convert it to her size — the little fairy, the little witch — to turn it into a child's tale —

I took her to my piano and she played with the keys, we found the music for that song and then other songs, and she laughed with pleasure. I had become strong, madame, and I realized it that day at the piano with the child Liliane, who is nothing to me and with whom I will henceforth live.

"Oh how blind we were —

"And blinder still after your parents' accident, although we finally did understand what had happened, Minor was so upset that he broke silence, he told us your brother was going to the dogs, but we didn't understand such things, Estelle, we didn't really understand, although now we're not quite so stupid —

"And I see now what Nicole must have been thinking, poor child, with nightmares of vengeance and retribution, she got upset so quickly, you know, and she lived inside her head so much —

"If she had come over to us that night we would have calmed her down, we would have reasoned with her, a father destroying his son, no, that just doesn't happen, and in any case it wasn't true, he did all he could for Dan, that man, Alwin, yes, Alwin, he never betrayed Mr. Helleur, he respected all of your lives, you poor little thing, everything was in league against you . . ."

"All these tears, I don't know where they come from, you know what your father used to say about Nicole and Tiresia —

" 'I wish they had your strength,' we used to speak to each other across the wall, and that expression of his made a deep impression on me . . . My husband has many good qualities, but he never compliments a person. 'My strength,' I really liked that, and what if your father could see me now . . ."

"Perhaps we seemed withdrawn, Estelle, and not too easygoing sometimes, but that's how it is in small towns — other people's secrets aren't your business — and my husband is even worse, 'You talk too much,' he said to me, he was silence itself, just like the Resistance —

"We were bound to you too closely to change, Estelle. My husband's arguments with Mr. Helleur, and his promise, they kept him alive, they kept him from slumping into depression, and I have to admit I was sometimes jealous of Nicole, even though I admired her. You couldn't help it, Nicole was not of this world —

"And Tiresia too . . . In the evening sometimes, when Mr. Neighbor was at the depot with his truck drivers, I'd go to the bottom of the garden and listen to her playing the piano. I bet you'd never have suspected that, you thought I was only interested in figures and saucepans, oh yes, I know you did —

"What she played made me sad and made me feel good, and when she gave up playing altogether I missed it . . .

"And when they were no longer there and you two had gone away, when everyone had left and the house next door was empty, I too felt empty, and so did my husband. We were no longer the same people. He's the one who said it: 'The Helleur house is empty and I'm no longer the same man . . . ' "

"Perhaps you think if we had spoken to you, your brother wouldn't have died, perhaps you think we really were cowardly and criminal —

"If I had known, Estelle, if I had known it was love between you, I swear I would have spoken. For me the love of the living is more important than the worries of the dead . . . I would have done it.

"I'm frightened for Adrien, Estelle, don't make him die, don't punish us . . ."

"You mustn't stay here, you must say farewell to them, do you hear me, Estelle, otherwise you too will soon be in your grave —

"Give me your hand, pass it over the stone, yes, over their names, gently" —

Andrew Helleur
Nicole Helleur
Dan Helleur
Thérèse Helleur

"Say farewell, Estelle."

SIXTY-THREE

Rest Your Cheek Against Mine

THAT WOMAN had seen us.

She walked below our window and saw us. She saw Adrien and me, embracing in the chill dawn, or perhaps naked in front of the fire.

"I couldn't sleep, Estelle, I got up and walked into your garden."

She talked and talked, our neighbor, oh, how she talked!

*   *   *

"She's my neighbor's wife, we talk across the garden wall . . ."

"A man needs a reliable woman, Mr. Helleur . . ."

Oh, Father, what could Mrs. Neighbor possibly have done for you?

You talked to her across the gap, and she talked to you, and then back you went through the garden, briefly relieved. Back you went to your duty cases, relieved that the Helleurs had good neighbors, relieved that the other side of the dividing wall harbored children from the now for your children from nowhere. Relieved to have this reliable woman for your own beautiful demented women, relieved to have this argumentative choleric man, owner of the N. Trucking Company, for a daily companion — even more so perhaps than your friend Doctor Minor . . . Oh, Father, they were your universe; you were delighted to have found such good neighbors in this secluded corner of the land of France, neighbors who condoned your sublime dream. Back you went to your study, your mind relieved for the moment . . .

Seen from the bend in the cemetery road on certain misty days, our two houses standing at the top of the rise seemed to be but one. The spire of the Helleur house, jutting prominently heavenward as a result of the amalgamation of the two roofs, appeared strangely high, and the windows jostling one another along the double facade had a fevered look. The Helleur house was the bigger of the two, but the other house seemed to hold it up: floating together in that way, the two houses made a fantastic and almost mobile whole . . . It only happened on certain days, and from one precise point along the cemetery road. A few steps farther and the two houses moved apart to become everyday small-town residences.

Mrs. Neighbor had seen us. Then she spoke.

She approached along the narrow cemetery pathways, out of breath after running up the road. It was still early morning. On the highway beyond our hills the rising sun glittered on Adrien's humiliated car. For one moment he had reverted to the superstitious child he had once been, and from the filling station, boiling with rage, he had called his parents. He had hurled my story at them. "Cowards, criminals," he had yelled. Then he had remained seated for a long while, watching the sun climb until at last the curse he felt in his heart evaporated in the light. The ambulance arrived but he refused it. He left in a rented vehicle, calm, already forgetting, already dreaming of a new and more splendid car. He did not yet know that the injury to his foot, painless at first and later operated on, would leave him with a slight limp.

And my mother's story had fallen upon this woman, our neighbor's wife.

"I have to explain, Estelle, you have to understand . . . if we had only been able to look ahead . . . all those deaths, my God, my head is bursting . . ."

I did not want her story, madame.

Please don't think I do not love this woman. She was our neighbor, a part of our childhood, but I did not want her story.

It was a story told by a village mourner, breathless and tearful. My mother was a woman of almost indestructible strength, a woman without tears.

I want an opera, madame. I want it to be not just a celebration of my dead but a celebration of all who came before, who stepped forward and fought the fight, alone and in dignity, their petty, magnificent fight —

For all such, madame, I seek celebration.

Those who girded themselves in arms and in rhetoric and who waged noisy war have no need of us. They have delirious crowds, thousands of bleeding bodies, history books, TV images . . .

In that ocean of images (and as we approach the second millennium the images proliferate and overlap) a catafalque rolled by. And all about that catafalque was a wave of human beings: they did not look human, madame; they looked like insects wiggling their thousands of feet around the one they mourned for, scrabbling at him with greedy feet, those people, madame — those dead and their attendant necrophiles — have no need of us.

They did not fight against life, but against men, only against men, so much noise to such little purpose. Against life there is only silence.

So it is the others we must celebrate, the unknown dead who answered life's summons without bluster.

Alone they marched out, with only their weak bodies and insignificant stories, to take their stand at the great dark wall.

We must celebrate the rising of their souls and the mustering of their forces to meet the incomprehensible summons. We must sing of how they remained steadfast in their small selves, and of how they responded, responded, and responded . . . until inevitable defeat.

In my time of love I had a talent. Then that talent died; it died with my brother. Now I have nothing left but my defenseless body and my insignificant story, and my pale beings drift on a disintegrating cloud. But I have not forsaken them, I am offering you the scenes that haunt me, the colors they blaze with, and the melodies that vibrate about them. You will not reject them, madame, you will not say, "This cannot be, this is monstrous": you will acknowledge the passage of life, the indescribable wake of fire and ashes that follows on the passage of life, and you will write a libretto, you will create music, dances, songs; you will erect a palace for my love. I have no idea who you are; you are very near yet unknown, but I have never stopped speaking to you, and you have given me strength . . .

When my resolution flagged, when the outside world raged past too swiftly, when Mrs. Neighbor's story devoured all other stories, when Phil arrived and I had to become Claire in order to hold on to that love, I spoke to you and you gave me strength . . .

I have spoken to you almost every day, as I once spoke to my dead brother, to my father and to Tiresia, who both tried to outwit evil, and to fair-headed Nicole, who wanted to dance in the sky, my pale ones, my most beloved ones . . . And from others — scarcely known, hated sometimes — I besought a god, Josepha's god, so poor and powerless in his divinity, and all the other gods, and still I spoke to my brother and always to you —

To you, madame —

My interlocutor —

And to you too, sir, of course.

When your pale loved ones sink into the regions of death, when your fingers stroke the names carved on their gravestones and a tearful and benevolent voice murmurs "Forget them, forget them," then you need an ally, all the allies in the world —

For he is mighty who stands before death's kingdom.

My Major has called, there was nothing I could do . . .

Oh, Doctor Minor, physicians may be helpless before him but the living possess a power, they have within them a sanctuary where celebrations can be held and where death cannot destroy all bodies.

A sanctuary in every living body, and if the opera I want is not performed on a stage it will be performed in this sanctuary. And if it is not an opera it will be something else, for every body has its resources, and I trust you, madame. All we must do is bring forward the offering.

We no longer have rites, we no longer know our souls, we cannot communicate with the dead.

Out on the street this morning a young man lithe as a tiger crossed through the traffic, resplendent among the long car bodies, landing with a bound right in front of me among the flower beds of the median strip. My breasts, the nipples I crushed you to just after you were born, stirred. The young man let out a great laugh of exultation; sweat glistened on his radiant face, and he looked at me, Dan, and then his gaze left me, it was not you, my love.

The plumes of desire still toss and wave, the erupting sun belches giant flames, a wheelchair-bound physicist is investigating the beginnings of time, and stains have appeared on my hands . . . Not stains of the disease that carried you off, but those that appear very early to plot the paths of age. Our Helleur home is no more, it was everything, my little brother, and it was nothing; the spots sit on my hands, my vagina quivers, oh, my brother, I am ready for death and I am ready for life.

I am going to live with Phil, I know he has a daughter, he knows Claire is not my name.

Our father gave us the fair Nicole for a mother, a woman with a body as whole and beautiful as an angel's to carry us into a new world, and I wanted to give Phil a transparent ever-cheerful woman to journey with into a new love — but in the end I was doing what our father did, Dan (*it all goes so much deeper, so much deeper*), and although our father was nothing to me by blood I resemble him, and I was following his path, the path that killed him . . .

But the child Liliane would not let me. Phil too wanted to take his stand against time, and that moved me, it finally moved something inside me. Now I am going to live with him. Perhaps my talent did not die, perhaps it will return; the child Liliane loves music and is